PENGUI

A DALGLIES

P. D. James was born in Oxford in 1920 and educated at Cambridge High School. From 1949 to 1968 she worked in the National Health Service as an administrator, and the experience she gained from her job helped her with the background for *Shroud for a Nightingale*, *The Black Tower* and *A Mind to Murder*. In 1968 she entered the Home Office as Principal, working first in the Police Department concerned with the forensic science service, and later in the Criminal Policy Department. She retired in 1979. She is a Fellow of the Royal Society of Literature and a Fellow of the Royal Society of Arts. She was a Governor of the BBC from 1988 to 1993 and was a member of the Board of the British Council from 1988 to 1993. She served on the Arts Council and was Chairman of its Literary Advisory Panel from 1988 to 1992. She has served as a magistrate in Middlesex and London. She has won awards for crime writing from Britain, America, Italy and Scandinavia, and has received honorary degrees from six universities. In 1983 she received the OBE and she was created a life peer in 1991. In 1997 she was elected President of the Society of Authors. She has been a widow for over twenty-five years and has two children and five grandchildren.

Her novels include *An Unsuitable Job for a Woman*, *Innocent Blood* and *The Skull Beneath the Skin* (also published as *Trilogy of Death*); *Shroud for a Nightingale*, *The Black Tower* and *Death of an Expert Witness* (also published as *A Dalgliesh Trilogy*); *A Taste for Death*, *A Mind to Murder* and *Devices and Desires* (also published as *A Second Dalgliesh Trilogy*); *Cover Her Face*; *Unnatural Causes*; *The Children of Men*; *Original Sin*; and *A Certain Justice*. She is co-author, with T. A. Critchley, of *The Maul and the Pear Tree*. All of her books are published by Penguin.

P. D. JAMES

A DALGLIESH TRILOGY

SHROUD FOR A NIGHTINGALE
THE BLACK TOWER
DEATH OF AN EXPERT WITNESS

PENGUIN BOOKS
IN ASSOCIATION WITH FABER & FABER

PENGUIN BOOKS

Published by the Penguin Group
Penguin Books Ltd, 27 Wrights Lane, London W8 5TZ, England
Penguin Putnam Inc., 375 Hudson Street, New York, New York 10014, USA
Penguin Books Australia Ltd, Ringwood, Victoria, Australia
Penguin Books Canada Ltd, 10 Alcorn Avenue, Toronto, Ontario, Canada M4V 3B2
Penguin Books (NZ) Ltd, Private Bag 102902, NSMC, Auckland, New Zealand

Penguin Books Ltd, Registered Offices: Harmondsworth, Middlesex, England

Shroud for a Nightingale first published by Faber & Faber 1971
Published by Penguin Books in association with Faber & Faber 1989

The Black Tower first published by Faber & Faber 1975
Published by Penguin Books in association with Faber & Faber 1989

Death of an Expert Witness first published by Faber & Faber 1977
Published by Penguin Books in association with Faber & Faber 1989

This collection first published by Penguin Books in association
with Faber & Faber 1991
14

Printed in England by Clays Ltd, St Ives plc

SHROUD FOR A NIGHTINGALE

For J. M. C.

CONTENTS

ONE

Demonstration of Death

I

On the morning of the first murder Miss Muriel Beale, Inspector of Nurse Training Schools to the General Nursing Council, stirred into wakefulness soon after six o'clock and into a sluggish early morning awareness that it was Monday, 12th January, and the day of the John Carpendar Hospital inspection. Already she had half registered the first familiar sounds of a new day: Angela's alarm silenced almost before she was conscious of hearing it; Angela herself padding and snuffling about the flat like a clumsy but benevolent animal; the agreeably anticipatory tinklings of early tea in preparation. She forced open her eyelids, resisting an insidious urge to wriggle down into the enveloping warmth of the bed and let her mind drift again into blessed unconsciousness. What on earth had prompted her to tell Matron Taylor that she would arrive shortly after nine a.m. in time to join the third-year students' first teaching session of the day? It was ridiculously, unnecessarily early. The hospital was in Heatheringfield on the Sussex/Hampshire border, a drive of nearly fifty miles, some of which would have to be done before daybreak. And it was raining, as it had rained with dreary insistence for the past week. She could hear the faint hiss of car tyres on the Cromwell Road and an occasional spatter against the window-pane. Thank God she had taken the trouble to check the map of Heatheringfield to find out exactly where the hospital lay. A developing market town, particularly if it were unfamiliar, could be a time-wasting maze to the motorist in the snarl of commuter traffic on a wet Monday morning. She felt instinctively that it was going to be a difficult day and stretched out under the bedclothes as if bracing herself to meet it. Extending her cramped fingers, she half relished the sharp momentary ache of her stretched joints. A touch of arthritis there. Well, it was to be expected. She was forty-nine after all. It was time she took life a little more gently. What on earth had led her to think she could get to Heatheringfield before half past nine?

The door opened, letting in a shaft of light from the passage. Miss Angela Burrows jerked back the curtains, surveyed the black January sky and the rain-spattered window and jerked them together again. 'It's raining,' she said with the gloomy relish of one who has prophesied rain and who cannot be held responsible for the ignoring of her warning. Miss Beale propped herself on her elbow, turned on the bed-side lamp, and waited. In a few seconds her friend returned and set down the early morning tray. The tray cloth was of stretched embroidered linen, the flowered cups were arranged with their handles aligned, the four biscuits on the matching plate were precisely placed, two of a kind, the teapot gave forth a delicate smell of freshly made Indian tea. The two women had a strong love of comfort and an addiction to tidiness and order. The standards which they had once enforced in the private ward of their teaching hospital were applied to their own comfort, so that life in the flat was not unlike that in an expensive and permissive nursing home.

Miss Beale had shared a flat with her friend since they had both left the same training school twenty-five years ago. Miss Angela Burrows was the Principal Tutor at a London teaching hospital. Miss Beale had thought her the paradigm of nurse tutors and, in all her inspections, subconsciously set her standard by her friend's frequent pronouncements on the principles of sound nurse teaching. Miss Burrows, for her part, wondered how the General Nursing Council would manage when the time came for Miss Beale to retire. The happiest marriages are sustained by such comforting illusions and Miss Beale's and Miss Burrows's very different, but essentially innocent, relationship was similarly founded. Except in this capacity for mutual but unstated admiration they were very different. Miss Burrows was sturdy, thick-set and formidable, hiding a vulnerable sensitivity under an air of blunt common sense. Miss Beale was small and birdlike, precise in speech and movement and threatened with an out-of-date gentility which sometimes brought her close to being thought ridiculous. Even their physiological habits were different. The heavy Miss Burrows awoke to instantaneous life at the first sound of her alarm, was positively energetic until teatime, then sank into sleepy lethargy as the evening advanced. Miss Beale daily opened her gummed eyelids with reluctance, had to force herself into early morning activity and became more brightly cheerful as the day wore on. They had managed to reconcile even this incompatibility. Miss Burrows was happy to brew the early morning tea and Miss Beale washed up after dinner and made the nightly cocoa.

Miss Burrows poured out both cups of tea, dropped two lumps of sugar in her friend's cup and took her own to the chair by the window. Early training forbade Miss Burrows to sit on the bed. She said: 'You need to be off early. I'd better run your bath. When does it start?'

Miss Beale muttered feebly that she had told Matron that she would arrive as soon as possible after nine o'clock. The tea was blessedly sweet and reviving. The promise to start out so early was a mistake but she began to think that she might after all make it by nine-fifteen.

'That's Mary Taylor, isn't it? She's got quite a reputation considering she's only a provincial matron. Extraordinary that she's never come to London. She didn't even apply for our job when Miss Montrose retired.' Miss Beale muttered incomprehensibly, which, since they had had this conversation before, her friend correctly interpreted as a protest that London wasn't everybody's choice and that people were too apt to assume that nothing remarkable ever came out of the provinces.

'There's that, of course,' conceded her friend. 'And the John Carpendar's in a very pleasant part of the world. I like that country on the Hampshire border. It's a pity you're not visiting it in the summer. Still, it's not as if she's matron of a major teaching hospital. With her ability she easily could be: she might have become one of the Great Matrons.' In their student days she and Miss Beale had suffered at the hands of one of the Great Matrons but they never ceased to lament the passing of that terrifying breed.

'By the way, you'd better start in good time. The road's up just before you strike the Guildford by-pass.'

Miss Beale did not inquire how she knew that the road was up. It was the sort of thing Miss Burrows invariably did know. The hearty voice went on:

'I saw Hilda Rolfe, their Principal Tutor, in the Westminster Library this week. Extraordinary woman! Intelligent, of course, and reputedly a first-class teacher, but I imagine she terrifies the students.'

Miss Burrows frequently terrified her own students, not to mention most of her colleagues on the teaching staff, but would have been amazed to be told it. Miss Beale asked:

'Did she say anything about the inspection?'

'Just mentioned it. She was only returning a book and was in a hurry so we didn't talk long. Apparently they've got a bad attack of influenza in the school and half her staff are off with it.'

Miss Beale thought it odd that the Principal Tutor should find time to visit London to return a library book if staffing problems were so difficult, but she didn't say so. Before breakfast Miss Beale reserved her energy for thought rather than speech. Miss Burrows came round the bed to pour out the second cups. She said:

'What with this weather and with half the training staff off sick, it looks as if you're in for a pretty dull day.'

As the two friends were to tell each other for years to come, with the cosy predilection for re-stating the obvious which is one of the pleasures of long intimacy, she could hardly have been more wrong. Miss Beale, expecting nothing worse of the day than a tedious drive, an arduous inspection, and a possible tussle with those members of the Hospital Nurse Education Committee who took the trouble to attend, dragged her dressing-gown around her shoulders, stubbed her feet into her bedroom slippers and shuffled off to the bathroom. She had taken the first steps on her way to witness a murder.

II

Despite the rain, the drive was less difficult than Miss Beale had feared. She made good time and was in Heatheringfield just before nine o'clock in time to meet the last surge of the morning rush to work. The wide Georgian High Street was blocked with vehicles. Women were driving their commuter husbands to the station or their children to school, vans were delivering goods, buses were discharging and loading their passengers. At the three sets of traffic lights the pedestrians streamed across the road, umbrellas slanted against the soft drizzle. The young had the spruce, over-uniformed look of the private-school child; the men were mostly bowler-hatted and carrying briefcases; the women were casually dressed with that nice compromise between town smartness and country informality, typical of their kind. Watching for the lights, the pedestrian crossing and the signpost to the hospital, Miss Beale had only a brief chance to notice the elegant eighteenth-century guildhall, the carefully preserved row of timber-fronted houses and the splendid crocketed spire of Holy Trinity church, but she gained an impression of a prosperous community which cared about preserving its architectural heritage even if the row of modern chain stores at the end of the High Street suggested that the caring might have begun thirty years earlier.

But here at last was the signpost. The road to the John Carpendar Hospital led upward from the High Street between a broad avenue of trees. To the left was a high stone wall which bounded the hospital grounds.

Miss Beale had done her homework. Her briefcase, plump on the back seat of the car, contained a comprehensive note on the hospital's history as well as a copy of the last General Nursing Council Inspector's report and the comments of the Hospital Management Committee on how far it had been possible to implement the inspector's optimistic recommendations. As she knew from her researches, the hospital had a long history. It had been founded in 1791 by a wealthy merchant who had been born in the town, had left it in youthful penury to seek his fortune in London, and had returned there in his retirement to enjoy patronizing and impressing his neighbours. He could have purchased fame and ensured his salvation by succouring the widows and fatherless or by rebuilding the church. But the age of science and reason was succeeding the age of faith and it had become fashionable to endow a hospital for the sick poor. And so, with the almost obligatory meeting in a local coffee-house, the John

Carpendar Hospital was born. The original house, of some architectural interest, had long since been replaced, first by a solid Victorian monument to ostentatious piety and then by the more functional gracelessness of the twentieth century.

The hospital had always flourished. The local community was predominantly middle-class and prosperous, with a well-developed charitable sense and too few objects on which to indulge it. Just before the Second World War a well-equipped private patients' wing had been added. Both before and after the advent of the National Health Service it had attracted wealthy patients, and consequently eminent consultants, from London and further afield. Miss Beale reflected that it was all very well for Angela to talk about the prestige of a London teaching hospital, but the John Carpendar had its own reputation. A woman might well think there were worse jobs than being Matron of a developing district general hospital, well thought of by the community it served, agreeably placed and fortified by its own local traditions.

She was at the main gates now. There was a porter's lodge on the left, an ornate doll's house in tessellated brick, a relic of the Victorian hospital, and – on the right – the doctors' car park. Already a third of the marked plots were occupied by the Daimlers and the Rollses. It had stopped raining and the dawn had given way to the grey normality of a January day. The lights were full on in the hospital. It lay before her like a great ship at anchor, brightly lit, latent with activity and power. To the left stretched the low glass-fronted buildings of the new out-patients' department. Already a thin stream of patients was making its dispirited way to the entrance.

Miss Beale drew up alongside the inquiry hatch of the lodge, wound down the car window, and announced herself. The porter, ponderous and uniformed in self-importance, deigned to come out to present himself.

'You'll be the General Nursing Council, Miss,' he stated grandiloquently. 'What a pity you decided to come in this gate. The Nurse Training School is in Nightingale House, only a 100 yards or so from the Winchester Road entrance. We always use the back entrance for Nightingale House.'

He spoke with reproachful resignation, as if deploring a singular lack of judgement which would cost him dear in extra work.

'But presumably I can get to the school this way?'

Miss Beale had no stomach for a return to the confusion of the High Street or intention of circling the hospital grounds in search of an elusive back entrance.

'Well you can, Miss.' The porter's tone implied that only the wilfully obstinate would try, and he settled himself against the car door as if to deliver confidential and complicated directions. They proved, however, remarkably simple. Nightingale House was in the hospital grounds at the rear of the new out-patients' department.

'Just take this road to the left, Miss, and keep straight on past the mortuary till you get to the resident medical quarters. Then turn to the right. There's a signpost where the road forks. You can't miss it.'

For once this notoriously unpropitious assertion seemed justified. The grounds of the hospital were extensive and well wooded, a mixture of formal garden, grass, and clumped unkempt trees which reminded Miss Beale of the grounds of an old mental hospital. It was rare to find a general hospital so well endowed with space. But the several roads were well signposted and only one led to the left of the new out-patients' department. The mortuary was easily identified, a squat, ugly little building tactfully sited among the trees and made more sinister by its strategic isolation. The medical officers' residence was new and unmistakable. Miss Beale had time to indulge her usual, frequently quite unjustified, resentment that Hospital Management Committees were always more ready to rehouse their doctors than to provide adequate accommodation for the nurse training school, before noting the promised sign. A white painted board pointed to the right and read 'Nightingale House, Nurse Training School'.

She changed gear and turned carefully. The new road was narrow and winding, banked high on each side with sodden leaves so that there was barely room for the single car. Everywhere was dampness and desolation. The trees grew close to the path and knitted themselves above it, ribbing the dark tunnel with their strong black boughs. From time to time a gust of wind brought down a spatter of raindrops on the car roof or flattened a falling leaf against the windscreen. The grass verge was scarred with flower beds, regular and oblong as graves and spiked with stunted bushes. It was so dark under the trees that Miss Beale switched on her side lamps. The road shone before her like an oiled ribbon. She had left the car window down and could smell, even above the inevitable car smell of petrol and warm vinyl, a sweet fungoid stench of decay. She felt strangely isolated in the dim quietness and suddenly she was touched with an irrational unease, a bizarre sensation of journeying out of time into some new dimension, borne onwards towards an uncomprehended and inescapable horror. It was only a second's folly and she quickly shook it off, reminding herself of the cheerful bustle of the High Street less than a mile away and the nearness of life and activity. But it had been an odd and disconcerting experience. Angry at herself at this lapse into morbid folly, she wound up the car window and stepped on the accelerator. The little car leaped forward.

Suddenly she found she had turned the last corner and Nightingale House was before her. She nearly stood on the brakes in surprise. It was an extraordinary house, an immense Victorian edifice of red brick, castellated and ornate to the point of fancy, and crowned with four immense turrets. It was brightly lit in the dark January morning and after the gloom of the road it blazed at her like a castle from some childhood mythology. An immense conservatory was grafted on to the right side of the house, looking, thought Miss Beale, more appropriate to Kew Gardens than to what had obviously once been a private residence. It was less brightly lit than the house but through the faintly luminous glass she could discern the sleek green leaves of aspidistras, the harsh red of poinsettias and the yellow and bronze blob of chrysanthemums.

Miss Beale's recent moment of panic under the trees was completely forgotten in her amazement at Nightingale House. Despite her normal confidence in her own taste, she was not entirely immune to the vagaries of fashion and she wondered uneasily whether in certain company it might not be proper to admire it. But it had become a habit with her to look at every building with an eye to its suitability as a nurse training school – she had once, on a Paris holiday, found herself to her horror rejecting the Elysée Palace as unworthy of further notice – and as a nurse training school Nightingale House was obviously quite impossible. She had only to look at it for the objections to spring to mind. Most of the rooms would be far too large. Where, for instance, would one find cosy offices for the principal tutor, clinical instructor or school secretary? Then the building would be extremely difficult to heat adequately and those oriel windows, picturesque no doubt if one liked that sort of thing, would keep out a great deal of light. Worse still, there was something forbidding, even frightening, about the house. When the Professional (Miss Beale, in defiance of an unfortunate comparison, always thought of it with a capital P) was climbing so painfully into the twentieth century, kicking away the stones of outworn attitudes and methods – Miss Beale was frequently required to make speeches and certain pet phrases tended to stick in her mind – it really was a pity to house young students in this Victorian pile. It would do no harm to incorporate a strong comment about the need for a new school in her report. Nightingale House was rejected even before she set foot in it.

But there was nothing to criticize in her welcome. As she reached the top step, the heavy door swung open letting out a gust of warm air and a smell of fresh coffee. A uniformed maid stood deferentially aside and behind her down the wide oak staircase, gleaming against the dark panelling like a Renaissance portrait in grey and gold, came the figure of Matron Mary Taylor, hand outstretched. Miss Beale assumed her bright professional smile, compounded of happy expectation and general reassurance, and stepped forward to meet her. The ill-fated inspection of the John Carpendar Training School had begun.

III

Fifteen minutes later, four people made their way down the main staircase to the demonstration room on the ground floor where they were to watch the first teaching session of the day. Coffee had been served in Matron's sitting-room in one of the turret blocks where Miss Beale had been introduced to the Principal Tutor, Miss Hilda Rolfe, and to a senior consultant surgeon, Mr

Stephen Courtney-Briggs. She knew both by reputation. Miss Rolfe's presence was necessary and expected, but Miss Beale was a little surprised that Mr Courtney-Briggs was prepared to devote so much of his morning to the inspection. He had been introduced as Vice-Chairman of the Hospital Nurse Education Committee and she would normally have expected to meet him with other members of the committee for the summing-up discussion at the end of the day. It was unusual for a senior surgeon to sit in at a teaching session and it was gratifying that he took such a personal interest in the school.

There was room for three to walk abreast in the wide wood-panelled corridors and Miss Beale found herself escorted by the tall figures of Matron and Mr Courtney-Briggs rather, she felt, like a diminutive delinquent. Mr Courtney-Briggs, stoutly impressive in the formal striped trousers of a consultant, walked on her left. He smelt of after-shave lotion. Miss Beale could discern it even above the pervading smell of disinfectant, coffee and furniture cream. She thought it surprising but not disagreeable. The Matron, tallest of the three, walked in serene silence. Her formal dress of grey gaberdine was buttoned high to the neck with a thin band of white linen around the throat and cuffs. Her corn-gold hair, almost indistinguishable in colour from her skin, was combed back from the high forehead and bound tight by an immense triangle of muslin, its apex reaching nearly to the small of her back. The cap reminded Miss Beale of those worn during the last war by Sisters of the Army Nursing Service. She had seldom seen it since. But its simplicity suited Miss Taylor. That face, with its high cheekbones and large, protuberant eyes – they reminded Miss Beale irreverently of pale veined gooseberries – could have looked grotesque under the fripperies of a more orthodox head-dress. Behind the three of them Miss Beale could sense the disturbing presence of Sister Rolfe, uncomfortably close on their heels.

Mr Courtney-Briggs was talking:

'This influenza epidemic has been a thorough nuisance. We've had to defer taking the next set off the wards and we thought at one time that this set would have to go back. It was a close thing.'

It would be, thought Miss Beale. Whenever there was a crisis in the hospital the first people to be sacrificed were the student nurses. Their training programme could always be interrupted. It was a sore point with her, but now was hardly the time to protest. She made a vaguely acquiescent noise. They started down the last staircase. Mr Courtney-Briggs continued his monologue:

'Some of the training staff have gone down with it too. The demonstration this morning is being taken by our clinical instructor, Mavis Gearing. We've had to recall her to the school. Normally, of course, she would be doing nothing but ward teaching. It's a comparatively new idea that there should be a trained instructor to teach the girls on the wards, using the patients as clinical material. Ward sisters just haven't the time these days. Of course the whole idea of the block system of training is relatively new. When I was a medical student the probationers, as we called them then, were taught entirely on the wards with occasional lectures in their own free time from the medical staff. There was little formal teaching and certainly no taking them off the wards each year for a period in the nurse training school. The whole concept of nurse training has altered.'

Miss Beale was the last person to require an explanation of the function and studies of a clinical instructor or the development of nurse training methods. She wondered whether Mr Courtney-Briggs had forgotten who she was. This elementary instruction was more suitable for new members of a Hospital Management Committee, who were generally as ignorant of nurse training as they were of anything else to do with hospitals. She had the feeling that the surgeon had something on his mind. Or was this merely the aimless chatter, unrelated to its hearer, of an egotist who could not tolerate even a moment without the comforting resonance of his own voice? If so, the sooner he got back to his out-patient session or ward round and let the inspection proceed without the benefit of his presence, the better for all concerned.

The little procession passed across the tessellated hall to a room at the front of the building. Miss Rolfe slipped forward to open the door and stood aside as the others entered. Mr Courtney-Briggs ushered Miss Beale in before him. Immediately she was at home. Despite the anomalies of the room itself – the two great windows with their spatter of coloured panes, the immense fireplace of carved marble with its draped figures supporting the chimney-piece, the high moulded ceiling desecrated with the three tubes of fluorescent light – it was happily evocative of her own student days, an utterly acceptable and familiar world. Here was all the paraphernalia of her profession: the rows of glass-fronted cabinets, with their instruments placed in shining precision; the wall charts showing in lurid diagram the circulation of the blood and the improbable processes of digestion; the wall-mounted blackboard smeared with the dust of past lecture notes imperfectly erased; the demonstration trolleys with their linen-covered trays; the two demonstration beds, one containing a life-sized doll propped among the pillows; the inevitable skeleton hanging from its gibbet in forlorn decrepitude. Pervading all was the astringent and potent smell of disinfectant. Miss Beale breathed it in like an addict. Whatever faults she might later find with the room itself, the adequacy of the teaching equipment, the lighting or the furniture, she never felt other than at home in this intimidating atmosphere.

She bestowed on students and teacher her brief smile of reassurance and encouragement and perched herself on one of the four chairs placed ready at the side of the room. Matron Taylor and Miss Rolfe seated themselves on either side of her as quietly and unobtrusively as possible in the face of Mr Courtney-Briggs's determination to be fussily gallant over pulling out the ladies' chairs. The arrival of the little party, however tactfully arranged, seemed temporarily to have disconcerted the nurse tutor. An inspection was hardly a natural teaching situation, but it was always interesting to see how long it took a tutor to re-establish *rapport* with her class. A first-class teacher, as Miss Beale knew from personal experience, could hold a class's interest even through a heavy bombing raid let alone the visit of a General Nursing Council Inspector; but she did not feel that Mavis Gearing was likely to prove one of that rare and dedicated band. The girl – or woman rather – lacked authority. She had a propitiatory air; she looked as though she might easily simper. And she was a great deal too heavily made up for a woman who should have her mind on less ephemeral arts. But she was, after all, merely the clinical instructor, not a qualified nurse tutor. She was taking the session at short notice and under difficulties. Miss Beale made a mental resolution not to judge her too harshly.

The class, she saw, were to practise feeding a patient by intragastric tube. The student who was to act as patient was already in one of the demonstration beds, her check dress protected by a mackintosh bib, her head supported by the back rest and a bank of pillows. She was a plain girl with a strong, obstinate and oddly mature face, her dull hair drawn back unbecomingly from a high nobbly forehead. She lay there immobile under the harsh strip lighting, looking a little ridiculous but strangely dignified as if concentrating on some private world and dissociating herself from the whole procedure by an effort of will. Suddenly it occurred to Miss Beale that the girl might be frightened. The thought was ridiculous but it persisted. She found herself suddenly unwilling to watch that resolute face. Irritated by her own unreasonable sensitivity, she turned her attention to the nurse tutor.

Sister Gearing cast an apprehensive and interrogative glance at the Matron, received a confirmatory nod and resumed her lesson.

'Nurse Pearce is acting the part of our patient this morning. We have just been going through her history. She is Mrs Stokes, the fifty-year-old mother of four children, wife of a council refuse collector. She has had a larynectomy for the treatment of cancer.' She turned to a student sitting on her right.

'Nurse Dakers, will you please describe Mrs Stokes's treatment so far.'

Nurse Dakers dutifully began. She was a pale, thin girl who blushed unbecomingly as she spoke. It was difficult to hear her but she knew her facts and presented them well. A conscientious little thing, thought Miss Beale, not outstandingly intelligent, perhaps, but hard-working and reliable. It was a pity that no one had done anything about her acne. She retained her air of bright professional interest whilst Nurse Dakers propounded the fictional medical history of Mrs Stokes and took the opportunity of a close look at the remaining students in the class, making her customary private assessment of their characters and ability.

The influenza epidemic had certainly taken its toll. There was a total of seven girls only in the demonstration room. The two who were standing one on each side of the demonstration bed made an immediate impression. They were obviously identical twins, strong, ruddy-faced girls, with copper-coloured hair clumped in a thick fringe above remarkable blue eyes. Their caps, the pleated crowns as saucers, were perched well forward, the two immense wings of white linen jutting behind. Miss Beale, who knew from her own student days what could be done with a couple of white-tipped hat pins, was nevertheless intrigued by the art which could so firmly attach such a bizarre and unsubstantial edifice on such a springing bush of hair. The John Carpendar uniform struck her as interestingly out of date. Nearly every hospital she visited had replaced these old-fashioned winged caps with the smaller American type which was easier to wear, quicker to make up, and cheaper to buy and launder. Some hospitals, to Miss Beale's regret, were even issuing disposable paper caps. But a hospital's nurse uniform was always jealously defended and changed with reluctance and the John Carpendar was obviously wedded to tradition. Even the uniform dresses were slightly old-fashioned. The twins' plump and speckled arms bulged from sleeves of check pink gingham which reminded Miss Beale of her own student days. Their skirt lengths paid no concession to modern fashion and their sturdy feet were planted in low-heeled black lace-up shoes.

She glanced quickly at the remaining students. There was a calm, bespectacled girl with a plain intelligent face. Miss Beale's immediate reaction was that she would be glad to have her on any ward. Next to her sat a dark, sulky-looking girl, rather over made-up and assuming an air of careful disinterest in the demonstration. Rather common, thought Miss Beale. Miss Beale, to her superiors' occasional embarrassment, was fond of such unfashionable adjectives, used them unashamedly and knew precisely what she meant by them. Her dictum 'Matron recruits a very nice type of girl' meant that they came of respectable middle-class families, had received the benefit of grammar school education, wore their skirts knee length or longer, and were properly aware of the privilege and responsibilities of being a student nurse. The last student in the class was a very pretty girl, her blonde hair worn in a fringe as low as her eyebrows above a pert, contemporary face. She was attractive enough for a recruiting poster, thought Miss Beale, but somehow it was the last face one would choose. While she was wondering why, Nurse Dakers came to the end of her recital.

'Right, Nurse,' said Sister Gearing. 'So we are faced with the problem of a post-operative patient, already seriously undernourished and now unable to take food by mouth. That means what? Yes, Nurse?'

'Intra-gastric or rectal feeding, Sister.'

It was the dark sulky-looking girl who answered, her voice carefully repressing any note of enthusiasm or even interest. Certainly not an agreeable girl, thought Miss Beale.

There was a murmur from the class. Sister Gearing raised an interrogative eyebrow. The spectacled student said:

'Not rectal feeding, Sister. The rectum can't absorb sufficient nourishment. Intra-gastric feeding by the mouth or nose.'

'Right, Nurse Goodale, and that's what the surgeon has ordered for Mrs Stokes. Will you carry on please, Nurse. Explain what you are doing at each step.'

One of the twins drew the trolley forward and demonstrated her tray of requirements: the gallipot containing sodium bicarbonate mixture for cleaning mouth or nostrils; the polythene funnel and eight inches of tubing to fit it; the connector; the lubricant; the kidney bowl with the tongue spatula, tongue forceps and gag. She held up the Jacques oesophageal tube. It dangled from her freckled hand obscenely like a yellow snake.

'Right, Nurse,' encouraged Sister Gearing. 'Now the feed. What are you giving her?'

'Actually, it's just warm milk, Sister.'

'But if we were dealing with a real patient?'

The twin hesitated. The spectacled student said with calm authority: 'We could add soluble protein, eggs, vitamin preparations and sugar.'

'Right. If tube feeding is to continue for more than forty-eight hours we must ensure that the diet is adequate in calories, protein and vitamins. At what temperature are you giving the feed, Nurse?'

'Body temperature, Sister, 38°C.'

'Correct. And as your patient is conscious and able to swallow we are giving her this feed by mouth. Don't forget to reassure your patient, Nurse. Explain simply to her what you are going to do and why. Remember this, girls, never begin any nursing procedure without telling your patient what is to happen.'

They were third-year students, thought Miss Beale. They should know this by now. But the twin, who no doubt would have coped easily enough with a real patient, found it embarrassingly difficult to explain her procedure to a fellow student. Suppressing a giggle she muttered a few words at the rigid figure in the bed and almost thrust the oesophageal tube at her. Nurse Pearce, still gazing fixedly ahead, felt for the tube with her left hand and guided it into her mouth. Then shutting her eyes she swallowed. There was a convulsive spasm of the throat muscles. She paused to take breath, and then swallowed again. The tube shortened. It was very silent in the demonstration room. Miss Beale was aware that she felt unhappy but was unsure why. It was a little unusual perhaps for gastric feeding to be practised on a student in this way but it was not unknown. In a hospital it might be more usual for a doctor to pass the tube but a nurse might well have to take the responsibility; it was better to learn on each other than on a seriously ill patient and the demonstration doll wasn't really a satisfactory substitute for a living subject. She had once acted as the patient in her own training school and had found swallowing the tube unexpectedly easy. Watching the convulsive movements of Nurse Pearce's throat and swallowing in an unconscious sympathy she could almost recall, after thirty years, the sudden chill as the tube slid over the soft palate and the faint shock of surprise at the ease of it all. But there was something pathetic and disturbing about that rigid white-faced figure on the bed, eyes tight closed, bibbed like a baby, the thin tube dragging and wriggling like a worm from the corner of her mouth. Miss Beale felt that she was watching gratuitous suffering, that the whole demonstration was an outrage. For a second she had to fight an urge to protest.

One of the twins was now attaching a 20-ml. syringe to the end of the tube, ready to aspirate some of the gastric juices to test that the end of the tube had reached the stomach. The girl's hands were quite steady. Perhaps it was just Miss Beale's imagination that the room was preternaturally silent. She glanced across at Miss Taylor. The Matron had her eyes fixed on Nurse Pearce. She was frowning slightly. Her lips moved and she shifted in her seat. Miss Beale wondered if she were about to expostulate. But the Matron made no sound. Mr Courtney-Briggs was leaning forward in his chair, his hands clasping his knees. He was gazing intently, not at Nurse Pearce, but at the drip as if mesmerized by the gentle swing of the tubing. Miss Beale could hear the heavy rasp of his breathing. Miss Rolfe sat bolt upright, her hands folded loosely in her lap, her black eyes expressionless. But Miss Beale saw that they were fixed, not on the girl in the bed, but on the fair pretty student. And for a fleeting second the girl looked back at her, equally expressionless.

The twin who was administering the feed, obviously satisfied that the end of the oesophageal tube was safely in the stomach, lifted the funnel high over Nurse Pearce's head and began slowly to pour the milky mixture down the tube. The class seemed to be holding its breath. And then it happened. There was a squeal, high-pitched, horribly inhuman, and Nurse Pearce precipitated herself from the bed as if propelled by an irresistible force. One second she was lying, immobile, propped against her mound of pillows, the next she was out of bed, teetering forward on arched feet in a parody of a ballet dancer, and clutching ineffectually at the air as if in frantic search of the tubing. And all the time she screamed, perpetually screamed, like a stuck whistle. Miss Beale, aghast, had hardly time to register the contorted face, the foaming lips, before the girl thudded to the floor and writhed there, doubled like a hoop, her forehead touching the ground, her whole body twitching in agony.

One of the students screamed. For a second no one moved. Then there was a rush forward. Sister Gearing tugged at the tube and tore it from the girl's mouth. Mr Courtney-Briggs moved resolutely into the mêlée, his arms wide. Matron and Sister Rolfe bent over the twitching figure hiding her from view. Then Miss Taylor rose and looked round at Miss Beale.

'The students . . . could you look after them please? There's an empty room next door. Keep them together.'

She was trying to keep calm but urgency made her voice sharp. 'Quickly please.'

Miss Beale nodded. The Matron bent again over the convulsed figure. The screaming had stopped now. It was succeeded by a piteous moaning and a dreadful staccato drumming of heels on the wooden floor. Mr Courtney-Briggs took off his coat, threw it to one side, and began to roll up his sleeves.

IV

Muttering gentle encouragement, Miss Beale shepherded the little group of students across the hall. One of them, she was not sure which, said in a high-pitched voice: 'What happened to her? What happened? What went wrong?' But no one replied. They moved in a shocked daze into the room next door. It was at the back of the house, a small, odd-shaped room which had obviously been partitioned from the original high-ceilinged drawing-room and which now served as the Principal Tutor's office. Miss Beale's first glance took in a business-like desk, a bank of green steel filing cabinets, a crowded notice-board, a small pegboard fitted with hooks from which hung a variety of keys, and a chart along the whole of one wall showing the teaching programme and the progress of each individual student. The partition wall cut the mullioned window in half so that the office, unpleasing in its proportions, was also inconveniently dark. One of the students clicked down the switch and the central bar of fluorescence began to flicker into light. Really, thought Miss Beale, her mind clutching desperately at the comfort of its normal preoccupations, it was a most unsuitable room for a Principal Tutor, or for any other tutor, come to that.

This brief remembrance of the purpose of her visit brought a second's comfort. But almost immediately the awful reality of the moment reasserted itself. The students – a pathetic and disorganized little bunch – had crowded together in the middle of the room as if incapable of action. Glancing quickly around, Miss Beale saw that there were only three chairs. For a moment she felt as embarrassed and nonplussed as a hostess who is not sure how she is going to seat all her guests. The concern wasn't altogether irrelevant. She would have to get the girls comfortable and relaxed if there were to be any chance of keeping their minds off what was happening next door; and they might be incarcerated for a long time.

'Come along,' she said brightly. 'Let's move Sister's desk back against the wall, then four of you can perch there. I'll take the desk chair and two of you can have the easy chairs.'

At least it was activity. Miss Beale saw that the thin, fair student was shaking. She helped her into one of the easy chairs and the dark, sulky-looking girl promptly took the other. Trust her to look after number one, thought Miss Beale. She busied herself helping the other students to clear the desk and push it back against the wall. If only she could send one of them to make some tea! Despite her intellectual assent to more modern methods of combating shock, Miss Beale still put her faith in warm strong sweet tea. But there wasn't a chance of any. It wouldn't do to upset and alert the kitchen staff.

'Now suppose we introduce ourselves,' she said encouragingly. 'My name is Miss Muriel Beale. There's no need to tell you I'm a G.N.C. Inspector. I know some of your names but I am not really sure who is who.'

Five pairs of eyes gazed at her with startled incomprehension. But the efficient student – as Miss Beale still thought of her – quietly identified them.

'The twins are Maureen and Shirley Burt. Maureen is the elder by about two minutes and has the most freckles. Otherwise we don't find it easy to tell them apart. Next to Maureen is Julia Pardoe. Christine Dakers is in one armchair and Diane Harper in the other. I'm Madeleine Goodale.'

Miss Beale, never good at remembering names, made her customary mental recapitulation. The Burt twins. Bonny and bouncing. It would be easy enough to remember their name, although impossible to decide which was which. Julia Pardoe. An attractive name for an attractive girl. Very attractive if one liked that blonde, rather feline prettiness. Smiling into the unresponsive violet-eyes, Miss Beale decided that some people, and not all of them men, might like it very much indeed. Madeleine Goodale. A good sensible name for a good sensible girl. She thought she would have no difficulty in remembering Goodale. Christine Dakers. Something very wrong here. The girl had looked ill throughout the brief demonstration and now seemed close to collapse. She had a poor skin, unusually so for a nurse. It was now drained of colour so that the spots around the mouth and over the forehead stood out in an angry rash. She was huddled deep into the armchair, her thin hands alternatively smoothing and plucking at her apron. Nurse Dakers was certainly the most affected of all the group. Perhaps she had been a particular friend of Nurse Pearce. Miss Beale superstitiously made a quick mental amendment of tense. Perhaps she was a particular friend. If only they could get the girl some hot reviving tea!

Nurse Harper, her lipstick and eye-shadow garish on the whitened face, said suddenly: 'There must have been something in the feed.'

The Burt twins turned to her simultaneously. Maureen said:

'Of course there was! Milk.'

'I mean something besides the milk.' She hesitated. 'Poison.'

'But there couldn't be! Shirley and I took a fresh bottle of milk out of the kitchen fridge first thing this morning. Miss Collins was there and saw us. We left it in the demo room and didn't pour it into the measuring jug until just before the demonstration, did we, Shirley?'

'That's right. It was a fresh bottle. We took it at about seven o'clock.'

'And you didn't add anything by mistake?'

'Like what? Of course we didn't.'

The twins spoke in unison, sounding sturdily confident, almost unworried. They knew exactly what they had done and when, and no one, Miss Beale saw, was likely to shake them. They weren't the type to be tormented by unnecessary guilt or fretted by those irrational doubts which afflict less stolid, more imaginative personalities. Miss Beale thought that she understood them very well.

Julia Pardoe said: 'Perhaps someone else mucked about with the feed.'

She looked round at her fellow students from under lowered lids, provocative, a little amused.

Madeleine Goodale said calmly: 'Why should they?'

Nurse Pardoe shrugged and pursued her lips into a little secret smile. She said: 'By accident. Or it might have been a practical joke. Or perhaps it was done on purpose.'

'But that would be attempted murder!' It was Diane Harper who spoke. She sounded incredulous. Maureen Burt laughed.

'Don't be daft, Julia. Who would want to murder Pearce?'

No one replied. The logic was apparently unassailable. It was impossible to imagine anyone wanting to murder Pearce. Pearce, Miss Beale realized, was either of the company of the naturally inoffensive or was too negative a personality to inspire the tormenting hatred which can lead to murder. Then Nurse Goodale said drily: 'Pearce wasn't everyone's cup of tea.'

Miss Beale glanced at the girl, surprised. It was an odd remark to come from Nurse Goodale, a little insensitive in the circumstances, disconcertingly out of character. She noted, too, the use of the past tense. Here was one student who didn't expect to see Nurse Pearce alive again.

Nurse Harper reiterated stoutly: 'It's daft to talk about murder. No one would want to kill Pearce.'

Nurse Pardoe shrugged: 'Perhaps it wasn't meant for Pearce. Jo Fallon was supposed to act as patient today, wasn't she? It was Fallon's name next on the list. If she hadn't been taken ill last night, it would have been Fallon in that bed this morning.'

They were silent. Nurse Goodale turned to Miss Beale.

'She's right. We take it in strict turn to act as patient; it wasn't really Pearce's turn this morning. But Josephine Fallon was taken into the sick bay last night – you've probably heard that we have an influenza epidemic – and Pearce was next on the list. Pearce was taking Fallon's place.'

Miss Beale was momentarily at a loss. She felt that she ought to put a stop to the conversation, that it was her responsibility to keep their minds off the accident, and surely it could only have been an accident. But she didn't know how. Besides, there was a dreadful fascination in getting at the facts. For her, there always had been. Perhaps, too, it was better that the girls should indulge this detached, investigatory interest, rather than sit there making unnatural and ineffective conversation. Already she saw that shock was giving way to that half-ashamed excitement which can follow tragedy, so long, of course, as it is someone else's tragedy.

Julia Pardoe's composed, rather childish voice went on: 'So if the victim was really meant to be Fallon, it couldn't have been one of us, could it? We all knew that Fallon wouldn't be acting the patient this morning.'

Madeleine Goodale said: 'I should think that everyone knew. Everyone at Nightingale House anyway. There was enough talk about it at breakfast.'

They were silent again, considering this new development. Miss Beale noted with interest that there were no protestations that no one would want to murder Fallon. Then Maureen Burt said:

'Fallon can't be all that sick. She was back here in Nightingale House this morning, just after eight-forty. Shirley and I saw her slipping out of the side door just before we went into the demo room after breakfast.'

Nurse Goodale said sharply: 'What was she wearing?' Maureen was unsurprised at this apparently irrelevant question.

'Slacks. Her top coat. That red headscarf she wears. Why?'

Nurse Goodale, obviously shaken and surprised, made an attempt to conceal it. She said:

'She slipped those on before we took her to the sick bay last night. I suppose she came back to fetch something she wanted from her room. But she shouldn't have left the ward. It was stupid. She had a temperature at 103.8 when she was warded. Lucky for her that Sister Brumfett didn't see her.'

Nurse Pardoe said maliciously: 'Funny though, isn't it?' No one replied. It was indeed funny, thought Miss Beale. She recalled her long damp drive from the hospital to the nurse training school. The road was a winding one; obviously there would be a short cut through the trees. But it was a strange journey for a sick girl to make on an early January morning. There must have been some compelling reason to bring her back to Nightingale House. After all, if she did want something from her room there was nothing to prevent her asking for it. Any of the students would gladly have taken it across to the sick bay. And this was the girl who should have played the patient that morning, who should, logically, be lying next door among the tangle of tubes and linen.

Nurse Pardoe said: 'Well, there's one person who knew that Fallon wouldn't be acting patient this morning. Fallon herself.'

Nurse Goodale, white-faced, looked across at her.

'If you want to be stupid and malicious I suppose I can't stop you. But, if I were you, I would stop short of slander.'

Nurse Pardoe looked unconcerned, even a little pleased. Catching sight of her sly, gratified smile, Miss Beale decided that it was time this talking stopped. She was searching for a change of topic when Nurse Dakers said faintly from the depths of her chair: 'I feel sick.'

There was immediate concern. Only Nurse Harper made no move to help. The rest gathered around the girl, glad of the chance to be doing something. Nurse Goodale said: 'I'll take her to the downstairs cloakroom.'

She supported the girl out of the room. To Miss Beale's surprise Nurse Pardoe went with her, their recent antagonism apparently forgotten as they supported Nurse Dakers between them. Miss Beale was left with the Burt twins and Nurse Harper. Another silence fell. But Miss Beale had learned her lesson. She had been unforgivably irresponsible. There was to be no more talk of death or murder. While they were here and in her charge they might as well work. She gazed sternly at Nurse Harper and invited her to describe the signs, symptoms and treatment of pulmonary collapse.

Ten minutes later the absent three returned. Nurse Dakers still looked pale but was composed. It was Nurse Goodale who looked worried. As if unable to keep it to herself, she said:

'The bottle of disinfectant is missing from the lavatory. You know the one I mean. It's always kept there on the little shelf. Pardoe and I couldn't find it.'

Nurse Harper interrupted her bored but surprisingly competent recital and said:

'You mean that bottle of milky-looking mixture? It was there after supper last night.'

'That's a long time ago. Has anyone been in that loo this morning?'

Apparently no one had. They looked at each other in silence.

It was then that the door opened. Matron came quietly in and shut it behind her. There was a creak of starched linen as the twins slipped from the desk and stood to attention. Nurse Harper rose gracelessly from her chair. All of them turned towards Miss Taylor.

'Children,' she said, and the unexpected and gentle word told them the truth before she spoke.

'Children, Nurse Pearce died a few minutes ago. We don't yet know how or why, but when something inexplicable like this happens we have to call the police. The Hospital Secretary is doing that now. I want you to be brave and sensible as I know you will be. Until the police arrive, I think it would be better if we don't talk about what has happened. You will collect your textbooks and Nurse Goodale will take you to wait in my sitting-room. I shall be ordering some strong hot coffee and it will be brought up to you soon. Is that understood?'

There was a subdued murmur of, 'Yes, Matron.'

Miss Taylor turned to Miss Beale.

'I'm so very sorry, but it will mean your waiting here too.'

'Of course, Matron, I quite understand.'

Across the heads of the students their eyes met in bewildered speculation and wordless sympathy.

But Miss Beale was a little horrified to remember afterwards the banality and irrelevance of her first conscious thought.

'This must be the shortest inspection on record. What on earth will I say to the General Nursing Council?'

V

A few minutes earlier the four people in the demonstration room had straightened up and looked at each other, white-faced, utterly exhausted. Heather Pearce was dead. She was dead by any criteria, legal or medical. They had known it for the last five minutes but had worked on, doggedly and without speaking, as if there were still a chance that the flabby heart would pulse again into life. Mr Courtney-Briggs had taken off his coat to work on the girl and the front of his waistcoat was heavily stained with blood. He stared at the thickening stain, brow creased, nose fastidiously wrinkled, almost as if blood were an alien substance to him. The heart massage had been messy as well as ineffectual. Surprisingly messy for Mr Courtney-Briggs, the Matron thought. But surely the attempt had been justified? There hadn't been time to get her over to the theatre. It was a pity that Sister Gearing had pulled out the oesophageal tube. It had, perhaps, been a natural reaction but it might have cost Pearce her only chance. While the tube was in place they could at least have tried an immediate stomach wash-out. But an attempt to pass another tube by the nostril had been frustrated by the girl's agonized spasms and, by the time these had ceased, it was too late and Mr Courtney-Briggs had been forced to open the chest wall and try the only measure left to him. Mr Courtney-Briggs's heroic efforts were well known. It was only a pity that they left the body looking so pathetically mangled and the demonstration room stinking like an abattoir. These things were better conducted in an operating theatre, shrouded and dignified by the paraphernalia of ritual surgery.

He was the first to speak.

'This wasn't a natural death. There was something other than milk in that feed. Well, that's obvious to all of us I should have thought. We'd better call the police. I'll get on to the Yard. I know someone there, as it happens. One of the Assistant Commissioners.'

He always did know someone, thought the Matron. She felt the need to oppose him. Shock had left an aftermath of irritation and, irrationally, it focused on him. She said calmly:

'The local police are the ones to call and I think that the Hospital Secretary should do it. I'll get Mr Hudson on the house telephone now. They'll call in the Yard if they think it necessary. I can't think why it should be. But that decision is for the Chief Constable, not for us.'

She moved over to the wall telephone, carefully walking round the crouched figure of Miss Rolfe. The Principal Tutor was still on her knees. She looked, thought the Matron, rather like a character from a Victorian melodrama with her smouldering eyes in a deathly white face, her black hair a little dishevelled under the frilly cap, and those reeking hands. She was turning them over slowly and studying the red mass with a detached, speculative interest as if she, too, found it difficult to believe that the blood was real. She said:

'If there's a suspicion of foul play ought we to move the body?'

Mr Courtney-Briggs said sharply:

'I have no intention of moving the body.'

'But we can't leave her here, not like this!' Miss Gearing was almost weeping in protest. The surgeon glared at her.

'My dear woman, the girl's dead! Dead! What does it matter where we have the body? She can't feel. She can't know. For God's sake don't start being sentimental about death. The indignity is that we die at all, not what happens to our bodies.'

He turned brusquely and went over to the window. Sister Gearing made a movement as if to follow him, and then sank into the nearest chair and began to cry softly like a snuffling animal. No one took any notice of her. Sister Rolfe got stiffly to her feet. Holding her hands raised in front of her in the ritual gesture of an operating theatre nurse she walked over to a sink in the corner, nudged on the tap with her elbow, and began to wash her hands. At the wall-mounted telephone the Matron was dialling a five-digit number. They heard her calm voice.

'Is that the Hospital Secretary's office? Is Mr Hudson there? It's Matron.' There was a pause. 'Good morning, Mr Hudson. I am speaking from the ground floor demonstration room in Nightingale House. Could you please come over immediately? Yes. Very urgent. I'm afraid something tragic and horrible has happened and it will be necessary for you to telephone the police. No, I'd rather not tell you on the telephone. Thank you.' She replaced the receiver and said quietly: 'He's coming at once. He'll have to put the Vice-Chairman in the picture, too – it's unfortunate that Sir Marcus is in Israel – but the first thing is to get the police. And now I had better tell the other students.'

Sister Gearing was making an attempt to control herself. She blew loudly into her handkerchief, replaced it in her uniform pocket, and raised a blotched face.

'I'm sorry. It's the shock, I suppose. It's just that it was all so horrible. Such an appalling thing to happen. And the first time I've taken a class too! And everyone sitting and watching it like that. The other students as well. Such a horrible accident.'

'Accident, Sister?' Mr Courtney-Briggs turned from the window. He strode over to her and bent his bull-like head close to hers. His voice was harsh, contemptuous as he almost spat the words into her face. 'Accident? Are you suggesting that a corrosive poison found its way into that feed by accident? Or that a girl in her right mind would choose to kill herself in that particularly horrible way? Come, come, Sister, why not be honest for once? What we've just witnessed was murder!'

TWO

Cease Upon the Midnight

I

It was late in the evening of Wednesday, 28th January, sixteen days after the death of Nurse Pearce and, in the students' sitting-room on the first floor of Nightingale House, Nurse Dakers was writing her mid-week letter to her mother. It was usual for her to finish it in time for the Wednesday evening post but, this week, she had lacked the energy and inclination to settle down to the task. Already the waste-paper basket at her feet held the screwed-up copies of the first two rejected drafts. And now she was trying again.

She was sitting at one of the twin writing-desks in front of the window, her left elbow almost brushing the heavy curtains which shut out the dank blackness of the night, her forearm curled protectively around the writing-pad. Opposite to her, the desk lamp shone on the bent head of Madeleine Goodale, so close that Nurse Dakers could see the clean white scalp at the hair parting and smell the almost imperceptible antiseptic tang of shampoo. Two textbooks were open before Goodale and she was making notes. Nothing, thought Nurse Dakers with resentful envy, was worrying her; nothing in the room or beyond it could disturb her quiet concentration. The admirable and secure Goodale was making sure that the John Carpendar Gold Medal for top marks in the final examination would eventually be pinned on her immaculate apron.

Frightened by the strength of this sudden and shaming antagonism, which she felt must communicate itself to Goodale, Nurse Dakers slid her eyes from the bent head so disconcertingly close to hers and gazed around the room. It was so familiar to her after nearly three years of training that normally she hardly noticed the details of architecture or furnishing. But tonight she saw it with an unexpected clarity, as if it had nothing to do with her or with her life. It was too large to be cosy and was furnished as if it had acquired odd items over the years and taken them to itself. It must once have been an elegant drawing-room, but the walls had long since lost their paper and were now painted and scruffy, due – it was rumoured – for redecoration when money allowed. The ornate fireplace of carved marble and surrounding oak was fitted with a large gas stove, old and ugly in design but still remarkably efficient, hissing a strong heat even into the dark corners of the room. The elegant mahogany table against the far wall with its jumble of magazines might have been bequeathed by John Carpendar himself. But it was scratched and dull now, dusted regularly but rarely polished, its surface scarred and ringed. To the left of the fireplace, in incongruous contrast, stood a large, modern television set, the gift of the Hospital League of Friends. In front of it was an immense cretonne-covered sofa with sagging springs, and a single matching armchair. The rest of the chairs were similar to those in the hospital out-patients' department but were now too old and shabby to be tolerated for the use of patients. The arm-rests of pale wood were grubby; the coloured vinyl seats were stretched and dented and now smelt unpleasantly in the heat from the fire. One of the chairs was empty. It was the red-seated one which Nurse Pearce had invariably used. Scorning the intimacy of the sofa, she would sit there, a little apart from the huddle of students around the television set, watching the screen with careful disinterest as if it were a pleasure she could easily forgo. Occasionally she would drop her eyes to a book in her lap as if the folly presented for her entertainment had become too much to bear. Her presence, thought Nurse Dakers, had always been a little unwelcome and oppressive. The atmosphere of the students' sitting-room had always been lighter, more relaxed without that upright and censorious figure. But the empty chair, the dented seat, was almost worse. Nurse Dakers wished that she had the courage to walk over to it, to swing it into line with the other chairs around the television set and settle herself nonchalantly into its sagging curves, exorcizing once and for all that oppressive ghost. She wondered if the other students felt the same. It was impossible to ask. Were the Burt twins, bunched together in the depths of the sofa, really as absorbed as they appeared by the old gangster film they were watching? They were each knitting one of the heavy sweaters which they invariably wore in winter, their fingers clicking away, their eyes never leaving the screen. Beside them Nurse Fallon lolled in the armchair, one trousered leg swung casually over the arm. It was her first day back in the school after her sick leave and she still looked pale and drawn. Was her mind really on the sleek-haired hero with his tall wide-ribboned and ridiculous trilby, his over-padded shoulders, whose raucous voice, punctuated with gunshots, filled the room? Or was she, too, morbidly conscious of that empty red chair, the dented seat, the rounded ends of the arm-rests polished by Pearce's hand?

Nurse Dakers shivered. The wall clock showed that it was already after nine-thirty. Outside the wind was rising. It was going to be a wild night. In the rare intervals of quiet from the television set she could hear the creaking and sighing of the trees and could picture the last leaves falling softly on grass and path, isolating Nightingale House in a sludge of silence and decay. She forced herself to pick up her pen. She really must get on! Soon it would be time for bed and, one by one, the students would say their good-nights and disappear leaving her to brave alone the poorly lit staircase and the dark corridor beyond. Jo Fallon would still be here of course. She never went to bed until the television programme closed for the night. Then she would make her lonely way upstairs to prepare her nightly hot whisky and lemon. Everyone knew Fallon's invariable habit. But Nurse Dakers felt that she could not face being left alone with Fallon. Hers was the last company she would choose, even in that lonely, frightening walk from the sitting-room to bed.

She began writing again.

'Now please, Mummy, don't keep on worrying about the murder.'

The impossibility of the sentence struck her as soon as she saw the words on the paper. Somehow she must avoid the use of that emotive, blood-stained word. She tried again. 'Now please, Mummy, don't start worrying about the things you read in the paper. There really isn't any need. I'm perfectly safe and happy and no one really believes that Pearce was deliberately killed.'

It wasn't true of course. Some people must think that Pearce had been deliberately killed or why would the police be here? And it was ridiculous to suppose that the poison could have got into the feed by accident or that Pearce, the god-fearing, conscientious and essentially dull Pearce, would have chosen to kill herself in that agonizing and spectacular way. She wrote on:

'We still have the local C.I.D. here, but they don't come in so often now. They have been very kind to us students and I don't think they suspect anyone. Poor Pearce wasn't very popular, but it's ridiculous to think that anyone here would want to harm her.'

Had the police really been kind? she wondered. They had certainly been very correct, very polite. They had produced all the usual reassuring platitudes about the importance of co-operating with them in solving this terrible tragedy, telling the truth at all times, keeping nothing back however trivial and unimportant it might seem. Not one of them had raised his voice; not one had been aggressive or intimidating. And all of them had been frightening. Their very presence in Nightingale House, masculine and confident, had been, like the locked door of the demonstration room, a constant reminder of tragedy and fear. Nurse Dakers had found Inspector Bailey the most frightening of them all. He was a huge, ruddy, moon-faced man whose encouraging and avuncular voice and manner were in unnerving contrast to his cold pig-like eyes. The questioning had gone on and on. She could still recall the interminable sessions, the effort of will necessary to meet that probing gaze.

'Now I'm told that you were the most upset of them all when Nurse Pearce died. She was a particular friend of yours perhaps?'

'No. Not really. Not a particular friend. I hardly knew her.'

'Well, there's a surprise! After nearly three years of training with her? Living and working so closely together, I should have thought that you all got to know each other pretty well.'

She had struggled to explain.

'In some ways we do. We know each other's habits. But I didn't really know what she was like; as a person, I mean.' A silly reply. How else could you know anyone except as a person? And it wasn't true. She had known Pearce. She had known her very well.

'But you got on well together? There hadn't been a quarrel or anything like that? No unpleasantness?'

An odd word, unpleasantness. She had seen again that grotesque figure, teetering forward in agony, fingers scrabbling at the ineffectual air, the thin tubing stretching the mouth like a wound. No, there had been no unpleasantness.

'And the other students? They got on well with Nurse Pearce too? There had been no bad blood as far as you know?'

Bad blood. A stupid expression. What was the opposite? she wondered. Good blood? There was only good blood between us. Pearce's good blood. She had answered:

'She hadn't any enemies as far as I know. And if anyone did dislike her, they wouldn't kill her.'

'So you all tell me. But someone did kill her, didn't they? Unless the poison wasn't intended for Nurse Pearce. She only played the part of the patient by chance. Did you know that Nurse Fallon had been taken ill that night?'

And so it had gone on. Questions about every minute of that last terrible demonstration. Questions about the lavatory disinfectant. The empty bottle, wiped clean of finger-prints, had been quickly found by the police lying among the bushes at the back of the house. Anyone could have thrown it from a bedroom window or bathroom window in the concealing darkness of that January morning. Questions about her movements from the moment of first awakening. The constant reiteration in that minatory voice that nothing should be held back, nothing concealed.

She wondered whether the other students had been as frightened. The Burt twins had seemed merely bored and resigned, obeying the Inspector's sporadic summons with a shrug of the shoulders and a weary, 'Oh, God, not again!' Nurse Goodale had said nothing when she was called for questioning and nothing afterwards. Nurse Fallon had been equally reticent. It was known that Inspector Bailey had interviewed her in the sick bay as soon as she was well enough to be seen. No one knew what had happened at that interview. It was rumoured that Fallon had admitted returning to Nightingale House early in the morning of the crime but had refused to say why. That would be very like Fallon. And now she had returned to Nightingale House to rejoin her set. So far she hadn't even mentioned Pearce's death. Nurse Dakers wondered if and when she would; and, morbidly sensitive to the hidden meaning in every word, struggled on with her letter:

'We haven't used the demonstration room since Nurse Pearce's death but otherwise the set is continuing to work according to plan. Only one of the students, Diane Harper, has left the school. Her father came to fetch her two days after Nurse Pearce died and the police didn't seem to mind her leaving. We all thought it was silly of her to give up so near to her finals but her father has never been keen on her training as a nurse and she is engaged to be married anyway, so I suppose she thought it didn't matter. No one else is thinking of leaving and there really isn't the slightest danger. So please, darling, do stop worrying about me. Now I must tell you about tomorrow's programme.'

There was no need to go on drafting now. The rest of the letter would be easy. She read over what she had written and decided that it would do. Taking a fresh sheet of paper from the pad she began to write the final letter. With any luck she would just get it finished before the film ended and the twins put away their knitting and went to bed.

She scribbled quickly on and, half an hour later, her letter finished, saw with relief that the film had come to the last holocaust and the final embrace. At the same moment Nurse Goodale removed her reading spectacles, looked up from her work, and closed her book. The door opened and Julia Pardoe appeared.

'I'm back,' she announced, and yawned. 'It was a lousy film. Anyone making tea?' No one answered but the twins stubbed their knitting needles into the balls of wool and joined her at the door, switching off the television on their way. Pardoe would never bother to make tea if she could find someone else to do it and the twins usually obliged. As she followed them out of the sitting-room Nurse Dakers looked back at the silent, immobile figure of Fallon alone now with Madeleine Goodale. She had a sudden impulse to speak to Fallon to welcome her back to the school, to ask after her health, or simply to say good night. But the words seemed to stick in her throat, the moment passed, and the last thing she saw as she closed the door behind her was Fallon's pale and individual face, blank eyes still fixed on the television set as if unaware that the screen was dead.

II

In a hospital, time itself is documented, seconds measured in a pulse beat, the drip of blood or plasma; minutes in the stopping of a heart; hours in the rise and fall of a temperature chart, the length of an operation. When the events of the night of 28th–29th January came to be documented there were few of the protagonists at the John Carpendar Hospital who were unaware what they had been doing or where they were at any particular moment of their waking hours. They might not choose to tell the truth, but at least they knew where the truth lay.

It was a night of violent but erratic storm, the wind varying in intensity and even in direction from hour to hour. At ten o'clock it was little more than a sobbing *obbligato* among the elms. An hour later it suddenly reached a crescendo of fury. The great elms around Nightingale House cracked and groaned under the onslaught, while the wind screamed among them like the cachination of devils. Along the deserted paths, the banks of dead leaves, still heavy with rain, shifted sluggishly then broke apart into drifts and rose in wild swirls like demented insects, to glue themselves against the black barks of the trees. In the operating theatre at the top of the hospital Mr Courtney-Briggs demonstrated his imperturbability in the face of crisis by muttering to his attendant registrar that it was a wild night before bending his head again to the satisfying contemplation of the intriguing surgical problem which throbbed between the retracted lips of the wound. Below him in the silent and dimly lit wards the patients muttered and turned in their sleep as if conscious of the tumult outside. The radiographer, who had been called from home to take urgent X-rays of Mr Courtney-Briggs's patient, replaced the covers on the apparatus, switched out the lights and wondered whether her small car would hold the road. The night nurses moved silently among their patients testing the windows, drawing the curtains more closely as if to keep out some threatening and alien force. The porter on duty in the main gate lodge shifted uneasily in his chair then rose cramped to his feet and put a couple more chunks of coal on the fire. He felt in need of warmth and comfort in his isolation. The little house seemed to shake with every gust of the wind.

But shortly before midnight the storm abated, as if sensing the approach of the witching hour, the dead of night when the pulse of man beats slowest and the dying patient slips most easily into the last oblivion. There was an eerie silence for about five minutes, succeeded by a soft rhythmic moaning as the wind swooped and sighed among the trees as if exhausted by its own fury. Mr Courtney-Briggs, the operation completed, peeled off his gloves and made his way into the surgeons' changing-room. As soon as he was disrobed he made a telephone call from the wall instrument to the Sisters' floor at Nightingale House and asked Sister Brumfett, the Sister in charge of the private ward, to return to the ward to supervise the care of his patient for the first critical hour. He noted with satisfaction that the wind had dropped. She could make her own way through the grounds as she had gone at his bidding countless times before. He need feel under no obligation to fetch her in his car.

Less than five minutes later Sister Brumfett plodded resolutely through the trees, her cloak folded around her like a flag whipped close to a flag pole, her hood drawn down over the frilly Sister's cap. It was curiously peaceful in this brief interlude of the storm. She moved silently over the sodden grass, feeling the pull of the rain-soaked earth through the thick sole of her shoes while, from time to time, a thin branch, torn by the storm, broke loose from its last thread of bark and thudded with gentle inadvertence at her feet. By the time she had gained the peace of the private ward and was helping the third-year student make up the post-operative bed and prepare the stand ready for the blood drip, the wind was rising again. But Sister Brumfett, absorbed in her task, no longer noticed it.

Shortly after half past twelve Albert Colgate, the porter on night duty in the main lodge, who was nodding over his evening paper, was jerked into consciousness by a band of light sweeping across the lodge window and the purr of an approaching car. It must, he thought, be Mr Courtney-Briggs's Daimler. So the operation was over. He expected the car to sweep out of the main gates but unexpectedly it stopped. There were two peremptory hoots on the horn. Muttering, the porter thrust his arms into his overcoat and made his way out of the lodge door. Mr Courtney-Briggs wound down the window and shouted at him through the wind.

'I tried to get out of the Winchester gate but there's a tree down across the path. I thought I'd better report it. Get it seen to as soon as you can.'

The porter thrust his head through the car window encountering an immediate and luxurious smell of cigar smoke, after-shave lotion and leather. Mr Courtney-Briggs recoiled slightly from his nearness. The porter said:

'That'll be one of those old elms no doubt, sir. I'll report it first thing in the morning. There's nothing I can do tonight, sir, not in this storm.'

Mr Courtney-Briggs began to wind up the window. Colgate's head made a sudden withdrawal.

The surgeon said: 'There's no need to do anything tonight. I've tied my white scarf on one of the boughs. I doubt whether anyone will use that road until the morning. If they do, they'll see the scarf. But you might warn anyone who drives in this way. Good night, Colgate.'

The large car purred out of the front gate and Colgate made his way back into the lodge. Meticulously he noted the time by the wall clock over the fireplace and made a record in his book. '12.32 Mr Courtney-Briggs reports fallen tree across the Winchester Road path.'

He had settled again into his chair and taken up his paper before the thought struck him that it was odd that Mr Courtney-Briggs should have tried to drive out through the Winchester gate. It wasn't on his quickest route home and it was a road he seldom used. Mr Courtney-Briggs invariably used the front entrance. Presumably, thought Colgate, he had a key to the Winchester Road gate. Mr Courtney-Briggs had a key to most parts of the hospital. But it was odd all the same.

Just before two o'clock on the silent second floor of Nightingale

House, Maureen Burt stirred in her sleep, muttered incoherently through her moist pursed lips and awoke to the disagreeable awareness that three cups of tea before bed had been two too many. She lay still for a moment, sleepily aware of the groaning of the storm, wondered whether she might not after all manage to get to sleep again, realized that her discomfort was too great to be reasonably borne and felt for the switch of her bedside lamp. The light was instantaneous and blinding, shocking her into full consciousness. She wriggled her feet into her bedroom slippers, threw her dressing-gown around her shoulders and padded out into the corridor. As she quietly closed her bedroom door behind her a sudden gust of wind billowed out the curtains at the far corridor window. She went across to shut it. Through the agitated tracery of boughs and their leaping shadows on the window-pane she could see the hospital riding the storm like a great ship at anchor, the ward windows only faintly luminous in comparison with the vertical line of brightly lit eyes marking the Sisters' offices and ward kitchens. She shut down the window carefully and, reeling slightly with sleep, felt her way down the passage to the cloakroom. Less than a minute later she came out again into the corridor, pausing momentarily to accustom her eyes to the gloom. From the confusion of shadows at the top of the stairs a deeper shadow detached itself, moved forward and was revealed as a cloaked and hooded figure. Maureen was not a nervous girl and in her somnolent state was conscious only of surprise that someone else should be awake and about. She saw at once that it was Sister Brumfett. Two piercing bespectacled eyes peered at her through the gloom. The Sister's voice was unexpectedly sharp.

'It's one of the Burt twins, isn't it? What are you doing here? Is anyone else up?'

'No, Sister. At least I don't think so. I've just been to the lavatory.'

'Oh I see. Well, as long as everyone's all right. I thought that the storm might have disturbed you all. I've just come back from my ward. One of Mr Courtney-Briggs's patients had a relapse and he had to operate urgently.'

'Yes, Sister,' said Nurse Burt, uncertain what else was expected of her. She was surprised that Sister Brumfett should bother to explain her presence to a mere student nurse, and she watched a little uncertainly as the Sister drew her long cloak more firmly around her and stumped briskly down the corridor towards the far stairs. Her own room was on the floor above, immediately next to Matron's flat. When she reached the bottom of the stairs, Sister Brumfett turned and seemed about to speak. It was at that moment that Shirley Burt's door opened slowly, and a tousled red head appeared.

'What's up?' it inquired sleepily.

Sister Brumfett walked towards them.

'Nothing, Nurse. I'm just on my way back to bed. I've come from my ward. And Maureen had to get up to go to the lavatory. There's nothing to worry about.'

Shirley gave no impression that she was or ever had been worried. She now trotted out on to the landing, pulling her dressing-gown around her. Resigned and a little complacent, she said:

'When Maureen wakes up I do too. We've always been like that ever since we were babies. You ask Mum!' A little unsteady with sleep but not ungratified that the family theurgy still worked, she closed her bedroom door behind her with the finality of one who, being up, intends to stay up.

'No use trying to get off again in this wind. I'm going to brew some cocoa. Can we bring you a mug, Sister? It'd help you to sleep.'

'No, thank you, Nurse. I don't think I shall have any trouble in sleeping. Be as quiet as you can. You don't want to disturb the others. And don't get cold.' She turned again towards the stairs. Maureen said: 'Fallon's awake. At least her bedside lamp's still on.'

The three of them looked down the corridor to where an eye of light from Nurse Fallon's keyhole pierced the darkness and threw a small luminous shadow on the linenfold panelling opposite.

Shirley said: 'We'll take her a mug then. She's probably awake and reading. Come on, Maureen! Good night, Sister.'

They shuffled off together down the corridor to the small utility room at the end. After a second's pause Sister Brumfett, who had been looking steadily after them, her face rigid and expressionless, turned finally towards the stairs and made her way up to bed.

Exactly one hour later but unheard and unrecorded by anyone in Nightingale House, a weakened pane of glass in the conservatory which had rattled spasmodically throughout the night, fell inwards to explode into splinters on the tessellated floor. The wind rushed in through the aperture like a questing animal. Its cold breath rustled the magazines on the wicker tables, lifted the fronds of the palms and sent the fern leaves gently waving. Finally it found the long white cupboard centred under the plant shelves. Early in the evening, the door had been left ajar by the desperate and hurried visitor who had thrust a hand into the cupboard depths. All night the door had stayed open, motionless on its hinges. But now the wind set it gently swinging to and fro, then as if wearying of the game, finally closed it with a soft, decisive thud.

And everything living under the roof of Nightingale House slept.

III

Nurse Dakers was woken by the whirr of the bedside alarm clock. The faintly luminous dial showed the time as 6.15. Even with the curtains drawn back the room was still completely dark. The square of faint light came, as she knew, not from the door but from the distant lights of the hospital where already the night staff would be taking round the first morning cups of tea. She lay still for a moment, adjusting to her own wakefulness, putting out tentative feelers to the day. She had slept well despite the storm of which she had been only briefly aware. She realized with a spring of joy that she could actually face the day with confidence. The misery and apprehension of the previous evening, of the previous weeks, seemed to have lifted. It seemed now no more than the effect of tiredness and temporary depression. She had passed down a tunnel of misery and insecurity since Pearce's death but this morning, miraculously, she had come out into daylight again. It was like Christmas morning in childhood. It was the beginning of a summer holiday from school. It was waking refreshed at the end of a febrile illness with the comfortable knowledge that Mummy was there and that all the solaces of convalescence lay ahead. It was familiar life restored.

The day shone before her. She catalogued its promises and pleasures. In the morning there would be the materia-medica lecture. This was important. She had always been weak on drugs and dosages. Then, after the coffee break, Mr Courtney-Briggs would give his third-year surgery seminar. It was a privilege that a surgeon of his eminence should take so much trouble with the student nurse training. She was a little afraid of him, particularly of his sharp staccato questions. But this morning she would be brave and speak up confidently. Then in the afternoon the hospital bus would take the set to the local maternity and child welfare clinic to watch the local authority staff at work. This, too, was important to someone who hoped in time to become a district nurse. She lay for a few moments contemplating this gratifying programme then she got out of bed, shuffled her feet into her slippers, struggled into her cheap dressing-gown and made her way along the passage to the students' utility room.

The Nightingale nurses were called promptly at seven each morning by one of the maids, but most students, accustomed to early waking when on the wards, set their alarm clocks at six-thirty to give themselves time for tea-making and gossip. The early arrivals were already there. The little room was brightly lit, cheerfully domestic, smelling, as always, of tea, boiled milk and detergent. The scene was reassuringly normal. The Burt twins were there, faces still puffy from sleep, each twin stoutly cocooned into a bright red dressing-gown. Maureen was carrying her portable wireless tuned to Radio 2 and was gently jerking hips and shoulders to the rhythm of the B.B.C.'s early morning syncopation. Her twin was setting their two immense mugs on a tray and rummaging in a tin for biscuits. The only other student present was Madeleine Goodale who, clad in an ancient plaid dressing-gown, was watching, teapot in hand, for the first spurt of steam from the kettle. In her mood of optimism and relief, Nurse Dakers could have hugged them all.

'Where's Fallon this morning?' asked Madeleine Goodale with no great interest.

Nurse Fallon was a notoriously late riser, but she was usually one of the first to make tea. It was her habit to carry it back to enjoy at leisure in bed, where she would stay until the last possible moment consistent with presenting herself at breakfast on time. But this morning her personal teapot and the matching cup and saucer were still on the cupboard shelf beside the canister of China tea which Fallon preferred to the strong brown brew which the rest of the set considered necessary before they could face the day.

'I'll give her a call,' suggested Nurse Dakers, happy to be of use and longing to celebrate her release from the strain of the last few weeks by general benevolence.

'Wait a moment, then you can take her a cuppa out of my pot,' said Maureen.

'She won't like Indian tea. I'll see if she's awake and just let her know the kettle's on the boil.'

For a moment it occurred to Nurse Dakers to make Fallon's tea for her. But the impulse faded. It was not that Fallon was particularly temperamental or unpredictable, but somehow people did not interfere with her personal things nor expect her to share them. She had few possessions but they were expensive, elegant, carefully chosen and so much part of her *persona* that they seemed sacrosanct.

Nurse Dakers almost ran along the passage to Fallon's room. The door was unlocked. That did not surprise her. Ever since one of the students had been taken ill in the night some years ago and had been too weak to creep across the room to unlock the door, there had been a rule forbidding girls to lock themselves in at night. Since Pearce's death one or two had taken to turning their keys, and if the Sisters suspected it they said nothing. Perhaps they, too, slept more soundly behind locked doors. But Fallon had not been afraid.

The curtains were closely drawn. The bedside lamp was on but with the adjustable shade tilted so that it threw a pale moon on the far wall and left the bed in shadow. There was a tangle of black hair on the pillow. Nurse Dakers felt along the wall for the light switch and paused before clicking it on. Then she pressed it down very gently as if it were possible softly and gradually to illuminate the room and spare Fallon that first fierce wakening. The room blazed into light. She blinked in the unexpected glare. Then she moved very quietly across to the bed. She didn't scream or faint. She stood absolutely still for a moment looking down at Fallon's body, and smiling a little as if surprised. She had no doubt that Fallon was dead. The eyes were still wide open but they were cold and opaque, like the eyes of dead fish. Nurse Dakers bent down and stared into them as if willing them into brightness or seeking in vain some trace of her own reflection. Then she slowly turned and left the room, switching off the light and closing the door behind her. She swayed like a sleepwalker along the passage, steadying her hands against the wall.

At first the students didn't notice her return. Then three pairs of eyes were suddenly fixed on her, three figures stood frozen in a tableau of puzzled inquiry. Nurse Dakers leaned against the door post and opened her mouth soundlessly. The words wouldn't come. Something seemed to have happened to her throat. Her whole jaw was trembling uncontrollably and her tongue was stuck to the roof of her mouth. Her eyes pleaded with them. It seemed minutes while they watched her struggle. When the words did come she sounded calm, gently surprised.

'It's Fallon. She's dead.'

She smiled like someone waking from a dream, patiently explaining: 'Someone's murdered Fallon.'

The room emptied. She wasn't aware of their concerted dash down the corridor. She was alone. The kettle was screeching now, the lid rattling under the force of the steam. Carefully she turned down the gas, frowning with concentration. Very slowly, like a child entrusted with a precious task, she took down the canister, the elegant teapot, the matching cup and saucer, and humming gently to herself, made Fallon's early morning tea.

THREE
Strangers in the House

I

'The pathologist is here, sir.'

A detective constable put his cropped head round the bedroom door and raised an interrogative eyebrow.

Chief Superintendent Adam Dalgliesh turned from his examination of the dead girl's clothes, his six feet two inches uncomfortably trapped between the foot of the bed and the wardrobe door. He looked at his watch. It was eight minutes past ten. Sir Miles Honeyman, as always, had made good time.

'Right, Fenning. Ask him to be good enough to wait for a moment, will you? We'll be finished in here in a minute. Then some of us can clear out and make room for him.'

The head disappeared. Dalgliesh closed the wardrobe door and managed to squeeze himself between it and the foot of the bed. Certainly there was no room for a fourth person at present. The huge bulk of the fingerprint man occupied the space between the bedside table and the window as, bent almost double, he brushed charcoal carefully on to the surface of the whisky bottle, turning it by its cork. Beside the bottle stood a glass plate bearing the dead girl's prints, the whorls and composites plainly visible.

'Anything there?' asked Dalgliesh.

The print man paused and peered more closely.

'A nice set of prints coming up, sir. They're hers all right. Nothing else, though. It looks as if the chap who sold it gave the bottle the usual wipe over before wrapping. It'll be interesting to see what we get from the beaker.'

He cast a jealously possessive glance at it as it lay where it had fallen from the girl's hand, lightly poised in a curve of the counterpane. Not until the last photograph had been taken would it be yielded up for his examination.

He bent again to his task on the bottle. Behind him the Yard photographer manoeuvred his tripod and camera – new Cambo monorail, Dalgliesh noticed – to the right-hand foot of the bed. There was a click, an explosion of light, and the image of the dead girl leapt up at them and lay suspended in air, burning itself on Dalgliesh's retina. Colour and shape were intensified and distorted in that cruel, momentary glare. The long black hair was a tangled wig against the whiteness of the pillows; the glazed eyes were ex-ophthalmic marbles, as if rigor mortis were squeezing them out of their sockets; the skin was very white and smooth, looking repulsive to the touch, an artificial membrane, tough and impermeable as vinyl. Dalgliesh blinked, erasing the image of a witch's play-thing, a grotesque puppet casually tossed against the pillow. When he next looked at her she was again a dead girl on a bed; no more and no less. Twice more the distorted image leapt up at him and lay petrified in air as the photographer took two pictures with the Polaroid Land camera to give Dalgliesh the immediate prints for which he always asked. Then it was over. 'That was the last. I'm through, sir,' said the photographer. 'I'll let Sir Miles in now.' He put his head around the door while the print man, grunting with satisfaction, lovingly lifted the drinking beaker from the counterpane with a pair of forceps and set it alongside the whisky bottle.

Sir Miles must have been waiting on the landing for he trotted in immediately, a familiar rotund figure with his immense head of black curling hair and eager beady eyes. He brought with him an air of music hall *bonhomie* and, as always, a faint smell of sour sweat. He was unfretted by the delay. But then Sir Miles, God's gift to forensic pathology or an amateur mountebank as you chose to take him, did not easily take offence. He had gained much of his reputation and also, possibly, his recent knighthood by adhering to the principle that you should never willingly offend anyone, however humble. He greeted the departing photographer and the fingerprint officer as if they were old friends, and Dalgliesh by his Christian name. But the socialities were perfunctory; his preoccupation preceded him like a miasma as he wriggled up close to the bed.

Dalgliesh despised him as a ghoul; hardly, he admitted, a rational cause for dislike. In a perfectly organized world, foot fetishists would, no doubt, become chiropodists; hair fetishists, hairdressers; and ghouls, morbid anatomists. It was surprising that so few of them did. But Sir Miles laid himself open to the implication. He approached each new corpse with eagerness, almost with glee; his macabre jokes had been heard at half the dining clubs in London; he was an expert in death who obviously enjoyed his work. Dalgliesh felt inhibited in his company by the consciousness of his dislike for the man. Antipathy seemed to crackle from him. But Sir Miles was oblivious of it. He liked himself too well to conceive that other men might find him less lovable, and this endearing naïvety gave him a kind of charm. Even those colleagues who most deplored his conceit, his publicity seeking, and the irresponsibility of most of his public utterances, found it hard to dislike him as much as they felt they should. Women were said to find him attractive. Perhaps he had a morbid fascination for them. Certainly, his was the infectious good humour of a man who necessarily finds the world an agreeable place since it contains himself.

He always tut-tutted over a body. He did so now, plucking back the sheet with a curiously mincing gesture of his pudgy fingers. Dalgliesh walked over to the window and gazed out at the tracery of boughs through which the distant hospital, still lit up, gleamed like an insubstantial palace suspended in air. He could hear the faint rustling of bed linen. Sir Miles would only be making a preliminary examination, but even to think of those pudgy fingers insinuating themselves into the body's tender orifices was enough to make one hope for a peaceful death in one's own bed. The real job would be done later on the mortuary table, that aluminium sink with its grim accessories of drains and sprays on which Josephine Fallon's body would be systematically dismembered in the cause of justice, or science, or curiosity, or what you will. And afterwards, Sir Miles's mortuary attendant would earn his guinea by stitching it up again into a decent semblance of humanity so that the family could view it without trauma. If there were a family. He wondered who, if anyone, would be Fallon's official mourners. Superficially there was nothing in her room – no photographs, no letters – to suggest that she had close ties with any living soul.

While Sir Miles sweated and muttered, Dalgliesh made a second tour of the room, carefully avoiding watching the pathologist. He knew this squeamishness to be irrational and was half ashamed of it. Post-mortem examinations did not upset him. It was this impersonal examination of the still warm female body which he couldn't stomach. A few short hours ago she would have been entitled to some modesty, to her own choice of doctor, free to reject those unnaturally white and eagerly probing fingers. A few hours ago she was a human being. Now she was dead flesh.

It was the room of a woman who preferred to be unencumbered. It contained the necessary basic comforts and one or two carefully chosen embellishments. It was as if she had itemized her needs and provided for them expensively but precisely and without extravagance. The thick rug by the bed was not, he thought, the kind provided by the Hospital Management Committee. There was only one picture but that was an original watercolour, a charming landscape by Robert Hills, hung where the light from the window lit it most effectively. On the window-sill stood the only ornament, a Staffordshire pottery figure of John Wesley preaching from his pulpit. Dalgliesh turned it in his hands. It was perfect; a collector's piece. But there were none of the small trivial impedimenta which those living in institutions often dispose about them to provide comfort or reassurance.

He walked over to the bookcase beside the bed and again examined the books. They, too, seemed chosen to minister to predictable moods. A collection of modern poetry, his own last volume included; a complete set of Jane Austen, well worn but in a leather binding and printed on India paper; a few books on philosophy nicely balanced between scholarship and popular appeal; about two dozen paperbacks of modern novels, Greene, Waugh, Compton-Burnett, Hartley, Powell, Cary. But most of the books were poetry. Looking at them, he thought, we shared the same tastes. If we had met we should at least have had something to say to each other. 'Everyman's death diminishes me.' But, of course, Doctor Donne. The over-exploited dictum had become a fashionable catch phrase in a crowded world where non-involvement was practically a social necessity. But some deaths still held their power to diminish more than others.

For the first time in years he was conscious of a sense of waste, of a personal irrational loss.

He moved on. At the foot of the bed was a wardrobe with a chest of drawers attached, a bastard contraption in pale wood, designed, if anyone had consciously designed an object so ugly, to provide the maximum of space in the minimum of room. The top of the chest was meant to serve as a dressing-table and held a small looking-glass. In front of it were her brush and comb. Nothing else.

He opened the small left-hand drawer. It held her make-up, the jars and tubes neatly arranged on a smaller papier-mâché tray. There was a great deal more than he had expected to find: cleansing cream, a box of tissues, foundation cream, pressed powder, eye shadow, mascara. She had obviously made up with care. But there was only one of each item. No experiments, no impulse buying, no half-used and discarded tubes with the make-up congealed round the stopper. The collection said: 'This is what suits me. This is what I need. No more and no less.'

He opened the right-hand drawer. It held nothing but a concertina file, each compartment indexed. He thumbed through the contents. A birth certificate. A certificate of baptism. A post office savings account book. The name and address of her solicitor. There were no personal letters. He tucked the file under his arm.

He moved on to the wardrobe and examined again the collection of clothes. Three pairs of slacks. Cashmere jumpers. A winter coat in bright red tweed. Four well-cut dresses in fine wool. They all spoke of quality. It was an expensive wardrobe for a student nurse.

He heard a final satisifed grunt from Sir Miles and turned round. The pathologist was straightening himself and peeling off his rubber gloves. They were so thin that it looked as if he were shedding his epidermis. He said:

'Dead, I should say, about ten hours. I'm judging mainly by rectal temperature and the degree of rigor in the lower limbs. But it's no more than a guess, my dear fellow. These things are chancy, as you know. We'll have a look at the stomach contents; that might give us a clue. At present, and on the clinical signs, I should say she died about midnight give or take an hour. Taking a common-sense view, of course, she died when she drank that nightcap.'

The fingerprint officer had left the whisky bottle and beaker on the table and was working now on the door handle. Sir Miles trotted round to them and without touching the beaker bent his head and placed his nose close to the rim.

'Whisky. But what else? That's what we're asking ourselves, my dear fellow. That's what we're asking ourselves. One thing, it wasn't a corrosive. No carbolic acid this time. I didn't do the P.M. on that other girl by the way. Rikki Blake did that little job. A bad business. I suppose you're looking for a connection between the two deaths?'

Dalgliesh said: 'It's possible.'

'Could be. Could be. This isn't likely to be a natural death. But we'll have to wait for the toxicology. Then we may learn something. There's no evidence of strangulation or suffocation. No external marks of violence come to that. By the way, she was pregnant. About three months gone, I'd say. I got a nice little *ballottement* there. Haven't found that sign since I was a student. The P.M. will confirm it of course.'

His little bright eyes searched the room. 'No container for the poison apparently. If it were poison, of course. And no suicide note?'

'That's not conclusive evidence,' said Dalgliesh.

'I know. I know. But most of them leave a little *billet doux*. They like to tell the tale, my dear fellow. They like to tell the tale. The mortuary van's here by the way. I'll take her away if you're finished with her.'

'I've finished,' said Dalgliesh.

He waited and watched while the porters manoeuvred their stretcher into the room and with brisk efficiency dumped the dead weight on to it. Sir Miles fretted around them with the nervous anxiety of an expert who has found a particularly good specimen and must carefully supervise its safe transport. It was odd that the removal of that inert mass of bone and tightening muscles, to which each in his different way had been ministering, should have left the room so empty, so desolate. Dalgliesh had noticed it before when the body was taken away; this sense of an empty stage, of props casually disposed and bereft of meaning, of a drained air. The recently dead had their own mysterious *charisma*; not without reason did men talk in whispers in their presence. But now she was gone, and there was nothing further for him to do in the room. He left his fingerprint man annotating and photographing his finds, and went out into the passage.

II

It was now after eleven o'clock but the corridor was still very dark, the one clear window at the far end discernible only as a square haze behind the drawn curtains. Dalgliesh could at first just make out the shape and colour of the three red fire buckets filled with sand and the cone of a fire extinguisher gleaming against the carved oak panelling of the walls. The iron staples, driven brutally into the woodwork, on which they were supported, were in incongruous contrast to the row of elegant light fittings in convoluted brass which sprang from the centres of the quatrefoil carvings. The fittings had obviously originally been designed for gas, but had been crudely adapted without imagination or skill to the use of electricity. The brass was unpolished and most of the delicate glass shades, curved in a semblance of flower petals, were missing or broken. In each of the deflowered clusters a single socket was now monstrously budded with one grubby and low-powered bulb whose faint and diffused light threw shadows across the floor and served only to accentuate the general gloom. Apart from the one small window at the end of the corridor there was little other natural light. The huge window over the well of the staircase, a Pre-Raphaelite representation in lurid glass of the expulsion from Eden, was hardly functional.

He looked into the rooms adjacent to that of the dead girl. One was unoccupied, with the bed stripped, the wardrobe door ajar and the drawers, lined with fresh newspaper, all pulled out as if to demonstrate the room's essential emptiness. The other was in use but looked as if it had been hurriedly left; the bedclothes were carelessly thrown back and the bedside rug was rumpled. There was a little pile of textbooks on the bedside table and he opened the flyleaf of the first to hand and read the inscription, 'Christine

Dakers'. So this was the room of the girl who had found the body. He inspected the wall between the two rooms. It was thin, a light partition of painted hardboard which trembled and let out a soft boom as he struck it. He wondered whether Nurse Dakers had heard anything in the night. Unless Josephine Fallon had died instantly and almost soundlessly some indication of her distress must surely have penetrated this insubstantial partition. He was anxious to interview Nurse Christine Dakers. At present she was in the nurses' sick bay suffering, so he was told, from shock. The shock was probably genuine enough, but even if it were not, there was nothing he could do about it. Nurse Dakers was for the moment effectively protected by her doctors from any questioning from the police.

He explored a little further. Opposite the rows of nurses' bedrooms was a suite of bathroom cubicles and lavatories leading out of a large square cloakroom fitted with four wash-basins, each surrounded by a shower curtain. Each of the bath cubicles had a small sash window fitted with opaque glass, inconveniently placed but not difficult to open. They gave a view of the back of the house and of the two short wings, each built above a brick cloister, which were incongruously grafted on to the main building. It was as if the architect, having exhausted the possibilities of Gothic revival and baroque, had decided to introduce a more contemplative and ecclesiastical influence. The ground between the cloisters was an overgrown jungle of laurel bushes and untended trees which grew so close to the house that some of the branches seemed to scrape the downstairs windows. Dalgliesh could see dim figures searching among the bushes and could hear the faint mutter of voices. The discarded bottle of disinfectant which had killed Heather Pearce had been found among these bushes and it was possible that a second container, its contents equally lethal, might also have been hurled in the dark hours from the same window. There was a nail brush on the bath rack and, reaching for it, Dalgliesh hurled it in a wide arc through the window and into the bushes. He could neither see nor hear its fall but a cheerful face appeared among the parted leaves, a hand was waved in salute and the two searching constables moved back deeper into the undergrowth.

He next made his way along the passage to the nurses' utility room at the far end. Detective Sergeant Masterson was there with Sister Rolfe. Together they were surveying a motley collection of objects laid out before them on the working surface rather as if they were engaged in a private Kim's game. There were two squeezed lemons; a bowl of granulated sugar; an assortment of mugs containing cold tea, the surface of the liquid mottled and puckered; and a delicate Worcester teapot with matching cup and saucer and milk jug. There was also a crumpled square of thin white wrapping paper bearing the words 'Scunthorpe's Wine Stores, 149, High Street, Heatheringfield' and a scribbled receipt smoothed out and held flat by a couple of tea canisters.

'She bought the whisky yesterday morning, sir,' Masterson said. 'Luckily for us, Mr Scunthorpe is punctilious about receipts. That's the bill and that's the wrapping paper. So it looks as if she first opened the bottle when she went to bed yesterday.'

Dalgliesh asked: 'Where was it kept?'

It was Sister Rolfe who replied. 'Fallon always kept her whisky in her bedroom.'

Masterson laughed.

'Not surprising with the stuff costing nearly three quid a bottle.'

Sister Rolfe looked at him with contempt.

'I doubt whether that would worry Fallon. She wasn't the type to mark the bottle.'

'She was generous?' asked Dalgliesh.

'No, merely unconcerned. She kept her whisky in her room because Matron asked her to.'

But brought it in here yesterday to prepare her late night drink, thought Dalgliesh. He stirred the sugar gently with his finger.

Sister Rolfe said: 'That's innocent. The students tell me that they all used it when they made their morning tea. And the Burt twins, at least, drank some of theirs.'

'But we'll send it and the lemon to the lab just the same,' said Dalgliesh.

He lifted the lid from the little teapot and looked inside. Answering his unspoken question, Sister Rolfe said:

'Apparently Nurse Dakers made early tea in it. The pot is Fallon's of course. No one else has early tea in antique Worcester.'

'Nurse Dakers made tea for Nurse Fallon before she knew that the girl was dead?'

'No, afterwards. It was a purely automatic reaction, I imagine. She must have been in shock. After all, she had just seen Fallon's body. She could hardly expect to cure rigor mortis with hot tea, even with the best China blend. I suppose you'll want to see Dakers, but you'll have to wait. She's in the sick bay at the moment. I think they told you. It's part of the private wing and Sister Brumfett is looking after her. That's why I'm here now. Like the police, we're a hierarchical profession and when Matron isn't in Nightingale House, Brumfett is next in the pecking order. Normally she would be dancing attendance on you, not I. You've been told, of course, that Miss Taylor is on her way back from a conference in Amsterdam. She had to deputize unexpectedly for the Chairman of the Area Nurse Training Committee, luckily for her. So at least there's one senior member of the staff with an alibi.'

Dalgliesh had been told, and more than once. The absence of the Matron seemed to be a fact which everyone he had met, however briefly, had found it necessary to mention, explain or regret. But Sister Rolfe was the first to make a snide reference to the fact that it gave Miss Taylor an alibi, at least for the time of Fallon's death.

'And the rest of the students?'

'They're in the small lecture room on the floor below. Sister Gearing, our clinical instructor, is taking them for a private study period. I don't suppose they're doing much reading. It would have been better to set them something more active but it's not easy at a moment's notice. Will you see them there?'

'No, later. And in the demonstration room where Nurse Pearce died.'

She glanced at him and then turned her eyes away quickly, but not so quickly that he missed the look of surprise and, he thought, disapproval. She had expected him to show more sensitivity, more consideration. The demonstration room had not been used since Nurse Pearce's death. To interview the students there so soon after this second tragedy would reinforce memory with fresh horror. If any of them were ready to be unnerved, this might do it and he had never considered using any other room. Sister Rolfe, he thought, was like all the rest of them. They wanted their murderers caught but only by the most gentlemanly means. They wanted them punished, but only if the punishment did not outrage their own sensibility.

Dalgliesh asked: 'How is this place locked at night?'

'Sister Brumfett, Sister Gearing, and myself take responsibility for a week at a time. It's Gearing's turn this week. We're the only three Sisters who are resident here. We lock and bolt the front door and the kitchen door at eleven o'clock promptly. There's a small side door with a Yale lock and an inside bolt. If any student or member of the staff has a late pass she is issued with a key to that door and bolts it when she comes in. Sisters have a key in their possession permanently. There's only one other door and that leads from Matron's flat on the third floor. She has a private staircase and, of course, her own key. Apart from that, there are the fire escape doors, but they are all kept locked on the inside. The place wouldn't be difficult to break into. I imagine that few institutions are. But we've never had a burglar so far as I know. Incidentally, there's a pane of glass out in the conservatory. Alderman Kealey, the Vice-Chairman, seems to think that Fallon's murderer got in that way. He's a great man for finding comfortable explanations for all life's embarrassing problems. It looks to me as if the pane blew in with the wind, but you'll no doubt form your own opinion.'

She's talking too much, he thought. Loquacity was one of the commonest reactions to shock or nervousness and one which any interrogating officer made the most of. Tomorrow she would despise herself for it, and become that much more difficult, that much less co-operative. In the meantime she was telling him more than she realized.

The broken pane would, of course, have to be looked at, the woodwork examined for marks of entry. But he thought it unlikely that Nurse Fallon's death had been the work of any intruder. He asked: 'How many people slept here last night?'

'Brumfett, Gearing and myself. Brumfett was out for part of the night. I understand she was recalled to the ward by Mr Courtney-Briggs. Miss Collins was here. She's the housekeeper. And there were five student nurses: Nurse Dakers, the Burt twins, Nurse Goodale, and Nurse Pardoe. And Fallon slept here of course. That is, if Fallon had time to sleep! Incidentally, her bedside light was on all night. The Burt twins were up brewing cocoa shortly after two and nearly took a cup in to Fallon. If they'd done so you might have got a clearer idea of the time of death. But it occurred to them that she might have fallen asleep with the light on and wouldn't exactly welcome being woken, even to the sight and smell of cocoa. The twins' invariable solace is food and drink, but at least they've lived long enough to realize that not everyone shares their preoccupation and that Fallon, in particular, might prefer sleep and privacy to cocoa and company.'

'I shall be seeing the Burt twins. What about the hospital grounds? Are they left open at night?'

'There's always a porter on duty at the front lodge. The main gates aren't locked because of the accident ambulances but he keeps an eye on anyone else who comes in or leaves. Nightingale House is much closer to the rear entrance to the grounds, but we don't usually go that way by foot because the path is ill-lit and rather frightening. Besides, it leads into Winchester Road which is almost two miles from the main part of the town. The back gate is locked at dusk summer and winter by one of the porters but all the Sisters and Matron have keys.'

'And the nurses with late passes?'

'They're expected to use the front gate and walk along the main path which skirts the hospital. There's a much shorter cut through the trees which we use in the daytime – it's only about two hundred yards – but not many people choose to come that way at night. I daresay Mr Hudson, he's the Hospital Secretary, can let you have a plan of the grounds and of Nightingale House. Incidentally, he and the Vice-Chairman are waiting for you now in the library. The Chairman, Sir Marcus Cohen, is in Israel. Even so, it's quite a reception committee. Even Mr Courtney-Briggs has deferred his out-patient session to welcome the Yard to Nightingale House.'

'Then,' said Dalgliesh, 'perhaps you'll be good enough to let them know that I'll be with them shortly.'

It was a dismissal. Sergeant Masterson, as if to soften it, said suddenly and loudly: 'Sister Rolfe has been very helpful.'

The woman gave a guttural snort of derision.

'Helping the police! Isn't there a sinister connotation about that phrase? Anyway, I don't think I can be particularly helpful. I didn't kill either of them. And last night I was at a film at the new arts cinema here. They're showing an Antonioni series. This week it's *L'Avventura*. I didn't get in until just before eleven and went straight to bed. I didn't even see Fallon.'

Dalgliesh recognized with weary resignation the first lie and wondered how many more, important and unimportant, would be spoken before the investigation was complete. But this wasn't the time to interrogate Sister Rolfe. She wasn't going to be an easy witness. She had answered his questions fully but with undisguised resentment. He wasn't sure whether it was he or his job which she disliked, or whether any man would have provoked this tone of angry contempt. Her angry face matched her personality, rebarbative and defensive. It was strong and intelligent but without softness or feminity. The deep-set and very dark eyes might have been attractive but they were set under a pair of perfectly straight black eyebrows, so dark and bushy that they gave to the face a faint suggestion of deformity. Her nose was large and open-pored, her lips a thin uncompromising line. It was the face of a woman who has never learnt to come to terms with life, and had, perhaps, given up trying. He thought suddenly that, if she proved to be a murderess and her photograph were at last published, other women, avidly searching that uncompromising mask for the marks of depravity, would profess themselves unsurprised. Suddenly he felt sorry for her with a mixture of irritation and compassion one might feel for the inadequate or the physically deformed. He turned quickly away so that she should not catch that sudden spasm of pity. To her it would, he knew, be the ultimate insult. And when he turned again to thank her formally for her help, he saw that she had gone.

III

Sergeant Charles Masterson was six feet three inches tall and broad-shouldered. He carried his bulk easily and all his movements were surprisingly controlled and precise for such an assertively masculine and heavy man. He was generally considered handsome, particularly by himself, and with his strong face, sensual lips and hooded eyes looked remarkably like a well-known American film actor of the guts-and-guns school. Dalgliesh occasionally suspected that the sergeant, aware, as he could hardly fail to be, of the resemblance, was helping it along by assuming a trace of an American accent.

'All right, Sergeant. You've had a chance to look at the place, you've talked to some of the people. Tell me about it.'

This invitation had been known to strike terror into the hearts of Dalgliesh's subordinates. It meant that the Superintendent now expected to hear a brief, succinct, accurate, elegantly phrased but comprehensive account of the crime which would give all the salient facts so far known to someone who came to it freshly. The ability to know what you want to say and to say it in the minimum of appropriate words is as uncommon in policemen as in other members of the community. Dalgliesh's subordinates were apt to complain that they hadn't realized that a degree in English was the new qualification for joining the C.I.D. But Sergeant Masterson was less intimidated than most. He had his weaknesses, but lack of confidence was not one of them. He was glad to be working on the case. It was well known at the Yard that Superintendent Dalgliesh couldn't tolerate a fool and that his definition of folly was individual and precise. Masterson respected him because Dalgliesh was one of the Yard's most successful detectives and for Masterson success was the only real criterion. He thought him very able, which is not to say that he thought Adam Dalgliesh as able as Charles Masterson. Most of the time, and for reasons which it seemed to him unprofitable to explore, he disliked him heartily. He suspected that the antipathy was mutual, but this didn't particularly worry him. Dalgliesh wasn't a man to prejudice a subordinate's career because he disliked him and was known to be meticulous, if judicious, in ascribing credit where it was due. But the situation would need watching, and Masterson intended to watch it. An ambitious man on his carefully planned climb to senior rank was a fool if he didn't early recognize that it was bloody daft to antagonize a senior officer. Masterson had no intention of being that kind of a fool. But a little co-operation from the Super in this campaign of mutual goodwill wouldn't be unwelcome. And he wasn't sure he was going to get it. He said:

'I'll deal with the two deaths separately, sir. The first victim . . .'

'Why talk like a crime reporter, Sergeant? Let's be sure we have a victim before we use that word.'

Masterson began: 'The first deceased . . . the first girl to die was a twenty-one-year-old student nurse, Heather Pearce.'

He went on to recite the facts of both girls' deaths, as far as they were known, taking care to avoid the more blatant examples of police jargon, to which he knew his Super to be morbidly sensitive, and resisting the temptation to display his recently acquired knowledge of intra-gastric feeding about which he had taken trouble to extract from Sister Rolfe a comprehensive, if grudging, explanation. He ended: 'So we have, sir, the possibilities that one or both of the deaths was suicide, that one or both was accidental, that the first was murder but that the wrong victim was killed, or that there were two murders with two intended victims. An intriguing choice, sir.'

Dalgliesh said: 'Or that Fallon's death was due to natural causes. Until we get the toxicology report we're theorizing in advance of the facts. But for the present we treat both deaths as murder. Well, let's go to the library and see what the Vice-Chairman of the Hospital Management Committee has to say to us.'

IV

The library, easily identified by a large painted sign above the door, was a pleasant high-ceilinged room on the first floor, next to the student nurses' sitting-room. One wall was entirely taken up with three ornate oriel windows, but the other three were book-lined to the ceiling, leaving the centre of the room bare. It was furnished with four tables ranged in front of the windows and two shabby sofas, one on each side of the stone fireplace, where now an ancient gas fire hissed its sinister welcome. In front of it, under the two strips of fluorescent lighting, a group of four men, muttering together conspiratorially, turned in one movement at the entrance of Dalgliesh and Masterson and watched them with wary curiosity. It was a familiar moment to Dalgliesh, compounded as always of interest, apprehension and hope – this first confrontation of the protagonists in a murder case with the outsider, the alien expert in violent death who has come among them, an unwelcome guest, to demonstrate his invidious talents.

Then the silence broke, the rigid figures relaxed. The two men Dalgliesh had already met – Stephen Courtney-Briggs and Paul Hudson, the Hospital Secretary – moved forward with formal welcoming smiles. Mr Courtney-Briggs, who apparently took charge of any situation dignified by his presence, made the introductions. The Group Secretary, Raymond Grout, shook hands damply. He had a gently lugubrious face, puckered now with distress like that of a child on the verge of crying. His hair lay in strands of silver silk over a high-domed forehead. He was probably younger than he appeared, thought Dalgliesh, but even so, he must be very near retirement.

Beside the tall, stooped figure of Grout, Alderman Kealey looked as perky as a terrier. He was a ginger-haired, foxy little man, bandy as a jockey and wearing a plaid suit, the awfulness of its pattern emphasized by the excellence of its cut. It gave him an anthropomorphic appearance, like an animal in a child's comic; and Dalgliesh almost expected to find himself shaking a paw.

'It was good of you to come, Superintendent, and so promptly,' he said.

The folly of the remark apparently struck him as soon as he had made it, for he darted a keen glance from under spiky ginger eyebrows at his companions, as if defying them to smirk. No one did, but the Group Secretary looked as humiliated as if the solecism had been his, and Paul Hudson turned his face away to hide an embarrassed grin. He was a personable young man who, on Dalgliesh's first arrival at the hospital, had shown himself as both efficient and authoritative. Now, however, the presence of his Vice-Chairman and the Group Secretary seemed to have inhibited his speech and he had the apologetic air of a man present on sufferance. Mr Courtney-Briggs said:

'It's too much to hope for any news yet, I suppose? We saw the mortuary van leaving, and I had a few words with Miles Honeyman. He couldn't commit himself at this stage, of course, but he'll be surprised if this was a natural death. The girl killed herself. Well, I should have thought that was obvious to anyone.'

Dalgliesh said: 'Nothing is obvious yet.'

There was a silence. The Vice-Chairman seemed to find it embarrassing for he cleared his throat noisily and said:

'You'll want an office, of course. The local C.I.D. worked from the police station here. They were really very little trouble to us. We hardly knew they were in the place.' He looked with faint optimism at Dalgliesh, as if hardly sanguine that the flying squad would be equally accommodating. Dalgliesh replied shortly:

'We shall want a room. It is possible to make one available in Nightingale House? That would be the most convenient.'

The request seemed to disconcert them. The Group Secretary said tentatively: 'If Matron were here . . . it's difficult for us to know what's free. She shouldn't be long now.'

Alderman Kealey grunted. 'We can't let everything wait for Matron. The Superintendent wants a room. Find him one.'

'Well there's Miss Rolfe's office on the ground floor, just next to the demonstration room.' The Group Secretary bent his sad eyes on Dalgliesh. 'You've met Miss Rolfe, our Principal Tutor, of course. Now if Miss Rolfe can move temporarily into her secretary's room . . . Miss Buckfield is off with flu, so it's free. It's rather cramped, only a cupboard really, but if Matron . . .'

'Get Miss Rolfe to move out any of her things she'll need. The porters can shift the filing cabinets.' Alderman Kealey turned and barked at Dalgliesh: 'Will that do?'

'If it's private, reasonably soundproof, has a lock on the door, is large enough to take three men and has a direct telephone to the exchange, it will do. If it also has running water, so much the better.'

The Vice-Chairman, chastened by this formidable list of requirements, said tentatively: 'There's a small cloakroom and lavatory on the ground floor opposite Miss Rolfe's room. That could be put at your disposal.'

Mr Grout's misery deepened. He glanced across at Mr Courtney-Briggs as if seeking an ally but the surgeon had been unaccountably silent for the last few minutes and seemed reluctant to meet his eyes. Then the telephone rang. Mr Hudson, apparently glad of a chance of activity, sprang to answer it. He turned to his Vice-Chairman.

'It's the *Clarion*, sir. They're asking for you personally.'

Alderman Kealey grasped the receiver resolutely. Having decided to assert himself he was apparently ready to take command of any situation, and this one was well within his capabilities. Murder might be outside his normal preoccupations but dealing tactfully with the local Press was something he understood.

'Alderman Kealey here. The Vice-Chairman of the Management Committee. Yes, we've got the Yard here. The victim? Oh, I don't think we want to talk about a victim. Not yet anyway. Fallon. Josephine Fallon. Age?' He placed his hand over the mouthpiece and turned to the Group Secretary. Oddly enough, it was Mr Courtney-Briggs who replied.

'She was thirty-one years, ten months,' he said. 'She was precisely twenty years younger than me to the day.'

Alderman Kealey, unsurprised by the gratuitous information, returned to his listener.

'She was thirty-one. No, we don't know yet how she died. No one knows. We are awaiting the post-mortem report. Yes, Chief Superintendent Dalgliesh. He's here now but he's too busy to talk. I hope to issue a Press statement this evening. We ought to have the autopsy report by then. No, there's no reason to suspect murder. The Chief Constable has called in the Yard as a precautionary measure. No, as far as we're aware, the two deaths aren't connected in any way. Very sad. Yes, very. If you care to telephone about six I may have some more information. All we know at present is that Nurse Fallon was found dead in her bed this morning shortly after seven. It could very well have been a heart attack. She was just recovering from flu. No, there wasn't a note. Nothing like that.'

He listened for a moment then again placed his hand over the mouthpiece and turned to Grout.

'They're asking about relatives. What do we know about them?'

'She hadn't any. Fallon was an orphan.' Again it was Mr Courtney-Briggs who replied.

Alderman Kealey passed on this information and replaced the receiver. Smiling grimly he gave Dalgliesh a look of mingled self-satisfaction and warning. Dalgliesh was interested to hear that the Yard had been called in as a precautionary measure. It was a new conception of the flying squad's responsibilities and one which he felt was unlikely to deceive the local Press boys, still less the London reporters who would soon be on the scent. He wondered how the hospital was going to cope with the publicity. Alderman Kealey was going to need some advice if the inquiry were not to be hampered. But there was plenty of time for that. Now all he wanted was to get rid of them, to get started with the investigation. These social preliminaries were always a time-consuming nuisance. And soon there would be a Matron to propitiate, to consult, possibly even to antagonize. From the Group Secretary's unwillingness to move a step without her consent, it looked as if she were a strong personality. He didn't relish the prospect of making it clear to her, tactfully, that there would be room for only one strong personality in this investigation.

Mr Courtney-Briggs, who had been standing at the window, staring out at the storm-wrecked garden, turned, shook himself free of his preoccupations and said:

'I'm afraid I can't spare any more time now. I have a patient to see in the private wing and then a ward round. I was due to lecture to the students here later this morning but that'll have to be cancelled now. You'll let me know, Kealey, if there's anything I can do.'

He ignored Dalgliesh. The impression given, and no doubt intended, was that he was a busy man who had already wasted too much time on a triviality. Dalgliesh resisted the temptation to delay him. Agreeable as it would be to tame Mr Courtney-Briggs's arrogance, it was an indulgence which he couldn't afford at present. There were more pressing matters.

It was then they heard the sound of a car. Mr Courtney-Briggs returned to the window and looked out, but did not speak. The rest of the little group stiffened and turned as if pulled by a common force to face the door. A car door slammed. Then there was silence for a few seconds followed by the clip of hurried footsteps on a tessellated floor. The door opened and Matron came in.

Dalgliesh's first impression was of a highly individual yet casual elegance and a confidence that was almost palpable. He saw a tall slender woman, hatless, with pale honey-gold skin and hair of almost the same colour, drawn back from a high forehead and swathed into an intricate coil at the nape of her neck. She was wearing a grey tweed coat with a bright-green scarf knotted at her neck and carrying a black handbag and a small travelling case. She came into the room quietly and, placing her case on the table, drew off her gloves and surveyed the little party silently. Almost instinctively, as if watching a witness, Dalgliesh noticed her hands. The fingers were very white, long and tapering but with unusually bony joints. The nails were clipped short. On the third finger of the right hand an immense sapphire ring in an ornate setting gleamed against the knuckle. He wondered irrelevantly whether she took it off when she was on duty and, if so, how she forced it over these nodular joints.

Mr Courtney-Briggs, after a brief, 'Good morning, Matron,' made his way to the door and stood there like a bored guest, demonstrating his anxiety to make a quick getaway. But the others crowded around her. There was an immediate sense of relief. Muttered introductions were made.

'Good morning, Superintendent.' Her voice was deep, a little husky, a voice as individual as herself. She seemed hardly aware of him, yet he was conscious of a swift appraisal from green exophthalmic eyes. Her handshake was firm and cool, but so momentary that it seemed a fleeting meeting of palms, nothing more.

The Vice-Chairman said: 'The police will want a room. We thought perhaps Miss Rolfe's office?'

'Too small, I think, and not private enough, so close to the main hall. It would be better if Mr Dalgliesh had the use of the visitors' sitting-room on the first floor and the cloakroom next door to it. The room has a key. There's a desk with lockable drawers in the general office and that can be moved up. That way the police will get some privacy and there'll be a minimum of interference with the work of the school.'

There was a murmur of assent. The men looked relieved. The Matron said to Dalgliesh: 'Will you need a bedroom? Do you want to sleep in the hospital?'

'That won't be necessary. We shall be staying in the town. But I would prefer to work from here. We shall probably be here late every night so that it would be helpful if we could have keys.'

'For how long?' asked the Vice-Chairman suddenly. It was on the face of it, a stupid question, but Dalgliesh noticed that all their faces turned to him as if it were one he could be expected to answer. He knew his reputation for speed. Did they perhaps know it too?

'About a week,' he said. Even if the case dragged on for longer, he would learn all he needed from Nightingale House and its occupants within seven days. If Nurse Fallon had been murdered – and he believed she had – the circle of suspects would be small. If the case didn't break within a week it might never break. He thought there was a small sigh of relief.

Matron said: 'Where is she?'

'They took the body to the mortuary, Matron.'

'I didn't mean Fallon. Where is Nurse Dakers? I understood it was she who found the body.'

Alderman Kealey replied. 'She's being nursed in the private ward. She was pretty shaken up so we asked Dr Snelling to take a look at her. He's given her a sedative and Sister Brumfett's looking after her.'

He added: 'Sister Brumfett was a little concerned about her. On top of that she's got rather a sick ward. Otherwise she would have met you at the airport. We all felt rather badly about your arriving with no one to meet you, but the best thing seemed to be to telephone a message for you, asking you to ring us here as soon as you landed. Sister Brumfett thought that the shock would be less if you learnt it in that way. On the other hand it seemed wrong not to have someone there. I wanted to send Grout but . . .'

The husky voice broke in with its quiet reproof: 'I should have thought that sparing me shock was the least of your worries.' She turned to Dalgliesh:

'I shall be in my sitting-room here on the third floor in about forty-five minutes' time. If it's convenient for you, I should be glad to have a word with you then.'

Dalgliesh, resisting the impulse to reply with a docile, 'Yes, Matron,' said that it would. Miss Taylor turned to Alderman Kealey.

'I'm going to see Nurse Dakers now. Afterwards the Superintendent will want to interview me and then I shall be in my main office in the hospital if you or Mr Grout want me. I shall, of course, be available all day.'

Without a further word or look she gathered up her travelling case and handbag and went out of the room. Mr Courtney-Briggs perfunctorily opened the door for her, then prepared to follow. Standing in the open doorway, he said with jovial belligerence:

'Well, now that Matron's back and the important matter of accommodation for the police has been settled, perhaps the work of the hospital can be permitted to continue. I shouldn't be late for your interview if I were you, Dalgliesh. Miss Taylor isn't accustomed to insubordination.'

He shut the door behind him. Alderman Kealey looked for a moment perplexed, then he said:

'He's upset, of course. Well, naturally. Wasn't there some kind of rumour . . .'

Then his eyes lit on Dalgliesh. He checked himself suddenly, and turned to Paul Hudson:

'Well, Mr Hudson, you heard what Matron said. The police are to use the visitors' sitting-room on this floor. Get on with it, my dear fellow. Get on with it!'

V

Miss Taylor changed into uniform before she went over to the private ward. At the time it seemed an instinctive thing to do, but, wrapping her cloak tightly around her as she walked briskly along the small footpath leading from Nightingale House to the hospital, she realized that the instinct had been prompted by reason. It was important to the hospital that Matron was back, and important that she should be seen to be back.

The quickest way to the private wing was through the out-patients' hall. The department was already buzzing with activity. The circles of comfortable chairs, carefully disposed to give an illusion of informality and relaxed comfort, were filling quickly. Volunteers from the ladies' committee of the League of Friends were already presiding at the steaming urn, serving tea to those regular patients who preferred to attend an hour before their appointments for the pleasure of sitting in the warmth, reading the magazines and chatting to their fellow habitués. As Matron passed she was aware of heads turning to watch her. There was a brief silence, followed by the customary murmur of deferential greeting. She was conscious of the white-coated junior medical staff standing briefly to one side as she passed, of the student nurses pressing themselves back against the wall.

The private ward was on the second floor of what still was called the new building, although it had been completed in 1945. Miss Taylor went up by the lift, sharing it with two radiographers and a young houseman. They murmured their formal, 'Good morning, Matron,' and stood in unnatural silence until the lift stopped, then stood back while she went out before them.

The private ward consisted of a suite of twenty single rooms, opening each side of a wide central corridor. The Sister's office, the kitchen and the utility room were just inside the door. As Miss Taylor entered, a young first-year student nurse appeared from the kitchen. She flushed when she saw Matron and muttered something about fetching Sister.

'Where is Sister, Nurse?'

'In room 7 with Mr Courtney-Briggs, Matron. His patient isn't too well.'

'Don't disturb them. Just tell Sister when she appears that I've come to see Nurse Dakers. Where is she?'

'In room 3, Matron.' She hesitated.

'It's all right, Nurse, I'll find my own way. Get on with what you are doing.'

Room 3 was at the far end of the corridor, one of six single rooms usually reserved for sick nurses. Only when these rooms were all occupied were the staff nursed in the side rooms of the wards. It was not, Miss Taylor noted, the room in which Josephine Fallon had been nursed. Room 3 was the sunniest and most pleasant of the six rooms reserved for nurses. A week ago it had been occupied by a nurse with pneumonia, a complication of influenza. Miss Taylor, who visited every ward in the hospital once a day and who received daily reports on every sick nurse, thought it unlikely that Nurse Wilkins was fit enough yet to be discharged. Sister Brumfett must have moved her to make room 3 available for Nurse Dakers. Miss Taylor could guess why. The one window gave a view of the lawns and smoothly forked flower beds at the front of the hospital; from this side of the ward it was impossible to glimpse Nightingale House even through the bare tracery of the winter trees. Dear old Brumfett! So unprepossessingly rigid in her views, but so imaginative when it came to the welfare and comfort of her patients. Brumfett, who talked embarrassingly of duty, obedience, loyalty, but who knew exactly what she meant by those unpopular terms and lived by what she knew. She was one of the best ward sisters that the John Carpendar had, or ever would have. But Miss Taylor was glad that devotion to duty had kept Sister Brumfett from meeting the plane at Heathrow. It was bad enough to come home to this further tragedy without the added burden of Brumfett's doglike devotion and concern.

She drew the stool from under the bed and seated herself beside the girl. Despite Dr Snelling's sedative, Nurse Dakers was not asleep. She was lying very still on her back gazing at the ceiling. Now her eyes turned to look at Matron. They were blank with misery. On the bedside locker there was a copy of a textbook, *Materia Medica for Nurses*. The Matron picked it up.

'This is very conscientious of you, Nurse, but just for the short time you are in here, why not have a novel from the Red Cross trolley or a frivolous magazine? Shall I bring one in for you?'

She was answered by a flood of tears. The slim figure twisted convulsively in the bed, buried her head in the pillow and clasped it with shaking hands. The bed shook with the paroxysm of grief. The Matron got up, moved over to the door and clicked across the board which covered the nurses' peephole. She returned quickly to her seat and waited without speaking, making no move except to place her hand on the girl's head. After a few minutes the dreadful shaking ceased and Nurse Dakers grew calmer. She began to mutter, her voice hiccuping with sobs, half muffled by the pillow:

'I'm so miserable, so ashamed.'

The Matron bent her head to catch the words. A chill of horror swept over her. Surely she couldn't be listening to a confession of murder? She found herself praying under her breath.

'Dear God, please not. Not this child! Surely not this child?'

She waited, not daring to question. Nurse Dakers twisted herself round and gazed up at her, her eyes reddened and swollen into two amorphous moons in a face blotched and formless with misery.

'I'm wicked, Matron, wicked. I was glad when she died.'

'Nurse Fallon.'

'Oh no, not Fallon! I was sorry about Fallon. Nurse Pearce.'

The Matron placed her hands on each of the girl's shoulders, pressing her back against the bed. She held the trembling body firmly and looked down into the drowned eyes.

'I want you to tell me the truth, Nurse. Did you kill Nurse Pearce?'

'No, Matron.'

'Nor Nurse Fallon?'

'No, Matron.'

'Or have anything at all to do with their deaths?'

'No, Matron.'

Miss Taylor let out her breath. She relaxed her hold on the girl and sat back.

'I think you'd better tell me all about it.'

So, calmly now, the pathetic story came out. It hadn't seemed like stealing at the time. It had seemed like a miracle. Mummy had so needed a warm winter coat and Nurse Dakers had been saving thirty shillings from her monthly salary cheque. Only the money had taken so long to save and the weather was getting colder; and Mummy, who never complained, and never asked her for anything, had to wait nearly fifteen minutes for the bus some mornings and caught cold so easily. And if she did catch cold she couldn't stay away from work because Miss Arkwright, the buyer in the department store, was only waiting for an opportunity to get her sacked. Serving in a store wasn't really the right job for Mummy, but it wasn't easy to find a job when you were over fifty and unqualified, and the young assistants in the department weren't very kind. They kept hinting that Mummy wasn't pulling her weight, which wasn't true. Mummy might not be as quick as they were but she really took trouble with the customers.

Then Nurse Harper had dropped the two crisp new £5 notes almost at her feet. Nurse Harper who had so much pocket money from her father that she could lose £10 without really worrying about it. It had happened about four weeks ago. Nurse Harper had been walking with Nurse Pearce from the Nurses' Home to the hospital dining-room for breakfast, and Nurse Dakers had been following a few feet behind. The two notes had fallen out of Nurse Harper's cape pocket and had lain there fluttering gently. Her first instinct had been to call after the other two students, but something about the sight of the money had stopped her. The notes had been so unexpected, so unbelievable, so beautiful in their pristine crispness. She had just stood looking at them for a second, and then she had realized that she was really looking at Mummy's new coat. And, by then, the other two students had passed almost out of sight, the notes were folded in her hand, and it was too late.

The Matron asked: 'How did Nurse Pearce know that you had the notes?'

'She said that she'd seen me. She just happened to glance round when I was bending to pick up the notes. It meant nothing to her at the time, but when Nurse Harper told everyone that she'd lost the money and that the notes must have fallen out of her cape pocket on the way over to breakfast, Nurse Pearce guessed what had happened. She and the twins went with Nurse Harper to search the path to see if they could find the money. I expect that was when she remembered about my stooping down.'

'When did she first talk to you about it?'

'A week later, Matron, a fortnight before our set came into block. I expect she couldn't bring herself to believe it before then. She must have been trying to make up her mind to speak to me.'

So Nurse Pearce had waited. The Matron wondered why. It couldn't have taken her a whole week to clarify her suspicions. She must have recalled seeing Dakers stoop to pick up the notes as soon as she heard that they were missing. So why hadn't she tackled the girl at once? Had it perhaps been more satisfying to her twisted ego to wait until the money was spent and the culprit safely in her power?

'Was she blackmailing you?' she demanded.

'Oh no, Matron!' The girl was shocked.

'She only took back five shillings a week, and that wasn't blackmail. She sent the money every week to a society for discharged prisoners. She showed me the receipts.'

'And did she, incidentally, explain why she wasn't repaying it to Nurse Harper?'

'She thought it would be difficult to explain without involving me and I begged her not to do that. It would have been the end of everything, Matron. I want to take a district nurse training after I'm qualified so that I can look after Mummy. If I could get a country district we could have a cottage together and perhaps even a car. Mummy will be able to give up the store. I told Nurse Pearce about that. Besides, she said that Harper was so careless about money that it wouldn't hurt her to learn a lesson. She sent the payments to the society for discharged prisoners because it seemed appropriate. After all, I might have gone to prison if she hadn't shielded me.'

The Matron said drily: 'That, of course, is nonsense and you should have known it was nonsense. Nurse Pearce seems to have been a very stupid and arrogant young woman. Are you sure she wasn't making any other demands on you? There is more than one kind of blackmail.'

'But she wouldn't do that, Matron!' Nurse Dakers struggled to lift her head from the pillow. 'Pearce was . . . well, she was good.' She seemed to find the word inadequate and puckered her brow as if desperately anxious to explain.

'She used to talk to me quite a lot and gave me a card with a passage out of the Bible which I had to read every day. Once a week she used to ask me about it.'

The Matron was swept by a sense of moral outrage so acute that she had to find relief in action. She got up from the stool and walked over to the window, cooling her flaring face against the pane. She could feel her heart bumping and noticed with almost clinical interest that her hands were shaking. After a moment she came back again to the bedside.

'Don't talk about her being good. Dutiful, conscientious, and well-meaning if you like, but not good. If ever you meet real goodness you will know the difference. And I shouldn't worry about being glad that she is dead. In the circumstances you wouldn't be normal if you felt differently. In time you may be able to pity her and forgive her.'

'But Matron, it's me who ought to be forgiven. I'm a thief.' Was there a suggestion of masochism in the whine of the voice, the perverse self-denigration of the born victim? Miss Taylor said briskly:

'You're not a thief. You stole once; that's a very different thing. Every one of us has some incident in our lives that we're ashamed and sorry about. You've recently learned something about yourself, about what you're capable of doing, which has shaken your confidence. Now you have to live with that knowledge. We can only begin to understand and forgive other people when we have learned to understand and forgive ourselves. You won't steal again. I know that, and so do you. But you did once. You are capable of stealing. That knowledge will save you from being too pleased with yourself, from being too self-satisfied. It can make you a much more tolerant and understanding person and a better nurse. But not if you go on indulging in guilt and remorse and bitterness. Those insidious emotions may be very enjoyable but they aren't going to help you or anyone else.'

The girl looked up at her.

'Will the police have to know?'

That, of course, was the question. And there could be only one answer.

'Yes. And you will have to tell them, just as you've told me.

But I shall have a word first with the Superintendent. He's a new detective, from Scotland Yard this time, and I think he's an intelligent and understanding man.'

Was he? How could she possibly tell? That first meeting had been so brief, merely a glance and a touching of hands. Was she merely comforting herself with a fleeting impression that here was a man with authority and imagination who might be able to solve the mystery of both deaths with a minimum of harm to the innocent and guilty alike. She had felt this instinctively. But was the feeling rational? She believed Nurse Dakers's story; but then she was disposed to believe it. How would it strike a police officer faced with a multiplicity of suspects but no other discernible motive? And the motive was there all right. It was Nurse Dakers's whole future, and that of her mother. And Dakers had behaved rather oddly. True she had been most distressed of all the students when Pearce had died, but she had pulled herself together remarkably quickly. Even under the intense police questioning she had kept her secret safe. What then had precipitated this disintegration into confession and remorse? Was it only the shock of finding Fallon's body? And why should Fallon's death be so cataclysmic if she had had no hand in it?

Miss Taylor thought again about Pearce. How little one really knew about any of the students. Pearce, if one thought about her at all, had typified the dull, conscientious, unattractive student who was probably using nursing to compensate for the lack of more orthodox satisfactions. There was usually one such in every nurse training school. It was difficult to reject them when they applied for training since they offered more than adequate educational qualifications and impeccable references. And they didn't on the whole make bad nurses. It was just that they seldom made the best. But now she began to wonder. If Pearce had possessed such a secret craving for power that she could use this child's guilt and distress as fodder for her own ego, then she had been far from ordinary or ineffective. She had been a dangerous young woman.

And she had worked it all out very cleverly. By waiting a week until she could be reasonably certain that the money had been spent, she had left Dakers no option. The child could hardly claim then that she had yielded to a sudden impulse but intended to return the money. And even if Dakers had decided to confess, perhaps to the Matron, Nurse Harper would have had to be told: Pearce would have seen to that. And only Harper could decide whether or not to prosecute. It might have been possible to influence her, to persuade her to mercy. But suppose it had not been possible? Nurse Harper would almost certainly have confided in her father, and the Matron couldn't see Mr Ronald Harper showing mercy to anyone who had helped herself to his money. Miss Taylor's acquaintance with him had been brief but revealing. He had arrived at the hospital two days after Pearce's death, a large, opulent-looking and aggressive man, top-heavy in his fur-lined motoring coat. Without preliminaries or explanation he had launched into his prepared tirade, addressing Matron as if she were one of his garage hands. He wasn't going to let his girl stay another minute in a house with a murderer at large, police or no police. This nurse training had been a damn fool idea in the first place, and now it was going to stop. His Diane didn't need a career anyway. She was engaged, wasn't she? A bloody good match too! His partner's son. They could put the marriage forward instead of waiting until the summer and, in the meantime, Diane could stay at home and help in the office. He was taking her away with him now, and he'd like to see anyone try to stop him.

No one had stopped him. The girl had made no objection. She had stood meekly in the Matron's office overtly demure, but smiling a little as if gratified by all the fuss, by her father's assertive masculinity. The police could not prevent her leaving, nor had they seemed concerned to try. It was odd, thought the Matron, that no one had seriously suspected Harper; and if the two deaths were the work of one hand, their instinct had been right. She had last seen the girl stepping into her father's immense and ugly car, legs spindly beneath the new fur coat he had bought her to compensate for her disappointment at cutting short her training, and turning to wave good-bye to the rest of the set like a film star condescending to her assembled fans. No, not a particularly attractive family. Miss Taylor would be sorry for anyone who was in their power. And yet, such were the vagaries of personality, Diane Harper had been an efficient nurse, a better nurse in many ways than Pearce.

But there was one more question which had to be asked, and it took her a second to summon the courage to ask it.

'Did Nurse Fallon know about this business?'

The girl answered at once, confident, a little surprised.

'Oh no, Matron! At least I don't think so. Pearce swore that she wouldn't tell a soul, and it wasn't as if she was particularly friendly with Fallon. I'm sure she wouldn't have told Fallon.'

'No,' said Matron. 'I don't suppose she would.'

Gently she lifted Nurse Dakers's head and smoothed the pillows.

'Now I want you to try and get some sleep. You'll feel a great deal better when you wake up. And try not to worry.'

The girl's face relaxed. She smiled up at the Matron and, putting out her hand, briefly touched Miss Taylor's face. Then she snuggled down into the sheets as if resolute for sleep. So that was all right. But of course it was. It always worked. How easy and how insidiously satisfying was this doling out of advice and comfort, each portion individually flavoured to personal taste! She might be a Victorian vicar's wife presiding over a soup kitchen. To each according to her need. It happened in the hospital every day. A ward Sister's brightly professional voice. 'Here's Matron to see you, Mrs Cox. I'm afraid Mrs Cox isn't feeling quite so well this morning, Matron.' A tired pain-racked face smiling bravely up from the pillow, mouth avid for its morsel of affection and reassurance. The Sisters bringing their problems, the perpetual unsolvable problems over work and incompatible personalities.

'Are you feeling happier about it now, Sister?'

'Yes, thank you, Matron. Much happier.'

The Group Secretary, desperately coping with his own inadequacies.

'I should feel better if we could have just a word about the problem, Matron.' Of course he would! They all wanted to have just a word about the problem. They all went away feeling better. Hear what comfortable words our Matron saith. Her whole working life seemed a blasphemous liturgy of reassurance and absolution. And how much easier both to give and to accept was this bland milk of human kindness than the acid of truth. She could imagine the blank incomprehension, the resentment with which they would greet her private credo.

'I haven't anything to offer. There isn't any help. We are all alone, all of us from the moment of birth until we die. Our past is our present and our future. We have to live with ourselves until there isn't any more time left. If you want salvation look to yourself. There's nowhere else to look.'

She sat for a few more minutes and then quietly left the room. Nurse Dakers gave a brief valedictory smile. As she entered the corridor she saw Sister Brumfett and Mr Courtney-Briggs coming out of his patient's room. Sister Brumfett bustled up.

'I'm sorry, Matron. I didn't know you were on the ward.'

She always used the formal title. They might spend the whole of their off-duty together driving or golfing; they might visit a London show once a month with the cosy, boring regularity of an old married couple; they might drink their early morning tea and late night hot milk together in indissoluble tedium. But in the hospital Brumfett always called her Matron. The shrewd eyes searched hers.

'You've seen the new detective, the man from the Yard?'

'Only briefly. I'm due for a session with him as soon as I get back.'

Mr Courtney-Briggs said: 'I know him as a matter of fact; not well but we have met. You'll find him reasonable and intelligent. He's got quite a reputation of course. He's said to work very quickly. As far as I'm concerned, that's a considerable asset. The hospital can stand only so much disruption. He'll want to see me I suppose, but he'll have to wait. Let him know that I'll pop across to Nightingale House when I've finished my ward round, will you, Matron?'

'I'll tell him if he asks me,' replied Miss Taylor calmly. She turned to Sister Brumfett.

'Nurse Dakers is calmer now, but I think it would be better if she were not disturbed by visitors. She'll probably manage to get some sleep. I'll send over some magazines for her and some fresh flowers. When is Dr Snelling due to see her?'

'He said he would come in before lunch, Matron.'

'Perhaps you would ask him to be good enough to have a word with me. I shall be in the hospital all day.'

Sister Brumfett said: 'I suppose that Scotland Yard detective will want to see me too. I hope he isn't going to take too long about it. I've got a very sick ward.'

The Matron hoped that Brum wasn't going to be too difficult. It would be unfortunate if she thought she could treat a Chief Superintendent of the Metropolitan Police as if he were a recalcitrant House Surgeon. Mr Courtney-Briggs, no doubt, would be his usual arrogant self, but she had a feeling that Superintendent Dalgliesh would be able to cope with Mr Courtney-Briggs.

They walked to the door of the ward together. Miss Taylor's mind was already busy with fresh problems. Something would have to be done about Nurse Dakers's mother. It would be some years before the child was fully qualified as a district nurse. In the meantime she must be relieved of the constant anxiety about her mother. It might be helpful to have a word with Raymond Grout. There might be a clerical job somewhere in the hospital which would suit her. But would that be fair? One couldn't indulge one's own urge to help at someone else's expense. Whatever problems of staff recruitment the hospital service might have in London, Grout had no difficulty in filling his clerical jobs. He had a right to expect efficiency; and the Mrs Dakers of this world, dogged by their own inadequacy as much as by ill-luck, could seldom offer that. She supposed she would have to telephone the woman; the parents of the other students too. The important thing was to get the girls out of Nightingale House. The training schedule couldn't be disrupted; it was tight enough as it was. She had better arrange with the House Warden for them to sleep in the Nurses' Home – there would be room enough with so many nurses in the sick bay – and they could come over each day to use the library and lecture room. And then there would be the Vice-Chairman of the Hospital Management Committee to consult and the Press to cope with, the inquest to attend and the funeral arrangements to be discussed. People would be wanting to get in touch with her continually. But first, and most important, she must see Superintendent Dalgliesh.

FOUR

Questions and Answers

I

The Matron and Sisters had their living-quarters on the third floor of Nightingale House. When he reached the top of the staircase Dalgliesh saw that the south-west wing had been cut off from the rest of the landing by a specially constructed partition in white-painted wood in which a door, meanly proportioned and insubstantial in contrast to the high ceiling and oak-lined walls, bore the legend 'Matron's Flat'. There was a bell push, but before pressing it he briefly explored the corridor. It was similar to the one below but fitted with a red carpet which, although faded and scuffed, gave an illusion of comfort to the emptiness of this upper floor.

Dalgliesh moved silently from door to door. Each bore a hand-written name card slotted into the brass holder. He saw that Sister Brumfett occupied the room immediately adjacent to Matron's flat. Next was a bathroom, functionally divided into three mean cubicles, each with its bath and lavatory. The slot on the next door bore Sister Gearing's name; the next two rooms were empty. Sister Rolfe was at the north end of the corridor immediately next to the kitchen and utility room. Dalgliesh had no authority to enter any of the bedrooms but he tentatively turned the handles on each of the doors. As he expected, they were locked.

The Matron herself opened the door of her flat to him within seconds of his ring, and he followed her into the sitting-room. Its size and magnificence caught the breath. It occupied the whole of the south-west turret, an immense white-painted octagonal room, the ceiling starred in patterns of gold and pale blue, and with two huge windows facing out towards the hospital. One of the walls was lined from ceiling to floor with white bookcases. Dalgliesh resisted the impertinence of walking casually towards them in the hope of assessing Miss Taylor's character by her taste in literature. But he could see from where he stood that there were no textbooks, no bound official reports or sloping banks of files. This was a living-room, not an office.

An open fire burnt in the grate, the wood still crackling with its recent kindling. It had as yet made no impression on the air of the room which was cold and very still. Matron was wearing a short scarlet cape over her grey dress. She had taken off her head-dress and the huge coil of yellow hair lay like a burden on the frail, etiolated neck.

She was fortunate, he thought, to have been born in an age which could appreciate individuality of feature and form, owing everything to bone structure and nothing to the gentle nuances of femininity. A century ago she would have been called ugly, even grotesque. But today most men would think her interesting, and some might even describe her as beautiful. For Dalgliesh she was one of the most beautiful women he had ever met.

Placed precisely in the middle of the three windows was a sturdy oak table bearing a large black-and-white telescope. Dalgliesh saw that this was no amateur's toy but an expensive and sophisticated instrument. It dominated the room. The Matron saw his eyes upon it and said:

'Are you interested in astronomy?'

'Not particularly.'

She smiled. '"*Le silence éternel de ces espaces infinis m'effraie*"?'

'Discomforts rather than terrifies. It's probably my vanity. I can't interest myself in anything which I not only don't understand but know that I have no prospect of ever understanding.'

'That for me is the attraction. It's a form of escapism, even of voyeurism, I suppose – this absorption in an impersonal universe which I can't do anything to influence or control and, better still, which no one expects me to. It's an abdication of responsibility. It restores personal problems to their proper proportion.'

She motioned Dalgliesh towards the black leather sofa in front of the fire. Before it, a low table held a tray with a coffee percolator, hot milk, crystal sugar and two cups.

As he seated himself, he smiled and said: 'If I want to indulge in humility or speculate on the incomprehensible, I prefer to look at a primrose. The expense is nugatory, the pleasure is more immediate, and the moral just as valid.'

The mobile mouth mocked him.

'And at least you restrict your indulgence in these dangerous philosophical speculations to a few short weeks in the spring.'

The conversation is, he thought, a verbal pavane. If I'm not careful I shall begin to enjoy it. I wonder when she will get down to business. Or is she expecting me to make the first move? And why not? It is I who am the suppliant, the intruder.

As if reading his thoughts, she said suddenly:

'It's odd that they should both have been such friendless girls, both orphans. It makes my task less onerous. There aren't any desolated parents to be comforted, thank God. Nurse Pearce only had the grandparents who brought her up. He's a retired miner and they live in some poverty in a cottage outside Nottingham. They belong to a very puritanical religious sect and their only reaction to the child's death was to say, "God's Will be Done." It seemed an odd response to a tragedy which was so obviously the will of man.'

'So you think Nurse Pearce's death was murder then?'

'Not necessarily. But I don't accuse God of tampering with the intra-gastric drip.'

'And Nurse Fallon's relatives?'

'None, as far as I know. She was asked for her next of kin when she first became a student and told us she was an orphan with no blood relations living. There was no reason to question it. It was probably true. But her death will be in the papers tomorrow and if there are any relatives or friends no doubt we shall be hearing from them. You've spoken to the students, I expect?'

'I've just had a preliminary talk with them as a group. I saw them in the demonstration room. It's been useful in giving me a background to the case. They've all agreed to be fingerprinted and that's being done now. I shall need the prints of everyone who was in Nightingale House last night and this morning, if only for elimination purposes. And I shall, of course, need to interview everyone separately. But I'm glad of this chance to see you first. After all, you were in Amsterdam when Nurse Fallon died. That means there's one less suspect for me to worry about.'

He saw with surprise her knuckles whiten around the handle of the coffee pot. Her face flushed. She closed her eyes and he thought he heard her sigh. He watched her a little disconcerted. What he had said must surely be obvious to a woman of her intelligence. He hardly knew why he had bothered to say it. If this second death were murder, then anyone with an alibi covering the whole of yesterday evening and night must be free of suspicion. As if sensing his surprise, she said:

'I'm sorry. I must seem obtuse. I know it's foolish to feel such relief at not being under suspicion when one knows anyway that one is innocent. Perhaps it's because none of us is innocent in any real sense. A psychologist could explain it, I'm sure. But ought you to be so confident? Couldn't the poison – if it were poison – have been put into Fallon's whisky bottle any time after she bought it, or another and poisoned bottle substituted for the one she purchased? That could have been done before I left for Amsterdam on Tuesday evening.'

'I'm afraid you must resign yourself to innocence. Miss Fallon bought this particular bottle of whisky from Scunthorpe's wine shop in the High Street yesterday afternoon, and took her first and only drink from it on the night she died. The bottle is still almost full, the whisky remaining is perfectly good whisky as far as we know, and the only prints on the bottle are Miss Fallon's own.'

'You've worked very fast. So the poison was put either into the glass after she'd poured her hot drink or into the sugar?'

'If she were poisoned. We can't be sure of anything till we get the P.M. report and perhaps not even then. The sugar is being tested but that is really only a formality. Most of the students helped themselves from that bowl when they had their early morning tea and at least two of the girls drank theirs. So that leaves us with the beaker of whisky and hot lemon. Miss Fallon made it very easy for a murderer. Apparently the whole of Nightingale House knew that, if she didn't go out in the evening, she watched the television until the programme closed down. She was a poor sleeper and never went to bed early. When the television ended she would go to her room and undress. Then in her bedroom slippers and dressing-gown she would go to the little pantry on the second floor and make her nightcap. She kept the whisky in her room but she couldn't make the drink there because there's no water laid on and no means of heating it. So it was her habit to take the insulated tumbler with the whisky poured out ready and add the hot lemon in the pantry. A supply of lemons was kept there in the cupboard with the cocoa, coffee, chocolate and other items with which the nurses tend to make their late night drinks. Then she would take the tumbler back to her room and leave it on the bedside locker while she had her bath. She always bathed quickly and she liked to get into bed immediately afterwards while she was still warm. I expect that's why she made her drink before she went into the bathroom. By the time she got back to her room and into bed, the drink was at precisely the right temperature. And apparently the routine never varied.'

The Matron said: 'It's rather frightening how much people get to know about each other's habits in a small closed community like this. But, of course, it's inevitable. There's no real privacy. How can there be? I knew about the whisky, of course, but it hardly seemed my business. The girl certainly wasn't an incipient alcoholic and she wasn't handing it out to the younger students. At her age she was entitled to her own choice of nightcap.'

Dalgliesh asked how the Matron had learned about the whisky.

'Nurse Pearce told me. She asked to see me and gave me the information in a spirit of "I don't want to tell tales but I think you ought to know." Drink and the devil were one and the same to Nurse Pearce. But I don't think Fallon made any secret of the whisky drinking. How could she? As I said, we know about each other's little habits. But there are some things, of course, that we don't know. Josephine Fallon was a very private person. I can't give you any information about her life outside the hospital and I doubt whether anyone here can.'

'Who was her friend here? She must have had someone she confided in, surely? Isn't that necessary for any woman in this kind of closed community?'

She looked at him a little strangely.

'Yes. We all need someone. But I think Fallon needed a friend less than most. She was remarkably self-sufficient. If she confided in anyone it would be Madeleine Goodale.'

'The plain one with the round face and large spectacles?'

Dalgliesh recalled her. It was not an unattractive face, mainly because of the good skin and the intelligence of those large grey eyes behind the thick horn rims. But Nurse Goodale could never be other than plain. He thought he could picture her future: the years of training willingly endured, the success in examinations; the gradually increasing responsibility until, at last, she too was a Matron. It was not unusual for such a girl to be friendly with a more attractive woman. It was one way of gaining at least a vicarious share in a more romantic, less dedicated life. As if reading his thoughts, Miss Taylor said:

'Nurse Goodale is one of our most efficient nurses. I was hoping that she would stay on after her training and take a post as staff nurse. But that is hardly likely. She's engaged to our local vicar and they want to marry next Easter.'

She glanced across at Dalgliesh a little maliciously.

'He is considered a most eligible young man. You seem surprised, Superintendent.'

Dalgliesh laughed: 'After over twenty years as a policeman I should have learned not to make superficial judgements. I think I had better see Nurse Goodale first. I understand the room you're making available isn't ready yet. I suppose we could go on using the demonstration room. Or are you likely to be needing it?'

'I would prefer you to see the girls somewhere else if you would. That room has very unhappy and dramatic memories for them. We're not even using it yet for teaching demonstrations. Until the small visitors' room on the first floor is ready I'd be happy for you to interview the students here.'

Dalgliesh thanked her. He replaced his coffee cup on the table.

She hesitated, then said: 'Mr Dalgliesh, there's one thing I want to say. I feel – I am – *in loco parentis* to my students. If ever any question . . . if you should begin to suspect that any one of them is involved, I can rely on you to let me know? They would then need protection. There would surely be the question of getting a solicitor.'

She hesitated again: 'Please forgive me if I'm being offensive.

One has so little experience of these matters. It's just that I shouldn't like them . . .'

'To be trapped?'

'To be rushed into saying things which might quite wrongly incriminate them or other members of the staff.'

Dalgliesh found himself unreasonably irritated.

'There are rules laid down, you know,' he said.

'Oh, rules! I know there are rules. But I'm sure you are both too experienced and too intelligent to let them hinder you over much. I'm just reminding you that these girls are less intelligent and in such matters not experienced at all.'

Fighting his irritation, Dalgliesh said formally:

'I can only tell you that the rules are there and that it's in our interests to keep them. Can't you imagine what a gift to the defending counsel any infringement would be? A young unprotected girl, a student nurse, bullied by a senior police officer with years of experience in trapping the unwary. Enough difficulties are placed in the path of the police in this country; we don't voluntarily add to them.'

She flushed and he was interested to see the wave of colour sweep from her neck over the pale honey-glow skin making her look momentarily as if the veins ran with fire. Then, instantaneously, it passed. The change was so sudden that he couldn't be sure that he had actually seen that tell-tale metamorphosis. She said composedly:

'We both have our responsibilities. We must hope that they don't conflict. In the meantime you must expect me to be as concerned with mine as you are with yours. And that brings me to some information which I have to give you. It concerns Christine Dakers, the student who discovered Nurse Fallon's body.'

She described briefly and succinctly what had happened during her visit to the private ward. Dalgliesh noted with interest that she made no comment, offered no opinion, and attempted no justification of the girl. He didn't ask her whether she believed the story. She was a highly intelligent woman. She must know that what she had handed him was the first motive. He asked when he would be able to interview Nurse Dakers.

'She's sleeping now. Dr Snelling, who is in charge of the nurses' health, is to see her later this morning. He will then report to me. If he agrees, it should be possible for you to see her this afternoon. And now I'll send for Nurse Goodale. That is, if there is nothing more I can tell you?'

'I shall need a great deal of information about people's ages, backgrounds and the time they've been at the hospital. Won't that be on their personal records? It would be helpful if I could have those.'

The Matron thought. Dalgliesh noticed that when she did so her face fell into absolute repose. After a moment she said:

'All the staff here have personal dossiers, of course. Legally these are the property of the Hospital Management Committee. The Chairman won't be back from Israel until tomorrow evening but I'll consult the Vice-Chairman. I imagine that he will ask me to look through the records, and if they contain nothing private which is irrelevant to your inquiry, to pass them over.'

Dalgliesh decided that it would be prudent not to press for the moment the question of who should decide what was irrelevant to his inquiry.

He said: 'There are personal questions I shall have to ask, of course. But it would be a great deal more convenient and would save time if I could get the routine information from the records.'

It was strange that her voice could be so agreeable and yet so obstinate.

'I can see that it would be a great deal more convenient; it would also be a check on the truth of what you are told. But the records can only be handed over under the conditions I have just stated.'

So she was confident that the Vice-Chairman would accept and endorse her view of what was right. And undoubtedly he would. Here was a formidable woman. Faced with a tricky problem she had given the matter thought, come to a decision and had stated it firmly without apology or wavering. An admirable woman. She would be easy to deal with as long, of course, as all her decisions were as acceptable as this.

He asked if he might use the telephone, recalled Sergeant Masterson from his supervision of the preparation of the small visitors' room to serve as an office; and prepared himself for the long tedium of the individual interviews.

II

Nurse Goodale was summoned by telephone and arrived within two minutes looking unhurried and composed. Miss Taylor seemed to think that neither explanation nor reassurance was necessary to this self-possessed young woman but simply said:

'Sit down, Nurse. Superintendent Dalgliesh wants to talk to you.'

Then she took up her cloak from the chair, swung it over her shoulders, and went out without another glance at either of them. Sergeant Masterson opened his notebook. Nurse Goodale seated herself in an upright chair at the table but, when Dalgliesh motioned her to an armchair before the fire, moved without demur. She sat stiffly on the very edge of the chair, her back straight, her surprisingly shapely and elegant legs planted modestly side by side. But the hands lying in her lap were perfectly relaxed and Dalgliesh, seated opposite, found himself confronting a pair of disconcertingly intelligent eyes. He said:

'You were probably closer to Miss Fallon than anyone else in the hospital. Tell me about her.'

She showed no surprise at the form of his first question, but paused for a few seconds before replying as if marshalling her thoughts. Then she said:

'I liked her. She tolerated me better than she did most of the other students but I don't think her feeling for me was much stronger than that. She was thirty-one after all, and we must all have seemed rather immature to her. She had a rather sarcastic tongue which didn't help, and I think some of the girls were rather afraid of her.

'She seldom spoke to me about her past but she did tell me that both her parents were killed in 1944 in a bombing raid in London. She was brought up by an elderly aunt and educated at one of those boarding-schools where they take children from an early age and keep them until they're ready to leave. Provided the fees are paid of course, but I got the impression that there wasn't any difficulty about that. She always wanted to be a nurse, but she got tuberculosis after she left school and had to spend two years in a sanatorium. I don't know where. After that, two hospitals turned her down on grounds of health, so she took a number of temporary jobs. She told me soon after we began our training that she had once been engaged but that it didn't work out.'

'You never asked her why?'

'I never asked her anything. If she had wanted to tell me she would have done so.'

'Did she tell you that she was pregnant?'

'Yes, she told me two days before she went sick. She must have suspected before then but the confirming report came that morning. I asked her what she intended doing about it and she said that she would get rid of the baby.'

'Did you point out that this was probably illegal?'

'No. She didn't care about legality. I told her that it was wrong.'

'But she still intended to go ahead with the abortion?'

'Yes. She said that she knew a doctor who would do it and that there wouldn't be any real risk. I asked her if she needed money and she said that she would be all right, that money was the least of her problems. She never told me who she was going to, and I didn't ask.'

'But you were prepared to help her with money had she needed it, even though you disapproved of getting rid of the baby?'

'My disapproval wasn't important. What was important was that it was wrong. But when I knew that she had made up her mind I had to decide whether to help her. I was afraid that she might go to some unqualified back street abortionist and risk her life and health. I know that the law has changed, that it's easier now to get a medical recommendation, but I didn't think she would qualify. I had to make a moral decision. If you are proposing to commit a sin it is as well to commit it with intelligence. Otherwise you are insulting God as well as defying Him, don't you think?'

Dalgliesh said gravely: 'It's an interesting theological point which I'm not competent to argue. Did she tell you who was the father of the child?'

'Not directly. I think it may have been a young writer she was friendly with. I don't know his name or where you can find him but I do know that Jo spent a week with him in the Isle of Wight last October. She had seven days' holiday due and she told me that she'd decided to walk in the island with a friend. I imagine he was the friend. It certainly wasn't anyone from here. They went during the first week and she told me that they'd stayed in a small inn about five miles south of Ventnor. That's all she did tell me. I suppose it's possible she became pregnant during that week?'

Dalgliesh said: 'The dates would fit. And she never confided in you about the father of the child?'

'No. I asked her why she wouldn't marry the father and she said that it would be unfair to the child to burden it with two irresponsible parents. I remember her saying: "He would be horrified at the idea, anyway, unless he had a sudden urge to experience fatherhood just to see what it was like. And he might like to see the baby born so that he could write a lurid account of childbirth some day. But he really isn't committed to anyone but himself."'

'But did she care for him?'

The girl paused a full minute before replying. Then she said:

'I think she did. I think that may have been why she killed herself.'

'What makes you think that she did?'

'I suppose because the alternative is even more unlikely. I never thought that Jo was the type to kill herself – if there is a type. But I really didn't know her. One never does really know another human being. Anything is possible for anyone. I've always believed that. And it's surely more likely that she killed herself than that someone murdered her. That seems absolutely incredible. Why should they?'

'I was hoping you might be able to tell me.'

'Well, I can't. She hadn't any enemies at the John Carpendar as far as I know. She wasn't popular. She was too reserved, too solitary. But people didn't dislike her. And even if they did, murder surely suggests something more than ordinary dislike. It seems so much more probable that she came back to duty too soon after influenza, was overcome by psychological depression, felt she couldn't cope with getting rid of the baby, and yet couldn't face up to having an illegitimate child and killed herself on impulse.'

'You said when I questioned you all in the demonstration room that you were probably the last person to see her alive. What exactly happened when you were together last night? Did she give you any idea that she might be thinking of suicide?'

'If she had, I should hardly have left her to go to bed alone. She said nothing. I don't think we exchanged more than half a dozen words. I asked her how she felt and she replied that she was all right. She obviously wasn't in the mood to chat so I didn't make myself a nuisance. After about twenty minutes I went up to bed. I never saw her again.'

'And she didn't mention her pregnancy?'

'She mentioned nothing. She looked tired, I thought, and rather pale. But then, Jo always was rather pale. It's distressing for me to think that she might have needed help and that I left her without speaking the words that might have saved her. But she wasn't a woman to invite confidences. I stayed behind when the others left because I thought she might want to talk. When it was plain that she wanted to be alone, I left.'

She talked about being distressed, thought Dalgliesh, but she neither looked nor sounded it. She felt no self-reproach. Why indeed should she? He doubted whether she felt particular grief. She had been closer to Josephine Fallon than any of the students. But she had not really cared. Was there anyone in the world who had? He asked:

'And Nurse Pearce's death?'

'I think that was essentially an accident. Someone put the poison in the feed as a joke or out of vague malice without realizing that the result would be fatal.'

'Which would be odd in a third-year student nurse whose programme of lectures presumably included basic information on corrosive poisons.'

'I wasn't suggesting that it was a nurse. I don't know who it was. I don't think you'll ever find out now. But I can't believe that it was wilful murder.'

That was all very well, thought Dalgliesh, but surely it was a little disingenuous in a girl as intelligent as Nurse Goodale. It was, of course, the popular, almost the official view. It exonerated everyone from the worst crime and indicted no one of anything more than malice and carelessness. It was a comforting theory, and unless he were lucky it might never be disproved. But he didn't believe it himself, and he couldn't accept that Nurse Goodale did. But it was even harder to accept that here was a girl to comfort herself with false theories or deliberately to shut her eyes to unpalatable facts.

Dalgliesh then asked her about her movements on the morning of Pearce's death. He already knew them from Inspector Bailey's notes and her previous statement and was not surprised when Nurse Goodale confirmed them without hesitation. She had got up at six forty-five and had drunk early morning tea with the rest of the set in the utility room. She had told them about Fallon's influenza since it was to her room that Nurse Fallon had come when she was taken ill in the night. None of the students had expressed particular concern but they had wondered how the demonstration would go now that the set was so decimated and had speculated, not without malice, how Sister Gearing would acquit herself in the face of a G.N.C. inspection. Nurse Pearce had drunk her tea with the rest of the set and Nurse Goodale thought that she remembered Pearce saying:

'With Fallon ill, I suppose I shall have to act the patient.' Nurse Goodale couldn't recall any comment or discussion about this. It was well accepted that the next student on the list substituted for anyone who was ill.

After she had drunk her tea, Nurse Goodale had dressed and had then made her way to the library to revise the treatment of larynectomy in preparation for the morning's session. It was important that there should be a quick and lively response to questions if the seminar were to be a success. She had settled herself to work at about seven-fifteen and Nurse Dakers had joined her shortly afterwards, sharing a devotion to study which, thought Dalgliesh, had at least been rewarded by an alibi for most of the time before breakfast. She and Dakers had said nothing of interest to each other while they had been working and had left the library at the same time and gone in to breakfast together. That had been at about ten minutes to eight. She had sat with Dakers and the Burt twins, but had left the breakfast room before them. That was at eight-fifteen. She had returned to her bedroom to make the bed, and then gone to the library to write a couple of letters. That done, she had paid a brief visit to the cloakroom and had made her way to the demonstration room just before a quarter to nine. Only Sister Gearing and the Burt twins were already there, but the rest of the set had joined them shortly afterwards; she couldn't remember in what order. She thought that Pearce had been one of the last to arrive.

Dalgliesh asked: 'How did Nurse Pearce seem?'

'I noticed nothing unusual about her, but then I wouldn't expect to. Pearce was Pearce. She made a negligible impression.'

'Did she say anything before the demonstration began?'

'Yes, she did as a matter of fact. It's odd that you should ask that. I haven't mentioned it before. I suppose because Inspector Bailey didn't ask. But she did speak. She looked round at us – the set had all assembled by then – and asked if anyone had taken anything from her bedroom.'

'Did she say what?'

'No. She just stood there with that accusing rather belligerent look she occasionally had and said: "Has anyone been to my room this morning or taken anything from it?"

'No one replied. I think we just all shook our heads. It wasn't a question we took particularly seriously. Pearce was apt to make a great fuss about trifles. Anyway, the Burt twins were busy with their preparations and the rest of us were chatting. Pearce didn't get a great deal of attention paid to her question. I doubt whether half of us heard her even.'

'Did you notice how she reacted? Was she worried or angry or distressed?'

'None of those things. It was odd really. I remember now. She looked satisfied, almost triumphant, as if something she suspected had been confirmed. I don't know why I noticed that, but I did. Sister Gearing then called us to order and the demonstration began.'

Dalgliesh did not immediately speak at the end of this recital and, after a little time, she took his silence for dismissal and rose to go. She got out of her chair with the same controlled grace as she had seated herself, smoothed her apron with a scarcely discernible gesture, gave him a last interrogatory glance and walked to the door. Then she turned as if yielding to an impulse.

'You asked me if anyone had a reason to kill Jo. I said I knew of no one. That is true. But I suppose a legal motive is something different. I ought to tell you that some people might think I have a motive.'

Dalgliesh said: 'Had you?'

'I expect you'll think so. I am Jo's heir, at least I think I am. She told me about three months ago that she had made her will and that she was leaving me all she had. She gave me the name and address of her solicitor. I can let you have the information. They haven't yet written to me but I expect they will, that is if Jo really made her will. But I expect she did. She wasn't a girl to make promises she didn't fulfil. Perhaps you would prefer to get in touch with the solicitors now? These things take time, don't they?'

'Did she say why she was making you her legatee?'

'She said that she had to leave her money to someone and that I would probably do most good with it. I didn't take the matter very seriously and neither, I think, did she. After all she was only thirty-one. She wasn't expecting to die. And she warned me that she'd probably change her mind long before she got old enough to make the legacy a serious prospect for me. After all she'd probably marry. But she felt she ought to make a will and I was the only person at the time who she cared to remember. I thought that it was only a formality. It never occurred to me that she might have much to leave. It was only when we had our talk about the cost of an abortion that she told me how much she was worth.'

'And what was it – is it – much?'

The girl answered calmly: 'About £16,000 I believe. It came from her parents' insurances.'

She smiled a little wrily.

'Quite worth having you see, Superintendent. I should think it would rank as a perfectly respectable motive, wouldn't you? We shall be able to put central heating in the vicarage now. And if you saw my fiancé's vicarage – twelve rooms, nearly all of them facing north or east – you would think I had quite a motive for murder.'

III

Sister Rolfe and Sister Gearing were waiting with the students in the library; they had moved from the nurses' sitting-room in order to occupy the waiting time with reading and revision. How much the girls were really taking in was problematic, but the scene certainly looked peaceful and studious enough. The students had seated themselves at the desks in front of the window and sat, books open before them, in apparent absorption. Sister Rolfe and Sister Gearing, as if to emphasize their seniority and solidarity, had withdrawn to the sofa in front of the fire and were seated side by side. Sister Rolfe was marking with green biro a pile of first-year students' exercises, picking up each notebook from a stack on the floor at her feet, and adding it, when dealt with, to the growing pile which rested against the back of the sofa. Sister Gearing was ostensibly making notes for her next lecture, but seemed unable to keep her eyes from her colleague's decisive hieroglyphics.

The door opened and Madeleine Goodale returned. Without a word she went back to her desk, took up her pen and resumed work.

Sister Gearing whispered: 'Goodale seems calm enough. Odd, considering she was supposed to be Fallon's best friend.'

Sister Rolfe did not raise her eyes. She said drily:

'She didn't really care about Fallon. Goodale has only a limited emotional capital and I imagine she expends it all on that extraordinarily dull person she's decided to marry.'

'He's good-looking, though. Goodale's lucky to get him, if you ask me.'

But the subject was of a secondary interest to Sister Gearing and she didn't pursue it. After a minute she said peevishly:

'Why haven't the police sent for someone else?'

'They will.' Sister Rolfe added another exercise book, liberally embellished in green, to a completed pile by her side. 'They're probably discussing Goodale's contribution.'

'They ought to have seen us first. After all, we're Sisters. Matron should have explained. And why isn't Brumfett here? I don't see why she should be treated any differently from us.'

Sister Rolfe: 'Too busy. Apparently a couple of the second-year students on the ward have now gone down with flu. She sent over some sort of note to Mr Dalgliesh by a porter, presumably giving information about her movements last night. I met him bringing it in. He asked me where he could find the gentleman from Scotland Yard.'

Sister Gearing's voice became petulant.

'That's all very well, but she ought to be here. God knows, we're busy too! Brumfett lives in Nightingale House; she had as much opportunity to kill Fallon as anyone.'

Sister Gearing said quietly: 'She had more chance.'

'What do you mean, more chance?'

Sister Gearing's sharp voice cut into the silence and one of the Burt twins lifted her head.

'She's had Fallon in her power in the sick bay for the last ten days.'

'But surely you don't mean . . .? Brumfett wouldn't!'

'Precisely,' said Sister coldly. 'So why make stupid and irresponsible remarks?'

There was a silence broken only by the rustle of paper and the hiss of the gas fire. Sister Gearing fidgeted.

'I suppose if Brumfett's lost another two nurses with flu she'll be pressing Matron to recall some of this block. She's got her eyes on the Burt twins, I know.'

'Then she'll be unlucky. This set have had their training disrupted enough already. After all, it's their last block before their finals. Matron won't let it be cut short.'

'I shouldn't be too sure. It's Brumfett, remember. Matron doesn't usually say no to her. Funny though, I did hear a rumour that they aren't going on holiday together this year. One of the pharmacists' assistants had it from Matron's secretary that Matron plans to motor in Ireland on her own.'

My God, thought Sister Rolfe. Isn't there any privacy in this place? But she said nothing, only shifting a few inches from the restless figure at her side.

It was then that the wall telephone rang. Sister Gearing leapt and went across to answer it. She turned to the rest of the group, her face creased with disappointment.

'That was Sergeant Masterson. Superintendent Dalgliesh would like to see the Burt twins next please. He's moved to the visitors' sitting-room on this floor.'

Without a word and with no signs of nervousness, the Burt twins closed their books and made for the door.

IV

It was half an hour later and Sergeant Masterson was making coffee. The visitors' sitting-room had been provided with a miniature kitchen, a large recess fitted with a sink and Formica-covered cupboard, on which stood a double gas-ring. The cupboard had been cleared of all its paraphernalia except for four large beakers, a canister of sugar and one of tea, a tin of biscuits, a large earthenware jug and strainer, and three transparent air-tight packets of fresh-ground coffee. By the side of the sink were two bottles of milk. The cream-line was easily discernible, but Sergeant Masterson prised the cap away from one of the bottles and sniffed at the milk suspiciously before heating a quantity in a saucepan. He warmed the earthenware jug with hot water from the tap, dried it carefully on the tea towel which hung by the side of the sink, spooned in a generous quantity of coffee and stood waiting for the kettle's first burst of steam. He approved of the arrangements that had been made. If the police had to work in Nightingale House this room was as convenient and comfortable as any and the coffee was an unexpected bonus which, mentally, he credited to Paul Hudson. The Hospital Secretary had struck him as an efficient and imaginative man. His couldn't be an easy job. The poor devil probably had one hell of a life, sandwiched between those two old fools, Kealey and Grout, and that high-handed bitch of a Matron.

He strained the coffee with meticulous care and carried a beaker over to his chief. They sat and drank companionably together, eyes straying to the storm-wrecked garden. Both of them had a strong dislike of badly cooked food or synthetic coffee and Masterson thought that they never got closer to liking each other than when they were eating and drinking together, deploring the inadequacies of the meals at the inn, or as now, rejoicing in good coffee. Dalgliesh comforted his hands around the beaker and thought that it was typical of Mary Taylor's efficiency and imagination to ensure that they had real coffee available. Hers couldn't be an easy job. That ineffectual couple, Kealey and Grout, wouldn't be much help to anyone, and Paul Hudson was too young to give much support.

After a moment of appreciative sipping, Masterson said:

'That was a disappointing interview, sir.'

'The Burt twins? Yes, I must say I had hoped for something more interesting. After all, they were at the centre of the mystery; they administered the fatal drip; they glimpsed the mysterious Nurse Fallon on her way out of Nightingale House; they met Sister Brumfett on her perambulations in the early hours. But we knew all that already. And we don't know any more now.'

Dalgliesh thought about the two girls. Masterson had drawn up a second chair on their entrance and they had sat there side by side, freckled hands ritualistically disposed in their laps, legs modestly crossed, each girl a mirror image of her twin. Their polite antiphonal answers to his questions, spoken in a West Country burr, were as agreeable to the ear as their shining good health to the eye. He had rather taken to the Burt twins. He might, of course, have been facing a couple of experienced accomplices in evil. Anything was possible. Certainly they had had the best opportunity to poison the drip and as good a chance as anyone in Nightingale House to doctor Fallon's nightcap. Yet they had seemed perfectly at ease with him, a little bored perhaps at having to repeat much of their story, but neither frightened nor particularly worried. From time to time they had gazed at him with a gentle speculative concern rather as if he were a difficult patient whose condition was beginning to give rise to some anxiety. He had noticed this intent and compassionate regard on the faces of other nurses during their first encounter in the demonstration room and had found it disconcerting.

'And you noticed nothing odd about the milk?'

They had answered almost in unison, rebuking him in the calm voice of common sense.

'Oh no! Well, we wouldn't have gone ahead with the drip if we had, would we?'

'Can you remember taking the cap off the bottle, was it loose?'

Two pairs of blue eyes looked at each other, almost as if in signal. Then Maureen replied:

'We don't remember that it was. But even if it had been, we wouldn't have suspected that someone had been at the milk. We would just have thought that the dairy put it on like that.'

Then Shirley spoke on her own:

'I don't think we would have noticed anything wrong with the milk anyway. You see, we were concentrating on the procedures for giving the drip, making sure that we had all the instruments and equipment we needed. We knew that Miss Beale and Matron would arrive at any minute.'

That, of course, was the explanation. They were girls who had been trained to observe, but their observation was specific and limited. If they were watching a patient they would miss nothing of his signs or symptoms, not a flicker of the eyelids or a change of pulse; anything else happening in the room, however dramatic, would probably be unnoticed. Their attention had been on the demonstration, the apparatus, the equipment, the patient. The bottle of milk presented no problems. They had taken it for granted. And yet they were farmer's daughters. One of them – it had been Maureen – had actually poured the stuff from the bottle. Could they really have mistaken the colour, the texture, the smell of milk?

As if reading his thoughts Maureen said:

'It wasn't as if we could smell the carbolic. The whole demo room stinks of disinfectant. Miss Collins throws the stuff around as if we're all lepers.'

Shirley laughed: 'Carbolic isn't effective against leprosy!'

They looked at each other, smiling in happy complicity.

And so the interview had gone on. They had no theories to propound, no suggestions to offer. They knew no one who could wish Pearce or Fallon dead, and yet both deaths – since they had occurred – seemed to cause them no particular surprise. They could recall every word of the conversation between Sister Brumfett and themselves in the small hours of that morning, yet the encounter apparently had made little impression on them. When Dalgliesh asked if the Sister had seemed unusually worried or distressed, they gazed at him simultaneously, brows creased in perplexity, before replying that Sister had seemed just the same as usual.

As if following his chief's thought, Masterson said:

'Short of asking them outright if Sister Brumfett looked as if she'd come straight from murdering Fallon you couldn't have put it much plainer. They're an odd uncommunicative couple.'

'At least they're sure of the time. They took that milk shortly after seven o'clock and went straight into the demonstration room with it. They stood the bottle unopened on the instrument trolley while they made preliminary preparations for the demonstration. They left the demonstration room at seven twenty-five for breakfast and the bottle was still on the trolley when they returned at about twenty to nine to complete their preparations. They then stood it, still unopened, in a jug of hot water to bring it to blood heat and it remained there until they poured the milk from the bottle into a measuring jug about two minutes before Miss Beale and Matron's party arrived. Most of the suspects were at breakfast together from eight until eight twenty-five, so that the mischief was either done between seven twenty-five and eight o'clock or in the short period between the end of breakfast and the twins' return to the demonstration room.'

Masterson said: 'I still find it strange that they noticed nothing odd about that milk.'

'They may have noticed more than they realize at present. After all, this is the umpteenth time they've told their story. During the weeks since Pearce's death, their first statements have become fixed in their minds as the immutable truth. That's why I haven't asked them the crucial question about the milk bottle. If they gave me the wrong answer now they'd never change it. They need to be shocked into total recall. They're not seeing anything that happened with fresh eyes. I dislike reconstructions of the crime; they always make me feel like a fictional detective.

But I think there may be a case for reconstruction here. I shall have to be in London early tomorrow, but you and Greeson can see to it. Greeson will probably enjoy himself.'

He told Masterson briefly what he proposed and ended:

'You needn't bother to include the Sisters. I expect you can get a supply of the disinfectant from Miss Collins. But for God's sake keep an eye on the stuff and chuck it away afterwards. We don't want another tragedy.'

Sergeant Masterson took up the two beakers and carried them to the sink. He said:

'Nightingale House does seem to be touched with ill-luck, but I can't see the killer having another go while we're around.'

It was to prove a singularly unprophetic remark.

V

Since her encounter with Dalgliesh in the nurses' utility room earlier that morning Sister Rolfe had had time to recover from shock and to consider her position. As Dalgliesh had expected she was now far less forthcoming. She had already given to Inspector Bailey a clear and unambiguous statement about the arrangements for the demonstration and the intra-gastric feeding and about her own movements on the morning that Nurse Pearce died. She confirmed the statement accurately and without fuss. She agreed that she had known that Nurse Pearce was to act the part of the patient and pointed out sarcastically that there would be little point in denying the knowledge since it was she whom Madeleine Goodale had called when Fallon was taken ill.

Dalgliesh asked: 'Did you have any doubt of the genuineness of her illness?'

'At the time?'

'Then or now.'

'I suppose you're suggesting that Fallon could have feigned influenza to ensure that Pearce took her place, and then sneaked back to Nightingale House before breakfast to doctor the drip? I don't know why she did come back, but you can put any idea that she was pretending to be ill out of your head. Even Fallon couldn't simulate a temperature of 103.8, a minor rigor and a racing pulse. She was a very sick girl that night, and she remained sick for nearly ten days.'

Dalgliesh pointed out that it was all the more odd that she should have been well enough to make her way back to Nightingale House next morning. Sister Rolfe replied that it was so odd that she could only assume that Fallon had had an imperative need to return. Invited to speculate on what that need could have been she replied that it wasn't her job to propound theories. Then, as if under a compulsion, she added:

'But it wasn't to murder Pearce. Fallon was highly intelligent, easily the most intelligent of her year. If Fallon came back to put the corrosive in the feed she would know perfectly well there was a considerable risk of her being seen in Nightingale House even if she weren't missed on the ward, and she'd have taken good care to have a story ready. It wouldn't have been difficult to think of something. As it is, I gather she merely declined to give Inspector Bailey any explanation.'

'Perhaps she was clever enough to realize that this extraordinary reticence would strike another intelligent woman in exactly that way.'

'A kind of double bluff? I don't think so. It would be banking too heavily on the intelligence of the police.'

She admitted calmly that she had no alibi for any of the time from seven o'clock when the twins had collected the bottle of milk from the kitchen until ten minutes to nine when she had joined the Matron and Mr Courtney-Briggs in Miss Taylor's sitting-room to await the arrival of Miss Beale, except for the period from eight to eight twenty-five when she had breakfasted at the same table as Sister Brumfett and Sister Gearing. Sister Brumfett had left the table first and she had followed at about eight twenty-five. She had gone first to her office next door to the demonstration room, but finding Mr Courtney-Briggs in occupation, had made her way at once to her bed-sitting-room on the third floor.

When Dalgliesh asked whether Sister Gearing and Sister Brumfett had appeared their usual selves at breakfast she replied drily that they exhibited no signs of impending homicidal mania if that was what he meant. Gearing had read the *Daily Mirror* and

Brumfett the *Nursing Times*, if that were of any significance, and the conversation had been minimal. She regretted she could offer no witness to her own movements before or after the meal but that was surely understandable; for some years now she had preferred to wash and go to the lavatory in private. Apart from that, she valued the free time before the day's work and preferred to spend it alone.

Dalgliesh asked: 'Were you surprised to find Mr Courtney-Briggs in your office when you went there after breakfast?'

'Not particularly. I took it for granted that he had spent the night in the medical officers' quarters and had come over early to Nightingale House to meet the G.N.C. Inspector. He probably wanted somewhere to write a letter. Mr Courtney-Briggs assumes the right to use any room in the John Carpendar as his private office if the fancy takes him.'

Dalgliesh asked her about her movements the previous night. She repeated that she had been to the cinema alone but added this time that she had met Julia Pardoe on the way out and that they had walked back to the hospital together. They had come in through the Winchester Road gate to which she had a key and had got back to Nightingale House shortly after eleven. She had gone immediately to her room and had seen no one. Nurse Pardoe, she assumed, had either gone straight to bed or had joined the rest of the set in the student nurses' sitting-room.

'So you have nothing to tell me, Sister? Nothing that can help?'

'Nothing.'

'Not even why, unnecessarily surely, you lied about going to the cinema alone?'

'Nothing. And I shouldn't have thought my private affairs were any concern of yours.'

Dalgliesh said calmly: 'Miss Rolfe, two of your students are dead. I'm here to find out how and why they died. If you don't want to co-operate, say so. You don't have to answer my questions. But don't try to tell me what questions I am to ask. I'm in charge of this investigation. I do it my way.'

'I see. You make up the rules as you go along. All we can do is say when we don't want to play. Yours is a dangerous game, Mr Dalgliesh.'

'Tell me something about these students. You're the Principal Nurse Tutor; you must have a good many girls through your hands. I think you're a good judge of character. We'll start with Nurse Goodale.'

If she felt surprise or relief at his choice she concealed it.

'Madeleine Goodale is confidently expected to take the Gold Medal as the best nurse of her year. She is less intelligent than Fallon – than Fallon was – but she's hard-working and extremely conscientious. She's a local girl. Her father is well known in the town, an extremely successful estate agent who inherited a long-established family business. He's a member of the Town Council and was on the Hospital Management Committee for a number of years. Madeleine went to the local grammar school and then came to us. I don't think she ever considered any other nurse training school. The whole family has a strong local loyalty. She is engaged to the young vicar of Holy Trinity and I understand they plan to marry as soon as she completes her training. Another good career lost to the profession, but she knows her own priorities I suppose.'

'The Burt twins?'

'Good sensible kindly girls, with more imagination and sensitivity than they are usually credited with. Their people are farmers near Gloucester. I'm not sure why they chose this hospital. I have an idea a cousin trained here and was happy enough. They are the kind of girls who would choose a training school on that kind of family basis. They aren't particularly intelligent but they aren't stupid. We don't have to take stupid girls here, thank God. Each of them has a steady boyfriend and Maureen is engaged. I don't think either of them looks on nursing as a permanent job.'

Dalgliesh said: 'You're going to have trouble finding leaders for the profession if this automatic resignation on marriage becomes the rule.'

She said drily: 'We're having trouble now. Who else are you interested in?'

'Nurse Dakers.'

'Poor kid! Another local girl, but with a very different background from Goodale. Father was a minor local government officer who died of cancer when she was twelve. Mother has been struggling on ever since with a small pension. The girl was educated at the same school as Goodale but they were never friendly as far as I know. Dakers is a conscientious hard-working student with a great deal of ambition. She'll do all right but she won't do better than all right. She tires easily, isn't really robust. People think of her as timid and highly strung, whatever that euphemism means. But Dakers is tough enough. She's a third-year student, remember. A girl doesn't get this far with her training if she's fundamentally weak, physically or mentally.'

'Julia Pardoe?'

Sister Rolfe had herself well under control now and there was no change in her voice as she went on.

'The only child of divorced parents. Mother is one of those pretty but selfish women who find it impossible to stay long with one husband. She's on her third now, I believe. I'm not sure that the girl really knows which is her father. She hasn't been often at home. Mother sent her off to a prep school when she was five. She had a stormy school career and came here straight from the sixth form of one of those independent girls' boarding-schools, where the girls are taught nothing but manage to learn a great deal. She first applied to one of the London teaching hospitals. She didn't quite measure up to their standard of acceptance either socially or academically but the Matron referred her here. Schools like ours have this kind of arrangement with the teaching hospitals. They get a dozen applications for every place. It's mostly snobbery and the hope of catching a husband. We're quite happy to take a number of their rejects; I suspect that they often make better nurses than the girls they accept. Pardoe was one of them. An intelligent but untrained mind. A gentle and considerate nurse.'

'You know a great deal about your students.'

'I make it my business to. But I take it I'm not expected to give an opinion of my colleagues.'

'Sister Gearing and Sister Brumfett? No. But I'd be glad of your opinion of Nurse Fallon and Nurse Pearce.'

'I can't tell you much about Fallon. She was a reserved, almost a secretive girl. Intelligent, of course, and more mature than the majority of students. I think I only had one personal conversation with her. That was at the end of her first year when I called her for an interview and asked her for her impressions of nursing. I was interested to know how our methods here struck a girl who was so different from the ordinary run of the straight-from-school student. She said that it wasn't fair to judge while one was still an apprentice and treated as if one were a sub-normal kitchen maid but that she still thought nursing was her job. I asked her what had attracted her to the profession and she said that she wanted to acquire a skill which would make her independent anywhere in the world, a qualification which would always be in demand. I don't think she had any particular ambition to get on in the profession. Her training was just a means to an end. But I could be wrong. As I said, I never really knew her.'

'So you can't say whether she had enemies?'

'I can't say why anyone should want to kill her, if that's what you mean. I should have thought that Pearce was a much more likely victim.'

Dalgliesh asked her why.

'I didn't take to Pearce. I didn't kill her, but then I'm not given to murdering people merely because I dislike them. But she was a strange girl, a mischief maker and a hypocrite. It's no use asking me how I know. I haven't any real evidence and, if I had, I doubt whether I should give it to you.'

'So you didn't find it surprising that she should have been murdered?'

'I found it astonishing. But I never for one moment thought her death was suicide or an accident.'

'And who do you suppose killed her?'

Sister Rolfe looked at him with a kind of grim satisfaction.

'You tell me, Superintendent. You tell me!'

VI

'So you went to the cinema last night and on your own?'

'Yes, I told you.'

'To see a revival of *L'Avventura*. Perhaps you felt that the subtleties of Antonioni could best be experienced without a companion? Or perhaps you couldn't find anyone willing to go with you?'

She couldn't, of course, resist that.

'There are plenty of people to take me to the movies if I want them to.'

The movies. It had been the flicks when Dalgliesh was her age. But the generation chasm was deeper than a matter of mere semantics, the alienation more complete. He simply didn't understand her. He hadn't the slightest clue to what was going on behind that smooth and childish forehead. The remarkable violet blue eyes, set wide apart under curved brows, gazed at him, wary but unconcerned. The cat's face with its small rounded chin and wide cheekbones expressed nothing but a vague distaste for the matter in hand. It was difficult, Dalgliesh thought, to imagine finding a prettier or more agreeable figure than Julia Pardoe beside one's sick bed; unless, of course, one happened to be in real pain or distress when the Burt twins' sturdy common sense or Madeleine Goodale's calm efficiency would be a great deal more acceptable. It might be a personal prejudice, but he couldn't imagine any man willingly exposing his weakness or physical distress to this pert and self-absorbed young woman. And what precisely, he wondered, was she getting out of nursing? If the John Carpendar had been a teaching hospital he could have understood it. That trick of widening the eyes when she spoke so that the hearer was treated to a sudden blaze of blue, of slightly parting moist lips above the neat eburnean teeth would go down very well with a gaggle of medical students.

It was not, he noticed, without its effects on Sergeant Masterson.

But what was it that Sister Rolfe had said of her?

'An intelligent but untrained mind; a gentle and considerate nurse.'

Well, it could be. But Hilda Rolfe was prejudiced. And so, in his own way, was Dalgliesh.

He pressed on with this interrogation, resisting the impulse to sarcasm, to the cheap jibes of antipathy.

'Did you enjoy the film?'

'It was all right.'

'And you returned to Nightingale House from this all right film when?'

'I don't know. Just before eleven, I suppose. I met Sister Rolfe outside the cinema and we walked back together. I expect she's told you.'

So they must have talked since this morning. This was their story and the girl was repeating it without even the pretence that she cared whether she were believed. It could be checked of course. The girl in the cinema box office might remember whether they had arrived together. But it was hardly worth the trouble of inquiry. Why indeed should it matter, unless they had spent the evening concocting murder as well as imbibing culture? And if they had, here was one partner in iniquity who wasn't apparently worried.

Dalgliesh asked: 'What happened when you got back?'

'Nothing. I went to the nurses' sitting-room and they were all watching the telly. Well, actually they switched it off as I came in. The Burt twins came to make tea in the nurses' kitchen and we took it into Maureen's room to drink it. Dakers came with us. Madeleine Goodale was left with Fallon. I don't know what time they came up. I went to bed as soon as I'd had my tea. I was asleep before twelve.'

So she might have been. But this had been a very simple murder. There had been nothing to prevent her waiting, perhaps in one of the lavatory cubicles, until she heard Fallon running her bath. Once Fallon was in the bathroom, Nurse Pardoe would know what all the other students knew; that a beaker of whisky and lemon would be waiting on Fallon's bedside table. How simple to slip into her room and add something to the drink. And what? It was maddening, this working in the dark with its inevitable tendency to theorize in advance of the facts. Until the autopsy was completed and the toxicology results available he couldn't even be sure that he was investigating a murder.

He suddenly changed tack, reverting to a previous course of questioning.

'Are you sorry about Nurse Pearce's death?'

Again the wide-opened eyes, the little *moue* of consideration, the suggestion that it was really rather a silly question.

'Of course.' A little pause. 'She never did me any harm.'

'Did she do anyone any harm?'

'You'd better ask them.' Another pause. Perhaps she felt that she had been imprudently foolish and rude. 'What harm could Pearce do to anyone?'

It was spoken with no tinge of contempt, almost with disinterest, a mere statement of fact.

'Someone killed her. That doesn't suggest that she was innocuous. Someone must have hated her enough to want her out of the way.'

'She could have killed herself. When she swallowed that tube she knew what was coming to her all right. She was terrified. Anyone watching her could see that.'

Julia Pardoe was the first student to have mentioned Nurse Pearce's fear. The only other person present to have noticed it had been the General Nursing Council Inspector, who, in her statement, had stressed the girl's look of apprehension, almost of endurance. It was interesting and surprising that Nurse Pardoe should have been so perceptive. Dalgliesh said:

'But do you really believe that she put a corrosive poison into the feed herself?'

The blue eyes met his. She gave her little secret smile.

'No. Pearce was always terrified when she had to act as patient. She hated it. She never said anything, but anyone could see what she was feeling. Swallowing that tube must have been particularly bad for her. She told me once that she couldn't bear the thought of a throat examination or operation. She'd had her tonsils out as a child and the surgeon – or it may have been a nurse – was rough with her and hurt her badly. Anyway, it had been a horrible experience and had left her with this phobia about her throat. Of course, she could have explained to Sister Gearing and one of us would have taken her place. She didn't have to act the patient. No one was forcing her. But I suppose Pearce thought it was her duty to go through with it. She was a great one for duty.'

So anyone present could have seen what Pearce was feeling. But in fact, only two of them had seen. And one of them had been this apparently insensitive young woman.

Dalgliesh was intrigued, but not particularly surprised, that Nurse Pearce should have chosen to confide in Julia Pardoe. He had met it before, this perverse attraction which the pretty and popular often held for the plain and despised. Sometimes it was even reciprocated; an odd mutual fascination which, he suspected, formed the basis of many friendships and marriages that the world found inexplicable. But if Heather Pearce had been making a pathetic bid for friendship or sympathy by a recital of childhood woes she had been unlucky. Julia Pardoe respected strength, not weakness. She would be impervious to a plea for pity. And yet – who knew? – Pearce might have got something from her. Not friendship, or sympathy, or pity even; but a modicum of understanding.

He said on a sudden impulse:

'I think you probably knew more about Nurse Pearce than anyone else here, probably understood her better. I don't believe her death was suicide, neither do you. I want you to tell me everything about her which would help me to a motive.'

There was a second's pause. Was it his imagination or was she really making up her mind to something? Then she said in her high, unemphatic, childish voice:

'I expect she was blackmailing someone. She tried it with me once.'

'Tell me about it.'

She looked up at him speculatively as if assessing his reliability or wondering whether the story was worth the trouble of telling. Then her lips curved in a little reminiscent smile. She said calmly:

'My boyfriend spent a night with me about a year ago. Not here; in the main nurses' home. I unlocked one of the fire escape doors and let him in. We did it for a lark really.'

'Was he someone from the John Carpendar?'

'Um, um. One of the surgical registrars.'

'And how did Heather Pearce find out about it?'

'It was the night before our preliminary – the first examination for State Registration. Pearce always got a stomach-ache before exams. I suppose she was prowling down the corridor to the loo and saw me letting Nigel in. Or she may have been on her way back to bed and listened at the door. Perhaps she heard us giggling or something. I expect she listened as long as she could. I wonder what she made of it. No one has ever wanted to make love to Pearce so I suppose she got a thrill just out of listening to someone else in bed with a man. Anyway, she tackled me about it next morning and then threatened to tell Matron and have me chucked out of the nurse training school.'

She spoke without resentment, almost with a touch of amusement. It hadn't bothered her at the time. It didn't bother her now.

Dalgliesh asked: 'And what price was she asking for her silence?'

He had no doubt that, whatever the price, it hadn't been paid.

'She said she hadn't made up her mind about that; she would have to think about it. It would have to be appropriate. You should have seen her face. It was all mottled and red like a disgusted turkey cock. I don't know how I kept a straight face. I pretended to be terribly worried and contrite and asked if we should talk about it that night. That was just to give me time to get in touch with Nigel. He lives with his widowed mother just outside the town. She adores him and I knew she wouldn't make any difficulty about swearing that he spent the night at home. She wouldn't even mind that we'd been together. She thinks that her precious Nigel's entitled to take just what he likes. But I didn't want Pearce to talk before I got that fixed up. When I saw her that evening I told her that both of us would deny the story absolutely and that Nigel would back it up with an alibi. She'd forgotten about his mother. There was something else she's forgotten too. Nigel is Mr Courtney-Briggs's nephew. So if she talked, all that would happen would be that Mr Courtney-Briggs would get her chucked out, not me. Pearce was terribly stupid, really.'

'You seem to have coped with admirable efficiency and composure. So you never learned what punishment Pearce had in store for you?'

'Oh yes I did! I let her talk about that before I told her. It was more amusing that way. It wasn't a question of punishment; it was more like blackmail. She wanted to come in with us, be one of my crowd.'

'Your crowd?'

'Well, me, Jennifer Blain and Diane Harper really. I was going with Nigel at the time and Diane and Jennifer had his friends You haven't met Blain; she's one of the students who are off with flu. Pearce wanted us to fix up a man for her so that she could make up a fourth.'

'Didn't you find that surprising? From what I've heard of her, Heather Pearce wasn't exactly the type to be interested in sex.'

'Everyone is interested in sex, in their own way. But Pearce didn't put it like that. She made out that the three of us weren't to be trusted and that we ought to have someone reliable to keep an eye on us. No prizes for guessing who! But I knew what she really wanted. She wanted Tom Mannix. He was the paediatric registrar at the time. He was spotty and rather a drip really, but Pearce fancied him. They both belonged to the hospital Christian Fellowship and Tom was going to be a missionary or something after his two years here were up. He'd have suited Pearce all right, and I daresay I could have made him go out with her once or twice if I'd pressed him. But it wouldn't have done her any good. He didn't want Pearce; he wanted me. Well, you know how it is.'

Dalgliesh did know. This, after all, was the commonest, the most banal of personal tragedies. You loved someone. They didn't love you. Worse still, in defiance of their own best interests and to the destruction of your peace, they loved another. What would half the world's poets and novelists do without the universal tragicomedy? But Julia Pardoe was untouched by it. If only, thought Dalgliesh, her voice had held a trace of pity, or even interest! But Pearce's desperate need, the longing for love which had led her to this pathetic attempt at blackmail, provoked in her victim nothing, not even an amused contempt. She couldn't even be bothered to ask him to keep the story a secret. And then, as if reading his thoughts, she told him why.

'I don't mind your knowing about it now. Why should I? After all, Pearce is dead. Fallon too. I mean, with two murders in the place, Matron and the Hospital Management Committee have something more important to worry about than Nigel and me in bed together. But when I think of that night! Honestly, it was hilarious. The bed was far too narrow and it kept creaking and Nigel and I were giggling so much we could hardly . . . And then to think of Pearce with one eye to the keyhole!

And then she laughed. It was a peal of spontaneous and reminiscent joy, innocent and infectious. Looking up at her, Masterson's heavy face coruscated into a wide indulgent grin and, for one extraordinary second, he and Dalgliesh had to restrain themselves from laughing aloud with her.

VII

Dalgliesh hadn't summoned the members of the little group in the library in any particular order and it wasn't with malice aforethought that he had left Sister Gearing to the last. But the long wait had been unkind to her. She had obviously found time, earlier in the morning, to make up her face with lavish care; an instinctive preparation, no doubt, for whatever traumatic encounters the day might bring. But the make-up had worn badly. The mascara had run and was now smudged into the eye shadow, there were beads of sweat along the forehead and a trace of lipstick in the cleft of her chin. Perhaps she had been unconsciously fiddling with her face. Certainly, she was finding it difficult to keep her hands still. She sat twisting her handkerchief through her fingers and crossing and recrossing her legs in fidgety discomfort. Without waiting for Dalgliesh to speak she broke into a high frenetic chatter.

'You and your sergeant are staying with the Maycrofts at the Falconer's Arms, aren't you? I hope they're making you comfortable. Sheila's a bit of a drag but Bob's good value when you get him on his own.'

Dalgliesh had taken very good care not to get Bob on his own. He had chosen the Falconer's Arms because it was small, convenient, quiet, and half empty; it had not taken long to understand why. Group Captain Robert Maycroft and his wife were more concerned to impress visitors with their own gentility than to minister to the comfort of their guests, and Dalgliesh fervently hoped to be out of the place by the end of the week. In the meantime he had no intention of discussing the Maycrofts with Sister Gearing and he guided her politely but firmly towards more relevant subjects.

Unlike the other suspects she found it necessary to waste the first five minutes in expressing her horror at the deaths of the two girls. It had been all too horrible, tragic, awful, ghastly, beastly, unforgettable, inexplicable. The emotion, thought Dalgliesh, was real enough even if its expression wasn't original. The woman was genuinely distressed. He suspected that she was also very frightened.

He took her through the events of Monday, 12th January. She had little new of interest to say and her account tallied with that already on the file. She had woken very late, dressed in a hurry, and had only just managed to get down to the dining-room by eight o'clock. There she had joined Sister Brumfett and Sister Rolfe for breakfast and had first heard from them that Nurse Fallon had been taken ill in the night. Dalgliesh asked her if she remembered which of the Sisters had given her the news.

'Well, I can't say I do really. I think it was Rolfe but I can't be sure. I was in a bit of a tizzy that morning what with one thing and another. It hadn't helped oversleeping like that, and I was naturally a bit nervous about the General Nursing Council inspection. After all, I'm not a qualified Sister Tutor. I was only deputizing for Sister Manning. And it's bad enough taking the first demonstration of a set without Matron and the G.N.C. Inspector, Mr Courtney-Briggs and Sister Rolfe all sitting there with their beady eyes on every move you make. It struck me that with Fallon absent, there would only be about seven students left in the set. Well, that suited me all right; the fewer the better as far as I was concerned. I only hoped the little beasts would answer up and show some intelligence.'

Dalgliesh asked her who had left the dining-room first.

'Brumfett did. Dead keen as usual to get back to her ward, I suppose. I left next. I took my papers through into the conservatory with a cup of coffee and sat down for ten minutes' read. Christine Dakers, Diane Harper and Julia Pardoe were there. Harper and Pardoe were chatting together and Dakers was sitting on her own reading a magazine. I didn't stay long and they were still there when I left. I went up to my room at about half past eight, collecting my post on the way, and then came down again and went straight into the demonstration room just before quarter to nine. The Burt twins were already there finishing their preparations and Goodale arrived almost immediately. The rest of the set came in together at about ten to nine, except Pearce, who didn't arrive until last. There was the usual girlish chatter before we got down to work but I can't remember any of it. The rest you know.'

Dalgliesh did know. But although he thought it unlikely that there was anything new to learn from Sister Gearing he took her again through the events of that traumatic demonstration. But she had nothing fresh to reveal. It had all been too awful, terrible, ghastly, frightful, unbelievable. She would never forget it as long as she lived.

Dalgliesh then turned to the death of Fallon. But here Sister Gearing had a surprise for him. She was the first suspect to produce an alibi, or what she obviously hoped was one, and she put it forward with understandable satisfaction. From eight o'clock until after midnight she had been entertaining a friend in her room. She gave Dalgliesh his name with coy reluctance. He was Leonard Morris, the chief pharmacist of the hospital. She had invited him to dinner, had produced a simple meal of spaghetti bolognaise in the Sisters' kitchen on the third floor and had served it in her sitting-room at eight o'clock, shortly after his arrival. They had been together for the whole of the four hours except for the few minutes when she had fetched the supper dish from the kitchen, and for a couple of minutes at about midnight when he had visited the lavatory, and a similar period earlier in the evening she had left him for the same purpose. Apart from that they had never been out of each other's sight. She added eagerly that Len – Mr Morris that was – would be only too happy to confirm her story. Len would remember the times perfectly well. Being a pharmacist he was precise and accurate about details. The only difficulty was that he wasn't in the hospital this morning, He had telephoned the pharmacy just before nine to say that he was sick. But he would be back at work tomorrow, she was sure of it. Len hated taking time off.

Dalgliesh asked at what hour he had actually left Nightingale House.

'Well, it couldn't have been long after midnight. I remember that when my clock struck twelve Len said that it was really time he was off. We went out about five minutes later, down the back staircase, the one leading from Matron's flat. I left the door open: Len collected his bicycle from where he'd left it and I walked with him to the first turn in the path. It wasn't exactly a night for a stroll but we'd still one or two matters about the hospital to discuss – Len lectures in pharmacology to the second-year students – and I thought I could do with a breath of air. Len didn't like to leave me to walk back alone so he came back as far as the door. I suppose it was about twelve-fifteen when we finally parted. I came in through Matron's door and locked it behind me. I went straight to my room, took the supper things into the kitchen to wash them up, went to the bathroom, and was in bed by a quarter to one. I didn't see Fallon all the evening. The next thing I knew was Sister Rolfe dashing in to wake me up with the news that Dakers had found Fallon dead in bed.'

'So you went out and returned through Miss Taylor's flat. Was her door left unlocked then?'

'Oh, yes! Matron usually leaves it open when she's away. She knows we find it convenient and more private to use her staircase. After all, we're grown women. We're not exactly forbidden to entertain friends in our rooms and it isn't particularly nice to have to show them out through the main house with every little student watching with her eyes out on stalks. Matron's awfully good like that. I think she even leaves her sitting-room unlocked when she's not in Nightingale House. I suppose that's so that Sister Brumfett can use it if she feels inclined. Brumfett, in case you hadn't heard, is Matron's spaniel. Most Matrons keep a little dog you know. Mary Taylor has Brumfett.'

The note of bitter cynicism was so unexpected that Masterson's head came up from his note-taking with a jerk and he looked at Sister Gearing as if she were an unpromising candidate who had suddenly revealed unexpected potentialities. But Dalgliesh let it pass. He asked:

'Was Sister Brumfett using Miss Taylor's flat last night?'

'At midnight! Not Brumfett! She goes to bed early unless she's in town gallivanting with Matron. She's usually brewing her last cuppa by ten-fifteen. Anyway, she was called out last night. Mr Courtney-Briggs rang her to go over to the private ward and receive one of his patients back from the theatre. I thought everyone knew. That was just before twelve.'

Dalgliesh asked if Sister Gearing had seen her.

'No, but my friend did. Len, I mean. He popped his head out of the door to see if the coast was clear to go to the loo before we left and saw Brumfett wrapped in her cloak, carrying that old bag of hers, disappearing down the staircase. It was obvious that she was going out, and I guessed that she had been called back to the ward. That's always happening to Brumfett. Mind you, it's partly her own fault. There's such a thing as being too conscientious.'

It was not, thought Dalgliesh, a fault to which Sister Gearing was likely to be prone. It was difficult to imagine her tramping through the grounds at midnight in the depth of winter at the casual summons of any surgeon, however eminent. But he felt rather sorry for her. She had given him a depressing glimpse into the stultifying lack of privacy, and of the small pettiness and subterfuges with which people living in unwelcome proximity try to preserve their own privacy or invade that of others. The thought of a grown man peeping surreptitiously around the door before coming out, of two adult lovers creeping furtively down a back staircase to avoid detection, was grotesque and humiliating. He remembered the Matron's words. 'We do get to know things here; there's no real privacy.' Even poor Brumfett's choice of nightcap and her usual hour for bed were common knowledge. Small wonder that Nightingale House bred its own brand of neurosis, that Sister Gearing found it necessary to justify a walk with her lover in the grounds, their obvious and natural wish to prolong the final good-night, with unconvincing twaddle about the need to discuss hospital business. He found it all profoundly depressing and he wasn't sorry when it was time to let her go.

VIII

Dalgliesh rather enjoyed his half-hour with the housekeeper, Miss Martha Collins. She was a thin, brown-skinned woman, brittle and nobbly as a dead branch who looked as if the sap had long since dried in her bones. She gave the appearance of having gradually shrunk in her clothes without having noticed it. Her working overall of thick fawn cotton hung in long creases from her narrow shoulders to mid-calf and was bunched around her waist by a schoolboy's belt of red and blue stripes clasped with a snake buckle. Her stockings were a concertina around her ankles, and either she preferred to wear shoes at least two sizes too large, or her feet were curiously disproportionate to the rest of her body. She had appeared as soon as summoned, had plonked herself down opposite Dalgliesh, her immense feet planted firmly astride, and had eyed him with anticipatory malevolence as if about to interview a particularly recalcitrant housemaid. Throughout the interview she didn't once smile. Admittedly there was nothing in the situation to provoke amusement but she seemed incapable of raising even the briefest smile of formal recognition. But despite these inauspicious beginnings the interview hadn't gone badly. Dalgliesh wondered whether her acidulated tone and perversely unattractive appearance were part of a calculated *persona*. Perhaps some forty years earlier she had decided to become a hospital character, the beloved tyrant of fiction, treating everyone from the Matron to the junior maid with equal irreverence, and had found the characterization so successful and satisfying that she had never managed to drop it. She grumbled incessantly but it was without malice, a matter of form. He suspected that, in fact, she enjoyed her work and was neither as unhappy nor discontented as she chose to appear. She would hardly have stayed in the job for forty years if it were as intolerable as she made it sound.

'Milk! Don't talk to me about milk. There's more trouble about milk in this house than the rest of the catering put together and that's saying something. Fifteen pints a day we're getting through even with half the house down with flu. Don't ask me where it's all going. I've stopped being responsible for it and so I told Matron. There's a couple of bottles go up first thing each morning to the Sisters' floor so they can make their own early tea. Two bottles between three I send up. You'd think that'd be enough for everyone. Matron is separate, of course. She gets a pint and not a drop grudged. But the trouble that milk causes! The first Sister to get at it takes all the cream, I suppose. Not very considerate, and so I told Matron. They're lucky to get a bottle or two of Channel Island milk; no one else in the house does. There's nothing but complaints. Sister Gearing going on because it's too watery for her and Sister Brumfett because it's not all Channel Island and Sister Rolfe wanting it sent up in half-pint bottles which she knows as well as I do you can't get any more. Then there's the milk for the students' early tea and that cocoa and stuff they brew themselves at night. They're supposed to sign for the bottles which they take from the fridge. The stuff isn't grudged, but that's the rule. Well, you take a look at the record book yourself! Nine times out of ten they can't be troubled. And then there are the empties. They're supposed to rinse them out and return them to the kitchen. You wouldn't think that would be too much bother. Instead they leave the bottles about the house, in their rooms, in the cupboards, and in the utility room – half rinsed too – until the place stinks. My girls have got enough to do without running around after the students and their empties, and so I told Matron.

'What do you mean, was I in the kitchen when the Burt twins took their pint? You know I was. I said so to the other policeman. Where else would I be at that hour of the day? I'm always in my kitchen by quarter to seven and it was nearly three minutes past when the Burt twins came in. No, I didn't hand the bottle to them. They helped themselves from the fridge. It's not my job to wait hand and foot on the students and so I told Matron. But there was nothing wrong with that milk when it left my kitchen. It wasn't delivered until six-thirty and I've got enough to do before breakfast without messing about putting disinfectant into the milk. Besides, I've got an alibi. I was with Mrs Muncie from six forty-five onwards. She's the daily woman who comes in from the town to lend a hand when I'm short. You can see her any time you like but I don't suppose you'll get much out of her. The poor soul hasn't got much between the ears. Come to think of it, I doubt whether she'd notice if I spent the whole morning poisoning the milk. But she was with me for what it's worth. And I was with her all the time. No popping out every other minute to the lavatory for me, thank you. I do all that sort of thing at the proper time.

'The lavatory disinfectant? I thought you'd be asking about that. I fill up the bottles myself from the big tin they send over once a week from the main hospital store. It's not really my job but I don't like to leave it to the housemaids. They're so careless. They'd only get the stuff slopped all over the lavatory floors. I refilled that bottle in the downstairs W.C. the day before Nurse Pearce died so it must have been nearly full. Some of the students bother to put a little down the bowl when they're finished with the lavatory but most of them don't. You'd think student nurses would be particular about little things like that, but they're no better than other young people. The stuff is mostly used by the maids when they've cleaned the W.C. bowl. All the lavatories get cleaned once a day. I'm very particular about having clean lavatories. The downstairs one was due to be cleaned by Morag Smith after lunch, but Nurse Goodale and Nurse Pardoe noticed that the bottle was missing before then. I'm told that the other policeman found it empty among the bushes at the back of the house. And who put it there, I'd like to know?

'No, you can't see Morag Smith. Didn't they tell you? She's on a day's leave. She went off after tea yesterday, lucky for her. They can't pin this latest spot of bother on Morag. No, I don't know whether she went home. I didn't inquire. The maids are enough responsibility when they're under my nose in Nightingale House. I don't concern myself with what they do on their days off. Just as well from some of the things I hear. She'll be back late tonight more than likely and Matron has left instructions that she's to move to the Resident Staff Hostel. This place is too dangerous for us now apparently. Well, no one's shifting me. I don't know how I'm supposed to manage in the morning if Morag doesn't show her face until just before breakfast. I can't control my staff if they're not under my eyes and so I told Matron. Not that Morag's much bother. She's as obstinate as they come but she's not a bad worker once you get her started. And if they try to tell you that Morag Smith interfered with the drip-feed, don't you believe them. The girl may be a bit dense but she's not a raving lunatic. I'll not have my staff slandered without cause.

'And now I'll tell you something, Mr Detective.' She raised her thin rump from her chair, leaned forward across the desk and fixed Dalgliesh with her beady eyes. He willed himself to meet them without blinking and they stared at each other like a couple of wrestlers before a bout.

'Yes, Miss Collins?'

She stuck a lean nodular finger and prodded him sharply in the chest. Dalgliesh winced.

'No one had any right to take that bottle out of the lavatory without my permission or to use it for any other purpose except for cleaning the lavatory bowl. Nobody!'

It was apparent where in Miss Collins's eyes the full enormity of the crime had laid.

IX

At twenty minutes to one, Mr Courtney-Briggs appeared. He knocked briskly at the door, came in without waiting for an invitation, and said curtly:

'I can give you a quarter of an hour now, Dalgliesh, if it's convenient.'

His tone assumed that it would be. Dalgliesh assented and indicated the chair. The surgeon looked across at Sergeant Masterson sitting impassively with his notebook at the ready, hesitated, then turned the chair so that its back was to the sergeant. Then he seated himself and slipped his hand into his waistcoat pocket. The cigarette case he drew out was of finely tooled gold and so slim that it hardly looked functional. He offered a cigarette to Dalgliesh but not to Masterson and seemed neither surprised nor particularly interested at the Superintendent's refusal. He lit his own. The hands cupped around the lighter were large, square-fingered; not the sensitive hands of a functional surgeon, but strong carpenter's hands, beautifully cared for.

Dalgliesh, overtly busy with his papers, observed the man. He was big but not yet fat. The formal suit fitted him almost too well, containing a sleek well-fed body and enhancing the effect of latent power only imperfectly controlled. He could still be called handsome. His long hair brushed straight back from a high forehead was strong and dark, except for one single white strand.

Dalgliesh wondered whether it were bleached. His eyes were too small for the large, rather florid face, but were well shaped and set wide apart. They gave nothing away.

Dalgliesh knew that it had been Mr Courtney-Briggs who had been mainly responsible for the Chief Constable calling in the Yard. From Inspector Bailey's somewhat bitter account during their brief colloquy when Dalgliesh had taken over the case, it was easy to understand why. The surgeon had made himself a nuisance from the beginning and his motives, if they were capable of rational explanation, raised interesting speculations. At first he had asserted vigorously that Nurse Pearce had obviously been murdered, that it was unthinkable that anyone connected with the hospital could have been concerned with the crime, and that the local police had a duty to proceed on this assumption and to find and arrest the killer with a minimum of delay. When their investigations yielded no immediate results, he became restive. He was a man used to exercising power and he was certainly not without it. There were eminent people in London who owed their lives to him and some of them had considerable nuisance value. Telephone calls, some tactful and half-apologetic, others frankly critical, were made both to the Chief Constable and to the Yard. As the Inspector in charge of the investigation became more convinced that Nurse Pearce's death was the result of a practical joke which had tragically misfired, so Mr Courtney-Briggs and his coagitators proclaimed more loudly that she had been murdered, and pressed more strongly for the case to be handed over to the Yard. And then Nurse Fallon had been found dead. It could be expected that the local C.I.D. would be galvanized into fresh activity, that the diffuse light which had played over the first crime would sharpen and focus on this second death. And it was at this moment that Mr Courtney-Briggs had chosen to telephone the Chief Constable to announce that no further activity was necessary, that it was obvious to him that Nurse Fallon had committed suicide, that this could only have been in remorse at the tragic result of the practical joke which had killed her colleague, and that it was now in the hospital's interest to close the case with the minimum of fuss before nurse recruitment and indeed the whole future of the hospital was jeopardized. The police are not unused to these sudden quirks of temperament, which is not to say that they welcome them. Dalgliesh thought that it must have been with considerable satisfaction that the Chief Constable decided that, in all the circumstances, it would be prudent to call in the Yard to investigate both the deaths.

During the week following Nurse Pearce's death, Courtney-Briggs had even rung up Dalgliesh, who had been his patient three years earlier. It had been a case of uncomplicated appendicitis, and although Dalgliesh's vanity was gratified by the smallness and neatness of the resultant scar, he felt that the surgeon's expertise had been adequately rewarded at the time. He had certainly no wish to be used for Courtney-Briggs's private ends. The telephone call had been embarrassing and he had resented it. He was interested to see that the surgeon had apparently decided that this was an incident it would be advisable for both of them to forget.

Without lifting his eyes from his papers, Dalgliesh said:

'I understand that you take the view that Miss Fallon killed herself?'

'Of course. It's the obvious explanation. You're not suggesting that someone else put stuff into her whisky? Why should they?'

'There's the problem, isn't there, of the missing container? That is, if it were poison. We shan't know until we get the autopsy report.'

'What problem? There's no problem. The beaker was opaque, heat insulated. She could have put the stuff into it earlier that evening. No one would have noticed. Or she could have carried a powder in a slip of paper and flushed it down the lavatory. The container's no problem. Incidentally, it wasn't a corrosive this time. That much was evident when I saw the body.'

'Were you the first doctor on the scene?'

'No. I wasn't in the hospital when they found her. Dr Snelling saw her. He's the general physician who looks after the nurses here. He realized at once that there was nothing to be done. I went across to have a look at the body as soon as I heard the news. I arrived at the hospital just before nine. By then the police had arrived, of course. The local people, I mean. I can't think why they weren't left to get on with it. I rang the Chief Constable to make my views known. Incidentally, Miles Honeyman tells me that she died about midnight. I saw him just as he was leaving. We were at medical school together.'

'So I understand.'

'You were wise to call him in. I gather he's generally considered to be the best.'

He spoke complacently, success condescending to recognize success. His criteria were hardly subtle, thought Dalgliesh. Money, prestige, public recognition, power. Yes, Courtney-Briggs would always demand the best for himself, confident of his ability to pay for it.

Dalgliesh said: 'She was pregnant. Did you know?'

'So Honeyman told me. No, I didn't know. These things happen, even today when birth control is reliable and easily obtained. But I should have expected a girl of her intelligence to be on the Pill.'

Dalgliesh remembered the scene that morning in the library when Mr Courtney-Briggs had known the girl's age to a day. He asked his next question without apology.

'Did you know her well?'

The implication was plain and the surgeon did not reply for a moment. Dalgliesh had not expected him to bluster or threaten and he did neither. There was an increased respect in the sharp look which he gave his interrogator.

'For a time, yes.' He paused. 'You could say I knew her intimately.'

'Was she your mistress?'

Courtney-Briggs looked at him, impassive, considering. Then he said:

'That's putting it rather formally. We slept together fairly regularly during her first six months here. Are you objecting?'

'It's hardly for me to object if she didn't. Presumably she was willing?'

'You could say that.'

'When did it end?'

'I thought I told you. It lasted until the end of her first year. That's a year and a half ago.'

'Did you quarrel?'

'No. She decided she'd, shall we say, exhausted the possibilities. Some women like variety. I do myself. I wouldn't have taken her on if I'd thought she was the type to make trouble. And don't get me wrong. I don't make it a practice to sleep with student nurses. I'm reasonably fastidious.'

'Wasn't it difficult to keep the affair secret? There's very little privacy in a hospital.'

'You have romantic ideas, Superintendent. We didn't kiss and cuddle in the sluice room. When I said I slept with her I meant just that. I don't use euphemisms for sex. She came to my Wimpole Street flat when she had a night off and we slept there. I haven't a resident man there and my house is near Selborne. The porter at Wimpole Street must have known, but he can keep his mouth shut. There wouldn't be many tenants left in the building if he couldn't. There wasn't any risk, provided that she didn't talk, and she wasn't a talker. Not that I would have minded particularly. There are certain areas of private behaviour in which I do as I like. You too no doubt.'

'So it wasn't your child?'

'No. I'm not careless. Besides the affair was over. But if it hadn't been I should hardly have killed her. That kind of solution causes more embarrassment than it prevents.'

Dalgliesh asked: 'What would you have done?'

'That would have depended on the circumstances. I should have had to be sure it was my child. But this particular problem is hardly uncommon and not insoluble if the woman is reasonable.'

'I've been told that Miss Fallon planned to get an abortion. Did she approach you?'

'No.'

'She might have done?'

'Certainly she might have done. But she didn't.'

'Would you have helped her if she had?'

The surgeon looked at him.

'That question is hardly within your terms of reference, I should have thought.'

Dalgliesh said: 'That's for me to judge. The girl was pregnant;

she apparently intended to get an abortion; she told a friend that she knew someone who would help her. I'm naturally interested to know who she had in mind.'

'You know the law. I'm a surgeon not a gynaecologist. I prefer to stick to my own speciality and to practise it legally.'

'But there are other kinds of help. Referring her to an appropriate consultant, helping with the fees.'

A girl with £16,000 to bequeath was hardly likely to want help with the fees for an abortion. But Miss Goodale's legacy was not being made public and Dalgliesh was interested to learn whether Courtney-Briggs knew about Fallon's capital. But the surgeon gave no sign.

'Well, she didn't come to me. She may have had me in mind but she didn't come. And if she had, I wouldn't have helped. I make it my business to assume my own responsibilities; but I don't take on other people's. If she chose to look elsewhere for her satisfaction she could look elsewhere for her help. I didn't impregnate her. Someone did. Let him look after her.'

'That would have been your response?'

'Certainly it would. And rightly.'

His voice held a note of grim satisfaction. Looking at him, Dalgliesh saw that his face was flushed. The man was controlling his emotion with difficulty. And Dalgliesh had little doubt of the nature of that emotion. It was hate. He went on with his interrogation.

'Were you in the hospital last night?'

'Yes. I was called to operate on an emergency. One of my patients relapsed. It wasn't altogether unexpected, but very serious. I finished operating at eleven forty-five p.m. The time will be noted in the theatre register. Then I rang Sister Brumfett at Nightingale House to ask her to be good enough to return to her ward for an hour or so. My patient was a private patient. After that I rang my home to say that I would be returning that night instead of sleeping here in the medical officers' quarters as I do occasionally after a late operation. I left the main building shortly after twelve. I intended driving out by the Winchester Road gate. I have my own key. However, it was a wild night, as you probably noticed, and I discovered that there was an elm down over the path. I was lucky not to drive into it. I got out of the car and knotted my white silk scarf round one of the branches to warn anyone who might be driving that way. It wasn't likely that anyone would, but the tree was an obvious danger and there was no chance of getting it moved before daylight. I reversed the car and left by the main entrance, reporting the fallen tree to the gate porter on my way out.'

'Did you notice the time then?'

'I didn't. He may have done. But, at a guess, it was probably about twelve fifteen, maybe later. I wasted a bit of time at the tree.'

'You would have had to drive past Nightingale House to reach the back gate. You didn't go in?'

'I had no reason to go in and I didn't go in, either to poison Nurse Fallon or for any other reason.'

'And you saw no one in the grounds?'

'After midnight and in the middle of a storm? No, I saw no one.'

Dalgliesh switched his questioning.

'You saw Nurse Pearce die, of course. I suppose there was never a real chance of saving her?'

'Never, I should say. I took pretty vigorous measures, but it isn't easy when you don't know what you're treating.'

'But you knew it was poison?'

'Pretty soon. Yes. But I didn't know what. Not that it would have made any difference. You've seen the post-mortem report. You knew what the stuff did to her.'

Dalgliesh asked: 'You were in Nightingale House from eight o'clock onwards on the morning that she died?'

'You know perfectly well that I was if, as I assume, you've taken the trouble to read my original statement. I arrived in Nightingale House shortly after eight. My contract here is for six notional half-days a week; I'm in the hospital all day on Monday, Thursday and Friday; but it's not uncommon for me to be called in to operate on an emergency; particularly if it's a private patient, and I occasionally do a Saturday morning session in the theatre if the lists are long. I'd been called out shortly after eleven o'clock on Sunday night for an emergency appendicectomy – one of my private patients – and it was convenient to spend the night in the medical officers' quarters.'

'Which are where?'

'In that deplorably designed new building near the out-patients' department. They serve breakfast at the ungodly hour of seven thirty.'

'You were here rather early surely. The demonstration wasn't due to begin until nine.'

'I wasn't here merely for the demonstration, Superintendent. You're really rather ignorant of hospitals, aren't you? The Senior Consultant Surgeon doesn't normally attend nurse training sessions unless he's actually lecturing the students. I only attended on January 12th because the G.N.C. Inspector was to be there and I'm Vice-Chairman of the Nurse Education Committee. It was a courtesy to Miss Beale to be here to meet her. I came in early because I wanted to work on some clinical notes which I had left in Sister Rolfe's office after a previous lecture. I also wanted to have a chat with Matron before the inspection began and to be sure that I was there in time to receive Miss Beale. I went up to Matron's flat at eight thirty-five and found her finishing breakfast. And, if you're thinking that I could have put the corrosive in the milk bottle any time between eight and eight thirty-five, you're perfectly right. As it happens, I didn't.'

He looked at his watch.

'And now if there's nothing else you need to ask I must get my lunch. I've another out-patients' session this afternoon and time's pressing. If it's really necessary, I can probably give you a few more minutes before I leave but I hope it won't be. I've already signed one statement about Pearce's death and I've nothing to add or to alter. I didn't see Fallon yesterday. I didn't even know she was discharged from the sick bay. She wasn't carrying my child, and even if she had been, I shouldn't have been foolish enough to kill her. Incidentally, what I told you about our previous relationship was naturally in confidence.'

He looked across meaningly at Sergeant Masterson.

'Not that I care whether it's made public. But, after all, the girl is dead. We may as well try to protect her reputation.'

Dalgliesh found it difficult to believe that Mr Courtney-Briggs was interested in anyone's reputation but his own. But, gravely, he gave the necessary assurance. He saw the surgeon leave without regret. An egotistical bastard whom it was agreeable, if childish, to provoke. But a murderer? He had the hubris, the nerve and the egotism of a killer. More to the point, he had had the opportunity. And the motive? Hadn't it been a little disingenuous of him to have confessed so readily to his relationship with Josephine Fallon? Admittedly he couldn't have hoped to keep his secret for long; a hospital was hardly the most discreet of institutions. Had he been making a virtue of necessity, ensuring that Dalgliesh heard the version of the affair before the inevitable gossip reached his ears? Or had it been merely the candour of conceit, the sexual vanity of a man who wouldn't trouble to conceal any exploit which proclaimed his attraction and virility?

Putting his papers together, Dalgliesh became aware that he was hungry. He had made an early start to the day and it had been a long morning. It was time to turn his mind from Stephen Courtney-Briggs and for him and Masterson to think about luncheon.

FIVE
Table Talk

I

The resident Sisters and students from Nightingale House took only their breakfast and afternoon tea in the dining-room at the school. For their main midday and evening meal they joined the rest of the staff in the hospital cafeteria where all but the consultants ate in institutionalized and noisy proximity. The food was invariably nourishing, adequately cooked, and as varied as was compatible with the need to satisfy the differing tastes of several hundred people, avoid outraging their religious or dietary susceptibilities, and keep within the catering officer's budget. The principles governing the menu planning were invariable. Liver and kidneys were never served on the days when the urinary surgeon operated, and the nurses were not faced with the same menu as that which they had just served to the patients.

The cafeteria system had been introduced at the John Carpendar Hospital against strong opposition from all grades of staff. Eight years ago there had been separate dining-rooms for the Sisters and nurses, one for the administrative and lay professional staff, and a canteen for the porters and artisans. The arrangements had suited everyone as making a proper distinction between grades and ensuring that people ate in reasonable quietness and in the company of those with whom they preferred to spend their lunch break. But now only the senior medical staff enjoyed the peace and privacy of their own dining-room. This privilege, jealously defended, was under perpetual attack from Ministry auditors, Government catering advisers and work study experts who, armed with costing statistics, had no difficulty in proving that the system was uneconomical. But so far the doctors had won. Their strongest argument was their need to discuss the patients in privacy. This suggestion that they never stopped working, even for meals, was greeted with some scepticism but was difficult to refute. The need to keep the patients' affairs confidential touched on that area of patient–doctor relationship which the doctors were always quick to exploit. Before this mystique even the Treasury auditors were powerless to prevail. Furthermore, they had had the support of Matron. Miss Taylor had made it known that she considered it eminently reasonable that the senior medical staff should continue to have their own dining-room. And Miss Taylor's influence over the Chairman of the Hospital Management Committee was so obvious and of such long standing that it had almost ceased to excite comment. Sir Marcus Cohen was a wealthy and personable widower and the only surprise now was that he and Matron hadn't married. This, it was generally accepted, was either because Sir Marcus, an acknowledged leader of the country's Jewish community, chose not to marry outside his faith or because Miss Taylor, wedded to her vocation, chose not to marry at all.

But the extent of Miss Taylor's influence over the Chairman and thus over the Hospital Management Committee was beyond speculation. It was known to be particularly irritating to Mr Courtney-Briggs since it considerably diminished his own. But in the matter of the consultants' dining-room it had been exercised in his favour and had proved decisive.

But if the rest of the staff had been forced into proximity they had not been forced into intimacy. The hierarchy was still apparent. The immense dining-room had been divided into smaller dining areas separated from each other by screens of latticework and troughs of plants, and in each of these alcoves the atmosphere of a private dining-room was re-created.

Sister Rolfe helped herself to plaice and chips, carried her tray to the table which, for the past eight years, she had shared with Sister Brumfett and Sister Gearing, and looked around at the denizens of this strange world. In the alcove nearest the door were the laboratory technicians in their stained overalls, noisily animated. Next to them was old Fleming, the out-patients' pharmacist, rolling bread pellets like pills in his nicotine-stained fingers. At the next table were four of the medical stenographers in their blue working overalls. Miss Wright, the senior secretary, who had been at the John Carpendar for twenty years, was eating with furtive speed as she always did, avid to get back to her typewriter. Behind the adjacent screen was a little clutch of the lay professional staff – Miss Bunyon, the head radiographer, Mrs Nethern, the head medical social worker, and two of the physiotherapists, carefully preserving their status by an air of calm unhurried efficiency, an apparent total disinterest in the food they were eating and the choice of a table as far removed as possible from that of the junior clerical staff.

And what were they all thinking about? Fallon probably. There couldn't be anyone in the hospital from the consultants to the ward maids who didn't know by now that a second Nightingale student had died in mysterious circumstances and that Scotland Yard had been called in. Fallon's death was probably the subject of gossip at most of the tables this morning. But it didn't prevent people from eating their lunch or from getting on with their jobs. There was so much to do; there were so many other pressing concerns; there was even so much gossip. It wasn't just that life had to go on; in hospital that cliché had particular relevance. Life did go on, carried forward by the imperative momentum of birth and death. New booked admissions came in; ambulances daily disgorged the emergencies; operation lists were posted; the dead were laid out and the healed discharged. Death, even sudden and unexpected death, was more familiar to these young fresh-faced students than it was to even the most experienced senior detective. And there was a limit to its power to shock. You either came to terms with death in your first year, or you gave up being a nurse. But murder? That was different. Even in this violent world, murder still held its macabre and primitive power to shock. But how many people in Nightingale House really believed that Pearce and Fallon had been murdered? It would take more than the presence of the Yard's wonder boy and his retinue to give credence to such an extraordinary idea. There were too many other possible explanations, all of them simpler and more believable than murder. Dalgliesh might believe as he chose; proving it would be another matter.

Sister Rolfe bent her head and began unenthusiastically to dissect her plaice. She felt no particular hunger. The strong smell of food was heavy on the air, stifling appetite. The noise of the cafeteria beat against her ears. It was ceaseless and inescapable, a confused continuum of discord in which individual sounds were scarcely distinguishable.

Next to her, her cloak folded neatly at the back of her chair and the shapeless tapestry bag which accompanied her everywhere dumped at her feet, Sister Brumfett was eating steamed cod and parsley sauce with belligerent intensity as if she resented the need to eat and was venting her irritation on the food. Sister Brumfett invariably chose steamed fish and Sister Rolfe felt suddenly that she couldn't face another lunch hour of watching Brumfett eat cod.

She reminded herself that there was no reason why she should. There was nothing to prevent her sitting somewhere else, nothing except this petrification of the will which made the simple act of carrying her tray three feet to a different table seem impossibly cataclysmic and irrevocable. On her left, Sister Gearing toyed with her braised beef, and chopped her wedge of cabbage into neat squares. When she actually began to eat she would shove the food in avidly like a greedy schoolgirl. But always there were finicky and salivatory preliminaries. Sister Rolfe wondered how many times she had resisted the urge to say, 'For God's sake, Gearing, stop messing about and eat it!' One day, no doubt, she would say it. And another middle-aged and unlikeable Sister would be pronounced 'getting very difficult. It's probably her age.'

She had considered living out of the hospital. It was permissible and she could afford it. The purchase of a flat or small house would be the best investment for her retirement. But Julia Pardoe had disposed of that idea in a few half-interested, destructive comments dropped like cold pebbles into the deep pool of her hopes and plans. Sister Rolfe could still hear that high, childish voice.

'Live out. Why should you want to do that? We shouldn't see so much of each other.'

'But we should, Julia. And in much greater privacy and without all this risk and deceit. It would be a comfortable and agreeable little house. You'd like it.'

'It wouldn't be as easy as slipping upstairs to see you when I feel like it.'

When she felt like it? Felt like what? Sister Rolfe had desperately fought off the question she never dared to let herself ask.

She knew the nature of her dilemma. It wasn't, after all, peculiar to herself. In any relationship there was one who loved and one who permitted himself or herself to be loved. This was merely to state the brutal economics of desire; from each according to his ability, to each according to his need. But was it selfish or presumptuous to hope that the one who took knew the value of the gift; that she wasn't wasting love on a promiscuous and perfidious little cheat who took her pleasure wherever she chose to find it? She had said:

'You could probably come twice or three times a week, perhaps more often. I wouldn't move far.'

'Oh, I don't see how I could manage that. I don't see why you want the work and bother of a house. You're all right here.'

Sister Rolfe thought: 'But I'm not all right here. This place is souring me. It isn't only the long-stay patients who become institutionalized. It's happening to me. I dislike and despise most of the people I'm required to work with. Even the job is losing its hold. The students get more stupid and worse educated with every intake. I'm not even sure any more of the value of what I'm supposed to be doing.'

There was a crash near the counter. One of the maids had dropped a tray of used crockery. Looking instinctively across, Sister Rolfe saw that the detective had just come in and taken up his tray at the end of the line. She watched the tall figure, disregarded by the chattering queue of nurses, as he began to move slowly down the line between a white-coated houseman and a pupil midwife, helping himself to a roll and butter, waiting for the girl to hand out his choice of main course. She was surprised to see him there. It had never occurred to her that he would eat in the hospital dining-hall or that he would be on his own. Her eyes followed him as he reached the end of the line, handed over his meal ticket and turned to look for a vacant seat. He seemed utterly at ease and almost oblivious of the alien world around him. She thought that he was probably a man who could never imagine himself at a disadvantage in any company since he was secure in his private world, possessed of that core of inner self-esteem which is the basis of happiness. She wondered what kind of a world his was, then bent her head to her plate at this unusual interest he aroused in her. Probably he would be thought handsome by most women, with that lean bony face, at once arrogant and sensitive. It was probably one of his professional assets, and being a man he would make the most of it. No doubt it was one of the reasons why he had been given this case. If dull Bill Bailey could make nothing of it, let the Yard's wonder boy take over. With a house full of women and the three middle-aged spinsters as his chief suspects, no doubt he fancied his chances. Well, good luck to him!

But she was not the only one at the table to notice his arrival. She felt rather than saw Sister Gearing stiffen and a second later heard her say:

'Well, well. The handsome sleuth! He'd better feed with us or he may find himself in a gaggle of students. Someone should have told the poor man how the system works.'

And now, thought Sister Rolfe, she'll give him one of her street corner come-hither looks and we shall be burdened with him for the rest of the meal. The look was given and the invitation not refused. Dalgliesh, carrying his tray nonchalantly and apparently completely at ease, threaded his way across the room and came up to their table. Sister Gearing said:

'What have you done with that handsome sergeant of yours? I thought policemen went about in pairs like nuns.'

'My handsome sergeant is studying reports and lunching on sandwiches and beer in the office while I enjoy the fruits of seniority with you. Is this chair taken?'

Sister Gearing moved her own chair closer to Sister Brumfett and smiled up at him:

'It is now.'

II

Dalgliesh sat down, well aware that Sister Gearing wanted him, that Sister Rolfe didn't, and that Sister Brumfett, who had acknowledged his arrival with a brief nod, didn't care whether he joined them or not. Sister Rolfe looked across at him unsmilingly and said to Sister Gearing:

'Don't imagine Mr Dalgliesh is sharing our table for the sake of your *beaux yeux*. The Superintendent plans to take in information with his braised beef.'

Sister Gearing giggled: 'My dear, it's no use warning me! I couldn't keep a thing to myself if a really attractive man set his mind to wangle it out of me. It would be quite useless for me to commit a murder. I haven't the brain for it. Not that I think for one moment that anyone has – committed murder I mean. Anyway, let's leave the grisly subject during lunch. I've had my grilling, haven't I, Superintendent?'

Dalgliesh disposed his cutlery around the plate of braised beef and tilting back his chair to save himself the trouble of rising, added his used tray to the stack on the nearby stand. He said:

'People here seem to be taking Nurse Fallon's death calmly enough.'

Sister Rolfe shrugged: 'Did you expect them to be wearing black armbands, talking in whispers, and refusing their lunch? The job goes on. Anyway, only a few will have known her personally, and still fewer knew Pearce.'

'Or liked her apparently,' said Dalgliesh.

'No, I don't think they did on the whole. She was too self-righteous, too religious.'

'If you can call it religious,' said Sister Gearing.

'It wasn't my idea of religion. *Nil nisi* and all that, but the girl was just a prig. She always seemed to be a damn sight more concerned with other people's shortcomings than she was with her own. That's why the other kids didn't like her. They respect genuine religious conviction. Most people do, I find. But they didn't like being spied on.'

'Did she spy on them?' asked Dalgliesh.

Sister Gearing seemed half to regret what she had said.

'Perhaps that's putting it a bit strongly. But if anything went wrong in the set you can bet Nurse Pearce knew all about it. And she usually managed to bring it to the notice of authority. Always with the best motives, no doubt.'

Sister Rolfe said drily: 'She had an unfortunate habit of interfering with other people for their own good. It doesn't make for popularity.'

Sister Gearing pushed her plate to one side, drew a bowl of plums and custard towards her and began to extract the stones from the fruit as carefully as if it were a surgical operation. She said:

'She wasn't a bad nurse, though. You could rely on Pearce. And the patients seemed to like her. I suppose they found that holier than thou attitude reassuring.'

Sister Brumfett looked up from her plate and spoke for the first time.

'You're not in a position to give an opinion on whether she was a good nurse. Nor is Rolfe. You only see the girls in the training school. I see them on the wards.'

'I see them on the wards too. I'm the clinical instructor, remember. It's my job to teach them on the ward.'

Sister Brumfett was unrepentant.

'Any student teaching that's done on my ward is done by me, as you know very well. Other ward Sisters can welcome the clinical instructor if they like. But on the private ward I do the teaching. And I prefer it that way when I see some of the extraordinary ideas you seem to put into their heads. And, by the way, I happen to know – Pearce told me, as a matter of fact – that you visited my ward when I was off duty on 7th January and conducted a teaching session. In future, please consult me before using my patients as clinical material.'

Sister Gearing flushed. She tried to laugh but her amusement sounded artificial. She glanced across at Sister Rolfe as if enlisting her aid but Sister Rolfe kept her eyes firmly on her plate. Then, belligerently and rather like a child determined to have the last word, she said with apparent irrelevance:

'Something happened to upset Pearce while she was on your ward.'

Sister Brumfett's sharp little eyes glared up at her.

'On my ward? Nothing upset her on my ward!'

The sturdy assertion conveyed unmistakably that no nurse worthy of the name could be upset by anything that happened on the private ward; that upsetting things just weren't permitted when Sister Brumfett was in charge.

Sister Gearing shrugged.

'Well, something upset her. It could have been something totally unconnected with the hospital, I suppose, but one never quite believes that poor Pearce had any real life outside these walls. It was the Wednesday of the week before this block went into school. I visited the chapel just after five o'clock to do the flowers – that's how I remember which day it was – and she was sitting there alone. Not kneeling or praying, just sitting. Well, I did what I had to do and then went out without speaking to her. After all, the chapel's open for rest and meditation and if one of the students wants to meditate that's all right by me. But when I went back nearly three hours later because I'd left my scissors in the sacristy she was still there, sitting perfectly still and in the same seat. Well, meditation's all very well, but four hours is a bit excessive. I don't think that the kid could have had any supper. She looked pretty pale too, so I went up to her and asked her if she was all right, if there was anything I could do for her. She didn't even look at me as she replied. She said: "No thank you, Sister. There was something troubling me which I had to think over very carefully. I did come here for help but not from you."'

For the first time during the meal Sister Rolfe sounded amused.

She said: 'Caustic little beast! Meaning, I suppose, that she'd come to consult a higher power than the clinical instructor.'

'Meaning mind your own business. So I did.'

Sister Brumfett said, as if feeling that her colleague's presence at a place of worship needed some explanation:

'Sister Gearing is very good at arranging flowers. That's why Matron asked her to look after the chapel. She sees to the flowers every Wednesday and Saturday. And she does very charming arrangements for the Annual Sisters' Dinner.' Sister Gearing stared at her for a second and then laughed.

'Oh, little Mavis isn't just a pretty face. But thanks for the compliment.'

A silence fell. Dalgliesh addressed himself to his braised beef. He wasn't disconcerted by the lack of conversation and had no intention of helping them out by introducing a fresh subject. But Sister Gearing seemed to feel that silence was reprehensible in the presence of a stranger. She said brightly:

'I see from the minutes that the Hospital Management Committee have agreed to introduce the Salmon Committee proposals. Better late than never. I suppose that means that Matron will be head of the nursing services over all the hospitals in the group. Chief Nursing Officer! It'll be a big thing for her, but I wonder how C.B. will take it. If he had his way, Matron would be given less authority not more. She's a big enough thorn in his flesh as it is.'

Sister Brumfett said: 'It's time something was done to wake up the psychiatric hospital and the geriatric units. But I don't know why they want to change the title. If Matron was good enough for Florence Nightingale it's good enough for Mary Taylor. I don't suppose she particularly wants to be called Chief Nursing Officer. It sounds like an army rank. Ridiculous.'

Sister Rolfe shrugged her thin shoulders.

'Don't expect me to get enthusiastic about the Salmon Report. I'm beginning to wonder what's happening to nursing. Every report and recommendation seems to take us further away from the bedside. We have dieticians to see to the feeding, physiotherapists to exercise the patients, medical social workers to listen to their troubles, ward orderlies to make the beds, laboratory technicians to take blood, ward receptionists to arrange the flowers and interview the relatives, operating theatre technicians to hand the surgeon the instruments. If we're not careful nursing will become a residual skill, the job which is left when all the technicians have had their turn. And now we have the Salmon Report with all its talk of first, second and third tiers of management. Management for what? There's too much technical jargon. Ask yourself what is the function of the nurse today. What exactly are we trying to teach these girls?'

Sister Brumfett said: 'To obey orders implicitly and be loyal to their superiors. Obedience and loyalty. Teach the students those and you've got a good nurse.'

She sliced a potato in two with such viciousness that the knife rasped the plate. Sister Gearing laughed.

'You're twenty years out of date, Brumfett. That was good enough for your generation, but these kids ask whether the orders are reasonable before they start obeying and what their superiors have done to deserve their respect. A good thing too on the whole. How on earth do you expect to attract intelligent girls into nursing if you treat them like morons? We ought to encourage them to question established procedures, even to answer back occasionally.'

Sister Brumfett looked as if she, for one, would willingly dispense with intelligence if its manifestations were so disagreeable.

'Intelligence isn't the only thing. That's the trouble nowadays. People think it is.'

Sister Rolfe said: 'Give me an intelligent girl and I'll make a good nurse of her whether she thinks she has a vocation or not. You can have the stupid ones. They may minister to your ego but they'll never make good professional women.' She looked at Sister Brumfett as she spoke and the undertone of contempt was unmistakable. Dalgliesh dropped his eyes to his plate and pretended more interest than he could feel in the careful separation of meat from fat and gristle. Sister Brumfett reacted predictably:

'Professional women! We're talking about nurses. A good nurse thinks of herself as a nurse first and last. Of course she's a professional woman! I thought we'd all accepted that by now. But there's too much thinking and talking of status nowadays. The important thing is to get on with the job.'

'But what job exactly? Isn't that precisely what we're asking ourselves?'

'You may be. I'm perfectly clear what I'm doing. Which, at the moment, is coping with a very sick ward.'

She pushed her plate to one side, flicked her cloak around her shoulders with brisk expertise, gave them a valedictory nod which was as much a warning as a good-bye, and strutted out of the dining-room with her brisk ploughman's waddle, the tapestry bag swinging at her side. Sister Gearing laughed and watched her go.

'Poor old Brum! According to her, she's always got a very sick ward.'

Sister Rolfe said drily: 'She invariably has.'

III

They finished the meal almost in silence. Then Sister Gearing left, first murmuring something about a clinical teaching session on the E.N.T. ward. Dalgliesh found himself walking back to Nightingale House with Sister Rolfe. They left the dining-room together and he retrieved his coat from the rack. They then passed down a long corridor and through the out-patients' department. It had obviously only recently been opened and the furniture and decoration were still bright and new. The large waiting-hall with its groups of Formica-topped tables and easy-chairs, its troughs of pot plants and unremarkable pictures was cheerful enough, but Dalgliesh had no wish to linger. He had the healthy man's dislike and disgust of hospitals, founded partly on fear and partly on repugnance, and he found this atmosphere of determined cheerfulness and spurious normality unconvincing and frightening. The smell of disinfectant, which to Miss Beale was the elixir of life, infected him with the gloomier intimations of mortality. He did not think that he feared death. He had come close to it once or twice in his career and it had not unduly dismayed him. But he did grievously fear old age, mortal illness and disablement. He dreaded the loss of independence, the indignities of senility, the yielding up of privacy, the abomination of pain, the glimpses of patient compassion in the faces of friends who knew that their indulgences would not be claimed for long. These things might have to be faced in time unless death took him quickly and easily. Well, he would face them. He was not arrogant enough to suppose himself secure from the lot of other men. But in the meantime, he preferred not to be reminded.

The out-patients' department was next to the casualty department entrance and as they passed it a stretcher was wheeled in. The patient was an emaciated old man; his moist lips spewed feebly above the rim of a vomit bowl, his immense eyes rolled uncomprehendingly in the skull-like head. Dalgliesh became aware that Sister Rolfe was looking at him. He turned his head in time to catch her glance of speculation and, he thought, contempt.

'You don't like this place, do you?' she asked.

'I'm not very happy in it, certainly.'

'Neither am I at present, but I suspect for very different reasons.'

They walked on for a minute in silence. Then Dalgliesh asked if Leonard Morris lunched in the staff dining-room when he was in the hospital.

'Not often. I believe he brings sandwiches and eats them in the pharmacy office. He prefers his own company.'

'Or that of Sister Gearing?'

She laughed contemptuously.

'Oh, you've got on to that have you? But of course! She was entertaining him last night, I hear. Either the food or the subsequent activity seems to have been rather more than the little man could take. What thorough little scavengers the police are! It must be a strange job, sniffing around for evil like a dog round trees.'

'Isn't evil a strong word for Leonard Morris's sexual preoccupations?'

'Of course. I was just being clever. But I shouldn't let the Morris–Gearing affair worry you. It's been hiccuping on for so long now that it's become almost respectable. It isn't even good for a gossip. She's the kind of woman who must have someone in tow, and he likes someone to confide in about the awfulness of his family and the beastliness of the hospital medical staff. They don't exactly take him at his own evaluation as an equal professional man. He's got four children, by the way. I imagine that if his wife decided to divorce him and he and Gearing were free to marry nothing would disconcert them more. Gearing would like a husband no doubt, but I don't think she's cast poor little Morris for the role. It's more likely . . .'

She broke off. Dalgliesh asked:

'You think she has a more eligible candidate in mind?'

'Why not try asking her? She doesn't confide in me.'

'But you are responsible for her work? The clinical instructor comes under the senior nurse tutor?'

'I'm responsible for her work not her morals.'

They had reached the far door of the casualty department and as Sister Rolfe put out her hand to push it open Mr Courtney-Briggs swept in. He was followed by a half-dozen chattering junior staff, white-coated and with stethoscopes slung round their necks. The two on each side of him were nodding in deferential attention as the great man spoke. Dalgliesh thought that he had the conceit, the patina of vulgarity and the slightly coarse *savoir-faire* which he associated with one type of successful professional man. As if reading his thoughts, Sister Rolfe said:

'They're not all alike, you know. Take Mr Molravey, our ophthalmic surgeon. He reminds me of a dormouse. Every Tuesday morning he patters in and stands for five hours in the theatre without speaking an unnecessary word, whiskers twitching and picking away with fastidious little paws at a succession of patients' eyes. Then he thanks everyone formally down to the most junior theatre nurse, peels off his gloves and patters away again to play with his collection of butterflies.'

'A modest little man, in fact.'

She turned towards him and he detected again in her eyes that uncomfortable elliptical flicker of contempt.

'Oh no! Not modest! He gives a different performance, that's all. Mr Molravey is just as convinced as is Mr Courtney-Briggs that he's a very remarkable surgeon. They are both vain in a professional sense. Vanity, Mr Dalgliesh, is a surgeon's besetting sin as subservience is a nurse's. I've never yet met a successful surgeon who wasn't convinced that he ranked only one degree lower than Almighty God. They're all infected with hubris.' She paused:

'Isn't that supposed to be true also of murderers?'

'Of one type of murderer. You must remember that murder is a highly individual crime.'

'Is it? I should have thought that the motives and the means would be monotonously familiar to you. But you, of course, are the expert.'

Dalgliesh said: 'You have little respect for men apparently, Sister?'

'A great deal of respect. I just don't happen to like them. But you have to respect a sex that has brought selfishness to such an art. That's what gives you your strength, this ability to devote yourselves entirely to your own interest.'

Dalgliesh said, a little maliciously, that he was surprised that Miss Rolfe, since she obviously resented the subservience of her job, hadn't chosen a more masculine occupation. Medicine perhaps? She laughed bitterly.

'I wanted to do medicine but I had a father who didn't believe in educating women. I'm forty-six, remember. When I was at school we didn't have universal free grammar school education. Father earned too much for me to get a free place, so he had to pay. He stopped paying as soon as he decently could, when I was sixteen.'

Dalgliesh found nothing appropriate to say. The confidence surprised him. She was hardly the woman, he would have thought, to expose a personal grievance to a stranger and he didn't flatter himself that she found him sympathetic. She would find no man sympathetic. The outburst was probably a spontaneous release of pent-up bitterness, but whether against her father, men in general or the limitations and subservience of her job it was hard to say.

They had left the hospital now and were passing along the narrow path which led to Nightingale House. Neither of them spoke another word until the house was reached. Sister Rolfe wrapped her long cloak tightly around her and pulled up her hood as if it could protect her from more than the bite of the wind. Dalgliesh was immersed in his private thoughts. And thus, with the width of the path between them, they paced together in silence under the trees.

IV

In the office Detective Sergeant Masterson was typing a report. Dalgliesh said:

'Immediately before she came into the school, Nurse Pearce was working on the private ward under Sister Brumfett. I want to know if anything significant happened there. And I want a detailed account of her last week's duty and an hour-by-hour account of what she did on her last day. Find out who the other nursing staff were, what her duties were, when she was off duty, how she appeared to the other staff. I want the names of the patients who were on the ward while she was nursing there and what happened to them. Your best plan is to talk to the other nurses and to work from the nursing reports. They're bound to keep a book which is written up daily.'

'Shall I get it from Matron?'

'No. Ask Sister Brumfett for it. We deal directly with her, and for God's sake be tactful. Have you those reports ready yet?'

'Yes, sir. They've been typed. Do you want to read them now?'

'No. Tell me if there's anything I ought to know. I'll look at them tonight. I suppose it's too much to expect that any of our suspects has a police record?'

'If they have, sir, it isn't noted on the personal dossiers. There's remarkably little information in most of them. Julia Pardoe was expelled from school, though. She seems to be the only delinquent among them.'

'Good God! What for?'

'Her dossier doesn't say. Apparently it was something to do with a visiting maths master. Her headmistress felt it right to mention it when she sent Matron a reference before the girl started here. It isn't very specific. She writes that Julia was more sinned against than sinning and that she hoped the hospital would give her the chance of training for the only career she has ever shown any interest in, or signs of being suited for.'

'A nice double-edged comment. So that's why the London teaching hospitals wouldn't take her. I thought Sister Rolfe was being a little disingenuous about the reasons. Anything about the others? Any previous connections between them?'

'Matron and Sister Brumfett trained together in the north at Nethercastle Royal Infirmary, did their midwifery training at the Municipal Maternity Hospital there and came here fifteen years ago, both as ward Sisters. Mr Courtney-Briggs was in Cairo during 1946–7 and so was Sister Gearing. He was a major in the R.A.M.C. and she was a nursing sister in the Q.A.R.N.S. There's no suggestion that they knew each other there.'

'If they did, you'd hardly expect to find the fact recorded on their personal records. But they probably did. Cairo in '46 was a chummy place, so my army friends tell me. I wonder if Miss Taylor served in the Q.A.R.N.S. That's an army nursing service cap which she wears.'

'If she did, sir, it isn't on her dossier. The earliest document is her reference from her training school when she came here as a Sister. They thought very highly of her at Nethercastle.'

'They think very highly of her here. Have you checked on Courtney-Briggs?'

'Yes, sir. The lodge porter makes a note of every car in and out after midnight. Mr Courtney-Briggs left at twelve thirty-two a.m.'

'Later than he led us to believe. I want to check on his schedule. The precise time he finished the operation will be in the operating theatre book. The junior doctor assisting him will probably know when he left – Mr Courtney-Briggs is the kind of man who gets escorted to his car. Then drive over the route and time him. They will have moved the tree by now but it should be possible to see where it came down. He can't have wasted more than a few minutes at the most tying on his scarf. Find out what happened to that. He'd hardly lie about something so easily disproved, but he's arrogant enough to think he can get away with anything, including murder.'

'Constable Greeson can do the checking, sir. He likes these reconstruction jobs.'

'Tell him to curb his urge for verisimilitude. There's no need for him to don an operating gown and go into the theatre. Not that they'd let him. Is there any news yet from Sir Miles or the lab?'

'No, sir, but we've got the name and address of the man Nurse Fallon spent that week in the Isle of Wight with. He's a G.P.O. night telephonist and lives in North Kensington. The local people got on to them almost at once. Fallon made it very easy for them. She booked in her own name and they had two single rooms.'

'She was a woman who valued her privacy. Still, she hardly got pregnant by staying in her own room. I'll see the man tomorrow morning after I've visited Miss Fallon's solicitor. Is Leonard Morris in the hospital yet, do you know?'

'Not yet, sir. I checked at the pharmacy that he telephoned this morning and said he wasn't well. Apparently he suffers from a duodenal ulcer. They assume that it's playing him up again.'

'It will play him up a great deal worse if he doesn't come back soon and get the interview over. I don't want to embarrass him by visiting his house, but we can't wait indefinitely to get Sister Gearing's story verified. Both these murders, if they were murders, hinge on the question of timing. We must know everyone's movements, if possible, to the minute. Time is crucial.'

Masterson said: 'That's what surprised me about the poisoned drip. The carbolic couldn't have been added to the milk without a great deal of care, particularly in replacing the bottle seal and making sure that the concentration was right and that the stuff had the texture and colour of milk. It couldn't have been done in a hurry.'

'I've no doubt a great deal of care and time were taken. But I think I know how it was done.'

He described his theory. Sergeant Masterson, cross with himself for having missed the obvious, said:

'Of course. It must have been done that way.'

'Not must, Sergeant. It was probably done that way.'

But Sergeant Masterson had seen an objection and voiced it.

Dalgliesh replied: 'But that wouldn't apply to a woman. A woman could do it easily and one woman in particular. But I admit it would be more difficult for a man.'

'So the assumption is that the milk was doctored by a woman?'

'The probability is that both girls were murdered by a woman. But it's still only a probability. Have you heard yet whether Nurse Dakers is well enough to be interviewed? Dr Snelling was supposed to be seeing her this morning.'

'Matron rang just before lunch to say that the girl is still asleep, but that she'll probably be fit enough once she wakes up. She's under sedation, so God knows when that'll be. Shall I take a look at her while I'm in the private wing?'

'No. I'll see her later. But you might check on this story that Fallon returned to Nightingale House on the morning of 12th January. Someone might have seen her leave. And where were her clothes while she was warded? Could anyone have got hold of them and impersonated her? It seems unlikely but it ought to be checked.'

'Inspector Bailey did check, sir. No one saw Fallon leave but they admit that she could have got out of the ward undetected. They were very busy and she had a private room. If it were found empty they would probably have assumed that she'd gone to the bathroom. Her clothes were hung in the wardrobe in her room. Anyone who had a right to be in the ward could have got at them, provided, of course, that Fallon was asleep or out of the room. But no one thinks it likely that anyone did.'

'Nor do I. I think I know why Fallon came back to Nightingale House. Nurse Goodale told us that Fallon had received the pregnancy confirmation only two days before she went sick. It's possible that she didn't destroy it. If so, it's the one possession in her room which she wouldn't want to leave for someone else to find. It certainly isn't among her papers. My guess is that she came back to retrieve it, tore it up, and flushed it down the lavatory.'

'Couldn't she have telephoned Nurse Goodale and asked her to destroy it?'

'Not without exciting suspicion. She couldn't be sure that she'd get Goodale herself when she rang and she wouldn't want to give anyone else a message. This insistence to speak to one particular nurse and the reluctance to accept help from anyone else would look rather odd. But it's no more than a theory. Is the search of Nightingale House completed?'

'Yes, sir. They've found nothing. No trace of poison and no container. Most of the rooms contain bottles of aspirin and Sister Gearing, Sister Brumfett and Miss Taylor all have a small supply of sleeping tablets. But surely Fallon didn't die of hypnotic or soporific poisoning?'

'No. It was quicker than that. We shall just have to possess ourselves in patience until we get the laboratory report.'

V

At two thirty-four p.m. precisely, in the largest and most luxurious of the private rooms, Sister Brumfett lost a patient. She always thought of death in that way. The patient was lost; the battle was over; she, Sister Brumfett, had been personally defeated. The fact that so many of her battles were foredoomed to failure, that the enemy, even if repulsed in the present skirmish, was always assured of final victory, never mitigated her sense of failure. Patients did not come into Sister Brumfett's ward to die; they came in to get better, and with Sister's indomitable will to fortify them, they usually did get better, often to their own surprise and occasionally despite their own wishes.

She had hardly expected to win this particular battle but it was only when Mr Courtney-Briggs lifted his hand to turn off the blood drip that she accepted failure. The patient had certainly fought well; a difficult patient, a demanding patient, but a good fighter. He had been a wealthy businessman whose meticulous plans for his future certainly didn't include dying at forty-two. She recalled the look of wild surprise, almost of outrage, with which he had greeted the realization that death was something neither he nor his accountant could fix. Sister Brumfett had seen too much of his young widow on that lady's daily visits to suppose that she would suffer much grief or inconvenience. The patient was the only one who would have been furious at the failure of Mr Courtney-Briggs's heroic and expensive efforts to save him, and happily for the surgeon, the patient was the one person in no position to demand either explanation or excuse.

Mr Courtney-Briggs would see the widow and offer her his customary carefully phrased condolences, his assurance that everything humanly possible had been done. In this case, the size of the bill would be a guarantee of that and a powerful antidote, no doubt, to the inevitable guilt of bereavement. Courtney-Briggs was really very good with the widows; and to do him justice, the poor as well as the rich received the consolation of his hand on their shoulder, of the stereotyped phrases of comfort and regret.

She drew the fold of the sheet up over the suddenly vacant face. Closing the dead eyes with practised fingers, she felt the eyeballs still warm under the wrinkled lids. She was conscious neither of grief nor anger. There was only, as always, this dragging weight of failure tugging like a physical load at the tired muscles of her stomach and back.

They turned away from the bed together. Glancing at the surgeon's face, Sister Brumfett was struck by his look of weariness. For the first time he, too, appeared threatened with failure and with age. It was, of course, unusual for a patient to die when he was there to see it happen. Still less frequently did they die on the operating table, even if the scramble from the theatre to the ward was sometimes a little undignified. But, unlike Sister Brumfett,

Mr Courtney-Briggs did not have to watch over his patients to the last gasp. All the same, she did not believe that this particular death had depressed him. It was, after all, not unexpected. He had nothing with which to reproach himself even if he had been given to self-criticism. She felt that he was stressed by some subtler worry, and she wondered whether it was something to do with Fallon's death. He's lost some of his bounce, thought Sister Brumfett. He looks suddenly ten years older.

He preceded her down the passage to her office. As they neared the ward kitchen there was the sound of voices. The door was open. A student nurse was setting a trolley with the afternoon tea trays. Sergeant Masterson was leaning against the sink and watching her with the air of a man completely at home. As the Sister and Mr Courtney-Briggs appeared in the doorway the girl flushed, muttered a low 'good afternoon, sir' and pushed the trolley past them into the corridor with clumsy haste. Sergeant Masterson gazed after her with tolerant condescension, then transferred his level gaze to the Sister. He appeared not to notice Mr Courtney-Briggs.

'Good afternoon, Sister, could I have a word with you?'

Baulked of the initiative, Sister Brumfett said repressively:

'In my office if you please, Sergeant. That is where you should have waited in the first place. People do not wander in and out of my ward just as they please, and that includes the police.'

Sergeant Masterson, unchastened, looked slightly gratified at this speech as if it confirmed something to his satisfaction. Sister Brumfett bustled into her office, tight-lipped and ready for battle. Rather to her surprise Mr Courtney-Briggs followed.

Sergeant Masterson said: 'I wonder, Sister, if I could see the ward report book covering the period when Nurse Pearce was on this ward? I'm particularly interested in her last week here.'

Mr Courtney-Briggs broke in roughly:

'Aren't they confidential records, Sister? Surely the police will have to apply for a subpoena before they can make you produce them?'

'Oh, I don't think so, sir.' Sergeant Masterson's voice, quiet, almost too respectful, yet held a tinge of amusement which wasn't lost on his hearer. 'Ward nursing records surely aren't medical in the proper sense. I merely want to see who was being nursed here during that period and whether anything happened which might be of interest to the Superintendent. It's been suggested that something occurred to upset Nurse Pearce while she was nursing on your ward. She went from here straight to the school, remember.'

Sister Brumfett, mottled and shaking with an anger which left small room for fear, found her voice.

'Nothing happened on my ward. Nothing! It's all stupid, malicious gossip. If a nurse does her job properly and obeys orders there's no need for her to be upset. The Superintendent is here to investigate a murder, not to interfere with my ward.'

Mr Courtney-Briggs broke in blandly:

'And even if she were – upset is the word I think you used, Sergeant – I don't see what relevance that has to her death.'

Sergeant Masterson smiled at him as if humouring a wilfully obstinate child.

'Anything that happened to Nurse Pearce in the week immediately before she was killed may have relevance, sir. That's why I'm asking to see the ward report book.'

As neither Sister Brumfett nor the surgeon made any move to comply, he added:

'It's only a matter of confirming information we already have. I know what she was doing on the ward during that week. I'm told she was devoting all her time to nursing one particular patient. A Mr Martin Dettinger. "Specializing" him, I think you call it. My information is that she seldom left his room while she was on duty here during the last week of her life.'

So, thought Sister Brumfett, he had been gossiping with the student nurses. But of course! That was how the police worked. It was pointless to try to keep anything private from them. Everything, even the medical secrets of her ward, the nursing care of her own patients, would be nosed out by this impertinent young man and reported to his superior officer. There was nothing in the ward book which he couldn't find out by more devious means; discover, magnify, misinterpret and use to make mischief. Inarticulate with anger and something close to panic she heard Mr Courtney-Briggs's bland and reassuring voice:

'Then you'd better hand the book over, Sister. If the police insist on wasting their own time there's no need for us to encourage them to waste ours.'

Without another word, Sister Brumfett went to her desk and, bending down, opened the deep right-hand drawer and took out a large, hard-backed book. Silently and without looking at him, she handed it to Sergeant Masterson. The Sergeant thanked her profusely and turned to Mr Courtney-Briggs:

'And now, sir, if the patient's still with you, I'd like to have a word with Mr Dettinger.'

Mr Courtney-Briggs made no attempt to keep the satisfaction out of his voice.

'I think that is likely to challenge even your ingenuity, Sergeant. Mr Martin Dettinger died on the day Nurse Pearce left this ward. If I remember rightly, she was with him when he died. So both of them are safely out of reach of your inquisition. And now, if you'd be good enough to excuse us, Sister and I have work to do.'

He held open the door and Sister Brumfett strutted out before him. Sergeant Masterson was left alone, holding the ward record book in his hand.

'Bloody bastard,' he said aloud.

He stood for a moment, thinking. Then he went in search of the medical records department.

VI

Ten minutes later he was back in the office. Under his arm was the ward report book and a buff-coloured file, stamped with a warning in black capital letters that it was not to be handed to the patient, and bearing the name of the hospital and Martin Dettinger's medical record number. He placed the book on the table and handed the file to Dalgliesh.

'Thank you. You got it without trouble?'

'Yes, sir,' said Masterson. He saw no reason to explain that the Medical Records Officer had been out of his department and that he had half persuaded, half bullied the junior clerk on duty into handing over the file on the grounds, which he didn't for a moment believe, that the rules about the confidentiality of medical records no longer applied when the patient was dead and that when a Superintendent of the Yard asked for a thing he was entitled to get it without fuss and without delay. They studied the file together. Dalgliesh said:

'Martin Dettinger. Aged forty-six. Gave his address as his London club. C. of E. Divorced. Next-of-kin, Mrs Louise Dettinger, 23 Saville Mansions, Marylebone. Mother. You had better see the lady, Masterson. Make an appointment for tomorrow evening. I shall need you here during the day while I'm in town. And take trouble with her. She must have visited her son pretty frequently when he was in hospital. Nurse Pearce was specializing him. The two women probably saw quite a lot of each other. Something happened to upset Pearce while she was working on the private ward during the last week of her life and I want to know what it was.'

He turned back to the medical record.

'There's a lot of paper here. The poor chap seems to have had a stormy medical history. He suffered from colitis for the past ten years, and before that there's a record of long spells of undiagnosed ill-health, perhaps a forerunner of the condition which killed him. He was in hospital for three periods during his army service, including a spell of two months in an army hospital in Cairo in 1947. He was invalided out of the army in 1952 and emigrated to South Africa. That doesn't seem to have done him much good. There are notes here from a hospital in Johannesburg. Courtney-Briggs wrote for them; he certainly takes trouble. His own notes are pretty copious. He took over the case a couple of years ago and seems to have been acting as a kind of general practitioner to Dettinger as well as his surgeon. The colitis became acute about a month ago, and Courtney-Briggs operated to remove a large part of the bowel on Friday, 2nd January. Dettinger survived the operation, although he was in a pretty bad state by then, and made some progress until the early afternoon of Monday, 5th January, when he relapsed. After that he was seldom conscious for long, and he died at five-thirty p.m. on Friday, 9th January.'

Masterson said: 'Nurse Pearce was with him when he died.'

'And apparently she nursed him almost single-handed for the last week of his life. I wonder what the nursing record tells us.'

But the nursing record was far less informative than the medical file. Nurse Pearce had entered in her careful schoolgirl's hand the details of her patient's temperature, respiration and pulse, his restlessness and brief hours of sleep, his medication and food. It could not be faulted as a meticulous record of nursing care. Beyond that it told them nothing.

Dalgliesh closed the book.

'You'd better return this to the ward and the medical folder to the proper department. We've learned all we can from them. But I feel in my bones that Martin Dettinger's death has something to do with this case.'

Masterson did not reply. Like all detectives who had worked with Dalgliesh, he had a healthy respect for the old man's hunches. Inconvenient, perverse and far-fetched they might seem, but they had been proved right too often to be safely ignored. And he had no objection to an evening trip to London. Tomorrow was Friday. The timetable on the hall notice-board showed that the students' sessions ended early on Friday. They would be free soon after five. He wondered whether Julia Pardoe would fancy a drive to town. After all, why not? Dalgliesh wouldn't be back by the time he was due to set out. It could be arranged with care. And there were some suspects it would be a positive pleasure to interview on their own.

VII

Just before half past four Dalgliesh, in defiance of convention and prudence, took tea alone with Sister Gearing in her bed-sitting-room. She had met him casually passing across the ground-floor hall as the students were filing out of the lecture room after the last seminar of the day. She had given the invitation spontaneously and without coyness, although Dalgliesh noted that Sergeant Masterson was not included. He would have accepted the invitation even had it been delivered on highly scented and pink writing-paper and accompanied by the most blatant of sexual innuendoes. What he wanted after the formal interrogation of the morning was to sit in comfort and listen to a flow of artless, candid and slightly malicious gossip; to listen with the surface of his mind soothed, uninvolved, even a little cynically amused, but with the sharp claws of the intelligence sharpened for their pickings. He had learned more about the Nightingale House Sisters from their conversation at luncheon than he had in all his formal interviews, but he couldn't spend all his time tagging along behind the nursing staff, picking up scraps of gossip like so many dropped handkerchiefs. He wondered whether Sister Gearing had something to tell or something to ask. Either way he didn't expect an hour in her company to be wasted.

Dalgliesh hadn't yet been in any of the rooms on the third floor except Matron's flat and he was struck by the size and pleasant proportions of Sister Gearing's room. From here, even in winter, the hospital couldn't be seen, and the room had a calm of its own, remote from the frenetic life of wards and departments. Dalgliesh thought that in summer it must be very pleasant with nothing but a curdle of tree tops breaking the view of the far hills. Even now, with the curtains drawn against the fading light and the gas fire giving out a merry hiss, it was welcoming and warm. Presumably the divan bed in the corner with its cretonne cover and carefully arranged bank of cushions had been provided by the Hospital Management Committee, as had the two comfortable armchairs similarly covered and the rest of the uninteresting but functional furniture. But Sister Gearing had imposed her own personality on the room. There was a long shelf along the far wall on which she had arranged a collection of dolls in different national costumes. On another wall was a smaller shelf holding an assortment of china cats of different sizes and breeds. There was one particularly repulsive specimen in spotted blue, bulging of eye and adorned with a bow of blue ribbon; and propped beside it was a greetings card. It showed a female robin, the sex denoted by a frilly apron and flowered bonnet, perched on a twig. At her feet, a male robin was spelling out the words 'Good luck' in worms. Dalgliesh hastily averted his eyes from this abomination and continued his tactful examination of the room.

The table in front of the window was presumably intended as a desk but about half a dozen photographs in silver frames effectively took up most of the working space. There was a record player in a corner with a cabinet of records beside it and a poster of a recent pop idol pinned on the wall above. There was a large number of cushions of all sizes and colours, three pouffes of unattractive design, an imitation tiger rug in brown-and-white nylon, and a coffee table on which Sister Gearing had set out the tea. But the most remarkable object in the room, in Dalgliesh's eyes, was a tall vase of winter foliage and chrysanthemums, beautifully arranged, standing on a side table. Sister Gearing was reputably good with flowers, and this arrangement had a simplicity of colour and line which was wholly pleasing. It was odd, he thought, that a woman with such an instinctive taste in flower arrangement should be content to live in this vulgarly overfurnished room. It suggested that Sister Gearing might be a more complex person than one would at first suppose. On the face of it, her character was easily read. She was a middle-aged, uncomfortably passionate spinster, not particularly well educated or intelligent, and concealing her frustrations with a slightly spurious gaiety. But twenty-five years as a policeman had taught him that no character was without its complications, its inconsistencies. Only the young or the very arrogant imagined that there was an identikit to the human mind.

Here in her own place Sister Gearing was less overtly flirtatious than she was in company. Admittedly she had chosen to pour the tea while curled on a large cushion at his feet, but he guessed from the number and variety of these cushions plumped around the room that this was her usual comfortable habit, rather than a kittenish invitation for him to join her. The tea was excellent. It was hot and freshly brewed, and accompanied by lavishly buttered crumpets with anchovy paste. There was an admirable absence of doilys and sticky cakes, and the cup handle could be comfortably held without dislocating one's fingers. She looked after him with quiet efficiency. Dalgliesh thought that Sister Gearing was one of those women who, when alone with a man, considered it their duty to devote themselves entirely to his comfort and the flattering of his ego. This may arouse fury in less dedicated women, but it is unreasonable to expect a man to object.

Relaxed by the warmth and comfort of her room and stimulated by tea, Sister Gearing was obviously in a mood for talk. Dalgliesh let her chatter on, only occasionally throwing in a question. Neither of them mentioned Leonard Morris. The artless confidences for which Dalgliesh hoped would hardly spring from embarrassment or restraint.

'Of course, what happened to that poor kid Pearce is absolutely appalling, however it was caused. And with the whole set looking on like that! I'm surprised that it hasn't upset their work completely, but the young are pretty tough these days. And it isn't as if they liked her. But I can't believe that any one of them put that corrosive into the feed. After all, these are third-year students. They know that carbolic acid taken straight into the stomach in that concentration is lethal. Damn it all, they had a lecture about poisons in their previous block. So it couldn't have been a practical joke that misfired.'

'All the same, that seems to be the general view.'

'Well, it's natural, isn't it? No one wants to believe that Pearce's death was murder. And if this were a first-year block I might believe it. One of the students might have tampered with the feed on impulse, perhaps with the idea that lysol is an emetic and that the demonstration might be enlivened by Pearce sicking up all over the G.N.S. Inspector. An odd idea of humour, but the young can be pretty crude. But these kids must have known what that stuff would do to the stomach.'

'And what about Nurse Fallon's death?'

'Oh, suicide I should think. After all, the poor girl was pregnant. She probably had a moment of intense depression and didn't see the point of going on. Three years of training wasted and no family to turn to. Poor old Fallon! I don't think she was really the suicidal type, but it probably happened on impulse. There has been a certain amount of criticism about Dr Snelling – he looks after the students' health – letting her come back to the block so soon after her influenza. But she hated being off and it wasn't as if she were on the wards. This is hardly the time of the year to send people away for convalescence. She was as well off in school as anywhere. Still, the flu couldn't have helped. It probably left her feeling pretty low. This epidemic is having some pretty nasty after-effects. If only she'd confided in someone. It's awful to think of her putting an end to herself like that with a houseful of people who would have been glad to help if only she'd asked. Here, let me give you another cup. And try one of those shortbreads. They're home-made. My married sister sends me them from time to time.'

Dalgliesh helped himself to a piece of shortbread from the proffered tin and observed that there were those who thought that Nurse Fallon might have had another reason for suicide, apart from her pregnancy. She could have put the corrosive in the feed. She had certainly been seen in Nightingale House at the crucial time.

He put forward the suggestion slyly, awaiting her reaction. It wouldn't, of course, be new to her; it must have occurred to everyone in Nightingale House. But she was too simple to be surprised that a senior detective should be discussing his case so frankly with her, and too stupid to ask herself why.

She dismissed this theory with a snort.

'Not Fallon! It would have been a foolish trick and she was no fool. I told you, any third-year nurse would know that the stuff was lethal. And if you're suggesting that Fallon intended to kill Pearce – and why on earth should she? – I'd say that she was the last person to suffer remorse. If Fallon decided to do murder she wouldn't waste time repenting afterwards, let alone kill herself in remorse. No, Fallon's death is understandable enough. She had post-flu depression and she felt she couldn't cope with the baby.'

'So you think they both committed suicide?'

'Well, I'm not so sure about Pearce. You'd have to be pretty crazy to choose that agonizing way of dying, and Pearce seemed sane enough to me. But it's a possible explanation, isn't it? And I can't see you proving anything else however long you stay.'

He thought he detected a note of smug complacency in her voice and glanced at her abruptly. But the thin face showed nothing but its usual look of vague dissatisfaction. She was eating shortbread, nibbling at it with sharp, very white teeth. He could hear them rasping against the biscuits. She said:

'When one explanation is impossible, the improbable must be true. Someone said something like that. G.K. Chesterton wasn't it? Nurses don't murder each other. Or anyone else for that matter.'

'There was Nurse Waddingham,' said Dalgliesh.

'Who was she?'

'An unprepossessing and unpleasant woman who poisoned with morphine one of her patients, a Miss Baguley. Miss Baguley had been so ill-advised as to leave Nurse Waddingham her money and property in turn for life-long treatment in the latter's nursing home. She struck a poor bargain. Nurse Waddingham was hanged.'

Sister Gearing gave a frisson of simulated distaste.

'What awful people you do get yourself mixed up with! Anyway, she was probably one of those unqualified nurses. You can't tell me that Waddingham was on the General Nursing Council's Register.'

'Come to think of it, I don't believe she was. And I wasn't mixed up with it. It happened in 1935.'

'Well, there you are then,' Sister Gearing said as if vindicated.

She stretched across to pour him a second cup of tea, then wriggled herself more comfortably into her cushion and leaned back against the arm of his chair, so that her hair brushed his knee. Dalgliesh found himself examining with mild interest the narrow band of darker hair each side of the parting where the dye had grown out. Viewed from above, her foreshortened face looked older, the nose sharper. He could see the latent pouch of skin under the bottom eyelashes and a spatter of broken veins high on the cheekbones, the purple threads only half disguised by make-up. She was no longer a young woman; that he knew. And there was a great deal more about her that he had gleaned from her dossier. She had trained at a hospital in the East End of London after a variety of unsuccessful and unprofitable office jobs. Her nursing career had been chequered and her references were suspiciously non-committal. There had been doubt about the wisdom of seconding her for training as a clinical instructor, a suggestion that she had been motivated less by a desire to teach than by the hope of an easier job than that of ward Sister. He knew that she was having difficulty with the menopause. He knew more about her than she realized, more than she would think he had any right to know. But he didn't yet know whether she was a murderess. Intent for a moment on his private thoughts, he hardly caught her next words.

'It's odd your being a poet. Fallon had your last volume of verse in her room, didn't she? Rolfe told me. Isn't it difficult to reconcile poetry with being a policeman?'

'I've never thought of poetry and police work as needing to be reconciled in that ecumenical way.'

She laughed coyly.

'You know very well what I mean. After all it is a little unusual. One doesn't think of policemen as poets.'

He did, of course, know what she meant. But it wasn't a subject he was prepared to discuss. He said:

'Policemen are individuals like people in any other job. After all, you three nursing Sisters haven't much in common have you? You and Sister Brumfett could hardly be more different personalities. I can't see Sister Brumfett feeding me on anchovy crumpets and home-made shortbread.'

She had reacted at once, as he had known she would.

'Oh, Brumfett's all right when you get to know her. Of course she's twenty years out of date. As I said at lunch, the kids today aren't prepared to listen to all that guff about obedience and duty and a sense of vocation. But she's a marvellous nurse. I won't hear a word against Brum. I had an appendicectomy here about four years ago. It went a bit wrong and the wound burst. Then I got an infection which was resistant to antibiotics. The whole thing was a mess. Not one of our Courtney-Briggs's most successful efforts. Anyway I felt like death. One night I was in ghastly pain and couldn't sleep and I felt absolutely sure I wouldn't see the morning. I was terrified. It was sheer funk. Talk about the fear of death! I knew what it meant that night. Then Brumfett came round. She was looking after me herself; she wouldn't let the students do a thing for me when she was on duty. I said to her: "I'm not going to die, am I?" She looked down at me. She didn't tell me not to be a fool or give me any of the usual comforting lies. She just said in that gruff voice of hers: "Not if I can help it you aren't." And immediately the panic stopped. I knew that if Brumfett was fighting on my side I'd win through. It sounds a bit daft and sentimental put like that, but that's what I thought. She's like that with all the really sick patients. Talk about confidence! Brumfett makes you feel that she'd drag you back from the edge of the grave by sheer will-power, even if all the devils in hell were tugging the other way; which in my case they probably were. They don't make them like that any more.'

Dalgliesh made appropriately assenting noises and paused briefly before picking up the references to Mr Courtney-Briggs. He asked rather naïvely whether many of the surgeon's operations went so spectacularly wrong. Sister Gearing laughed:

'Lord, no! Courtney-Briggs's operations usually go the way he wants. That's not to say they go the way the patient would choose if he knew the whole of it. C.B. is what they call a heroic surgeon. If you ask me, most of the heroism has to be shown by the patients. But he does an extraordinary good job of work. He's one of the last remaining great general surgeons. You know, take anything on, the more hopeless the better. I suppose a surgeon is rather like a lawyer. There's no glory to be had in getting someone off if he's obviously innocent. The greater the guilt the greater the glory.'

'What is Mrs Courtney-Briggs like? I presume he's married. Does she show herself at the hospital?'

'Not very often, although she's supposed to be a member of the League of Friends. She gave the prizes away last year when the Princess couldn't come at the last moment. Blonde, very smart. Younger than C.B. but beginning to wear a bit now. Why do you ask? You don't suspect Muriel Courtney-Briggs surely? She wasn't even in the hospital the night Fallon died. Probably tucked up in bed in their very nice little place near Selborne. And she certainly hadn't any motive for killing poor Pearce.'

So she did have a motive for getting rid of Fallon. Mr Courtney-Briggs's liaison had probably been more noticed than he had realized. Dalgliesh wasn't surprised that Sister Gearing should know about it. Her sharp nose would be adept at smelling out sexual scandal.

He said: 'I wondered if she were jealous.'

Sister Gearing, unaware of what she had told, rambled happily on.

'I don't suppose she knew. Wives don't usually. Anyway, C.B. wasn't going to break up his marriage to wed Fallon. Not him! Mrs C.B. has plenty of money of her own. She's the only child of Price of Price and Maxwell, the building firm – and what with C.B.'s earnings and Daddy's ill-gotten gains, they're very comfortable. I don't think Muriel worries much what he does as long as he behaves himself properly to her and the money keeps rolling in. I know I wouldn't. Besides, if rumour's correct, our Muriel doesn't exactly qualify for the League of Purity.'

'Anyone here?' asked Dalgliesh.

'Oh no, nothing like that. It's just that she goes around with quite a smart set. She usually gets her picture in every third issue of the social glossies. And they're in with the theatrical crowd too. C.B. had a brother who was an actor, Peter Courtney. He hanged himself about three years ago. You must have read about it.'

Dalgliesh's job gave him few opportunities to see a play and theatre-going was one of the pleasures he missed most. He had seen Peter Courtney act only once but it had been a performance not easily forgotten. He had been a very young Macbeth, as introspective and sensitive as Hamlet, in thrall sexually to a much older wife, and whose physical courage was compounded of violence and hysteria. It had been a perverse but interesting interpretation, and it had very nearly succeeded. Thinking of the performance now, Dalgliesh imagined that he could detect a likeness between the brothers, something to do with the set of the eyes perhaps. But Peter must have been the younger by nearly twenty years. He wished he knew what the two men, so widely separated in age and talent, had made of each other.

Suddenly and irrelevantly Dalgliesh asked:

'How did Pearce and Fallon get on together?'

'They didn't. Fallon despised Pearce. I don't mean she hated her or would have harmed her; she just despised her.'

'Was there any particular reason?'

'Pearce took it upon herself to tell Matron about Fallon's little tipple of whisky at nights. Self-righteous little beast. Oh, I know she's dead and I ought not to have said that. But really, Pearce could be insufferably self-righteous. Apparently what happened was that Diane Harper – she's left the training school now – had a bad cold about a fortnight before the set came into the block, and Fallon fixed her a hot whisky and lemon. Pearce could smell the stuff half-way along the corridor and concluded that Fallon was attempting to seduce her juniors with the demon drink. So she appeared in the utility room – they were in the main nurses' home then, of course – in her dressing-gown, sniffing the air like an avenging angel, and threatened to report Fallon to Matron unless she promised more or less on her knees never to touch the stuff again. Fallon told her where to go and what to do with herself when she got there. She had a picturesque turn of phrase when roused, had Fallon. Nurse Dakers burst into tears. Harper lost her temper and the general noise brought the House Sister on to the scene. Pearce reported it to Matron all right, but no one knows with what result, except that Fallon started keeping her whisky in her own room. But the whole thing caused a great deal of feeling in the third year. Fallon was never popular with the set, she was too reserved and sarcastic. But they liked Pearce a damn sight less.'

'And did Pearce dislike Fallon?'

'Well, it's difficult to say. Pearce never seemed to concern herself with what other people thought of her. She was an odd girl, pretty insensitive too. For example, she might disapprove of Fallon and her whisky-drinking but that didn't prevent her from borrowing Fallon's library ticket.'

'When did this happen?'

Dalgliesh leaned across and replaced his teacup on the tray. His voice was level, unconcerned. But he felt again that spring of excitement and anticipation, the intuitive sense that something important had been said. It was more than a hunch; it was, as always, a certainty. It might happen several times during a case if he were lucky, or not at all. He couldn't will it to happen and he was afraid to examine its roots too closely since he suspected that it was a plant easily withered by logic.

'Just before she came into block, I think. It must have been the week before Pearce died. The Thursday, I think. Anyway, they hadn't yet moved into Nightingale House. It was just after supper time in the main dining-room. Fallon and Pearce were walking out of the door together and I was just behind them with Goodale. Then Fallon turned to Pearce and said; "Here's the library token I promised you. I'd better give it to you now as I don't suppose we'll see each other in the morning. You'd better take the reader's ticket too, or they may not let you have the book." Pearce mumbled something and grabbed the token rather ungraciously I thought, and that was that. Why? It isn't important, is it?'

'I can't think why it should be,' said Dalgliesh.

VIII

He sat through the next fifteen minutes in exemplary patience. Sister Gearing couldn't have guessed from his courteous attention to her chattering and the leisurely way in which he drank his third and last cup of tea, that every moment was now grudged. When the meal was over, he carried the tray for her into the small Sisters' kitchen at the end of the corridor while she fretted at his heels, bleating her protests. Then he said: 'Thank you,' and left.

He went at once to the cell-like bedroom which still held nearly all the possessions Nurse Pearce had owned at the John Carpendar. It took him a moment to select the correct key from the heavy bunch in his pocket. The room had been locked after her death and was still locked. He went in, switching on the light. The bed was stripped and the whole room was very tidy and clean as if it, too, had been laid out for burial. The curtains were drawn back so that, from outside, the room would look no different from any other. The window was open but the air held a faint tang of disinfectant as if someone had tried to obliterate the memory of Pearce's death by a ritual purification.

He had no need to refresh his memory. The detritus of this particular life was pathetically meagre. But he went through her leavings again, turning them in careful hands as if the feel of cloth and leather could transmit their own clues. It didn't take long. Nothing had been altered since his first inspection. The hospital wardrobe, identical to that in Nurse Fallon's room, was more than adequate for the few woollen dresses, unexciting in colour and design, which, under his questing hand, swung from their padded hangers and gave out a faint smell of cleaning fluid and mothballs. The thick winter coat in fawn was of good quality but obviously old. He sought once more in the pockets. There was nothing except the handkerchief which had been there on his first examination, a crumpled ball of white cotton smelling of sour breath.

He moved to the chest of drawers. Here again the space provided had been more than sufficient. The two top drawers were filled with underclothes, strong sensible vests and knickers, comfortably warm no doubt for an English winter but with no concessions to glamour or fashion. The drawers were lined with newspaper. The sheets had been taken out once already, but he ran his hand under them and felt nothing but the gritty surface of bare unpolished wood. The remaining three drawers held skirts, jumpers and cardigans; a leather handbag, carefully wrapped in tissue paper; a pair of best shoes in a string bag; an embroidered handkerchief sachet with a dozen handkerchiefs carefully folded; an assortment of scarves; three pairs of identical nylon stockings still in their wrappers.

He turned again to the bedside locker and the small shelf fixed above it. The locker held a bedside lamp, a small alarm clock in a leather case which had long since run down, a packet of paper handkerchiefs with one crumpled tissue half-pulled through the slit, and an empty water carafe. There was also a leather-bound Bible and a writing-case. Dalgliesh opened the Bible at the flyleaf and read again the inscription in careful copper plate. 'Awarded to Heather Pearce for attendance and diligence. St Mark's Sunday School.' Diligence. An unfashionable, intimidating word but one, he felt, of which Nurse Pearce would have approved.

He opened the writing-case, but with little hope of finding what he sought. Nothing had changed since his first examination. Here still was the half-finished letter to her grandmother, a dull recital of the week's doings written as impersonally as a ward report, and a quarto-sized envelope, posted to her on the day of her death and obviously slipped into the writing-case by someone who, having opened it, couldn't think of what else to do with it. It was an illustrated brochure on the work of a home in Suffolk for German war refugees apparently sent in the hope of a donation.

He turned his attention to the small collection of books on the wall shelf. He had seen them before. Then, as now, he was struck by the conventionality of her choice and the meagreness of this personal library. A school prize for needlework. Lambs' *Tales from Shakespeare*. Dalgliesh had never believed that any child read them and there was no evidence that Nurse Pearce had done so. There were two travel books, *In the Steps of St Paul* and *In the Steps of the Master*. In both the girl had carefully inscribed her name. There was a well-known but out-of-date edition of a nursing textbook. The date on the flyleaf was nearly four years old. He wondered whether she had bought it in anticipation of her training, only to find that its advice on applying leeches and administering enemas had become out of date. There was a copy of Palgrave's *Golden Treasury*, also a school prize, but this time inappropriately for deportment. This, too, showed little sign of having been read. Lastly there were three paperbacks – novels by a popular woman writer, each advertised as 'The Book of the Film' – and a fictional and highly sentimental account of the wanderings across Europe of a lost dog and cat which Dalgliesh remembered had been a best-seller some five years previously. This was inscribed, 'To Heather, with love from Auntie Edie, Christmas 1964'. The whole collection told him little about the dead girl, except that her reading had apparently been as restricted as her life. And nowhere he found what he was seeking.

He didn't go again to look in Nurse Fallon's room. The scene-of-crime officer had searched every inch of it, and he himself could have described the room in minute detail and given an accurate inventory of all its contents. Wherever the library ticket and the token were, he could be sure that they weren't here. Instead he ran lightly up the wide staircase to the floor above where he had noticed a wall-mounted telephone when carrying Sister Gearing's tea tray to the utility room. A card listing the internal extensions hung beside it and, after a moment's thought, he rang the nurses' sitting-room. Maureen Burt answered. Yes, Nurse Goodale was still there. Almost immediately Dalgliesh heard her voice and he asked her to come up to see him in Nurse Pearce's room.

She came so promptly that he had hardly reached the door before he saw the self-assured, uniformed figure at the top of the stairs. He stood aside and she moved into the room before him and silently surveyed the stripped bed, the silent bedside clock, the closed Bible, letting her gaze rest briefly on each object with gentle uninquisitive interest. Dalgliesh moved to the window and, both standing, they regarded each other wordlessly across the bed. Then he said:

'I'm told that Nurse Fallon lent a library ticket to Nurse Pearce sometime during the week before she died. You were leaving the dining-room with Sister Gearing at the time. Can you remember what happened?'

Nurse Goodale was not given to showing surprise.

'Yes, I think so. Fallon had told me earlier that day that Pearce wanted to visit one of the London libraries and had asked to borrow her reader's ticket and the token. Fallon was a member of the Westminster library. They've got a number of branches in the City but you aren't really supposed to belong unless you either live or work in Westminster. Fallon had a flat in London before she became a student here and had kept her reader's card and token. It's an excellent library, much better than we've got here, and it's useful to be able to borrow books. I think Sister Rolfe is a member too. Fallon took her reader's ticket and one of the tokens across to lunch and handed them to Pearce as we were leaving the dining-room.'

'Did Nurse Pearce say why she wanted them?'

'Not to me. She may have told Fallon. I don't know. Any of us could borrow one of Fallon's tokens if we wanted to. Fallon didn't require an explanation.'

'What precisely are those tokens like?'

'They're small oblongs of pale blue plastic with the City Arms stamped on them. The library usually gives four to every reader and you hand one in every time you take out a book, but Jo only had three. She may have lost the fourth. There's also the reader's ticket. That's the usual small piece of cardboard with her name, address and date of expiry. Sometimes the assistant asks to see the reader's ticket and I suppose that's why Jo handed it over with the token.'

'Do you know where the other two are?'

'Yes, in my room. I borrowed them about a fortnight ago when I went up to town with my fiancé to attend a special service in the Abbey. I thought we might have time to visit the Great Smith Street branch to see whether they had the new Iris Murdoch. However, we met some friends from Mark's theological college after the service and never got to the library. I meant to return the tokens to Jo but I slipped them in my writing-case and forgot about them. She didn't remind me. I can show them to you if it would be helpful.'

'I think it would. Did Heather Pearce use her token, do you know?'

'Well, I assume she did. I saw her waiting for the Green Line bus to town that afternoon. We were both off duty so it must have been the Thursday. I imagine that she had it in mind to visit the library.'

She looked puzzled.

'Somehow I feel quite sure that she did take out a library book but I can't think why I should be so certain.'

'Can't you? Think very hard.'

Nurse Goodale stood silently, her hands folded composedly as if in prayer over the white stiffness of her apron. He did not hurry her. She gazed fixedly ahead and then turned her eyes to the bed and said quietly:

'I know now. I saw her reading a library book. It was the night when Jo was taken ill, the night before Pearce herself died. I went into her bedroom just after half past eleven to ask her to go and look after Jo while I fetched Sister. She was sitting up in bed with her hair in two plaits and she was reading. I remember now. It was a large book, bound in a dark colour, dark blue I think, and with a reference number stamped in gold at the foot of the spine. It looked an old and rather heavy book. I don't think it was fiction. She was holding it propped up against her knees I remember. When I appeared she closed it quickly and slipped it under her pillow. It was a strange thing to do but it didn't mean anything to me at the time. Pearce was always oddly secretive. Besides, I was too concerned about Jo. But I remember it now.'

She stood again in silence for a few moments. Dalgliesh waited. Then she said quietly:

'I know what's worrying you. Where's that book now? It wasn't among her things when Sister Rolfe and I tidied her room and made a list of her belongings after her death. The police were with us and we didn't find a book anything like it. And what happened to the ticket? It wasn't among Fallon's things either.'

Dalgliesh asked:

'What exactly happened that night? You said you went in to Nurse Fallon shortly after eleven thirty. I thought she didn't go to bed before midnight.'

'She did that night. I suppose it was because she wasn't feeling well and hoped that an early bed would put her right. She didn't tell anyone she was ill. Jo wouldn't. And I didn't go in to her. She came in to me. Shortly after eleven thirty she woke me up. She looked ghastly. She was obviously in a high fever and she could hardly stand. I helped her back to her bed, went in to ask Pearce to stay with her, and then rang Sister Rolfe. She's generally responsible for us when we're in Nightingale House. Sister came to look at Jo and then telephoned the private wing and asked for an ambulance to come over for her. Then she rang Sister Brumfett to let her know what had happened. Sister Brumfett likes to know what's happening on her ward even when she's off duty. She wouldn't have been pleased to arrive in the hospital next morning and find that Jo had been warded without her being told. She came down to have a look at Jo but didn't go over in the ambulance with her. It wasn't really necessary.'

'Who did accompany her?'

'I did. Sister Rolfe and Sister Brumfett went back to their rooms and Pearce returned to hers.'

So the book could hardly have been removed that night, thought Dalgliesh. Pearce would certainly have noticed its absence. Even if she had decided not to continue reading it, she would hardly settle to sleep with a heavy book under her pillow. So the probability was that someone had taken it after her death. One thing was certain. A particular book had been in her possession late on the night before she died yet was not in her room when the police, Miss Rolfe and Nurse Goodale examined it for the first time at about ten past ten the next morning. Whether or not that book had come from Westminster library, it was missing, and if the book wasn't from the library, then what had happened to the token and the reader's ticket? Neither was among her things. And if she had decided not to use them and handed them back to Fallon, why weren't they among Fallon's possessions?

He asked Nurse Goodale what had happened immediately after Nurse Pearce's death.

'Matron sent us students up to her sitting-room and asked us to wait there. Sister Gearing joined us after about half an hour and then some coffee came and we drank that. We stayed there together talking and trying to read until Inspector Bailey and Matron arrived. That must have been about eleven o'clock, perhaps a little earlier.'

'And were you all together in that room for the whole of that time?'

'Not all the time. I went out to the library to fetch a book I wanted and was away about three minutes. Nurse Dakers left the room too. I'm not sure why but I think she muttered something about going to the lavatory. Otherwise, as far as I can remember, we all stayed together. Miss Beale, the G.N.C. Inspector, was with us.'

She paused.

'You think that this missing library book has something to do with Pearce's death, don't you? You think it's important.'

'I think that it may be. That's why I want you to say nothing about our conversation.'

'Of course, if that's what you want.' She paused.

'But couldn't I try to find out what has happened to the book? I could ask the other students quite casually if they had the ticket and token. I could pretend that I wanted to use them.'

Dalgliesh smiled: 'Leave the detecting to me. I'd much prefer you to say nothing.'

He saw no reason to suggest to her that in a murder investigation too much knowledge could be dangerous. She was a sensible girl. She would think it out for herself soon enough. Taking his silence for dismissal she turned to go. When she reached the door she hesitated and turned:

'Superintendent Dalgliesh, forgive me if I'm interfering. I can't believe that Pearce was murdered. But if she was, then surely the library book could have been taken from her room any time after five to nine when Pearce went into the demo room. The murderer would know that she wouldn't come out of that room alive and that it would be safe for him, or her, to remove it. If the book were taken after Pearce's death it could have been taken by anyone and for a perfectly innocent reason. But if it were taken before she died then it was taken by her killer. That would be true even if the book itself had nothing to do with the reason why she was killed. And Pearce's question to us all about something missing from her room suggests that the book was taken before she died. And why should the murderer bother to remove it if it wasn't in some way connected with the crime?'

'Exactly,' said Dalgliesh. 'You're a very intelligent young woman.'

For the first time he saw Nurse Goodale disconcerted. She blushed, looking at once as pink and pretty as a young bride, then smiled at him, turned quickly and was gone. Dalgliesh, intrigued by the metamorphosis, decided that the local vicar had shown much sense and discernment in choosing his wife. What the parochial church council would make of her uncompromising intelligence was another matter. And he hoped that he wouldn't have to arrest her for murder before they had a chance to make up their minds.

He followed her into the corridor. As usual it was gloomily obscure, lit only by the two bulbs high in a cluster of entwined brass. He had reached the top of the staircase when instinct made him pause and then retrace his steps. Switching on his torch he bent low and moved the beam slowly over the surface of sand in the two fire buckets. The nearer one was caked and grey with dust; it had obviously not been disturbed since it was filled. But the surface of the second one bore a fresher look. Dalgliesh put on his thin cotton searching gloves, fetched from Nurse Pearce's bedroom a sheet of newspaper from one of the drawers, spread it on the corridor floor and slowly tipped out the sand in a rising pyramid. He found no hidden library ticket. But there tumbled out a squat, screw-topped tin, with a stained label. Dalgliesh brushed off the grains of sand to reveal the black print of a skull and the word POISON in capitals. Underneath were the words: 'Plant Spray. Death to Insects, Harmless to Plants. Use carefully in accordance with instructions.'

He did not need to read the instructions to know what he had found. This stuff was almost pure nicotine. The poison which had killed Nurse Fallon was at last in his hands.

SIX

Long Day's Ending

I

Five minutes later Dalgliesh, having spoken to the forensic science laboratory director and to Sir Miles Honeyman, looked up at a sulkily defensive Sergeant Masterson.

'I'm beginning to see why the Force is so keen on training civilian searchers. I told the scene-of-crime officer to stick to the bedroom, that we'd see to the rest of the house. I thought for some reason that policemen could use their eyes.'

Sergeant Masterson, the more furious because he knew the rebuke to be justified, controlled himself with difficulty. He found any criticism difficult to take; from Dalgliesh it was almost impossible. He stiffened to attention like an old soldier on a charge, knowing full well that Dalgliesh would be exasperated rather than mollified by this punctilio, and contrived to sound at the same time both aggrieved and contrite.

'Greeson is a good searcher. I haven't known Greeson miss anything before. He can use his eyes all right, sir.'

'Greeson has excellent eyesight. The trouble is that there's no connection between his eyes and his brain. And that's where you come in. The damage is done now. There's no point in holding a post-mortem. We don't know whether this tin was in the bucket or not when Fallon's body was discovered this morning. But at least we've found it now. The laboratory has the viscera by the way. Sir Miles called in with it about an hour ago. They're already putting some of the stuff through the gas chromatograph. Now that they know what they're looking for it should speed things. We'd better get this tin off to them as soon as possible. But we'll have a look at it first.'

He went over to his murder bag for the fingerprint powder, insufflator and lens. The squat little tin became sooty under his careful hands. But there were no prints, only a few amorphous smudges on the faded label.

'Right,' he said. 'Find the three Sisters, will you, Sergeant? They're the ones most likely to know where this tin came from. They live here. Sister Gearing is in her sitting-room. The others should be somewhere around. And if Sister Brumfett is still on her ward she'll have to leave it. Anyone who dies in the next hour must do so without her assistance.'

'Do you want to see them separately or together?'

'Either. It doesn't matter. Just get them. Gearing's the one most likely to help. She looks after the flowers.'

Sister Gearing arrived first. She came in jauntily, her face perked with curiosity and flushed with the lingering euphoria of a successful hostess. Then her eyes lit on the tin. The transformation was so immediate and startling that it was almost comic. She gasped, 'Oh, no!', shot her hand to her mouth and sank into the chair opposite Dalgliesh, deathly pale.

'Where did you . . . Oh my God! You're not telling me that Fallon took nicotine?'

'Took, or was given. You recognize this tin, Sister?'

Sister Gearing's voice was almost inaudible.

'Of course. It's my . . . isn't it the tin of rose spray? Where did you find it?'

'Somewhere about the place. Where and when did you see it last?'

'It's kept in that white cupboard under the shelf in the conservatory, just to the left of the door. All my gardening stuff is there. I can't remember when I saw it last.'

She was on the edge of tears; happy confidence completely dissolved.

'Honestly, it's just too awful! It's frightful! I feel dreadful about it. I really do. But how was I to tell that Fallon would know the stuff was there and use it? I didn't even remember about it myself. If I had, I'd have gone to check that it was still there. I suppose there's no doubt about it? She did die of nicotine poisoning?'

'There's a great deal of doubt until we get the toxicology report. But taking the common-sense view, it looks as if this stuff killed her. You bought it when?'

'Honestly, I can't remember. Sometime early last summer, just before the roses were due. One of the other Sisters might remember. I'm responsible for most of the plants in the conservatory here. At least, I'm not really responsible; it's never been an official arrangement. But I like flowers and there's no one else to bother so I do what I can. I was trying to establish a small rose bed outside the dining-room, too, and I needed the stuff to kill pests. I bought it from Bloxham's Nurseries on the Winchester Road. Look, you can see the address stamped on the label. And I kept it with my other gardening things, gloves and string and the watering cans and trowels and so on, in the corner cupboard in the conservatory.'

'Can you remember when you last saw it?'

'Not really. But I went to the cupboard for my gloves last Saturday morning. We had a special service at the chapel on Sunday and I went to do the flowers. I thought I might be able to find some interesting boughs, bits of autumn foliage or seed pods in the garden to help the decoration. I don't remember seeing the tin there on Saturday but I think I might have noticed if it were actually missing. But I'm not sure. I haven't used it for months.'

'Who else knew that it was there?'

'Well, anyone could have known. I mean, the cupboard isn't locked and there was nothing to stop people looking inside. I suppose I ought to have locked it but one doesn't expect . . . I mean if people are going to kill themselves they'll find a way somehow. I feel absolutely awful but I won't be made to feel responsible! I won't! It isn't fair! She could have used anything. Anything!'

'Who could?'

'Well, Fallon. If Fallon did kill herself. Oh, I don't know what I'm saying.'

'Did Nurse Fallon know about the nicotine?'

'Not unless she looked in the cupboard and found it. The only people I can say for certain who did know are Brumfett and Rolfe. I remember that they were sitting in the conservatory when I put the tin into the cupboard. I held it up and said something daft about having enough poison there to kill the lot of them, and Brumfett told me that I ought to lock it up.'

'But you didn't?'

'Well, I put it straight away in the cupboard. There isn't a lock so I couldn't do anything about it. Anyway, the tin's labelled clearly enough. Anyone can see that it's poison. And one doesn't expect people to kill themselves. Besides, why the nicotine? Nurses have plenty of opportunity to get hold of drugs. It's not fair to blame me. After all, the disinfectant which killed Pearce was just as lethal. No one complained because that was left in the lavatory. You can't run a nurse training school like a psychiatric unit. I'm not going to be blamed. People here are supposed to be sane, not homicidal maniacs. I won't be made to feel guilty. I won't!'

'If you didn't use the stuff on Nurse Fallon there's no reason why you should feel guilty. Did Sister Rolfe say anything when you brought in the tin?'

'I don't think so. Just looked up from her book. But I can't really remember. I can't even tell you exactly when it was. But it was a warm sunny day. I do remember that. I think it was probably in late May or early June. Rolfe may remember and Brumfett certainly will.'

'We'll ask them. In the meantime I'd better have a look at this cupboard.'

He left the tin of nicotine for Masterson to pack for despatch to the laboratory, told him to send Sister Brumfett and Sister Rolfe to the conservatory, and followed Sister Gearing out of the room. She led him down to the ground floor, still muttering her indignant protests. They passed into the empty dining-room. The discovery that the door into the conservatory was locked shook Sister Gearing from her mood of frightened resentment.

'Damn! I'd forgotten. Matron thought we'd better keep it locked after dark because some of the glass isn't too secure. You remember that a pane fell out during the storm? She's afraid someone could get in this way. Usually we don't bother to lock it until we do the final locking up last thing at night. The key will be on the board in Rolfe's office. Wait here. I won't be a jiffy.'

She returned almost immediately and fitted the large old-fashioned key into the lock. They passed into the warm fungoid smell of the conservatory. Sister Gearing unerringly reached for the switch, and the two long tubes of fluorescent light, suspended from the high concave ceiling, flickered erratically, then burst into brilliance, revealing the arboreal jungle in all its lushness. The conservatory was a remarkable sight. Dalgliesh had thought so on his first tour of the house, but now, dazzled by the fierce glare on leaves and glass, he blinked in wonder. Around him a minor forest of greenery twined, sprouted, crept and burst in menacing profusion while, outside, its pale reflection hung in the evening air and stretched, motionless and insubstantial into a green infinity.

Some of the plants looked as if they had flourished in the conservatory since the day it was built. They sprang like mature if miniature palm trees from ornate urns, spreading a canopy of glistening leaves under the glass. Others, more exotic, sprouted bursts of foliage from their scarred and dentate stalks or, like giant cacti, lifted rubber lips, spongy and obscene, to suck the humid air. Between them the ferns sprayed a green shadow, their fragile fronds moving in the draught from the door. Around the sides of the great room were white shelves on which stood pots of the more domestic and agreeable plants which were Sister Gearing's care – red, pink and white chrysanthemums, and African violets. The conservatory should have evoked a tender scene of Victorian domesticity, of fluttering fans and whispered confidences behind the palms. But for Dalgliesh, no corner of Nightingale House was free of the oppressive atmosphere of evil; the very plants seemed to be sucking their manna from a tainted air.

Mavis Gearing went straight over to a low, four-foot-long cupboard in white-painted wood, fitted underneath the wall shelf on the left of the door and hardly visible behind the curtain of waving ferns. It had one inadequate door fitted with a small knob and no lock. Together they crouched to look in it. Although the overhead fluorescent lights were unpleasantly garish, the recesses of the cupboard were dim and their view obstructed by the shadow of their heads. Dalgliesh switched on his torch. Its beam revealed the usual paraphernalia of the indoor gardener. He made a mental inventory. There were balls of green twine, a couple of watering cans, a small spray, packets of seed, some opened and half-used with their tops pressed back, a small plastic bag of potting compost and one of fertilizer, about two dozen flower pots of various sizes, a small stack of seed trays, pruning shears, a trowel and small fork, a disorderly pile of seedsmen's catalogues, three clothbound books on gardening, their covers stained and dirty, an assortment of flower vases, and bundles of tangled wire.

Mavis Gearing pointed to a space in the far corner.

'That's where it was. I put it well back. It couldn't have been a temptation to anyone. You wouldn't even notice it, just opening the door. It was quite hidden really. Look, that's the space – you can see where it was.'

She spoke with urgent self-justification, as if the empty space acquitted her of all responsibility. Then her voice changed. It dropped a tone and became huskily pleading like an amateur actress playing a seduction scene.

'I know it looks bad. First, I was in charge of the demonstration when Pearce died. And now this. But I haven't touched the stuff since I used it last summer. I swear I haven't! I know some of them won't believe me. They'll be glad – yes glad – and relieved if suspicion falls on me and Len. It'll let them out. Besides they're jealous. They've always been jealous. It's because I've got a man and they haven't. But you believe me don't you? You've got to believe me!'

It was pathetic and humiliating. She pressed her shoulder against his, as they knelt huddled together in a ridiculous parody of prayer. He could feel her breath against his cheek. Her right hand, the fingers twitching nervously, crept across the floor towards his hand.

Then her mode broke. They heard Sister Rolfe's voice from the door. 'The Sergeant told me to meet you here. Am I interrupting anything?'

Dalgliesh felt the pressure on his shoulder immediately released, and Sister Gearing scrambled gracelessly to her feet. He got up more slowly. He neither felt nor looked embarrassed, but he was not sorry that Miss Rolfe had chosen that moment to appear.

Sister Gearing broke into explanation:

'It's the rose spray. That stuff containing nicotine. Fallon must have taken it. I feel absolutely ghastly about it, but how was I to know? The Superintendent has found the tin.'

She turned to Dalgliesh.

'You didn't say where?'

'No,' Dalgliesh said. 'I didn't say where.' He spoke to Miss Rolfe.

'Did you know the stuff was kept in this cupboard?'

'Yes, I saw Gearing put it there. Sometime last summer wasn't it?'

'You didn't mention this to me.'

'I didn't think of it until now. It never occurred to me that Fallon might have taken nicotine. And, presumably, we don't yet know that she did.'

Dalgliesh said: 'Not until we get the toxicology report.'

'And even then, Superintendent, can you be sure that the drug came from this tin? There are other sources of nicotine at the hospital surely? This could be a blind.'

'Of course, although it seems to me highly unlikely. But the forensic science laboratory should be able to tell us that. This nicotine is mixed with a proportion of concentrated detergent. It will be identifiable by gas chromatography.'

She shrugged.

'Well, that should settle it then.'

Mavis Gearing cried out: 'What do you mean, other sources of supply? Who are you getting at? Nicotine isn't kept in the pharmacy, as far as I know. And anyway Len had left Nightingale House before Fallon died.'

'I wasn't accusing Leonard Morris. But he was on the spot when both of them died, remember, and he was here in this room when you put the nicotine in the cupboard. He's a suspect like the rest of us.'

'Was Mr Morris with you when you bought the nicotine?'

'Well, he was as a matter of fact. I'd forgotten it or I would have told you. We'd been out together that afternoon and he came back here to tea.'

She turned angrily to Sister Rolfe.

'It's nothing to do with Len, I tell you! He hardly knew Pearce or Fallon. Pearce hadn't anything on Len.'

Hilda Rolfe said calmly: 'I wasn't aware that she had anything on anyone. I don't know whether you're trying to put ideas into Mr Dalgliesh's head, but you're certainly putting them into mine.'

Sister Gearing's face disintegrated into misery. Moaning, she jerked her head from side to side as if desperately seeking help or asylum. Her face, sickly and surrealist, was suffused with the green light of the conservatory.

Sister Rolfe gave Dalgliesh one sharp look, then ignoring him, moved over to her colleague and said with unexpected gentleness:

'Look, Gearing, I'm sorry. Of course I'm not accusing Leonard Morris or you. But the fact that he was here would have come out anyway. Don't let the police fluster you. It's how they work. I don't suppose the Superintendent cares a damn whether you or I or Brumfett killed Pearce and Fallon so long as he can prove someone did. Well, let him get on with it. Just answer his questions and keep calm. Why not get on with your job and let the police get on with theirs?'

Mavis Gearing wailed like a child seeking reassurance:

'But it's all so awful!'

'Of course it is! But it won't last for ever. And in the meantime, if you must confide in a man, find yourself a solicitor, a psychiatrist or a priest. At least you can be reasonably sure that they'll be on your side.'

Mavis Gearing's worried eyes moved from Dalgliesh to Rolfe. She looked like a child hesitating to decide where her allegiance lay. Then the two women moved imperceptibly together and gazed at Dalgliesh, Sister Gearing in puzzled reproach and Sister Rolfe with the tight satisfied smile of a woman who has just brought off a successful piece of mischief.

II

At that moment Dalgliesh caught the sound of approaching footsteps. Someone was moving across the dining-room. He turned to the door, expecting to find that Sister Brumfett had at last come to be interviewed. The conservatory door opened but, instead of her squat figure, he saw a tall bare-headed man wearing a belted raincoat and with a gauze patch tied across his left eye. A peevish voice spoke from the doorway:

'What's happened to everyone? This place is like a morgue.'

Before anyone could reply, Miss Gearing had darted forward and seized his arm. Dalgliesh saw with interest his frown and twitch of involuntary recoil.

'Len, what is it? You're hurt! You never told me! I thought it was your ulcer. You never said anything about hurting your head!'

'It was my ulcer. But this didn't help it.'

He spoke directly to Dalgliesh:

'You must be Chief Superindendent Dalgliesh of New Scotland Yard. Miss Gearing told me that you wanted to see me. I'm on my way to my general practitioner's surgery but I'm at your disposal for half an hour.'

But Sister Gearing was not to be diverted from her concern.

'But you never said anything about an accident! How did it happen? Why didn't you tell me about it when I rang?'

'Because we had other things to discuss and because I didn't want you to fuss.'

He shook off her detaining arm and sat himself down in a wicker chair. The two women and Dalgliesh moved in close to him. There was a silence. Dalgliesh revised his unreasonably preconceived notions of Miss Gearing's lover. He should have looked ridiculous, sitting there in his cheap raincoat with his patched eye and bruised face and speaking in that grating sarcastic voice. But he was curiously impressive. Sister Rolfe had somehow conveyed the impression of a little man, nervous, ineffectual and easily intimidated. This man had force. It might be only the manifestation of pent-up nervous energy; it might be the obsessive resentment born of failure or unpopularity. But his was certainly not a comfortable or negligible personality.

Dalgliesh asked: 'When did you learn that Josephine Fallon was dead?'

'When I rang my pharmacy office just after nine-thirty this morning to say that I wouldn't be in. My assistant told me. I suppose the news was all over the hospital by then.'

'How did you react to the news?'

'React? I didn't react. I hardly knew the girl. I was surprised, I suppose. Two deaths in the same house and so close together in time; well, it's unusual to say the least of it. It's shocking really. You could say I was shocked.'

He spoke like a successful politician condescending to express an attributable opinion to a cub reporter.

'But you didn't connect the two deaths?'

'Not at the time. My assistant just said that another Nightingale – we call the students Nightingales when they are in block – that another Nightingale, Jo Fallon, had been found dead. I asked him how and he said something about a heart attack following influenza. I thought it was a natural death. I suppose that's what everyone thought at first.'

'When did you think otherwise?'

'I suppose when Miss Gearing rang me an hour later to say that you were here.'

So Sister Gearing had telephoned Morris at his home. She must have wanted to reach him urgently to have risked that. Was it perhaps to warn him, to agree their story? While Dalgliesh was wondering what excuse, if any, she had given to Mrs Morris, the pharmacist answered the unspoken question.

'Miss Gearing doesn't usually ring me at home. She knows that I like to keep my professional and my private life absolutely separate. But she was naturally anxious about my health when she rang the laboratory after breakfast and was told that I wasn't in. I suffer from a duodenal ulcer.'

'Your wife, no doubt, was able to reassure her.'

He replied calmly but with a sharp glance at Sister Rolfe, who had moved to the periphery of the group:

'My wife takes the children to her mother's all day on Fridays.'

As Mavis Gearing would no doubt have known. So they had, after all, had a chance to consult each other, to decide on their story. But if they were concocting an alibi, why fix it for midnight? Because they knew for the best or worst of reasons that Fallon had died at that hour? Or because, knowing her habits, they judged that midnight was the most likely time? Only the killer, and perhaps not even he, could know precisely when Fallon had died. It could have been before midnight. It could have been as late as two-thirty. Even Miles Honeyman with his thirty years' experience couldn't time the death precisely from clinical signs alone. The only certain thing was that Fallon was dead and that she had died almost immediately after drinking her whisky. But when exactly had that been? It was her usual habit to prepare her late night drink as soon as she went upstairs to bed. But no one admitted to having seen her after she left the nurses' sitting-room. Fallon could, just possibly, have been alive when Sister Brumfett and the Burt twins saw her light shining through the keyhole just after two a.m. And if she had been alive then what had she been doing between midnight and two o'clock? Dalgliesh had been concentrating on those people who had access to the school. But suppose Fallon had left Nightingale House that night, perhaps to keep an assignation. Or suppose she had deferred making her nightly drink of whisky and lemon because she was expecting a visitor. The front and back doors of Nightingale House had been found bolted in the morning, but Fallon could have let her visitor out any time during the night and bolted the door behind him.

But Mavis Gearing was still preoccupied with her lover's damaged head and bruised face.

'What happened to you, Len? You've got to tell me. Did you come off your bicycle?'

Sister Rolfe laughed unkindly. Leonard Morris bestowed on her a measured glance of intimidating contempt, then turned to Sister Gearing.

'If you must know Mavis, yes I did. It happened after I left you last night. There was one of the big elms down across the path and I cycled right into it.'

Sister Rolfe spoke for the first time.

'Surely you could see it in the light of your bicycle lamp?'

'My bicycle lamp, Sister, not unreasonably, is fixed to shine on the road. I saw the tree trunk. What I didn't see in time was one of the highly jutting boughs. I was lucky not to lose an eye.'

Sister Gearing, predictably, gave an anguished yelp.

Dalgliesh asked: 'What time did this happen?'

'I've just told you. Last night after I had left Nightingale House. Oh, I see! You're asking what time precisely? As it happens I can answer that. I came off my bicycle under the impact and was afraid that my watch had been broken. Fortunately it hadn't. The hands stood at twelve-seventeen a.m. precisely.'

'Wasn't there some warning – a white scarf – tied to the branch?'

'Of course not, Superintendent. If there had been I should hardly have ridden straight into it.'

'If it were tied high up on a bough you might not have noticed it.'

'It wasn't there to notice. After I'd picked up my bicycle and recovered a little from the shock I inspected the tree carefully. My first thought was that I might be able to shift it at least slightly and leave part of the road clear. That was obviously impossible. The job was going to need a tractor and tackle. But there was no scarf on any part of that tree at twelve-seventeen a.m.'

'Mr Morris,' said Dalgliesh, 'I think it's time you and I had a little talk.'

But Sister Brumfett was waiting for him outside the interview room. Before Dalgliesh could speak she said accusingly:

'I was summoned to see you in this room. I came promptly at some inconvenience to my ward. When I arrive I'm told that you're not in your room and will I please go down to the conservatory. I don't propose to chase around Nightingale House for you. If you want to see me I can spare you half an hour now.'

'Sister Brumfett,' said Dalgliesh, 'you seem determined by your behaviour to give me the impression that you killed these girls. It's possible you did. I shall come to a conclusion about that as soon as I reasonably can. In the meantime, please curb your enthusiasm for antagonizing the police and wait until I can see you. That will be when I'm finished talking to Mr Morris. You can wait here outside the office or go to your own room, whichever suits you. But I shall want you in about thirty minutes and I, too, have no intention of chasing over the house to find you.'

He had no idea how she would take this rebuke. Her reaction was surprising. The eyes behind the thick spectacles softened and twinkled. Her face broke into a momentary grin and she gave a satisfied little nod as if she had at least succeeded in provoking a particularly docile student into showing a flash of spirit.

'I'll wait here.' She plonked herself down on the chair outside the office door then nodded towards Morris.

'And I shouldn't let him do all the talking or you'll be lucky to be through in half an hour.'

III

But the interview took less than thirty minutes. The first couple were spent by Morris in making himself comfortable. He took off his shabby raincoat, shaking it and smoothing down the folds as if it had somehow become contaminated in Nightingale House, then folded it with fussy precision over the back of his chair. Then he seated himself opposite Dalgliesh and took the initiative.

'Please don't fire questions at me, Superintendent. I don't like being interrogated. I prefer to tell my story in my own way. You needn't worry about it being accurate. I'd hardly be chief pharmacist of an important hospital if I hadn't the head for detail and a good memory for facts.'

Dalgliesh said mildly: 'Then could I have some facts please, starting perhaps with your movements last night.'

Morris continued as if he hadn't heard this eminently reasonable request.

'Miss Gearing has given me the privilege of her friendship for the past six years. I've no doubt that certain people here, certain women living in Nightingale House, have placed their own interpretation on that friendship. That is to be expected. When you get a community of middle-aged spinsters living together you're bound to get sexual jealousy.'

'Mr Morris,' said Dalgliesh gently. 'I'm not here to investigate your relationship with Miss Gearing or hers with her colleagues. If those relationships have anything to do with the deaths of these two girls, then tell me about them. Otherwise let's leave out the amateur psychology and get down to the material facts.'

'My relationship with Miss Gearing is germane to your inquiry in that it brought me into this house at about the time Nurse Pearce and Nurse Fallon died.'

'All right. Then tell me about those two occasions.'

'The first was the morning when Nurse Pearce died. You are, no doubt, aware of the details. Naturally I reported my visit to Inspector Bailey since he caused a notice to be appended to all the hospital notice-boards inquiring the names of people who had visited Nightingale House on the morning on which Nurse Pearce died. But I have no objection to repeating the information. I called in here on my way to the pharmacy to leave Miss Gearing a note. It was in fact a card, one of those "good luck" cards which it is customary to send friends before some important event. I knew that Miss Gearing would have to take the first demonstration of the day, indeed the first demonstration of this school, as Sister Manning, who is Miss Rolfe's assistant, is sick with flu. Miss Gearing was naturally nervous, particularly as the General Nursing Council Inspector was to be present. Unfortunately I missed the previous evening's post. I was anxious for her to get my card before she went in to the demonstration so I decided to slip it into her cubbyhole myself. I came to work especially early, arrived at Nightingale House shortly after eight, and left almost immediately. I saw no one. Presumably the staff and students were at breakfast. I certainly didn't enter the demonstration room. I wasn't particularly keen to draw attention to myself. I merely inserted the card in its envelope into Miss Gearing's cubbyhole and withdrew. It was rather an amusing card. It showed two robins, the male bird forming the words "Good luck" in worms at the feet of the female. Miss Gearing may well have kept the card; she has a fancy for such trifles. No doubt she would show it to you on request. It would corroborate my story of what I was doing in Nightingale House.'

Dalgliesh said gravely: 'I have already seen the card. Did you know what the demonstration would be about?'

'I knew that it was on intra-gastric feeding but I didn't know that Nurse Fallon had been taken ill in the night or who was to act the part of the patient.'

'Have you any idea at all how the corrosive poison got into the drip?'

'If you would just let me take my own time. I was about to tell you. I have none. The most likely explanation is that someone was playing a stupid joke and didn't realize that the result would be fatal. That, or an accident. There are precedents. A new-born baby was killed in the maternity wing of a hospital – happily not one of ours – only three years ago when a bottle of disinfectant was mistaken for milk. I can't explain how the accident here could have occurred or who in Nightingale House could have been so ignorant and stupid as to think that the result of putting a corrosive poison in the milk feed would entertain anyone.'

He paused as if defying Dalgliesh to interrupt with another question. Meeting only a bland interrogatory gaze, he went on:

'So much for Nurse Pearce's death. I can't help you further there. It's rather a different matter with Nurse Fallon.'

'Something that happened last night; someone you saw?'

The irritation snapped out: 'Nothing to do with last night, Superintendent, Miss Gearing has already told you about last night. We saw no one. We left her room immediately after twelve o'clock and went out down the back stairs through Miss Taylor's flat. I retrieved my bicycle from the bushes at the rear of the house – I see no reason why my visits here should be advertised to every mean-minded female in the neighbourhood – and we walked together to the first turn in the path. Then we paused to talk and I escorted Miss Gearing back to Nightingale House and watched her in through the back door. She had left it open. I finally rode off and, as I have told you, got to the fallen elm at twelve-seventeen a.m. If anyone passed that way after me and fixed a white scarf to a branch, I can only say that I didn't see him. If he came by car it must have been parked at the other side of Nightingale House. I saw no car.'

Another pause. Dalgliesh made no sign, but Masterson permitted himself a sigh of weary resignation as he rustled over a page of his note pad.

'Now, Superintendent, the event which I am about to relate took place last spring when this present set of students, including Nurse Fallon, were in their second-year block. As was customary, I gave them a lecture on poisons. At the end of my talk all the students except Nurse Fallon had gathered up their books and left. She came up to the desk and asked me for the name of a poison which could kill painlessly and instantaneously and which an ordinary person might be able to obtain. I thought it an unusual question but saw no reason why I should refuse to answer it. It never occurred to me for one moment that the question had any personal application and, in any case, it was information she could have obtained from any book in the hospital library on materia medica or forensic medicine.'

Dalgliesh said: 'And what exactly did you tell her, Mr Morris?'

'I told her that one such poison was nicotine and that it could be obtained from an ordinary rose spray.'

Truth or a lie? Who could tell? Dalgliesh fancied that he could usually detect lying in a suspect; but not this suspect. And if Morris stuck to his story, how could it ever be disproved? And if it were a lie, its purpose was plain – to suggest that Josephine Fallon had killed herself. And the obvious reason why he should wish to do that was to protect Sister Gearing. He loved her. This slightly ridiculous, pedantic man; that silly, flirtatious, ageing woman – they loved each other. And why not. Love wasn't the prerogative of the young and desirable. But it was a complication in any investigation – pitiable, tragic or ludicrous, as the case might be, but never negligible. Inspector Bailey, as he knew from the notes on the first crime, had never fully believed in the story of the greetings card. It was in his opinion a foolish and childish gesture for a grown man, and particularly out of character for Morris; therefore he distrusted it. But Dalgliesh thought differently. It was at one with Morris's lonely, unromantic cycle rides to visit his mistress; the machine hidden ignominiously in the bushes behind Nightingale House; the slow walk together through the cold of a January midnight prolonging those last precious minutes; his clumsy but strangely dignified defence of the woman he loved. And this last statement, true or false, was inconvenient to say the least. If he stuck to it it would be a powerful argument for those who preferred to believe that Fallon had died by her own hand. And he would stick to it. He looked at Dalgliesh now with the steadfast, exalted gaze of a prospective martyr, holding his adversary's eyes, daring him to disbelieve. Dalgliesh sighed:

'All right,' he said. 'We won't waste time in speculation. Let's go once again over the timing of your movements last night.'

IV

Sister Brumfett, true to her promise, was waiting outside the door when Masterson let Leonard Morris out. But her previous mood of cheerful acquiescence had vanished and she settled herself down opposite Dalgliesh as if to do battle. Before that matriarchal glare he felt something of the inadequacy of a junior student nurse newly arrived on the private ward; and something stronger and horribly familiar. His mind traced the surprising fear unerringly to its source. Just so had the Matron of his prep school once looked at him, producing in the homesick eight-year-old the same inadequacy, the same fear. And for one second he had to force himself to meet her gaze.

It was the first opportunity he had to observe her closely and on her own. It was an unattractive and yet an ordinary face. The small shrewd eyes glared into his through steel spectacles, their bridge half embedded in the deep fleshy cleft above the mottled nose. Her iron-grey hair was cut short, framing in ribbed waves the pump marsupial cheeks and the obstinate line of the jaw. The elegant gophered cap which on Mavis Gearing looked as delicate as a meringue of spun lace and which flattered even Hilda Rolfe's androgynous features was bound low on Sister Brumfett's brow like a pie frill circling a particularly unappetizing crust. Take that symbol of authority away and replace it by an undistinguished felt hat, cover the uniform with a shapeless fawn coat, and you would have the prototype of a middle-aged suburban housewife strutting through the supermarket, shapeless bag in hand, eyes shrewd for this week's bargain. Yet here, apparently, was one of the best ward Sisters John Carpendar had ever had. Here, more surprisingly, was Mary Taylor's chosen friend.

Before he could begin to question her, she said:

'Nurse Fallon committed suicide. First she killed Pearce and then herself. Fallon murdered Pearce. I happen to know that she did. So why don't you stop worrying Matron and let the work of the hospital go on? There's nothing you can do to help either of them now. They're both dead.'

Spoken in that authoritative and disconcertingly evocative tone the statement had the force of a command. Dalgliesh's reply was unreasonably sharp. Damn the woman! He wouldn't be intimidated.

'If you know that for certain, you must have some proof. And anything you know ought to be told. I'm investigating murder, Sister, not the theft of a bedpan. You have a duty not to withhold evidence.'

She laughed; a sharp, derisive hoot like an animal coughing.

'Evidence! You wouldn't call it evidence. But I know!'

'Did Nurse Fallon speak to you when she was being nursed on your ward? Was she delirious?'

It was no more than a guess. She snorted her derision.

'If she did, it wouldn't be my duty to tell you. What a patient lets out in delirium isn't gossip to be bandied about. Not on my ward anyway. It isn't evidence either. Just accept what I tell you and stop fussing. Fallon killed Pearce. Why do you think she came back to Nightingale House that morning, with a temperature of 103? Why do you think she refused to give the police a reason? Fallon killed Pearce. You men like to make things so complicated. But it's all so simple really. Fallon killed Pearce, and there's no doubt she had her reasons.'

'There are no valid reasons for murder. And even if Fallon did kill Pearce, I doubt whether she killed herself. I've no doubt your colleagues have told you about the rose spray. Remember that Fallon hadn't been in Nightingale House since that tin of nicotine was placed in the conservatory cupboard. Her set haven't been in Nightingale House since the spring of last year and Sister Gearing bought the rose spray in the summer. Nurse Fallon was taken ill on the night that this block began and didn't return to Nightingale House until the evening before she died. How do you account for the fact that she knew where to find the nicotine?'

Sister Brumfett looked surprisingly undisconcerted. There was a moment's silence and then she muttered something unintelligible. Dalgliesh waited. Then she said defensively:

'I don't know how she got hold of it. That's for you to discover. But it's obvious that she did.'

'Did you know where the nicotine had been put?'

'No. I don't have anything to do with the garden or the conservatory. I like to get out of the hospital on my free days. I usually play golf with Matron or we go for a drive. We try to arrange our off-duty together.'

Her tone was smug with satisfaction. She made no attempt to hide her complacency. What was she trying to convey? he wondered. Was this reference to the Matron her way of telling him that she was teacher's pet, to be treated with deference?

He said: 'Weren't you in the conservatory that evening last summer when Miss Gearing came in with the stuff?'

'I don't remember.'

'I think you'd better try to remember, Sister. It shouldn't be difficult. Other people remember perfectly well.'

'If they say I was there, I probably was.'

'Miss Gearing says that she showed you all the bottle and made a facetious remark about being able to poison the whole school with a few drops. You told her not to be childish and to make sure the tin was locked away. Do you remember now?'

'It's the sort of silly remark Mavis Gearing would make and I daresay I did tell her to be careful. It's a pity she didn't take notice of me.'

'You take these deaths very calmly, Sister.'

'I take every death very calmly. If I didn't I couldn't do my job. Death is happening all the time in a hospital. It's probably happening now on my ward as it did this afternoon to one of my patients!'

She spoke with sudden and passionate protest, stiffening as if in outrage that the dread finger could touch anyone for whom she was responsible. Dalgliesh found the sudden change of mood disconcerting. It was as if this thickening, unattractive body housed the temperament of a *prima donna*, passionate and irrational. At one moment the eyes, small and unremarkable behind their thick lenses, met his in dull resentment, the obstinate little mouth snapped out its grievances. And then, suddenly, there was this metamorphosis. She blazed at him, her face flaming with indignation so that it came fiercely alive. He had a glimpse of that fervent and possessive love with which she encompassed those in her care. Here was a woman, outwardly unremarkable, who had dedicated her life to a single aim with formidable determination. If something – or someone – got in the way of what she regarded as the greater good, how far would that determination carry her? She seemed to Dalgliesh a fundamentally intelligent woman. But murder was frequently the last resort of the unintelligent. And were these murders, for all their complexity, the work of a clever woman? A bottle of disinfectant quickly seized; a tin of nicotine readily available. Didn't both these deaths speak of a sudden uncontrolled impulse, an unthinking reliance on the easiest means? Surely in a hospital there were more subtle methods of disposal?

The shrewd eyes were regarding him with watchful dislike. The whole interrogation was an outrage to her. It was hopeless to try to propitiate such a witness and he had no stomach to try. He said:

'I want to go through your movements on the morning Nurse Pearce died, and last night.'

'I've already told Inspector Bailey about the morning Pearce died. And I've sent you a note.'

'I know. Thank you for it. Now I want you to tell me yourself.'

She made no further protest but recited the sequence of her movements and actions as if they were a railway timetable.

Her account of her movements on the morning of Heather Pearce's death agreed almost exactly with the written statement she had already given to Inspector Bailey. She described only her own actions, put forward no theories, gave no opinion. After that first revealing outburst she had apparently decided to stick to facts.

She had woken at six-thirty on Monday, 12th January, and had then joined the Matron for early morning tea which it was their habit to drink together in Miss Taylor's flat. She had left Matron at seven-fifteen and had then bathed and dressed. She had stayed in her own room until about ten minutes to eight when she had collected her paper from the rack in the hall and had gone in to breakfast. She had seen no one on the stairs or in the hall. Sister Gearing and Sister Rolfe had joined her in the dining-room and they had breakfasted together. She had finished her breakfast and had left the room first; she was unable to say precisely when but it was probably not later than twenty-past eight, had returned briefly to her sitting-room on the third floor, and had then walked over to the hospital where she had arrived on her ward shortly before nine o'clock. She had known about the General Nursing Council Inspection since, obviously, Matron had talked to her about it. She had known about the demonstration since details of the nurse training programme were on the hall notice-board. She had known about Josephine Fallon's illness since Sister Rolfe telephoned her during the night. She had not, however, known that Nurse Pearce was to take Fallon's place. She agreed that she could have discovered this easily by a glance at the notice-board, but she had not troubled to look. There was no reason why she should be concerned. Taking an interest in the general nurse training programme was one thing, bothering to check on who was to act as the patient was quite another.

She had not known that Nurse Fallon had returned to Nightingale House that morning. Had she done so, she would have reprimanded the girl severely. By the time she had reached the ward Nurse Fallon was in her room and in bed. No one in the ward had noticed her absence. Apparently the Staff Nurse had thought she was in the bathroom or the lavatory. It was reprehensible of the Staff Nurse not to have checked, but the ward was particularly busy and one did not expect patients, particularly student nurses, to behave like idiots. Nurse Fallon had probably only left the ward for about twenty minutes. Her walk through the dark morning had apparently done her no harm. She had made a quick recovery from the influenza and there had been no complications. She had not seemed particularly depressed while she was in the ward, and if there was anything worrying her, she had not confided in Sister Brumfett. In Sister Brumfett's opinion, the girl had been perfectly well enough on discharge from the ward to rejoin her set in Nightingale House.

Next she went through her movements on the previous night, in the same dull, unemphatic voice. Matron had been in Amsterdam at the International Conference so she had spent the evening alone watching television in the Sisters' sitting-room. She had gone to bed at ten p.m. and had been awakened at about quarter to twelve by Mr Courtney-Briggs's telephone call. She had made her way across to the hospital by a short cut through the trees and had helped the student nurse on duty to prepare the bed for the patient's return. She had stayed with her patient until satisfied that the oxygen and drip were being satisfactorily administered and that his general condition was as good as could be expected. She had returned to Nightingale House shortly after two a.m. and on her way up to her room had seen Maureen Burt coming out of the lavatory. The other twin had appeared almost immediately and she had had a brief conversation with them. She had declined their offer to make her cocoa and had gone straight up to her room. Yes, there was a light shining through Fallon's keyhole at that time. She had not gone into Fallon's room and had no way of knowing whether the girl was alive or dead. She had slept well and had awoken just after seven o'clock when Sister Rolfe had come rushing in with the news that Fallon's body had been discovered. She hadn't seen Fallon since the girl was discharged from the ward after supper on the Tuesday.

At the end of the recital there was a silence, then Dalgliesh asked:

'Did you like Nurse Pearce, Sister? Or Nurse Fallon?'

'No. I didn't dislike them either. I don't believe in having personal relationships with the student nurses. Like and dislike don't come into it. They're either good nurses or they aren't.'

'And were they good nurses?'

'Fallon was better than Pearce. She had more intelligence and more imagination. She wasn't an easy colleague but the patients liked her. Some people thought her callous but you wouldn't find a patient who said so. Pearce tried too hard. She went about looking like a young Florence Nightingale, or so she thought. Always thinking of the impression she was making. A silly girl fundamentally. But you could rely on her. She always did what was correct. Fallon did what was right. That takes instinct as well as training. Wait until you're dying, my good man. You'll know the difference.'

So Josephine Fallon had been both intelligent and imaginative. He could believe it. But these were the last two qualities he would have expected Sister Brumfett to praise. He recalled the conversation at luncheon, her insistence on the need for unquestioning obedience. He said carefully:

'I'm surprised that you should rank imagination among the

virtues of a student nurse. I thought that you valued absolute obedience above all. It's difficult to reconcile imagination, which is surely individual, even iconoclastic, with the submission to authority of the good subordinate. I'm sorry if I sound presumptuous. This conversation hasn't much to do with my business here, I know. But I'm curious.'

It had a great deal to do with his business there; his curiosity wasn't irrelevant. But she wasn't to know that. She said gruffly:

'Obedience to rightful authority comes first. You're in a disciplined service; you shouldn't need telling. It's only when the obedience is automatic, when the discipline is accepted and even welcomed, that one learns the wisdom and courage that can safely step outside the rules when the moment comes. Imagination and intelligence are dangerous in nursing if they aren't founded on discipline.'

So she wasn't as simple or as obstinately conformist as she appeared, or chose to appear to her colleagues. And she, too, had imagination. Was this the Brumfett, he wondered, that Mary Taylor knew and valued? And yet, he was convinced that his first impressions hadn't been wrong. Fundamentally, she wasn't an intelligent woman. Was she, even now, voicing the theory, the very words perhaps, of another? 'The wisdom and courage to step outside the rules.' Well, someone in Nightingale House had stepped outside them, someone hadn't lacked the courage. They looked at each other. He was beginning to wonder if Nightingale House had put some kind of spell on him, if its threatening atmosphere had begun to affect his judgement. For behind the thick spectacles he thought he saw the eyes change, thought he detected an urgency to communicate, to be understood, even a plea for help. And then the illusion passed. He was facing again the most ordinary, the most uncompromising, the least complex of all his suspects. And the interview was at an end.

V

It was now after nine o'clock but Dalgliesh and Masterson were still together in the office. There were at least a couple of hours' work ahead before they could break for the night, checking and comparing statements, searching for the tell-tale discrepancy, planning tomorrow's activity. Dalgliesh decided to let Masterson get on with it and dialling the internal number of Matron's flat, he asked if she could give him twenty minutes of her time. Courtesy and policy both dictated that he should keep her informed, but there was another reason for seeing her before he left Nightingale House.

She had left the door of the flat open for him and he passed straight down the corridor to the sitting-room, knocked and entered. He walked into peace, quietness, light. And coldness. The room was surprisingly chilly. A bright fire was burning in the grate but its warmth hardly reached the far corners of the room. As he went across to her he saw that she was appropriately dressed, her long legs encased in brown velvet slacks topped by a high-necked cashmere sweater in pale fawn, the sleeves pushed back from brittle wrists. A silk scarf in bright green was knotted around her throat.

They sat down together on the sofa. Dalgliesh saw that she had been working. There was an open briefcase propped against the leg of the coffee table and a spread of papers across its surface. A coffee pot stood in the grate, and the comforting scent of warm wood and coffee pervaded the room.

She offered him coffee or whisky; nothing else. He accepted the coffee and she rose to fetch a second cup. When she had returned, the coffee poured, he said:

'They've told you, I expect, that we've found the poison.'

'Yes. Gearing and Rolfe both came to see me after you'd finished questioning them. I suppose this means that it must be murder?'

'I think so, unless Nurse Fallon hid the tin herself. But somehow that seems unlikely. To make a deliberate mystery of suicide with the object of causing the maximum of trouble would be the action of an exhibitionist or a neurotic. This girl seems to me to have been neither, but I wanted your view.'

'I agree with you. Fallon, I would have said, was essentially a rational person. If she decided to kill herself it would be for reasons which seemed good to her at the time and I would expect her to leave a brief but lucid note explaining them. A great many suicides kill themselves to make trouble for other people. But not Fallon.'

'That would be my assessment, but I wanted to ask someone who had actually known her.'

She asked: 'What does Madeleine Goodale say?'

'Madeleine Goodale thinks that her friend killed herself; but that was before we found the nicotine.'

He didn't say where and she didn't ask. He had no intention of telling anyone in Nightingale House where the tin had been found. But one person would know where it had been hidden and with luck might inadvertently reveal their guilty knowledge.

He went on: 'There is another matter. Miss Gearing tells me she entertained a friend in her room last night; she says that she let him out through your door. Does that surprise you?'

'No. I leave the flat open when I'm not here so that the Sisters can use the back staircase. It gives them at least the illusion of privacy.'

'At the cost, surely, of your own?'

'Oh, I think it's understood that they don't come into the flat. I trust my colleagues. Even if I didn't, there's nothing here to interest them. I keep all official papers in my office over at the hospital.'

She was right of course. There was nothing here to interest anyone except him. The sitting-room for all its individuality was almost as plain as his own flat high above the Thames at Queenhithe. Perhaps that was one reason why he felt so at home. Here were no photographs to invite speculation; no bureau bursting with its accumulated hoard of trivia; no pictures to betray a private taste; no invitations to advertise the diversity, the existence even, of a social life. He held his own flat inviolate; it would have been intolerable to him to think that people could walk in and out at will. But here was an even greater reticence; the self-sufficiency of a woman so private that even her personal surroundings were permitted to give nothing away.

He said: 'Mr Courtney-Briggs tells me that he was Josephine Fallon's lover for a short period during her first year. Did you know that?'

'Yes. I knew it in the same way that I know Mavis Gearing's

visitor yesterday was almost certainly Leonard Morris. In a hospital, gossip spreads by a kind of osmosis. One can't always remember being told the latest scandal; one just gets to know.'

'And is there much to know?'

'More perhaps than in less sensational institutions. Is that so very surprising? Men and women who have to watch daily what the body can suffer in agony and degradation aren't likely to be too scrupulous about availing themselves of its solace.'

When, and with whom, he wondered, did she find her consolation? In her job; in the power which that job undoubtedly gave her? In astronomy, tracing through long nights the paths of the movable stars? With Brumfett? Surely to God not with Brumfett!

She said: 'If you're thinking that Stephen Courtney-Briggs might have killed to protect his reputation, well, I don't believe it. I got to know about the affair. So did half the hospital, I've no doubt. Courtney-Briggs isn't particularly discreet. Besides, such a motive would only apply to a man vulnerable to public opinion.'

'Every man is vulnerable in some way to public opinion.'

She gave him a sudden keen glance from those extraordinary exophthalmic eyes.

'Of course. No doubt Stephen Courtney-Briggs is as capable of killing to prevent personal disaster or public disgrace as any of us. But not, I think, to prevent people knowing that a young and attractive woman was willing to go to bed with him; or that middle-aged as he may be, he is still able to take his sexual pleasure where he finds it.'

Was there a trace of contempt, of resentment almost, in her voice? For a moment he caught an echo of Sister Rolfe.

'And Hilda Rolfe's friendship with Julia Pardoe? You knew about that?'

She smiled a little bitterly.

'Friendship? Yes, I know, and I think that I understand. But I'm not sure that you do. The orthodox reaction, if the affair became known, would be that Rolfe is corrupting Pardoe. But if that young woman has been corrupted, I suspect that it happened before she came to the John Carpendar. I don't propose to interfere. The affair will settle itself. Julia Pardoe should qualify as a State Registered Nurse in a few months' time. I happen to know that she has plans for her future and they certainly don't include staying on here. I'm afraid there is a great deal of unhappiness ahead for Sister Rolfe. But we must meet that when it comes.'

Her voice told him that she knew, that she was watching, that she had the situation under control. And that it was not a matter for further discussion.

He finished his coffee in silence, then rose to go. There was nothing else he needed to ask at present and he found himself disagreeably sensitive to every nuance in her voice, every silence which might imply that his presence was irksome. It could hardly be welcome, he knew that. He was used to being the harbinger, at best of ill news, at worst of disaster. But at least he could avoid forcing his company on her a minute more than was necessary.

As she rose to accompany him to the door he made a casual reference to the architecture of the house and asked how long it had been in the possession of the hospital. She said:

'It's a tragic and rather horrible story. The place was built in 1880 by a Thomas Nightingale, a local string and rope manufacturer who had come up in the world and wanted a house to dignify his new position. The name is fortuitously appropriate; it has nothing to do with Florence or with the bird. Nightingale lived here with his wife, they had no children, until 1886. In the January of that year the body of one of the maidservants, a nineteen-year-old girl called Nancy Gorringe, who had been taken by Mrs Nightingale from an orphanage, was found hanging from one of the trees in the grounds. When the body was cut down it was apparent that she had been systematically ill-treated, beaten, tortured even, over a period of months. It had been calculated sadism. One of the most horrible features of the case was that the other members of the staff must have had some idea of what was going on, but did nothing. They were apparently well treated; they paid touching tribute at the trial to Nightingale as a just and considerate master. It must have been similar to some of these modern cases of child cruelty where only one member of the family is singled out for violence and neglect and the others acquiesce in the ill-treatment. A taste for vicarious sadism, I suppose, or just the desperate hope of preserving their own safety. And yet it's odd. Not one of them turned against Nightingale, not even when local feeling was at its height in the weeks following the trial. He and his wife were both convicted and spent many years in prison. I have an idea that they died there. Anyway, they never returned to Nightingale House. It was sold to a retired boot manufacturer who lived here for only two years before deciding that he didn't like it. He sold it to one of the governors of the hospital, who spent the last twelve years of his life here and bequeathed it to the John Carpendar. It has always been something of an embarrassment to the hospital; no one has been quite sure what to do with it. It's not really suitable as a nurse training school, but it's difficult to see what exactly it would be suitable for. There's a story that Nancy Gorringe's ghost can be heard weeping in the grounds after dark at this time of year. I've never heard her and it's a tale we try to keep from the students. But it's never been a happy house.'

And it was less happy than ever now, thought Dalgliesh, as he made his way back to the office. Now there were two murders to add to the history of the violence and hate.

He told Masterson that he could go off duty, then settled down for a last solitary study of the papers. Hardly had the sergeant left when the outside telephone rang. It was the director of the forensic science laboratory to say that the tests were complete. Josephine Fallon had died of nicotine poisoning and the nicotine had come from the tin of rose spray.

VI

It was two hours before he finally locked the side door of Nightingale House behind him and set out to walk back to the Falconer's Arms.

The path was lit by the old-fashioned type of street lamp, but the lamps were widely spaced and dim so that for most of the time he walked in darkness. He met no one and could well believe that this lonely path was unpopular with the students once night had fallen. The rain had stopped but the wind was rising, shaking down the last drops from the interlocking branches of the elms. He could feel them spitting against his face and seeping under the collar of his coat, and felt a momentary regret that he had decided that morning not to use his car. The trees grew very close to the path, separated from it by a narrow verge of sodden turf. It was a warm night despite the rising wind, and a light mist moved among the trees and coiled around the lamps. The pathway was about ten feet wide. It must have been once a main drive to Nightingale House, but it wound inconsequently among the clumps of elms and birch as if the original owner of the house had hoped to increase his self-importance by the length of his drive.

As he walked he thought about Christine Dakers. He had seen the girl at three forty-five p.m. The private ward had been very quiet at that time and, if Sister Brumfett were about, she had taken care to keep out of his way. The Staff Nurse had received him and had shown him into Nurse Dakers's room. The girl had been sitting up against the pillows looking as flushed and triumphant as a newly delivered mother and had welcomed him as if she expected congratulations and an offering of flowers. Someone had already supplied her with a vase of daffodils and there were two pots of chrysanthemums beside the tea tray on the overbed table, and a spatter of magazines strewn over the bedcover.

She had tried to appear unconcerned and contrite as she told her story but the acting had been unconvincing. In truth she had been radiant with happiness and relief. And why not? Matron had visited her. She had confessed and had been forgiven. She was filled now with the sweet euphoria of absolution. More to the point, he thought, the two girls who might have menaced her had gone for good. Diane Harper had left the hospital. And Heather Pearce was dead.

And to what exactly had Nurse Dakers confessed? Why this extraordinary liberation of spirit? He wished he knew. But he had come out of her room little wiser than when he went in. But at least, he thought, she had confirmed Madeleine Goodale's evidence of their study time together in the library. Unless there was collusion, which seemed unlikely, they had given each other an alibi for the time before breakfast. And, after breakfast, she had taken her final cup of coffee into the conservatory where she had sat reading the *Nursing Mirror* until it was time to join the demonstration. Nurse Pardoe and Nurse Harper had been with her. The three girls had left the conservatory at the same time, had paid a brief visit to the bathroom and lavatories on the second floor, and then had made their way straight to the demonstration room. It was very difficult to see how Christine Dakers could have poisoned the feed.

Dalgliesh had covered about fifty yards when he stopped in mid-stride, frozen into immobility by what, for one unbelievable second, he thought was the sound of a woman crying. He stood still, straining to distinguish that desperate alien voice. For a moment all was silent, even the wind seemed to have dropped. Then he heard it again, this time unmistakably. This wasn't the night cry of an animal or the figment of a tired but over-stimulated brain. Somewhere in the cluster of trees to his left a woman was howling in misery.

He was not superstitious, but he had the imaginative man's sensitivity to atmosphere. Standing alone in the darkness and hearing that human voice wailing in descant to the rising wind he felt a frisson of awe. The terror and helplessness of that nineteenth-century maidservant touched him briefly as if with her own cold finger. He entered for one appalling second into her misery and hopelessness. The past fused with the present. The terror was eternal. The last desperate act was here and now. Then the moment passed. This was a real voice, a living woman. Pressing on his torch, he turned from the path into the utter darkness of the trees.

About twenty yards from the edge of the turf he could see a wooden hut about twelve feet square, its one dimly lit window casting a square of light on the bark of the nearest elm. He strode over to it, his feet soundless on the sodden earth, and pushed open the door. The warm, rich smell of wood and of paraffin wafted out to meet him. And there was something else. The smell of human life. Sitting huddled in a broken wicker chair, with a storm lantern on the upturned box beside her, was a woman.

The impression of an animal trapped in its lair was immediate and inevitable. They gazed at each other soundlessly. Despite her wild crying, cut off instantaneously at his entrance as if it had been simulated, the eyes which peered keenly into his were unclouded and bright with menace. This animal might be in distress but it was on its own ground and all its senses were alert. When she spoke she sounded gloomily belligerent but with no trace of curiosity or fear.

'Who are yer?'

'My name's Adam Dalgliesh. What's yours?'

'Morag Smith.'

'I've heard about you, Morag. You must have got back to the hospital this evening.'

'That's right. And told by Miss Collins to report to the resident staff hostel if yer please. I asked to go back to the medical officers' quarters if I couldn't stay in Nightingale House. But oh no! No bloody fear! Got on too well with the doctors I did. So it's off to the 'ostel. They bugger you about properly in this place, they do. I asked to see Matron but Sister Brumfett said she wasn't to be worried.'

She paused in her recital of woes to fiddle with the wick of the lantern. The light increased. She screwed up her eyes at him.

'Adam Dalgliesh. Funny name. You're new around 'ere, aren't yer?'

'I only arrived this morning. I expect they've told you about Nurse Fallon. I'm a detective. I'm here to find out how she and Nurse Pearce died.'

At first he thought that the news was going to precipitate another bout of wailing. She opened her mouth wide but then, thinking better of it, gave a little gasp and closed it sharply again. She said gruffly:

'I never killed 'er.'

'Nurse Pearce? Of course not. Why should you?'

'That's not what the other one thought.'

'What other one?'

'That Inspector, Inspector bloody Bill Bailey. I could see what 'e was thinking. Asking all them questions, and his eyes fixed on yer all the bleeding time. What were yer doing from the moment you got up? What the 'ell did he think I was doing? Working! That's what I was doing. Did you like Nurse Pearce? Was she ever unkind to you? I'd 'ave liked to see 'er try. Anyway, I never even knew 'er. Well, I 'adn't been over to Nightingale 'ouse for more than a week. But I could see what 'e was after. It's always the same. Blame the poor bloody maid.'

Dalgliesh moved into the hut and seated himself on a bench against the wall. He would have to question Morag Smith and this seemed as good a time as any. He said:

'I think you're wrong, you know. Inspector Bailey didn't suspect you. He told me so.'

She gave a derisive snort.

'Yer don't want to believe everything the police tell yer. Blimey, didn't yer dad tell yer that? 'e suspected me all right. Bloody Bugger Bailey. My God, my dad could tell you some things about the police.'

No doubt the police could tell a lot about dad, thought Dalgliesh, but rejected that line of conversation as unlikely to be profitable. The inspector's name lent itself to alliterative abuse and Morag was in the mood to relish it. Dalgliesh hastened to defend his colleague.

'Inspector Bailey was only doing his job. He didn't mean to upset you. I'm a policeman too, and I shall have to ask questions. We all do. I shan't get anywhere unless you help. If Nurse Pearce and Nurse Fallon were killed, then I'm going to find out who did it. They were young, you know. Nurse Pearce was about your age. I don't suppose they wanted to die.'

He was not sure how Morag would react to this nicely judged appeal to justice and sentiment but he could see the sharp little eyes probing through the semi-darkness.

''elp yer!' Her voice was full of scorn. 'Don't kid me. Your sort don't need 'elp. Yer know 'ow the milk got into the coconut all right.'

Dalgliesh considered this startling metaphor and decided, in the absence of contrary evidence, that it was intended as a compliment. He balanced his torch upright on the bench so that it threw one bright pool of light on the roof, wriggled his thighs more firmly against the wall, and cushioned his head on a thick bundle of raffia which hung from a nail above him. He was surprisingly comfortable. He asked conversationally:

'Do you come here often?'

'Only when I'm upset.' Her tone suggested that this was an

eventuality for which any reasonable woman would make provision.

'It's private 'ere.' She added defensively: 'It used to be private, anyway.'

Dalgliesh felt rebuked.

'I'm sorry. I won't come here again.'

'Oh, I don't mind you. You can come again if you like.'

The voice might be ungracious but the compliment was unmistakable. They sat for a moment in curiously companionable silence.

The stout walls of the hut enclosed them, insulating them in an unnatural silence from the moaning of the wind. Inside, the air was cold but musty, smelling pungently of wood, paraffin and humus. Dalgliesh looked around him. The place was not uncomfortable. There was a bale of straw in the corner, a second old cane chair similar to that in which Morag was curled, and an upturned packing-case covered with oil-cloth which served as a table. On it he could just make out the shape of a primus oil stove. One of the wall shelves held a white aluminium teapot and a couple of mugs. He guessed that the gardener had once used the place as a comfortable retreat from the ardours of work as well as a potting and storage shed. In spring and summer, isolated in the quiet of the trees and surrounded by bird song, it must, Dalgliesh thought, be an agreeable hiding-place. But this was mid-winter. He said:

'Forgive my asking, but wouldn't it be more comfortable to be upset in your own room? And more private?'

'It isn't cosy over in Nightingale 'ouse. And it isn't cosy in the resident staff 'ostel either. I like it 'ere. It smells like my dad's shed on the allotment. And nobody comes after dark. They're all afraid of the ghost.'

'And you aren't?'

'I don't believe in 'em.'

It was, thought Dalgliesh, the ultimate vindication of sturdy scepticism. You didn't believe in a thing, therefore it didn't exist. Untortured by imagination, you could enjoy the reward of your own certainty even if it were only the undisputed possession of a garden shed when you were feeling upset. He found this admirable. He wondered whether he ought to inquire the cause of her grief, suggest perhaps that she could confide in Matron. Had that wild crying really been caused by nothing more than Bill Bailey's passionately resented attentions? Bailey was a good detective, but not particularly subtle with people. One couldn't afford to be critical. Every detective, however competent, knew what it was unwittingly to antagonize a witness. Once this happened it was the devil to get anything useful out of her – and it usually was a woman – even if the antipathy were partly subconscious. Success in a murder investigation depended largely on making people want to help you, getting them to talk. Bill Bailey had singularly failed with Morag Smith. Adam Dalgliesh, too, had failed in his time.

He remembered what Inspector Bailey, in that brief hour's colloquy when the case had been handed over, had told him about the two maids.

'They're out of it. The old one, Miss Martha Collins, has been at the hospital for forty years and if she had homicidal tendencies they would have shown before now. She's mainly concerned about the theft of the lavatory disinfectant. Seems to regard it as a personal affront. Probably takes the view that the lavatory is her responsibility and the murder isn't. The young girl, Morag Smith, is half dotty if you ask me, and as obstinate as an army mule. She might have done it, I suppose, but I can't for the life of me see why. Heather Pearce hadn't done anything to upset her as far as I know. And in any case she hardly had the time. Morag was only transferred from the doctors' residence to Nightingale House on the day before Pearce died. I gather that she wasn't too pleased about the change, but that's scarcely a motive to kill off the student nurses. Besides, the girl isn't frightened. Obstinate, but not frightened. If she did it, I doubt whether you'll ever prove it.'

They sat on in silence. He wasn't anxious to probe into her grief and suspected that she had been indulging an irrational need for a good cry. She had chosen her secret place for it and was entitled to emotional privacy even if her physical privacy had been invaded. He was too reticent himself to have any stomach for the emotional prying which gives so many people the comforting illusion that they care. He seldom did care. Human beings were perpetually interesting to him, and nothing about them surprised him any more. But he didn't involve himself. He wasn't surprised that she should like the shed, smelling as it did of home.

He became aware of a confused background mumbling. She had returned to a recital of her grievance.

'Kept looking at me all the time 'e did. And asking the same old thing over and over again. Stuck up too. You could see that he fancied himself.'

Suddenly she turned to Dalgliesh.

'You feeling sexy?'

Dalgliesh gave the question serious attention.

'No. I'm too old to feel sexy when I'm cold and tired. At my age you need the creature comforts if you're to perform with any pleasure to your partner or credit to yourself.'

She gave him a look in which disbelief struggled with commiseration.

'You're not that old. Thanks for the 'anky anyway.'

She gave one last convulsive blow before handing it back. Dalgliesh slipped it quickly into his pocket, resisting the temptation to drop it unobtrusively behind the bench. Stretching his legs ready to move, he only half heard her next words.

'What did you say?' he asked, careful to keep his voice level, uninquisitorial.

She answered sulkily.

'I said that 'e never found out about me drinking the milk anyway, bugger 'im. I never told 'im.'

'Was that the milk used for the demonstration feed? When did you drink it?'

He tried to sound conversational, only mildly interested. But he was aware of the silence in the hut and the two sharp eyes staring at him. Could she really be unaware of what she was telling him?

'It was at eight o'clock, maybe a minute before. I went into the demo room to see if I'd left my tin of polish there. And there was this bottle of milk on the trolley and I drank some of it. Just a bit off the top.'

'Just out of the bottle?'

'Well, there wasn't any cup 'andy was there? I was thirsty and I saw the milk and I just fancied a bit. So I took a swig.'

He asked the crucial question.

'You just had the cream off the top?'

'There wasn't any cream. It wasn't that kind of milk.'

His heart leapt.

'And what did you do then?'

'I didn't do nothing.'

'But weren't you afraid that Sister Tutor would notice that the bottle wasn't full?'

'The bottle was full. I filled it up with the water from the tap. Anyway, I only took a couple of gulps.'

'And replaced the seal on top of the bottle?'

'That's right. Careful like, so they wouldn't notice.'

'And you never told anyone?'

'No one asked me. That Inspector asked me if I'd been in the demo room and I said only before seven o'clock when I did a bit of cleaning. I wasn't going to tell 'im nothing. It wasn't 'is bloody milk anyway; 'e never paid for it.'

'Morag, you are quite, quite sure of the time?'

'Eight o'clock. The demo clock said eight anyway. I looked at it because I was supposed to help serve the breakfasts, the dining-room maids being off with flu. Some people think you can be in three places at once. Anyway, I went into the dining-room where the Sisters and the students had all started eating. Then Miss Collins gave me one of 'er looks. Late again, Morag! So it must 'ave been eight. The students always start breakfast at eight.'

'And were they all there?'

'Of course they was all there! I told yer! They was at their breakfast.'

But he knew that they had been there. The twenty-five minutes from eight until eight twenty-five was the only time in which all the female suspects had been together, eating under the eye of Miss Collins and full in each other's gaze. If Morag's story were true, and he didn't for one moment doubt it, then the scope of the inquiry had been dramatically narrowed. There were only six people who had no firm alibi for the whole of the period from eight o'clock until the class assembled at eight-forty. He would have to check the statements of course, but he knew what he would find. This was the sort of information he had been trained to recall at will and the names came obediently to mind. Sister Rolfe, Sister Gearing, Sister Brumfett, Nurse Goodale, Leonard Morris and Stephen Courtney-Briggs.

He pulled the girl gently to her feet.

'Come on, Morag, I'm going to see you back to the hostel. You're a very important witness and I don't want you to get pneumonia before I've had a chance to take your statement.'

'I don't want to write nothing down. I'm no scholar.'

'Someone will write it down for you. You'll only have to sign it.'

'I don't mind doing that. I'm not daft. I can sign my name, I 'ope.'

And he would have to be there to see that she did. He had a feeling that Sergeant Masterson would be no more successful than Inspector Bailey in dealing with Morag. It would be safer to take her statement himself even if it meant a later start than he had planned for his journey to London.

But it would be time well spent. As he turned to pull the shed door firmly behind them – it had no lock – he felt happier than at any time since the finding of the nicotine. Now he was making progress. On the whole, it hadn't been too bad a day.

SEVEN

Danse Macabre

I

It was five minutes to seven the next morning. Sergeant Masterson and Detective Constable Greeson were in the kitchen at Nightingale House with Miss Collins and Mrs Muncie. It seemed like the middle of the night to Masterson, dark and cold. The kitchen smelt agreeably of new-baked bread, a country smell, nostalgic and comforting. But Miss Collins was no prototype of the buxom and welcoming cook. She watched, lips tight and arms akimbo, as Greeson placed a filled milk bottle in the front of the middle shelf of the refrigerator, and said:

'Which one are they supposed to take?'

'The first bottle to hand. That's what they did before, didn't they?'

'So they say. I had something better to do than sit and watch them. I've got something better to do now.'

'That's okay by us. We'll do the watching.'

Four minutes later the Burt twins came in together. No one spoke. Shirley opened the refrigerator door and Maureen took out the first bottle to hand. Followed by Masterson and Greeson the twins made their way to the demonstration room through the silent and echoing hall. The room was empty and the curtains drawn. The two fluorescent lights blazed down on a semicircle of vacant chairs and on the high narrow bed where a grotesque demonstration doll, round mouthed, nostrils two black and gaping apertures, was propped against the pillows. The twins set about their preparations in silence. Maureen set down the bottle on the trolley, then dragged out the drip-feed apparatus and positioned it by the side of the bed. Shirley collected instruments and bowls from the various cupboards and set them out on the trolley. The two policemen watched. After twenty minutes Maureen said:

'That's as much as we did before breakfast. We left the room just like it is now.'

Masterson said: 'Okay. Then we'll put forward our watches to eight-forty when you come back here. There's no point in hanging about. We can call the rest of the students in now.'

Obediently the twins adjusted their pocket watches while Greeson rang the library where the remaining students were waiting. They came almost immediately and in the order of their original appearance. Madeleine Goodale first, followed by Julia Pardoe and Christine Dakers who arrived together. No one made any attempt to talk and they took their places silently on the semicircle of chairs, shivering a little as if the room were cold. Masterson noticed that they kept their eyes averted from the grotesque doll in the bed. When they had settled themselves he said:

'Right, Nurse. You can go ahead with the demonstration now. Start heating the milk.'

Maureen looked at him, puzzled.

'The milk? But no one's had a chance to . . .' Her voice died away.

Masterson said: 'No one's had a chance to poison it? Never mind. Just go ahead. I want you to do precisely what you did last time.'

She filled a large jug with hot water from the tap then stood the unopened bottle in it for a few seconds to warm the milk. Receiving Masterson's impatient nod to get on with it, she prised the cap off the bottle and poured the liquid into a glass measuring jug. Then she took a glass thermometer from the instrument trolley and checked the temperature of the liquid. The class watched in fascinated silence. Maureen glanced at Masterson. Receiving no sign, she took up the oesophageal tube and inserted it into the rigid mouth of the doll. Her hand was perfectly steady. Lastly she lifted a glass funnel high over her head and paused. Masterson said:

'Go ahead, Nurse. It isn't going to hurt the doll to get a bit damp. That's what it's made for. A few ounces of warm milk isn't going to rot its guts.'

Maureen paused. This time the fluid was visible and all their eyes were on the white curving stream. Then suddenly the girl paused, arm still poised high, and stood motionless, like a model awkwardly posed.

'Well,' said Masterson: 'Is it or isn't it?'

Maureen lowered the jug to her nostrils, then without a word passed it to her twin. Shirley sniffed and looked at Masterson.

'This isn't milk, is it? It's a disinfectant. You wanted to test whether we really could tell!'

Maureen said: 'Are you telling us that it was disinfectant last time; that the milk was poisoned before we took the bottle out of the fridge?'

'No. Last time the milk was all right when you took it out of the fridge. What did you do with the bottle once the milk had been poured into the measuring jug?'

Shirley said: 'I took it over to the sink in the corner and rinsed it out. I'm sorry I forgot. I should have done that earlier.'

'Never mind. Do it now.'

Maureen had placed the bottle on the table by the side of the sink, its crumpled cap at its side. Shirley picked it up. Then she paused. Masterson said very quietly:

'Well?'

The girl turned to him, perplexed.

'There's something different, something wrong. It wasn't like this.'

'Wasn't it? Then think. Don't worry yourself. Relax. Just relax and think.'

The room was preternaturally silent. Then Shirley swung round to her twin.

'I know now, Maureen! It's the bottle top. Last time we took one of the homogenized bottles from the fridge, the kind with the silver cap. But when we came back into the demonstration room after breakfast it was different. Don't you remember? The cap was gold. It was Channel Island milk.'

Nurse Goodale said quietly from her chair: 'Yes. I remember too. The only cap I saw was gold.'

Maureen looked across at Masterson in puzzled inquiry.

'So someone must have changed the cap?'

Before he had a chance to reply they heard Madeleine Goodale's calm voice.

'Not necessarily the cap. Somebody changed the whole bottle.'

Masterson did not reply. So the old man had been right! The solution of disinfectant had been made up carefully and at leisure and the lethal bottle substituted for the one from which Morag Smith had drunk. And what had happened to the original bottle? Almost certainly it had been left in the small kitchen on the Sisters' floor. Wasn't it Sister Gearing who had complained to Miss Collins that the milk was watery?

II

Dalgliesh's business at the Yard was quickly completed and by eleven o'clock he was in North Kensington.

Number 49 Millington Square, W.10, was a large dilapidated Italianate house fronted with crumbling stucco. There was nothing remarkable about it. It was typical of hundreds in this part of London. It was obviously divided into bed-sitting-rooms since every window showed a different set of curtains, or none, and it exuded that curious atmosphere of secretive and lonely over-occupation which hung over the whole district. Dalgliesh saw that there was no bank of bellpushes in the porch and no neat list of the tenants. The front door was open. He pushed through the glass-panelled door which led to the hall and was met at once by a smell of sour cooking, floor polish and unwashed clothes. The walls of the hall had been papered with a thick encrusted paper, now painted dark brown, and glistening as if it exuded grease and perspiration. The floor and staircase were laid with a patterned linoleum, patched with a brighter newer design where the tears would have been dangerous, but otherwise torn and unmended. The paintwork was an institutional green. There was no sign of life but, even at this time of the day, he felt its presence behind the tightly closed and numbered doors as he made his way unchallenged to the upper floors.

Number 14 was on the top floor at the back. As he approached the door he heard the sharp staccato clatter of typing. He knocked loudly and the sound stopped. There was a wait of more than a minute before the door half opened and he found himself facing a pair of suspicious and unwelcoming eyes.

'Who are you? I'm working. My friends know not to call in the mornings.'

'But I'm not a friend. May I come in?'

'I suppose so. But I can't spare you much time. And I don't think it'll be worth your while. I don't want to join anything; I haven't the time. And I don't want to buy anything because I haven't the money. Anyway, I've got everything I need.' Dalgliesh showed his card.

'I'm not buying or selling; not even information, which is what I'm here for. It's about Josephine Fallon. I'm a police officer and I'm investigating her death. You, I take it, are Arnold Dowson.'

The door opened wider.

'You'd better come in.' No sign of fear but perhaps a certain wariness in the grey eyes.

It was an extraordinary room, a small attic with a sloping roof and a dormer window, furnished almost entirely with crude and unpainted wooden boxes, some still stencilled with the name of the original grocer or wine merchant. They had been ingeniously fitted together so that the walls were honeycombed from floor to ceiling with pale wooden cells, irregular in size and shape and containing all the impedimenta of daily living. Some were stacked close with hard-backed books; others with orange paperbacks. Another framed a small two-bar electric fire, perfectly adequate to heat so small a room. In another box was a neat pile of clean but unironed clothes. Another held blue-banded mugs and other crockery, and yet another displayed a group of *objets trouvés*, sea-shells, a Staffordshire dog, a small jam jar of bird feathers. The single bed, blanket-covered, was under the window. Another upturned box served as a table and desk. The only two chairs were the folding canvas type sold for picnicking. Dalgliesh was reminded of an article once seen in a Sunday colour supplement on how to furnish your bed-sitting-room for under £50. Arnold Dowson had probably done it for half the price. But the room was not unpleasing. Everything was functional and simple. It was perhaps too claustrophobic for some tastes and there was something obsessional in the meticulous tidiness and the way in which every inch of space had been used to the full which prevented it from being restful. It was the room of a self-sufficient, well-organized man who, as he had told Dalgliesh, plainly had everything he wanted.

The tenant suited the room. He looked almost excessively tidy. He was a young man, probably not much over twenty, Dalgliesh thought. His fawn polo-neck sweater was clean, with each cuff neatly turned back to match its fellow, and the collar of a very white shirt visible at the neck. His blue jeans were faded but unstained and had been carefully washed and ironed. There was a crease down the centre of each leg and the ends had been turned up and stitched carefully into place. It gave an oddly incongruous effect to such an informal outfit. He wore leather sandals of the buckled style normally seen on children, and no socks. His hair was very fair and was brushed into a helmet which framed his face in the manner of a medieval page. The face beneath the sleek fringe was bony and sensitive, the nose crooked and too large, the mouth small and well shaped with a hint of petulance. But his most remarkable features were his ears. They were the smallest Dalgliesh had ever seen on a man, and were without colour even at the tips. They looked as if they were made of wax. Sitting on an upturned orange box with his hands held loosely between his knees and his watchful eyes on Dalgliesh, he looked like the centrepiece of a surrealist painting; singular and precise against the multi-cellular background. Dalgliesh pulled out one of the boxes and seated himself opposite the boy. He said:

'You knew that she was dead, of course?'

'Yes. I read about it in this morning's papers.'

'Did you know that she was pregnant?'

This at least produced emotion. The boy's tight face whitened. His head jerked up and he stared at Dalgliesh silently for a moment before replying.

'No. I didn't know. She didn't tell me.'

'She was nearly three months' pregnant. Could it have been your child?'

Dowson looked down at his hands.

'It could have been, I suppose. I didn't take any precautions, if that's what you mean. She told me not to worry, that she'd see to that. After all, she was a nurse. I thought she knew how to take care of herself.'

'That was something I suspect she never did know. Hadn't you better tell me about it?'

'Do I have to?'

'No. You don't have to say anything. You can demand to see a solicitor and make any amount of fuss and trouble and cause a great deal of delay. But is there any point? No one is accusing you of murdering her. But someone did. You knew her and presumably you liked her. For some of the time, anyway. If you want to help you can best do it by telling me everything you knew about her.'

Dowson got slowly to his feet. He seemed as slow-moving and clumsy as an old man. He looked round as if disoriented. Then he said:

'I'll make some tea.'

He shuffled over to a double gas ring, fitted to the right of the meagre and unused fireplace, lifted the kettle as if testing by weight that it held sufficient water, and lit the gas. He took down two of the jugs from one of the boxes and set them out on a further box which he dragged between himself and Dalgliesh. It held a number of neatly folded newspapers which looked as if they hadn't been read. He spread one over the top of the box and set out the blue mugs and a bottle of milk as formally as if they were about to drink from Crown Derby. He didn't speak again until the tea was made and poured. Then he said:

'I wasn't her only lover.'

'Did she tell you about the others?'

'No, but I think one of them was a doctor. Perhaps more than one. That wouldn't be surprising in the circumstances. We were talking once about sex and she said that a man's nature and character were always completely revealed when he made love. That if he were selfish or insensitive or brutal he couldn't conceal it in bed whatever he might do with his clothes on. Then she said that she had once slept with a surgeon and it was only too apparent that most of the bodies he came into contact with had been anaesthetized first; that he was so busy admiring his own technique that it never occurred to him that he was in bed with a conscious woman. She laughed about it. I don't think she minded very much. She laughed about a great many things.'

'But you don't think she was happy?'

He appeared to be considering. Dalgliesh thought: And for God's sake don't answer, 'Who is?'

'No, not really happy. Not for most of the time. But she did know how to be happy. That was the important thing.'

'How did you meet her?'

'I'm learning to be a writer. That's what I want to be and I've never wanted to be anything else. I have to earn some money to live while I get my first novel finished and published, so I work at night as a continental telephone operator. I know enough French to make it possible. The pay isn't bad. I don't have many friends because there isn't time and I never went to bed with any woman until I met Jo. Women don't seem to like me. I met her last summer in St James's Park. She was there on one of her off-duty days and I was there to watch the ducks and see what the park looked like. I wanted to set one of the scenes in my book in St James's Park in July, and I went there to make some notes. She was lying on her back on the grass staring at the sky. She was quite alone. One of the pages of my notebook got detached and blew across into her face. I went after it and apologized, and we chased it together.'

He was holding the mug of tea looking at it as if staring again into the summer surface of the lake.

'It was an odd day – very hot, sunless and blustery. The wind blew in warm gusts. The lake looked heavy like oil.'

He paused for a moment, and when Dalgliesh didn't speak, went on:

'So we met and talked, and I asked her to come back for tea. I don't know what I expected. After tea we talked more and she made love to me. She told me weeks later that she didn't have that in mind when she came here but I don't know. I don't even know why she came back. Perhaps she was bored.'

'Did you have it in mind?'

'I don't know that either. Perhaps. I know that I wanted to make love to a woman. I wanted to know what it was like. That's one experience you can't write about until you know.'

'And sometimes not even then. And how long did she continue to provide you with copy?'

The boy seemed unaware of the irony. He said:

'She used to come here about once a fortnight on her day off. We never went out together except to a pub occasionally. She would bring in some food and cook a meal and afterwards we would talk and go to bed.'

'What did you talk about?'

'I suppose I did most of the talking. She didn't tell me much about herself, only that both her parents had been killed while she was a child and that she had been brought up in Cumberland by an elderly aunt. The aunt is dead now. I don't think Jo had a very happy childhood. She always wanted to be a nurse but she got T.B. when she was seventeen. It wasn't very bad and she spent eighteen months in a sanatorium in Switzerland and was cured. But the doctors advised her not to train as a nurse. So she did a number of other jobs. She was an actress for about three years; but that wasn't much of a success. Then she was a waitress and a shop assistant for a time. Then she became engaged but nothing came of it. She broke it off.'

'Did she say why?'

'No, except that she found something out about the man which made it impossible to marry him.'

'Did she say what it was or who the man was?'

'No, and I didn't ask. But I think he may have been some kind of sexual pervert.'

Seeing Dalgliesh's face he added quickly:

'I don't really know. She never told me. Most of the things I know about Jo just came up casually in conversation. She never really talked about herself for long. It's just an idea I have. There was a kind of bitter hopelessness about the way she spoke of her engagement.'

'And after that?'

'Well, apparently she decided that she might as well go back to her original idea of being a nurse. She thought she could get through the medical examination with luck. She chose the John Carpendar Hospital because she wanted to be near London but not actually in it, and thought that a small hospital would be less arduous. She didn't want her health to break down, I suppose.'

'Did she talk about the hospital?'

'Not much. She seemed happy enough there. But she spared me the intimate details of the bedpan rounds.'

'Do you know whether she had an enemy?'

'She must have had, mustn't she, if somebody killed her? But she never told me about it. Perhaps she didn't know.'

'Do these names mean anything to you?'

He went through the names of all the people, students, sisters, surgeon, pharmacist, who had been in Nightingale House the night Josephine Fallon had died.

'I think she mentioned Madeleine Goodale to me. I've a feeling they were friendly. And the Courtney-Briggs name seems familiar. But I can't remember any details.'

'When did you last see her?'

'About three weeks ago. She came on her night off and cooked supper.'

'How did she seem then?'

'She was restless and she wanted to make love rather badly. Then just before she left she said that she wouldn't see me again. A few days later I got a letter. It merely said, "I meant what I said. Please don't try to get in touch. It's nothing you've done so don't worry. Good-bye and thank you. Jo."'

Dalgliesh asked if he had kept the letter.

'No. I only keep important papers. I mean, there isn't room here to hoard letters.'

'And did you try to get in touch with her again?'

'No. She'd asked me not to and there didn't seem much point in it. I suppose if I'd known about the child I might have done. But I'm not sure. There's nothing I could have done. I couldn't have had a child here. Well, you can see that. How could I? She wouldn't want to marry me and I never considered marrying her. I don't want to marry anyone. But I don't think she killed herself because of the baby. Not Jo.'

'All right. You don't think she killed herself. Tell me why.'

'She wasn't the type.'

'Oh, come now! You can do better than that.'

The boy said belligerently: 'It's true enough. I've known two people in my life who killed themselves. One was a boy in my last year at school when we were sitting for our G.C.E.s. The other was a manager of a dry-cleaning firm I worked for. I drove the delivery van. Well, in both cases, everyone said all the usual things about how dreadful and how surprising it was. But I wasn't really surprised. I don't mean that I was expecting it or anything like that. I just wasn't really surprised. When I thought about both deaths I could believe that they had actually done it.'

'Your sample is too small.'

'Jo wouldn't kill herself. Why should she?'

'I can think of reasons. She hadn't made much success of her life so far. She hadn't any relatives to care about her, and very few friends. She didn't sleep easily at night, wasn't really happy. She had at last succeeded in training to be a nurse and was within a few months of her final examination. And then she finds herself pregnant. She knows that her lover won't want the child, that it's no use looking to him for comfort or support.'

Dowson cried out in vehement protest.

'She never looked to anyone for comfort or support! That's what I'm trying to tell you! She slept with me because she wanted to. I'm not responsible for her. I'm not responsible for anyone. Anyone! I'm only responsible for myself. She knew what she was doing. It wasn't as if she were a young, inexperienced girl who needed kindness and protection.'

'If you believe that only the young and innocent need comfort and protection you're thinking in clichés. And if you begin by thinking in clichés you end by writing them.'

The boy said sullenly: 'Maybe. But that's what I believe.'

Suddenly he got up and went over to the wall. When he came back to the centre box Dalgliesh saw that he held a large smooth stone. It fitted snugly into his curved palm, a perfect ovoid. It was a pale grey, flecked like an egg. Dowson let it slide from his hand on to the table, where it rocked gently into stillness. Then he sat down again and bent forward, his head in his hands. Together they looked at the stone. Dalgliesh did not speak. Suddenly the boy said:

'She gave it to me. We found it together on the beach at Ventnor, in the Isle of Wight. We went there together last October. But of course you know. That must have been how you traced me. Lift it. It's surprisingly heavy.'

Dalgliesh took the stone in his hands. It was satisfying to touch, smooth and cool. He took pleasure in the sea-washed perfection of its shape, in the hard unyielding roundness of it which yet fitted with such gentleness into the palm of his hand.

'I never had a holiday by the sea when I was a boy. Dad died before I was six and the old woman hadn't the money. So I missed out on the seaside. Jo thought it would be fun to go there together. It was very warm last October. Remember? We took the ferry from Portsmouth and there were only half a dozen people on it besides ourselves. The island was empty too. We could walk from Ventnor to St Catherine's Lighthouse without meeting a soul. It was warm enough and deserted enough to bathe naked. Jo found this stone. She thought it would do as a paper-weight. I wasn't going to tear my pocket carrying that weight home but she did. Then, when we got back here, she gave it to me as a keepsake. I wanted her to have it but she said that I'd forget the holiday long before she did. Don't you see? She knew how to be happy. I'm not sure that I do. But Jo did. If you're like that you don't kill yourself. Not when you know how marvellous living can be. Colette knew about that. She wrote about "a compelling fierce and secret *rapport* with the earth and everything that gushes from its breasts".' He looked at Dalgliesh.

'Colette was a French writer.'

'I know. And you believe that Josephine Fallon could feel that?'

'I know she could. Not for long. Not often. But when she was happy she was marvellous. If you once know that kind of happiness you don't kill yourself. While you live there's a hope it could happen again. So why cut yourself off from the hope of it for ever?'

Dalgliesh said: 'You cut yourself off from the misery too. That might seem more important. But I think you're right. I don't believe Josephine Fallon killed herself. I believe she was murdered. That's why I'm asking if there's anything else you can tell me.'

'No. I was on duty at the Exchange the night she died. I had better give you the address. I suppose you'll want to check.'

'There are reasons why it's extremely unlikely to have been

anyone who wasn't familiar with Nightingale House. But we shall check.'

'Here's the address then.'

He tore a corner from the newspaper covering the table and, taking a pencil from his trouser pocket, wrote down the address in a crabbed hand, his head nearly touching the paper. Then he folded it as if the message were secret, and pushed it across the table.

'Take the stone too. I'd like you to have it. No, take it. Please take it. You think I'm heartless, that I'm not grieving for her. But I am. I want you to find out who killed her. It won't do any good to her or to the man, but I want you to find out. And I am sorry. It's just that I can't let myself feel too much. I can't let myself get involved. You understand?'

Dalgliesh took the stone in his hand and rose to go.

'Yes,' he said: 'I understand.'

III

Mr Henry Urquhart of Messrs Urquhart, Wimbush and Portway was Josephine Fallon's solicitor. Dalgliesh's appointment with him was for twelve twenty-five p.m., a time disobligingly chosen, he felt, to intimate that every minute of the solicitor's time was valuable and that he was prepared to spare the police no more than half an hour before lunch. Dalgliesh was admitted immediately. He doubted whether a detective sergeant would have been received so promptly. This was one of the minor advantages of his passion for doing the job himself, controlling the investigation from his office with a small army of detective constables, scenes-of-crime men, photographers, fingerprint experts and scientists ministering to his ego and effectively cutting him off from all but the main protagonists of the crime. He knew that he had a reputation for solving his cases very fast, but he never grudged time on jobs which some of his colleagues thought more appropriate to a detective constable. As a result he was sometimes given information which a less experienced interrogator would have missed. He hardly expected this happy bonus from Mr Henry Urquhart. This interview was likely to be little more than the formal and punctilious exchange of relevant facts. But it had been necessary for him to visit London. There were matters which he had to attend to at the Yard. And it was always a pleasure to visit on foot and in the fitful sunlight of a winter morning these secluded corners of the City.

Messrs Urquhart, Wimbush and Portway were one of the most respected and successful of the City's firms of solicitors. Dalgliesh felt that few of Mr Urquhart's clients could have been mixed up in a murder investigation. They might have their little difficulties from time to time with the Queen's proctor; they might, against all advice, indulge in imprudent litigation or obstinately persist in devising unwise wills; they might require their solicitor's services to devise technical defences to the drink and driving laws; it might indeed be necessary to extricate them from all manner of folly and imprudence. But their killing would be done legally.

The room into which he was shown could have served as a stage set for a successful solicitor's office. The coal fire was banked high in the grate. From above the mantelshelf the portrait of the founder gazed down in approval on his great-grandson. The desk at which the great-grandson sat was of the same period as the portrait and displayed the same qualities of durability, fitness for the task in hand, and a sturdy opulence which stopped just short of ostentation. On the other wall there was a small oil. Dalgliesh thought that it looked very like a Jan Steen. It proclaimed to the world that the firm knew a good picture when it saw one and could afford to display it on the wall.

Mr Urquhart, tall, ascetic, discreetly grey at the temples and with the air of a reserved dominie, was well cast for the role of successful solicitor. He was wearing an exceedingly well-cut suit, but in lovat tweed as if the more orthodox pin stripe would have verged on caricature. He received Dalgliesh without apparent curiosity or concern but the Superintendent noted with interest that Miss Fallon's box was already on the table before him. Dalgliesh stated his business briefly and ended:

'Can you tell me anything about her? In a murder inquiry anything we can learn about the past life and personality of the victim is helpful.'

'And this, you are now confident, is murder?'

'She was killed by taking nicotine in her late night beaker of whisky. As far as we know, she wasn't aware that the tin of rose spray was in the conservatory cupboard, and if she knew and it occurred to her to use it, I doubt whether she would subsequently have hidden the tin.'

'I see. And there is, too, the suggestion that the poison administered to the first victim – Heather Pearce wasn't it – was intended for my client?'

Mr Urquhart sat for a moment finger to finger with his head slightly bent as if consulting either his own subconscious, a higher power, or the ghost of his former client before divulging what he knew. Dalgliesh thought he could have saved the time. Urquhart was a man who knew perfectly well how far he was prepared to go, professionally or otherwise. The pantomime was unconvincing. And his story, when it came, did nothing to clothe the dry bones of Josephine Fallon's life. The facts were there. He consulted the pages in front of him, and presented them logically, unemotionally, lucidly. The time and place of her birth; the circumstances of her parents' death; her subsequent upbringing by an elderly aunt, who together with him had been a trustee until Miss Fallon's majority; the date and circumstance of that aunt's death from cancer of the uterus; the money left to Josephine Fallon and the exact way in which it had been invested; the girl's movements after her twenty-first birthday, in so far as, he pointed out drily, she had troubled to inform him of them.

Dalgliesh said: 'She was pregnant. Did you know?'

It could not be said that this news disconcerted the solicitor although his face creased into the vaguely pained look of a man who can never quite reconcile himself to the messiness of the world.

'No. She didn't tell me. But then I would not expect her to do so, unless, of course, she was thinking of applying for an affiliation order. I gather that was not in question.'

'She told her friend, Madeleine Goodale, that she intended to have an abortion.'

'Indeed. An expensive and to my mind, despite the recent legislation, a dubious business. I speak morally, of course, not legally. The recent legislation . . .'

Dalgliesh said: 'I am aware of the recent legislation. So there is nothing else you can tell me?'

The solicitor's tone held a tinge of reproof.

'I have already told you a great deal about her background and financial position in so far as they were known to me. I am afraid I can't supply you with any more recent or intimate information. Miss Fallon consulted me seldom. Indeed she had no reason to do so. The last time was about her will. You are, I believe, already apprised of its terms. Miss Madeleine Goodale is the sole legatee. The estate is likely to amount to approximately twenty thousand pounds.'

'Was there a previous will?'

Was it Dalgliesh's imagination, or did he detect the slight stiffening of facial muscles, the almost imperceptible frown which greeted an unwelcome question?

'There were two, but the second of these was never signed. The first, made soon after her majority, left everything to medical charities, including cancer research. The second she proposed to execute on the occasion of her marriage. I have the letter here.'

He handed this across to Dalgliesh. It was addressed from a flat in Westminster and was written in a confident upright and unfeminine hand.

'Dear Mr Urquhart, This is to let you know that I shall be married on 14th March at St Marylebone Registry Office to Peter Courtney. He is an actor; you may have heard of him. Will you please draw up a will for me to sign on that date. I shall leave everything to my husband. His full name incidentally is Peter Albert Courtney Briggs. No hyphen. I expect you'll need to know that to draw up the will. We shall be living at this address.

'I shall also need some money. Could you please ask Warranders to make two thousand pounds available to me by the end of the month? Thank you. I hope that you and Mr Surtees are keeping well. Yours sincerely, Josephine Fallon.'

A cool letter, thought Dalgliesh. No explanations. No justification. No expressions of happiness or hope. And come to that, no invitation to the wedding.

Henry Urquhart said: 'Warranders were her stockbrokers. She always dealt with them through us, and we kept all her official papers. She preferred us to do so. She said she preferred to travel unencumbered.'

He repeated the phrase, smiling complacently as if he found it in some way remarkable, and glanced at Dalgliesh as if expecting him to comment.

He went on: 'Surtees is my clerk. She always asked after Surtees.'

He seemed to find that fact more puzzling than the terms of the letter itself.

Dalgliesh said: 'And Peter Courtney subsequently hanged himself.'

'That is so, three days before the wedding. He left a note for the coroner. It wasn't read out at the inquest, I'm thankful to say. It was quite explicit. Courtney wrote that he had planned to marry to extricate himself from certain financial and personal difficulties, but at the last moment had found he couldn't face it. He was a compulsive gambler apparently. I am informed that uncontrolled gambling is, in fact, a disease akin to alcoholism. I know little of the syndrome but can appreciate that it could be tragic in its consequences, particularly for an actor whose earnings, although large, are erratic. Peter Courtney was very heavily in debt and totally unable to extricate himself from a compulsion which daily made that debt worse.'

'And the personal difficulties? I believe he was a homosexual. There was gossip about it at the time. Do you know whether your client knew?'

'I have no information. It seems unlikely that she should not have known since she committed herself so far as to become engaged. She may, of course, have been so sanguine or so unwise as to suppose that she could help to cure him. I should have advised her against the marriage had she consulted me, but as I have said she did not consult me.'

And shortly afterwards, thought Dalgliesh, a matter of months only, she had begun her training at the John Carpendar and was sleeping with Peter Courtney's brother. Why? Loneliness? Boredom? A desperate need to forget? Payment for services rendered? What service? Simple sexual attraction, if physical need were ever simple, for a man who physically was a coarse edition of the fiancé she had lost? The need to reassure herself that she could attract heterosexual desire? Courtney-Briggs himself had suggested that it was she who had taken the initiative. It was certainly she who had brought the affair to an end. There had been no mistaking the surgeon's bitter resentment of a woman who had had the temerity to reject him before he had chosen to reject her.

As he rose to go Dalgliesh said: 'Peter Courtney's brother is a consultant surgeon at the John Carpendar Hospital. But perhaps you knew?'

Henry Urquhart smiled his tight, unamused smile.

'Oh yes, I know. Stephen Courtney-Briggs is a client of mine. Unlike his brother, he has acquired a hyphen to his name and a more permanent success.' He added with apparent irrelevance:

'He was holidaying in a friend's yacht in the Mediterranean when his brother died. He came home immediately. It was, of course, a great shock as well as being a considerable embarrassment.'

It must have been, thought Dalgliesh. But Peter dead was decidedly less embarrassing than Peter living. It would no doubt have suited Stephen Courtney-Briggs to have had a well-known actor in the family, a younger brother who, without competing in his own field, would have added his lustre to the patina of success and given Courtney-Briggs an entrée to the extravagantly egotistical world of the stage. But the asset had become a liability; the hero an object of derision or, at best, of pity. It was a failure his brother would find hard to forgive.

Five minutes later Dalgliesh shook hands with Urquhart and left. As he passed through the hall the girl at the switchboard, hearing his footsteps, glanced round, flushed, and paused in momentary confusion, plug in hand. She had been well trained, but not quite well enough. Unwilling to embarrass her further, Dalgliesh smiled and passed swiftly out of the building. He had no doubt that, on Henry Urquhart's instructions, she was ringing Stephen Courtney-Briggs.

IV

Saville Mansions was a block of late Victorian flats close to Marylebone Road, respectable, prosperous but neither ostentatious nor opulent. Masterson had the expected trouble in finding a vacant lot to park his car and it was after seven-thirty before he entered the building. The entrance hall was dominated by a grille-encased lift of ornate design and a reception desk presided over by a uniformed porter. Masterson, who had no intention of stating his business, nodded to him casually and ran lightly up the stairs. Number 23 was on the second floor. He pressed the bell and prepared for a brief wait.

But the door opened immediately and he found himself almost embraced by an extraordinary apparition, painted like the caricature of a stage whore and wearing a short evening dress of flame-coloured chiffon which would have looked incongruous on a woman half her age. The bodice was so low that he could glimpse the fold between the sagging breasts bunched high into the cups of her brassière, and could see where the powder lay caked in the cracks of dry yellow skin. Her lashes were weighted with mascara; the brittle hair, dyed an improbable blonde, was dressed in lacquered swathes around the raddled face; her carmine-painted mouth hung open in incredulous dismay. Their surprise was mutual. They stared at each other as if unable to believe their eyes. The change in her face from relief to disappointment was almost comic.

Masterson recovered first and announced himself:

'You remember,' he said, 'I telephoned early this morning and made an appointment?'

'I can't see you now. I'm just going out. I thought you were my dancing partner. You said you'd come early in the evening.'

A shrill nagging voice made sharper by disappointment. She looked as if she might close the door in his face. Quickly he slid one foot across the threshold.

'I was unavoidably detained. I'm sorry.'

Unavoidably detained. Too right, he had been. That frantic but ultimately satisfying interlude in the back of the car had occupied more of the evening than he had anticipated. It had taken longer, too, to find a sufficiently secluded spot even on a dark winter's evening. The Guildford Road had offered few promising turnings into open country with its prospect of grass verges and unfrequented lanes. Julia Pardoe had been fussy too.

Every time he slowed the car at a likely spot he had been met with her quiet, 'not here'. He had first seen her as she was about to step off the pavement on to the pedestrian crossing which led to the entrance of Heatheringfield station. He had slowed the car for her but, instead of waving her on, had leaned over and opened the passenger door. She had paused for only a second before walking over to him, coat swinging above the knee-length boots, and had slipped into the seat beside him without a word or glance. He had said:

'Coming up to town?'

She had nodded and had smiled secretively, eyes fixed on the windscreen. It had been as simple as that. She had hardly spoken a dozen words throughout the drive. The tentative or more overt preliminaries which he felt the game demanded of him had met with no response. He might have been a chauffeur with whom she was driving in unwelcome proximity. In the end, pricked by anger and humiliation, he had begun to wonder whether he could have been mistaken. But there had been the reassurance of that concentrated stillness, the eyes which, for minutes at a time, had watched with blue intensity his hands stroking the wheel or busy with the gears. She had wanted it all right. She had wanted it as much as he. But you could hardly call it a quick lay. One thing, surprisingly, she had told him. She was on her way to meet Hilda Rolfe; they were going to a theatre together after an early dinner. Well, either they would have to go without dinner or miss the first act; she was apparently unconcerned either way.

Amused and only slightly curious he had asked:

'How are you going to explain your lateness to Sister Rolfe? Or won't you bother now to turn up?'

She had shrugged.

'I shall tell her the truth. It might be good for her.' Seeing his sudden frown she had added with contempt:

'Oh, don't worry! She won't sneak to Mr Dalgliesh. Hilda isn't like that.'

Masterson hoped she was right. This was something Dalgliesh wouldn't forgive.

'What will she do?' he had asked.

'If I tell? Chuck in her job I imagine; leave the John Carpendar.

She's pretty fed up with the place. She only stays on because of me.'

Wrenching his mind from the memory of that high, merciless voice into the present, Masterson forced himself to smile at the very different woman now confronting him and said in a propitiatory tone:

'The traffic you know . . . I had to drive from Hampshire. But I shan't keep you long.'

Holding out his warrant card with that slightly furtive air inseparable from the gesture, he edged himself into the flat. She didn't try to stop him. But her eyes were blank, her mind obviously elsewhere. As she closed the door, the telephone rang. Without a murmur she left him standing in the hall and almost ran into a room to the left. He could hear her voice rising in protest. It seemed to be expostulating, then pleading. Then there was a silence. He moved quietly up the hall and strained his ears to hear. He thought he detected the clicking of the dial. Then she was speaking again. He couldn't hear the words. This time the conversation was over in seconds. Then came another click of the dial. Another wail. In all she rang four numbers before she reappeared in the hall.

'Is anything wrong?' he asked. 'Can I help?'

She screwed up her eyes and regarded him intently for a second like a housewife assessing the quality and price of a piece of beef. Her reply when it came was peremptory and astonishing.

'Can you dance?'

'I was the Met. police champion for three years running,' he lied. The Force, not surprisingly, held no dancing championships but he thought it unlikely that she would know this and the lie, like most of his lies, came easily and spontaneously.

Again that speculative, intent gaze.

'You'll need a dinner-jacket. I've still got Martin's things here. I'm going to sell them but the man hasn't come yet. He promised he'd come this afternoon but he didn't. You can't rely on anyone these days. You look about the same size. He was quite broad before his illness.'

Masterson resisted the temptation to laugh aloud. He said gravely:

'I'd like to help you out if you're in a difficulty. But I'm a policeman. I'm here to get information, not to spend the night dancing.'

'It isn't the whole night. The ball stops at eleven thirty. It's the Delaroux Dancing Medal Ball at the Athenaeum Ballroom off the Strand. We could talk there.'

'It would be easier to talk here.' Her sullen face set in obstinacy.

'I don't want to talk here.'

She spoke with the peevish insistence of a whining child. Then her voice hardened for the ultimatum.

'It's the ball or nothing.'

They faced one another in silence. Masterson considered. The idea was grotesque, of course, but he wasn't going to get anything out of her tonight unless he agreed. Dalgliesh had sent him to London for information and his pride wouldn't let him return to Nightingale House without it. But would his pride permit him to spend the rest of the evening escorting this painted hag in public? There was no difficulty about the dancing. That was one of the skills, although not the most important, that Sylvia had taught him. She had been a randy blonde, ten years older than himself, with a dull bank manager husband whom it had been a positive duty to cuckold. Sylvia had been crazy on ballroom dancing and they had progressed together through a series of bronze, silver and gold medal competitions before the husband had become inconveniently menacing, Sylvia had begun to hint about divorce, and Masterson had prudently decided that the relationship had outlasted its usefulness, not to say his capacity for indoor exercise, and that the police service offered a reasonable career for an ambitious man who was looking for an excuse for a period of comparative rectitude. Now his taste in women and dancing had changed and he had less time for either. But Sylvia had had her uses. As they told you at Detective Training School, no skill is ever wasted in police work.

No, there would be no difficulty about the dancing. Whether she was equally expert was another matter. The evening would probably be a fiasco and whether he went with her or not she would probably talk in time. But when would that be? Dalgliesh liked to work fast. This was one of those cases where the number of suspects was limited to a small, closed community and he didn't normally expect to spend more than a week on them. He wouldn't exactly thank his subordinate for a wasted evening. And then there was that time in the car to be accounted for somehow. It wouldn't be a good night to return empty-handed. And what the hell! It would make a good story for the boys. And if the evening became too impossible he could always ditch her. He'd better remember to take his own clothes in the car in case he needed to make a quick escape.

'All right,' he said. 'But it's got to be worth my while.'

'It will be.'

Martin Dettinger's dinner-jacket fitted him better than he had feared. It was strange, this ritual of dressing up in another man's clothes. He found himself searching in the pockets as if they too could hold some kind of clue. But he found nothing. The shoes were too small and he made no effort to force them on his feet. Luckily he was wearing black shoes with leather soles. They were too heavy for dancing and looked incongruous with the dinner-jacket but they would have to do. He bundled his own suit in a cardboard box reluctantly provided by Mrs Dettinger and they set off.

He knew that there would be little chance of finding a space for the car in or near the Strand so drove over to the South Bank and parked next to County Hall. Then they walked to Waterloo Station and hired a taxi. That part of the evening wasn't too bad. She had wrapped herself in a voluminous, old-fashioned fur coat. It smelt strong and sour as if a cat had got at it, but at least it was concealing. For the whole of the journey neither of them spoke a word.

The dance had already started when they arrived shortly after eight and the great hall was unpleasantly full. They made their way to one of the few remaining empty tables under the balcony. Masterson noticed that each of the male instructors sported a red carnation; the women a white one. There was a great deal of promiscuous kissing and caressing pats of shoulders and arms. One of the men minced up to Mrs Dettinger with little bleats of welcome and congratulation.

'You're looking marvellous, Mrs D. Sorry to hear that Tony's ill. But I'm glad you found a partner.'

The glance at Masterson was perfunctorily curious. Mrs Dettinger received this greeting with a clumsy jerk of the head and a slight leer of gratification. She made no attempt to introduce Masterson.

They sat out the next two dances and Masterson contented himself with looking round the hall. The whole atmosphere was drearily respectable. A huge bunch of balloons hung from the ceiling, ready no doubt to descend for some orgiastic climax to tonight's festivities. The band wore red jackets with gold epaulettes and had the gloomily resigned look of men who have seen it all before. Masterson looked forward to an evening of cynical uninvolvement, the gratification of observing the folly of others, the insidious pleasure of disgust. He recalled the description of a French diplomat of the English dancing '*avec les visages si tristes, les derrières si gais*'. Here the bottoms were positively staid, but the faces were fixed in grins of simulated delight so unnatural that he wondered whether the school had taught the approved facial expression with the correct steps. Away from the dance floor all the women looked worried, their expressions ranging from slight apprehension to almost frantic anxiety. They greatly outnumbered the men and some of them were dancing together. The majority were middle-aged or older and the style of dress was uniformly old-fashioned, the bodices tight and low cut, the immense circular skirts studded with sequins.

The third dance was a quick step. She turned to him suddenly and said, 'We'll dance this.' Unprotesting, he led her on to the floor and clasped her rigid body with his left arm. He resigned himself to a long and exhausting evening. If this old harpy had anything useful to tell – and the old man seemed to think she had – then, by God, she would tell it even if he had to jangle her round this bloody floor until she dropped. The notion was pleasing and he indulged it. He could picture her, disjointed as a puppet loosed from its cords, the brittle legs sprawled awkwardly, the arms swinging into the final exhaustion. Except that he would probably drop first. That half-hour with Julia Pardoe hadn't been the best possible preparation for a night on the dance floor. But the old bitch had plenty of life in her. He could taste and feel the beads of sweat tickling the corners of his mouth, but she was hardly breathing faster and her hands were cool and dry. The face close to his was intent, the eyes glazed, the lower lip sagging open. It was like dancing with an animated bag of bones.

The music crashed to a stop. The conductor swung round and flashed his artificial smile over the floor. The players relaxed, permitting themselves a brief smile. The kaleidoscope of colour in the middle of the floor coalesced then flowed into new patterns as the dancers disengaged and minced back to their tables. A waiter was hovering for orders. Masterson crooked his finger.

'What will you have?'

He sounded as ungracious as a miser forced into standing his round. She asked for a gin and tonic and when it came accepted it without thanks or apparent gratification. He settled for a double whisky. It was to be the first of many. Spreading the flame-coloured skirt around her chair, she began to survey the hall with that look of disagreeable intensity which he was beginning to know so well. He might not have been there. Careful, he thought, don't get impatient. She wants to keep you here. Let her.

'Tell me about your son,' he said quietly, careful to keep his voice even and unemphatic.

'Not now. Some other evening. There's no hurry.'

He nearly shouted aloud with exasperation. Did she really think that he planned to see her again? Did she expect him to dance with her for ever on the half promise of a titbit of information? He pictured them, capering grotesquely through the years, involuntary participants in a surrealist charade. He put down his glass.

'There won't be another time. Not unless you can help me. The Superintendent isn't keen on spending public money when there's nothing to be learned. I have to justify every minute of my time.'

He instilled into his voice the right degree of resentment and self-righteousness. She looked at him for the first time since they had sat down.

'There might be something to be learned. I never said there wasn't. What about the drinks?'

'The drinks?' He was momentarily nonplussed.

'Who pays for the drinks?'

'Well, normally they are on expenses. But when it's a question of entertaining friends, like tonight for example, naturally I pay myself.'

He lied easily. It was one of the talents which he thought helped most in his job.

She nodded as if satisfied. But she didn't speak. He was wondering whether to try again when the band crashed into a cha-cha. Without a word she rose and turned towards him. They took the floor again.

The cha-cha was succeeded by a mamba, the mamba by a waltz, the waltz by a slow fox-trot. And still he had learned nothing. Then there was a change in the evening's programme. The lights suddenly dimmed and a sleek man, glistening from head to toe as if he had bathed in hair oil, appeared in front of the microphone and adjusted it for his height. He was accompanied by a languid blonde, her hair elaborately dressed in a style already five years out of date. The spotlight played upon them. She dangled a chiffon scarf negligently from her right hand and surveyed the emptying dance floor with a proprietorial air. There was an anticipatory hush. The man consulted a list in his hand.

'And now, ladies and gentlemen, the moment we have all been waiting for. The exhibition dances. Our medallists for the year will demonstrate for our delight the dances which won them their awards. Mrs Dettinger, dancing' – he consulted the list – 'dancing the tango.'

He swept a chubby hand around the floor. The band crashed into a discordant fanfare. Mrs Dettinger rose, dragging Masterson with her. Her claw was like a vice round his wrist. The spotlight swung round and settled on them. There was a little burst of applause. The sleek man continued:

'Mrs Dettinger is dancing with – could we have the name of your new partner, Mrs Dettinger?' Masterson called out loudly:

'Mr Edward Heath.'

The sleek man paused, then decided to take it at its face value. Forcing enthusiasm into his voice, he proclaimed:

'Mrs Dettinger, silver medallist, dancing the tango with Mr Edward Heath.'

The cymbals clashed, there was a further spatter of applause. Masterson led his partner on to the floor with exaggerated courtesy. He was aware that he was slightly drunk and was glad of it. He was going to enjoy himself.

He clasped his hand to the small of her back and assumed an expression of lecherous expectancy. It won an immediate giggle from the nearest table. She frowned and he watched fascinated while an unbecoming crimson flowed over her face and neck. He realized with delight that she was intensely nervous, that this pathetic charade actually mattered to her. It was for this moment that she had dressed so carefully, painted her raddled face. The Delaroux Medal Ball. The demonstration tango. And then her partner had failed her. Lost courage probably, the poor sap. But fate had provided her with a personable and competent substitute. It must have seemed like a miracle. It was for this moment that he had been enticed to the Athenaeum Hall, kept dancing here hour after tedious hour. The knowledge was exhilarating. By God, he had her now. This was to be her big moment. He would see that she didn't forget it in a hurry.

The slow rhythm began. He noted with irritation that it was the same old tune for this dance that they had played most of the evening. He hummed the words in her ear. She whispered:

'We're supposed to be dancing the Delaroux tango.'

'We're dancing the Charles Masterson tango, sweetheart.'

Clasping her tightly he marched her belligerently across the floor in a strutting parody of the dance, swung her viciously around so that her lacquered hair nearly brushed the floor and he heard her bones cracking, and held her in the pose while he bestowed a smile of surprised gratification on the party at the nearest table. The giggle was louder now, more prolonged. As he jerked her upright and waited for the next beat she hissed:

'What do you want to know?'

'He recognized someone, didn't he? Your son. When he was in the John Carpendar Hospital. He saw someone he knew?'

'Will you behave yourself and dance properly?'

'Perhaps.'

They were moving again in an orthodox tango. He could feel her relaxing a little in his arms, but he still kept a firm hold on her.

'It was one of the Sisters. He'd seen her before.'

'Which Sister?'

'I don't know, he didn't tell me.'

'What did he tell you?'

'After the dance.'

'Tell me now if you don't want to end on the floor. Where had he seen her before?'

'In Germany. She was in the dock. It was a war trial. She got off but everybody knew she was guilty.'

'Where in Germany?'

He mouthed the words through lips stretched into the fatuous smile of a professional dancing partner.

'Felsenheim. It was a place called Felsenheim.'

'Say it again. Say that name again!'

'Felsenheim.'

The name meant nothing to him but he knew he would remember it. With luck he would get the details later but the salient facts must be torn from her now while he had her in his power. It might not be true, of course. None of it might be true. And if true it might not be relevant. But this was the information he had been sent to get. He felt a surge of confidence and good humour. He was even in danger of enjoying the dance. He decided that it was time for something spectacular and led her into a complicated routine beginning with a progressive link and ending with a close promenade that took them diagonally across the hall. It was faultlessly executed and the applause was loud and sustained. He asked:

'What was her name?'

'Irmgard Grobel. She was only a young girl then, of course. Martin said that was why she got off. He never had any doubt she was guilty.'

'Are you sure he didn't tell you which Sister it was?'

'No. He was very ill. He told me about the trial when he came home from Europe, so I already knew about it. But he was unconscious most of the time in hospital. And when he wasn't he was mostly delirious.'

So he could have made a mistake, thought Masterson. It was an unlikely enough story. And surely it would be hard to recognize a face after over twenty-five years; except that he must have watched that particular face with fascinated intensity all through the trial. It must have made an impression on a young and probably sensitive man. Enough, perhaps, for him to relive it in his delirium and delude himself that one of the faces bending over him in those few moments of consciousness and lucidity was the face of Irmgard Grobel. But supposing, just supposing, he had been right. If he had told his mother he might well have told his special nurse or blurted it out in his delirium. And what use had Heather Pearce made of her knowledge?

He whisphered softly into her ear: 'Who else have you told?'

'Nobody. I haven't told anybody. Why should I?'

Another rock swing. Then an over swing. Very nice. More applause. He tightened his hold on her and made his voice husky with menace beneath the fixed grin.

'Who else? You must have told someone.'

'Why should I?'

'Because you're a woman.'

It was a lucky reply. The mulish obstinacy on her face softened. She glanced up at him for a second, then fluttered her sparse mascara-coated eyelashes in a travesty of flirtation. Oh God, he thought, she's going to be coy.

'Oh well . . . perhaps I did tell just one person.'

'I know bloody well you did. I'm asking who?'

Again the deprecatory glance, the little moue of submission. She had decided to enjoy this masterful man. For some reason, perhaps the gin, perhaps the euphoria of the dance, her resistance had crumbled. It was going to be hunky-dory from now on.

'I told Mr Courtney-Briggs, Martin's surgeon. Well, it seemed only right.'

'When?'

'Last Wednesday. The Wednesday of last week, I mean. At his consulting rooms in Wimpole Street. He had just left the hospital on the Friday when Martin died so I couldn't see him earlier. He's only at the John Carpendar on Monday, Thursday and Friday.'

'Did he ask to see you?'

'Oh no! The staff nurse who was taking Sister's place said that he would be very glad to have a talk with me if I thought it would be helpful and that I could phone Wimpole Street to make an appointment. I didn't then. What was the use? Martin was dead. But then I got his bill. Not very nice, I thought, so soon after Martin had passed away. Two hundred guineas! I thought it was monstrous. After all, it's not as if he did any good. So I thought I'd just pop into Wimpole Street and see him and mention what I knew. It wasn't right for the hospital to employ a woman like that. A murderess really. And then to charge all that money. There was a second bill from the hospital for his maintenance you know, but it wasn't anything like Mr Courtney-Briggs's two hundred guineas.'

The sentences were disjointed. She spoke them close into his ear as opportunity offered. But she was neither breathless nor incoherent. She had plenty of energy for both the dance and the talk. And it was Masterson who was feeling the strain. Another progressive link leading into the *doré* and ending with a close promenade. She didn't put a foot wrong. The old girl had been well taught even if they couldn't give her grace or *élan*.

'So you trotted along to tell him what you knew and suggested that he took a slice off his profits?'

'He didn't believe me. He said that Martin was delirious and mistaken and that he could personally vouch for all the Sisters. But he took £50 off the bill.'

She spoke with grim satisfaction. Masterson was surprised. Even if Courtney-Briggs had believed the story there was no reason why he should deduct a not inconsiderable amount from his bill. He wasn't responsible for recruiting or appointing the nursing staff. He had nothing to worry about. Masterson wondered whether he had believed the story. He had obviously said nothing, either to the Chairman of the Hospital Management Committee or to the Matron. Perhaps it was true that he could vouch personally for all the Sisters and the £50 deduction had merely been a gesture to keep a tiresome woman quiet. But Courtney-Briggs hadn't struck Masterson as the kind of man to submit himself to blackmail or to relinquish a penny of what he thought was due to him.

It was at that moment that the music crashed to a finish.

Masterson smiled benevolently on Mrs Dettinger, and led her back to their table. The applause lasted until they reached it and then was cut off abruptly as the sleek man announced the next dance. Masterson looked around for the waiter and beckoned.

'Well, now,' he said to his partner, 'that wasn't so bad, was it? If you behave yourself nicely for the rest of the evening I might even take you home.'

He did take her home. They left early but it was well past midnight before he finally left the Baker Street flat. By then he knew he had as much of the story as she could tell him. She had grown maudlin after their return, a reaction, he felt, to triumph and gin. He had kept her supplied with the latter through the rest of the evening, not enough to make her unmanageably drunk but sufficient to keep her talkative and pliable. But the journey home had been a nightmare, not made easier by the cab driver's glances of mingled amusement and contempt as he drove them from the hall to the South Bank car park, and by the disapproving superciliousness of the hall porter when they arrived at Saville Mansions. Once in the flat he had coaxed, comforted and bullied her into coherence, making black coffee for them both in the unbelievably squalid kitchen – a slut's kitchen he thought, glad of one more reason to despise her – and giving it to her with promises that, of course, he wouldn't leave her, that he would call for her again the following Saturday, that they would be permanent dancing partners. By midnight he had got out of her all he wanted to know about Martin Dettinger's career and his stay in the John Carpendar Hospital. There wasn't a great deal to be learned about the hospital. She hadn't visited often during the week he was there. Well, what was the point of it? There wasn't anything she could do for him. He was unconscious most of the time and didn't really know her even when he woke. Except that once, of course. She had hoped then for a little word of comfort and appreciation, but all she had got was that odd laugh and the talk about Irmgard Grobel. He had told her that story years before. She was tired of hearing it. A boy ought to be thinking of his mother when he was dying. It had been a terrible effort to sit there watching. She was a sensitive person. Hospitals upset her. The late Mr Dettinger hadn't understood how sensitive she was.

There was apparently a great deal that the late Mr Dettinger hadn't understood, his wife's sexual needs among them. Masterson listened to the story of her marriage without interest. It was the usual story of an unsatisfied wife, a hen-pecked husband and an unhappy and sensitive child. Masterson heard it without pity. He wasn't particularly interested in people. He divided them into two broad groups, the law-abiding and the villains and the ceaseless war which he waged against the latter fulfilled, as he knew, some inarticulated need of his own nature. But he was interested in facts. He knew that, when anybody visited the scene of a crime, some evidence was left behind or some was taken away. It was the detective's job to find that evidence. He knew that fingerprints hadn't yet been known to lie and that human beings did frequently, irrationally, whether they were innocent or guilty. He knew that facts stood up in court and people let you down. He knew that motive was unpredictable although he had honesty enough sometimes to recognize his own. It had struck him at the very moment of entering Julia Pardoe that his act, in its anger and exaltation, was in some way directed against Dalgliesh. But it never occurred to him to ask why. That would have seemed profitless speculation. Nor did he wonder whether, for the girl also, it had been an act of malice and private retribution.

'You'd think a boy would want his mother when he was dying. It was terrible to sit there and hear that dreadful breathing, first soft and then dreadfully loud. Of course he had a private room. That's why the hospital was able to charge. He wasn't National Health. But the other patients must have heard the noise all over the ward.'

'Cheyne–Stokes's breathing,' said Masterson. 'It comes before the death rattle.'

'They should have done something about it. It upset me dreadfully. That special nurse he had should have done something about it. The plain one. I suppose she was doing her duty, but she never gave a thought to me. After all, the living need some attention. There wasn't anything else she could do for Martin.'

'That was Nurse Pearce. The one who died.'

'Yes, I remember you told me. So she's dead too. I hear of nothing but death. It's all around me. What did you call that breathing?'

'Cheyne–Stokes. It means that you're going to die.'

'They should have done something about it. That girl should have done something about it. Did she breathe like that before she died?'

'No, she screamed. Someone poured disinfectant into her stomach and burned it out.'

'I don't want to hear about it! I don't want to hear about it any more! Tell me about the dance. You will come back next Saturday, won't you?'

And so it had gone on. It had been tedious and exhausting and, in the end, almost frightening. The triumphant glow of getting what he wanted had faded before midnight and he was aware of hatred and disgust. While he listened to her babblings he toyed with imagined violence. It was easy to see how these things happened. A handy poker. The silly face smashed into pulp. Blow on blow on blow. The bones splintering. A gush of blood. An orgasm of hatred. Imagining it, he found it hard to keep his breathing even. He took her hand gently.

'Yes,' he said. 'Yes, I'll come again. Yes. Yes.'

The flesh was dry and hot now. She might have been in a fever. The painted nails were ridged. On the back of the hands the veins stood out like purple cords. He traced with a caressing finger the brown stains of age.

Shortly after midnight her voice burbled into incoherency, her head sank forward, and he saw that she was asleep. He waited for a moment, then disengaged his hand and tiptoed into the bedroom. It took him only a couple of minutes to change his clothes. Then he tiptoed into the bathroom and washed his face and the hand which had touched hers, washed them over and over again. Finally he left the flat, shutting the door quietly behind him as if afraid to wake her, and went out into the night.

V

Fifteen minutes later, Masterson's car passed the flat where Miss Beale and Miss Burrows, cosily dressing-gowned, were sipping their late night cocoa before the dying fire. They heard it as one brief crescendo in the intermittent flow of traffic, and broke off their chatter to speculate with desultory interest on what brought people out in the small hours of the morning. It was certainly unusual for them to be still up at this hour, but tomorrow was Saturday and they could indulge their fondness for late night conversation in the comfortable knowledge that they could lie in next morning.

They had been discussing the visit that afternoon of Chief Superintendent Dalgliesh. Really, they agreed, it had been a success, almost a pleasure. He had seemed to enjoy his tea. He had sat there, deep in their most comfortable armchair, and the three of them had talked together as if he were as harmless and familiar as the local vicar.

He had said to Miss Beale: 'I want to see Nurse Pearce's death through your eyes. Tell me about it. Tell me everything you saw and felt from the moment you drove through the hospital gates.'

And Miss Beale had told him, taking a shameful pleasure in her half-hour of importance, in his obvious appreciation that she had observed so carefully and could describe with such clarity. He was a good listener, they conceded. Well, that was part of his job. He was clever, too, at making people talk. Even Angela, who had sat in watchful silence for most of the time, couldn't explain why she had felt drawn to mention her recent encounter with Sister Rolfe in the Westminster library. And his eyes had flickered with interest, interest which had faded into disappointment when she told him the date. The friend agreed that they couldn't have been mistaken. He had been disappointed. Sister Rolfe had been seen in the library on the wrong day.

VI

It was after eleven o'clock when Dalgliesh turned the key in his desk drawer, locked the office behind him and let himself out of the side door of Nightingale House to walk back to the Falconer's Arms. At the turn of the path where it narrowed before losing itself in the dark shadows of the trees, he looked back at the gaunt pile of the house, enormous and sinister, with its four turrets black against the night sky. The house was in almost total darkness. There was only one lighted window and it took him a minute to identify the room. So Mary Taylor was in her bedroom but not yet asleep. The light was merely a faint glow, perhaps from a bedside lamp, and as he watched it went out.

He made his way towards the Winchester Gate. The trees here were very close to the path. Their black boughs arched over his head shutting out the faint light from the nearest lamp. For about fifty yards he walked in absolute darkness, treading swiftly and silently over the mush of dead leaves. He was in that state of physical tiredness when the mind and body seem detached, the body, conditioned to reality, moving half consciously in the familiar physical world, while the liberated mind swings into uncontrolled orbit in which fantasy and fact show an equally ambiguous face. Dalgliesh was surprised that he was so tired. This job was no more arduous than any other. He was working long hours, but then a sixteen-hour day was normal for him when he was on a case. And this extraordinary weariness wasn't the exhaustion of frustration or failure. The case would break by tomorrow morning. Later tonight Masterson would be back with another piece of the jigsaw and the picture would be complete. In two days at the latest he would have left Nightingale House. In two days' time he would have seen the last of that gold and white room in the south-west turret.

Moving like an automaton he heard, too late, the sudden muted footfall at his back. Instinctively, he threw himself round to face his adversary and felt the blow glance from his left temple to his shoulder. There was no pain, only a crack as if his whole cranium had split, a numbness of his left arm, and after a second which seemed an eternity, the warm, almost comforting, gush of blood. He gave one gasp and crumpled forward. But he was still conscious. Blinded by blood and fighting against nausea, he tried to rise, feeling for the earth with both hands, willing himself to get up and fight. But his feet scrabbled ineffectively in the moist earth and there was no strength in his arms. His eyes were blinded by his own blood. The suffocating smell of damp humus pressed against his nose and mouth, pungent as an anaesthetic. He lay there, helplessly retching, waking pain with every spasm, and waited in angry impotence for the final annihilating blow.

But nothing happened. He sank, unresisting, into unconsciousness. A few seconds later he was recalled to reality by a hand gently shaking his shoulder. Someone was bending over him. He heard a woman's voice.

'It's me. What's 'appened? Somebody cosh yer?'

It was Morag Smith. He struggled to answer, to warn her to get away quickly. The two of them would be no match for a determined killer. But his mouth seemed incapable of forming words. He was aware that somewhere very close a man was groaning, then realized with bitter humour that the voice was his. He seemed to have no control over it. He was aware of hands moving around his head. Then she shuddered like a child.

'Ugh! Yer all over blood!'

Again he tried to talk. She bent her head nearer. He could see the dark strands of hair and the white face hovering in front of him. He struggled to rise and this time managed to get to his knees.

'Did you see him?'

'Not really – 'e 'eard me coming through. Made off towards Nightingale 'ouse. Blimey, you don't 'alf look a bloody mess. 'Ere, lean on me.'

'No. Leave me and get help. He may be back.'

'Not 'im. Anyway, we're better together. I don't fancy going it alone. Ghosts is one thing, bloody murderers is another. Come on, I'll give yer a 'and.'

He could feel the sharp bones in her thin shoulders, but the fragile body was remarkably wiry and she stood his weight well. He forced himself to his feet and stood there swaying. He asked:

'Man or woman?'

'Didn't see. Could've been either. Never mind about that now. Think yer can make it to Nightingale 'ouse? That'd be the nearest.'

Dalgliesh felt remarkably better now that he was on his legs. He could scarcely see the path but he took a few tentative steps forward, his hand supported by her shoulder.

'I think so. The back door would be the nearest. It can't be more than fifty yards. Ring the bell of Matron's flat. I know she's there.'

Together they shuffled slowly along the path, obliterating, as Dalgliesh realized bitterly, any footprints he might otherwise have hoped to find next morning. Not that these sodden leaves would yield many clues. He wondered what had happened to the weapon. But this was pointless speculation. He could do nothing until it was light. He felt a wave of gratitude and affection for the tough little person whose brittle arm lay weightless as a child's around his hips. We must look an odd pair, he thought. He said:

'You probably saved my life, Morag. He only ran off because he heard you coming.'

He, or was it she? If only Morag had been in time to glimpse whether it were a man or a woman. He could scarcely catch her reply.

'Don't talk bloody daft.'

He heard, without surprise, that she was crying. She made no attempt to suppress or check her sobbing and it didn't impede their progress. Perhaps, to Morag, crying was almost as natural as walking. He made no effort to comfort her except to press on her shoulders. She took that as a plea for more support and tightened her arm around his hips, leaning against him, helping him on this way. And thus incongruously they passed under the shadows of the trees.

VII

The light in the demonstration room was bright, too bright. It pierced even his gummed eyelids and he moved his head restlessly from side to side to escape the shaft of pain. Then his head was being steadied by cool hands. Mary Taylor's hands. He heard her speaking to him, telling him that Courtney-Briggs was in the hospital. She had sent for Courtney-Briggs. Then the same hands were taking off his tie, undoing the buttons of his shirt, slipping his arms out of his jacket with practised skill.

'What happened?'

It was Courtney-Briggs's voice, harsh and masculine. So the surgeon had arrived. What had he been doing in the hospital? Another emergency operation? Courtney-Briggs's patients seemed curiously prone to relapse. What alibi had he for the last half-hour? Dalgliesh said:

'Someone was lying in wait for me. I've got to check who's in Nightingale House.'

A firm grip was on his arm. Courtney-Briggs was pressing him back into his chair. Two swinging blobs of grey hovered over him. Her voice again.

'Not now. You can hardly stand. One of us will go.'

'Go now.'

'In a minute. We've locked all the doors. We shall know if anyone returns. Rely on us. Just relax.'

So reasonable. Rely on us. Relax. He gripped the metal arms of the chair, taking hold on reality.

'I want to check for myself.'

Half blinded by blood, he sensed rather than saw their mutual glance of concern. He knew that he sounded like a petulant child, beating his insistence against the implacable calm of the grown-ups. Maddened with frustration, he tried to rise from the chair. But the floor tipped sickeningly, then rose up to meet him through whorls of screaming colour. It was no good. He couldn't stand.

'My eyes,' he said.

Courtney-Briggs's voice, annoyingly reasonable: 'In one moment. I must look first at your head.'

'But I want to see!'

His blindness infuriated him. Were they doing this to him deliberately? He put up a hand and began to pick at the caked eyelids. He could hear them talking together, low voiced, in the muttered idiom of their craft from which he, the patient, was excluded. He was conscious of new sounds, the hiss of a sterilizer, a jingle of instruments, the closing of a metal lid. Then the smell of disinfectant sharpened. Now she was cleaning his eyes. A pad, deliciously cool, was wiped across each lid, and he opened them blinking to see more clearly the sheen of her dressing-gown and the long plait of hair falling over her left shoulder. He spoke to her directly.

'I must know who's in Nightingale House. Could you check now, please?'

Without another word or a further glance at Mr Courtney-Briggs, she slipped out of the room. As soon as the door was closed, Dalgliesh said:

'You didn't tell me that your brother was once engaged to Josephine Fallon.'

'You didn't ask me.'

The surgeon's voice was deliberate, uninterested, the response of a man with his mind on his job. There was a snip of scissors, a momentary chill of steel against the skull. The surgeon was clipping Dalgliesh's hair around the wound.

'You must have known that I should be interested.'

'Oh, interested! You're interested all right. Your kind have an infinite capacity for taking an interest in other people's affairs. But I confined myself to satisfying your curiosity only so far as the deaths of these two girls were concerned. You can't complain that I've held anything relevant back. Peter's death isn't relevant – merely a private tragedy.'

Not so much a private tragedy thought Dalgliesh as a public embarrassment. Peter Courtney had violated his brother's first principle, the necessity of being successful. Dalgliesh said:

'He hanged himself.'

'As you said, he hanged himself. Not a very dignified or pleasant way to go, but the poor boy hadn't my resources. The day when they make my final diagnosis I shall have more appropriate measures available than doing myself to death on the end of a rope.'

His egotism, thought Dalgliesh, was astounding. Even his brother's death had to be seen in relationship to himself. He stood complacently secure at the hub of his private universe while other people – brother, mistress, patient – revolved round the central sun existing by virtue of its warmth and light, obedient to its centripetal force. But wasn't that how most people saw themselves? Was Mary Taylor less self-absorbed? Was he himself? Wasn't it merely that she and he pandered more subtly to their essential egotism?

The surgeon moved over to his black instrument case and took out a mirror mounted on a metal band which he clipped around his head. He came back to Dalgliesh, ophthalmoscope in hand and settling himself into a chair opposite his patient. They sat confronting each other, foreheads almost touching. Dalgliesh could sense the metal of the instrument against his right eye. Courtney-Briggs commanded:

'Look straight ahead.'

Dalgliesh stared obediently at the pinpoint of light. He said:

'You left the main hospital building at about midnight. You spoke to the porter at the main gate at twelve thirty-eight a.m. Where were you between those times?'

'I told you. There was a fallen elm blocking the path back. I spent some minutes examining the scene and making sure that other people didn't injure themselves on it.'

'One person did precisely that. That was at twelve seventeen a.m. There was no warning scarf tied on the branches at that time.'

The ophthalmoscope moved to the other eye. The surgeon's breathing was perfectly regular.

'He was mistaken.'

'He doesn't think so.'

'So you deduce that I arrived at the fallen tree later than twelve seventeen a.m. It may have been so. As I wasn't concocting an alibi, I didn't check the time every two minutes.'

'But you're not suggesting that it took you over seventeen minutes to drive from the main hospital to that particular place.'

'Oh, I think I could make out quite a case for the delay, don't you know. I could claim that I needed, in your deplorable police jargon, to obey a call of nature and left my car to meditate among the trees.'

'And did you?'

'I may have done. When I've dealt with your head, which incidentally is going to need about a dozen stitches, I'll give some thought to the matter. You'll forgive me if I concentrate now on my own job.'

The matron had quietly returned. She took up her stance next to Courtney-Briggs like an acolyte waiting for orders. Her face was very white. Without waiting for her to speak the surgeon handed her the ophthalmoscope. She said:

'Everyone who should be in Nightingale House is in her room.'

Courtney-Briggs was running his hands over Dalgliesh's left shoulder causing pain with every thrust of the strong probing fingers. He said:

'The collar-bone seems all right. Badly bruised but not fractured. Your attacker must have been a tall woman. You're over six feet yourself.'

'If it were a woman. Or she may have had a long weapon, a golf club perhaps.'

'A golf club. Matron, what about your clubs? Where do you keep them?'

She answered dully: 'In the hall at the bottom of my staircase. The bag is usually left just inside the door.'

'Then you'd better check them now.'

She was gone for less than two minutes and they awaited her return in silence. When she came back she spoke directly to Dalgliesh.

'One of the irons is missing.'

The news seemed to hearten Courtney-Briggs. He said almost jovially:

'Well, there's your weapon for you! But there's not much point in searching for it tonight. It'll be lying about somewhere in the grounds. Your men can find it and do everything necessary to it tomorrow; test it for fingerprints, look for blood and hair, all the usual tricks. You're not in any fit state to bother yourself tonight. We've got to get this wound sutured. I shall have to get you over to the out-patients' theatre. You'll need an anaesthetic.'

'I don't want an anaesthetic.'

'Then I can give you a local. That just means a few injections around the wound. We could do this here, Matron.'

'I don't want any anaesthetic. I just want it stitched.'

Courtney-Briggs explained patiently as if to a child.

'It's a very deep cut and it's got to be sutured. It's going to hurt badly if you won't accept an anaesthetic.'

'I tell you I don't want one. And I don't want a prophylactic injection of penicillin or anti-tetanus. I just want it sutured.'

He felt them look at each other. He knew that he was being obstinately unreasonable but he didn't care. Why couldn't they get on with it? Then Courtney-Briggs spoke, curiously formal:

'If you'd prefer another surgeon . . .'

'No, I just want you to get on with it.'

There was a moment's silence. Then the surgeon spoke:

'All right. I'll be as quick as I can.'

He was aware that Mary Taylor had moved behind him. She drew his head back against her breast, supported it between cold, firm hands. He shut his eyes like a child. The needle felt immense, an iron rod simultaneously ice cold and red hot which pierced his skull time and time again. The pain was an abomination, made bearable only by anger and by his obstinate determination not to betray weakness. He set his features into a rigid mask. But it was infuriating to feel involuntary tears seeping under his eyelids.

After an eternity he realized that it was over. He heard himself say:

'Thank you. And now I'd like to get back to my office. Sergeant Masterson has instructions to come on here if I'm not in the hotel. He can drive me home.'

Mary Taylor was winding a crêpe bandage around his head. She didn't speak. Courtney-Briggs said:

'I'd prefer you to go straight to bed. We can let you have a room in the Medical Officers' quarters for tonight. I'll arrange for an X-ray first thing in the morning. Then I'd like to see you again.'

'You can arrange what you like for tomorrow. Just now I'd like to be left alone.'

He got up from the chair. She put a hand on his arm, supporting him. But he must have made some kind of gesture for she dropped her arm. He felt surprisingly light on his feet. It was odd that such an insubstantial body could support the weight of so heavy a head. He put up an exploring hand and felt the scrape of the bandage; it seemed an immense distance from his skull. Then, focusing his eyes carefully, he walked unhindered across the room to the door. As he reached it, he heard Courtney-Briggs's voice.

'You will want to know where I was at the time of the attack. I was in my room in the Medical Officers' quarters. I'm staying there for tonight ready for an early operating session. I'm sorry I can't oblige you with an alibi. I can only hope that you realize that, if I want to put anyone out of the way, I have subtler methods at my disposal than a golf iron.'

Dalgliesh didn't reply. Without looking round and without a further word he left them and closed the door of the demonstration room quietly behind him. The stairs looked a formidable climb and, at first, he was afraid that he wouldn't be able to make it. But he grasped the banister resolutely and, step by careful step, made his way back to the office and settled down to wait for Masterson.

EIGHT
A Circle of Burnt Earth

I

It was nearly two in the morning when the gate porter waved Masterson through the main entrance of the hospital. The wind was rising steadily as he drove along the twisting path to Nightingale House between an avenue of black rumbustious trees. The house was in darkness except for the one lit window where Dalgliesh was still working. Masterson scowled at it. It had been irritating and disconcerting to discover that Dalgliesh was still at Nightingale House. He expected to have to give his report on the day's activities; the prospect wasn't unpleasing since he was fortified by success. But it had been a long day. He hoped that they weren't in for one of the Superintendent's all-night sessions.

Masterson let himself in at the side door, double locking it behind him. The silence of the vast entrance hall received him, eerie and portentous. The house seemed to be holding its breath. He smelt again the alien but now familiar amalgam of disinfectant and floor polish, unwelcoming and faintly sinister. As if afraid to stir the sleeping house – half empty as it was – he did not switch on the light but made his way across the hall by the beam of his electric torch. The notices on the hall board gleamed white reminding him of mourning cards in the vestibule of some foreign cathedral. Of your charity pray for the soul of Josephine Fallon. He found himself tiptoeing up the stairs as if afraid to wake the dead.

In the first-floor office Dalgliesh was sitting at his desk with the file open before him. Masterson stood stock-still in the doorway, concealing his surpise. The Superintendent's face was drawn and grey under an immense cocoon of white crêpe bandage. He was sitting bolt upright, forearms resting on the desk, palms spread lightly each side of the page. The pose was familiar. Masterson reflected, not for the first time, that the Superintendent had remarkable hands and knew how to display them to advantage.

He had long decided that Dalgliesh was one of the proudest men he knew. This essential conceit was too carefully guarded to be generally recognized, but it was gratifying to catch him out in one of the lesser vanities. Dalgliesh looked up without smiling.

'I expected you back two hours ago, Sergeant. What were you doing?'

'Extracting information by unorthodox means, sir.'

'You look as if the unorthodox means have been used on you.'

Masterson bit back the obvious retort. If the old man chose to be mysterious about his injury he wasn't going to give him the gratification of showing curiosity.

'I was dancing until nearly midnight, sir.'

'At your age that shouldn't be too exhausting. Tell me about the lady. She seems to have made an impression on you. You had an agreeable evening?'

Masterson could have retorted with reason that he had had one hell of an evening. He contented himself with an account of what he had learned. The exhibition tango was prudently forgotten. Instinct warned him that Dalgliesh might think it neither funny nor clever. But he gave an otherwise accurate account of the evening. He tried to keep it factual and unemotional but became aware that he was enjoying some of the telling. His description of Mrs Dettinger was concise but caustic. Towards the end he hardly troubled to conceal his contempt and disgust of her. He felt that he was making rather a good job of it.

Dalgliesh listened in silence. His cocooned head was still bent over the file and Masterson got no hint of what he was feeling. At the end of the recital Dalgliesh looked up.

'Do you enjoy your work, Sergeant?'

'Yes sir, for most of the time.'

'I thought you might say that.'

'Was the question intended as a rebuke, sir?'

Masterson was aware that he was entering on dangerous ground but was unable to resist his first tentative step.

Dalgliesh didn't answer the question. Instead he said:

'I don't think it's possible to be a detective and remain always kind. But if you ever find that cruelty is becoming pleasurable in itself, then it's probably time to stop being a detective.'

Masterson flushed and was silent. This from Dalgliesh! Dalgliesh who was so uncaring about his subordinates' private life as to seem unaware that they had any; whose caustic wit could be as devastating as another man's bludgeon. Kindness! And how kind exactly was he himself? How many of his notable successes had been won with kindness? He would never be brutal, of course. He was too proud, too fastidious, too controlled, too bloody inhuman in fact for anything so understandable as a little down-to-earth brutality. His reaction to evil was a wrinkle of the nose not a stamp of the foot. But kindness! Tell that to the boys, thought Masterson.

Dalgliesh went on talking as if he had said nothing remarkable.

'We'll have to see Mrs Dettinger again, of course. And we'll want a statement. Did you think she was telling the truth?'

'It's difficult to tell. I can't think why she should lie. But she's a strange woman and she wasn't feeling too pleased with me at the time. It might give her some kind of perverse satisfaction to mislead us. She might have substituted Grobel's name for one of the other defendants, for example.'

'So that the person her son recognized on the ward could have been any one of the Felsenheim defendants, those who are still alive and unaccounted for. What exactly did her son tell her?'

'That's the problem, sir. Apparently he gave her to understand that this German woman, Irmgard Grobel, was employed at the John Carpendar but she can't recall his exact words. She thinks he said something like: '"This is a funny kind of hospital, ma, they've got Grobel here, working as one of the Sisters."'

Dalgliesh said: 'Suggesting that it wasn't the Sister who was actually nursing him, otherwise he'd presumably have said so. Except, of course, that he was unconscious most of the time and may not have seen Sister Brumfett previously or appreciated that she was in charge of the ward. He wasn't in any state to recognize the niceties of the hospital hierarchy. According to his medical record he was either delirious or unconscious most of the time, which would make his evidence suspect even if he hadn't inconveniently died. Anyway, his mother at first didn't apparently take the story too seriously. She didn't mention it to anyone at the hospital? Nurse Pearce, for example?'

'She says not. I think at the time Mrs Dettinger's main concern was to collect her son's belongings and the death certificate and claim on the insurance.'

'Bitter, Sergeant?'

'Well, she's paying nearly £2,000 a year for dancing lessons and she's come to the end of her capital. These Delaroux people like payments in advance. I heard all about her finances when I took her home. Mrs Dettinger wasn't out to make trouble. But then she received Mr Courtney-Briggs's bill, and it occurred to her that she might use her son's story to get a reduction. And she got one too. Fifty quid.'

'Which suggests that Mr Courtney-Briggs is either more charitable than we had supposed or thought that the information was worth the money. Did he pay it over at once?'

'She says not. She first visited him at his Wimpole Street consulting rooms on the evening of Wednesday, 21st January. She didn't get much joy on that occasion so she rang him up last Saturday morning. The receptionist told her that Mr Courtney-Briggs was out of the country. She intended to ring again on the Monday but the cheque for fifty pounds came by the first post. There was no letter and no explanation, merely his compliment slip. But she got the message all right.'

'So he was out of the country last Saturday. Where, I wonder? Germany? That's something to check, anyway.'

Masterson said, 'It all sounds so unlikely, sir. And it doesn't really fit.'

'No. We're pretty certain who killed both those girls. Logically all the facts point to one person. And as you say, this new evidence doesn't really fit in. It's disconcerting when you scramble around in the dirt for a missing piece of the jigsaw and then find it's part of a different puzzle.'

'So you don't think it's relevant, sir? I should hate to think that my evening's exertions with Mrs Dettinger were in vain.'

'Oh, it's relevant. It's exceedingly relevant. And we've found some corroboration. We've traced the missing library book. Westminster City Library were very helpful. Miss Pearce went to the Marylebone branch on the afternoon of Thursday, 8th January, when she was off duty and asked if they had a book dealing with

German war trials. She said she was interested in a trial at Felsenheim in November 1945. They couldn't find anything in stock but they said they would make inquiries of other London libraries and suggested that she should come back or telephone them in a day or two. She telephoned on the Saturday morning. They told her that they'd been able to trace a book which dealt with the Felsenheim trial among others, and she called in for it that afternoon. On each visit she gave her name as Josephine Fallon and presented Fallon's ticket and the blue token. Normally, of course, they wouldn't have noticed the name and address. They did so because the book had to be specially obtained from another library.'

'Was the book returned, sir?'

'Yes, but anonymously, and they can't say exactly when. It was probably on the Wednesday after Pearce died. Someone left it on the non-fiction trolley. When the assistant went to fill up the trolley with recently returned books she recognized it and took it back to the counter to be registered and put on one side ready for return to its parent library. No one saw who returned it. The library is particularly busy and people come in and out at will. Not everyone has a book to return or calls at the counter. It would be easy enough to bring in a book in a basket or a pocket and slip it among the others on the trolley. The assistant who found it had been on counter duty for most of the morning and afternoon and one of the junior staff had been replenishing the trolley. The girl was getting behind with the work so her senior went to give a hand. She noticed the book at once. That was at four-thirty approximately. But it could have been put there at any time.'

'Any prints, sir?'

'Nothing helpful. A few smudges. It had been handled by quite a number of the library staff and God knows how many of the public. And why not? They weren't to know that it was part of the evidence in a murder inquiry. But there's something interesting about it. Have a look.'

He opened one of the desk drawers and brought out a stout book bound with a dark blue cloth and embossed with a library catalogue number on the spine. Masterson took it and laid it on the table. He seated himself and opened it carefully, taking his time. It was an account of various war trials in Germany from 1945 onwards, apparently carefully documented, unsensational in treatment and written by a Queen's Counsel who had once been on the staff of the Judge Advocate General. There were only a few plates and of these only two related to the Felsenheim trial. One showed a general view of the Court with an indistinct glimpse of the doctor in the dock, and the other was a photograph of the camp commandant. Dalgliesh said:

'Martin Dettinger is mentioned, but only briefly. During the war he served in the King's Wiltshire Light Infantry and in November 1945 he was appointed as a member of a military Court set up in West Germany to try four men and one woman accused of war crimes. These Courts were established under a Special Army Order of June 1945 and this one consisted of a President who was a Brigadier of the Grenadier Guards, four army officers of whom Dettinger was one, and the Judge Advocate appointed by the Judge Advocate General to the Forces. As I said, they had the job of trying five people who, it was alleged – you'll find the indictment on page 127 – "acting jointly and in pursuance of a common intent and acting for and on behalf of the then German Reich did on or about 3rd September 1944 wilfully, deliberately and wrongfully aid, abet and participate in the killing of 31 human beings of Polish and Russian nationality".'

Masterson was not surprised that Dalgliesh should be able to quote the indictment word for word. This was an administrator's trick, this ability to memorize and present facts with accuracy and precision. Dalgliesh could do it better than most, and if he wanted to exercise his technique it was hardly for his Sergeant to interrupt. He said nothing. He noticed that the Superintendent had taken up a large grey stone, a perfect ovoid, and was rolling it slowly between his fingers. It was something that had caught his eye in the grounds, presumably, and which he had picked up to serve as a paper-weight. It certainly hadn't been on the office desk that morning. The tired, strained voice went on.

'These 31 men, women and children were Jewish slave workers in Germany and were said to have been suffering from tuberculosis. They were sent to an institution in Western Germany which was originally designed to care for the mentally sick but which since the summer of 1944 had been dedicated, not to curing, but to the business of killing. There is no evidence to how many German mentally ill patients were done to death there. The staff had been sworn to secrecy about what went on, but there were plenty of rumours in the neighbouring districts. On 3rd September 1944, a transport of Polish and Russian nationals were sent to the institution. They were told they were to receive treatment for tuberculosis. That night they were given lethal injections – men, women and children – and by the morning they were dead and buried. It was for this crime, not for the murder of the German nationals, that the five accused were on trial. One was the head doctor Max Klein, one a young pharmacist Ernst Gumbmann, one the chief male nurse Adolf Straub, and one a young, untrained female nurse aged 18, Irmgard Grobel. The head doctor and the chief male nurse were found guilty. The doctor was condemned to death and the male nurse to twenty-three years' imprisonment. The pharmacist and the woman were acquitted. You can find what her counsel said on page 140. You had better read it out.'

Surprised, Masterson took up the book in silence and turned to page 140. He began reading. His voice sounded unnaturally loud.

'This court is not trying the defendant Irmgard Grobel for participation in the death of German nationals. We know now what was happening at Steinhoff Institution. We know, too, that it was in accordance with German law as proclaimed by Adolf Hitler alone. In accordance with orders handed down from the highest authority, many thousands of insane German people were put to death with perfect legality from 1940 onward. On moral grounds one can judge this action as one pleases. The question is not whether the staff at Steinhoff thought it wrong or whether they thought it merciful. The question is whether they thought it was lawful. It has been proved by witnesses that there was such a law in existence. Irmgard Grobel, if she were concerned with the deaths of these people, acted in accordance with this law.

'But we are not concerned with the mentally ill. From July

1944 this same law was extended to cover incurably tubercular foreign workers. It might be contended that the accused would be in no doubt of the legality of such killings when she had seen German nationals put out of their misery in the interests of the State. But that is not my contention. We are not in a position to judge what the accused thought. She was not implicated in the only killings which are the concern of this Court. The transport of Russians and Poles arrived at Steinhoff on 3rd September 1944 at half past six in the evening. On that day Irmgard Grobel was returning from her leave. The Court has heard how she entered the nurses' quarters at half past seven and changed into her uniform. She was on duty from nine o'clock. Between the time of entering the Institution and arriving in the nurses' duty room in E Block she spoke only to two other nurses, witnesses Willig and Rohde. Both these women have testified that they did not tell Grobel of the arrival of the transport. So Grobel enters the duty room. She has had a difficult journey and is tired and sick. She is hesitating whether or not to seek permission to go off duty. It is then that the telephone rings and Doctor Klein speaks to her. The Court has heard the evidence of witnesses to this conversation. Klein asks Grobel to look in the drug store and tell him how much evipan and phenol there is in stock. You have heard how the evipan was delivered in cartons, each carton containing 25 injections and each injection consisting of one capsule of evipan in powder form and one container of sterile water. The evipan and phenol, together with other dangerous drugs, were kept in the nurses' duty room. Grobel checks the amounts and reports to Klein that there are two cartons of evipan and about 150 c.c. of liquid phenol in stock. Klein then orders her to have all the available evipan and phenol ready to hand over to male nurse Straub, who will fetch it. He also orders her to hand over twelve 10 c.c. syringes and a quantity of strong needles. The accused claimed that at no time did he state for what purpose these drugs were required and you have heard from the accused Straub that he, also, did not enlighten her.

'Irmgard Grobel did not leave the duty room until she was carried back to her quarters at nine-twenty that night. The Court has heard how Nurse Rohde coming late on duty found her in a faint on the floor. For five days she was confined to her bed with acute vomiting and fever. She did not see the Russians and Poles enter E Block, she did not see their bodies carried out in the early hours of 4th September. When she returned to duty the corpses had been buried.

'Mr President, this Court has heard witnesses who have testified to the kindness of Irmgard Grobel, to her gentleness with the child patients, to her skill as a nurse; I would remind the Court that she is young, hardly more than a child herself. But I do not ask for an acquittal on the grounds of her youth nor her sex but because she, alone of the accused, is manifestly innocent of this charge. She had no hand in the deaths of these 31 Russians and Poles. She did not even know that they existed. The Defence has nothing further to add.'

Dalgliesh's bitter voice broke in on the silence.

'The usual Teutonic plea of legality you note, Sergeant. They didn't waste much time with their killings, did they? Admitted at six-thirty and injected soon after nine. And why evipan? They couldn't be sure that death would be instantaneous unless they injected a heavy dose. I doubt whether less than 20 c.c. would kill immediately. Not that it would worry them. What saved Grobel was being on leave until late that evening. The Defence claimed that she was never told that the foreign prisoners had arrived, that no one knew until the morning of the 4th. That same plea gave the pharmacist his freedom. Technically they were both innocent, if you can use that word of anyone who worked at Steinhoff.'

Masterson was silent. It was all so long ago. Grobel had been a girl. Ten years younger than he was now. The war was old history. It had no more relevance to his life than had the Wars of the Roses, less since it did not even evoke the faintly romantic and chivalrous overtones of the history learned in his boyhood. He had no particular feelings about the Germans, or indeed about any race other than the few he regarded as culturally and intellectually inferior. The Germans were not among these. Germany to him meant clean hotels and good roads, *rippchen* eaten with the local wine at the Apfel Wine Stuben Inn, the Rhine curving below him like a silver ribbon, the excellence of the camping ground at Koblenz.

And if any of the accused from Felsenheim were alive they

would be well into middle age now. Irmgard Grobel herself would be forty-three. It was all such old history. It had relevance only because it touched this present case. He said:

'It happened so long ago. Is a secret like that worth killing to preserve? Who really cares now? Isn't the official policy to forgive and forget?'

'We English are good at forgiving our enemies; it releases us from the obligation of liking our friends. Take a look at this book, Masterson. What do you notice?'

Masterson let the pages fall apart, shook them gently, lifted the book to eye level and examined the binding. Then he replaced it on the table and pressed back the middle pages. There, embedded deep in the fold were a few grains of sand.

Dalgliesh said: 'We've sent a sample to the lab for analysis, but the result isn't much in doubt. It's almost certainly from one of the fire buckets in Nightingale House.'

'So that's where it was hidden until he, or she, could return it to the library. The same person hid the book and the tin of rose spray. It all hangs together very neatly, sir.'

'A little too neatly, don't you think?' said Dalgliesh.

But Sergeant Masterson had remembered something else.

'That brochure, the one we found in Pearce's room! Wasn't it about the work of a Suffolk Refuge for Fascist War Victims? Suppose Pearce sent for it? Is this another example of making the punishment fit the crime?'

'I think so. We'll get in touch with the place in the morning and find out what, if anything, she promised them. And we'll talk again to Courtney-Briggs. He was in Nightingale House at about the time Fallon died. When we know who he came to see and why, we shall be close to solving this case. But all that must wait for tomorrow.'

Masterson stifled a yawn. He said: 'It's been tomorrow, sir, for nearly three hours.'

II

If the night porter of the Falconer's Arms was surprised at the return of the two guests in the small hours of the morning, one obviously ill and with his head ostentatiously bandaged, he was trained not to show it. His inquiry whether there was anything he could get for the gentlemen was perfunctory; Masterson's reply barely civil. They climbed the three flights of stairs to their floor since the old-fashioned lift was erratic and noisy. Dalgliesh, obstinately determined not to betray his weakness to his Sergeant, made himself take each step without grasping the banister. He knew it to be a foolish vanity and by the time he had gained his room he was paying for it. He was so weak that he had to lean against the closed door for a minute before weaving his unsteady way over to the wash-basin. Grasping the taps for support, he retched painfully and ineffectually, his forehead resting on his forearms. Without lifting his head he twisted on the right-hand tap. There was a gush of ice-cold water. He swilled it over his face and gulped it down from cupped hands. Immediately he felt better.

He slept fitfully. It was difficult to rest his cocooned head comfortably on the pillows, and loss of blood seemed to have left his mind preternaturally active and lucid, militating against sleep. When he did doze it was only to dream. He was walking in the grounds of the hospital with Mavis Gearing. She was skipping girlishly between the trees, brandishing her garden shears and saying kittenishly:

'It's wonderful what you can find to make a show even in this dead time of the year.'

It didn't strike him as incongruous that she was snipping full blown red roses from the dead branches, or that neither of them remarked on the body of Mary Taylor, white neck encircled by the hangman's noose, as she swung gently from one of the boughs.

Towards morning he slept more deeply. Even so, the harsh incessant ring of the telephone woke him to instant consciousness. The illuminated dial of his travelling clock showed five forty-nine a.m. He shifted his head with difficulty from the hollowed pillow and felt for the receiver. The voice was instantly recognizable. But then he knew that he could have distinguished it from any other woman's voice in the world.

'Mr Dalgliesh? This is Mary Taylor. I'm sorry to disturb you but I thought you'd prefer me to ring. We have a fire here. Nothing dangerous; it's only in the grounds. It seems to have started in a disused gardener's hut about fifty yards from Nightingale House. The house itself isn't in any danger but the fire spread very quickly among the trees.'

He was surprised how clearly he could think. His wound no longer ached. He felt literally light-headed and it was necessary to touch the rough gauze of the bandage to reassure himself that it was still there. He said:

'Morag Smith. Is she all right? She used that hut as a kind of refuge.'

'I know. She told me so this evening after she'd brought you in. I gave her a bed here for the night. Morag is safe. That was the first thing I checked.'

'And the others in Nightingale House?'

There was a silence. Then she spoke, her voice sharper.

'I'll check now. It never occurred to me . . .'

'Of course not. Why should it? I'll come over.'

'Is that necessary? Mr Courtney-Briggs was insistent that you should rest. The fire brigade have things under control. At first they were afraid that Nightingale House was threatened but they've axed some of the nearer trees. The blaze should be out in half an hour. Couldn't you wait till morning?'

'I'm coming over now,' he said.

Masterson was lying flat on his back, drugged with tiredness, his heavy face vacant with sleep, his mouth half-open. It took nearly a minute to rouse him. Dalgliesh would have preferred to leave him there in his stupor, but he knew that, in his present weakened state, it wouldn't be safe for him to drive. Masterson, shaken at last into wakefulness, listened to his Superintendent's instructions without comment, then pulled on his clothes in resentful silence. He was too prudent to question Dalgliesh's decision to return to Nightingale House, but it was obvious by his sullen manner that he thought the excursion unnecessary, and the short drive to the hospital was spent in silence.

The fire was visible as a red glow on the night sky long before they came in sight of the hospital, and as they drove through the open Winchester Road gate they could hear the staccato crackle of burning trees and could smell the rich evocative scent of smouldering wood, strong and sweet on the cold air. It broke Masterson's mood of sullen resentment. He breathed it in with noisy enjoyment and said in happy candour:

'I like that smell, sir. It reminds me of boyhood, I suppose. Summer camps with the Boy Scouts. Huddled in a blanket around the camp fire with the sparks soaring off into the night. Bloody marvellous when you're thirteen and being patrol leader is more power and glory than you're every likely to feel again. You know, sir.'

Dalgliesh didn't know. His solitary and lonely boyhood had been devoid of these tribal delights. But it was an interesting and curiously touching glimpse into Masterson's character. Patrol leader in the Boy Scouts! Well, why not? Given a different heritage, a different twist of fate and he could have easily been a leader in a street gang, his essential ambition and ruthlessness channelled into less conformist paths.

Masterson drove the car under the trees at a safe distance and they walked towards the blaze. As if by unspoken consent, they halted and stood together in the shadow of the trees watching in silence. No one appeared to notice them and no one approached. The firemen were getting on with their job. There was only one appliance and they were apparently running the hose from Nightingale House. The fire was by now well under control but it was still spectacular. The shed had gone completely with nothing but a ring of black earth to show where it had once stood, and the surrounding trees were blackened gibbets, stunted and twisted as if with the agony of their burning. On the periphery a few saplings still burned fiercely, crackling and spluttering in the jets from the fire hose. A single flame, writhing and twisting in the stiff breeze, leapt from tree top to tree top and burned there with the clear incandescent light of a candle before it was scotched by one unerring jet from the hose. As they watched, a tall conifer burst into instantaneous fire and exploded in a shower of golden needles. There was a soft gasp of appreciation, and Dalgliesh saw that a little group of black-cloaked students who had been watching at a distance had crept imperceptibly forward into the light of the fire. It shone momentarily on their faces and he thought he recognized Madeleine Goodale and Julia Pardoe. Then he saw the tall unmistakable figure of Matron move across to them. She spoke a few words and the little group turned and reluctantly melted into the trees. It was then that she saw Dalgliesh. For a moment she stood absolutely still. Wrapped in her long black cloak, the hood thrown back, she stood against a single sapling like a victim at the stake, the fire glow dancing behind her and the light flaming her pale skin. Then she walked slowly across to him. He saw then that her face was very white. She said:

'You were right. She wasn't in her room. She's left me a letter.'

Dalgliesh didn't reply. His mind was so clear that it seemed to be operating outside his own volition, not so much ranging over all the clues of the crime, but seeing it as from a great height; a landscape without shadows spread out beneath him, comprehensible, unambiguous. He knew it all now. Not just how the two girls had been murdered; not just when and why; not just by whom. He knew the essential truth of the whole crime, for it was one crime. He might never be able to prove it; but he knew.

Half an hour later the fire was out. The spent hoses crept and thudded on the blackened earth as they were wound in, sending up little spurts of acrid smoke. The last of the onlookers had melted away and the cacophony of fire and wind was replaced by a gentle background hiss broken only by the orders of the fire officer and the blurred voices of his men. Even the wind had died a little and its touch on Dalgliesh's face was gentle and warm as it passed over the steaming earth. Everywhere there hung the reek of charred wood. The headlights of the fire engine were turned on the smoking circle where the hut had stood. Dalgliesh walked over to it, Masterson on his left, Mary Taylor on his right. The heat struck uncomfortably through the soles of his shoes. There was little to be seen; a grotesquely twisted piece of metal which might once have been part of a stove; the charred shape of a metal teapot – one kick would disintegrate it beyond recognition. And there was something else, a shape, nothing more, which even in death's extreme desecration, was still horribly human. They stood looking down in silence. It took them a few minutes to identify the few details; the pelvic girdle ridiculously small when denuded of its animate wrappings of muscle and flesh; the skull upturned and innocent as a chalice; the stain where the brain had burst away.

Dalgliesh said: 'Get a screen around this place and see that it's kept guarded, then ring Sir Miles Honeyman.'

Masterson said: 'There's a pretty problem of identification for him here, sir.'

'Yes,' replied Dalgliesh, 'if we didn't know already who it was.'

III

They went by tacit consent and without exchanging a word through the quiet house to the Matron's flat. No one followed them. As they entered the sitting-room the carriage clock on the mantelpiece struck half past six. It was still very dark and in contrast to the fire-warmed air of the grounds the room was bitterly cold. The curtains had been drawn back and the casement window left open. Matron went quickly across to close it, drew the curtains together with a swift defensive sweep of her arms and turned to look at Dalgliesh steadily and compassionately, as if seeing him for the first time.

'You look desperately tired and cold. Come over to the fire and sit down.'

He walked over and leaned against the fireplace, fearing that if he once sat down he might never be able to get up again. But the mantelpiece felt unstable, the marble slippery as ice. He let himself down into the armchair, and watched while she knelt on the hearth rug and added the dry sticks of kindling to the still warm ashes of the previous evening's fire. The sticks blazed into life. She added a few nuggets of coal, holding out her hands to the blaze. Then without getting up she reached into the pocket of her cloak and handed him a letter.

A pale blue envelope unsealed and addressed in a round, childish but firm hand 'to whom it may concern'. He took out the letter. Cheap, blue paper, perfectly ordinary, unruled, but with the lines of writing so straight that she must have used the ruled sheet as a guide.

'I killed Heather Pearce and Josephine Fallon. They had discovered something about my past, something which was no concern of theirs, and were threatening to blackmail me. When Sister Gearing rang to tell me Fallon had been taken ill and was warded I knew that Nurse Pearce would act the patient in her place. I collected the bottle of disinfectant very early that morning and filled one of the empty milk bottles from the Sisters' utility room. I replaced the cap carefully and took the bottle with me to breakfast in my tapestry bag. All I had to do was to slip into the demonstration room after I had finished breakfast and substitute the bottle of poison for the bottle of milk on the trolley. If anyone had been in the room I should have made an excuse and tried another time and in another way. But the room was empty. I took the bottle of milk upstairs to the Sisters' utility room and threw the empty bottle of disinfectant out of one of the bathroom windows.

'I was in the conservatory when Sister Gearing produced her tin of nicotine rose spray and I thought of it when it came to killing Fallon. I knew where the key to the conservatory was kept and I wore surgical gloves so that there would be no fingerprints. It was an easy matter to pour the poison into Fallon's beaker of lemon and whisky while she was in the bathroom and the drink was cooling on her bedside table. Her nightly routine never varied. I intended to keep the tin, then place it on her bedside table later that night so that it would look as if she had killed herself. I knew it would be important to impress her fingerprints on the tin but that wouldn't be difficult. I had to change my plan because Mr Courtney-Briggs telephoned shortly before twelve to call me back to my ward. I couldn't keep the tin in my possession since it wouldn't be possible to have my bag always with me on the ward and I didn't think it would be safe to leave it in my room. So I hid it in the sand bucket opposite Nurse Fallon's room with the intention of retrieving it and placing it on her bedside table when I returned to Nightingale House. That plan, too, proved impossible. As I got to the top of the stairs the Burt twins came out of their rooms. There was a light shining through Nurse Fallon's keyhole and they said they would take her some cocoa. I expected the body to be discovered that night. There was nothing I could do but to go upstairs to bed. I lay there waiting, expecting every minute to hear the alarm raised. I wondered if the twins had changed their plan and if Fallon had fallen asleep before drinking her whisky and lemon. But I didn't dare to go down and see. If I had been able to place the tin of nicotine by Fallon's bed no one would ever have suspected that she was murdered and I should have committed two perfect crimes.

'There is nothing else to say except that no one knew what I intended to do and no one helped me.

Ethel Brumfett.'

Mary Taylor said: 'It's her handwriting, of course. I found it on her mantelshelf when I came back after I had telephoned you to check that everyone was safe. But is it true?'

'Oh yes, it's true. She killed both of them. Only the murderess could have known where the tin of nicotine was hidden. It was obvious that the second death was meant to look like suicide. Why then wasn't the tin left on the bedside table? It could only have been because the killer was interrupted in her plan. Sister Brumfett was the only person in Nightingale House who was called out that night and who was prevented on her return from going into Fallon's room. But she was always the first suspect. The bottle of poison must have been prepared at leisure and by someone who had access to milk bottles and to the disinfectant and who could carry the lethal bottle about with her undetected. Sister Brumfett went nowhere without that large tapestry bag. It was bad luck for her that she happened to choose a bottle with the wrong coloured cap. I wonder if she even noticed. Even if she did, there wouldn't be time to change it. The whole plan depended on a substitution which would take merely a second. She would have to hope that no one noticed. And, in fact, no one did. And there is one way in which she was unique among the suspects. She was the only one who wasn't present to witness either of the deaths. She couldn't lift a hand against Fallon while the girl was her patient. That would have been impossible for her. And she preferred to watch neither murder. It takes a psychopathic killer or a professional willingly to watch their victim die.'

She said: 'We know that Heather Pearce was a potential blackmailer. I wonder what pathetic incident from poor Brumfett's dreary past she'd raked up for her entertainment.'

'I think you know that, just as I know. Heather Pearce had found out about Felsenheim.'

She seemed to freeze into silence. She was curled on the edge of the armchair at his feet, her face turned away from him. After a moment she turned and looked at him.

'She wasn't guilty, you know. Brumfett was conforming, authoritarian, trained to think of unquestioning obedience as a nurse's first duty. But she didn't kill her patients. The verdict of that court at Felsenheim was just. And even if it wasn't, it was the verdict of a properly constituted court of law. She is officially innocent.'

Dalgliesh said: 'I'm not here to question the verdict at Felsenheim.'

As if he had not spoken she went on eagerly, as if willing him to believe.

'She told me about it when we were both students together at Nethercastle General Infirmary. She lived in Germany most of her childhood but her grandmother was English. After the trial she naturally went free and eventually in 1944 married an English sergeant, Ernest Brumfett. She had money and it was a marriage of convenience only, a way of getting out of Germany and into England. Her grandmother was dead by now and she still had some ties with this country. She went to Nethercastle as a ward orderly and was so efficient that, after eighteen months, there was no difficulty in getting the Matron to take her on as a student. It was a clever choice of hospital. They weren't likely to delve too carefully into anyone's past, particularly into the past of a woman who had proved her worth. The hospital is a large Victorian building, always busy, chronically understaffed. Brumfett and I finished our training together, went together to the local maternity hospital to train as midwives, came south together to the John Carpendar. I've known Ethel Brumfett for nearly twenty years. I've watched her pay over and over again for anything that happened at the Steinhoff Institution. She was a girl then. We can't show what happened to her during those childhood years in Germany. We can only know what the grown woman did for this hospital and for her patients. The past has no relevance.'

Dalgliesh said: 'Until the thing which she must always have subconsciously dreaded happened at last. Until someone from that past recognized her.'

She said: 'Then all the years of work and striving would come to nothing. I can understand that she felt it necessary to kill Pearce. But why Fallon?'

'For four reasons. Nurse Pearce wanted some proof of Martin Dettinger's story before she spoke to Sister Brumfett. The obvious way to get it seemed to be to consult a record of the trial. So she asked Fallon to lend her a library ticket. She went up to the Westminster library on the Thursday and again on the Saturday when the book was produced. She must have shown it to Sister Brumfett when she spoke to her, must have mentioned where she got the ticket. Sooner or later Fallon would want that ticket back. It was essential that no one ever found out why Nurse Pearce had wanted it or the name of the book she had borrowed from the library. That was one of several significant facts which Sister Brumfett chose to omit from her confession. After she had substituted the bottle of poison for the one of milk, she came upstairs, took the library book from Nurse Pearce's room, and hid it in one of the fire buckets until she had an opportunity to return it anonymously to the library. She knew only too well that Pearce would never come out of that demonstration room alive. It was typical of her to choose the same hiding place later for the tin of nicotine. Sister Brumfett wasn't an imaginative woman.

'But the problem of the library book wasn't the main reason for killing Nurse Fallon. There were three others. She wanted to confuse the motives, to make it look as if Fallon were the intended victim. If Fallon died there would always be the probability that Pearce had been killed by mistake. It was Fallon who was listed to act as patient on the morning of the inspection. Fallon was a more likely victim. She was pregnant; that alone might provide a motive. Sister Brumfett had nursed her and could have known or guessed about the pregnancy. I don't think there were many signs or symptoms that Sister Brumfett missed in her patients. Then there was the possibility that Fallon would be held responsible for Pearce's death. After all, she had admitted returning to Nightingale House on the morning of the murder and had refused to give any explanation. She could have put the poison in the drip. Then afterwards, tormented by remorse perhaps, she killed herself. That explanation would dispose very neatly of both mysteries. It's an attractive theory from the hospital's point of view and quite a number of people preferred to believe it.'

'And the last reason? You said there were four. She wanted to avoid inquiries about the library ticket; she wanted to suggest that Fallon had been the intended victim; alternatively she wanted to implicate Fallon in Pearce's death. What was the fourth motive?'

'She wanted to protect you. She always wanted that. It wasn't easy with the first murder. You were in Nightingale House; you had as much opportunity as anyone to interfere with the drip-feed. But at least she could ensure that you had an alibi for the time of Fallon's death. You were safely in Amsterdam. You couldn't possibly have killed the second victim. Why, therefore, should you have killed the first? From the beginning of this investigation I decided that the two murders were connected. It was too much of a coincidence to postulate two killers in the same house at the same time. And that automatically excluded you from the list of suspects.'

'But why should anyone suspect me of killing either girl?'

'Because the motive we've imputed to Ethel Brumfett doesn't make sense. Think about it. A dying man came momentarily out of unconsciousness and saw a face bending over him. He opened his eyes and through his pain and delirium he recognized a woman. Sister Brumfett? Would you recognize Ethel Brumfett's face after twenty-five years? Plain, ordinary, inconspicuous Brumfett? There's only one woman in a million who has a face so beautiful and so individual that it can be recognized even in a fleeting glance across twenty-five years of memory. Your face. It was you and not Sister Brumfett who was Irmgard Grobel.'

She said quietly: 'Irmgard Grobel is dead.'

He went on as if she had not spoken.

'It's not surprising that Nurse Pearce never suspected for one moment that Grobel could be you. You're the Matron, protected by a quasi-religious awe from that taint of human weakness, let alone human sin. It must have been psychologically impossible for her to think of you as a killer. And then, there were the words used by Martin Dettinger. He said it was one of the Sisters. I think I know how he made that mistake. You visit every ward in the hospital once a day, speak to nearly all the patients. The face he saw bending over him was not only clearly the face of Irmgard Grobel. He saw a woman wearing what to him was a Sister's uniform, the short cape and wide triangular cap of the army nursing service. To his drug-muddled mind that uniform meant a Sister. It still means a Sister to anyone who has been nursed in an army hospital, and he had spent months in them.'

She said again quietly: 'Irmgard Grobel is dead.'

'So he told Nurse Pearce much the same as he told his own mother. Mrs Dettinger wasn't particularly interested. Why should she be? And then she received a hospital account and thought that there might be a way of saving herself a few pounds. If Mr Courtney-Briggs hadn't been greedy I doubt whether she would have taken it any further. But she did, and Courtney-Briggs was given an intriguing piece of information which he thought it worth taking some time and trouble to verify. We can guess what Heather Pearce thought. She must have experienced much the same triumph and sense of power as when she saw Nurse Dakers stooping to pick up those pound notes fluttering on the path in front of her. Only this time someone a great deal more important and interesting than a fellow student would be in her power. It never occurred to her that the patient could be referring to a woman other than the Sister nursing him. But she knew she had to get proof, or at least assure herself that Dettinger, who after all was a dying man, wasn't deluded or hallucinating. So she spent her half-day on Thursday visiting the Westminster library and asked them for a book about the Felsenheim trial. They had to borrow it for her from another branch and she returned for it on Saturday. I think she learned enough from that book to convince herself that Martin Dettinger knew what he was talking about. I think that she spoke to Sister Brumfett on the Saturday night and that the Sister didn't deny the charge. I wonder what price Pearce was asking? Nothing as commonplace or understandable or as reprehensible as direct payment for her silence. Pearce liked to exercise power; but even more she enjoyed indulging in moral rectitude. It must have been on Sunday morning that she wrote to the Secretary of the League for the Assistance of Fascist Victims. Sister Brumfett would be made to pay, but the money would go in regular instalments to the League. Pearce was a great one for making the punishment fit the crime.'

This time she was silent, sitting there with her hands folded gently in her lap and looking expressionless into some unfathomable past. He said gently:

'It can all be checked, you know. We haven't much of her body left but we don't need it while we have your face. There will be records of the trial, photographs, the record of your marriage to a Sergeant Taylor.'

She spoke so quietly that he had to bend his head to hear:

'He opened his eyes very wide and looked at me. He didn't speak. There was a wildness, a desperation about that look. I thought that he was becoming delirious, or perhaps that he was afraid. I think he knew in that moment that he was going to die. I spoke to him a little and then his eyes closed. I didn't recognize him. Why should I?

'I'm not the same person as that child in Steinhoff. I don't mean I think of Steinhoff as if it happened to someone else. It did happen to someone else. I can't even remember now what exactly happened in that court at Felsenheim; I can't recall a single face.'

But she had had to tell someone. That must have been part of becoming another person, of putting Steinhoff out of her thoughts. So she had told Ethel Brumfett. They had both been young student nurses at Nethercastle and Dalgliesh supposed that Brumfett represented something to her: kindness, reliability, devotion. Otherwise, why Brumfett? Why on earth choose her as a confidante? He must have been speaking his words aloud because she said eagerly as if it were important to make him understand:

'I told her because she was so ordinary. There was a security about her ordinariness. I felt that if Brumfett could listen and believe me and still like me, then nothing that had happened was so very terrible after all. You wouldn't understand that.'

But he did understand. There had been a boy in his prep school like that, so ordinary, so safe, that he was a kind of talisman against death and disaster. Dalgliesh remembered the boy. Funny, but he hadn't thought of him now for over thirty years. Sproat Minor with his round, pleasant, spectacled face, his ordinary conventional family, his unremarkable background, his blessed normality. Sproat Minor, protected by mediocrity and insensitivity from the terrors of the world. Life could not be wholly frightening while it had a Sproat Minor. Dalgliesh wondered briefly where he was now.

He said: 'And Brumfett had stuck to you ever since. When you came here she followed. That impulse to confide, the need to have at least one friend who knew all about you, put you in her power. Brumfett, the protector, adviser, confidante. Theatres with Brumfett; morning golf with Brumfett; holidays with Brumfett; country drives with Brumfett; early morning tea and late-night drinks with Brumfett. Her devotion must have been real enough. After all, she was willing to kill for you. But it was blackmail all the same. A more orthodox blackmailer, merely demanding a regular tax-free income, would have been infinitely preferable to Brumfett's intolerable devotion.'

She said sadly: 'It's true. It's all true. How can you possibly know?'

'Because she was essentially a stupid and dull woman and you are not.'

He could have added: 'Because I know myself.'

She cried out in vehement protest.

'And who am I to despise stupidity and dullness? What right had I to be so particular? Oh, she wasn't clever! She couldn't even kill for me without making a mess of it. She wasn't clever enough to deceive Adam Dalgliesh, but when is that to be the criteria for intelligence? Have you ever seen her doing her job? Seen her with a dying patient or a sick child? Have you ever watched this stupid and dull woman, whose devotion and company it is apparently proper for me to despise, working all night to save a life?'

'I've seen the body of one of her victims and read the autopsy report on the other. I'll take your word for her kindness to children.'

'Those weren't her victims. They were mine.'

'Oh no,' he said. 'There has only been one victim of yours in Nightingale House and she was Ethel Brumfett.'

She rose to her feet in one swift movement and stood facing him; those astonishing green eyes, speculative and unwavering, gazed into his. Part of his mind knew that there were words he ought to speak. What were they, those over-familiar phrases of statutory warning, the professional spiel which came almost unbidden to the lips at the moment of confrontation? They had slipped away, a meaningless irrelevancy, into some limbo of his mind. He knew that he was a sick man, still weak from loss of blood, and that he ought to stop now, to hand over the investigation to Masterson, and get to his bed. He, the most punctilious of detectives, had already spoken as if none of the rules had been formulated, as if he were facing a private adversary. But he had to go on. Even if he could never prove it, he had to hear her admit what he knew to be the truth. As if it were the most natural question in the world he asked quietly:

'Was she dead when you put her into the fire?'

IV

It was at that moment that someone rang the doorbell of the flat. Without a word Mary Taylor swung her cape around her shoulders and went to open it. There was a brief murmur of voices; then Stephen Courtney-Briggs followed her into the sitting-room. Glancing at the clock, Dalgliesh saw that the hands stood at seven twenty-four a.m. The working day had almost begun.

Courtney-Briggs was already dressed. He showed no surprise at Dalgliesh's presence and no particular concern at his obvious weakness. He spoke to them both impartially:

'I'm told there was a fire in the night. I didn't hear the engines.'

Mary Taylor, her face so white that Dalgliesh thought she might faint, said calmly:

'They came in at the Winchester Road entrance and kept the bell silent so as not to wake the patients.'

'And what's this rumour that they found a burnt body in the ashes of the garden shed? Whose body?'

Dalgliesh said: 'Sister Brumfett's. She left a note confessing to the murders of Nurse Pearce and Nurse Fallon.'

'Brumfett killed them! Brumfett!'

Courtney-Briggs looked at Dalgliesh belligerently, his large handsome features seeming to disintegrate into irritated disbelief.

'Did she say why? Was the woman mad?'

Mary Taylor said: 'Brumfett wasn't mad and no doubt she believed that she had a motive.'

'But what's going to happen to my ward today? I start operating at nine o'clock. You know that, Matron. And I've got a very long list. Both the staff nurses are off with flu. I can't trust dangerously sick patients to first- and second-year students.'

The Matron said calmly: 'I'll see to it at once. Most of the day nurses should be up by now. It isn't going to be easy but, if necessary, we'll have to withdraw someone from the school.'

She turned to Dalgliesh: 'I prefer to do my telephoning from one of the Sisters' sitting-rooms. But don't worry. I realize the importance of our conversation. I shall be back to complete it.'

Both men looked after her as she went out of the door and closed it quietly behind her. For the first time Courtney-Briggs seemed to notice Dalgliesh. He said brusquely:

'Don't forget to go over to the radiography department and get that head X-rayed. You've no right to be out of bed. I'll examine you as soon as I've finished my list this morning.' He made it sound like a tedious chore which he might find time to attend to.

Dalgliesh asked: 'Who did you come to visit in Nightingale House the night Josephine Fallon was murdered?'

'I told you. No one. I never entered Nightingale House.'

'There are at least ten minutes unaccounted for, ten minutes when the back door leading to Matron's flat was unlocked. Sister Gearing had let her friend out that way and was walking with him in the grounds. So you thought that the Matron must be in despite the absence of lights and made your way up the stairs to her flat. You must have spent some time there. Why? I wonder. Curiosity? Or were you searching for something?'

'Why should I visit the Matron? She wasn't there. Mary Taylor was in Amsterdam that night.'

'But you didn't know that at the time, did you? Miss Taylor wasn't accustomed to attending International Conferences. For reasons we can guess she didn't want her face to be too widely known. This reluctance to undertake public duties was thought becomingly modest in a woman so able and so intelligent. She was only asked late on Tuesday to go to Amsterdam to deputize for the Chairman of the Area Nurse Training Committee. Your sessions are on Mondays, Thursdays and Fridays. Then, on Wednesday night, you were called to operate on a private patient. I don't suppose that the operating-theatre staff, busy with an emergency, thought to mention that the Matron wasn't in the hospital. Why should they?' He paused.

Courtney-Briggs said: 'And when am I supposed to have planned to visit the Matron at midnight? You're not supposing that I would have been a welcome visitor? You're not suggesting that she was expecting me?'

'You came to see Irmgard Grobel.'

There was a moment's silence. Then Courtney-Briggs said:

'How do you know about Irmgard Grobel?'

'From the same person who told you, Mrs Dettinger.'

Another silence. Then he said with the obstinate finality of a man who knows he won't be believed:

'Irmgard Grobel is dead.'

'Is she?' asked Dalgliesh. 'Didn't you expect to find her in the Matron's flat? Wasn't this your first opportunity to confront her with what you knew? And you must have been looking forward to it. The exercise of power is always pleasurable, isn't it?'

Courtney-Briggs said calmly: 'You should know that.'

They stood looking at each other in silence. Dalgliesh asked:

'What had you in mind?'

'Nothing. I didn't connect Grobel with the deaths of Pearce or Fallon. Even if I had, I doubt whether I should have spoken. This hospital needs Mary Taylor. As far as I'm concerned Irmgard Grobel doesn't exist. She was tried once and found not guilty. That was good enough for me. I'm a surgeon, not a moral theologian. I should have kept her secret.'

Of course he would, thought Dalgliesh. Its value would be lost to him once the truth were known. This was very special, very important information, gained at some cost, and he would use it in his own way. It put Mary Taylor for ever in his power. The

Matron who so frequently and irritatingly opposed him; whose power was increasing; who was about to be appointed Director of Nursing Services over all the hospitals in the Group; who influenced the Chairman of the Hospital Management Committee against him. Sir Marcus Cohen. How much influence would she retain with that dedicated Jew once he learned about the Steinhoff Institution? It had become fashionable to forget these things. But would Sir Marcus Cohen forgive?

He thought of Mary Taylor's words. There are more ways than one of blackmail. Heather Pearce and Ethel Brumfett both knew that. And perhaps the most subtly pleasurable was the blackmail which made no financial demands but enjoyed its secret knowledge under the cloak of generosity, kindness, complicity or moral superiority. Sister Brumfett hadn't asked much after all, only a room next to her idol; the prestige of being known as the Matron's friend; a companion for her off-duty hours. Poor stupid Pearce had asked only a few shillings a week and a verse or two of scripture. But how they must have relished their power. And how infinitely more gratifying would Courtney-Briggs have found his. No wonder that he had been determined to keep the secret to himself, that he hadn't welcomed the thought of the Yard descending on Nightingale House.

Dalgliesh said: 'We can prove that you flew to Germany last Friday night. And I think I can guess why. It was a quicker and surer way of getting the information you wanted than pestering the Judge Advocate's Department. You probably consulted the newspaper files and the record of the trial. That's what I would have done. And, no doubt, you have useful contacts. But we can find out where you went and what you did. You can't slip in and out of the country anonymously, you know.'

Courtney-Briggs said: 'I admit that I knew. I admit, too, that I came to Nightingale House to see Mary Taylor on the night Fallon died. But I've done nothing illegal, nothing which could put me in jeopardy.'

'I can believe that.'

'Even if I'd spoken earlier I should have been too late to save Pearce. She was dead before Mrs Dettinger came to see me. I've nothing with which to reproach myself.'

He was beginning to defend himself clumsily like a schoolboy. Then they heard the soft footfall and looked around. Mary Taylor had returned. She spoke directly to the surgeon.

'I can let you have the Burt twins. I'm afraid it means the end of this block but there's no choice. They'll have to be recalled to the wards.'

Courtney-Briggs said grudgingly: 'They'll do. They're sensible girls. But what about a Sister?'

'I thought that Sister Rolfe might take over temporarily. But I'm afraid that's impossible. She's leaving the John Carpendar.'

'Leaving! But she can't do that!'

'I don't see how I can prevent her. But I don't think I shall be given the opportunity to try.'

'But why is she leaving? What's happened?'

'She won't say. I think something about the police investigation has upset her.'

Courtney-Briggs swung round at Dalgliesh.

'You see! Dalgliesh, I realize you're only doing your job, that you were sent here to clear up these girls' deaths. But, for God's sake, doesn't it ever occur to you that your interference makes things a bloody sight worse?'

'Yes,' said Dalgliesh. 'And in your job? Does it ever occur to you?'

V

She went with Courtney-Briggs to the front door. They didn't linger. She was back in less than a minute, and walking briskly over to the fire, she slipped her cloak from her shoulders and laid it tidily over the back of the sofa. Then, kneeling, she took up a pair of brass tongs and began to build up the fire, coal carefully disposed on coal, each licking flame fed with its gleaming nugget. Without looking up at Dalgliesh, she said:

'We were interrupted in our conversation, Superintendent. You were accusing me of murder. I have faced that charge once before, but at least the court at Felsenheim produced some evidence. What evidence have you?'

'None.'

'Nor will you ever find any.'

She spoke without anger or complacency but with an intensity, a quiet finality that had nothing to do with innocence. Looking down on the gleaming head burnished by the firelight Dalgliesh said:

'But you haven't denied it. You haven't lied to me yet and I don't suppose you'll trouble to begin now. Why should she have killed herself in that way? She liked her comfort. Why be uncomfortable in death? Suicides seldom are unless they're too psychotic to care. She had access to plenty of pain-killing drugs. Why not use one of them? Why trouble to creep away to a cold dark garden shed to immolate herself in lonely agony? She wasn't even fortified by the gratifications of a public show.'

'There are precedents.'

'Not many in this country.'

'Perhaps she was too psychotic to care.'

'That will be said of course.'

'She may have realized that it was important not to leave an identifiable body if she wanted to convince you that she was Grobel. Faced with a written confession and a heap of charred bones, why should you bother any further? There was no point in killing herself to protect me if you could confirm her real identity without trouble.'

'A clever and far-sighted woman might argue like that. She was neither. But you are. It must have seemed just worth a try. And even if we never found out about Irmgard Grobel and Felsenheim, it had become important to get rid of Brumfett. As you've said, she couldn't even kill without making a mess of it. She had already panicked once when she tried to murder me. She might easily panic again. She had been an encumbrance for years; now she had become a dangerous liability. You hadn't asked her to kill for you. It wasn't even a reasonable way out of the difficulty. Pearce's threats could have been dealt with if Sister Brumfett had only kept her head and reported the matter to you. But she had to demonstrate her devotion in the most spectacular way she knew. She killed to protect you. And those two deaths bound you and she together indissolubly for life. How could you ever be free or secure while Brumfett lived?'

'Aren't you going to tell me how I did it?'

They might, Dalgliesh thought, be two colleagues talking over a case together. Even through his weakness he knew that this bizarre conversation was dangerously unorthodox, that the woman kneeling at his feet was an enemy, that the intelligence opposed to his was inviolate. She had no hope now of saving her reputation, but she was fighting for freedom, perhaps even for her life. He said:

'I can tell you how I would have done it. It wasn't difficult. Her bedroom was the one nearest the door of your flat. I suppose she asked for that room, and nothing Sister Brumfett wanted could be denied. Because she knew about the Steinhoff Institution? Because she had a hold over you? Or merely because she had lumbered you with the weight of her devotion and you hadn't the ruthlessness to break free? So she slept close to you.

'I don't know how she died. It could have been a tablet, an injection, something you administered on the pretence that it would help her to sleep. She had already, at your request, written the confession. I wonder how you persuaded her to do that? I don't suppose she thought for one moment that it was going to be used. It isn't addressed to me or to any particular person. I imagine you told her that there ought to be something in writing just in case anything happened to her or to you and it was necessary sometime in the future to have a record of what really happened, proof that would protect you. So she wrote that plain note, probably at your dictation. It has a directness and lucidity that has little, I imagine, to do with Sister Brumfett.

'And so she dies. You have only to carry her body two yards to gain the safety of your door. Even so, this is the most risky part of your plan. Suppose Sister Gearing or Rolfe should appear? So you prop open Sister Brumfett's door and the door of your flat and listen carefully to make sure that the corridor is clear. Then you hoist the body over your shoulder and move swiftly into your flat. You lay the body on the bed and go back to shut her bedroom door and to shut and lock your own front door. She was a plump but short woman. You are tall and strong and have been trained to lift helpless patients. That part wasn't so difficult.

'But now you must move her to your car. It's convenient having access to your garage from the downstairs hall and a private stairway. With both the outside and inside doors of the flat locked you can work without fear of interruption. The body is hoisted into the back of your car and covered with a travelling rug. Then you drive out through the grounds and reverse the car under the trees, as close as possible to the garden shed. You keep the engine running. It is important to make a quick getaway, be back in your flat before the fire is seen. This part of the plan is a little risky but the Winchester Road path is seldom used after dark. The ghost of Nancy Gorringe sees to that. It would be inconvenient but not catastrophic if you were seen. After all, you are the Matron, there is nothing to prevent you taking a night drive. If anyone passes, you will have to drive on and choose another place or another time. But no one does pass. The car is deep under the trees; the lights are out. You carry the body to the shed. Then there is a second journey with the can of petrol. And after that there is nothing to do but souse the body and the surrounding furniture and piles of wood and throw in a lighted match from the open doorway.

'It takes only a moment to get in the car and to drive straight back through the garage doors. Once they are closed behind you, you are safe. Certainly you know that the fire will burn with such fierceness that it will be seen almost at once. But by then you are back in your own flat, ready to receive the telephone call which tells you that the fire engine is on its way, ready to ring me. And the suicide note which she left in your charge, perhaps never to be used, is ready to be handed over.'

She asked quietly: 'And how will you prove it?'

'Probably never. But I know that is how it happened.'

She said: 'But you will try to prove it, won't you? After all, failure would be intolerable for Adam Dalgliesh. You will try to prove it no matter what the cost to yourself or anyone else. And after all, there is a chance. There isn't much hope of finding tyre marks under the trees of course. The effects of the fire, the wheels of the fire engine, the trampling of the men, will have obliterated any clues on the ground. But then you will examine the inside of the car surely, particularly the rug. Don't neglect the car rug,

Superintendent. There may be fibres from the clothes, even a few hairs, perhaps. But that wouldn't be surprising. Miss Brumfett often drove with me; the car rug actually belongs to her; it's probably covered with her hairs. But what about clues in my flat? If I carried her body down the narrow back staircase surely there will be marks on the walls where they were grazed by her shoes? Unless, of course, the woman who killed Brumfett had sufficient sense to remove the victim's shoes and carry them separately, perhaps slung by the laces around her neck. They couldn't be left in the flat. You might check on the number of pairs that Brumfett owned. After all, someone in Nightingale House could tell you. We have so little privacy from each other. And no woman would walk through the woods barefoot to her death.

'And the other clues in the flat? If I killed her, ought there not to be a syringe, a bottle of pills, something to indicate how I did it? But her medicine cupboard and mine both contain a supply of aspirin and sleeping tablets. Suppose I gave her those? Or simply stunned or suffocated her? Any method would be as good as another provided it didn't make a mess. How can you possibly prove how she died when all you have for the autopsy are a few charred bones? And there's the suicide note, a note in her own handwriting and containing facts which only the killer of Pearce and Fallon could have known. Whatever you may choose to believe, Superintendent, are you going to tell me that the Coroner won't be satisfied that Ethel Brumfett intended that note as a confession before burning herself to death?'

Dalgliesh knew that he could no longer stay upright. He was fighting sickness now as well as weakness. The hand which grasped the mantelshelf for support was colder than the marble and slippery with sweat, and the marble itself was soft and yielding as putty. His wound was beginning to throb painfully, and the dull headache which up to now had been little more than vague discomfort was sharpening and localizing into needles of pain behind his left eye. To drop in a faint at her feet would be unforgettably humiliating. He reached out his arm and found the back of the nearest chair. Then gently he lowered himself into it. Her voice seemed to be coming from a long way off, but at least he could hear the words and knew that his own voice was still steady.

She said: 'Suppose I told you that I could manage Stephen Courtney-Briggs, that no one but the three of us need ever know about Felsenheim? Would you be willing to leave my past out of your report so that at least those girls need not have died entirely in vain? It is important for this hospital that I stay on as Matron. I'm not asking you for mercy. I'm not concerned for myself. You will never prove that I killed Ethel Brumfett. Aren't you going to make yourself look ridiculous if you try? Isn't the most courageous and sensible course to forget that this conversation ever took place, to accept Brumfett's confession for the truth which it is, and to close the case?'

He said: 'That's not possible. Your past is part of the evidence. I can't suppress evidence or omit relevant facts from my report because I don't choose to like them. If I once did that I should have to give up my job. Not just this particular case, my job. And for always.'

'And you couldn't do that, of course. What would a man like you be without his job, this particular job? Vulnerable like the rest of us. You might even have to begin living and feeling like a human being.'

'You can't touch me like that. Why humiliate yourself trying? There are regulations, orders, and an oath. Without them no one could safely do police work. Without them Ethel Brumfett wouldn't be safe, you wouldn't be safe, and Irmgard Grobel wouldn't be safe.'

'Is that why you won't help me?'

'Not altogether. I don't choose to.'

She said sadly: 'That's honest, anyway. And you haven't any doubts?'

'Of course I have. I'm not as arrogant as that. There are always doubts.' And so there were. But they were intellectual and philosophical doubts, untormenting and uninsistent. It had been many years since they had kept him awake at night.

'But there are the regulations, aren't there? And the orders. An oath even. They're very convenient shields to shelter behind if the doubts become troublesome. I know. I sheltered behind them once myself. You and I are not so very different after all, Adam Dalgliesh.'

She took up her cloak from the back of the chair and threw it around her shoulders. She came over and stood in front of him, smiling. Then, seeing his weakness, she held out both her hands and grasping his, helped him to his feet. They stood there facing each other. Suddenly there was a ring of her front doorbell and almost simultaneously the harsh insistent burr of the telephone. For both of them the day had begun.

NINE
Summer Epilogue

I

It was shortly after nine o'clock when the call came through to him, and Dalgliesh walked out of the Yard and across Victoria Street through an early morning haze, a sure harbinger of yet another hot August day. He found the address without difficulty. It was a large red-brick building between Victoria Street and Horseferry Road, not particularly sordid but depressingly dull, a functional oblong with the front punctuated with meanly proportioned windows. There was no lift and he walked unchallenged up the three linoleum-covered flights of stairs to the top floor.

The landing smelt of sour sweat. Outside the flat a grossly fat middle-aged woman in a flowered apron was expostulating to the police constable on duty in an adenoidal whine. As Dalgliesh approached she turned to him, spieling forth a flood of protest and recrimination. What was Mr Goldstein going to say? She wasn't really allowed to sub-let a room. She had only done it to oblige the lady. And now this. People had no consideration.

He passed her without speaking and went into the room. It was a square box, stuffy and smelling of furniture polish, and over-furnished with the heavy prestige symbols of an earlier decade. The window was open and the lace curtains drawn back but there was little air. The police surgeon and the attendant constable, both large men, seemed to have used all there was.

One corpse more to be viewed; only this one wasn't his responsibility. He need only glance, as if verifying a memory, at the stiffening body on the bed, noting with detached interest that the left arm hung loosely over the side, long fingers curled, and that the hypodermic syringe was still attached to the underarm, a metallic insect with its fang deeply embedded in the soft flesh. Death hadn't robbed her of individuality, not yet anyway. That would come soon enough with all the grotesque indignities of decay.

The police surgeon, shirt-sleeved and sweating, was apologetic as if concerned that he might have done the wrong thing. As he turned from the bed Dalgliesh was aware that he was speaking:

'And as New Scotland Yard is so close and the second note was addressed personally to you' . . . he paused uncertainly.

'She injected herself with evipan. The first note is quite explicit. It's a clear case of suicide. That's why the constable didn't want to ring you. He thought it wasn't worth your trouble to come. There's really nothing here of interest.'

Dalgliesh said: 'I'm glad you did ring. And it isn't any trouble.'

There were two white envelopes, one sealed and addressed to himself; the other unsealed and bearing the words, 'To anyone whom it may concern.' He wondered if she had smiled when she wrote that phrase. Watched by the police surgeon and the constable, Dalgliesh opened the letter. The writing was perfectly firm, black and spiky. He realized with a kind of shock that it was the first time he had seen her handwriting.

'They wouldn't believe you but you were right. I killed Ethel Brumfett. It was the first time I had ever killed; it seems important that you should know that. I injected her with evipan, just as I shall shortly do myself. She thought I was giving her a sedative. Poor trusting Brumfett! She would have easily taken nicotine from my hand and it would have been as appropriate.

'I thought it might be possible for me to make some kind of a useful life. It hasn't been, and I haven't the temperament to live with failure. I don't regret what I did. It was best for the hospital, best for her, best for me. I wasn't likely to be deterred because Adam Dalgliesh sees his job as the embodiment of the moral law.'

She was wrong, he thought. They hadn't disbelieved him, they had just demanded, reasonably enough, that he find some proof. He found none, either at the time or later, although he had pursued the case as if it were a personal vendetta, hating himself and her. And she had admitted nothing; not for one moment had she been in any danger of panicking.

There had been very little left unexplained at the resumed inquest on Heather Pearce and the inquest on Josephine Fallon and Ethel Brumfett. Perhaps the Coroner felt that there had been enough rumours and speculation. He had sat with a jury and had made no attempt to inhibit their questions to witnesses, or even to control the proceedings. The story of Irmgard Grobel and the Steinhoff Institution had come out, and Sir Marcus Cohen had sat with Dalgliesh at the back of the court and listened with a face rigid with pain. After the inquest Mary Taylor walked across the room to him, handed him her letter of resignation, and turned away without a word. She had left the hospital the same day. And that, for the John Carpendar, had been the end. Nothing else had come out. Mary Taylor had gone free; free to find this room, this death.

Dalgliesh walked over to the fireplace. The small grate, tiled in bilious green, was filled with a dusty fan and a jam jar of dried leaves. Carefully he moved them out of the way. He was aware of the police surgeon and the uniformed constable watching him expressionlessly. What did they think he was doing? Destroying evidence? Why should they worry? They had their piece of paper ready to be docketed, produced as evidence, filed away for oblivion. This concerned only him.

He shook the note open in the chimney recess and, striking a match, set light to one of the corners. But there was little draught and the paper was tough. He had to hold it, shaking it gently, until the tips of his fingers scorched before the blankened sheet drifted from his grasp, disappeared into the darkness of the chimney recess and was wafted upwards towards the summer sky.

II

Ten minutes later on the same day Miss Beale drove through the front entrance gate of the John Carpendar Hospital and drew up at the porter's lodge. She was greeted by an unfamiliar face, a new youngish porter, shirt-sleeved in his summer uniform.

'The General Nursing Council Inspector? Good morning, miss. I'm afraid this entrance isn't very convenient for the new school of nursing. It's just a temporary building at present, miss, built on a cleared part of the grounds where we had the fire. It's quite close to where the old school was. If you just take this first turn . . .'

'It's all right, thank you,' said Miss Beale. 'I know the way.'

There was an ambulance standing at the entrance to the casualty department. As Miss Beale drove slowly past, Nurse Dakers, wearing the lace-trimmed cap and blue belt of a staff nurse, came out of the hospital, conferred briefly with the attendants, and stood supervising the transfer of the patient. She seemed to Miss Beale's eyes to have grown in stature and authority. There was no trace of the terrified student nurse about this confident figure. So Nurse Dakers had qualified. Well, that was to be expected. Presumably the Burt twins, equally elevated, were working somewhere in the hospital. But there had been changes. Nurse Goodale had married; Miss Beale had seen the notice in the national Press. And Hilda Rolfe, so Angela reported, was nursing somewhere in Central Africa. There would be a new Principal Tutor to meet this morning. And a new Matron. Miss Beale wondered briefly about Mary Taylor. She would be earning a good living somewhere if not in nursing. The Mary Taylors of the world were natural survivors.

She drove down the familiar path between the parched summer lawns, the flower beds blotched with overblown roses, and turned into the green tunnel of the trees. The air was still and warm, the narrow road chequered with the first bright sunlight of the day. And here was the last remembered corner. Nightingale House, or what was left of it, was before her.

Once again she stopped the car and gazed. The house looked as if it had been clumsily cut in two by a giant's cleaver, a living thing wantonly mutilated, with its shame and its nakedness exposed to every gaze. A staircase, bereft of its banister and brutally hacked, reeled into nothingness; on the second landing a delicate light filament hung by a thread of flex against the cracked panelling; downstairs the front arched windows, empty of glass, were an elegant arcade of carved stone giving a view of faded wallpaper with lighter patches where pictures and mirrors had once hung. From the remaining ceilings, naked wires sprouted like the bristles of a brush. Propped against a tree at the front of the house was a motley collection of fireplaces, mantelshelves, and sections of carved panelling, obviously selected for preservation. On top of what remained of the rear wall, a figure silhouetted against the sky was picking in a desultory way at the loose bricks. They tumbled one by one into the rubble of the interior of the house, sending up small spurts of dust.

In front of the building another workman, naked to the waist and burnt bronze, was operating a tractor mounted with a crane from which hung an immense iron ball and chain. As Miss Beale watched, hands taut on the steering-wheel as if bracing herself against an instinctive recoil of protest, the ball swung forward and crashed against all that remained of the front wall. For a moment there was nothing but the reverberation of hideous noise. Then the wall buckled gently and collapsed inwards with a roar of cascading bricks and mortar, sending up a monstrous cloud of yellow dust through which the lonely figure on the skyline could be seen dimly like some supervising demon.

Miss Beale paused for a moment, then gently let in the clutch and steered the car to the right to where the low, functional, clean-looking lines of the new temporary school could be glimpsed between the trees. Here was normality, sanity, a world she recognized and knew. This emotion, suspiciously like regret, at witnessing the violent destruction of Nightingale House was really too ridiculous. She fought against it resolutely. It was a horrible house; an evil house. It should have been pulled down fifty years ago. And it had never been in the least suitable as a nurse training school.

THE BLACK TOWER

CONTENTS

AUTHOR'S NOTE

Lovers of Dorset will, I hope, forgive me for the liberties I have taken with the topography of their beautiful county and in particular for my temerity in erecting my twin follies of Toynton Grange and the black tower on the Purbeck coast. They will learn with relief that, although the scenery is borrowed, the characters are completely my own and bear no resemblance to any person living or dead.

ONE

Sentence of Life

It was to be the consultant physician's last visit and Dalgliesh suspected that neither of them regretted it, arrogance and patronage on one side and weakness, gratitude and dependence on the other being no foundation for a satisfactory adult relationship however transitory. He came into Dalgliesh's small hospital room preceded by Sister, attended by his acolytes, already dressed for the fashionable wedding which he was to grace as a guest later that morning. He could have been the bridegroom except that he sported a red rose instead of the customary carnation. Both he and the flower looked as if they had been brought and burnished to a peak of artificial perfection, gift-wrapped in invisible foil, and immune to the chance winds, frosts and ungentle fingers which could mar more vulnerable perfections. As a final touch, he and the flower had both been lightly sprayed with an expensive scent, presumably an aftershave lotion. Dalgliesh could detect it above the hospital smell of cabbage and ether to which his nose had become so inured during the past weeks that it now hardly registered on the senses. The attendant medical students grouped themselves round the bed. With their long hair and short white coats they looked like a gaggle of slightly disreputable bridesmaids.

Dalgliesh was stripped by Sister's skilled impersonal hands for yet another examination. The stethoscope moved, a cold disc, over his chest and back. This last examination was a formality but the physician was, as always, thorough; nothing he did was perfunctory. If, on this occasion, his original diagnosis had been wrong his self-esteem was too secure for him to feel the need for more than a token excuse. He straightened up and said:

'We've had the most recent path. report and I think we can be certain now that we've got it right. The cytology was always obscure, of course, and the diagnosis was complicated by the pneumonia. But it isn't acute leukaemia, it isn't any type of leukaemia. What you're recovering from – happily – is an atypical mononucleosis. I congratulate you, Commander. You had us worried.'

'I had you interested; you had me worried. When can I leave here?'

The great man laughed and smiled at his retinue, inviting them to share his indulgence at yet one more example of the ingratitude of convalescence. Dalgliesh said quickly:

'I expect you'll be wanting the bed.'

'We always want more beds than we can get. But there's no great hurry. You've a long way to go yet. Still, we'll see. We'll see.'

When they had left him he lay flat on his back and let his eyes range round the two cubic feet of anaesthetized space, as if seeing the room for the first time. The wash basin with its elbow-operated taps; the neat functional bedside table with its covered water jug; the two vinyl-covered visitors' chairs; the earphones curled above his head; the window curtains with their offensive flowered pattern, the lowest denominator of taste. They were the last objects he had expected to see in life. It had seemed a meagre, impersonal place in which to die. Like a hotel room, it was designed for transients. Whether its occupants left on their own feet or sheeted on a mortuary trolley, they left nothing behind them, not even the memory of their fear, suffering and hope.

The sentence of death had been communicated, as he suspected such sentences usually were, by grave looks, a certain false heartiness, whispered consultations, a superfluity of clinical tests, and, until he had insisted, a reluctance to pronounce a diagnosis or prognosis. The sentence of life, pronounced with less sophistry when the worst days of his illness were over, had certainly produced a greater outrage. It was, he had thought, uncommonly inconsiderate if not negligent of his doctors to reconcile him so thoroughly to death and then change their minds. It was embarrassing now to recall with what little regret he had let slip his pleasures and preoccupations, the imminence of loss revealing them for what they were, at best only a solace, at worst a trivial squandering of time and energy. Now he had to lay hold of them again and believe that they were important, at least to himself. He doubted whether he would ever again believe them important to other people. No doubt, with returning strength, all that would look after itself. The physical life would re-assert itself given time. He would reconcile himself to living since there was no alternative and, this perverse fit of resentment and accidie conveniently put down to weakness, would come to believe that he had had a lucky escape. His colleagues, relieved of embarrassment, would congratulate him. Now that death had replaced sex as the great unmentionable it had acquired its own pudency; to die when you had not yet become a nuisance and before your friends could reasonably raise the ritual chant of 'happy release' was in the worst of taste.

But, at present, he wasn't sure that he could reconcile himself to his job. Resigned as he had become to the role of spectator – and soon not even to be that – he felt ill-equipped to return to the noisy playground of the world and, if it had to be, was minded to find for himself a less violent corner of it. It wasn't something he had thought about deeply during his periods of consciousness; there hadn't been time. It was more a conviction than a decision. The time had come to change direction. Judges' Rules, rigor mortis, interrogation, the contemplation of decomposing flesh and smashed bone, the whole body business of manhunting, he was finished with it. There were other things to do with his time. He wasn't yet sure which things but he would find them. He had over two weeks of convalescence ahead, time to formulate a decision, rationalize it, justify it to himself and, more difficult, find the words with which he would attempt to justify it to the Commissioner. It was a bad time to leave the Yard. They would see it as desertion. But then, it would always be a bad time.

He wasn't sure whether this disenchantment with his job was caused solely by his illness, the salutary reminder of inevitable death, or whether it was the symptom of a more fundamental malaise, that latitude in middle-life of alternate doldrums and uncertain winds when one realizes that hopes deferred are no longer realizable, that ports not visited will now never be seen, that this journey and others before it may have been a mistake, that one has no longer even confidence in charts and compass. More than his job now seemed to him trivial and unsatisfactory. Lying sleepless as so many patients must have done before him in that bleak impersonal room, watching the headlamps of passing cars sweep across the ceiling, listening to the secretive and muted noises of the hospital's nocturnal life, he took the dispiriting inventory of his life. His grief for his dead wife, so genuine, so heart-breaking at the time – how conveniently personal tragedy had excused him from further emotional involvement. His love affairs, like the one which at present spasmodically occupied a little of his time and somewhat more of his energy, had been detached, civilized, agreeable, undemanding. It was understood that his time was never completely his own but that his heart most certainly was. The women were liberated. They had interesting jobs, agreeable flats, they were adept at settling for what they could get. Certainly they were liberated from the messy, clogging, disruptive emotions which embroiled other female lives. What, he wondered, had those carefully spaced encounters, both participants groomed for pleasure like a couple of sleek cats, to do with love, with untidy bedrooms, unwashed dishes, babies' nappies, the warm, close, claustrophobic life of marriage and commitment. His bereavement, his job, his poetry, all had been used to justify self-sufficiency. His women had been more amenable to the claims of his poetry than of his dead wife. They had small regard for sentiment, but an exaggerated respect for art. And the worst of it – or perhaps the best – was that he couldn't now change even if he wanted and that none of it mattered. It was absolutely of no importance. In the last fifteen years he hadn't deliberately hurt a single human being. It struck him now that nothing more damning could be said about anyone.

Well, if none of that could be changed, his job could. But first there was one personal commitment to fulfil, one from which perversely he had been relieved that death would so conveniently excuse him. It wasn't going to excuse him now. Propping himself on his elbow he reached out and took Father Baddeley's letter from his locker drawer and read it carefully for the first time. The old man must be nearly eighty now; he hadn't been young when, thirty years ago, he had first come to the Norfolk village as curate to Dalgliesh's father, timid, ineffective, maddeningly inefficient, muddling in everything but the essentials, but never less than his uncompromising self. This was only the third letter which Dalgliesh had received from him. It was dated 11th September and read:

My dear Adam,

I know that you must be very busy but I would very much welcome a visit from you as there is a matter on which I would be glad of your professional advice. It isn't really urgent, except that my heart seems to be wearing out before the rest of me so that I ought not to rest too confidently on the thought of tomorrow. I am here every day, but perhaps a weekend would suit you best. I ought to tell you, so that you will know what to expect, that I am Chaplain to Toynton Grange, a private home for the young disabled, and that I live here in Hope Cottage on the estate through the kindness of the Warden, Wilfred Anstey. Usually I eat my midday and evening meal at the Grange but this may not be agreeable to you and it would, of course, lessen our time together. So I shall take the opportunity of my next visit to Wareham to lay in a store of provisions. I have a small spare room into which I can move so that there will be a room for you here.

Could you send me a card to let me know when you will arrive? I have no car but if you come by train William Deakin, who has a car hire service about five minutes from the station (the station staff will direct you), is very reliable and not expensive. The buses from Wareham are infrequent and don't come beyond Toynton Village. There is then a mile and a half to walk which is quite pleasant if the weather is good but which you may wish to avoid at the end of a long journey. If not, I have drawn a map on the back of this letter.

The map could be guaranteed to confuse anyone accustomed to depend on the orthodox publications of the National Survey rather than on early seventeenth-century charts. The wavy lines presumably represented the sea. Dalgliesh felt the omission of a spouting whale. The Toynton bus station was clearly marked, but the tremulous line thereafter meandered uncertainly past a diversity of fields, gates, pubs and copses of triangular, serrated firs, sometimes retreating upon itself as Father Baddeley realized that metaphorically he had lost his way. One tiny phallic symbol on the coast, and seemingly included as a landmark, since it was nowhere near the marked path, bore the legend 'the black tower'.

The map affected Dalgliesh much as a child's first drawing might affect an indulgent father. He wondered to what depth of weakness and apathy he must have sunk to reject its appeal. He fumbled in the drawer for a postcard and wrote briefly that he would arrive by car early in the afternoon of Monday, 1st October. That should give him plenty of time to get out of hospital and return to his Queenhythe flat for the first few days of convalescence. He signed the card with his initials only, stamped it for first-class delivery and propped it against his water jug so that he shouldn't forget to ask one of the nurses to post it.

There was one other small obligation and one he felt less competent to handle. But it could wait. He must see or write to Cordelia Gray and thank her for her flowers. He didn't know how she discovered that he was ill except perhaps through police friends. Running Bernie Pryde's Detective Agency – if it hadn't by now collapsed, as it should have done by all the laws of justice and economics – probably meant that she was in touch with one or two policemen. He believed, too, that there had been a casual mention of his inconvenient illness in the London evening papers when they had commented on recent losses in the higher echelons of the Yard.

It had been a small, carefully arranged, personally picked bouquet, as individual as Cordelia herself, a charming contrast to his other offerings of hothouse roses, over-large chrysanthemums shaggy as dust mops, forced spring flowers and artificial-looking gladioli, pink plastic flowers smelling of anaesthetic rigid on their fibrous stems. She must have been recently in a country garden; he wondered where. He wondered too, illogically, whether she was getting enough to eat, but immediately put this ridiculous thought from him. There had, he remembered clearly, been silver discs of honesty, three sprigs of winter heather, four rosebuds, not the starved tight buds of winter but furls of orange and yellow, gentle as the first buds of summer, delicate sprigs of outdoor chrysanthemums, orange-red berries, one bright dahlia like a jewel in the centre, the whole bouquet surrounded by the grey furry leaves he remembered from his childhood as rabbits' ears. It had been a touching, very young gesture one knew that an older or more sophisticated woman would never have made. It had arrived with only a brief note to say that she had heard of his illness and had sent the flowers to wish him well again. He must see or write to her and thank her personally. The telephone call which one of the nurses had made on his behalf to the Agency was not enough.

But that, and other more fundamental decisions, could wait. First he must see Father Baddeley. The obligation was not merely pious or even filial. He discovered that, despite certain foreseen difficulties and embarrassments, he was looking forward to seeing the old priest again. He had no intention of letting Father Baddeley, however unwittingly, entice him back to his job. If this were really police work, which he doubted, then the Dorset Constabulary could take it over. And, if this pleasant early autumn sunshine continued unbroken, Dorset would be as agreeable a place as any in which to convalesce.

But the stark oblong of white, propped against his water jug, was oddly intrusive. He felt his eyes constantly drawn towards it as if it were a potent symbol, a written sentence of life. He was glad when the staff nurse came in to say that she was now going off duty, and took it away to post.

TWO

Death of a Priest

I

Eleven days later, still weak and with his hospital pallor but euphoric with the deceptive well-being of convalescence, Dalgliesh left his flat high above the Thames at Queenhythe just before the first light and drove south-west out of London. He had finally and reluctantly parted with his ancient Cooper Bristol two months before the onset of his illness and was now driving a Jensen Healey. He was glad that the car had been run in and that he was already almost reconciled to the change. To embark symbolically on a new life with a totally new car would have been irritatingly banal. He put his one case and a few picnic essentials including a corkscrew in the boot and, in the pocket, a copy of Hardy's poems, *The Return of the Native* and Newman and Pevsner's guide to the buildings of Dorset. This was to be a convalescent's holiday: familiar books; a brief visit to an old friend to provide an object for the journey; a route left to each day's whim and including country both familiar and new; even the salutary irritant of a personal problem to justify solitude and self-indulgent idleness. He was disconcerted when, taking his final look round the flat, he found his hand reaching for his scene-of-crime kit. He couldn't remember when last he had travelled without it, even on holiday. But now to leave it behind was the first confirmation of a decision which he would dutifully ponder from time to time during the next fortnight but which he knew in his heart was already made.

He reached Winchester in time for late breakfast at a hotel in the shadow of the Cathedral, then spent the next two hours rediscovering the city before finally driving into Dorset via Wimborne Minster. Now he sensed in himself a reluctance to reach journey's end. He meandered gently, almost aimlessly, north-west to Blandford Forum, bought there a bottle of wine, buttered rolls, cheese and fruit for his lunch and a couple of bottles of Amontillado for Father Baddeley, then wandered south-east through the Winterbourne villages through Wareham to Corfe Castle.

The magnificent stones, symbols of courage, cruelty and betrayal, stood sentinel at the one cleft of the ridge of the Purbeck Hills as they had for a thousand years. As he ate his solitary picnic, Dalgliesh found his eyes constantly drawn to those stark embattled slabs of mutilated ashlar silhouetted high against the gentle sky. As though reluctant to drive under their shadow and unwilling to end the solitude of this peaceful undemanding day he spent some time searching unsuccessfully for marsh gentians in the swampy scrubland before setting off on the last five miles of his journey.

Toynton village; a thread of terraced cottages, their undulating grey stone roofs glittering in the afternoon sun; a not too picturesque pub at the village end; the glimpse of an uninteresting church tower. Now the road, bordered with a low stone wall, rose gently between sparse plantations of fir and he began to recognize the landmarks on Father Baddeley's map. Soon the road would branch, one narrow route turning westward to skirt the headland, the other leading through a barrier gate to Toynton Grange and the sea. And here, predictably, it was, a heavy iron gate set into a wall of flat, uncemented stones. The wall was up to three feet thick, the stones intricately and skilfully fitted together, bound with lichen and moss and crowned with waving grasses, and it formed a barrier as permanent as the headland from which it seemed to have grown. On each side of the gate was a notice painted on board. The one on the left read:

OF YOUR CHARITY PLEASE RESPECT OUR PRIVACY

The one on the right was more didactic, the lettering faded but more professional.

KEEP OUT
THIS LAND IS STRICTLY PRIVATE
DANGEROUS CLIFFS NO ACCESS TO BEACH
CARS AND CARAVANS PARKED HERE WILL BE MOVED

Under the notice was fixed a large postbox.

Dalgliesh thought that any motorist unmoved by this nicely judged mixture of appeal, warning and threats would hesitate before risking his car springs. The track deteriorated sharply beyond the gate and the contrast between the comparative smoothness of the approach road and the boulder-edged and stony way ahead was an almost symbolic deterrent. The gate, too, although unlocked, had a heavy latch of intricate design, the manipulation of which gave an intruder ample time in which to repent of his rashness. In his still weakened state, Dalgliesh swung back the gate with some difficulty. When he had driven through and finally closed it behind him it was with a sense of having committed himself to an enterprise as yet imperfectly understood and probably unwise. The problem would probably be embarrassingly unrelated to any of his skills, something that only an unworldly old man – and he perhaps getting senile – could have imagined that a police officer could solve. But at least he had an immediate objective. He was moving, even if reluctantly, back into a world in which human beings had problems, worked, loved, hated, schemed for happiness, and since the job he had determined to relinquish would go on despite his defection, killed and were killed.

Before he turned again to the car his eye was caught by a small clump of unknown flowers. The pale pinkish white heads rose from a mossy pad on top of the wall and trembled delicately in the light breeze. Dalgliesh walked over and stood stock still, regarding in silence their unpretentious beauty. He smelt for the first time the clean half-illusory salt tang of the sea. The air moved warm and gentle against his skin. He was suddenly suffused with happiness and, as always in these rare transitory moments, intrigued by the purely physical nature of his joy. It moved along his veins, a gentle effervescence. Even to analyse its nature was to lose hold of it. But he recognized it for what it was, the first clear intimation since his illness that life could be good.

The car bumped gently over the rising track. When some two hundred yards further on he came to the summit of the rise he expected to see the English Channel spread blue and wrinkled before him to the far horizon and experienced all the remembered disappointment of childhood holidays when after so many false hopes, the eagerly awaited sea still wasn't in sight. Before him was a shallow rock-strewn valley, criss-crossed with rough paths, and to his right what was obviously Toynton Grange.

It was a powerfully built square stone house dating, he guessed, from the first half of the eighteenth century. But the owner had been unlucky in his architect. The house was an aberration, unworthy of the name of Georgian. It faced inland, north-east he estimated, thus offending against some personal and obscure canon of architectural taste which, to Dalgliesh, decreed that a house on the coast should face the sea. There were two rows of windows above the porch, the main ones with gigantic keystones, the row above unadorned and mean in size as if there had been difficulty in fitting them beneath the most remarkable feature of the house, a huge Ionic pediment topped by a statue, a clumsy and, at this distance, unidentifiable lump of stone. In the centre was one round window, a sinister cyclops eye glinting in the sun. The pediment debased the insignificant porch and gave a lowering and cumbersome appearance to the whole façade. Dalgliesh thought that the design would have been more successful if the façade had been balanced by extended bays, but either inspiration or money had run out and the house looked curiously unfinished. There was no sign of life behind the intimidating frontage. Perhaps the inmates – if that was the right word for them – lived at the back. And it was only just three-thirty, the dead part of the day as he remembered from hospital. Probably they were all resting.

He could see three cottages, a pair about a hundred yards from the Grange and a third standing alone higher on the foreland. He thought there was a fourth roof just visible to seaward, but couldn't be sure. It might be only an excrescence of rock. Not knowing which was Hope Cottage it seemed sensible to make first for the nearer pair. He had briefly turned off his car engine while deciding what next to do and now, for the first time, he heard the sea, that gentle continuous rhythmic grunt which is one of the most nostalgic and evocative of sounds. There was still no sign that his approach was observed; the headland was silent, birdless. He sensed something strange and almost sinister in its emptiness and loneliness which even the mellow afternoon sunlight couldn't dispel.

His arrival at the cottages produced no face at the window, no cassock-clad figure framed in the front porch. They were a pair of old, limestone single-storeyed buildings, whose heavy stone roofs, typical of Dorset, were patterned with bright cushions of emerald moss. Hope Cottage was on the right, Faith Cottage on the left, the names comparatively recently painted. The third more distant cottage was presumably Charity, but he doubted whether Father Baddeley had had any hand in this eponymous naming. He didn't need to read the name on the gate to know which cottage housed Father Baddeley. It was impossible to associate his remembered almost total uninterest in his surroundings with those chintzy curtains, that hanging basket of trailing ivy and fuchsia over the door of Faith Cottage or the two brightly painted yellow tubs still garish with summer flowers which had been artfully placed one each side of the porch. Two mushrooms, looking mass-produced in concrete, stood each side of the gate, seeming so cosily suburban that Dalgliesh was surprised that they weren't crowned with squatting gnomes. Hope Cottage, in contrast, was starkly austere. There was a solid oak bench in front of the window serving as a seat in the sun, and a conglomeration of sticks and an old umbrella littered the front porch. The curtains, apparently of some heavy material in a dull red, were drawn across the windows.

No one answered to his knock. He had expected no one. Both cottages were obviously empty. There was a simple latch on the door and no lock. After a second's pause he lifted it and stepped into the gloom inside to be met with a smell, warm, bookish, a little musty, which immediately took him back thirty years. He drew back the curtains and light streamed into the cottage. And now his eyes recognized familiar objects: the round single-pedestal rosewood table, dull with dust, set in the middle of the room; the roll-top desk against one wall; the high-backed and winged armchair, so old now that the stuffing was pushing through the frayed cover and the dented seat was worn down to the wood. Surely it couldn't be the same chair? This stab of memory must be a nostalgic delusion. But there was another object, equally familiar, equally old. Behind the door hung Father Baddeley's black cloak with, above it, the battered and limp beret.

It was the sight of the cloak that first alerted Dalgliesh to the possibility that something was wrong. It was odd that his host wasn't here to greet him, but he could think of a number of explanations. His postcard might have gone astray, there might have been an urgent call to the Grange, Father Baddeley might have gone into Wareham to shop and missed the return bus. It was even possible that he had completely forgotten the expected arrival of his guest. But if he were out, why wasn't he wearing his cloak? It was impossible to think of him in summer or winter wearing any other garment.

It was then that Dalgliesh noticed what his eye must have already seen but disregarded, the little stack of service sheets on top of the bureau printed with a black cross. He took the top one over to the window as if hoping that a clearer light would show him mistaken. But there was, of course, no mistake. He read:

Michael Francis Baddeley, Priest
Born 29th October 1896
Died 21st September 1974 R.I.P.
Buried at St Michael & All Angels,
Toynton, Dorset
26th September 1974

He had been dead eleven days and buried five. But he would have known that Father Baddeley had died recently. How else could one account for that sense of his personality still lingering in the cottage, the feeling that he was so close that one strong call could bring his hand to the latch? Looking at the familiar faded cloak with its heavy clasp – had the old man really not changed it in thirty years? – he felt a pang of regret, of grief even, which surprised him by its intensity. An old man was dead. It must have been a natural death; they had buried him quickly enough. His death and burial had been unpublicized. But there had been something on his mind and he had died without confiding it. It was suddenly very important that he should be reassured that Father Baddeley had received his postcard, that he hadn't died believing that his call for help had gone unregarded.

The obvious place to look was in the early Victorian bureau which had belonged to Father Baddeley's mother. Father Baddeley, he remembered, had kept this locked. He had been the least secretive of men, but any priest had to have at least one drawer or desk private from the prying eyes of cleaning women or over-curious parishioners. Dalgliesh could remember Father Baddeley fumbling in the deep pockets of his cloak for the small antique key, secured by string to an old-fashioned clothes peg for easier handling and identification, which opened the lock. It was probably in one of the cloak pockets still.

He dug his hand into both pockets with a guilty feeling of raiding the dead. The key wasn't there. He went over to the bureau and tried the lid. It opened easily. Bending down he examined the lock, then fetched his torch from the car and looked again. The signs were unmistakable: the lock had been forced. It had been quite a neat job and one requiring little strength. The lock was decorative but unsubstantial, intended as a defence against the idly curious but not against determined assault. A chisel or knife, probably the blade of a penknife, had been forced between the desk and the lid and used to pry the lock apart. It had done surprisingly little damage, but the scratch marks and the broken lock itself told their story.

But not who had been responsible. It could have been Father Baddeley himself. If he had lost the key there would have been no chance of replacing it, and how in this remote spot would he have found a locksmith? A physical assault on the desk lid was an unlikely expedient for the man, Dalgliesh remembered; but it wasn't impossible. Or it might have been done after Father Baddeley's death. If the key couldn't be found, someone at Toynton Grange would have had to break open the lock. There might have been documents or papers which they needed; a health insurance card; names of friends to be notified; a will. He shook himself free from conjecture, irritated to find that he had actually considered putting on his gloves before looking further, and made a rapid examination of the contents of the desk drawers.

There was nothing of interest there. Father Baddeley's concern with the world had apparently been minimal. But one thing immediately recognizable caught his eye. It was a neatly stacked row of quarto-size child's exercise books bound in pale green.

These, he knew, contained Father Baddeley's diary. So the same books were still being sold, the ubiquitous pale-green exercise books, the back cover printed with arithmetical tables, as evocative of primary school as an ink-stained ruler or india rubber. Father Baddeley had always used these books for his diary, one book for each quarter of the year. Now, with the old black cloak hanging limply on the door, its musty ecclesiastical smell in his nose, Dalgliesh recalled the conversation as clearly as if he were still that ten-year-old boy and Father Baddeley, middle-aged then but already seeming ageless, sitting at his desk.

'It's just an ordinary diary then, Father? It isn't about your spiritual life?'

'This is the spiritual life; the ordinary things one does from hour to hour.'

Adam had asked with the egotism of the young:

'Only what you do? Aren't I in it?'

'No. Just what I do. Do you remember what time the Mothers' Union met this afternoon? It was your mother's drawing-room this week. The time was different, I think.'

'It was two forty-five p.m. instead of three p.m., Father. The Archdeacon wanted to get away early. But do you have to be accurate?'

Father Baddeley had seemed to ponder this question, briefly but seriously as if it were new to him and unexpectedly interesting.

'Oh, yes, I think so. I think so. Otherwise it would lose its point.'

The young Dalgliesh, to whom the point was already lost beyond ken, had wandered away to pursue his own more interesting and immediate concerns. The spiritual life. It was a phrase he had often heard on the lips of his father's more ultra-mundane parishioners although never on the Canon's own. He had occasionally tried to visualize this mysterious other existence. Was it lived at the same time as the ordinary regulated life of getting up, meal times, school, holidays; or was it an existence on some other plane to which he and the uninitiated had no access but into which Father Baddeley could retreat at will? Either way it had surely little to do with this careful recording of daily trivia.

He picked up the last book and looked through it. Father

Baddeley's system had not been changed. It was all here, two days to the page, neatly ruled off. The times at which he had daily said morning prayer and evensong; where he had walked and how long it had taken; the monthly trip by bus into Dorchester; the weekly trip to Wareham; his hours spent helping at Toynton Grange; odd treats baldly recorded; the methodical account of how he had disposed of every hour of his working day year after unremarkable year, documented with the meticulousness of a book-keeper. 'But this is the spiritual life; the ordinary things that one does from day to day.' Surely it couldn't be as simple as that?

But where was the current diary, the book for the third quarter of 1974? It had been Father Baddeley's habit to keep old copies of his diary covering the last three years. There should have been fifteen books here; there were only fourteen. The diary stopped at the end of June 1974. Dalgliesh found himself searching almost feverishly through the desk drawers. The diary wasn't there. But he did find something. Pushed beneath three receipted bills for coal, paraffin and electricity was a sheet of cheap rather thin paper with Toynton Grange printed inexpertly and lopsidedly at the top. Underneath someone had typed:

'Why don't you get out of the cottage you silly old hypocrite and let someone have it who would really be some use here? Don't think we don't know what you and Grace Willison get up to when you're supposed to be hearing her confession. Don't you wish you could really do it? And what about that choir boy? Don't think we don't know.'

Dalgliesh's first reaction was to be more irritated by the note's silliness than angered by its malice. It was a childish piece of gratuitous spite but without even the dubious merit of verisimilitude. Poor old seventy-seven-year-old Father Baddeley, accused simultaneously of fornication, sodomy and impotence! Could any reasonable man have taken this puerile nonsense seriously enough even to be hurt by it? Dalgliesh had seen plenty of poison pen letters in his professional life. This was a comparatively mild effort; he could almost suppose that the writer's heart hadn't been in it. 'Don't you wish you could really do it?' Most poison pen writers could find a more graphic description of that implied activity. And the belated reference to the choir boy, no name, no date. That hadn't been dredged from any real knowledge. Could Father Baddeley really have been concerned enough to have sent for a professional detective and one he hadn't seen for nearly thirty years just to advise on or investigate this petty nastiness? Perhaps. This might not be the only letter. If the trouble were endemic at Toynton Grange, then it was more serious. A poison pen at work in a closed community could cause real trouble and distress, occasionally he or she could literally be a killer. If Father Baddeley suspected that others had received similar letters he might well have looked around for professional help. Or, and this was more interesting, had someone intended Dalgliesh to believe precisely that? Had the note been deliberately planted for him to find? It was odd, surely, that no one had discovered and destroyed it after Father Baddeley's death. Someone from Toynton Grange must have looked through his papers. This was hardly a note one would leave for others to read.

He folded it away in his wallet and began to wander around the cottage. Father Baddeley's bedroom was much as he had expected. A mean window with a dingy cretonne curtain, a single bed still made-up with sheets and blankets but with the counterpane pulled taut over the single lumpy pillow; books lining two walls; a small bedside table with a shoddy lamp; a Bible; a cumbersome and gaudily decorated china ashtray bearing an advertisement for beer. Father Baddeley's pipe still rested in its bowl and beside it Dalgliesh saw a half-used booklet of cardboard matches, the kind given away in restaurants and bars. This bore an advertisement for Ye Olde Tudor Barn near Wareham. One single used match was in the ashtray; it had been shredded down to the burnt-out tip. Dalgliesh smiled. So this small personal habit, too, had survived over thirty years. He could recall Father Baddeley's small squirrel-like fingers delicately shredding the sliver of thin cardboard as if attempting to beat some previous personal record. Dalgliesh picked up the match and smiled; six segments. Father Baddeley had excelled himself.

He wandered into the kitchen. It was small, ill-equipped, neat but not very clean. The small gas stove of old-fashioned design looked as if it would soon qualify for a folk museum. The sink under the window was of stone fitted on one side with a scarred and discoloured wooden draining board smelling of stale fat and sour soap. The faded cretonne curtains faintly patterned with overblown roses and daffodils unseasonably intertwined were pulled back to show an inland view of the far Purbeck hills. Clouds tenuous as smoke puffs were drifting and dissolving in the limitless blue sky and the sheep lay like white slugs on their distant pasture.

He explored the pantry. Here at least was evidence that he was expected. Father Baddeley had indeed bought extra food and the tins were a dispiriting reminder of what for him had constituted an adequate diet. Pathetically, he had obviously provided for two, one of whom he confidently expected to have a larger appetite. There was one large tin and one small of many of the staple provisions: baked beans, tuna fish, Irish stew, spaghetti, rice pudding.

Dalgliesh went back to the sitting-room. He was aware of weariness, that the journey had tired him more than he had expected. He saw by the heavy oak clock over the fireplace, still ticking solidly on, that it was still not four o'clock, but his body protested that this had already been a long hard day. He craved tea. There had been a caddy of tea in the pantry but no milk. He wondered whether the gas was still on.

It was then that he heard the footfall at the door, the clank of the latch. There was a woman's figure framed against the afternoon light. He heard a gravelly deep but very feminine voice with a trace, no more, of an Irish accent.

'For God's sake! A human being and a male at that. What are you doing here?'

She came into the room leaving the door open behind her and he saw her clearly. She was about thirty-five, he guessed, sturdy, long-legged, her mane of yellow hair, visibly darker at the roots, worn in a long sweep to her shoulders. Her eyes were full-lidded and narrow in the square face, her mouth wide. She was wearing brown ill-fitting slacks with a strap under the foot, dirty, grass-stained white plimsoles and a sleeveless white cotton top, low-necked, which showed a brown and mottled triangle of sunburn. She wore no brassière and the full, heavy breasts swung loose under the thin cotton. Three wooden bangles clanked on her left forearm. The total impression was of a raffish but not unattractive sexuality, so strong that, although she wore no scent, she brought into the room her own female and individual smell.

He said: 'My name's Adam Dalgliesh. I came here intending to visit Father Baddeley. It seems that it won't now be possible.'

'Well, that's one way of putting it. You're exactly eleven days late. Eleven days too late to see him and five days too late to bury him. Who are you, a chum? We didn't know that he had any. But then, there were quite a number of things we didn't know about our Reverend Michael. He was a secretive little man. He certainly kept you hidden.'

'We hadn't met except briefly since I was a boy and I only wrote to tell him I was coming the day before he died.'

'Adam. I like that. They call a lot of kids that nowadays. It's getting trendy again. But you must have found it a bit of a drag when you were at school. Still, it suits you. I can't think why. You aren't exactly of the earth, earthy are you? I know about you now. You've come to collect the books.'

'Have I?'

'The ones Michael left you in his will. To Adam Dalgliesh, only son of the late Canon Alexander Dalgliesh, all my books to keep or dispose of as he sees fit. I remember it exactly because I thought the names were so unusual. You haven't lost much time, have you? I'm surprised that the solicitors have even got round to writing to you. Bob Loder isn't usually that efficient. But I shouldn't get too excited if I were you. They never looked particularly valuable to me. A lot of dry old theological tomes. By the way, you weren't expecting to be left any of his money, were you? If so, I've got news for you.'

'I didn't know that Father Baddeley had any money.'

'Nor did we. That was another of his little secrets. He left £19,000. Not a great fortune, but useful. He left it all to Wilfred for the benefit of Toynton Grange, and it came just in time from all I hear. Grace Willison is the only other legatee. She got that old bureau. At least she will get it when Wilfred bothers to have it moved.'

She had settled down in the fireside chair, her hair thrown

back against the headrest, both legs splayed wide. Dalgliesh pulled out one of the wheel-backed chairs and sat facing her.

'Did you know Father Baddeley well?'

'We all know each other well here, that's half our trouble. Are you thinking of staying here?'

'In the district perhaps for a day or two. But it doesn't seem possible now to stay here. . .'

'I don't see why not if you want to. The place is empty, at least until Wilfred finds another victim – tenant, I should say. I shouldn't think that he'd object. Besides you'll have to sort out the books, won't you? Wilfred will want them out of the way before the next incumbent moves in.'

'Wilfred Anstey owns the cottage then?'

'He owns Toynton Grange and all the cottages except Julius Court's. He's further out on the headland, the only one with a sea view. Wilfred owns all the rest of the property and he owns us.'

She looked at him appraisingly.

'You haven't any useful skills, have you? I mean you're not a physiotherapist or a male nurse or doctor, or even an accountant? Not that you look like one. Anyway, if you are I'd advise you to keep away before Wilfred decides that you're too useful to let go.'

'I don't think that he'd find my particular skills of much use.'

'Then I should stay on if it suits you. But I'd better put you in the picture. You might then change your mind.'

Dalgliesh said:

'Start with yourself. You haven't told me who you are.'

'Good God, nor have I! Sorry. I'm Maggie Hewson. My husband is resident medical officer at the Grange. At least, he lives with me in a cottage provided by Wilfred and appropriately named Charity Cottage, but he spends most of his time at Toynton Grange. With only five patients left you'd wonder what he finds to amuse him. Or would you? What do you suppose he finds to amuse him, Adam Dalgliesh?'

'Did your husband attend Father Baddeley?'

'Call him Michael, we all did except Grace Willison. Yes, Eric looked after him when he was alive and signed the death certificate when he died. He couldn't have done that six months ago, but now that they've graciously restored him to the Medical

Register he can actually put his name to a piece of paper to say that you're properly and legally dead. God, what a bloody privilege.'

She laughed, and fumbling in the pockets of her slacks produced a packet of cigarettes and lit one. She handed the packet to Dalgliesh. He shook his head. She shrugged her shoulders and blew a puff of smoke towards him.

Dalgliesh asked:

'What did Father Baddeley die of?'

'His heart stopped beating. No, I'm not being facetious. He was old, his heart was tired and on 21st September it stopped. Acute myocardiac infarction complicated by mild diabetes, if you want the medical jargon.'

'Was he alone?'

'I imagine so. He died at night, at least he was last seen alive by Grace Willison at seven forty-five p.m. when he heard her confession. I suppose he died of boredom. No, I can see I shouldn't have said that. Bad taste, Maggie. She says he seemed as usual, a bit tired of course, but then he'd only been discharged from hospital that morning. I came in at nine o'clock the next day to see if he wanted anything from Wareham – I was taking the eleven o'clock bus; Wilfred doesn't allow private cars – and there he lay, dead.'

'In bed?'

'No, in that chair where you're sitting now, slumped back with his mouth open and his eyes closed. He was wearing his cassock and a purple ribbon thing round his neck. All quite seemly. But very, very dead.'

'So it was you who first found the body?'

'Unless Millicent from next door came pussy-footing in earlier, didn't like the look of him and tiptoed home again. She's Wilfred's widowed sister in case you're interested. Actually, it's rather odd that she didn't come in, knowing that he was ill and alone.'

'It must have been a shock for you.'

'Not really. I was a nurse before I married. I've seen more dead bodies than I can remember. And he was very old. It's the young ones – the kids particularly – who get you down. God, am I glad to be finished with all that messy business.'

'Are you? You don't work at Toynton Grange then?'

She got up and moved over to the fireplace before replying. She blew a cloud of smoke against the looking glass over the mantelpiece then moved her face close to the glass as if studying her reflection.

'No, not when I can avoid it. And by God, do I try to avoid it. You may as well know. I am the delinquent member of the community, the non-co-operator, the drop-out, the heretic. I sow not, neither do I reap. I am impervious to the charms of dear Wilfred. I close my ears to the cries of the afflicted. I do not bend the knee at the shrine.'

She turned towards him with a look half challenging, half speculative. Dalgliesh thought that the outburst had been less than spontaneous, the protest had been made before. It sounded like a ritual justification and he suspected that someone had helped her with the script. He said:

'Tell me about Wilfred Anstey.'

'Didn't Michael warn you? No, I suppose he wouldn't. Well, it's an odd story but I'll try to make it short. Wilfred's great-grandfather built Toynton Grange. His grandfather left it in trust jointly to Wilfred and his sister Millicent. Wilfred bought her out when he started the Home. Eight years ago Wilfred developed multiple sclerosis. It progressed very swiftly; within three months he was chairbound. Then he went on a pilgrimage to Lourdes and got himself cured. Apparently he made a bargain with God. You cure me and I'll devote Toynton Grange and all my money to serving the disabled. God obliged, and now Wilfred's busy fulfilling his part of the bargain. I suppose he's afraid to back out of the agreement in case the disease returns. I don't know that I blame him. I'd probably feel the same myself. We're all superstitious at heart, particularly about disease.'

'And is he tempted to back out?'

'Oh, I don't think so. This place gives him a sensation of power. Surrounded by grateful patients, regarded as a half-superstitious object of veneration by the women, Dot Moxon – the matron so-called – fussing round him like an old hen. Wilfred's happy enough.'

Dalgliesh asked:

'When exactly did the miracle happen?

'He claims, when they dipped him in the well. As he tells it, he experienced an initial shock of intense cold followed immediately by a tingling warmth which suffused his whole body, and a feeling of great happiness and peace. That's exactly what I get after my third whisky. If Wilfred can produce it in himself by bathing in ice-cold germ-laden water, then all I can say is, he's bloody lucky. When he got back to the hospice he stood on his legs for the first time in six months. Three weeks later he was skipping around like a young ram. He never bothered to return to St Saviour's Hospital in London where he was treated, so that they could record the miraculous cure on his medical record. It would have been rather a joke if he had.'

She paused as if about to say something further and then merely added:

'Touching, isn't it?'

'It's interesting. How does he find the money to fulfil his part of the bargain?'

'The patients pay according to means and some of them are sent here under contractual arrangements by local authorities. And then, of course, he's used his own capital. But things are getting pretty desperate, or so he claims. Father Baddeley's legacy came just in time. And, of course, Wilfred gets the staff on the cheap. He doesn't exactly pay Eric the rate for the job. Philby, the odd job man, is an ex-convict and probably otherwise unemployable; and the matron, Dot Moxon, wouldn't exactly find it easy to get another job after that cruelty investigation at her last hospital. She must be grateful to Wilfred for taking her on. But then, we're all terribly, terribly grateful to dear Wilfred.'

Dalgliesh said:

'I suppose I'd better go up to the Grange and introduce myself. You say there are only five patients left?'

'You're not supposed to refer to them as patients, although I don't know what else Wilfred thinks you can call them. Inmates sounds too much like a prison although, God knows, it's appropriate enough. But there are only five left. He's not admitting from the waiting list until he's made up his mind about the Home's future. The Ridgewell Trust's angling for it and Wilfred's considering handing the whole place over to them, lock, stock and gratis. Actually, there were six patients a fortnight or so ago, but that was before Victor Holroyd threw himself over Toynton Head and smashed himself on the rocks.'

'You mean he killed himself?'

'Well, he was in his wheelchair ten feet from the cliff-edge and either he slipped the brakes and let himself be carried over or Dennis Lerner, the male nurse with him, pushed him. As Dennis hasn't the guts to kill a chicken let alone a man, the general feeling is that Victor did it himself. But as that notion is distressing to dear Wilfred's feelings we're all busy pretending that it was an accident. I miss Victor, I liked him. He was about the only person here I could talk to. But the rest hated him. And now, of course, they've all got bad consciences wondering if they may have misjudged him. There's nothing like dying for putting people at a disadvantage. I mean, when a chap keeps on saying that life isn't worth living you take it that he's just stating the obvious. When he backs it up with action you begin to wonder if there wasn't more to him than you thought.'

Dalgliesh was spared the need to reply by the sound of a car on the headland. Maggie, whose ears were apparently as keen as his own, sprang from her chair and ran outside. A large black saloon was approaching the junction of the paths.

'Julius,' Maggie called back to him in brief explanation and began a boisterous semaphoring.

The car stopped and then turned towards Hope Cottage. Dalgliesh saw that it was a black Mercedes. As soon as it slowed down Maggie ran like an importunate schoolgirl beside it, pouring her explanation through the open window. The car stopped and Julius Court swung himself lightly out.

He was a tall, loose-limbed young man dressed in slacks and a green sweater patched army fashion on the shoulders and elbows. His light brown hair, cut short, was shaped to his head like a pale glinting helmet. It was an authoritative, confident face but with a trace of self-indulgence in the perceptible pouches under the wary eyes and the slight petulance of the small mouth set in a heavy chin. In middle age he would be heavy, even gross. But now he gave an immediate impression of slightly arrogant good looks, enhanced rather than spoilt by the white triangular scar like a colophon above his right eyebrow.

He held out his hand and said:

'Sorry you missed the funeral.'

He made it sound as if Dalgliesh had missed a train. Maggie wailed:

'But darling, you don't understand! He hasn't come for the funeral. Mr Dalgliesh didn't even know that the old man had snuffed out.'

Court looked at Dalgliesh with slightly more interest.

'Oh, I'm sorry. Perhaps you'd better come up to the Grange. Wilfred Anstey will be able to tell you more about Father Baddeley than I. I was at my London flat when the old man died so I can't even provide interesting death-bed revelations. Hop in, both of you. I've got some books in the back for Henry Carwardine from the London Library. I may as well deliver them now.'

Maggie Hewson seemed to feel that she had been remiss in not affecting a proper introduction; she said belatedly:

'Julius Court. Adam Dalgliesh. I don't suppose you've come across each other in London. Julius used to be a diplomat, or is it diplomatist?'

As they got into the car Court said easily:

'Neither is appropriate at the comparatively lowly level I reached in the service. And London is a large place. But don't worry, Maggie. Like the clever lady in the TV panel game, I think I can guess what Mr Dalgliesh does for a living.'

He held open the car door with elaborate courtesy. The Mercedes moved slowly towards Toynton Grange.

II

Georgie Allan looked up from the narrow bed in the sick bay. His mouth began to work grotesquely. The muscles of his throat stood out hard and taut. He tried to raise his head from the pillow.

'I'll be all right for the Lourdes pilgrimage, won't I? You don't think I'll be left behind?

The words came out in a hoarse, discordant wail. Helen

Rainer lifted up the edge of the mattress, tucked the sheet neatly back into place in the orthodox hospital-approved style and said briskly:

'Of course you won't be left behind. You'll be the most important patient on the pilgrimage. Now stop fretting, that's a good boy, and try to rest before your tea.'

She smiled at him, the impersonal, professionally reassuring smile of the trained nurse. Then lifted her eyebrow at Eric Hewson. Together they went over to the window. She said quietly:

'How long can we go on coping with him?'

Hewson replied:

'Another month or two. It would upset him terribly to have to leave now. Wilfred too. In a few months' time both of them will be readier to accept the inevitable. Besides, he's set his heart on this Lourdes trip. Next time we go I doubt whether he will be alive. He certainly won't be here.'

'But he's really a hospital case now. We aren't registered as a nursing home. We're only a home for the young chronic sick and disabled. Our contract is with the local authorities not the National Health Service. We don't pretend to offer a full medical nursing service. We aren't even supposed to. It's time Wilfred gave up or made up his mind what he's trying to do here.'

'I know.' He did know, they both did. This wasn't a new problem. Why, he wondered, had so much of their conversation become a boring repetition of the obvious, dominated by Helen's high didactic voice?

Together they looked down at the small paved patio, bordered by the two new single-storey wings which contained the bedrooms and dayrooms, where the little group of remaining patients had gathered for the last sit in the sun before tea. The four wheelchairs were carefully placed a little apart and faced away from the house. The two watchers could see only the back of the patients' heads. Unmoving they sat looking fixedly toward the headland. Grace Willison, her grey untidy hair ruffled by the light breeze; Jennie Pegram, her neck sunk into her shoulders, her aureole of yellow hair streaming over the back of her wheelchair as if bleaching in the sun; Ursula Hollis's small round poll on its thin neck, high and motionless as a decapitated head on a pole; Henry Carwardine's dark head on its twisted neck, slumped sideways like a broken puppet. But then, they were all puppets. Dr Hewson had a momentary and insane picture of himself rushing on to the patio and setting the four heads nodding and wagging, pulling invisible strings at the back of the necks so that the air was filled with their loud, discordant cries.

'What's the matter with them?' he asked suddenly. 'Something's wrong about this place.'

'More than usual?'

'Yes. Haven't you noticed?'

'Perhaps they're missing Michael. God knows why. He did little enough. If Wilfred's determined to carry on here he can find a better use for Hope Cottage now. As a matter of fact, I thought about suggesting that he let me live there. It would be easier for us.'

The thought appalled him. So that was what she had been planning. The familiar depression fell on him, physical as a lead weight. Two positive, discontented women, both wanting something that he couldn't give. He tried to keep the panic from his voice.

'It wouldn't do. You're needed here. And I couldn't come to you at Hope Cottage, not with Millicent next door.'

'She hears nothing once she's switched on the TV. We know that. And there's a back door if you do have to make quick getaway. It's better than nothing.'

'But Maggie would suspect.'

'She suspects now. And she's got to know some time.'

'We'll talk about it later. It's a bad time to worry Wilfred just now. We've all been on edge since Victor died.'

Victor's death. He wondered what perverse masochism had made him mention Victor. It reminded him of those early days as a medical student when he would uncover a suppurating wound with relief because the sight of blood, inflamed tissue and pus was so less frightening than the imagination of what lay beneath the smooth gauze. Well, he had got used to blood. He had got used to death. In time he might even get used to being a doctor.

They moved together into the small clinical room at the front of the building. He went to the basin and began methodically sluicing his hands and forearms as if his brief examination of young Georgie had been a messy surgical procedure requiring a thorough cleansing. Behind his back he could hear the clink of instruments. Helen was unnecessarily tidying the surgical cupboard yet once more. With a sinking heart he realized that they were going to have to talk. But not yet. Not yet. And he knew what she would say. He had heard it all before, the old insistent arguments spoken in that confident school prefect's voice. 'You're wasted here. You're a doctor, not a dispensing chemist. You've got to break free, free of Maggie and Wilfred. You can't put loyalty to Wilfred before your vocation.' His vocation! That was the word his mother had always used. It made him want to break into hysterical laughter.

He switched on the tap to full and the water came gushing out, swirling round the basin, filling his ears like the sound of the incoming tide. What had it been like for Victor, that hurtle into oblivion? Had the clumsy wheelchair, heavy with its own momentum, sailed into space like one of those ridiculous flying contraptions in a James Bond film, the little manikin secure among his gadgets, ready to pull the lever and sport wings? Or had it twisted and tumbled through the air, bouncing off the rock face, with Victor confined in canvas and metal, flailing impotent arms, adding his screams to the cry of the gulls? Had his heavy body broken free of the strap in mid-air, or had the canvas held until that final annihilating crash against the flat-iron rocks, the first sucking wave of the relentless unthinking sea? And what had been in his mind? Exaltation or despair, terror or a blessed nothingness? Had the clean air and the sea wiped it all away, the pain, the bitterness, the malice?

It was only after his death that the full extent of Victor's malice had been known, in the codicil to his will. He had taken trouble to let the other patients know that he had money, that he paid the full fee at Toynton Grange, modest though that was, and wasn't, as were all the others except Henry Carwardine, dependent upon the benevolence of a local authority. He had never told them the source of his wealth – he had, after all, been a schoolmaster and they were hardly well paid – and they still didn't know. He might have told Maggie of course. There were a number of things he might have told Maggie. But on this she had been unaccountably silent.

Eric Hewson didn't believe that Maggie had taken an interest in Victor simply because of the money. They had, after all, had something in common. They had both made no secret that they hated Toynton Grange, that they were there of necessity not of choice, that they despised their companions. Probably Maggie found Victor's rebarbative malice to her liking. They had certainly spent a great deal of time together. Wilfred had seemed almost to welcome it, almost as if he thought Maggie was at last finding her proper place at Toynton. She had taken her turn at wheeling Victor in his heavy chair to his favourite spot. He had found some kind of peace in sight of the sea. Maggie and he had spent hours together, out of sight of the house, high on the edge of the cliff. But it hadn't worried him. He knew, none better, that Maggie could never love a man who couldn't satisfy her physically. He welcomed her friendship. At least it gave her something to occupy her time, kept her quiet.

He couldn't remember exactly when she had begun to become excited about the money. Victor must have said something. Maggie had changed almost overnight. She had become animated, almost gay. There had been a kind of feverish and suppressed excitement about her. And then Victor had suddenly demanded that he be driven to London for an examination at St Saviour's Hospital and to consult his solicitor. It was then that Maggie had hinted to him about the will. He had caught something of her excitement. He wondered now what either of them had hoped for. Had she seen the money as a release merely from Toynton Grange, or also from him? Either way, surely, it would have brought salvation for them both. And the idea wasn't absurd. It was known that Victor had no relatives except a sister in New Zealand to whom he never wrote. No, he thought, reaching for the towel and beginning to dry his hands, it hadn't been an absurd dream; less absurd than the reality.

He thought of that drive back from London; the warm, enclosed world of the Mercedes; Julius silent, his hands resting lightly on the wheel; the road a silver reel punctuated with stars slipping endlessly under the bonnet; road signs leaping out of darkness to pattern the blue-black sky; small petrified animals, fur erect, briefly glorified in the headlamps; the road verges drained pale gold in their glare. Victor had sat with Maggie in the back, wrapped in his plaid cloak and smiling, always smiling. And the air had been heavy with secrets, shared and unshared.

Victor had indeed altered his will. He had added a codicil to the bequest which left the whole of his fortune to his sister, a final testimony of petty malice. To Grace Willison, a bar of toilet soap; to Henry Carwardine, a mouthwash; to Ursula Hollis, body deodorant; to Jennie Pegram, a toothpick.

Eric reflected that Maggie had taken it very well. Really very well indeed; if you could call that wild, ringing, uncontrolled laughter taking it well. He recalled her now, reeling about their small stone sitting-room, helpless with hysteria, throwing back her head and baying out her laughter so that it echoed harshly back from the walls, like a menagerie, and rang out over the headland so that he was afraid they would hear it as far as Toynton Grange.

Helen was standing by the window. She said, her voice sharp:

'There's a car outside Hope Cottage.'

He walked over to her. Together they looked out. Slowly their eyes met. She took his hand, and her voice was gentle, the voice he had heard when they had first made love.

'You've got nothing to worry about, darling. You know that, don't you? Nothing to worry about at all.'

III

Ursula Hollis closed her library book, shut her eyes against the afternoon sun and entered into her private daydream. To do so now in the brief fifteen minutes before teatime was an indulgence, and quick as always to feel guilty at so ill-disciplined a pleasure, she was at first afraid that the magic wouldn't work. Usually, she made herself wait until she was in bed at night, wait even until Grace Willison's rasping breath, heard through the unsubstantial partition, had gentled into sleep before she allowed herself to think of Steve and the flat in Bell Street. The ritual had become an effort of will. She would lie there hardly daring to breathe because the images, however clearly conjured up, were so sensitive, so easily dispelled. But now it was happening beautifully. She concentrated, seeing the amorphous shapes and the changing patterns of colour focus into a picture, clearly as a developing negative, tuning in her ears to the sounds of home.

She saw the brick wall of the nineteenth-century house opposite with the morning sun lighting its dull façade so that each brick was individually distinct, multi-coloured, a pattern of light. The pokey two-roomed flat above Mr Polanski's delicatessen, the street outside, the crowded heterogeneous life of that square mile of London between Edgware Road and Marylebone Station had absorbed and enchanted her. She was back there now, walking again with Steve through Church Street market on Saturday morning, the happiest day of the week. She saw the local women in their flowered overalls and carpet slippers, heavy wedding rings sunk into their bulbous toil-scarred fingers, their eyes bright in amorphous faces, as they sat gossiping beside their prams of second-hand clothes; the young people, joyfully garbed, squatting on the curbstone behind their stalls of bric-à-brac; the tourists cheerfully impulsive or cautious and discerning by turns, conferring over their dollars or displaying their bizarre treasures. The street smelt of fruit, flowers and spice, of sweating bodies, cheap wine and old books. She saw the black women with their jutting buttocks and high barbaric staccato chatter, heard their sudden deep-throated laughter, as they crowded round the stall of huge unripe bananas and mangoes as large as footballs. In her dreams she moved on, her fingers gently entwined with Steve's like a ghost passing unseen down familiar paths.

The eighteen months of her marriage had been a time of intense but precarious happiness, precarious because she could never feel that it was rooted in reality. It was like becoming another person. Before, she had taught herself contentment and had called it happiness. After, she realized that there was a world of experience, of sensation, of thought even, for which nothing in those first twenty years of life in the Middlesbrough suburb, or the two and a half years in the Y.W.C.A. hostel in London, had prepared her. Only one thing marred it, the fear which she could never quite suppress that it was all happening to the wrong person, that she was an imposture of joy.

She couldn't imagine what it was about her that had so capriciously caught Steve's fancy that first time when he had called at the inquiry desk in the Council offices to ask about his rates. Was it the one feature which she had always thought of as close to a deformity; the fact that she had one blue and one brown eye? Certainly it was an oddity which had intrigued and amused him, had given her, she realized, an added value in his eyes. He had changed her appearance, making her grow her hair shoulder length, bringing home for her long gaudy skirts in Indian cotton found in the street markets or the shops in the back streets of Edgware Road. Sometimes, catching a glimpse of herself in a shop window, so marvellously altered, she would wonder again which strange predilection had led him to choose her, what possibilities undetected by others, unknown to herself, he had seen in her. Some quality in her had caught his eccentric fancy as did the odd items of bric-à-brac on the Bell Street stalls. Some object, unregarded by the passers-by, would catch his eye and he would turn it to the light this way and that in the palm of his hand, suddenly enchanted. She would make a tentative protest.

'But darling, isn't it rather hideous?'

'Oh, no, it's amusing. I like it. And Mogg will love it. Let's buy it for Mogg.'

Mogg, his greatest and, she sometimes thought, his only friend, had been christened Morgan Evans but preferred to use his nickname, regarding it as more appropriate to a poet of the people's struggle. It was not that Mogg struggled greatly himself; indeed Ursula had never met anyone who drank and ate so resolutely at other people's expense. He chanted his confused battle cries to anarchy and hatred in local pubs where his hairy and sad-eyed followers listened in silence or spasmodically banged the table with their beer mugs amid grunts of approval. But Mogg's prose style had been more comprehensible. She had read his letter only once before returning it to the pocket in Steve's jeans, but she could recall every word. Sometimes she wondered whether he had intended her to find it, whether it was fortuitous that he had forgotten to clear out the pockets of his jeans on the one evening when she always took their dirty clothes to the washeteria. It was three weeks after the hospital had given her a firm diagnosis.

'I would say I told you so except that this is my week for abjuring platitudes. I prophesied disaster, but not total disaster. My poor bloody Steve! But isn't it possible for you to get a divorce? She must have had some symptoms before you married. You can – or could – get a divorce for V.D. existing at the time of marriage and what's a dose of clap compared with this? It astounds me, the irresponsibility of the so-called establishment about marriage. They bleat about its sanctity, about protecting it as a staple foundation of society, and then let people acquire a wife with less physical check-up than they would give to a second-hand car. Anyway, you do realize that you must break free, don't you? It will be the end of you if you don't. And don't take refuge in the cowardice of compassion. Can you really see yourself wheeling her invalid chair and wiping her bottom? Yes, I know some men do it. But you never did get much of a kick out of masochism, did you? Besides, the husbands who can do that know something about loving, and even you, my darling Steve, wouldn't presume to claim that. By the way, isn't she an R.C.? As you married in a Registry Office I doubt whether she considers herself properly married at all. That could be a way out for you. Anyway, see you in the Paviours Arms, Wednesday eight p.m. I will celebrate your misfortune with a new poem and a pint of bitter.'

She hadn't really expected him to wheel her chair. She hadn't wanted him to perform the simplest, least intimate physical service for her. She had learnt very early in their marriage that any illness, even transitory colds and sickness, disgusted and frightened him. But she had hoped that the disease would spread very slowly, that she could continue to manage on her own at least for a few precious years. She had schemed how it might be possible. She would get up early so that he needn't be offended by her slowness and ungainliness. She could move the furniture just a few inches, he probably wouldn't even notice, to provide unobtrusive supports so that she needn't take too quickly to sticks and callipers. Perhaps they could find an easier flat, one on the ground floor. If she could have a front door ramp she could get out in the daytime to do her shopping. And there would still be the nights together. Surely nothing could change those?

But it had quickly become evident that the disease, moving inexorably along her nerves like a predator, was spreading at its own pace, not hers. The plans she had made, lying stiffly beside him, distanced in the large double bed, willing that no spasm of muscle should disturb him, had become increasingly unrealistic. Watching her pathetic efforts, he had tried to be considerate and kind. He hadn't reproached her except by his withdrawal, hadn't condemned her growing weakness except by demonstrating his lack of strength. In her nightmares she drowned; thrashing and choking in a limitless sea, she clutched at a floating bough and felt it sink, sponge soft and rotten, beneath her hands. She sensed morbidly that she was acquiring the propitiatory simperingly pathetic air of the disabled. It was hard to be natural with him, harder still to talk. She remembered how he used to lie full length on the sofa watching her while she read or sewed, the creature of his selection and creation, draped and celebrated with the eccentric clothes which he had chosen for her. Now he was afraid for their eyes to meet.

She remembered how he had broken the news to her that he had spoken to the medical social worker at the hospital and that there might be a vacancy soon at Toynton Grange.

'It's by the sea, darling. You've always liked the sea. Quite a small community too, not one of those huge impersonal institutions. The chap who runs it is very highly regarded and it's basically a religious foundation. Anstey isn't a Catholic himself but they do go regularly to Lourdes. That will please you; I mean that you've always been interested in religion. It's one of the subjects that we haven't really seen eye to eye about. I probably wasn't as understanding about your needs as I ought to have been.'

He could afford now to be indulgent of that particular foible. He had forgotten that he had taught her to do without God. Her religion had been one of those possessions that, casually, neither understanding them nor valuing them, he had taken from her. They hadn't really been important to her, those consoling substitutes for sex, for love. She couldn't pretend that she had relinquished them with much of a struggle, those comforting illusions taught in St Matthew's Primary School, assimilated behind the draped terylene curtains of her aunt's front sitting-room in Alma Terrace, Middlesbrough, with its holy pictures, its photograph of Pope John, its framed papal blessing of her aunt and uncle's wedding. All were part of that orphaned, uneventful, not unhappy childhood which was as remote now as a distant once-visited alien shore. She couldn't return because she no longer knew the way.

In the end she had welcomed the thought of Toynton Grange as a refuge. She had pictured herself with a group of patients sitting in their chairs in the sun and looking at the sea; the sea, constantly changing but eternal, comforting and yet frightening, speaking to her in its ceaseless rhythm that nothing really mattered, that human misery was of small account, that everything passed in time. And it wasn't, after all, to be a permanent arrangement. Steve, with the help of the local authority social services department, planned to move into a new and more suitable flat; this was only to be a temporary separation.

But it had lasted now for eight months; eight months in which she had become increasingly unhappy. She had tried to conceal it since unhappiness at Toynton Grange was a sin against the Holy Ghost, a sin against Wilfred. And for most of the time she thought that she had succeeded. She had little in common with the other patients. Grace Willison, dull, middle-aged, pious. Eighteen-year-old Georgie Allan with his boisterous vulgarity; it had been a relief when he became too ill to leave his bed. Henry Carwardine, remote, sarcastic, treating her as if she were a junior clerk. Jennie Pegram, for ever fussing with her hair and smiling her stupid secret smile. And Victor Holroyd, the terrifying Victor, who had hated her as much as he hated everyone at Toynton Grange. Victor who saw no virtue in concealing unhappiness, who frequently proclaimed that if people were dedicated to the practice of charity they might as well have someone to be charitable about.

She had always taken it for granted that it was Victor who had typed the poison pen letter. It was a letter as traumatic in its way as the one she had found from Mogg. She felt for it now, deep in a side pocket in her skirt. It was still there, the cheap paper limp with much handling. But she didn't need to read it. She knew it now by heart, even the first paragraph. She had read that once, and then had turned the paper over at the top so that the words were hidden. Even to think about them burnt her cheek. How could he – it must be a man surely? – know how she and Steve had made love together, that they had done those particular acts and in that way? How could anyone know? Had she, perhaps, cried out in her sleep, moaning her need and her longing? But, if so, only Grace Willison could possibly have heard from the adjoining bedroom, and how could she have understood?

She remembered reading somewhere that obscene letters were usually written by women, particularly by spinsters. Perhaps it hadn't been Victor Holroyd after all. Grace Willison, dull, repressed, religious Grace. But how could she have guessed what Ursula had never admitted to herself?

'You must have known you were ill when you married him. What about those tremors, the weakness in your legs, the clumsiness in the mornings? You knew you were ill, didn't you? You cheated him. No wonder he seldom writes, that he never visits. He's not living alone, you know. You didn't really expect him to stay faithful, did you?'

And there the letter broke off. Somehow she felt that the writer hadn't really come to the end, that some more dramatic and revelationary finish was intended. But perhaps he or she had been interrupted; someone might have come into the office unexpectedly. The note had been typed on Toynton Grange paper, cheap and absorbent and with the old Remington typewriter. Nearly all the patients and staff occasionally typed. She thought she could remember seeing most of them use the Remington at one time or another. Of course, it was really Grace's machine; it was recognized as primarily hers; she used it to type the stencils for the quarterly newsletter. Often she worked alone in the office when the rest of the patients considered that they had finished the working day. And there would be no difficulty in ensuring that it reached the right recipient.

Slipping it into a library book was the surest way of all. They all knew what the others were reading, how could they help it? Books were laid down on tables, on chairs, were easily accessible to anyone. All the staff and patients must have known that she was reading the latest Iris Murdoch. And, oddly enough, the poison letter had been placed at exactly the page she had reached.

At first she had taken it for granted that this was just a new example of Victor's power to hurt and humiliate. It was only since his death that she had felt these doubts, had glanced surreptitiously at the faces of her fellow inmates, had wondered and feared. But surely this was nonsense? She was tormenting herself unnecessarily. It must have been Victor and, if it were Victor, then there would be no more letters. But how could even he have known about her and Steve; except that Victor did mysteriously know things. She remembered the scene when she and Grace Willison had been sitting with him here in the patients' patio. Grace lifting her face to the sun and wearing that silly, gentle smile had begun to talk of her happiness, about the next Lourdes pilgrimage. Victor had broken in roughly:

'You're cheerful because you're euphoric. It's a feature of your disease, D.S. patients always have this unreasonable happiness and hope. Read the textbooks. It's a recognized symptom. It's certainly no virtue on your part and it's bloody irritating for the rest of us.'

She recalled Grace's voice already tremulous with hurt.

'I wasn't claiming happiness as a virtue. But even if it's only a symptom, I can still give thanks for it; it's a kind of grace.'

'As long as you don't expect the rest of us to join in, give thanks by all means. Thank God for the privilege of being no bloody use to yourself or anyone else. And while you're about it, thank Him for some of the other blessings of His creation; the millions toiling to get a living out of barren soil swept by flood, burnt by drought; for pot-bellied children; for tortured prisoners; for the whole doomed, bloody, pointless mess.'

Grace Willison had protested quietly through the first smart of her tears:

'But Victor, how can you talk like that? Suffering isn't the whole of life; you can't really believe that God doesn't care. You come with us to Lourdes.'

'Of course I do. It's the one chance to get out of this boring crack-brained penitentiary. I like movement, I like travel, I like the sight of the sun shining on the Pyrenees, I enjoy the colour. I even get some kind of satisfaction from the blatant commercialism of it all, from the sight of thousands of my fellow beings who are more deluded than I.'

'But that's blasphemy!'

'Is it? Well, I enjoy that too.'

Grace persisted: 'If only you would talk to Father Baddeley, Victor. I'm sure that he would help you. Or perhaps to Wilfred. Why not talk to Wilfred?'

He had burst into raucous laughter, jeering but strangely and frighteningly shot through with genuine amusement.

'Talk to Wilfred! My God, I could tell you something about our saintly Wilfred that would give you a laugh, and one day, if he irritates me enough, I probably shall. Talk to Wilfred!'

She thought she could still hear the distant echo of that laughter. 'I could tell you something about Wilfred.' Only he hadn't told them, and now he never would. She thought about Victor's death. What impulse had led him on that particular afternoon to make his final gesture against fate? It must have been an impulse: Wednesday wasn't his normal day for an outing and Dennis hadn't wanted to take him. She remembered clearly the scene on the patio. Victor, importunate, insistent, exerting every effort of will to get what he wanted. Dennis flushed, sulky, a recalcitrant child, finally giving way but with a poor grace. And so, they had left together for that final walk, and she had never seen Victor again. What was he thinking of when he released those brakes and hurled himself and the chair towards annihilation? Surely it must have been the impulse of a moment. No one could choose to die with such spectacular horror while there were gentler means available. And surely there were gentler means; sometimes she found herself thinking about them, about those two most recent deaths, Victor's and Father Baddeley's. Father Baddeley, gentle, ineffectual, had passed away as if he had never been; his name now was hardly mentioned. It was Victor who seemed to be still among them. It was Victor's bitter uneasy spirit which hung over Toynton Grange. Sometimes, particularly at dusk, she dared not turn her face towards an adjacent wheelchair in case she should see, not the expected occupant, but Victor's heavy figure shrouded in his heavy plaid cloak, his dark sardonic face with its fixed smile like a rictus. Suddenly, despite the warmth of the afternoon sun, Ursula shivered. Releasing the brakes on her chair she turned and wheeled herself towards the house.

IV

The front door of Toynton Grange was open and Julius Court led the way into a high square hall, oak panelled and with a chequered black and white marble floor. The house struck very warm. It was like passing through an invisible curtain of hot air. The hall smelt oddly; not with the usual institutional smell of bodies, food and furniture polish overlaid with antiseptic, but sweeter and strangely exotic as if someone had been burning incense. The hall was as dimly lit as a church. An impression reinforced by the two front windows of Pre-Raphaelite stained glass one on each side of the main door. To the left was the expulsion from Eden, to the right the sacrifice of Isaac. Dalgliesh wondered what aberrant fancy had conceived that effeminate angel with his curdle of yellow hair under the plumed helmet or the sword embellished with glutinous lozenges in ruby, bright blue and orange with which he was ineffectively barring the two delinquents from an apple-orchard Eden. Adam and Eve, their pink limbs tactfully if improbably entwined with laurel, wore expressions respectively of spurious spirituality and petulant remorse. On the right the same angel swooped like a metamorphosized batman over Isaac's bound body, watched from the thicket by an excessively woolly ram whose face, understandably, bore an expression of the liveliest apprehension.

There were three chairs in the hall, bastard contraptions in painted wood covered with vinyl, themselves deformities, one with an unusually high seat, two very low. A folded wheelchair rested against the far wall and a wooden rail was screwed waist high into the panelling. To the right an open door gave a glimpse of what could be a business room or cloakroom. Dalgliesh could see the fold of a plaid cloak hanging on the wall, a pegboard of keys and the edge of a heavy desk. A carved hall table bearing a brass tray of letters and surmounted by a huge fire bell stood to the left of the door.

Julius led the way through a rear door and into a central vestibule from which rose a heavily carved staircase, its banister half cut away to accommodate the metal cage of a large modern lift. They came to a third door. Julius threw it dramatically open and announced:

'A visitor for the dead. Adam Dalgliesh.'

The three of them passed into the room together. Dalgliesh, flanked by his two sponsors, had the unfamiliar sensation of being under escort. After the dimness of the front hall and the central vestibule the dining-room was so bright that he blinked. The tall mullioned windows gave little natural light but the room was harshly lit by two tubes of fluorescent lighting incongruously suspended from the moulded ceiling. Images seemed to fuse together and then parted and he saw clearly the inhabitants of Toynton Grange grouped like a tableau round the oak refectory table at tea.

His arrival seemed to have struck them momentarily into silent surprise. Four of them were in wheelchairs, one a man. The two remaining women were obviously staff; one was dressed as a matron except for the customary status symbol of a cap. Without it, she looked curiously incomplete. The other, a fair-haired younger woman, was wearing black slacks and a white smock but succeeded, despite this unorthodox uniform, in giving an immediate impression of slightly intimidating competence. The three able-bodied men all wore dark-brown monk's habits. After a second's pause, a figure at the head of the table rose and came with ceremonial slowness towards them with hands held out.

'Welcome to Toynton Grange, Adam Dalgliesh. My name is Wilfred Anstey.'

Dalgliesh's first thought was that he looked like a bit-player acting with practised conviction the part of an ascetic bishop. The brown monk's habit suited him so well that it was impossible to imagine him in any other garb. He was tall and very thin, the wrists from which the full woollen sleeves fell away were brown and brittle as autumn sticks. His hair was grey but strong and shaved very short revealing the boyish curve of the skull. Beneath it the thin long face was mottled brown as if the summer tan were fading unevenly; two shining white patches on the left temple had the appearance of diseased skin. It was difficult to guess his age; fifty perhaps. The gentle questioning eyes with their suggestion of other people's suffering meekly borne were young eyes, the blue irises very clear, the whites opaque as milk. He smiled, a singularly sweet lopsided smile spoilt by the display of uneven and discoloured teeth. Dalgliesh wondered why it was that philanthropists so often had a reluctance to visit their dentist.

Dalgliesh held out his hand and felt it imprisoned between Anstey's two palms. It took an effort of will not to flinch from this clammy encounter of moist flesh. He said:

'I had hoped to pay a few days' visit to Father Baddeley. I'm an old friend. I didn't know until I arrived that he was dead.'

'Dead and cremated. His ashes were buried last Wednesday in the churchyard of St Michael's, Toynton. We knew that he would wish them to lie in consecrated ground. We didn't announce his death in the papers because we didn't know that he had friends.'

'Except us here.' It was one of the women patients who added the gentle but firm correction. She was older than the other patients, grey-haired and angular as a Dutch doll propped in her chair. She looked at Dalgliesh steadily with kind and interested eyes.

Wilfred Anstey said:

'Of course. Except us here. Grace was, I think, closer to Michael than anyone else and was with him on the night he died.'

Dalgliesh said:

'He died alone, Mrs Hewson tells me.'

'Unhappily yes. But so at the last do we all. You'll join us for tea, I hope. Julius, you too, and Maggie of course. And did you say that you hoped to stay with Michael? Then you must, of course, spend the night here.'

He turned to the matron.

'Victor's room, I think, Dot. Perhaps, after tea, you would prepare it for our guest.'

Dalgliesh said:

'That's very kind of you, but I don't want to be a nuisance. Would there be any objection if, after tonight, I spent a few days in the cottage? Mrs Hewson tells me that Father Baddeley left me his library. It would be helpful if I could sort and pack the books while I'm here.'

Was it his imagination that the suggestion wasn't entirely welcome? But Anstey hesitated only for a second before saying:

'Of course, if that is what you prefer. But first let me introduce you to the family.'

Dalgliesh followed Anstey in a formal charade of greetings. A succession of hands, dry, cold, moist, reluctant or firm clasped his. Grace Willison, the middle-aged spinster; a study in grey; skin, hair, dress, stockings, all of them slightly dingy so that she looked like an old-fashioned, stiffly jointed doll neglected too long in a dusty cupboard. Ursula Hollis; a tall, spotty-faced girl dressed in a long skirt of Indian cotton who gave him a tentative smile and brief, reluctant handshake. Her left hand lay limply in her lap as if wearied by the weight of the thick wedding ring. He was aware of something odd about her face but had moved on before he realized that she had one blue eye, one brown. Jennie Pegram; the youngest patient but probably older than she looked with a pale, sharp face and mild lemur-like eyes. She was so short-necked that she seemed hunched into her wheelchair. Corn-gold hair, parted in the middle, hung like a crimped curtain around the dwarfish body. She cringed deprecatingly at his touch, gave him a sickly smile and whispered 'hullo' on a gasp of intaken breath. Henry Carwardine; a handsome, authoritative face but cut with deep lines of strain; a high beaky nose and long mouth. The disease had wrenched his head to one side so that he looked like a supercilious bird of prey. He took no notice of Dalgliesh's proffered hand but said a brief 'how do you do' with an uninterest amounting almost to discourtesy. Dorothy Moxon, the matron; sombre, stout and gloomy-eyed under the dark fringe. Helen Rainer; large, slightly protruding green eyes under lids as thin as grape skins and a shapely figure which even the loose-fitting smock couldn't wholly disguise. She would, he thought, be attractive were it not for the disconnected droop of the slightly marsupial cheeks. She shook hands firmly with Dalgliesh and gave him a minatory glance as if welcoming a new patient from whom she expected trouble. Dr Eric Hewson; a fair, good-looking man with a boyish vulnerable face, mud-brown eyes fringed with remarkably long lashes. Dennis Lerner; a lean, rather weak face, eyes blinking nervously behind the steel-rimmed spectacles, a moist handshake. Anstey added, almost as if he thought Lerner needed a word of explanation, that Dennis was the male nurse.

'The two remaining members of our family, Albert Philby, our handyman, and my sister Millicent Hammitt you will meet later, I hope. But I mustn't, of course, forget Jeoffrey.' As if catching his name, a cat, who had been slumbering on a window seat, uncurled himself, dropped ponderously to the floor and stalked towards them, tail erect. Anstey explained:

'He is named after Christopher Smart's cat. I expect you remember the poem.

"For I will consider my cat Jeoffrey.
For he is the servant of the living God, duly
and daily serving him,
For he counteracts the powers of darkness by his
electric skin and glaring eyes,
For he counteracts the Devil, who is death, by
brisking about the life."'

Dalgliesh said that he knew the poem. He could have added that if Anstey had destined his cat for this hieratic role, then he had been unlucky in his choice of the litter. Jeoffrey was a barrel-shaped tabby with a tail like a fox's brush who looked as if his life were dedicated less to the service of his creator than to the gratification of feline lusts. He gave Anstey a disagreeable look compounded of long suffering and disgust and leapt with lightness and precision on to Carwardine's lap, where he was ill-received. Gratified at Carwardine's obvious reluctance to acquire him, he settled down with much purring and foot padding and permitted his eyes to close.

Julius Court and Maggie Hewson had settled themselves at the far end of the long table. Suddenly Julius called out:

'Be careful what you say to Mr Dalgliesh, it may be taken down and given in evidence. He chooses to travel incognito but actually he's Commander Adam Dalgliesh of New Scotland Yard. His job is catching murderers.'

Henry Carwardine's cup began an agitated rattle in its saucer. He tried ineffectively to steady it with his left hand. No one looked at him. Jennie Pegram gave an apprehensive gasp, then looked complacently round the table as if she had done something clever. Helen Rainer said sharply:

'How do you know?'

'I live in the world, my darlings, and occasionally read the newspapers. There was a notorious case last year which gained the Commander some public notice.'

He turned to Dalgliesh:

'Henry will be drinking wine with me after dinner tonight and listening to some music. You may care to join us. You could perhaps wheel him over. Wilfred will excuse you, I know.'

The invitation hardly seemed courteous, excluding as it did all but two of the company and peremptorily claiming the new arrival with no more than a token acknowledgement to his host. But no one seemed to mind. Perhaps it was usual for the two men to drink together when Court was at his cottage. After all, there was no reason why the patients should be compelled to share each other's friends, or those friends obliged to issue a general invitation. Besides, Dalgliesh was obviously invited to provide an escort. He said a brief thank-you and sat down at the table between Ursula Hollis and Henry Carwardine.

It was a plain, boarding-school tea. There was no cloth. The scarred oak table, reamed with scorch marks, held two large brown teapots wielded by Dorothy Moxon, two plates of thickly cut brown bread, thinly spread with what Dalgliesh suspected was margarine, a jar of honey and one of Marmite, a dish of rock buns, home-made and pebbled with an excrescence of bullet black currants. There was also a bowl of apples. They looked like windfalls. Everyone was drinking from brown earthenware mugs. Helen Rainer went over to a cupboard set under the window and brought over three similar mugs and matching plates for the visitors.

It was an odd tea party. Carwardine ignored the guest except to push the plate of bread and butter towards him, and Dalgliesh at first made little headway with Ursula Hollis. Her pale intense face was turned perpetually towards him, the two discordant eyes searched his. He felt uncomfortably that she was making some demand on him, desperately hoping to evoke a response of interest, of affection even, which he could neither recognize nor was competent to give. But, by happy chance, he mentioned London. Her face brightened, she asked him if he knew Marylebone, the Bell Street market? He found himself involved in a lively, almost obsessive discussion about London's street markets. She became animated, almost pretty and, strangely, it seemed to give her some comfort.

Suddenly Jennie Pegram leaned forward across the table and said with a moue of simulated distaste:

'A funny job catching murderers and getting them hanged. I don't see how you fancy it.'

'We don't fancy it, and nowadays they don't get hanged.'

'Well, shut up for life then. I think that's worse. And I bet some of those you caught when you were younger got hanged.'

He detected the anticipatory, almost lascivious gleam in her eyes. It wasn't new to him. He said quietly:

'Five of them. It's interesting that those are the ones people always want to hear about.'

Anstey smiled his gentle smile and spoke as one determined to be fair.

'It isn't only a question of punishment though, Jennie, is it? There is the theory of deterrence; the need to mark public abhorrence of violent crime; the hope of reforming and rehabilitating the criminal; and, of course, the importance of trying to ensure that he doesn't do it again.'

He reminded Dalgliesh of a school master he had much disliked who was given to initiating frank discussion as a matter of duty but always with the patronizing air of permitting a limited expression of unorthodox opinion provided the class came back within the allotted time to a proper conviction of the rightness of his own views. But now Dalgliesh was neither compelled nor disposed to co-operate. He broke into Jennie's simple, 'Well, they can't do it again if they're hanged, can they?' by saying:

'It's an interesting and important subject, I know. But forgive me if I don't personally find it fascinating. I'm on holiday – actually I'm convalescing – and I'm trying to forget about work.'

'You've been ill?' Carwardine, with the deliberate care of a child uncertain of its powers, reached across and helped himself to honey.

'I hope your call here isn't, even subconsciously, on your own behalf. You aren't looking for a future vacancy? You haven't a progressive incurable disease?'

Anstey said:

'We all suffer from a progressive incurable disease. We call it life.'

Carwardine gave a tight self-congratulatory smile, as if he had scored a point in some private game. Dalgliesh, who was beginning to feel himself part of a mad hatter's tea party, wasn't sure whether the remark was spuriously profound or merely silly. What he was sure was that Anstey had made it before. There was a short, embarrassed silence, then Anstey said:

'Michael didn't let us know he was expecting you.' He made it sound like a gentle reproof.

'He may not have received my postcard. It should have arrived on the morning of his death. I couldn't find it in his bureau.'

Anstey was peeling an apple, the yellow rind curved over his thin fingers. His eyes were intent on his task. He said:

'He was brought home by the ambulance service. It wasn't convenient that morning for me to fetch him. I understand that the ambulance stopped at the postbox to collect any letters, probably at Michael's request. He later handed a letter to me and one to my sister, so he should have received your card. I certainly found no postcard when I looked in the bureau for his will and for any other written instructions he may have left. That was early on the morning after his death. I may, of course, have missed it.'

Dalgliesh said easily:

'In which case it would still be there. I expect Father Baddeley threw it away. It's a pity you had to break into the bureau.'

'Break into?' Anstey's voice expressed nothing but a polite, unworried query.

'The lock has been forced.'

'Indeed. I imagine that Michael must have lost the key and was forced to that extremity. Forgive the pun. I found the bureau open when I looked for his papers. I'm afraid I didn't think to examine the lock. Is it important?'

'Miss Willison may think so. I understand that the bureau is now hers.'

'A broken lock does, of course, reduce its value. But you will find that we place little store on material possessions at Toynton Grange.'

He smiled again, dismissing a frivolity, and turned to Dorothy Moxon. Miss Willison was concentrating on her plate. She didn't look up. Dalgliesh said:

'It's probably foolish of me, but I wish I could be sure that Father Baddeley knew that I hoped to visit him. I thought he might have slipped my postcard into his diary. But the last volume isn't in his desk.'

This time Anstey looked up. The blue eyes met the dark brown, innocent, polite, unworried.

'Yes, I noticed that. He gave up keeping a diary at the end of June apparently. The surprise is that he kept one, not that he gave up the habit. In the end one grows impatient of the egotism which records trivia as if it had a permanent value.'

'It's unusual surely after so many years to stop in mid-year.'

'He had just returned from hospital after a grave illness and can't have been in much doubt about the prognosis. Knowing that death could not be far off, he may have decided to destroy the diaries.'

'Beginning with the last volume?'

'To destroy a diary must be like destroying a memory. One would begin with the years one could best endure to lose. Old memories are tenacious. He made a start by burning the last volume.'

Grace Willison again spoke her gentle but firm correction:

'Not by burning, Wilfred. Father Baddeley used his electric fire when he got home from hospital. The grate is filled with a jam pot of dried grasses.'

Dalgliesh pictured the sitting-room of Hope Cottage. She was, of course, right. He recalled the old-fashioned grey stone jar, the crumpled bunch of dried leaves and grasses filling the narrow fireplace and thrusting their dusty and soot-laden stalks between the bars. They probably hadn't been disturbed for the best part of a year.

The animated chatter at the other end of the table died into speculative silence as it does when people suddenly suspect that something interesting is being said which they ought to hear.

Maggie Hewson had seated herself so close to Julius Court that Dalgliesh was surprised that he had room to drink his tea and had been overtly flirting with him during the meal, whether for her husband's discomfiture or Court's gratification it was difficult to say. Eric Hewson, when he glanced towards them, had the shame-faced look of an embarrassed schoolboy. Court, perfectly at his ease, had distributed his attention among all the women present, with the exception of Grace. Now Maggie looked from face to face and said sharply:

'What's the matter? What did she say?'

No one replied. It was Julius who broke the moment of sudden and inexplicable tension:

'I forgot to tell you. You're doubly privileged in your visitor. The Commander doesn't confine his talents to catching murderers, he publishes verse. He's Adam Dalgliesh, the poet.'

This announcement was met with a confused congratulatory murmur during which Dalgliesh fastened on Jennie's comment of 'how nice' as the most irritatingly inept. Wilfred smiled encouragingly and said:

'Of course. We are certainly privileged. And Adam Dalgliesh comes at an opportune time. We are due to hold our monthly family social evening on Thursday. May we hope that our guest will recite some of his poems for our pleasure?'

There were a number of answers to that question but, in the present disadvantaged company, none of them seemed either kind or possible.

Dalgliesh said:

'I'm sorry but I don't travel with copies of my own books.'

Anstey smiled.

'That will present no problem. Henry has your last two volumes. I am sure he will lend them.'

Without looking up from his plate, Carwardine said quietly:

'Given the lack of privacy in this place, I've no doubt you could provide a verbal catalogue of my whole library. But, since you've shown a complete lack of interest in Dalgliesh's work until now, I have no intention of lending my books so that you can blackmail a guest into performing for you like a captive monkey!'

Wilfred flushed slightly and bent his head over his plate.

There was nothing further to be said. After a second's silence, the talk flowed on, innocuous, commonplace. Neither Father Baddeley nor his diary was mentioned again.

V

Anstey was obviously unworried by Dalgliesh's expressed wish after tea to talk to Miss Willison in private. Probably the request struck him as no more than the pious protocol of courtesy and respect. He said that Grace had the task of feeding the hens and collecting the eggs before dusk. Perhaps Adam could help her?

The two larger wheels of the chair were fitted with a second interior wheel in chrome which could be used by the occupant to drive the chair forward. Miss Willison grasped it and began to make slow progress down the asphalt path jerking her frail body like a marionette. Dalgliesh saw that her left hand was deformed and had little power so that the chair tended to swivel, and progress was erratic. He moved to her left and, while walking beside her, he laid his hand unobtrusively on the back of the chair and gently helped it forward. He hoped he was doing the acceptable thing. Miss Willison might rescnt his tact as much as she did the implied pity. He thought that she sensed his embarrassment and had resolved not to add to it even by smiling her thanks.

As they walked together he was intensely aware of her, noting the details of her physical presence as keenly as if she were a young and desirable woman and he on the verge of love. He watched the sharp bones of her shoulders jerking rhythmically under the thin grey cotton of her dress; the purple tributaries of the veins standing like cords on her almost transparent left hand, so small and fragile in contrast to its fellow. This, too, looked deformed in its compensating strength and hugeness as she gripped the wheel as powerfully as a man. Her legs, clad in wrinkled woollen stockings, were thin as sticks; her sandalled feet, too large surely for such inadequate supports, were clamped to the footrest of her chair as if glued to the metal. Her grey hair flecked with dandruff had been combed upward in a single heavy plait fixed to the crown of her head with a plastic white comb, not particularly clean. The back of her neck looked dingy either with fading suntan or inadequate washing. Looking down he could see the lines on her forehead contracting into deeper furrows with the effort of moving the chair, the eyes blinking spasmodically behind the thin-framed spectacles.

The hen house was a large ramshackle cage bounded by sagging wire and creosoted posts. It had obviously been designed for the disabled. There was a double entry so that Miss Willison could let herself in and fasten the door behind her before opening the second door into the main cage, and the smooth asphalt path, just wide enough for a wheelchair, ran along each side and in front of the nesting boxes. Inside the first door a rough wooden shelf had been nailed waist high to one of the supports. This held a bowl of prepared meal, a plastic can of water and a wooden spoon riveted to a long handle, obviously for the collection of eggs. Miss Willison took them in her lap with some difficulty and reached forward to open the inner door. The hens, who had unaccountably bunched themselves in the far corner of the cage like the nervous virgins, lifted their beady spiteful faces and instantly came squawking and swooping towards her as if determined on a feathered hecatomb. Miss Willison recoiled slightly and began casting handfuls of meal before them with the air of a neophyte propitiating the Furies. The hens began an agitated pecking and gulping. Scraping her hand against the rim of the bowl Miss Willison said:

'I wish I could get more fond of them, or they of me. Both sides might get more out of this activity. I thought that animals developed a fondness for the hand that feeds them but it doesn't seem to apply to hens. I don't see why it should really. We exploit them so thoroughly, first take their eggs and when they're past laying wring their necks and consign them to the pot.'

'I hope you don't have to do the wringing.'

'Oh, no, Albert Philby has that unpleasant job; not that I

think he finds it altogether unpleasant. But I eat my share of the boiled fowl.'

Dalgliesh said:

'I feel rather the same. I was brought up in a Norfolk vicarage and my mother always had hens. She was fond of them and they seemed fond of her but my father and I thought they were a nuisance. But we liked the fresh eggs.'

'Do you know, I'm ashamed to tell you that I can't really tell the difference between these eggs and the ones from the supermarket. Wilfred prefers us not to eat any food which hasn't been naturally produced. He abhors factory farming and, of course, he's right. He would really prefer Toynton Grange to be vegetarian, but that would make the catering even more difficult than it is now. Julius did some sums and proved to him that these eggs cost us two and a half times more than the shop ones, not counting of course for my labour. It was rather discouraging.'

Dalgliesh asked:

'Does Julius Court do the book-keeping here then?'

'Oh, no! Not the real accounts, the ones included in the annual report. Wilfred has a professional accountant for those. But Julius is clever with finance and I know Wilfred looks to him for advice. It's usually rather disheartening advice, I'm afraid; we run on a shoe-string really. Father Baddeley's legacy was a real blessing. And Julius has been very kind. Last year the van which we hired to drive us back from the port after our return from Lourdes had an accident. We were all very shaken. The wheelchairs were in the back and two of them got broken. The telephone message that reached here was rather alarmist; it wasn't as bad as Wilfred thought. But Julius drove straight to the hospital where we had been taken for a check-up, hired another van, and took care of everything. And then he bought the specially adapted bus which we have now so that we're completely independent. Dennis and Wilfred between them can drive us all the way to Lourdes. Julius never comes with us, of course, but he's always here to arrange a welcome home party for us when we return after the pilgrimage.'

This disinterested kindness was unlike the impression that, even after a short acquaintanceship, Dalgliesh had formed of Court. Intrigued he asked carefully:

'Forgive me if I sound crude but what does Julius Court get out of it, this interest in Toynton?'

'Do you know, I've sometimes asked myself that. But it seems an ungracious question when it's so apparent what Toynton Grange gets out of him. He comes back from London like a breath of the outside world. He cheers us all. But I know that you want to talk about your friend. Shall we just collect the eggs and then find somewhere quiet?'

Your friend. The quiet phrase, quietly spoken, rebuked him. They filled up the water containers and collected the eggs together, Miss Willison scooping them up in her wooden spoon with the expertise born of long practice. They found only eight. The whole procedure, which an able-bodied person could have completed in ten minutes, had been tedious, time-consuming and not particularly productive. Dalgliesh saw no merit in work for the sake of work, wondered what his companion really thought about a job which had obviously been designed in defiance of economics to give her the illusion of being useful.

They made their way back to the little courtyard behind the house. Only Henry Carwardine was sitting there, a book on his lap but his eyes staring towards the invisible sea. Miss Willison gave him a quick worried glance and seemed about to speak. But she said nothing until they had settled themselves some thirty yards from the silent figure; Dalgliesh at the end of one of the wooden benches and she at his side. Then she said:

'I can never get used to being so close to the sea and yet not being able to look at it. One can hear it so plainly sometimes as we can now. We're almost surrounded by it, we can sometimes smell it and listen to it, but we might be a hundred miles away.'

She spoke wistfully but without resentment. They sat for a moment in silence. Dalgliesh could indeed hear the sea clearly now, the long withdrawing rasp of the shingled tide borne to him on the onshore breeze. To the inmates of Toynton Grange that ceaseless murmur must evoke the tantalizingly close but unobtainable freedom of wide blue horizons, scudding clouds, white wings falling and swooping through the moving air. He could understand how the need to see it might grow into an obsession. He said deliberately:

'Mr Holroyd managed to get himself wheeled to where he could watch the sea.'

It had been important to see her reaction and he realized at once that to her the remark had been worse than tactless. She was deeply shaken and distressed. Her right hand tightened on the arm of the chair. Her face crimsoned in an unlovely wave, and then became very pale. For a moment he almost wished that he hadn't spoken. But the regret was transitory. It was returning despite himself, he thought with sardonic humour, this professional itch to seek out the facts. They were seldom discovered without some cost, however irrelevant or important they finally proved to be, and it wasn't usually he who paid. He heard her speaking so quietly that he had to bend his head to catch the words.

'Victor had a special need to get away by himself. We understood that.'

'But it must have been very difficult to push a light wheelchair like this over the rough turf and up to the edge of the cliff.'

'He had a chair which belonged to him, like this type but larger and stronger. And it wasn't necessary to push him up the steep part of the headland. There's an inland path which leads, I understand, to a narrow sunken lane. You can get to the cliff edge that way. Even so it was hard on Dennis Lerner. It took him half an hour hard pushing each way. But you wanted to talk about Father Baddeley.'

'If it won't distress you too much. It seems that you were the last person to see him alive. He must have died very soon after you left the cottage since he was still wearing his stole when Mrs Hewson found his body next morning. Normally he would surely have taken it off very soon after hearing a confession.'

There was a silence as if she were making up her mind to something. Then she said:

'He did take it off, as usual, immediately after he'd given me absolution. Folded it up and placed it over the arm of his chair.'

This, too, was a sensation which in the long dog days in hospital he had thought never to experience again, the frisson of excitement along the blood at the first realization that something important had been said, that although the quarry wasn't yet in sight nor his spore detectable, yet he was there. He tried to reject this unwelcome surge of tension but it was as elemental and involuntary as the touch of fear. He said:

'But that means that Father Baddeley put on his stole again after you had left. Why should he do that?'

Or someone else had put it on for him. But that thought was best unspoken and its implications must wait.

She said quietly:

'I assume that he had another penitent; that is the obvious explanation.'

'He wouldn't wear it to say his evening Office?'

Dalgliesh tried to remember his father's practice in these matters on the very rare occasions when the rector did not say his Office in church; but memory provided only the unhelpful boyhood picture of them both holed up in a hut in the Cairngorms during a blizzard, himself watching, half bored, half fascinated, the patterns of the swirling snow against the windows, his father in leggings, anorak and woollen cap quietly reading from his small black prayer book. He certainly hadn't worn a stole then.

Miss Willison said:

'Oh no! He would wear it only when administering a sacrament. Besides, he had said Evensong. He was just finishing when I arrived and I joined him in a last Collect.'

'But if someone followed you, then you weren't the last person to see him alive. Did you point that out to anyone when you were told of his death?'

'Should I have done? I don't think so. If the person himself – or herself – didn't choose to speak it wasn't for me to invite conjecture. Of course, if anyone but you had realized the significance of the stole it wouldn't have been possible to avoid speculation. But no one did, or if they did, they said nothing. We gossip too much at Toynton, Mr Dalgliesh. It's inevitable perhaps, but it isn't – well – healthy morally. If someone other than I went to confession that night, it's nobody's business but theirs and Father Baddeley's.'

Dalgliesh said:

'But Father Baddeley was still wearing his stole next morning. That suggests that he might have died while his visitor was actually with him. If that happened surely the first reaction, however private the occasion, would be to summon medical help?'

'The visitor might have had no doubts that Father Baddeley had died and was beyond that kind of help. If so there might be a temptation to leave him there sitting peaceably in his chair and slip away. I don't think Father Baddeley would call that a sin, and I don't think you could call it a crime. It might seem callous but would it necessarily be so? It could argue an indifference to form and decorum perhaps, but that isn't quite the same thing, is it?'

It would argue, too, thought Dalgliesh, that the visitor had been a doctor or a nurse. Was that what Miss Willison was hinting? The first reaction of a lay person would surely be to seek help, or at least confirmation that death had actually occurred. Unless, of course, he knew for the best or worst of reasons that Baddeley was dead. But that sinister possibility seemed not to have occurred to Miss Willison. Why, indeed, should it? Father Baddeley was old, he was sick, he was expected to die and he had died. Why should anyone suspect the natural and the inevitable? He said something about determining the time of death and heard her gentle, inexorable reply.

'I expect that in your job the actual time of death is always important and so you get used to concentrating on that fact. But in real life does it matter? What matters is whether one dies in a state of grace.'

Dalgliesh had a momentary and impious picture of his detective sergeant punctiliously attempting to determine and record this essential information about a victim in an official crime report and reflected that Miss Willison's nice distinction between police work and real life was a salutary reminder of how other people saw his job. He looked forward to telling the Commissioner about it. And then he remembered that this wasn't the kind of casual professional gossip which they would exchange in that final slightly formal and inevitably disappointing interview which would mark the end of his police career.

Ruefully, he recognized in Miss Willison the type of unusually honest witness whom he had always found difficult. Paradoxically, this old-fashioned rectitude, this sensitivity of conscience, were more difficult to cope with than the prevarications, evasions, or flamboyant lying which were part of a normal interrogation. He would have liked to have asked her who at Toynton Grange was likely to have visited Father Baddeley for the purpose of confession, but recognized that the question would only prejudice confidence between them and that, in any case, he wouldn't get a reply. But it must have been one of the able-bodied. No one else could have come and gone in secret, unless, of course, he or she had an accomplice. He was inclined to dismiss the accomplice. A wheelchair and its occupant, whether pushed from Toynton Grange or brought by car, must surely have been seen at some stage of the journey.

Hoping that he wasn't sounding too much like a detective in the middle of an interrogation he asked:

'So when you left him he was – what?'

'Just sitting there quietly in the fireside chair. I wouldn't let him get up. Wilfred had driven me down to the cottage in the small van. He said that he would visit his sister at Faith Cottage while I was with Father Baddeley and be outside again in half an hour unless I knocked on the wall first.'

'So you can hear sounds between the two cottages? I ask because it struck me that if Father Baddeley had felt ill after you'd left, he might have knocked on the wall for Mrs Hammitt.'

'She says that he didn't knock, but she might not have heard if she had the television on very loudly. The cottages are very well built, but you can hear sounds through that interior wall, particularly if voices are raised.'

'You mean that you could hear Mr Anstey talking to his sister?'

Miss Willison seemed to regret that she had gone so far, and she said quickly:

'Well, just now and then. I remember that I had to make an effort of will to prevent it disturbing me. I wished that they would keep their voices lower, and then felt ashamed of myself for being so easily distracted. It was good of Wilfred to drive me to the cottage. Normally, of course, Father Baddeley would come up to the house to see me and we would use what is called the quiet room next to the business room just inside the front door. But Father Baddeley had only been discharged from hospital that morning and it wasn't right that he should leave the cottage. I could have postponed my visit until he was stronger but he wrote to me from hospital to say that he hoped I would come and precisely at what time. He knew how much it meant to me.'

'Was he fit to be alone? It seems not.'

'Eric and Dot – that's Sister Moxon – wanted him to come here and be looked after at least for the first night, but he insisted on going straight back home. Then Wilfred suggested that someone should sleep in his spare room in case he wanted help in the night. He wouldn't agree to that either. He really was adamant that he should be left alone that night; he had great authority in his quiet way. Afterwards I think Wilfred blamed himself for not having been more firm. But what could he do? He couldn't bring Father Baddeley here by force.'

But it would have been simpler for all concerned if Father Baddeley had agreed to spend at least his first night out of hospital at Toynton Grange. It was surely untypically inconsiderate of him to resist the suggestion so strenuously. Was he expecting another visitor? Was there someone he wanted to see, urgently and in private, someone to whom, like Miss Willison, he had written to give a precisely timed appointment? If so, whatever the reason for the visit, that person must have come on his own feet. He asked Miss Willison if Wilfred and Father Baddeley had spoken together before she had left the cottage.

'No. After I'd been with Father Baddeley about thirty minutes he knocked on the wall with the poker and, soon afterwards, Wilfred honked on the horn. I manoeuvred my chair to the front door just as Wilfred arrived to open it. Father Baddeley was still in his chair. Wilfred called out goodnight to him, but I don't think he answered. Wilfred seemed in rather a hurry to get home. Millicent came out to help push my chair into the back of the van.'

So neither Wilfred nor his sister had spoken to Michael before driving away that evening, neither had seen him closely. Glancing down at Miss Willison's strong right hand Dalgliesh toyed momentarily with the possibility that Michael was already dead. But that notion, apart from its psychological unlikelihood, was of course, nonsense. She couldn't have relied on Wilfred not coming into the cottage. Come to think of it, it was odd that he hadn't done so. Michael had only returned from hospital that morning. Surely it would have been natural to come in and inquire how he was feeling, to spend at least a few minutes in his company. It was interesting that Wilfred Anstey had made so quick a getaway, that no one had admitted visiting Father Baddeley after seven forty-five.

He asked:

'What lighting was there in the cottage when you were with Father Baddeley?' If the question surprised her, she didn't show it.

'Only the small table lamp on the bureau top behind his chair. I was surprised that he could see to say Evensong, but the prayers, of course, would be familiar to him.'

'And the lamp was off next morning?'

'Oh yes, Maggie said that she found the cottage in darkness.'

Dalgliesh said:

'I find it rather strange that no one looked in later that night to inquire how Father Baddeley was or help him get to bed.'

She said quickly:

'Eric Hewson thought that Millicent was going to look in last thing and she had somehow got the impression that Eric and Helen – Nurse Rainer, you know – had agreed to do so. They all blamed themselves very much the next day. But, as Eric told us, medically it could have made no difference. Father Baddeley died quite peaceably soon after I left.'

They sat in silence for a minute. Dalgliesh wondered whether this was the right time to ask her about the poison pen letter. Remembering her distress over Victor Holroyd, he was reluctant to embarrass her further. But it was important to know. Looking sideways at the thin face with its look of resolute tranquillity, he said:

'I looked in Father Baddeley's writing bureau very soon after I arrived, just in case there was a note or unposted letter for me. I found a rather unpleasant poison pen letter under some old receipts. I wondered whether he had spoken to anyone about it, whether anyone else at Toynton Grange had received one.'

She was even more distressed by the question than he had feared. For a moment she could not speak. He stared straight ahead until he heard her voice. But, when at last she answered, she had herself well in hand.

'I had one, about four days before Victor died. It was . . . it was obscene. I tore it into small fragments and flushed it down the lavatory.'

Dalgliesh said with robust cheerfulness:

'Much the best thing to do with it. But, as a policeman, I'm always sorry when the evidence is destroyed.'

'Evidence?'

'Well, sending poison pen letters can be an offence; more important, it can cause a great deal of unhappiness. It's probably best always to tell the police and let them find out who's responsible.'

'The police! Oh, no! We couldn't do that. It isn't the kind of problem the police can help us with.'

'We aren't as insensitive as people sometimes imagine. It isn't inevitable that the culprit would be prosecuted. But it is important to put a stop to this kind of nuisance, and the police have the best facilities. They can send the letter to the forensic science laboratory for examination by a skilled document examiner.'

'But they would need to have the document. I couldn't have shown the letter to anyone.'

So it had been as bad as that. Dalgliesh asked:

'Would you mind telling me what kind of letter it was? Was it handwritten, typed, on what kind of paper?'

'The letter was typed on Toynton Grange paper, in double spacing, on our old Imperial. Most of us here have learned typewriting. It's one of the ways in which we try to be self-supporting. There was nothing wrong with the punctuation or spelling. There were no other clues that I could see. I don't know who typed it, but I think the writer must have been sexually experienced.'

So, even in the middle of her distress, she had applied her mind to the problem. He said:

'There are only a limited number of people with access to that machine. The problem wouldn't have been too difficult for the police.'

Her gentle voice was stubborn.

'We had the police here over Victor's death. They were very kind, very considerate. But it was terribly upsetting. It was horrible for Wilfred – for all of us. I don't think we could have stood it again. I'm sure that Wilfred couldn't. However tactful the police are, they have to keep on asking questions until they've solved the case, surely? It's no use calling them in and expecting them to put people's sensitivities before their job.'

This was undeniably true and Dalgliesh had little to argue against it. He asked her what, if anything, she had done apart from flushing away the offending letter.

'I told Dorothy Moxon about it. That seemed the most sensible thing to do. I couldn't have spoken about it to a man. Dorothy told me that I shouldn't have destroyed it, that no one could do anything without the evidence. But she agreed that we ought to say nothing at present. Wilfred was particularly worried about money at the time and she didn't want him to have anything else on his mind. She knew how much it would distress him. Besides, I think she had an idea who might have been responsible. If she was right, then we shan't be getting any more letters.'

So Dorothy Moxon had believed, or had pretended to believe, that Victor Holroyd was responsible. And if the writer now had the sense and self-control to stop, it was a comfortable theory which, in the absence of the evidence, no one could disprove.

He asked whether anyone else had received a letter. As far as she knew, no one had. Dorothy Moxon hadn't been consulted by anyone else. The suggestion seemed to distress her. Dalgliesh realized that she had seen the note as a single piece of gratuitous spite directed against herself. The thought that Father Baddeley had also received one, was distressing her almost as much as the original letter. Knowing only too well from his experience the kind of letter it must have been, he said gently:

'I shouldn't worry too much about Father Baddeley's letter. I don't think it would have distressed him. It was very mild really, just a spiteful little note suggesting that he wasn't of much help to Toynton Grange and that the cottage could be more usefully occupied by someone else. He had too much humility and sense to be bothered by that kind of nonsense. I imagine that he only kept the letter because he wanted to consult me in case he wasn't the only victim. Sensible people put these things down the W.C. But we can't always be sensible. Anyway, if you do receive another letter, will you promise to show it to me?'

She shook her head gently but didn't speak. But Dalgliesh saw that she was happier. She put out her withered left hand and placed it momentarily over his, giving it a slight press. The sensation was unpleasant, her hand was dry and cold, the bones felt loose in the skin. But the gesture was both humbling and dignified.

It was getting cold and dark in the courtyard; Henry Carwardine had already gone in. It was time for her to move inside. He thought quickly and then said:

'It isn't important, and please don't think that I take my job with me wherever I go. But if during the next few days you can recall how Father Baddeley spent the last week or so before he went into hospital, it would be helpful to me. Don't ask anyone else about this. Just let me know what he did from your own memory of him, the times he came to Toynton Grange, where else he may have spent his hours. I should like to have a picture in my mind of his last ten days.'

She said:

'I know that he went into Wareham on the Wednesday before he was taken ill, he said to do some shopping and to see someone on business. I remember that because he explained on the Tuesday that he wouldn't be visiting the Grange as usual next morning.'

So that, thought Dalgliesh, was when he had bought his store of provisions, confident that his letter wouldn't go unanswered. But then he had been right to be confident.

They sat for a minute not speaking. He wondered what she had thought of so odd a request. She hadn't seemed surprised. Perhaps she saw it as perfectly natural, this wish to build up a picture of a friend's last ten days on earth. But suddenly he had a spasm of apprehension and caution. Ought he perhaps to stress that his request was absolutely private? Surely not. He had told her not to ask anyone else. To make more of it would only arouse suspicion. And what danger could there be? What had he to go on? A broken bureau lock, a missing diary, a stole replaced as if for confession. There was no real evidence here. With an effort of will he reasoned away this inexplicable spasm of apprehension, strong as a premonition. It was too disagreeable a reminder of those long nights in hospital when he had struggled in restless half-consciousness against irrational terrors and half-understood fears. And this was equally irrational, equally to be resisted by sense and reason, the ridiculous conviction that a simple, almost casual and not very hopeful request had sounded so clearly a sentence of death.

THREE

A Stranger for the Night

I

Before dinner Anstey suggested that Dennis Lerner should show Dalgliesh round the house. He apologized for not escorting the guest himself, but he had an urgent letter to write. The post was delivered and collected shortly before nine o'clock each morning from the box on the boundary gate. If Adam had letters to send he had only to leave them on the hall table, and Albert Philby would take them to the box with the Toynton Grange letters. Dalgliesh thanked him. There was one urgent letter he needed to write, to Bill Moriarty at the Yard, but he proposed to post that himself later in the day at Wareham. He had certainly no intention of leaving it exposed to the curiosity or speculation of Anstey and his staff.

The suggestion for a tour of the Grange had the force of a command. Helen Rainer was helping the patients wash before dinner and Dot Moxon had disappeared with Anstey, so that he was taken round only by Lerner accompanied by Julius Court. Dalgliesh wished the tour were over, or better still, that it could have been avoided without giving hurt. He recalled with discomfort a visit he had paid as a boy with his father to a geriatric hospital on Christmas Day; the courtesy with which the patients accepted yet one more invasion of their privacy, the public display of pain and deformity, the pathetic eagerness with which the staff demonstrated their small triumphs. Now, as then, he found himself morbidly sensitive to the least trace of revulsion in his voice and thought that he detected what was more offensive, a note of patronizing heartiness. Dennis Lerner didn't appear to notice it and Julius walked jauntily with them looking round with lively curiosity as if the place were new to him. Dalgliesh wondered whether he had come to keep an eye on Lerner or on Dalgliesh himself.

As they passed from room to room, Lerner lost his first diffidence and became confident, almost voluble. There was something endearing about his naïve pride in what Anstey was trying to do. Anstey had certainly laid out his money with some imagination. The Grange itself, with its large, high rooms and cold marble floors, its oppressively panelled dark oak walls and mullioned windows, was a depressingly unsuitable house for disabled patients. Apart from the dining-room and the rear drawing-room, which had become a TV and communal sitting-room, Anstey had used the house mainly to accommodate himself and his staff and had built on to the rear a one-storey stone extension to provide ten individual patients' bedrooms on the ground floor and a clinical room and additional bedrooms on the floor above. This extension had been joined to the old stables which ran at right angles to it, providing a sheltered patio for the patients' wheelchairs. The stables themselves had been adapted to provide garages, a workshop and a patients' activity room for woodwork and modelling. Here, too, the handcream and bath powder which the Home sold to help with finances were made and packed at a workbench behind a transparent plastic screen, erected, presumably, to indicate respect for the principle of scientific cleanliness. Dalgliesh could see, hanging on the screen, the white shadows of protective overalls.

Lerner said:

'Victor Holroyd was a chemistry teacher and he gave us the prescription for the handcream and powder. The cream is really only lanolin, almond oil and glycerine but it's very effective and people seem to like it. We do very well with it. And this corner of the workroom is given over to modelling.'

Dalgliesh had almost exhausted his repertoire of appreciative comments. But now he was genuinely impressed. In the middle of the workbench and mounted on a low wooden base was a clay head of Wilfred Anstey. The neck, elongated and sinewy, rose tortoise-like from the folds of the hood. The head was thrust forward and held a little to the right. It was almost a parody, and yet it had an extraordinary power. How, Dalgliesh wondered, had the sculptor managed to convey the sweetness and the obstinacy of that individual smile, to model compassion and yet reduce it to self-delusion, to show humility garbed in a monk's habit and yet convey an overriding impression of the puissance of evil. The plastic-wrapped lumps and rolls of clay which lay, disorderly, on the workbench only emphasized the force and technical achievement of this one finished work.

Lerner said:

'Henry did the head. Something's gone a little wrong with the mouth, I think. Wilfred doesn't seem to mind it but no one else thinks that it does him justice.'

Julius put his head on one side and pursed his lips in a parody of critical assessment.

'Oh, I wouldn't say that. I wouldn't say that. What do you think of it, Dalgliesh?'

'I think it's remarkable. Did Carwardine do much modelling before he came here?'

It was Dennis Lerner who answered:

'I don't think he did any. He was a senior civil servant before his illness. He modelled this about a couple of months ago without Wilfred giving him a sitting. It's quite good for a first effort, isn't it?'

Julius said:

'The question which interests me is did he do it intentionally, in which case he's a great deal too talented to waste himself here, or were his fingers merely obeying his subconscious? If so, it raises interesting speculations about the origin of creativity and even more interesting ones about Henry's subconscious.'

'I think it just came out like that,' said Dennis Lerner simply. He looked at it with puzzled respect, clearly seeing nothing in it either for wonder or explanation.

Lastly, they went into one of the small rooms at the end of the extension. It had been arranged as an office and was furnished with two wooden ink-stained desks which looked as if they were rejects from a government office. At one Grace Willison was typing names and addresses on a perforated sheet of sticky labels. Dalgliesh saw with some surprise that Carwardine was typing what looked like a private letter at the other desk. Both the typewriters were very old. Henry was using an Imperial; Grace a Remington. Dalgliesh stood over her and glanced at the list of names and addresses. He saw that the newsletter was widely distributed. Apart from local rectories, and other homes for the chronic sick, it went to addresses in London and even to two in the United States and one near Marseilles. Flustered at his interest, Grace jerked her elbow clumsily and the bound list of names and addresses from which she was working fell to the floor. But Dalgliesh had seen enough; the unaligned small e, the smudged o, the faint almost indecipherable capital w. There was no doubt that this was the machine on which Father Baddeley's note had been typed. He picked up the book and handed it to Miss Willison. Without looking at him, she shook her head and said:

'Thank you, but I don't really need to look at it. I can type all the sixty-eight names by heart. I've done it for so long you see. I can imagine what the people are like just from their names and the names they give their houses. But I've always been good at remembering names and addresses. It was very useful to me when I worked for a charity to help discharged prisoners and there were so many lists to type. This is quite short, of course. May I add your name so that you get our quarterly magazine? It's only ten pence. I'm afraid with postage so expensive we have to charge more than we'd like.'

Henry Carwardine looked up and spoke:

'I believe this quarter we have a poem by Jennie Pegram which begins:

"Autumn is my favourite time,
I love its glowing tints."

It's worth ten pence to you Dalgliesh, I should have thought, to discover how she tackles that little problem of rhyming.'

Grace Willison smiled happily.

'It's only an amateur production I know, but it does keep the League of Friends in touch with what is going on here; our personal friends too, of course.'

Henry said:

'Not mine. They know I've lost the use of my limbs but I've no wish to suggest that I've lost the use of my mind. At best the newsletter reaches the literary level of a parish magazine; at worst, which is three issues out of four, it's embarrassingly puerile.'

Grace Willison flushed and her lip trembled. Dalgliesh said quickly:

'Please add my name. Would it be easier if I paid for a year now?'

'How kind! Perhaps six months would be safer. If Wilfred does decide to transfer the Grange to the Ridgewell Trust they may have different plans for the newsletter. I'm afraid the future is very uncertain for all of us at present. Would you write your address here? Queenhythe. That's by the river, isn't it? How pleasant for you. You won't be wanting any of the handcream or bath powder, I suppose, although we do send the powder to one or two gentlemen customers. But this is really Dennis's department. He sees to the distribution and does most of the packing himself. I'm afraid our hands are too shaky to be much use. But I'm sure he could spare you some of the bath powder.'

Dalgliesh was saved from the need to reply to this wistful inquiry by the booming of the gong. Julius said:

'The warning gong. One more boom and dinner will be on the table. I shall return home and see what my indispensable Mrs Reynolds has left for me. By the way, have you warned the Commander that dinner at Toynton Grange is eaten Trappist fashion in silence? We don't want him to break the rule with inconvenient questions about Michael's will or what possible reason a patient in this abode of love could have for hurling himself over the cliff.'

He disappeared at some speed as if afraid that any tendency to linger would expose him to the risk of an invitation to dine.

Grace Willison was obviously relieved to see him go but she smiled bravely at Dalgliesh.

'We do have a rule that no one talks during the evening meal. I hope that it won't inconvenience you. We take it in turns to read from any work we choose. Tonight it's Wilfred's turn so we shall have one of Donne's sermons. They're very fine of course – Father Baddeley enjoyed them, I know – but I do find them rather difficult. And I don't really think that they go well with boiled mutton.'

II

Henry Carwardine wheeled his chair to the lift, drew back the steel grille with difficulty, clanged the gate closed and pressed the button to the floor above. He had insisted on having a room in the main building, firmly rejecting the unsubstantial, meanly proportioned cells in the annexe, and Wilfred, despite what Henry thought were obsessive, almost paranoid fears that he might be trapped in a fire, had reluctantly agreed. Henry had confirmed his committal to Toynton Grange by moving one or two chosen pieces of furniture from his Westminster flat and virtually all his books. The room was large, high ceilinged and pleasantly proportioned, its two windows giving a wide view south-west across the headland. Next door was a lavatory and shower which he shared only with any patient being nursed in the sickroom. He knew, without the least qualm of guilt, that he had the most comfortable quarters in the house. Increasingly he was retreating into this tidy and private world, closing the heavy carved door against involvement, bribing Philby to bring up occasional meals on a tray, to buy for him in Dorchester special cheeses, wines, pâté and fruit to augment the institutional meals which the staff of the Grange took it in turns to cook. Wilfred had apparently thought it prudent not to comment on this minor insubordination, this trespass against the law of togetherness.

He wondered what had provoked him to that spatter of malice against harmless, pathetic Grace Willison. It wasn't the first time since Holroyd's death that he had caught himself speaking with Holroyd's voice. The phenomenon interested him. It set him thinking again about that other life, the other one he had so prematurely and resolutely renounced. He had noticed it when chairing committees, how the members played their individual roles, almost as if these had been allocated in advance. The hawk; the dove; the compromiser; the magisterial elder statesman; the unpredictable maverick. How swiftly, if one were absent, a colleague modified his views, subtly adapted even his voice and manner to fill the gap. And so, apparently, he had assumed the mantle of Holroyd. The thought was ironic and not unsatisfying. Why not? Who else at Toynton Grange better fitted that rebarbative, non-conforming role?

He had been one of the youngest Under Secretaries of State ever appointed. He was confidently spoken of as the future head of a Department. That was how he saw himself. And then the disease, touching nerves and muscles at first with tentative fingers, had struck at the roots of confidence, at all the carefully laid plans. Dictating sessions with his personal assistant had become mutual embarrassments to be dreaded and deferred. Every telephone conversation was an ordeal; that first insistent, anxiety-pitched ring was enough to set his hand trembling. Meetings which he had always enjoyed and chaired with a quiet if abrasive competence had become unpredictable contests between mind and unruly body. He had become unsure where he had been most confident.

He wasn't alone in misfortune. He had seen others, some of them in his own Department, being helped from their grotesquely graceless invalid cars into their wheelchairs, accepting a lower grade and easier work, moving to a division which could afford to carry a passenger. The Department would have balanced expediency and the public interest with proper consideration and compassion. They would have kept him on long after his usefulness justified it. He could have died, as he had watched others die, in official harness, harness lightened and adjusted to his frail shoulders, but nevertheless harness. He accepted that there was a kind of courage in that. But it wasn't his kind.

It had been a joint meeting with another Department, chaired by himself, that had finally decided him. He still couldn't think of the shambles without shame and horror. He saw himself again, feet impotently padding, his stick beating a tattoo on the floor as he strove to take one step towards his chair, the mucus spluttering out with his welcoming words to shower over his neighbour's papers. The ring of eyes around the table, animals' eyes, watchful, predatory, embarrassed, not daring to meet his. Except for one boy, a young good-looking Principal from the Treasury. He had looked fixedly at the Chairman, not with pity but with an almost clinical interest, noting for future reference one more manifestation of human behaviour under stress. The words had come out at last, of course. Somehow he had got through the meeting. But for him, it had been the end.

He had heard of Toynton Grange as one did hear of such places, through a colleague whose wife received the Home's quarterly newsletter and contributed to the funds. It had seemed to offer an answer. He was a bachelor without family. He couldn't hope indefinitely to look after himself, nor on a disability pension could he buy a permanent nurse. And he had to get out of London. If he couldn't succeed, then he would opt out completely, retire to oblivion, away from the embarrassed pity of colleagues, from noise and foul air, from the hazards and inconveniences of a world aggressively organized for the healthy and able bodied. He would write the book on decision-making in Government planned for his retirement, catch up on his Greek, re-read the whole of Hardy. If he couldn't cultivate his own garden, at least he could avert fastidious eyes from the lack of cultivation in everyone else's.

And for the first six months it had seemed to work. There were disadvantages which, strangely, he hadn't expected or considered; the unenterprising, predictable meals; the pressures of discordant personalities; the delay in getting books and wine delivered; the lack of good talk; the self-absorption of the sick, their preoccupation with symptoms and bodily functions; the awful childishness and spurious joviality of institutional life. But it had been just supportable and he had been reluctant to admit failure since all alternatives seemed worse. And then Peter had arrived.

He had come to Toynton Grange just over a year ago. He was a polio victim, the seventeen-year-old only child of a haulage contractor's widow from the industrial Midlands who had made three preparatory visits of officious and ill-informed inspection before calculating whether she could afford to accept the vacancy. Henry suspected that, panicked by the loneliness and debased status of the early months of widowhood, she was already looking for a second husband and was beginning to realize that a seventeen-year-old chair-bound son was an obstacle to be carefully weighed by likely candidates against her late husband's money, her own ageing and desperate sexuality. Listening to her spate of obstetric and marital intimacies, Henry had realized once again that the disabled were treated as a different breed. They posed no threat, sexual or otherwise, offered no competition.

As companions they had the advantage of animals; literally anything could be spoken in front of them without embarrassment.

So Dolores Bonnington had expressed herself satisfied and Peter had arrived. The boy had made little impression on him at first. It was only gradually that he had come to appreciate his qualities of mind. Peter had been nursed at home with the help of district nurses and had been driven, when his health permitted, to the local comprehensive school. There he had been unlucky. No one, least of all his mother, had discovered his intelligence. Henry Carwardine doubted whether she was capable of recognizing it. He was less ready to acquit the school. Even with the problem of understaffing and over-large classes, the inevitable logistic difficulties of a huge city comprehensive, someone on the staff of that over-equipped and ill-disciplined menagerie, he thought with anger, ought to have been able to recognize a scholar. It was Henry who conceived the idea that they might provide for Peter the education he had lost; that he might in time enter a university and become self-supporting.

To Henry's surprise, preparing Peter for his 'O' levels had provided the common concern, the sense of unity and community at Toynton Grange which none of Wilfred's experiments had achieved. Even Victor Holroyd helped.

'It seems that the boy isn't a fool. He's almost totally uneducated, of course. The staff, poor sods, were probably too busy teaching race relations, sexual technique and other contemporary additions to the syllabus and preventing the barbarians from pulling the school down around their ears to have time for someone with a mind.'

'He ought to have maths and one science, Victor, at least at 'O' level. If you could help . . .'

'Without a lab?'

'There's the clinical room, you could fix something up there. He wouldn't be taking a science as a main subject at 'A' level?'

'Of course not. I realize my disciplines are included merely to provide an illusion of academic balance. But the boy ought to be taught to think scientifically. I know the suppliers of course. I could probably fix something up.'

'I shall pay, of course.'

'Certainly. I could afford it myself but I'm a great believer in people paying for their own gratifications.'

'And Jennie and Ursula might be interested.'

Henry had been amazed to find himself making the suggestion. Affection – he had not yet come to use the word love – had made him kind.

'God forbid! I'm not setting up a kindergarten. But I'll take on the boy for maths and general science.'

Holroyd had given three sessions a week each of a carefully measured hour. But there had been no doubt about the quality of his teaching.

Father Baddeley had been pressed into service to teach Latin. Henry himself took English literature and history and undertook the general direction of the course. He discovered that Grace Willison spoke French better than anyone else at Toynton Grange and after some initial reluctance, she agreed to take French conversation twice a week. Wilfred had watched the preparations indulgently, taking no active part but raising no objections. Everyone was suddenly busy and happy.

Peter himself was accepting rather than dedicated. But he proved incredibly hard-working, gently amused perhaps by their common enthusiasm but capable of the sustained concentration which is the mark of a scholar. They found it almost impossible to overwork him. He was grateful, biddable, but detached. Sometimes Henry, looking at the calm girlish face, had the frightening feeling that the teachers were all seventeen-year-old children and the boy alone burdened with the sad cynicism of maturity.

Henry knew that he would never forget that moment when, at last, and joyfully, he had acknowledged love. It had been a warm day in early spring; was it really only six months ago? They had been sitting together where he sat now in the early afternoon sunshine, books on their laps ready to begin the two-thirty history lesson. Peter had been wearing a short-sleeved shirt, and he had rolled up his own sleeves to feel the first warmth of the sun pricking the hairs of his forearm. They had been sitting in silence as he was sitting now. And then, without turning to look at him, Peter had lain the length of his soft inner forearm against Henry's and deliberately, as if every movement were part of a ritual, an affirmation, had twined their fingers together so that their palms too were joined flesh against flesh. Henry's nerves and blood remembered that moment and would do until he died. The shock of ecstasy, the sudden realization of joy, a spring of sheer unalloyed happiness which for all its surging excitement was yet paradoxically rooted in fulfilment and peace. It seemed in that moment as if everything which had happened in life, his job, his illness, coming to Toynton Grange, had led inevitably to this place, this love. Everything – success, failure, pain, frustration – had led to it and was justified by it. Never had he been so aware of another's body: the beat of the pulse in the thin wrist; the labyrinth of blue veins lying against his, blood flowing in concert with his blood; the delicate unbelievably soft flesh of the forearm; the bones of the childish fingers confidently resting between his own. Besides the intimacy of this first touch all previous adventures of the flesh had been counterfeit. And so they had sat silently, for unmeasured unfathomable time, before turning to look, at first gravely and then smilingly, into each other's eyes.

He wondered now how he could have so underestimated Wilfred. Happily secure in the confidence of love acknowledged and returned, he had treated Wilfred's innuendoes and expostulations – when they pierced his consciousness – with pitying contempt, seeing them as no more real or threatening than the bleatings of a timid, ineffectual schoolmaster obsessively warning his boys against unnatural vice.

'It's good of you to give so much time to Peter, but we ought to remember that we are one family at Toynton Grange. Other people would like a share of your interest. It isn't perhaps kind or wise to show too marked a preference for one person. I think that Ursula and Jennie and even poor Georgie sometimes feel neglected.'

Henry had hardly heard; had certainly not bothered to reply.

'Henry, Dot tells me that you've taken to locking your door when giving Peter his lessons. I would prefer that you didn't. It is one of our rules that doors are never locked. If either of you needed medical help suddenly, it could be very dangerous.'

Henry had continued to lock his door keeping the key always

with him. He and Peter might have been the only two people at Toynton Grange. Lying in bed at night he began to plan and to dream, at first tentatively and then with the euphoria of hope. He had given up too early and too easily. There was still some future before him. The boy's mother hardly visited him, seldom wrote. Why shouldn't the two of them leave Toynton Grange and live together? He had his pension and some capital. He could buy a small house, at Oxford or Cambridge perhaps, and get it adapted for their two wheelchairs. When Peter was at university he would need a home. He made calculations, wrote to his bank manager, schemed how it might be organized so that the plan in its ultimate reasonableness and beauty could be presented to Peter. He knew that there were dangers. He would get worse; with luck Peter might even slightly improve. He must never let himself be a burden to the boy. Father Baddeley had only once spoken to him directly of Peter. He had brought over to Toynton Grange a book from which Henry had planned to set a passage of précis. On leaving he had said gently, as always not baulking the truth:

'Your disease is progressive, Peter's isn't. One day he's going to have to manage without you. Remember that, my son.' Well, he would remember.

In early August Mrs Bonnington arranged for Peter to spend a fortnight with her at home. She called it taking him for a holiday. Henry had said:

'Don't write. I never expect anything good from a letter. I shall see you again in two weeks.'

But Peter hadn't come back. The evening before he was due to return Wilfred had announced the news at dinner, eyes carefully avoiding Henry's.

'You'll be glad for Peter's sake to hear that Mrs Bonnington has found a place for him nearer his home and that he won't be returning to us. She hopes to marry again fairly soon and she and her husband want to visit Peter more frequently and have him home for occasional weekends. The new home will make arrangements for Peter's education to continue. You have all worked so hard with him. I know you'll be glad to hear that it won't be wasted.'

It had been very cleverly planned; he had to give Wilfred that credit. There must have been discreet telephone calls and letters to the mother, negotiations with the new home. Peter must have been on the waiting list for weeks, possibly months. Henry could imagine the phrases.

'Unhealthy interests; unnatural affection; driving the boy too hard; mental and psychological pressure.'

Hardly anyone at Toynton Grange had spoken to him about the transfer. They had avoided the contamination of his misery. Grace Willison had said, shrinking from his angry eyes:

'We shall all miss him, but his own mother . . . It's natural that she should want him close to her.'

'Of course. By all means let us defer to the sacred rights of motherhood.'

Within a week they had apparently forgotten Peter and returned to their old pursuits as easily as children discarding new and unwanted Christmas toys. Holroyd had disconnected his apparatus and packed it away.

'Let it be a lesson to you, my dear Henry. Put not your trust in pretty boys. We can hardly expect that he was dragged to the new home by force.'

'He may have been.'

'Oh, come now! The boy is practically of age. He has the use of brain and speech. He can hold a pen. We have to face it that our company here was less fascinating than we had deluded ourselves. Peter is amenable. He made no objections when he was dumped here and I've no doubt he made none when he was dragged away.'

Henry, on impulse, had grasped Father Baddeley's arm as he passed and asked him:

'Did you collude in this triumph for morality and mother-love?'

Father Baddeley had briefly shaken his head, a gesture so slight that it was hardly discernible. He had seemed about to speak and then, with one pressure on Henry's shoulder, had moved on, for once at a loss, offering no comfort. But Henry had felt a spurt of anger and resentment against Michael as he hadn't against anyone else at Toynton Grange. Michael, who had the use of his legs and voice, who wasn't reduced by anger into a jibbering, slobbering buffoon. Michael, who could surely have prevented this monstrous thing if he hadn't been inhibited by timidity, by his fear and disgust of the flesh. Michael, who had no place at Toynton Grange if not to affirm love.

There had been no letter. Henry had been reduced to bribing Philby to collect the post. His paranoia had reached the stage when he believed that Wilfred might be intercepting letters. He didn't write himself. Whether or not to do so was a preoccupation which took most of his waking hours. But, less than six weeks later, Mrs Bonnington had written to Wilfred to say that Peter was dead of pneumonia. It could, Henry knew, have happened anywhere at any time. It didn't necessarily mean that the medical and nursing care at the new home had been less than at Toynton Grange. Peter had always been peculiarly at risk. But in his heart Henry knew that he could have kept Peter safe. In scheming his transfer from Toynton Grange Wilfred had killed him.

And Peter's murderer went about his business, smiled his indulgent lop-sided smile, ceremoniously drew the folds of his cloak around him to preserve him from the contamination of human emotion, surveyed complacently the flawed objects of his beneficence. Was it his imagination, Henry wondered, that Wilfred had become afraid of him? Now they seldom spoke. Naturally solitary, Henry had become morose since Peter's death. Except for meal times he spent most of his days in his room, looking out over the desolate headland, neither reading nor working, possessed by a profound ennui. He knew that he hated rather than felt hatred. Love, joy, anger, grief even, were emotions too powerful for his diminished personality. He could entertain only their pale shadows. But hatred was like a latent fever dormant in the blood; sometimes it could flare into terrifying delirium. It was during one such a mood that Holroyd had whispered to him, had wheeled his chair across the patio and manoeuvred it close to Henry. Holroyd's mouth, pink and precise as a girl's, a neat, suppurating wound in the heavy blue jaw, puckered to discharge its venom. Holroyd's breath sour in his nostrils.

'I have learnt something of interest about our dear Wilfred. I shall share it with you in time but you must forgive me if I savour it alone for a little longer. There will be a right moment for disclosure. One strives always for the maximum dramatic effect.' Hatred and boredom had reduced them to secrets together, planning their petty stratagems of vengeance and betrayal.

He looked out of the tall, curved window westward over the rising headland. The darkness was falling. Somewhere out there the restless tide was scouring the rocks, rocks washed clean for ever of Holroyd's blood. Not even a twist of torn cloth remained for the barnacles to fasten on. Holroyd's dead hands like floating weeds moving sluggishly in the tide, sand-filled eyes turned upwards to the swooping gulls. What was that poem of Walt Whitman which Holroyd had read at dinner on the night before he died:

> 'Approach strong deliveress,
> When it is so, when thou hast taken them I joyously
> sing the dead,
> Lost in the loving floating ocean of thee,
> Laved in the flood of thy bliss O death.
>
> The night in silence under many a star,
> The ocean shore and the husky whispering wave
> whose voices I know,
> And the soul turning to thee O vast and well-veiled
> death,
> And the body gratefully nestling close to thee.'

Why that poem, in its sentimental resignation, at once so alien to Holroyd's embattled spirit, and yet so prophetically apposite? Was he telling them, even subconsciously, that he knew what must happen, that he embraced and welcomed it? Peter and Holroyd. Holroyd and Baddeley. And now this policeman friend of Baddeley's had arrived out of his past. Why, and for what? He might learn something when they drank together after dinner with Julius. And so, of course, might Dalgliesh. 'There is no art to find the mind's construction in the face.' But Duncan was wrong. There was a great deal of art and one in which a Commander of the Metropolitan Police would be better practised than most. Well, if that was what he had come for, he could make a beginning after dinner. Tonight he, Henry, would dine in his room. Philby when summoned would bring up his tray and plonk it unceremoniously and grudgingly in front of him. It wasn't possible to buy civility from Philby but it was possible, he thought with grim exultation, to buy almost anything else.

III

'My body is my prison; and I would be so obedient to the Law, as not to break prison; I would not hasten my death by starving or macerating this body. But if this prison be burnt down by continual fevers, or blown down with continual vapours, would any man be so in love with the ground upon which that prison stood, as to desire rather to stay there than to go home?'

It wasn't so much, thought Dalgliesh, that the Donne didn't go with the stewed mutton, as that the mutton didn't go with the home-brewed wine. Neither was in itself unpalatable. The mutton, cooked with onions, potatoes and carrots, and flavoured with herbs, was unexpectedly good if a little greasy. The elderberry wine was a nostalgic reminder of duty visits paid with his father to house-bound and hospitable parishioners. Together they tasted lethal. He reached for the water carafe.

Opposite him sat Millicent Hammitt, her square slab of a face softened by the candlelight, her absence during the afternoon explained by the pungent scent of lacquer which was wafted to him from the stiff, corrugated waves of greying hair. Everyone was present except the Hewsons, dining presumably in their own cottage, and Henry Carwardine. At the far end of the table, Albert Philby sat a little apart, a monkish Caliban in a brown habit, half crouching over his food. He ate noisily, tearing his bread into crusts and wiping them vigorously around his plate. All the patients were being helped to eat. Dalgliesh, despising his squeamishness, tried to shut his ears to the muted slobbering, the staccato rattle of spoon against plate, the sudden retching, unobtrusively controlled.

'If thou didst depart from that Table in peace, thou canst depart from this world in peace. And the peace of that Table is to come to it in peace desiderii, with a contented minde . . .'

Wilfred stood at a reading desk at the head of the table, flanked by two candles in metal holders. Jeoffrey, distended with food, lay ceremoniously curved at his feet. Wilfred had a good voice and knew how to use it. An actor manqué? Or an actor who had found his stage and played on, happily oblivious of the dwindling audience, of the creeping paralysis of his dream? A neurotic driven by obsession? Or a man at peace with himself, secure at the still centre of his being?

Suddenly the four table candles flared and hissed. Dalgliesh's ears caught the faint squeak of wheels, the gentle thud of metal against wood. The door was slowly swinging open. Wilfred's voice faltered, and then broke off. A spoon rasped violently against a plate. Out of the shadows came a wheelchair, its occupant, head bent, swaddled in a thick plaid cloak. Miss Willison gave a sad moan and scratched the sign of the cross on her grey dress. There was a gasp from Ursula Hollis. No one spoke. Suddenly Jennie Pegram screamed, thin and insistent as a tin whistle. The sound was so unreal that Dot Moxon jerked her head round as if uncertain where the sound was coming from. The scream subsided into a giggle. The girl clamped her hand against her mouth. Then she said:

'I thought it was Victor! That's Victor's cloak.'

No one else moved or spoke. Glancing along the table, Dalgliesh let his eyes rest speculatively on Dennis Lerner. His face was a mask of terror which slowly disintegrated into relief, the features seeming to droop and crumble, amorphous as a smudged painting. Carwardine wheeled his chair to the table. He had some difficulty in getting out his words. A globule of mucus gleamed like a yellow jewel in the candle light and dribbled from his chin. At last he said in his high distorted voice:

'I thought I might join you for coffee. It seemed discourteous to absent myself on our guest's first night.'

Dot Moxon's voice was sharp:

'Did you have to wear that cloak?'

He turned to her:

'It was hanging in the business room and I felt cold. And we hold so much in common. Need we exclude the dead?'

Wilfred said:

'Shall we remember the Rule?'

They turned their faces to him like obedient children. He waited until they had again begun to eat. The hands which gripped the sides of the reading desk were steady, the beautiful voice perfectly controlled.

'That so riding at Anchor, and in that calme, whether God enlarge thy voyage, by enlarging thy life, or put thee into the harbour by the breath, by the breathlesnesse of Death, either way, East or West, thou maist depart in peace . . .'

IV

It was after eight-thirty before Dalgliesh set out to wheel Henry Carwardine to Julius Court's cottage. The task wasn't easy for a man in the first stages of convalescence. Carwardine, despite his leanness, was surprisingly heavy and the stony path wound uphill. Dalgliesh hadn't liked to suggest using his car since to be hoisted through the narrow door might be more painful and humiliating for his companion than the customary wheelchair. Anstey had been passing through the hall as they left. He had held open the door and helped guide the wheelchair down the ramp, but had made no attempt to assist, nor did he offer the use of the patients' bus. Dalgliesh wondered whether it was his imagination that detected a note of disapproval of the enterprise in Anstey's final goodnight.

Neither man spoke for the first part of the journey. Carwardine rested a heavy torch between his knees and tried to steady its beam on the path. The circle of light, reeling and spinning before them with every lurch of the chair, illumined with dazzling clarity a secret night world of greenness, movement and scurrying life. Dalgliesh, a little light-headed with tiredness, felt disassociated from his physical surroundings. The two thick rubber hand-grips, slippery to the touch, were loose and twisted irritatingly beneath his hands, seeming to have no relation to the rest of the chair. The path ahead was real only because its stones and crevices jarred the wheels. The night was still and very warm for autumn, the air heavy with the smell of grass and the memory of summer flowers. Low clouds had obscured the stars and they moved forwards in almost total darkness towards the strengthening murmur of the sea and the four oblongs of light which marked Toynton Cottage. When they were close enough for the largest oblong to reveal itself as the rear door of the cottage, Dalgliesh said on impulse:

'I found a rather disagreeable poison pen letter in Father Baddeley's bureau. Obviously someone at Toynton Grange didn't like him. I wondered whether this was personal spite or whether anyone else had received one.'

Carwardine bent his head upwards. Dalgliesh saw his face intriguingly foreshortened, his sharp nose a spur of bone, the jaw hanging loose as a marionette's below the shapeless void of mouth. He said:

'I had one about ten months ago, placed inside my library book, I haven't had one since, and I don't know of anyone else who has. It's not the kind of thing people talk about, but I think the news would have got around if the trouble had been endemic. Mine was, I suppose, the usual muck. It suggested what methods of somewhat acrobatic sexual self-gratification might be open to me supposing I still had the physical agility to perform them. It took the desire to do so for granted.'

'It was obscene, then, rather than merely offensive?'

'Obscene in the sense of calculated to disgust rather than to deprave or corrupt, yes.'

'Have you any idea who was responsible?'

'It was typed on Toynton Grange paper and on an old Remington machine used chiefly by Grace Willison to send out the quarterly newsletter. She seemed the most likely candidate. It wasn't Ursula Hollis; she didn't arrive until two months later. And aren't these things usually sent by respectable middle-aged spinsters?'

'In this case I doubt it.'

'Oh, well – I defer to your greater experience of obscenity.'

'Did you tell anyone?'

'Only Julius. He counselled against telling anyone else and suggested I tear the note up and flush it down the WC. As that advice coincided with my own inclination, I took it. As I said, I haven't had another. I imagine that the sport loses its thrill if the victim shows absolutely no sign of concern.'

'Could it have been Holroyd?'

'It didn't really seem his style. Victor was offensive but not, I should have thought, in that particular way. His weapon was the voice, not the pen. Personally I didn't mind him as much as some of the others did. He hit out rather like an unhappy child. There was more personal bitterness than active malice. Admittedly, he added a somewhat childish codicil to his will the week before he died; Philby and Julius's housekeeper, Mrs Reynolds, witnessed it. But that was probably because he'd made up his mind to die and wanted to relieve us all of any obligation to remember him with kindness.'

'So you think he killed himself?'

'Of course. And so does everyone else. How else could it have happened? It seems the most likely hypothesis. It was either suicide or murder.'

It was the first time anyone at Toynton Grange had used that portentous word. Spoken in Carwardine's pedantic, rather high voice it sounded as incongruous as blasphemy on the lips of a nun.

Dalgliesh said:

'Or the chair brakes could have been defective.'

'Given the circumstances, I count that as murder.'

There was silence for a moment. The chair lurched over a small boulder and the torch light swung upwards in a wide arc, a miniature and frail searchlight. Carwardine steadied it and then said:

'Philby oiled and checked the chair brakes at eight-fifty on the night before Holroyd died. I was in the workroom messing about with my modelling clay at the time. I saw him. He left the workroom shortly afterwards and I stayed on until about ten o'clock.'

'Did you tell the police that?'

'Since they asked me, yes. They inquired with heavy tact where exactly I had spent the evening and whether I had touched Holroyd's chair after Philby had left. Since I would hardly have admitted the fact if I had, the question was naïve. They questioned Philby, although not in my presence, and I've no doubt that he confirmed my story. I have an ambivalent attitude towards the police; I confine myself strictly to answering their questions, but on the premise that they are, in general, entitled to the truth.'

They had arrived. Light streamed from the rear door of the cottage and Julius Court, a dark silhouette, emerged to meet them. He took the wheelchair from Dalgliesh and pushed it along the short stone passage leading into the sitting-room. On the way Dalgliesh just had time to glimpse through an open door the pine-covered walls, red-tiled floor and gleaming chrome of Julius's kitchen, a kitchen too like his own where a woman, overpaid and underworked to assuage her employer's guilt for hiring her at all, cooked the occasional meal to gratify one person's over-fastidious taste.

The sitting-room occupied the whole of the front ground floor of what had obviously been two cottages. A fire of driftwood crackled on the open hearth but both the long windows were open to the night. The stone walls vibrated with the thudding of the sea. It was disconcerting to feel so close to the cliff edge and yet not know precisely how close. As if reading his thoughts, Julius said:

'We're just six yards from the forty-foot drop to the rocks. There's a stone patio and low wall outside; we might sit there later if it's warm enough. What will you drink, spirits or wine? I know Henry's preference is for claret.'

Dalgliesh didn't repent of his choice when he saw the labels on the three bottles which were standing, two already uncorked, on the low table near the hearth. He was surprised that wine of such quality should be produced for two casual guests. While Julius busied himself with the glasses, Dalgliesh wandered about the room. It contained enviable objects, if one were in a mood to prize personal possessions. His eyes lit on a splendid Sunderland lustre-ware jug commemorating Trafalgar, three early Staffordshire figures on the stone mantelpiece, a couple of agreeable seascapes on the longest wall. Above the door leading to the cliff edge was a ship's figure-head finely and ornately carved in oak; two cherubs supported a galleon topped with a shield and swathed with heavy seaman's knots. Seeing his interest, Julius called out:

'It was made about 1660 by Grinling Gibbons, reputedly for

Jacob Court, a smuggler in these parts. As far as I can discover, he was absolutely no ancestor of mine, worse luck. It's probably the oldest merchant ship figure-head known to exist. Greenwich think they have one earlier, but I'd give mine the benefit of a couple of years.'

Set on a pedestal at the far end of the room and faintly gleaming as if luminous was the marble bust of a winged child holding in his chubby hand a posy of rosebuds and lilies of the valley. The marble was the colour of pale coffee except over the lids of the closed eyes, which were tinged with a faint pink. The unveined hands held the flowers with the upright, unselfconscious grip of a child; the boy's lips were slightly parted in a half-smile, tranquil and secretive. Dalgliesh stretched out a finger and gently stroked the cheek; he could imagine it warm to his touch. Julius came over to him carrying two glasses.

'You like my marble? It's a memorial piece, of course, seventeenth or very early eighteenth century and derived from Bernini. Henry, I suspect, would like it better if it were Bernini.'

Henry called out:

'I wouldn't like it better. I did say I'd be prepared to pay more for it.'

Dalgliesh and Court moved back to the fireplace and settled down for what was obviously intended to be a night of serious drinking. Dalgliesh found his eyes straying around the room. There was no bravura, no conscious striving after originality or effect. And yet, trouble had been taken; every object was in the right place. They had, he thought, been bought because Julius liked them; they weren't part of a careful scheme of capital appreciation, nor acquired out of an obsessive need to add to his collection. Yet Dalgliesh doubted whether any had been casually discovered or cheaply bought. The furniture, too, betrayed wealth. The leather sofa and the two winged and back-buttoned leather chairs were perhaps too opulent for the proportions and basic simplicity of the room, but Julius had obviously chosen them for comfort. Dalgliesh reproached himself for the streak of puritanism which compared the room unfavourably with the snug, unindulgent shabbiness of Father Baddeley's sitting-room.

Carwardine, sitting in his wheelchair and staring into the fire above the rim of his glass, asked suddenly:

'Did Baddeley warn you about the more bizarre manifestations of Wilfred's philanthropy, or was your visit here unpremeditated?'

It was a question Dalgliesh had been expecting. He sensed that both men were more than casually interested in his reply.

'Father Baddeley wrote to say that he would be glad to see me. I decided to come on impulse. I've had a spell in hospital and it seemed a good idea to spend a few days of my convalescence with him.'

Carwardine said:

'I can think of more suitable places than Hope Cottage for convalescence, if the inside is anything like the exterior. Had you known Baddeley long?'

'Since boyhood; he was my father's curate. But we last met, and only briefly, when I was at university.'

'And having been content to know nothing of each other for a decade or so, you're naturally distressed to find him so inconveniently dead.'

Unprovoked, Dalgliesh replied equably:

'More than I would have expected. We seldom wrote except to exchange cards at Christmas but he was a man more often in my thoughts, I suppose, than some people I saw almost daily. I don't know why I never bothered to get in touch. One makes the excuse of busyness. But, from what I remember of him, I can't quite see how he fitted in here.'

Julius laughed:

'He didn't. He was recruited when Wilfred was going through a more orthodox phase, I suppose to give Toynton Grange a certain religious respectability. But in recent months I sensed a coolness between them, didn't you, Henry? Father Baddeley was probably no longer sure whether Wilfred wanted a priest or a guru. Wilfred picks up any scraps of philosophy, metaphysics and orthodox religion which take his fancy to make his Technicolor dreamcoat. As a result, as you'll probably discover if you stay long enough, this place suffers from the lack of a coherent ethos. There's nothing more fatal to success. Take my London club, dedicated simply to the enjoyment of good food and wine and the exclusion of bores and pederasts. It's unstated of course, but we all know where we stand. The aims are simple and comprehensible and, therefore, realizable. Here the poor dears don't know whether they're in a nursing home, a commune, a hotel, a monastery or a particularly dotty lunatic asylum. They even have meditation sessions from time to time. I'm afraid Wilfred may be getting a touch of the Zens.'

Carwardine broke in:

'He's muddled, but which of us isn't? Basically he's kind and well meaning, and at least he's spent his own personal fortune at Toynton Grange. In this age of noisy and self-indulgent commitment when the first principle of private or public protest is that it mustn't relate to anything for which the protestor can be held in the least responsible or involve him in the slightest personal sacrifice that, at least, is in his favour.'

'You like him?' asked Dalgliesh.

Henry Carwardine answered with surprising roughness.

'As he's saved me from the ultimate fate of incarceration in a long-stay hospital and gives me a private room at a price I can afford, I'm naturally bound to find him delightful.'

There was a short, embarrassed silence. Sensing it, Carwardine added:

'The food is the worst thing about Toynton, but that can be remedied, even if I do occasionally feel like a greedy schoolboy feasting alone in my room. And listening to my fellow inmates read their favourite bleeding chunks from popular theology and the less enterprising anthologies of English verse is a small price to pay for silence at dinner.'

Dalgliesh said:

'Staffing must be a difficulty. According to Mrs Hewson, Anstey chiefly relies on an ex-convict and an otherwise unemployable matron.'

Julius Court reached out for the claret and refilled the three glasses. He said:

'Dear Maggie, discreet as always. It's true that Philby, the handyman, has some kind of record. He's not exactly an advertisement for the place, but someone has to sluice the foul linen, slaughter the chickens, clean the lavatories and do the other jobs which Wilfred's sensitive soul cringes at. Besides, he's passionately devoted to Dot Moxon, and I've no doubt that helps to keep her happy. Since Maggie has let slip so much, you may as well know the truth about Dot. Perhaps you remember something of the case – she was that notorious staff nurse at Nettingfield Geriatric Hospital. Four years ago she struck a patient. It was only a light blow but the old woman fell, knocking her head against a bedside locker and nearly died. Reading between the lines at the subsequent inquiry report, she was a selfish, demanding, foul-mouthed virago who would have tempted a saint. Her family would have nothing to do with her – didn't even visit – until they discovered that there was a great deal of agreeable publicity to be made out of righteous indignation. Perfectly proper too, no doubt. Patients, however disagreeable, are sacrosanct and it's in all our ultimate interests to uphold that admirable precept. The incident sparked off a spate of complaints about the hospital. There was a full-dress inquiry covering the administration, medical services, food, nursing care, the lot. Not surprisingly, they found plenty to inquire into. Two male nurses were subsequently dismissed and Dot left of her own accord. The inquiry, while deploring her loss of control, exonerated her from any suspicion of deliberate cruelty. But the damage was done; no other hospital wanted her. Apart from the suspicion that she wasn't exactly reliable under stress, they blamed her for provoking an inquiry which did no one any good and lost two men their jobs. Afterwards, Wilfred tried to get in touch with her; he thought from the accounts of the inquiry that she'd been hard done by. He took some time to trace her, but succeeded in the end and invited her here as a kind of matron. Actually, like the rest of the staff, she does anything that's needed from nursing to cooking. His motives weren't entirely beneficent. It's never easy to find nursing staff for a remote specialized place like this, apart from the unorthodoxy of Wilfred's methods. If he lost Dorothy Moxon he wouldn't easily find a replacement.'

Dalgliesh said:

'I remember the case but not her face. It's the young blonde girl – Jennie Pegram, isn't it? – who looks familiar.'

Carwardine smiled; indulgent, a little contemptuous.

'I thought you might ask about her. Wilfred ought to find a

way of using her for fund-raising, she'd love it. I don't know anyone who's better at assuming that expression of wistful, uncomprehending, long-suffering fortitude. She'd make a fortune for the place properly exploited.'

Julius laughed:

'Henry, as you have gathered, doesn't like her. If she looks familiar, you may have seen her on television about eighteen months ago. It was the month for the media to lacerate the British conscience on behalf of the young chronic sick, and the producer sent out his underlings to scavenge for a suitable victim. They came up with Jennie. She had been nursed for twelve years, and very well nursed, in a geriatric unit, partly, I gather, because they couldn't find a more suitable place for her, partly because she rather liked being the petted favourite of the patients and visitors, and partly because the hospital had group physiotherapy and occupational therapy facilities of which our Jennie took advantage. But the programme, as you can imagine, made the most of her situation – "Unfortunate twenty-five-year-old girl incarcerated among the old and dying; shut away from the community; helpless; hopeless." All the most senile patients were carefully grouped round her for the benefit of the camera with Jennie in the middle doing her stuff magnificently. Shrill accusations against the inhumanity of the Department of Health, the regional hospital board, the hospital managers. Next day, predictably, there was a public outburst of indignation which lasted, I imagine, until the next protest programme. The compassionate British public demanded that a more suitable place be found for Jennie. Wilfred wrote offering a vacancy here, Jennie accepted, and fourteen months ago she arrived. No one quite knows what she makes of us. I should give a lot to look into what passes for Jennie's mind.'

Dalgliesh was surprised that Julius had such an intimate knowledge of the patients at Toynton Grange, but he asked no more questions. He dropped unobtrusively out of the chatter and sat drinking his wine, half listening to the desultory voices of his companions. It was the quiet, undemanding talk of men who had acquaintances and interests in common, who knew just enough about each other and cared just sufficiently to create an illusion of companionship. He had no particular wish to share it. The wine deserved silence. He realized that this was the first fine wine he had drunk since his illness. It was reassuring that yet another of life's pleasures still held its power to solace. It took him a minute to realize that Julius was talking to him directly.

'I'm sorry about the proposed poetry reading. But I'm not altogether displeased. It illustrates one thing that you'll realize about Toynton. They exploit. They don't mean to, but they can't help it. They say that they want to be treated as ordinary people, and then make demands no ordinary person would dream of making, and naturally one can't refuse. Now, perhaps, you won't think too harshly of those of us who seem less than enthusiastic about Toynton.'

'Us?'

'The little group of normals anyway, in thrall to the place.'

'Are you?'

'Oh, yes! I get away to London or abroad so that the spell never really has a chance to take hold. But think of Millicent, stuck in that cottage because Wilfred lets her have it rent-free. All she wants is to get back to the bridge tables and cream cakes of Cheltenham Spa. So why doesn't she? And Maggie. Maggie would say that all she wanted was a bit of life. Well, that's what we all want, a bit of life. Wilfred tried to get her interested in bird-watching. I remember her reply. "If I have to watch another bloody seagull shitting on Toynton Head I'll run screaming into the sea." Dear Maggie. I rather take to Maggie when she's sober. And Eric? Well, he could break away if he had the courage. Looking after five patients and medically supervising the production of hand lotion and bath powder is hardly an honourable job for a registered medical practitioner, even one with an unfortunate predilection for little girls. And then there's Helen Rainer. But I rather fancy that our enigmatic Helen's reason for staying is more elemental and understandable. But they're all a prey of boredom. And now I'm boring you. Would you like to hear some music? We usually listen to records when Henry's here.'

The claret, unaccompanied by speech or music, would have contented Dalgliesh. But he could see that Henry was as anxious to hear a record as Julius probably was to demonstrate the superiority of his stereo equipment. Invited to choose Dalgliesh asked for Vivaldi. While the record was playing he strolled out into the night. Julius followed him and they stood in silence at the low barricade of stone at the cliff edge. The sea lay before them, faintly luminous, ghostly under a scatter of high, unemphatic stars. He thought that the tide was on the ebb but it still sounded very close, thudding against the rocky beach in great chords of sound, a base accompaniment to the high, sweet counterpoint of the distant violins. Dalgliesh thought that he could feel the spume light on his forehead, but when he put up his hand he found it was only a trick of the freshening breeze.

So there must have been two poison-pen writers, only one genuinely committed to his or her obscene trade. It was obvious from Grace Willison's distress and Carwardine's laconic disgust that they had received a very different type of letter from the one found at Hope Cottage. It was too great a coincidence that two poison pens should be operating at the same time in so small a community. The assumption was that Father Baddeley's note had been planted in the bureau after his death, with small attempt at concealment, for Dalgliesh to find. If this were so, then it must have been put there by someone who knew about at least one of the other letters; had been told that it was typed on a Toynton Grange machine and on Toynton Grange paper, but who hadn't actually seen it. Grace Willison's letter had been typed on the Imperial machine and she had confided only in Dot Moxon. Carwardine's, like Father Baddeley's, had been typed on the Remington, and he had told Julius Court. The inference was obvious. But how could a man as intelligent as Court expect such a childish ruse to deceive a professional detective, or even an enthusiastic amateur? But then, had it been intended to? Dalgliesh had signed his postcard to Father Baddeley only with his initials. If it had been found by someone with a guilty secret as he searched feverishly through the bureau it would have told him nothing except that Father Baddeley was expecting a visitor on the afternoon of 1st October, a visitor who was probably as innocuous as a fellow clergyman or an old parishioner. But, just in case Father Baddeley had confided that something was on his mind, it might have seemed worthwhile to concoct and plant a false clue. Almost certainly, it had been placed in the bureau shortly before his arrival. If Anstey were telling the truth about looking through Father Baddeley's papers on the morning after his death, it was impossible that he should have missed the poison pen note or failed to remove it.

But even if all this were an elaborate and over-sophisticated edifice of conjecture, and Father Baddeley had indeed received the poison pen note, Dalgliesh now felt certain that it wasn't the reason for his summons. Father Baddeley would have felt perfectly competent both to discover the sender and to deal with him. He was unworldly but not naïve. Unlike Dalgliesh, he had probably seldom become involved professionally with the more spectacular sins but that didn't mean they were outside his comprehension or, for that matter, his compassion. It was arguable, anyway, that those were the sins which did least damage. Of the more corrosive, petty, mean-minded delinquencies in all their sad but limited variety he, like any other parish priest, would have had his fill. He had his answer ready, compassionate but inexorable, offered, Dalgliesh remembered wryly, with all the gentle arrogance of absolute certainty. No, when Father Baddeley wrote he wanted professional advice he meant just that; advice which he could only get from a police officer on a matter which he felt unable to deal with himself. And that was unlikely to include the detection of a spiteful but not particularly vicious poison pen writer operating in a small community of which every member must have been known intimately to him.

The prospect of trying to discover the truth filled Dalgliesh with a profound depression. He was at Toynton Grange merely as a private visitor. He had no standing, no facilities, no equipment even. The task of sorting Father Baddeley's books could be stretched to cover a week, perhaps longer. After that, what excuse would he have to remain? And he had discovered nothing which would justify bringing in the local police. What did these vague suspicions, this sense of foreboding amount to? An old man, dying of heart disease, suffering his final and expected attack peacefully in his fireside chair, reaching perhaps in his last conscious moment for the familiar feel of his stole, lifting it over his head for the last time for reasons, probably only half understood, of comfort, of reassurance, of symbolism, of the simple affirmation of his priesthood or his faith. One could think of a dozen explanations, all simple, all more plausible than the secret visit of a murderous mock penitent. The missing diary; who could ever prove that Father Baddeley hadn't himself destroyed it before his admission to hospital? The forced bureau lock; nothing but the diary was missing and, as far as he knew, nothing valuable had been stolen. In the absence of other evidence, how could he possibly justify an official inquiry into a mislaid key and a broken lock?

But Father Baddeley had sent for him. There had been something on his mind. If Dalgliesh, without too great involvement, inconvenience or embarrassment, could discover in the next week or ten days what it had been, then he would do so. He owed that at least to the old man. But there it would end. Tomorrow he would pay a duty visit to the police and to Father Baddeley's solicitor. If anything came to light, then the police could deal with it. He was finished with police work, professional or amateur, and it would take more than the death of one old priest to change that decision.

V

When they got back to Toynton Grange shortly after midnight Henry Carwardine said roughly:

'They'll be relying on you to help me to bed, I'm afraid. Dennis Lerner usually wheels me to Toynton Cottage and calls for me at midnight, but since you're here . . . As Julius said, we're great exploiters at Toynton Grange. And I'd better shower. Dennis is off duty tomorrow morning and I can't stomach Philby. My room is on the first floor. We take the lift.'

Henry knew that he sounded ungracious but that, he guessed, would be more acceptable to his silent companion than humility or self-pity. It struck him that Dalgliesh looked as if he could have done with help himself. Perhaps the man had been more sick than they realized. Dalgliesh said calmly:

'Another half-bottle and I suspect we would both have needed help. But I'll do my best. Put down my clumsiness to inexperience and the claret.'

But he was surprisingly gentle and competent, getting Henry out of his clothes, supporting him to the lavatory, and finally wheeling him under the shower. He spent a little time examining the hoist and equipment and then used them intelligently. When he didn't know what was needed, he asked. Apart from these brief and necessary exchanges, neither spoke. Henry thought that he had seldom been put to bed with such imaginative gentleness. But, catching a glimpse in the bathroom mirror of his companion's drawn preoccupied face, of the dark secretive eyes cavernous with fatigue, he wished suddenly that he hadn't asked for help, that he had tumbled unshowered and fully dressed on to his bed, free from the humiliating touch of these competent hands. He sensed that, behind the disciplined calm, every contact with his naked body was a disagreeable duty. And for Henry himself, illogically and surprisingly, the touch of Dalgliesh's cool hands was like the touch of fear. He wanted to cry out:

'What are you doing here? Go away; don't interfere; leave us in peace.' The urge was so strong that he could almost believe that he had spoken the words aloud. And when, at last, he was comfortably bedded by his temporary nurse and Dalgliesh said an abrupt goodbye and immediately left him without another word, he knew that it was because he couldn't bear to hear even the most perfunctory and least gracious word of thanks.

FOUR

The Dreadful Shore

I

He awoke sluggishly soon before seven to disagreeably familiar noises; intrusive plumbing, the clang of apparatus, the squeal of chair wheels, sudden hurrying footsteps, determinedly cheerful exhortatory voices. Telling himself that the bathrooms would be needed for the patients, he shut his eyes resolutely on the bleak, impersonal room and willed himself to sleep again. When he woke an hour later after a fitful doze the annexe was silent. Someone – he dimly remembered a brown cloaked figure – had placed a mug of tea on his bedside table. It was cold, the greyish surface mottled with milk. He dragged on his dressing gown and went in search of the bathroom.

Breakfast at Toynton Grange was, as he had expected, laid out in the communal dining-room. But, at eight-thirty, he was either too early or too late for the majority of the inmates. Only Ursula Hollis was breakfasting when he arrived. She gave him a shy good-morning, then returned her eyes to the library book precariously propped against a jar of honey. Dalgliesh saw that the breakfast was simple, but adequate. There was a bowl of stewed apples; home-made muesli consisting mostly of porridge oats, bran and shredded apple; brown bread and margarine, and a row of boiled eggs each in its eggcup and individually named. The two remaining were cold. Presumably they were all cooked together earlier in the morning, and those who wanted their egg warm took the trouble to be on time. Dalgliesh helped himself to the egg pencilled with his name. It was glutinous at the top and very hard at the bottom, a result which he felt must have taken some perverse culinary skill to achieve.

After breakfast he went in search of Anstey to thank him for his overnight hospitality and to ask if there was anything he wanted from Wareham. He had decided that some of the afternoon had better be given over to shopping if he were to make himself comfortable in Michael's cottage. A short search of the seemingly deserted house found Anstey with Dorothy Moxon in the business room. They were seated together at the table with an open ledger before them. As he knocked and entered they looked up simultaneously with something of the air of guilty conspirators. It seemed to take a couple of seconds before they realized who he was. Anstey's smile, when it came, was as sweet as ever but his eyes were perfunctory. Dalgliesh sensed that he wouldn't be sorry to see him go. Anstey might see himself in the role of a welcoming medieval abbot, always ready with the bread and ale, but what he really craved were the gratifications of hospitality without the inconvenience of a guest. He said there was nothing he wanted in Wareham and then asked Dalgliesh how long he expected to be in the cottage. There was absolutely no hurry, of course. Their guest wasn't to feel himself at all in the way. When Dalgliesh replied that he would stay only until Father Baddeley's books were sorted and packed, it was difficult for him to conceal his relief. He offered to send Philby to Hope Cottage with some packing cases. Dorothy Moxon said nothing. She continued to stare fixedly at Dalgliesh as if determined not to betray her irritation at his presence and her desire to get back to the ledger by so much as a flicker of her sombre eyes.

It was comforting to be back in Hope Cottage, to smell again the familiar faintly ecclesiastical smell and to look forward to a long exploratory walk along the cliff before setting out for Wareham. But he had scarcely had time to unpack his case and change into stout walking shoes when he heard the patients' bus stopping outside and, going to the window, saw Philby unloading the first of the promised packing cases. Swinging it on his shoulder, he marched up the short path, kicked open the door, bringing with him into the room a powerful smell of stale sweat, and dropped the case at Dalgliesh's feet with a brusque:

'There's a couple more in the back.'

It was an obvious invitation to help unload them, and Dalgliesh took the hint. It was the first time he had seen the handyman in the full light, and the sight wasn't agreeable. He had, in fact, seldom encountered a man whose physical appearance so repelled him. Philby was only a little over five feet and stockily built with short plump arms and legs as pale and shapeless as peeled tree trunks. His head was round and his skin, despite his outdoor life, was pink and glossy and very smooth as if blown up with air. His eyes would have been remarkable in a more attractive face. They were slightly slanted and the irises were large and blue-black in colour. His black hair was scanty and combed straight back over the domed skull to end in an untidy and greasy fringe. He was wearing sandals, the right one fastened with string; a pair of dirty white shorts, so brief that they were almost indecent; and a grey vest, stained with sweat. Over this he wore, loosely open and held together only by a cord at the waist, his brown monk's habit. Without this incongruous garb he would have looked merely dirty and disreputable. With it he looked positively sinister.

As he made no attempt to go once the cases were unloaded, Dalgliesh deduced that he expected a tip. The proffered coins were slipped into the pocket of the habit with sly expertise but with no thanks. Dalgliesh was interested to learn that, despite the expensive experiment with home-produced eggs, not all the economic laws were defunct in this unworldly abode of brotherly love. Philby gave the three boxes a vicious valedictory kick as if to earn his tip by demonstrating that they were sound. As they disappointingly remained intact, he gave them a final look of sour displeasure and then departed. Dalgliesh wondered where Anstey had recruited this particular member of the staff. To his prejudiced eye the man looked like a category 'A' rapist on licence, but perhaps that was going a little too far even for Wilfred Anstey.

His second attempt to set out was frustrated by a second visitor, this time Helen Rainer, who had cycled the short distance from Toynton Grange with her bicycle basket piled high with linen from his bed. She explained that Wilfred was concerned in case the sheets at Hope Cottage were inadequately aired. It surprised Dalgliesh that she hadn't taken the opportunity to come with Philby in the bus. But perhaps, understandably, she found his proximity distasteful. She came in quietly but briskly and without too obviously making Dalgliesh feel he was a nuisance, unmistakably conveyed the impression that this wasn't a social visit, that she hadn't come to chat, and that there were more important duties awaiting her. They made the bed together, Nurse Rainer flicking the sheets into place and neatly mitring each corner with such brisk expertise that Dalgliesh, a second or two behind her, felt himself slow and incompetent. At first they worked in silence. He doubted whether this was the time to ask, however tactfully, how the misunderstanding had arisen over the neglected visit to Father Baddeley on the last night of his life. His stay in hospital must have intimidated him. It took an effort of will to say:

'I'm probably being over-sensitive, but I wish that someone had been with Father Baddeley when he died, or at least had looked in on him later that night to see that all was well.'

She could with justice, he thought, reply to this implied criticism by pointing out that it came inappropriately from someone who had shown no concern for the old man for nearly thirty years. But she said without rancour, almost eagerly:

'Yes, that was bad. It couldn't have made any difference medically, but the misunderstanding shouldn't have happened, one of us ought to have looked in. Do you want this third blanket? If not, I'll take it back to Toynton Grange, it's one of ours.'

'Two will be enough. What exactly happened?'

'To Father Baddeley? He died of acute myocarditis.'

'I mean, how did the misunderstanding arise?'

'I served him a cold lunch of chicken and salad when he arrived back from hospital and then settled him for his afternoon rest. He was ready for it. Dot took him his afternoon tea and helped him to wash. She got him into his pyjamas and he insisted on wearing his cassock on top. I cooked scrambled eggs for him in the kitchen here shortly after six-thirty. He was absolutely insistent that he wanted to spend the evening undisturbed, except, of course, for Grace Willison's visit, but I told him that someone would come in about ten and he seemed perfectly happy with that. He said that he'd rap on the wall with the poker if he were in any distress. Then I went next door to ask Millicent to listen for him and she offered to look in on him last thing. At least, that's what I understood. Apparently she thought that Eric or I would come. As I said, it shouldn't have happened. I blame myself. It wasn't Eric's fault. As his nurse, I should have ensured that he was seen again professionally before he went to bed.'

Dalgliesh said:

'This insistence on being alone; did you get the impression that he was expecting a visitor?'

'What visitor could he be expecting, other than poor Grace? I think he'd had enough of people while he was in hospital and just wanted some peace.'

'And you were all here at Toynton Grange that night?'

'All except Henry, who hadn't got back from London. Where else could we be?'

'Who unpacked his case for him?'

'I did. He was admitted to hospital as an emergency and had very few things with him, only those which we found by his bed and packed.'

'His Bible, prayer book and his diary?'

She looked up at him briefly, her face expressionless, before bending again to tuck in a blanket.

'Yes.'

'What did you do with them?'

'I left them on the small table beside his chair. He may have moved them later.'

So the diary had been with Father Baddeley in hospital. That meant that the record would have been up to date. And if Anstey were not lying about its being missing next morning, then it had been removed some time within those twelve hours.

He wondered how he could phrase his next question without arousing her suspicions. Keeping his voice light, he said:

'You may have neglected him in life but you looked after him very thoroughly after he died. First cremation and then burial. Wasn't that a little over-conscientious?'

To his surprise she burst out as if he had invited her to share a justified indignation:

'Of course it was! It was ridiculous! But that was Millicent's fault. She told Wilfred that Michael had frequently expressed his strong wish to be cremated. I can't think when or why. Although they were neighbours, she and Michael didn't exactly live in each other's pockets. But that's what she said. Wilfred was equally sure that Michael would want an orthodox Christian burial, so the poor man got both. It meant a lot of extra trouble and expense and Dr McKeith from Wareham had to sign a medical certificate as well as Eric. All that fuss just because Wilfred had a bad conscience.'

'Did he? About what?'

'Oh, nothing. I just got the impression that he felt that Michael had been a bit neglected one way and another, the usual self-indulgent compunction of the bereaved. Is this pillow going to be adequate? It feels very lumpy to me, and you look as if you could do with a good night's rest. Don't forget to come up to the Grange if there's anything you need. The milk is delivered to the boundary gate. I've ordered a pint for you each day. If that's too much, we can always use it. Now, have you everything you need?'

With the sensation of being under firm discipline Dalgliesh said meekly that he had. Nurse Rainer's briskness, her confidence, her concentration on the job in hand, even her reassuring smile of farewell, all relegated him to the status of a patient. As she wheeled her bicycle down the path and remounted, he felt that he had been visited by the district nurse. But he felt an increased respect for her. She hadn't appeared to resent his questions, and she had certainly been remarkably forthcoming. He wondered why.

II

It was a warm misty morning under a sky of low cloud. As he left the valley and began to trudge up the cliff path a reluctant rain began to fall in slow heavy drops. The sea was a milky blue, sluggish and opaque, its sloping waves pitted with rain and awash with shifting patterns of floating foam. There was a smell of autumn as if someone far off, undetected even by a wisp of smoke, was burning leaves. The narrow path rose higher skirting the cliff edge, now close enough to give him a brief vertiginous illusion of danger, now twisting inland between a tatter of bronzed bracken crumpled with the wind, and low tangles of bramble bushes, their red and black berries tight and meagre compared with the luscious fruit of inland hedgerows. The headland was dissected by low broken walls of stone and studded with small limestone rocks. Some, half buried, protruded tipsily from the soil like the relics of a disorderly graveyard.

Dalgliesh walked warily. It was his first country walk since his illness. The demands of the job meant that walking had always been a rare and special pleasure. Now he moved with something of the uncertainty of those first tentative steps of convalescence, muscles and senses rediscovering remembered pleasures, not with keen delight but with the gentle acceptance of familiarity. The brief metallic warble and churling note of stonechats, busy among the brambles; a solitary black-headed gull motionless as a ship's figure-head on a promontory of rock; clumps of rock samphire, their umbels stained with purple; yellow dandelions, pinpoints of brightness on the faded autumnal grass.

After nearly ten minutes of walking the cliff path began to slope gently downhill and was eventually dissected by a narrow lane running inland from the cliff edge. About six yards from the sea it broadened into a gently sloping plateau of bright-green turf and moss. Dalgliesh stopped suddenly as if stung by memory. This, then, must be the place where Victor Holroyd had chosen to sit, the spot from which he had plunged to his death. For a moment he wished that it hadn't lain so inconveniently in his path. The thought of violent death broke disagreeably into his euphoria. But he could understand the attraction of the spot. The lane was secluded and sheltered from the wind, there was a sense of privacy and peace; a precarious peace for a man captive in a wheelchair and with only the power of his brakes holding the balance between life and death. But that may have been part of the attraction. Perhaps only here, poised above the sea on this secluded patch of bright moss, could Holroyd, frustrated and chairbound, gain an illusion of freedom, of being in control of his destiny. He might always have intended to make here his final bid for release, insisting month after month on being wheeled to the same spot, biding his time so that no one at Toynton Grange suspected his real purpose. Instinctively, Dalgliesh studied the ground. Over three weeks had passed since Holroyd's death but he thought he could still detect the faint indentation of the soft turf where the wheels had rested and, less plainly, marks where the short grass had been matted with the scuffle of policemen's feet.

He walked to the cliff edge and looked down. The view, spectacular and frightening, made him catch his breath. The cliffs had changed and here the limestone had given place to an almost vertical wall of blackish clay larded with calcareous stone. Almost a hundred and fifty feet below, the cliff tumbled into a broad fissured causeway of boulders, slabs and amorphous chunks of blue-black rock which littered the foreshore as if hurled in wild disorder by a giant hand. The tide was out and the oblique line of foam moved sluggishly among the furthest rocks. As he looked down on this chaotic and awe-inspiring waste of rock and sea and tried to picture what the fall must have done to Holroyd, the sun moved fitfully from behind the clouds and a band of sunlight moved across the headland lying warm as a hand on the back of his neck, gilding the bracken, marbling the strewn rocks at the cliff edge. But it left the foreshore in shadow, sinister and unfriendly. For a moment Dalgliesh believed that he was looking down on a cursed and dreadful shore on which the sun could never shine.

Dalgliesh had been making for the black tower marked on Father Baddeley's map, less from a curiosity to see it than from the need to set an object for his walk. Still musing on Victor Holroyd's death, he came upon the tower almost unexpectedly. It was a squat intimidating folly, circular for about two-thirds of its height but topped with an octagonal cupola like a pepperpot pierced with eight glazed slit windows, compass points of reflected light which gave it something of the look of a lighthouse. The tower intrigued him and he moved round it touching the black walls. He saw that it had been built of limestone blocks but faced with the black shale as if capriciously decorated with pellets of polished jet. In places the shale had flaked away giving the tower a mottled appearance; black nacreous scales littered the base of the walls and gleamed among the grasses. To the north, and sheltered from the sea, was a tangle of plants as if someone had once tried to plant a garden. Now nothing remained but a dishevelled clump of Michaelmas daisies, patches of self-seeded antirrhinums, marigolds and nasturtiums, and a single etiolated rose with two white, starved buds, its stem bent double against the stone as if resigned to the first frost.

To the east was an ornate stone porch above an iron-bound oak door. Dalgliesh lifted the heavy handle and twisted it with difficulty. But the door was locked. Looking up he saw that there was a rough stone plaque set in the wall of the porch with a carved inscription:

IN THIS TOWER DIED
WILFRED MANCROFT ANSTEY
27th OCTOBER 1887 AGED 69 YEARS
CONCEPTIO CULPA NASCI PENA
LABOR VITA NECESSI MORI
ADAM OF ST. VICTOR AD 1129

A strange epitaph for a Victorian landed gentleman and a bizarre place in which to die. The present owner of Toynton Grange had perhaps inherited a degree of eccentricity. CONCEPTIO CULPA: the theology of original sin had been discarded by modern man with other inconvenient dogma; even in 1887 it must have been on the way out. NASCI PENA: anaesthesia had mercifully done something to vitiate that dogmatic assertion. LABOR VITA: not if twentieth-century technological man could help it. NECESSI MORI: ah, there was still the rub. Death. One could ignore it, fear it, even welcome it, but never defeat it. It remained as obtrusive but more durable than these commemorative stones. Death: the same yesterday, today and for ever. Had Wilfred Mancroft Anstey himself chosen and taken comfort from this stark memento mori?

He continued walking along the cliff edge, skirting a small pebbled bay. About twenty yards ahead was a rough path to the beach, steep and probably treacherous in wet weather but obviously partly the result of a felicitous natural arrangement of the rock face and partly the work of man. Immediately beneath him, however, the cliff fell away in an almost vertical face of limestone. He saw with surprise that even at this early hour there were two roped climbers on the rock. The upper and bareheaded figure was instantly recognizable as Julius Court. When the second looked up Dalgliesh glimpsed the face under the red climbing helmet and saw that his companion was Dennis Lerner.

They were climbing slowly but competently, so competently

that he felt no temptation to move back in case the unexpected sight of a spectator should break their concentration. They had obviously done this climb before; the route, the techniques were familiar to them. Now they were on the last pitch. Watching Court's smooth unhurrying movements, the splayed limbs leech-like on the rock face, he found himself reliving some of the climbs of his boyhood and making the ascent with them, mentally documenting each stage. Traverse right about fifteen feet with peg protection; step up with difficulty; then on to a small pinnacle block; gain the next ledge by a mantelshelf; climb the groove with the aid of two pegs and one sling to the horizontal crack; follow the groove again to a small ledge in the corner; finally climb with the aid of two pegs to the top.

Ten minutes later Dalgliesh strolled slowly round to where Julius was heaving his shoulders over the edge of the cliff. He drew himself up and stood, slightly panting, beside Dalgliesh. Without speaking he banged a peg into the crack of the rock beside one of the larger boulders, clipped a sling through the peg and into his waistline and started hauling in the rope. There was a cheerful shout from the rock face. Julius settled himself back against the boulder, rope around his waist, shouted 'Climb when you're ready,' and began inching the rope through careful hands. Less than fifteen minutes later, Dennis Lerner stood beside him and began coiling the rope. Blinking rapidly Dennis took off his steel-rimmed spectacles, rubbed away what could have been spray or rain drops from his face and twisted the ends behind his ears with shaking fingers. Julius looked at his watch:

'One hour twelve minutes, our best so far.'

He turned to Dalgliesh.

'There aren't many climbs on this part of the coast because of the shale, so we try to improve our time. Do you climb? I could lend you some gear.'

'I haven't done much since I left school and judging from what I've just seen, I'm not in your class.'

He didn't bother to explain that he was still too convalescent to climb safely. Once he might have found it necessary to justify his reluctance, but it had been some years now since he bothered how other people judged his physical courage. Julius said:

'Wilfred used to climb with me but about three months ago we discovered that someone had deliberately frayed one of his ropes. We were about to tackle this particular climb, incidentally. He refused to try to discover who was responsible. Someone at the Grange expressing a personal grievance, I suppose. Wilfred must expect these occasional contretemps. It's an occupational hazard for playing God. He was never in real danger. I always insist on checking equipment before we start. But it unnerved him, perhaps gave him the excuse he was looking for to give up climbing. He was never much good. Now I depend on Dennis when he has a day off, as today.'

Lerner turned and smiled directly at Dalgliesh. The smile transformed his face, releasing it from strain. He looked suddenly boyish, confiding:

'I'm just as terrified as Wilfred most of the time but I'm learning. It's fascinating; I'm getting to love it. There's a mild climb about half a mile back, guillemot ledge. Julius started me off there. It's really quite gentle. We could tackle that if you'd like to try.'

His naïve eagerness to communicate and share his pleasure was endearing.

Dalgliesh said:

'I hardly think I shall be long enough at Toynton to make it worthwhile.'

He intercepted their quick glance at each other, an almost imperceptible meeting of eyes in what? Relief? Warning? Satisfaction?

The three men stood silently while Dennis finished coiling the rope. Then Julius nodded towards the black tower.

'Ugly, isn't it? Wilfred's great-grandfather built it shortly after he rebuilt the Grange. It replaced – the Grange I mean – a small Elizabethan manor house which originally stood on the site and was destroyed by fire in 1843. A pity. It must have been more agreeable than the present house. Great-grandfather had no eye for form. Neither the house nor the folly have quite come off, have they?'

Dalgliesh asked:

'How did he die here, by design?'

'You could say that. He was one of those unamiable and obstinate eccentrics which the Victorian age seemed to breed. He invented his own religion, based, I understand, on the Book of Revelation. In the early autumn of 1887 he walled himself up inside the tower and starved himself to death. According to the somewhat confused testament he left, he was waiting for the second coming. I hope it arrived for him.'

'And no one stopped him?'

'They didn't know he was here. The old man was crazy but cunning. He made his secret preparations here, stones and mortar and so on, and then pretended to set off to winter in Naples. It was over three months before they found him. Long before that he'd torn his fingers to the bone trying to claw himself out. But he'd done his brick and mortar work too well, poor devil.'

'How horrible!'

'Yes. In the old days before Wilfred closed the headland, the locals tended to avoid the place, and so to be honest do I. Father Baddeley used to come here occasionally. According to Grace Willison, he said some prayers for great-grandfather's soul, sprinkled holy water around and that decontaminated the tower as far as he was concerned. Wilfred uses it for meditation, or so he says. Personally I think it's to get away from the Grange. The sinister family association doesn't seem to worry him. But then, it doesn't really touch him personally. He was adopted. But I expect Millicent Hammitt has told you about that.'

'Not yet. I've hardly spoken to her.'

'She will, she will.'

Dennis Lerner said surprisingly:

'I like the black tower, particularly in summer when the headland is peaceful and golden and the sun glints on the black stone. It's a symbol really, isn't it? It looks magical, unreal, a folly built to amuse a child. And underneath there's horror, pain, madness and death. I said that to Father Baddeley once.'

'And what did he reply?' asked Julius.

'He said, "Oh, no my son. Underneath there's the love of God."'

Julius said roughly:

'I don't need a phallic symbol erected by a Victorian eccentric to remind me of the skull under my skin. Like any reasonable man I prepare my own defences.'

Dalgliesh asked:

'What are they?'

The quiet question, even in his own ears, sounded stark as a command. Julius smiled:

'Money and the solace it can buy. Leisure, friends, beauty, travel. And when they fail, as your friend Father Baddeley would have reminded me they inevitably will, and Dennis's four horses of the apocalypse take over, three bullets in a Luger.' He looked up once more at the tower.

'In the meantime, I can do without reminders. My half-Irish blood makes me superstitious. Let's go down to the beach.'

They slid and clambered cautiously down the cliff path. At the foot of the cliff Dennis Lerner's brown monk's habit lay neatly folded, topped by a rock. He corded it round himself, exchanged his climbing boots for sandals taken from the pocket of the cloak and, thus metamorphosed and with his climbing helmet tucked under his arm, joined his companions as they trudged through the shingle.

All three seemed weary and no one spoke until the cliffs changed and they passed under the shadow of the black shale. The shore was even more remarkable seen close-to, a wide shining platform of boulder-strewn clay, fractured and crevassed as if by an earthquake, a bleak uncompromising shore. The pools were blue-black pits festooned with slimy seaweed; surely no northern sea bred such an exotic green? Even the ubiquitous litter of the shore – tarred splinters of wood, cartons in which the foam bubbled like brown scum, bottles, ends of tarred rope, the fragile bleached bones of sea birds – looked like the sinister debris of catastrophe, the sad sludge of a dead world.

As if by common consent they moved closer together and picked their way cautiously over the viscous rocks and Dennis Lerner had to hitch up his cloak. Suddenly Julius paused and turned towards the rock face. Dalgliesh turned with him, but Dennis still looked steadfastly out to sea.

'The tide was coming in fast. It must have reached about here. I got down to the beach by the path we used. It took some minutes of hard running but it was the nearer, really the only way. I didn't see either him or the chair as I plunged and scrambled through the shingle. When I reached the black cliff I had to force myself to look at him. At first I could see nothing unusual, only the sea boiling between the rocks. Then I caught sight of one of the wheels of his chair. It was lying in the centre of a flat rock, the sun gleaming on the chrome and the metal spokes. It looked so decorative, so precisely placed, it couldn't surely have landed there by chance. I suppose that it bounced off with the shock of impact and finally rolled on to the stone. I remember that I picked it up and hurled it towards the shore, laughing aloud. Shock, I suppose. The sound echoed back from the rock face.'

Lerner, without turning, said in a stifled voice:

'I remember. I heard you. I thought it was Victor laughing; it sounded like Victor.'

Dalgliesh asked:

'You saw the accident, then?'

'From a distance of about fifty yards. I'd got back to the cottage from London after lunch and decided to have a swim. It was an exceptionally warm day for September. I was just coming over the headland when I saw the chair lurch forward. There was nothing I, or anyone, could do. Dennis was lying on the grass about ten yards from Holroyd. He scrambled to his feet and ran after the chair hooting like a banshee. Then he ran backwards and forwards along the cliff edge, flailing his arms like a great brown demented crow.'

Lerner said through tight lips:

'I know that I didn't behave with much courage.'

'It wasn't exactly an occasion for courage, dear boy. No one could expect you to hurl yourself over the cliff after him, although, for a second, I thought you were going to.'

He turned to Dalgliesh.

'I left Dennis lying prone on the grass in what I suppose was a state of shock, paused long enough to yell at him to get help from Toynton Grange, and made for the cliff path. It took Dennis about ten minutes to pull himself together and get moving. It might have been more sensible if I'd paid more attention to him and then got him down here with me to help with the corpse. I nearly lost it.'

Dalgliesh said:

'The chair must have come over the cliff with considerable speed if he landed as far out as here.'

'Yes, odd isn't it? I was looking for him further inshore. Then I saw a tangle of metal about twenty feet to the right already being washed by the tide. And lastly I saw Holroyd. He looked like a great stranded fish rolling in the tide. His face was pale and bloated, even when he was alive poor devil; something to do with the steroids Eric was giving him. Now he looked grotesque. He must have parted from the chair before impact; anyway he was some distance from the wreckage. He was wearing only slacks and a cotton shirt when he died, and now the shirt had been torn away by the rocks and the sea so that all I could see was this great white torso turning and rising as the tide washed over him. He had gashed open his head and cut the neck artery. He must have bled copiously, and the sea had done the rest. By the time I reached him the foam was still stained pink, pretty as a bubble bath. He looked bloodless, as if he had been in the sea for months. A bloodless corpse, half naked, wallowing in the tide.'

A bloodless corpse. A bloodless murder.

The phrase fell unbidden into Dalgliesh's mind. He asked, making his voice unemphatic, hardly interested:

'How did you manage to get hold of him?'

'It wasn't easy. As I've said, the tide was coming in fast. I managed to get my bathing towel under his belt and tried to haul him on to one of the higher rocks, an undignified clumsy business for both of us. He was considerably heavier than I and his waterlogged trousers added to the weight. I was afraid they would come off. I suppose it wouldn't have mattered if they had, but it seemed important at the time to preserve some dignity for him. I took advantage of each onrush of wave to heave him further to shore and managed to get him on to this rock here, as far as I can remember. I was soaking myself and shivering despite the heat. I remember thinking it odd that the sun didn't seem to have the power to dry my clothes.'

Dalgliesh had glanced at Lerner's profile during this recital. A pulse in the thin sun-reddened neck was beating like a pump. He said coolly:

'We must hope that Holroyd's death was less distressing for him than it obviously was for you.'

Julius Court laughed:

'You must remember that not everyone has your professional predilection for these entertainments. When I'd got him this far I just hung on grimly like a fisherman to his catch until the party from Toynton Grange arrived with a stretcher. They came stumbling along the beach, the quicker way, strung out, falling over the stones, overladen like a disorganized picnic party.'

'What about the wheelchair?'

'I only remembered it when we got back to Toynton. It was a write-off, of course. We all knew that. But I thought that the police might want to examine it to see if the brakes were defective. Rather clever of me wasn't it? The idea didn't seem to occur to anyone else. But when a party from the Grange came back to look they could only find the two wheels and the main part of the body. The two side pieces with the ratchet hand-brakes were missing. The police searched more thoroughly next morning but with no better luck.'

Dalgliesh would have liked to have asked who it was from Toynton Grange who had done the searching. But he was determined not to betray real curiosity. He told himself that he had none. Violent death was no longer his concern and, officially, this violent death never would be. But it was odd that the two vital pieces of the wheelchair hadn't been found. And this rocky shore, with its deep crevices, its pools, its numerous hiding places would have been an ideal place in which to conceal them. But the local police would have thought of that. It was, he supposed, one of the questions he would tactfully have to ask them. Father Baddeley had written to ask for his help the day before Holroyd had died, but that didn't mean that the two events were totally unconnected. He asked:

'Was Father Baddeley very distressed about Holroyd's death? I imagine so.'

'Very much, when he knew. But that wasn't until a week later. We'd had the inquest by then and Holroyd had been buried. I thought Grace Willison would have told you. Michael and Victor between them gave us quite a day. When Dennis arrived back at the Grange with his news, the rescue party set out without saying anything to the patients. It was understandable but unfortunate. When we all staggered through the front door about forty minutes later, with what remained of Holroyd half slipping off the stretcher, Grace Willison was wheeling herself through the hall. Just to add to the excitement, she collapsed with shock. Anyway, Wilfred thought that Michael might start earning his money, and sent Eric off to Hope Cottage. Eric found Father Baddeley in the throes of his heart attack. So yet another ambulance was summoned – we thought it might finish Michael off if he had to share his journey to the hospital with what remained of Victor – and the old man went off in happy ignorance. The ward sister broke the news about Victor as soon as the doctors thought he was well enough to take it. According to her, he took it quietly, but was obviously upset. He wrote to Wilfred I believe; a letter of condolence. Father Baddeley had the professional knack of taking other people's death in his stride, and he and Holroyd weren't exactly close. It was the idea of suicide which upset his professional susceptibilities, I imagine.'

Suddenly Lerner said in a low voice:

'I feel guilty because I feel responsible.'

Dalgliesh said:

'Either you pushed Holroyd over the cliff or you didn't. If you didn't, guilt is an indulgence.'

'And if I did?'

'Then it's a dangerous indulgence.'

Julius laughed:

'Victor committed suicide. You know it, I know it, so does everyone who knew Victor. If you're going to start fantasizing about his death, it's lucky for you that I decided to swim that afternoon and came over the brow of the hill when I did.'

The three of them, as if by common consent, began squelching their way along the shingled shore. Looking at Lerner's pale face, the twitch of muscle at the corner of the slack mouth, the perpetually anxious blinking eyes, Dalgliesh felt they'd had enough of Holroyd. He began to ask about the rock. Lerner turned to him eagerly.

'It's fascinating isn't it? I love the variety of this coast. You get the same shale further to the west at Kimmeridge; there it's known as Kimmeridge coal. It's bituminous you know, you can actually burn it. We did try at Toynton Grange; Wilfred liked the idea that we might be self-supporting even for heating. But the stuff smelt so offensive that we had to give it up. It practically stank us out. I believe people have tried to exploit it from the middle of the eighteenth century but no one's managed yet to deodorize it. The blackstone looks a bit dull and uninteresting now, but if it's polished with beeswax it comes up like jet. Well, you saw the effect on the black tower. People used to make ornaments of it as far back as Roman times. I've got a book on the geology of this coast if you're interested and I could show you my collection of fossils. Wilfred thinks that I ought not to take them now that the cliffs are so denuded, so I've given up collecting. But I've got quite an interesting collection. And I've got what I think is part of an Iron Age shale armlet.'

Julius Court was grating through the shingle a few feet ahead. He turned and shouted back at them:

'Don't bore him with your enthusiasm for old rocks, Dennis. Remember what he said. He won't be long enough at Toynton to make it worthwhile.'

He smiled at Dalgliesh. He made it sound like a challenge.

III

Before setting out for Wareham, Dalgliesh wrote to Bill Moriarty at the Yard. He gave such brief information as he had about the staff and patients at Toynton Grange and asked whether anything was officially known. He thought that he could imagine Bill's reaction to the letter, just as he could predict the style of his reply. Moriarty was a first-class detective but, except mercifully in official reports, he affected a facetious, spuriously jovial style when talking or writing about his cases as if nervously anxious to decontaminate violence with humour, or to demonstrate his professional sang-froid in the face of death. But if Moriarty's style was suspect, his information was invariably detailed and accurate. What was more, it would come quickly.

Dalgliesh, when stopping in Toynton village to post his letter, had taken the precaution of telephoning the police before calling in at divisional headquarters. His arrival was, therefore, expected and provided for. The Divisional Superintendent, called away unexpectedly to a meeting with his Chief Constable, had left apologies and instructions for the entertainment of the visitor. His final words to Detective Inspector Daniel, deputed to do the honours, had been:

'I'm sorry to miss the Commander. I met him last year when he lectured at Bramshill. At least he tempers the arrogance of the Met. with good manners and a plausible show of humility. It's refreshing to meet someone from the smoke who doesn't treat provincial forces as if we recruit by lurking outside the hill caves with lumps of raw meat on a pole. He may be the Commissioner's blue-eyed boy but he's a good copper.'

'Doesn't he write verse, Sir?'

'I shouldn't try to ingratiate yourself by mentioning that. I invent crossword puzzles for a hobby, which probably requires much the same level of intellectual skill, but I don't expect people to compliment me on it. I got his last book from the library. *Invisible Scars*. Do you suppose, given the fact that he's a copper, that the title is ironic?'

'I couldn't say, Sir, not having read the book.'

'I only understood one poem in three but I may have been flattering myself. I suppose he didn't say why we're being honoured.'

'No, Sir, but as he's staying at Toynton Grange he may be interested in the Holroyd case.'

'I can't see why; but you'd better arrange for Sergeant Varney to be available.'

'I've asked Varney to join us for lunch, Sir. The usual pub, I thought.'

'Why not? Let the Commander see how the poor live.'

And so Dalgliesh found himself, after the usual polite preliminaries, invited to lunch at the Duke's Arms. It was an unprepossessing pub, not visible from the High Street, but approached down a dark alleyway between a corn merchant and one of those general stores common in country towns where every possible garden implement and an assortment of tin buckets, hip baths, brooms, twine, aluminium tea pots and dogs' leads swing from the ceiling above a pervading smell of paraffin and turpentine. Inspector Daniel and Sergeant Varney were greeted with uneffusive but evident satisfaction by the burly, shirt-sleeved landlord, who was obviously a publican who could afford to welcome the local police to his bar without the fear of giving it a bad name. The saloon bar was crowded, smoky and loud with the burr of Dorset voices. Daniel led the way down the narrow passage smelling strongly of beer and faintly of urine and out into an unexpected and sun-filled cobbled yard. There was a cherry tree in the centre, its trunk encircled by a wooden bench, and half a dozen sturdy tables and slatted wooden chairs set out on the paved stones which surrounded the cobbles. The yard was deserted. The regulars probably spent too much of their working lives in the open air to see it as a desirable alternative to the camaraderie of the snug, smoke-filled bar, while tourists who might have valued it were unlikely to penetrate to the Duke's Arms.

Without being summoned the publican brought out two pints of beer, a plate of cheese-filled rolls, a jar of home-made chutney and a large bowl of tomatoes. Dalgliesh said he would have the same. The beer proved excellent, the cheese was English Cheddar, the bread had obviously been baked locally and was not the gutless pap of some mass-produced oven. The butter was unsalted and the tomatoes tasted of the sun. They ate together in companionable silence.

Inspector Daniel was a stolid six-footer, with a jutting comb of strong undisciplined grey hair and a ruddy sun-tanned face. He looked close to retirement age. His black eyes were restless, perpetually moving from face to face with an amused, indulgent, somewhat self-satisfied expression as if he felt himself personally responsible for the conduct of the world and was, on the whole, satisfied that he wasn't making too bad a job of it. The contrast between these glittering unquiet eyes and his unhurried movements and even more deliberate countryman's voice was disconcerting.

Sergeant Varney was two inches shorter with a round, bland, boyish face on which experience had so far left no trace. He looked very young, the prototype of that officer whose boyish good looks provoke the perennial middle-aged complaint that the policemen get younger each year. His manner to his superiors was easy, respectful, but neither sycophantic nor deferential. Dalgliesh suspected that he enjoyed an immense self-confidence which he was at some pains to conceal. When he talked about his investigation of Holroyd's death, Dalgliesh could understand why. Here was an intelligent and highly competent young officer who knew exactly where he was going and how he proposed to get there.

Dalgliesh carefully understated his business.

'I was ill at the time Father Baddeley wrote and he was dead when I arrived. I don't suppose he wanted to consult me about anything important, but I have something of a conscience about having let him down. It seemed sensible to have a word with you and see whether anything was happening at Toynton Grange which might have worried him. I must say it seems to me highly unlikely. I've been told about Victor Holroyd's death, of course, but that happened the day after Father Baddeley wrote to me. I did wonder, though, whether there was anything leading up to Holroyd's death which might have worried him.'

Sergeant Varney said:

'There was no evidence that Holroyd's death concerned anyone but himself. As I expect you know, the verdict at the inquest was accidental death. Dr Maskell sat with a jury and if you ask me he was relieved at the verdict. Mr Anstey is greatly respected in the district even if they do keep themselves very much to themselves at Toynton Grange, and no one wanted to add to his distress. But in my opinion, Sir, it was a clear case of suicide. It looks as if Holroyd acted pretty much on impulse. It wasn't his usual day to be wheeled to the cliff top and he seemed to make up his mind to it suddenly. We had the evidence of Miss Grace Willison and Mrs Ursula Hollis, who were sitting with Holroyd on the patients' patio, that he called Dennis Lerner over to him and more or less nagged him into wheeling him out. Lerner testified that he was in a particularly difficult mood on the journey and when they got to their usual place on the cliff he became so offensive that Lerner took his book and lay some little distance from the chair. That is where Mr Julius Court saw him when he breasted the hill in time to see the chair jerk forward and hurtle down the slope and over the cliff. When I examined the ground next morning I could see by the broken flowers and pressed grass exactly where Lerner had been lying and his library book, *The Geology of the Dorset Coast*, was still on the grass where he'd dropped it. It looks to me, Sir, as if Holroyd deliberately taunted him into moving some distance away so that he wouldn't be able to get to him in time once he'd slipped the brakes.'

'Did Lerner explain in court exactly what it was that Holroyd said to him?'

'He wasn't specific, Sir, but he more or less admitted to me that Holroyd taunted him with being a homosexual, not pulling his weight at Toynton Grange, looking for an easy life, and being an ungentle and incompetent nurse.'

'I would hardly describe that as unspecific. How much truth is there in any of it?'

'That's difficult to say, Sir. He may be all of those things including the first; which doesn't mean to say that he'd welcome Holroyd telling him so.'

Inspector Daniel broke in:

'He's not an ungentle nurse and that's for certain. My sister Ella is a staff nurse at the Meadowlands Nursing Home outside Swanage. Old Mrs Lerner – over eighty she is now – is a patient over there. Her son visits her regularly and isn't above lending a hand when they're busy. It's odd that he doesn't take a post there, but perhaps it's no bad thing to keep your professional and private life separate. Anyway, they may not have a vacancy for a male nurse. And no doubt he feels some loyalty to Wilfred Anstey. But Ella thinks very highly of Dennis Lerner. A good son, is how she describes him. And it must take the best part of his salary to keep Mum at Meadowlands. Like all the really good places, it's not cheap. No, I'd say that Holroyd was a pretty impossible chap. The Grange will be a good deal happier without him.'

Dalgliesh said:

'It's an uncertain way of committing suicide, I should have thought. What surprises me is that he managed to move that chair.'

Sergeant Varney took a long drink of his beer.

'It surprised me too, Sir. We weren't able to get the chair intact so I couldn't experiment with it. But Holroyd was a heavy chap, about half a stone heavier than I am, I estimate, and I experimented with one of the older chairs at Toynton Grange as close as possible to the model of his. Provided it were on fairly firm ground and the slope was more than one in three, I could get it moving with a sharp jerk. Julius Court testified that he saw Holroyd's body jerk although he couldn't say from that distance whether the chair was being thrust forward or whether it was spontaneous reaction on Holroyd's part to the shock of finding himself moving. And one has to remember, Sir, that other methods of killing himself weren't readily at hand. He was almost entirely helpless. Drugs would have been the easiest way, but those are kept locked in the clinical room on the upper floor; he hadn't a hope of getting to anything really dangerous without help. He might have tried hanging himself with a towel in the bathroom but there are no locks on the bathroom or lavatory doors. That, of course, is a precaution against patients collapsing and being too ill to summon assistance, but it does mean that there's a lack of privacy about the place.'

'What about a possible defect of the chair?'

'I thought about that, Sir, and it was, of course, brought out at the inquest. But we only recovered the seat of the chair and one of the wheels. The two side pieces with the handbrakes and the cross-bar with the ratchets have never been found.'

'Exactly the parts of the chair where any defects of the brakes, whether natural or deliberately produced, might have been apparent.'

'If we could have found the pieces in time, Sir, and the sea hadn't done too much damage. But we never found them. The body had broken free of the chair in mid-air or on impact and Court naturally concentrated on retrieving the body. It was being tumbled by the surf, the trousers were waterlogged and it was too heavy for him to shift far. But he got his bathing towel into Holroyd's belt and managed to hold on until help, in the persons of Mr Anstey, Dr Hewson, Sister Moxon and the handyman Albert Philby, arrived with a stretcher. Together they managed to get the body on to it and struggled back along the beach to Toynton Grange. It was only then that they rang us. It occurred to Mr Court as soon as they reached the Grange that the chair ought to be retrieved for examination and he sent Philby back to look for it. Sister Moxon volunteered to go with him. The tide had gone out about twenty yards by then and they found the main part of the chair, that is the seat and the back, and one of the wheels.'

'I'm surprised that Dorothy Moxon went to search, I would have expected her to stay with the patients.'

'So should I, Sir. But Anstey refused to leave Toynton Grange and Dr Hewson apparently thought that his place was with the body. Nurse Rainer was off duty for the afternoon, and there was no one else to send unless you count Mrs Millicent Hammitt, and I don't think anyone thought of counting Mrs Hammitt. It did seem important that two pairs of eyes should be looking for the chair before the light faded.'

'And what about Julius Court?'

'Mr Court and Mr Lerner thought they ought to be at Toynton Grange to meet us when we arrived, Sir.'

'A very proper thought. And by the time you did arrive no doubt it was too dark to make an effective search.'

'Yes, Sir, it was seven fourteen when we got to Toynton Grange. Apart from taking statements and arranging for the body to be removed to the mortuary, there was very little we could do until the morning. I don't know whether you've seen that shore at low tide, Sir. It looks like a great sheet of black treacle toffee which some prodigious giant has amused himself by smashing-up with a gigantic hammer. We searched pretty thoroughly over a wide area but if the metal pieces are lodged in the crevasses between any of those rocks it would take a metal detector to find them – and we'd be lucky then – and lifting tackle to retrieve them. It's most likely, I think, that they've been dragged down under the shingle. There's a great deal of turbulence there at high tide.'

Dalgliesh said:

'Was there any reason to suppose that Holroyd had suddenly become suicidal, I mean – why choose that particular moment?'

'I asked about that, Sir. A week earlier, that is on 5th September, Mr Court with Dr Hewson and Mrs Hewson had taken him in Court's car up to London to see his solicitors and a consultant at St Saviour's Hospital. That's Dr Hewson's own training hospital. I gather that Holroyd wasn't given much hope that anything more could be done for him. Dr Hewson said that the news didn't seem to depress him unduly. He hadn't expected anything else. Dr Hewson more or less told me that Holroyd had insisted on the consultation just for the trip to London. He was a restless man and liked an excuse to get away from Toynton Grange occasionally. Mr Court was travelling up anyway and offered the use of his car. That matron, Mrs Moxon, and Mr Anstey were both adamant that Holroyd hadn't come back particularly depressed; but then they've got something of a vested interest in discrediting the suicide theory. The patients told me a rather different story. They noticed a change in Holroyd after his return. They didn't describe him as depressed, but he certainly wasn't any easier to live with. They described him as excited. Miss Willison used the word elated. She said that he seemed to be making up his mind to something. I don't think that she has much doubt that Holroyd killed himself. When I questioned her she was obviously shocked by the idea and distressed on Mr Anstey's account. She didn't want to believe it. But I think that she did.'

'What about Holroyd's visit to his solicitor? Did he learn anything there to distress him I wonder?'

'It's an old family firm, Holroyd and Martinson in Bedford Row. Holroyd's elder brother is now the senior partner. I did ring him to ask but I didn't get far. According to him, the visit was almost entirely social and Victor was no more depressed than usual. They were never close but Mr Martin Holroyd did visit his brother occasionally at Toynton Grange, particularly when he wanted to talk to Mr Anstey about his affairs.'

'You mean that Holroyd and Martinson are Anstey's solicitors?'

'They've acted for the family for over 150 years I understand. It's a very old connection. That's how Victor Holroyd came to hear about the Grange. He was Anstey's first patient.'

'What about Holroyd's wheelchair? Could anyone at Toynton Grange have sabotaged that, either on the day Holroyd died or on the evening before?'

'Philby could, of course. He had the best opportunity. But a number of people could have done it. Holroyd's rather heavy chair, the one which was used for these outings, was kept in the workroom at the end of the passage in the southern extension. I don't know whether you know it, Sir, but it's perfectly accessible even to wheelchairs. Basically it's Philby's workshop. He has the usual standard equipment and tools for carpentry and some metal work there. But the patients can use it too and are, in fact, encouraged either to help him or to indulge in their own hobbies. Holroyd used to do some fairly simple carpentry before he got too ill and Mr Carwardine occasionally models in clay. The women patients don't usually use it but there'd be nothing surprising to see one of the men there.'

Dalgliesh said:

'Carwardine told me that he was in the workroom when Philby oiled and checked the brakes at eight forty-five.'

'That's rather more than he told me. He gave me the impression that he hadn't really seen what Philby was up to. Philby was a bit coy about whether he could actually remember testing the brakes. I wasn't surprised. It was pretty obvious that they all wanted it to look like an accident if that could be done without provoking the coroner into too many strictures about carelessness. I had a bit of luck, however, when I questioned them about the actual morning of Holroyd's death. After breakfast Philby went back to the workroom shortly after eight forty-five. He was there for just an hour and when he left he locked the place up. He was glueing some repairs and didn't want them disturbed. I got the impression that Philby thinks of the workroom as his domain and doesn't exactly welcome the patients being allowed to use it. Anyway, he pocketed the key and didn't unlock the room until Lerner came fussing to ask for the key shortly before four o'clock so that he could get Holroyd's wheelchair. Assuming that Philby was telling the truth, the only people at Toynton Grange without alibis for the time when the workroom was unlocked and unoccupied early on the morning of 12th September are Mr Anstey,

Holroyd himself, Mr Carwardine, Sister Moxon and Mrs Hewson. Mr Court was in London and didn't arrive back at his cottage until just before Lerner and Holroyd set out. Lerner is clear too. He was busy with the patients at all the relevant times.'

That was all very well, thought Dalgliesh, but it proved very little. The workroom had been unlocked the previous evening after Carwardine and Philby had left and, presumably, also during the night. He said:

'You were very thorough, Sergeant. Did you manage to discover all this without alarming them too much?'

'I think so, Sir. I don't think they thought for a moment that I was checking up on what opportunity Holroyd had to muck about with the chair himself. And if it were deliberately damaged, then my bet is he did it. He was a malicious man, from what I hear. It probably amused him to think that, when the chair was recovered from the sea and the damage discovered, then everyone at Toynton Grange would be under suspicion. That's the kind of final thought that would give him quite a kick.'

Dalgliesh said:

'I just can't believe that both brakes failed simultaneously and accidentally. I've seen those wheelchairs at the Grange. The brakes system is very simple but it's effective and safe. And it's almost as difficult to imagine that there was deliberate sabotage. How could the murderer possibly rely on the brakes failing at that particular moment? Lerner or Holroyd might easily have tested them before starting out. The defect might be discovered when the chair was braked on the cliff top or even on the journey. Besides, no one apparently knew that Holroyd was going to insist on an outing that afternoon. What did exactly happen on the cliff top, by the way? Who braked the chair?'

'According to Lerner, Holroyd did. Lerner admits that he never looked at the brakes. All he can say is that he noticed nothing wrong with the chair. The brakes weren't used until they reached their usual stopping place.'

For a moment there was silence. They had finished eating and Inspector Daniel felt in the pocket of his tweed jacket and produced a pipe. As he stroked its bowl with his thumb before filling it, he said quietly:

'Nothing was worrying you about the old gentleman's death was it, Sir?'

'He was medically diagnosed as a dying man and somewhat inconveniently for me he died. I worry that I didn't visit him in time to hear what was on his mind; but that's a private worry. Speaking as a policeman, I should rather like to know who saw him last before he died. Officially, it was Grace Willison, but I've a feeling he had a later visitor than she; another patient. When he was found dead next morning he was wearing his stole. His diary was missing, and someone broke into his bureau. As I haven't seen Father Baddeley for over twenty years it's probably unreasonable of me to be so sure that it wasn't he.'

Sergeant Varney turned to his Inspector.

'What would be the theological position, Sir, if someone confessed to a priest, got absolution and then killed him to make sure that he kept his mouth shut. Would the confession take as it were?'

The young face was preternaturally grave, it was impossible to tell whether the inquiry had been serious, whether this was a private joke directed against the Inspector, or made with some more subtle motive. Daniel took his pipe from his mouth:

'God, you young men are an ignorant lot of heathens! When I was a kid in Sunday School I put pennies in the collection plate for black bambinos not half as ignorant as your lot. Take it from me, lad, it would do you no good theologically or otherwise.'

He turned to Dalgliesh.

'Wearing his stole, was he? Now that's interesting.'

'I thought so.'

'And yet, is it so unnatural? He was alone and may have known he was dying. Maybe he just felt more comfortable with the feel of it around his neck. Wouldn't you say that, Sir?'

'I don't know what he'd do, or what he'd feel. I've been content not to know for the past twenty years.'

'And the forced bureau. Maybe he'd decided to make a start with destroying his papers and couldn't remember where he'd put the key.'

'It's perfectly possible.'

'And he was cremated?'

'Cremated, on the insistence of Mrs Hammitt, and his ashes buried with the appropriate rite of the Church of England.'

Inspector Daniel said nothing more. There was, Dalgliesh thought bitterly as they rose to go, nothing else to say.

IV

Father Baddeley's solicitors, the firm of Loder and Wainwright, occupied a simple but harmonious house of red brick facing directly on to South Street and typical, Dalgliesh thought, of the more agreeable houses which were built after the old town was virtually destroyed by fire in 1762. The door was propped open by a brass doorstop shaped like a miniature cannon, its dazzling muzzle pointing intimidatingly towards the street. Apart from this bellicose symbol the house and its furnishings were reassuringly welcoming, producing an atmosphere of solid affluence, tradition and professional rectitude. The white painted hall was hung with prints of eighteenth-century Dorchester and smelt of furniture polish. To the left, an open door led to a large waiting-room with an immense circular table on a carved pedestal, half a dozen carved mahogany chairs heavy enough to accommodate a robust farmer in upright discomfort, and an oil painting of an unnamed Victorian gentleman, presumably the founder of the firm, bewhiskered and beribboned and displaying the seal of his watch chain between a delicate thumb and finger as if anxious that the painter should not overlook it. It was a house in which any of Hardy's more prosperous characters would have felt themselves at home, could with confidence have discussed the effects of the abolition of the corn laws or the perfidy of the French privateers. Opposite the waiting-room was a partitioned office occupied by a young girl, dressed up to the waist in black boots and a long skirt like a Victorian governess and above the waist like a pregnant milkmaid. She was laboriously typing at a speed which could have explained Maggie Hewson's strictures about the firm's dilatoriness. In response to Dalgliesh's inquiry she glanced up at him through a curtain of lank hair and said that Mr Robert was out at present but was expected back in ten minutes. Taking his time over lunch, thought Dalgliesh, and resigned himself to a half-hour wait.

Loder returned some twenty minutes later. Dalgliesh heard him galumphing happily into the reception office; there was the murmur of voices and a second later he appeared in the waiting-room and invited his visitor into his office at the rear of the house. Neither the room – poky, stuffy and untidy – nor its owner were quite what Dalgliesh had expected. Neither suited the house. Bob Loder was a swarthy, heavily built, square-faced man with a blotched skin and unhealthy pallor and small, discouraged eyes. His sleek hair was uniformly dark – too dark to be entirely natural – except for a thin line of silver at the brow and sides. His moustache was dapper and trim above lips so red and moist that they looked about to ooze blood. Noting the lines at the corner of the eyes and the sagging muscles of the neck Dalgliesh suspected that he was neither as young nor as vigorous as he was at pains to suggest.

He greeted Dalgliesh with a heartiness and *bonhomie* which seemed as unsuited to his personality as it was to the occasion. His manner recalled to Dalgliesh something of the desperate heartiness of ex-officers of his acquaintance who hadn't adjusted themselves to civilian life, or perhaps of a car salesman with little confidence that the chassis and engine will hang together long enough to complete the sale.

Dalgliesh briefly explained the ostensible reason for his visit.

'I didn't know that Father Baddeley was dead until I arrived at Toynton and the first I heard about his bequest to me was from Mrs Hewson. That isn't important. You probably haven't had a chance to write yet. But Mr Anstey wants the cottage cleared for the new occupant and I thought that I'd better check with you before removing the books.'

Loder put his head outside the door and yelled for the file. It was produced in a surprisingly quick time. After a perfunctory examination he said:

'That's OK. Perfectly. Sorry about no letter. It wasn't so much the lack of time as no address, don't know you. The dear old chap didn't think of that. Name familiar, of course. Ought I to know you?'

'I don't think so. Perhaps Father Baddeley mentioned my name when he visited you. I believe he did call in a day or so before the start of his last illness.'

'That's right, on Wednesday 11th p.m. That was only the second time we'd met, come to think of it. He first consulted me about three years ago, soon after he arrived at Toynton Grange. That was to make his will. He didn't have much but, then, he hadn't been spending much and it had accumulated into quite a nice little sum.'

'How did he hear of you?'

'He didn't. The dear old chap wanted to make his will, knew that he'd need a solicitor and just took the bus into Wareham, and walked into the first solicitor's office he came to. I happened to be here at the time so I got him. I drew up the will there and then since that was what he wanted and two of the staff here signed it. I'll say this for the old dear, he was the easiest client I've ever had.'

'I wondered whether his visit on 11th was to consult you about anything that was worrying him. From his last letter to me I rather gathered that he had something on his mind. If there's anything I ought to do . . .'

He let his voice trail away in a long interrogation.

Loder said cheerfully:

'The dear old chap came in some perturbation of the spirit. He was thinking of changing his will but hadn't quite made up his mind. He seemed to have got the idea that I could somehow put the money into limbo for him while he came to a decision. I said: "My dear Sir, if you die tonight the money goes to Wilfred Anstey and Toynton Grange. If you don't want that to happen, then you'll have to make up your mind what you do want and I'll draw up a new will. But the money exists. It won't disappear. And if you don't cancel the old will or change it, then it stands." '

'Did he strike you as sensible?'

'Oh, yes, muddled perhaps but more in his imagination than his comprehension if you get me. As soon as I pointed out the facts he understood them. Well, he always had understood them. It's just that he wished for a moment that the problem wasn't there. Don't we all know the feeling?'

'And a day later he went into hospital, and less than a fortnight later the problem was solved for him.'

'Yes, poor old dear. I suppose he would have said that providence decided it for him. Providence certainly made its views known in no uncertain way.'

'Did he give you any idea what was on his mind? I don't want to pry into professional confidences, but I did get a strong impression that he wanted to consult me about something. If he had a commission for me I'd like to try to carry it out. And I suppose I have the policeman's curiosity to find out what he wanted, to clear up unfinished business.'

'A policeman?'

Was the flicker of surprise and polite interest in those tired eyes a little too obvious to be natural?

Loder said:

'Did he invite you as a friend or in a professional capacity?'

'Probably a bit of both.'

'Well, I don't see what you can do about it now. Even if he'd told me his intentions about the will and I knew whom he wanted to benefit it's too late to do anything about it now.'

Dalgliesh wondered whether Loder seriously thought that he had been hoping for the money himself and was inquiring into a possible way of upsetting Father Baddeley's will.

He said:

'I know that. I doubt whether it was anything to do with his will. It's odd, though, that he never wrote to tell me about my legacy, and he left the main beneficiary in the same ignorance apparently.' It was entirely a shot in the dark but it found its mark. Loder spoke carefully, a trifle too carefully.

'Did he? I'd rather thought that that particular embarrassment was part of the old chap's dilemma, the reluctance to disappoint when he'd promised.'

He hesitated, seeming to think that he had said either too much or too little, and added:

'But Wilfred Anstey could confirm that.'

He paused again as if disconcerted by some subtle implication in his words and, obviously irritated at the devious paths into which the conversation was leading him, said more strongly:

'I mean if Wilfred Anstey says he didn't know that he was the principal legatee then he didn't know and I'm wrong. Are you staying long in Dorset?'

'Rather less than a week, I imagine. Just long enough to sort out and pack the books.'

'Oh, yes, the books, of course; perhaps that's what Father Baddeley meant to consult you about. He may have thought that a library of theological tomes would be more of a liability than an acceptable bequest.'

'It's possible.' The conversation seemed to have died. There was a brief, somewhat embarrassed pause before Dalgliesh said, rising from his chair:

'So there was nothing else worrying him as far as you know except this problem of the disposal of his money? He didn't consult you about anything else?'

'No, nothing. If he had, it might have been something I wouldn't have felt able to tell you without breaking a professional confidence. But, as he didn't, I don't see why you shouldn't know that. And what would he have to consult me over, poor old gentleman? No wife, no children, no relatives, as far as I know, no family troubles, no car, a blameless life. What would he need a solicitor for except to draw up his will?'

It was a little late to talk about professional confidence thought Dalgliesh. There was really no need for Loder to have confided that Father Baddeley had been thinking of changing his will. Given the fact that he hadn't in fact done so that was the kind of information which a prudent solicitor would feel was best left undisclosed. As Loder walked with him to the door, Dalgliesh said casually:

'Father Baddeley's will probably gave nothing but satisfaction. One can hardly say as much of Victor Holroyd's.'

The dull eyes were suddenly sharp, almost conspiratorial. Loder said:

'So you've heard about that, have you?'

'Yes. But I'm surprised that you have.'

'Oh, news gets around, don't you know, in a country district. As a matter of fact I have friends at Toynton. The Hewsons. Well, Maggie really. We met at the Conservative dance here last winter. It's a pretty dull life stuck there on the cliff for a lively girl.'

'Yes. It must be.'

'She's quite a lass is our Maggie. She told me about Holroyd's will. I gather that he went up to London to see his brother and it was rather taken for granted that he wanted to discuss his will. But it looks as if big brother didn't much like what Victor proposed and suggested that he thought again. In the event, Holroyd drew up the codicil himself. It wouldn't exactly present any problem for him. All the family have been brought up in the law and Holroyd started reading for the Bar himself before he decided to switch to school-teaching.'

'I understand that Holroyd and Martinson act for the Anstey family.'

'That's right, and have for four generations. It's a pity grandfather Anstey didn't consult them before drawing up his will. That case was quite a lesson in the unwisdom of trying to act as your own lawyer. Well, good afternoon, Commander. I'm sorry I couldn't be of more help.'

As he looked back when turning out of South Street, Dalgliesh could see Loder still watching after him, the brass cannon shining like a toy at his feet. There were a number of things about the solicitor which he found interesting. Not the least was how Loder had learned his rank.

But there was one other task before he turned his mind to his shopping. He called at the early nineteenth-century hospital, Christmas Close. But here he was unlucky. The hospital knew nothing of Father Baddeley; they admitted only chronic cases. If his friend had suffered a heart attack he would almost certainly have been admitted to the acute ward of a district general hospital despite his age. The courteous porter suggested that he should try either Poole General Hospital, Blandford or the Victoria Hospital at Wimborne, and helpfully directed him to the nearest public telephone.

He tried Poole Hospital first as being the nearest. And here he was luckier than he could have hoped. The clerk who answered the telephone was efficient. Given the date of Father Baddeley's discharge he was able to confirm that the Reverend Baddeley had been a patient and to put Dalgliesh through to the right ward. The staff nurse answered. Yes, she remembered Father Baddeley. No, they hadn't heard that he had died. She spoke the conventional words of regret and was able to make them sound sincere. Then she fetched Nurse Breagan to the telephone. Nurse Breagan usually offered to post the patients' letters. Perhaps she could help Commander Dalgliesh.

His rank, he knew, had something to do with their helpfulness, but not all. They were kindly women who were disposed to take trouble, even with a stranger. He explained his dilemma to Nurse Breagan.

'So you see, I didn't know my friend had died until I arrived yesterday at Toynton Grange. He promised to return the papers we were working on to me, but they're not among his things. I wondered whether he posted them back to me from hospital, either to my London address or to the Yard.'

'Well now, Commander, the Father wasn't a great one for writing. Reading, yes; but not writing. But I did post two letters for him. They were both local as far as I can remember. I have to look at the addresses, you see, so that I post them in the right box. The date? Well, I couldn't remember that. But he did hand them to me together.'

'Would those be the two letters he wrote to Toynton, one to Mr Anstey and one to Miss Willison?'

'Come to think of it, Commander, I do seem to remember those names. But I couldn't be sure, you understand.'

'It's very clever of you to remember so much. And you're quite sure you only posted those two?'

'Oh, quite sure. Mind you, one of the other nurses might have posted a letter for him, but I couldn't find out for you without difficulty. Some of them have changed wards. But I don't think so. It's usually me that takes the letters. And he wasn't one for writing. That's how I remember the two letters he did send.'

It could mean something or nothing. But the information had been worth the trouble. If Father Baddeley had made an appointment for the night of his return home, he must have done so either by telephoning from the hospital once he was well enough, or by letter. And only Toynton Grange itself, the Hewsons and Julius Court were on the telephone. But it might have been more convenient for him to write. The letter to Grace Willison would have been the one arranging her appointment for confession. The one to Anstey might have been the letter of condolence on Holroyd's death to which she had referred. But, on the other hand, it might not.

Before ringing off he asked whether Father Baddeley had made any telephone calls from the hospital.

'Well, he made one, that I do know. That was when he was up and about. He went down to make it from the out-patients' waiting-hall and he asked me if there'd be a London directory there. That's how I remember.'

'At what time was this?'

'The morning. Just before I went off duty at twelve.'

So Father Baddeley had needed to make a London call, to a number he had to look up. And he had made it, not during the evening, but in office hours. There was one obvious inquiry Dalgliesh could make. But not yet. He told himself that as yet he had learned nothing which could justify even his unofficial involvement. And even if he had, where would all the suspicions, all the clues, ultimately lead? Only to a few fistfuls of ground bones in Toynton churchyard.

V

It wasn't until after an early dinner at the inn near Corfe Castle that Dalgliesh drove back to Hope Cottage and settled down to begin sorting Father Baddeley's books. But first there were small but necessary domestic chores to tackle. He replaced the dim bulb in the table lamp with a higher wattage; cleaned and adjusted the pilot light on the gas boiler over the sink; cleared a space in the food cupboard for his provisions and wine; and discovered in the outside shed by the aid of his torch a pile of driftwood for kindling, and a tin bath. There was no bathroom at Hope Cottage. Father Baddeley had probably taken his baths at Toynton Grange. But Dalgliesh had every intention of stripping and sluicing himself in the kitchen. Austerity was a small price to pay to avoid the bathroom at Toynton with its hospital smell of strong disinfectant, its intrusive reminders of sickness and deformity. He put a match to the dried grasses in the grate and watched them flare instantaneously into black needles in one sweet-smelling flame. Then he lit a small experimental fire and found to his relief that the chimney was clear. With a wood fire, a good light, books, food and a stock of wine he saw no reason to wish himself elsewhere.

He estimated that there were between two hundred and three hundred books on the sitting-room shelves and three times as many in the second bedroom; indeed the books had so taken over the room that it was impossible to get to the bed. The books presented very few surprises. Many of the theological tomes might be of interest to one of the London theological libraries; some, he thought, his aunt might be glad to give a home to; some were destined for his own shelves. There was H. B. Swete's *Greek Old Testament* in three volumes, Thomas à Kempis's *Imitation of Christ*; William Law's *Serious Call*; a leather-bound *Life and Letters of Eminent 19th Century Divines* in two volumes; a first edition of Newman's *Parochial and Plain Sermons*. But there was also a representative collection of the major English novelists and poets and, since Father Baddeley had indulged himself by buying an occasional novel, there was a small but interesting collection of first editions.

At a quarter to ten he heard approaching footsteps and the squeak of wheels, there was a peremptory knock on the door, and Millicent Hammitt entered bringing with her an agreeable smell of fresh coffee and wheeling after her a laden trolley. There was a sturdy banded blue jug of coffee, a similar jar of hot milk, a bowl of brown sugar, two blue banded mugs, and a plate of digestive biscuits.

Dalgliesh felt that he could hardly object when Mrs Hammitt cast an appreciative glance at the wood fire, poured out two mugs of coffee and made it obvious that she was in no hurry to go.

Dalgliesh had been briefly introduced to her before dinner the previous evening, but there had been time for only half a minute's conversation before Wilfred had taken his stance at the reading desk and the ordained silence fell. She had taken the opportunity to discover, by the expedient of a blunt interrogation with no attempt at finesse, that Dalgliesh was holidaying alone because he was a widower and that his wife had died in childbirth with her baby. Her response to this had been, 'Very tragic. And unusual, surely, for these days?' spoken with an accusatory glance across the table and in a tone which suggested that someone had been inexcusably careless.

She was wearing carpet slippers and a thick tweed skirt, incongruously topped by an open-work jumper in pink wool, liberally festooned with pearls. Dalgliesh suspected that her cottage was a similar unhappy compromise between utility and fussiness, but had no inclination to find out. To his relief she made no attempt to help with the books but sat squatting on the edge of the chair, coffee mug cradled in her lap, her legs planted firmly apart to reveal twin balloons of milky white and varicosed thigh above the bite of the stockings. Dalgliesh continued with his job, coffee mug on the floor at his side. He shook each volume gently before allocating it to its pile in case some message should drop out. If it did, Mrs Hammitt's presence would be embarrassing. But he knew that the precaution was merely his professional habit of leaving nothing to chance. This wouldn't be Father Baddeley's way.

Meanwhile Mrs Hammitt sipped her coffee and talked, encouraged in her volubility and occasional indiscretion by the belief which Dalgliesh had noticed before that a man who is physically working only hears half what is said to him.

'No need to ask you if you had a comfortable night. Those beds of Wilfred's are notorious. A certain amount of hardness is supposed to be good for disabled patients but I like a mattress I can sink into. I'm surprised that Julius didn't invite you to sleep at his cottage, but he never does have visitors. Doesn't want to put Mrs Reynolds out I suppose. She's the village constable's widow from Toynton village and she does for Julius whenever he's here. Grossly overpaid, of course. Well, he can afford it. And you'll be sleeping here tonight, I understand. I saw Helen Rainer coming in with the bed linen. I suppose it won't worry you, sleeping in Michael's bed. No, of course it wouldn't, being a policeman. You aren't sensitive or superstitious about things like that. Quite right too; our death is but a sleep and a forgetting. Or do I mean life? Wordsworth anyway. I used to be very fond of poetry when I was a girl but I can't get along with these modern poets. Still, I should have quite looked forward to your reading.'

Her tone suggested that it would have been a solitary and eccentric pleasure. But Dalgliesh had momentarily stopped listening to her. He had found the first edition of *Diary of a Nobody* with an inscription written in a boyish hand, on the title page.

> To Father Baddeley for his Birthday with love from Adam. I bought this from Mr Snelling in Norwich and he let me have it cheap because of the red stain on page twenty. But I've tested it and it isn't blood.

Dalgliesh smiled. So he'd tested it, had he, the arrogant little blighter. What mysterious concoction of acids and crystals from the remembered chemistry set had resulted in that confident scientific pronouncement? The inscription reduced the value of the book rather more than the stain, but he didn't think that Father Baddeley thought so. He placed it on the pile reserved for his own shelves and again let Mrs Hammitt's voice pierce his consciousness.

'And if a poet can't take the trouble to make himself intelligible to the educated reader, then the educated reader had better leave him alone, that's what I always say.'

'I'm sure you do, Mrs Hammitt.'

'Call me Millicent, won't you? We're supposed to be one happy family here. If I have to put up with Dennis Lerner and Maggie Hewson and even that appalling Albert Philby calling me by my Christian name – not that I give him much opportunity, I assure you – I don't see why you shouldn't. And I shall try to call you Adam but I don't think it's going to come easily. You aren't a Christian-name person.'

Dalgliesh carefully dusted the volumes of Maskell's *Monumenta Ritualica Ecclesiae Anglicanae* and said that, from what he had heard, Victor Holroyd hadn't done much towards promoting the concept of one happy family.

'Oh, you've heard about Victor then? Maggie gossiping, I suppose. He really was an extremely difficult man, inconsiderate in life and in death. I managed to get on with him fairly well. I think he respected me. He was a very clever man and full of useful information. But no one at the Grange could stand him. Even Wilfred more or less gave up in the end and left him alone.

Maggie Hewson was the exception. Odd woman; she always has to be different. Do you know, I believe she thought Victor had willed his money to her. Of course we all knew that he had money. He took good care to let us know that he wasn't one of those patients paid for by the local authority. And I suppose she thought that if she played her cards right some of it might come to her. She more or less hinted to me once. Well, she was half drunk at the time. Poor Eric! I give that marriage another year at the most. Some men might find her physically attractive, I suppose, if you like that dyed blonde, blowzy, over-sexed type. Of course, her affair, if you can call it an affair, with Victor was just indecent. Sex is for the healthy. I know that the disabled are supposed to have feelings like the rest of us but you'd think that they'd put that sort of thing behind them when they get to the wheelchair stage. That book looks interesting. The binding's good anyway. You might get a shilling or two for that.'

Placing a first edition of *Tracts for the Times* out of reach of Millicent's nudging foot and among the books selected for himself, Dalgliesh recognized with transitory self-disgust that, however much he deplored Mrs Hammitt's uninhibited expression, the sentiment wasn't far from his own thoughts. What, he wondered, must it be like to feel desire, love, lust even, and be imprisoned in an unresponsive body? Or worse, a body only too responsive to some of its urges, but uncoordinated, ugly, grotesque. To be sensitive to beauty, but to live always with deformity. He thought that he could begin to understand Victor Holroyd's bitterness. He asked:

'What happened in the end to Holroyd's money?'

'It all went to his sister in New Zealand, all sixty-five thousand of it. Very right too. Money ought to be kept in the family. But I daresay Maggie had her hopes. Probably Victor more or less promised her. It's the sort of thing he would do. He could be very spiteful at times. But at least he left his fortune where it ought to go. I should be very displeased indeed if I thought that Wilfred had bequeathed Toynton Grange to anyone but me.'

'But would you want it?'

'Oh, the patients would have to go, of course. I can't see myself running Toynton Grange as it is now. I respect what Wilfred's trying to do, but he has a particular need to do it. I expect you've heard about his visit to Lourdes and the miracle. Well, that's all right by me. But I haven't had a miracle, thank God, and I've no intention of putting myself in the way of one. Besides, I've done quite enough for the chronic sick already. Half the house was left to me by father and I sold out to Wilfred so that he could start the Home. We had a proper valuation made at the time, naturally, but it wasn't very high. At the time large country houses were a drag on the market. Now, of course, it's worth a fortune. It's a beautiful house isn't it?'

'It's certainly interesting architecturally.'

'Exactly. Regency houses of character are fetching fantastic prices. Not that I'm set on selling. After all, it was our childhood home and I have an affection for it. But I should probably get rid of the land. As a matter of fact, Victor Holroyd knew someone locally who would be interested in buying, someone who wants to set up another holiday caravan camp.'

Dalgliesh said involuntarily:

'What a horrible thought!'

Mrs Hammitt was unabashed. She said complacently:

'Not at all. A very selfish attitude on your part, if I may say so. The poor need holidays just like the rich. Julius wouldn't like it, but I'm under no obligation to consider Julius. He'd sell his cottage and get out I suppose. He owns that acre and a half of the headland, but I can't see him driving through a caravan park every time he comes here from London. Besides, they'd more or less have to pass his windows to get down to the beach. That's the only spot with a beach at high tide. I can see them, can't you; knobbly-kneed fathers in natty little shorts carrying the picnic bag, mum following with a blaring transistor, squealing kids, yelling babies. No, I can't see Julius staying here.'

'Does everyone here know that you stand to inherit Toynton Grange?'

'Of course; it's no secret. Who else should get it? As a matter of fact, the whole estate should belong to me by right. Perhaps you know that Wilfred isn't really an Anstey, that he was adopted?'

Dalgliesh said cautiously that he thought someone had mentioned as much.

'Then you may as well know the whole of it. It's quite interesting if you're concerned with the law.'

Mrs Hammitt refilled her mug and wriggled back into her chair as if settling herself for a complicated dissertation.

'My father was particularly anxious for a son. Some men are like that, daughters don't really count with them. And I can quite see that I was a disappointment. If a man really wants a son, the only thing that reconciles him to a daughter is her beauty. And that I've never had. Luckily, it didn't seem to worry my husband. We suited very well.'

As the only possible answer to this announcement was a vague, congratulatory murmur, Dalgliesh made the appropriate sound.

'Thank you,' said Mrs Hammitt, as if acknowledging a compliment. She went on happily:

'Anyway, when the doctors told father that my mother couldn't bear another child, he decided to adopt a son. I believe he got Wilfred from a children's home, but I was only six at the time and I don't think I was ever told how and when they found him. Illegitimate, of course. People minded more about that kind of thing in 1920 and you could take your pick of unwanted babies. I remember how excited I was at the time to have a brother. I was a lonely child and with more than my share of natural affection. At the time, I didn't see Wilfred as a rival. I was very fond of Wilfred when we were young. I still am. People forget that sometimes.'

Dalgliesh asked what happened.

'It was my grandfather's will. The old man distrusted lawyers, even Holroyd and Martinson who were the family solicitors, and he drew up his own will. He left a life interest in the estate to my parents and the whole property in equal shares to his grandchildren. The question was, did he intend to include Wilfred? In the end we had to go to law about it. The case made quite a stir at the time and raised the whole question of rights of adopted children. Perhaps you remember the case?'

Dalgliesh did have a vague memory of it. He asked:

'When was your grandfather's will made, I mean in relation to your brother's adoption?'

'That was the vital part of the evidence. Wilfred was legally adopted on 3rd May 1921, and grandfather signed his will exactly ten days later on 13th May. It was witnessed by two servants, but they were dead by the time the case was fought. The will was perfectly clear and in order, except that he didn't put in the names. But Wilfred's lawyers could prove that grandfather knew about the adoption and was happy about it. And the will did say children, in the plural.'

'But he might have had it in mind that your mother would die first and your father remarry.'

'How clever of you! I can see that you've a lawyer's devious mind. That's exactly what my counsel argued. But it was no good. Wilfred won. But you can understand my feelings over the Grange. If grandfather had only signed that will before 3rd May things would be very different, I can tell you.'

'But you did get half the value of the estate?'

'That didn't last long I'm afraid. My dear husband got through money very quickly. It wasn't women, I'm glad to say. It was horses. They're just as expensive and even more unpredictable but a less humiliating rival for a wife. And, unlike another woman, you can at least be glad when they win. Wilfred always said that Herbert became senile when he retired from the army, but I didn't complain. I rather preferred him that way. But he did get through the money.'

Suddenly she glanced around the room, leaned forward and gave Dalgliesh a sly conspiratorial glance.

'I'll tell you something that no one at Toynton Grange knows, except Wilfred. If he does sell out I shall get half the sale price. Not just half the extra profit, fifty per cent of what he gets. I've got an undertaking from Wilfred, properly signed and witnessed by Victor. Actually it was Victor's suggestion. He thought it would stand up in law. And it isn't kept where Wilfred can get his hands on it. It's with Robert Loder, a solicitor in Wareham. I suppose Wilfred was so confident that he'd never need to sell, that he didn't care what he signed or perhaps he was arming himself against temptation. I don't think for one minute that he will sell. He cares too much about the place for that. But if he should change his mind, then I shall do very nicely.'

Dalgliesh said, greatly daring:

'When I arrived, Mrs Hewson said something about the Ridgewell Trust. Hasn't Mr Anstey got it in mind to transfer the Home?'

Mrs Hammitt took the suggestion more calmly than he had expected. She retorted robustly:

'Nonsense! I know Wilfred talks about it from time to time, but he'd never just hand over Toynton Grange. Why should he? Money's tight, of course, but money always is tight. He'll just have to put up the fees or get the local authorities to pay more for the patients they send. There's no reason why he should subsidize the local authorities. And if he still can't make the place pay, then he'd do better to sell out, miracle or no miracle.'

Dalgliesh suggested that, in all the circumstances, it was surprising that Anstey hadn't become a Roman Catholic. Millicent seized on the thought with vehemence.

'It was quite a spiritual struggle for him at the time.' Her voice deepened and throbbed with the echo of cosmic forces linked in mortal struggle. 'But I was glad that he decided to remain in our church. Our father' – her voice boomed out in such a sudden access of hortatory fervour that Dalgliesh, startled, half expected that she was about to launch into the Lord's prayer – 'would have been so very distressed. He was a great churchman, Commander Dalgliesh. Evangelical of course. No, I was glad that Wilfred didn't go over.'

She spoke as if Wilfred, faced with the Jordan river, had neither liked the look of the water nor had confidence in his boat.

Dalgliesh had already asked Julius Court about Anstey's religious allegiance and had received a different and, he suspected, a more accurate explanation. He recalled their conversation on the patio before they had rejoined Henry; Julius's amused voice: 'Father O'Malley, who was supposed to be instructing Wilfred, made it plain that his church would in future proclaim on a number of matters that Wilfred had seen as coming within his personal jurisdiction. It occurred to dear Wilfred that he was on the point of joining a very large organization and one which thought that, as a convert, he was receiving rather that bestowing benefit. In the end, after what I have no doubt was a gratifying struggle, he decided to remain in a more accommodating fold.'

'Despite the miracle?' Dalgliesh had asked.

'Despite the miracle. Father O'Malley is a rationalist. He admits the existence of miracles but prefers the evidence to be submitted to the proper authorities for thorough examination. After a seemly delay the Church in her wisdom will then pronounce. To go about proclaiming that one has been the recipient of special grace smacks to him of presumption. Worse, I suspect he thinks it in poor taste. He's a fastidious man, is Father O'Malley. He and Wilfred don't really get on. I'm afraid that Father O'Malley has lost his church a convert.'

'But the pilgrimages to Lourdes still go on?' Dalgliesh had asked.

'Oh, yes. Twice a year regularly. I don't go. I used to when I first came here but it isn't, in the contemporary idiom, exactly my scene. But I usually make it my business to provide a slap-up tea to welcome them all back.'

Dalgliesh, his mind recalled to the present, was aware that his back was beginning to ache. He straightened up just as the clock on the mantelshelf struck the three-quarters. A charred log tumbled from the grate shooting up a final cascade of sparks. Mrs Hammitt took it as a signal that it was time to go. Dalgliesh insisted first on washing up the coffee mugs and she followed him into the kitchen.

'It has been a pleasant hour, Commander, but I doubt whether we shall repeat it. I'm not one of those neighbours who keep dropping in. Thank God I can stand my own company. Unlike poor Maggie, I have resources. And I'll say one thing for Michael Baddeley, he did keep himself to himself.'

'Nurse Rainer tells me that you persuaded him of the advantages of cremation.'

'Did she say that? Well, I daresay she's right. I may have mentioned it to Michael. I strongly disapprove of wasting good ground to bury putrifying bodies. As far as I remember the old man didn't care what happened to him as long as he ended up in consecrated earth with the proper words said over him. Very sensible. My view entirely. And Wilfred certainly didn't object to the cremation. He and Dot Moxon agreed with me absolutely. Helen protested over the extra trouble, but what she didn't like was having to get a second doctor's signature. Thought it cast some kind of aspersion on dear Eric's clinical judgement, I suppose.'

'But surely no one was suggesting that Dr Hewson's diagnosis was wrong?'

'Of course not! Michael died of a heart attack, and even Eric was competent to recognize that, I should hope. No, don't bother to see me home, I've got my torch. And if there's anything you need at any time, just knock on the wall.'

'But would you hear? You didn't hear Father Baddeley.'

'Naturally not, since he didn't knock. And after about nine-thirty I wasn't really listening for him. You see, I thought someone had already visited to settle him for the night.'

The darkness outside was cool and restless, a black mist, sweet-tasting and smelling of the sea, not the mere absence of light but a positive, mysterious force. Dalgliesh manoeuvred the trolley over the doorstep. Walking beside Millicent down the short path, and steadying the trolley with one hand, he asked with careful uninterest:

'Did you hear someone, then?'

'Saw, not heard. Or so I thought. I was thinking of making myself a hot drink and I wondered whether Michael would like one. But when I opened my front door to call in and ask, I thought I saw a figure in a cloak disappearing into the darkness. As Michael's light was off – I could see that the cottage was completely dark – naturally I didn't want to disturb him. I know now that I was mistaken. Either that or I'm going potty. It wouldn't be difficult in this place. Apparently no one did visit him and now they've all got a bad conscience about it. I can see how I was deceived. It was a night like this. Just a slight breeze but the darkness seeming to move and form itself into shapes. And I heard nothing, not even a footfall. Just a glimpse of a bent head, hooded and a cloak swirling into the darkness.'

'And this was at about nine-thirty?'

'Or a little later. Perhaps it was about the time he died. A fanciful person could frighten herself imagining that she'd seen his ghost. That was what Jennie Pegram actually suggested when I told them at Toynton Grange. Ridiculous girl!'

They had almost reached the door of Faith Cottage. She hesitated and then said as if on impulse, and, he thought, with some embarrassment:

'They tell me that you're worried about the broken lock of Michael's bureau. Well, it was all right the night before he came back from hospital. I found I'd run out of envelopes and I had an urgent letter to write. I thought that he wouldn't mind if I took a look in the bureau. It was locked then.'

Dalgliesh said:

'And broken when your brother looked for the will shortly after the body was found.'

'So he says, Commander. So he says.'

'But you have no proof that he broke it?'

'I've no proof that anyone did. The cottage was full of people running in and out. Wilfred, the Hewsons, Helen, Dot, Philby, even Julius when he arrived from London; the place was like a wake. All I know is that the bureau was locked at nine o'clock on the night before Michael died. And I've no doubt that Wilfred was keen to get his eyes on that will and see if Michael really had left Toynton Grange all he possessed. And I do know that Michael didn't break the lock himself.'

'How, Mrs Hammitt?'

'Because I found the key, just after lunch on the day he died. In the place where, presumably, he always kept it – that old tea tin on the second shelf of the food cupboard. I didn't think he'd mind my having any little bits of food he'd left. I slipped it into my pocket in case it got lost when Dot cleared the cottage. After all, that old bureau desk is quite valuable and the lock ought to be repaired. As a matter of fact, if Michael hadn't left it to Grace in his will, I would have moved it into here and looked after it properly.'

'So you still have the key?'

'Of course. No one has ever bothered about it but you. But, as you seem so interested you may as well take it.'

She dug her hand into the pocket of her skirt and he felt the cold metal pressed into his palm. She had opened the door of her cottage now and had reached for the light switch. In the sudden glare he blinked, and then saw it clearly, a small silver key, delicate as filigree, but tied now with thin string to a red plastic clothes peg, the red so bright that, for a dazzled second, it looked as if his palm were stained with blood.

FIVE
Act of Malice

I

When he looked back on his first weekend in Dorset, Dalgliesh saw it as a series of pictures, so different from the later images of violence and death that he could almost believe that his life at Toynton Head had been lived on two levels and at different periods of time. These early and gentle pictures, unlike the later harsh black and white stills from some crude horror film, were suffused with colour and feeling and smell. He saw himself plunging through the sea-washed shingle of Chesil Bank, his ears loud with bird cries and the grating thunder of the tide to where Portland reared its dark rocks against the sky; climbing the great earthworks of Maiden Castle and standing, a solitary windblown figure, where four thousand years of human history were compassed in numerous contours of moulded earth; eating a late tea in Judge Jeffrey's lodgings in Dorchester as the mellow autumn afternoon faded into dusk; driving through the night between a falling tangle of golden bracken and high untrimmed hedgerows to where the stone-walled pub waited with lighted windows on some remote village green.

And then, late at night when there could be small risk of a visitor from Toynton Grange disturbing him, he would drive back to Hope Cottage to the familiar and welcoming smell of books and a wood fire. Somewhat to his surprise, Millicent Hammitt was faithful to her promise not to disturb him after that first visit. He soon guessed why; she was a television addict. As he sat drinking his wine and sorting Father Baddeley's books, he could hear through the chimney breast the faint and not disagreeable sounds of her nightly entertainment; the sudden access of a half-familiar advertising jingle; the antiphonal mutter of voices; the bark of gun shots; feminine screams; the blaring fanfare to the late-night film.

He had a sense of living in a limbo between the old life and the new, excused by convalescence from the responsibility of immediate decision, from any exertion which he found disagreeable. And he found the thought of Toynton Grange and its inmates disagreeable. He had taken what action he could. Now he was waiting on events. Once, looking at Father Baddeley's empty and shabby chair, he was reminded irreverently of the fabled excuse of the distinguished atheist philosopher, ushered after death to his astonishment into the presence of God.

'But Lord, you didn't provide sufficient evidence.'

If Father Baddeley wanted him to act he would have to provide more tangible clues than a missing diary and a broken lock.

He was expecting no letters except Bill Moriarty's reply since he had left instructions that none were to be forwarded. And he intended to collect Bill's letter himself from the postbox. But it arrived on the Monday, at least a day earlier than he had thought possible. He had spent the morning in the cottage and hadn't walked to the postbox until after his lunch at two-thirty when he had taken back his milk bottles for collection.

The postbox contained the one letter, a plain envelope with a W.C. postmark; the address was typed but his rank omitted. Moriarty had been careful. But as he slipped his thumb under the flap, Dalgliesh wondered if he himself had been careful enough. There was no obvious sign that the letter had been opened; the flap was intact. But the glue was suspiciously weak, and the flap slid open a little too easily under the pressure of his thumb. And the postbox was otherwise empty. Someone, probably Philby, must already have the Toynton Grange post. It was odd that he hadn't delivered this letter at Hope Cottage. Perhaps he should have used a poste restante in Toynton village or Wareham. The thought that he had been careless irritated him. The truth is, he thought, that I don't know what, if anything, I'm investigating, and I only spasmodically care. I haven't the stomach to do the job properly or the will and courage to leave it alone. He was in the mood to find Bill's prose style more than usually irritating.

'Nice to see your elegant handwriting again. There's general relief here that the reports of your impending decease were exaggerated. We're keeping the wreath contributions for a celebration party. But what are you doing anyway gum-shoeing in Dorset among such a questionable group of weirdies? If you pine for work there's plenty here. However, here's the gen.

'Two of your little lot have records. You know, apparently, something about Philby. Two convictions for G.B.H. in 1967 and 1969, four for theft in 1970 and a miscellany of earlier misdemeanours. The only extraordinary thing about Philby's criminal history is the leniency with which judges have sentenced him. Looking at his C.R.O. I'm not altogether surprised. They probably felt that it was unjust to punish too harshly a man who was following the only career for which physiognomy and talents had fitted him. I did manage to have a word with "the open door" about him. They admit his faults, but say that he is capable, given affection, of a ferocious loyalty. Watch out that he doesn't take a fancy to you.

'Millicent Hammitt was convicted twice for shoplifting by the Cheltenham Magistrates in 1966 and 1968. In the first case there was the usual defence of menopausal difficulties, and she was fined. She was lucky to escape so easily the second time. But that was a couple of months after her husband, a retired army major, had died and the court was sympathetic. They were probably influenced too by Wilfred Anstey's assurances that she was coming to live with him at Toynton Grange and would be under his eye. There's been no trouble since so I assume that Anstey's surveillance has been effective, the local shopkeepers more accommodating, or Mrs Hammitt more skilful in lifting the goods.

'That's all the official gen. The rest of them are clean, at least as far as the C.R.O. is concerned. But if you're looking for an interesting villain – and I hardly suppose that Adam Dalgliesh is wasting his talents on Albert Philby – then may I recommend Julius Court? I got a line on him from a man I know who works at the F.C.O. Court is a bright grammar-school boy from Southsea who entered the foreign service after university equipped with all the usual elegant appurtenances but rather short on cash. He was at the Paris Embassy in 1970 when he gave evidence in the notorious murder trial when Alain Michonnet was accused of murdering Poitaud the racing driver. You may remember the case. There was a fair amount of publicity in the English press. It was pretty clear-cut, and the French police were salivating happily at the thought of nailing Michonnet. He's the son of Theo d'Estier Michonnet, who owns a chemical manufacturing plant near Marseilles, and they've had their eyes on père and fils for quite a time. But Court gave his chum an alibi. The odd thing was that they weren't really chums – Michonnet is aggressively heterosexual as the media make only too boringly plain – and the horrid word blackmail was hissed round the Embassy. No one believed Court's story; but no one could shake it. My informant thinks that Court's motive was nothing more sinister than a desire to amuse himself and to get his superiors twisting their knickers. If that was his motive he certainly succeeded. Eight months later his godfather conveniently died leaving him £30,000 and he chucked the service. He's said to have been rather clever with his investments. Anyway, that's all water under the bridge. Nothing is known to his discredit as they say, except, perhaps, a tendency to be a little too accommodating to his friends. But I give you the story for what it's worth.'

Dalgliesh folded the letter and stuffed it into his jacket pocket. He wondered how much, if any, of either story was known at Toynton Grange. Julius Court was unlikely to worry. His past was his own affair; he was independent of Wilfred's suffocating hold. But Millicent Hammitt had a double weight of gratitude. Who else except Wilfred knew, he wondered, about these two discreditable and pathetic incidents? How much would she care if the story became generally known at Toynton Grange? He wished again that he had used a poste restante.

A car was approaching. He looked up. The Mercedes, driven very fast, was coming down the coast road. Julius stepped on the brakes and the car rocked to a stop, its front bumper inches from the gate. He wrenched himself out and began tugging at the gate, calling out to Dalgliesh.

'The black tower's on fire! I saw smoke from the coast road. Have you a rake at Hope Cottage?'

Dalgliesh put his shoulder to the gate.

'I don't think so. There's no garden. But I found a yard broom – a besom – in the shed.'

'Better than nothing. D'you mind coming? It may take the two of us.'

Dalgliesh slipped quickly into the car. They left the gate open. Julius drove to Hope Cottage with little regard for the car springs or his passenger's comfort. He opened the boot while Dalgliesh ran to the yard shed. There among the paraphernalia of past occupants were the remembered besom, two empty sacks and, surprisingly, an old shepherd's crook. He threw them into the capacious boot. Julius had already turned the car and the engine was running. Dalgliesh got in beside him and the Mercedes leapt forward.

As they swung on to the coast road Dalgliesh asked:

'Is anyone there do you know? Anstey?'

'Could be. That's the worry. He's the only one who goes there now. And I can't see otherwise how the fire started. We can get closest to the tower this way, but it means foot slogging it over the headland. I didn't try when I first spotted the smoke. It's no use without something to tackle the fire.'

His voice was tight, the knuckles on the wheel shone white. In the driving mirror Dalgliesh saw that the irises of his eyes were large and bright. The triangular scar above the right eye, normally almost invisible, had deepened and darkened. Above it he could see the insistent beat of the temple pulse. He glanced at the speedometer; they were doing over a hundred but the Mercedes, beautifully handled, held the narrow road easily. Suddenly the road twisted and rose and they caught a glimpse of the tower. The broken panes in the slitted windows below the cupola were belching puff-balls of greyish smoke like miniature cannonfire. They tumbled merrily over the headland until the wind shook them into shredded dusters of cloud. The effect was absurd and picturesque, as innocuous as a child's entertainment. And then the road dipped and the tower was lost to view.

The coast road, wide enough only for a single car, was bounded to the seaward by a drystone wall. Julius was sure of his way. He had swung the car to the left even before Dalgliesh noticed the narrow gap, gateless but still bounded by two rotting posts. The car bumped to a standstill in a deep hollow to the right of the entry. Dalgliesh seized the crook and sacks and Julius the broom.

Thus ridiculously lumbered, they began running across the headland.

Julius had been right; this was the quickest way. But they had to do it on foot. Even had he been willing to drive over this rough, rock-strewn ground it wouldn't have been possible. The headland was crossed with fragmented stone walls, low enough to leap over and with plenty of gaps, but none wide enough for a vehicle. The ground was deceptive. At one minute the tower seemed to recede, separated from them by interminable barriers of tumbling stone. Then it was upon them.

The smoke, acrid as a damp bonfire, was rolling strongly from the half-open door. Dalgliesh kicked it wide and leapt to one side as the gusts billowed out. There was an immediate roar and the tongue of flame fanged out at him. With the crook he began raking out the burning debris, some still identifiable – long dried grass and hay, rope ends, what looked like the remains of an old chair – the years of accumulated rubbish since the headland had been public land and the black tower, unlocked, used as a shepherd's shelter or a night lodging for tramps. As he raked out the burning malodorous clumps he could hear Julius behind him frantically beating them out. Little fires started and crawled like red tongues among the grasses.

As soon as the doorway was clear Julius rushed in stamping down the smouldering remnants of grass and hay with the two sacks. Dalgliesh could see his smoke-shrouded figure coughing and reeling. He dragged him unceremoniously out and said:

'Keep back until I've cleared it. I don't want the two of you on my hands.'

'But he's there! I know he is. He must be. Oh, God! The bloody fool!'

The last smouldering clump of grass was out now. Julius, pushing Dalgliesh aside, ran up the stone stairway which circled the walls. Dalgliesh followed. A wooden door to a middle chamber was ajar. Here there was no window, but in the smoke-filled darkness they could see the huddled sack-like figure against the far wall. He had drawn the hood of the monk's cloak over his head and had swathed himself into its folds like a human derelict wrapped against the cold. Julius's feverish hands got lost in the folds. Dalgliesh could hear him cursing. It took seconds before Anstey's arms were freed and, together, they dragged him to the door and, with difficulty, supported and manoeuvred the inert body between them down the narrow stairs and into the fresh-smelling air.

They laid him prone on the grass. Dalgliesh had dropped to his knees, ready to turn him and start artificial respiration. Then Anstey slowly stretched out both arms and lay in an attitude both theatrical and vaguely blasphemous. Dalgliesh, relieved that he wouldn't now have to fasten his mouth over Anstey's, got to his feet. Anstey drew up his knees and began to cough convulsively in hoarse whooping gasps. He turned his face to one side, his cheek resting on the headland. The moist mouth, coughing out saliva and bile, seemed to be sucking at the grass as if avid for nourishment. Dalgliesh and Court knelt and raised him between them. He said weakly:

'I'm all right. I'm all right.'

Dalgliesh asked:

'We've got the car on the coast road. Can you walk?'

'Yes. I'm all right, I tell you. I'm all right.'

'There's no hurry. Better rest for a few minutes before we start.'

They lowered him against one of the large boulders and he sat there a little apart from them, still coughing spasmodically, and looking out to sea. Julius paced the cliff edge, restlessly as if fretting at the delay. The stench of the fire was blown gently from the blackened headland like the last waves of a fading pestilence.

After five minutes Dalgliesh called:

'Shall we start now?'

Together and without speaking, they raised Anstey and supported him between them across the headland and to the car.

II

No one spoke on the drive back to Toynton Grange. As usual, the front of the house seemed deserted, the tessellated hall was empty, unnaturally silent. But Dorothy Moxon's sharp ears must have heard the car, perhaps from the clinical room at the front of the house. Almost immediately she appeared at the top of the stairs.

'What is it? What happened?'

'It's all right. Wilfred managed to set fire to the black tower with himself inside. He isn't hurt, just shocked. And the smoke hasn't done his lungs any good.'

She glanced accusingly from Dalgliesh to Julius as if it were their fault, then put both her arms round Anstey in a gesture fiercely maternal and protective and began to urge him gently up the stairs, muttering encouragement and remonstration into his ear in a soft grumbling monotone which, to Dalgliesh, sounded like an endearment. Anstey, he noticed, seemed less capable of supporting himself now than he had been on the headland and they made slow progress. But when Julius came forward to help, a glance from Dorothy Moxon made him draw back. With difficulty she got Anstey into his small white-painted bedroom at the back of the house and helped him on to the narrow bed. Dalgliesh made a swift mental inventory. The room was much as he had expected. One small table and chair set under the window giving a view of the patients' rear courtyard; a well-stocked bookcase; one rug; a crucifix over the bed; a bedside table with a simple lamp and a carafe of water. But the thick mattress bounced gently as Wilfred rolled on to it. The towel hanging beside the wash basin looked luxuriantly soft. The bedside rug, plain in design, was no strip of worn, discarded carpet. The hooded dressing-gown in white towelling hanging behind the door had a look of simplicity, almost austerity; but Dalgliesh did not doubt that it was agreeably soft to the skin. This might be a cell, but it lacked none of the essential comforts.

Wilfred opened his eyes and fixed his blue gaze on Dorothy Moxon. It was interesting, Dalgliesh thought, how he managed to combine humility with authority in one look. He held out a suppliant hand.

'I want to talk to Julius and Adam, Dot dear. Just for a moment. Will you?'

She opened her mouth, clamped it shut again, and stomped out without a word, closing the door firmly behind her. Wilfred closed his eyes again and appeared mentally to withdraw himself from the scene. Julius looked down at his hands. His right palm was red and swollen and a blister had already formed over the bowl of the thumb. He said with a note of surprise:

'Funny! My hand's burnt. I never felt it at the time. Now it's beginning to hurt like hell.'

Dalgliesh said:

'You should get Miss Moxon to dress it. And it might be as well to let Hewson have a look at it.'

Julius took a folded handkerchief from his pocket, soaked it in cold water at the wash basin and wrapped it inexpertly round his hand.

He said:

'It can wait.'

The realization that he was in pain appeared to have soured his temper. He stood over Wilfred and said crossly:

'Now that a definite attack has been made on your life and damn nearly succeeded, I suppose you'll act sensibly for once and send for the police.'

Wilfred did not open his eyes, he said weakly:

'I have a policeman here.'

Dalgliesh said:

'It isn't for me. I can't undertake an official investigation for you. Court is right, this is a matter for the local police.'

Wilfred shook his head.

'There's nothing to tell them. I went to the black tower because there were things I needed to think over in peace. It's the only place where I can be absolutely alone. I was smoking; you know how you all complain about my smelly old pipe. I remember knocking it out against the wall as I went up. It must have been still alight. All that dried grass and straw would have gone up at once.'

Julius said grimly:

'It did. And the outside door? I suppose you forgot to lock it after you, despite all the fuss you make about never leaving the black tower open. You're a careless lot at Toynton Grange aren't you? Lerner forgets to check the wheelchair brakes and Holroyd goes over the cliff. You knock out your pipe above a floor strewn with highly combustible dry straw, leave the door open to provide a draught, and bloody nearly immolate yourself.'

Anstey said:

'That's how I prefer to believe it happened.'

Dalgliesh said quickly:

'Presumably there's a second key to the tower. Where is it kept?'

Wilfred opened his eyes and stared into space as if patiently dissociating himself from this dual interrogation.

'Hanging on a nail on the keyboard in the business room. It was Michael's key, the one I brought back here after his death.'

'And everyone knows where it's hung?

'I imagine so. All the keys are kept there and the one to the tower is distinctive.'

'How many people at Toynton Grange knew that you planned to be in the tower this afternoon?

'All of them. I told them my plans after prayers. I always do. People have to know where to find me in an emergency. Everyone was there except Maggie and Millicent. But what you're suggesting is ridiculous.'

'Is it?' asked Dalgliesh.

Before he could move, Julius, who was nearer the door had slipped out. They waited in silence. It was another two minutes before he returned. He said with grim satisfaction:

'The business room is empty and the key isn't there. That means whoever took it hasn't yet had the chance to put it back. Incidentally, I called Dot on my way back. She's lurking in her surgical hell sterilizing enough equipment for a major operation. It's like confronting a harpy through a hiss of steam. Anyway, she claims with bad grace that she was in the business room continually from 2 p.m. until about five minutes before we got back. She can't remember whether the tower key was on the keyboard. She didn't notice it. I'm afraid I've made her suspicious, Wilfred, but it seemed important to establish some facts.'

Dalgliesh thought that the facts could have been established without direct questioning. But it was too late now to initiate inquiries and in any case he had neither the heart nor stomach to undertake them. Certainly he had no wish to pit the claims of orthodox detection against Julius's enthusiastic amateurism. But he asked:

'Did Miss Moxon say whether anyone had come into the business room while she was there? They may have made an attempt to replace the key.'

'According to her, the place was – untypically – like a railway station. Henry wheeled himself in shortly after two, and then went out again. No explanation. Millicent dropped in about half an hour ago looking, so she said, for you, Wilfred. Dennis arrived a few minutes later to look up an unspecified telephone number. Maggie arrived just before we did. Again, no explanation. She didn't stay, but she did ask Dot whether she'd seen Eric. The only safe deduction from all this is that Henry couldn't have been on the headland at the material time. But then, we know he wasn't. Whoever started that fire had the use of a pair of very sound legs.'

His own, or someone else's, thought Dalgliesh.

He spoke again directly to the quiet figure on the bed.

'Did you see anyone when you were in the tower, either before or after the fire started?'

Wilfred paused before replying.

'I think so.'

Seeing Julius's face, he went on quickly:

'I'm sure I did, but only very briefly. When the fire started I was sitting at the southern window, the one overlooking the sea. I smelt smoke and went down into the middle chamber. I opened the door to the base of the tower and saw the hay smouldering and a sudden tongue of flame. I could have got out then, but I panicked. I'm terrified of fire. It isn't a rational fear. It goes well beyond that. I suppose you'd call it a phobia. Anyway, I scrambled ignominiously back into the top room and began running from window to window looking hopelessly for help. It was then I saw – unless it was an hallucination – a figure in a brown habit slipping between that clump of boulders to the south-west.'

Julius said:

'From which he could escape unrecognized by you either to the road or down the cliffs to the beach. That's if he were agile enough for the cliff path. What sort of figure, a man or a woman?'

'Just a figure. I only had a glimpse. I shouted but the wind was against me and he obviously didn't hear. I never thought of it being a woman.'

'Well, think now. The hood was up, I suppose?'

'Yes. Yes it was.'

'And on a warm afternoon! Think it out for yourself, Wilfred. Incidentally, there are three brown habits hanging in the business room. I felt in the pockets for the key. That's why I noticed. Three habits. How many do you have altogether?'

'Eight of the lightweight summer ones. They're always kept hanging in the business room. Mine has rather different buttons, but otherwise we have them in common. We're not really particular which one we take.'

'You're wearing yours; presumably Dennis and Philby are wearing theirs. That means two are missing.'

'Eric may be wearing one, he does occasionally. And Helen sometimes slips into one if the day is chilly. I seem to remember that one is in the sewing room being mended. And I think one was missing just before Michael died, but I can't be sure. It may have turned up again. We don't really keep a check on them.'

Julius said:

'So it's practically impossible to know whether one is missing. I suppose what we ought to be doing, Dalgliesh, is to check up on them now. If she hasn't had a chance to replace the key, presumably she's still got the habit.'

Dalgliesh said:

'We've no proof that it was a woman. And why hang on to the habit? It could be discarded anywhere in Toynton Grange without suspicion.'

Anstey propped himself up and said with sudden strength:

'No, Julius, I forbid it! I won't have people questioned and cross-examined. It was an accident.'

Julius, who seemed to be relishing his role of chief inquisitor, said:

'All right. It was an accident. You forgot to lock the door. You knocked out your pipe before it was dead and started the fire smouldering. The figure you saw was just someone from Toynton Grange taking an innocent stroll on the headland, somewhat overclad for the time of year and so immersed in the beauty of nature that he, or she, neither heard your shout, smelt the fire nor noticed the smoke. What happened then?'

'You mean, after I saw the figure? Nothing. I realized of course that I couldn't get out of the windows and I climbed down to the middle room. I opened the door to the bottom of the tower. The last thing I remember was a great billow of choking smoke and a sheet of flame. The smoke was suffocating me. The flames seemed to be searing my eyes. I hadn't even time to shut the door again before I was overcome. I suppose I should have kept both doors shut and sat tight. But it isn't easy to make sensible decisions in a state of panic.'

Dalgliesh asked:

'How many people here knew that you are abnormally afraid of fire?'

'Most of them suspect, I think. They may not know just how obsessive and personal a fear it is, but they do know that fire worries me. I insist on all the patients sleeping on the ground floor. I've always worried about the sick room, and I was reluctant to let Henry have an upper room. But someone had to sleep in the main part of the house, and we must have a sick room close to the clinical room and the nurses' bedrooms in case there's an emergency at night. It's sensible and prudent to fear fire in a place like this. But prudence has nothing to do with the terror I feel at the sight of smoke and flame.'

He put one hand up to his eyes and they saw that he had begun to tremble. Julius looked down at the shaking figure with almost clinical interest.

Dalgliesh said:

'I'll get Miss Moxon.'

He had hardly turned to the door when Anstey shot out a protesting hand. They saw that the trembling had stopped. He said, looking at Julius:

'You do believe that the work I'm doing here is worthwhile?'

Dalgliesh wondered if only he had noticed a fraction of a second's pause before Julius replied evenly:

'Of course.'

'You're not just saying that to comfort me, you believe it?'

'I wouldn't say it otherwise.'

'Of course not, forgive me. And you agree that the work is more important than the man?'

'That's more difficult. I could argue that the work is the man.'

'Not here. This place is established now. It could go on without me if it had to.'

'Of course it could, if it's adequately endowed, and if the local authorities continue to send contractual patients. But it won't have to go on without you if you act sensibly instead of like the reluctant hero of a third-rate TV drama. It doesn't suit you, Wilfred.'

'I'm trying to be sensible and I'm not being brave. I haven't much physical courage you know. It's the virtue I most regret. You two have it – no, don't argue. I know, and I envy you for it. But I don't really need courage for this situation. You see, I can't believe that someone is really trying to kill me.' He turned to Dalgliesh.

'You explain, Adam. You must see what I'm getting at.'

Dalgliesh said carefully:

'It could be argued that neither of the two attempts were serious. The frayed climbing rope? It's hardly a very certain method, and most people here must know that you wouldn't start a climb without checking your equipment and that you certainly wouldn't climb alone. This afternoon's little charade? You would probably have been safe enough if you'd closed both the doors and stayed in the top room; uncomfortably hot probably, but in no real danger. The fire would have burnt itself out in time. It was opening the middle door and gasping in a lungful of smoke which nearly did for you.'

Julius said:

'But suppose the grass had burnt fiercely and the flames had caught the wooden floor of the first storey? The whole of the middle tower would have gone up in a matter of seconds; the fire must have reached the top room. If it had, nothing could have saved you.' He turned to Dalgliesh:

'Isn't that true?'

'Probably. That's why you ought to tell the police. A practical joker who takes risks like that has to be taken seriously. And the next time there mightn't be someone handy to rescue you.'

'I don't think there will be a next time. I think I know who's responsible. I'm not really quite as foolish as I seem. I'll take care, I promise. I have a feeling that the person responsible won't be here with us much longer.'

Julius said:

'You're not immortal, Wilfred.'

'I know that, too, and I could be wrong. So I think it's time I spoke to the Ridgewell Trust. The Colonel is overseas, visiting his homes in India, but he's due back on the 18th. The trustees would like my answer by the end of October. It's a question of tying up capital for future developments. I wouldn't hand it over to them without a majority agreement from the family. I propose to hold a family council. But, if someone is really trying to frighten me into breaking my vow, then I'll see that my work here is made indestructible, whether I'm alive or dead.'

Julius said:

'If you hand the whole property over to the Ridgewell Trust, it isn't going to please Millicent.'

Wilfred's face set into a mask of obstinacy. Dalgliesh was interested to see how the features changed. The gentle eyes became stern and glazed as if unwilling to see, the mouth set into an uncompromising line. And yet the whole expression was one of petulant weakness.

'Millicent sold out to me perfectly willingly and at a fair valuation. She can't reasonably complain. If I'm driven out of here, the work goes on. What happens to me isn't important.'

He smiled at Julius.

'You aren't a believer, I know, so I'll find another authority for you. How about Shakespeare? "Be absolute for death; either death or life shall thereby be the sweeter."'

Julius Court's eyes briefly met Dalgliesh's over Wilfred's head. The message simultaneously passed was simultaneously understood. Julius had some difficulty in controlling his mouth. At last he said dryly:

'Dalgliesh is supposed to be convalescent. He's already practically passed out with the exertion of saving you. I may look healthy enough but I need my strength for the pursuit of my own personal pleasures. So if you are determined to hand over to the

Ridgewell Trust by the end of the month, try being absolute for life, at least for the next three weeks, there's a good chap.'

III

When they were outside the room Dalgliesh asked:

'Do you believe he's in real danger?'

'I don't know. It was probably a closer thing this afternoon than someone intended.' He added with affectionate scorn:

'Silly old pseud! Absolute for death! I thought we were about to move on to *Hamlet* and be reminded that the readiness is all. One thing is certain though, isn't it? He isn't putting on a show of courage. Either he doesn't believe that someone at Toynton Grange has it in for him, or he thinks he knows his enemy and is confident that he can deal with him, or her. Or, of course, he started the fire himself. Wait until I've had this hand bandaged and then come in for a drink. You look as if you need it.'

But there were things Dalgliesh had to do. He left Julius, volubly apprehensive, to the mercies of Dorothy Moxon and walked back to Hope Cottage to collect his torch. He was thirsty, but there was no time for anything but cold water from the kitchen tap. He had left the cottage windows open but the little sitting-room, insulated by thick stone walls, was as warm and stuffy as on the day he arrived. As he closed the door, Father Baddeley's cassock swung against it and he caught again the musty, faintly ecclesiastical smell. The crochet chair back and arm covers were sleekly in place uncrumpled by Father Baddeley's head and hands. Something of his personality still lingered here, although already Dalgliesh felt its presence less strongly. But there was no communication. If he wanted Father Baddeley's counsel he would have to seek it in paths familiar but unaccustomed and to which he no longer felt that he had any right of way.

He was ridiculously tired. The cool, rather harsh-tasting water only brought him to a clearer realization of just how tired. The thought of the narrow bed upstairs, of throwing himself down upon its hardness, was almost irresistible. It was ridiculous that so comparatively little exertion could so exhaust him. And it seemed to have become insufferably hot. He drew a hand over his brow and felt the sweat, clammy and cold on his fingers. Obviously he had a temperature. He had, after all, been warned by the hospital that the fever might recur. He felt a surge of anger against his doctors, against Wilfred Anstey, against himself.

It would be easy now to pack his things and get back to the London flat. It would be cool and unencumbered there high above the Thames at Queenhythe. People would leave him alone supposing him to be still in Dorset. Or he could leave a note for Anstey and drive away now; the whole of the West Country was open to him. There were a hundred better places for convalescence than this claustrophobic, self-regarding community dedicated to love and self-fulfilment through suffering, where people sent each other poison pen letters, played at childish and malicious pranks or got tired of waiting for death and hurled themselves into annihilation. And there was nothing to keep him at Toynton; he told himself so with stubborn insistence, resting his head against the coolness of the small square of glass over the sink which had obviously served Father Baddeley as a shaving mirror. It was probably some freak aftermath of illness that made him at once so indecisive and so stubbornly reluctant to leave. For someone who had made up his mind never to go back to detection, he was giving a good imitation of a man committed to his job.

He saw no one as he left the cottage and began the long trudge up the cliff. It was still a bright day on the headland with that sudden almost momentary intensification of light which comes before the setting of the autumn sun. The cushions of moss on the fragmented walls were an intense green, dazzling the eye. Each individual flower was bright as a gem, its image shimmering in the gently moving air. The tower, when at last he came up to it, glistened like ebony and seemed to shiver in the sun. He felt that if he touched it it would reel and dissolve. Its long shadow lay like a monitory finger across the headland.

Taking advantage of the light, since the torch would be more use inside the tower, he began his search. The burnt straw and blackened debris lay in untidy heaps close to the porch, but the light breeze, never absent from this peak of the headland, had already begun to shift the humps and had strewn odd strands almost to the edge of the cliff. He began by scrutinizing the ground close to the walls, then moved out in widening circles. He found nothing until he reached the clump of boulders about fifty yards to the south-west. They were a curious formation, less a natural outcrop of the headland than an artefact, as if the builder of the tower had transported to the site double the weight of stone needed and had amused himself by arranging the surplus in the form of a miniature mountain range. The stones formed a long semi-circle about forty yards long, the peaks, from six to eight feet high, linked by smaller, more rounded uplands. There was adequate cover here for a man to escape undetected either to the cliff path or by way of the rapidly falling ground to the north-west to within a couple of hundred yards of the road.

It was here, behind one of the larger boulders, that Dalgliesh found what he had expected to find, a lightweight brown monk's habit. It was tightly rolled into a bolster and wedged into the crevice between two smaller stones. There was nothing else to be seen, no discernible footprints in the firm dry turf, no tin smelling of paraffin. Somewhere he expected to find a tin. Although the straw and dry grass in the base of the tower would have burned quickly enough once a fire was well established, he doubted whether a thrown match could have been relied upon to start a blaze.

He tucked the habit under his arm. If this were a murder hunt the forensic scientists would examine it for traces of fibre, for dust, for paraffin, for any biological or chemical link with someone at Toynton Grange. But it wasn't a murder hunt; it wasn't even an official investigation. And even if fibres were identified on the habit which matched those from a shirt, a pair of slacks, a jacket, a dress even, of someone at Toynton Grange, what did that prove? Apparently any of the helpers had a right to array themselves in Wilfred's curious idea of a working uniform. The fact that the habit had been abandoned, and at that point, suggested that the wearer had chosen to escape down the cliff rather than by way of the road; otherwise why not continue to rely on its camouflage? Unless, of course, the wearer were a woman and one who didn't normally thus array herself. In that case, to be seen by chance on the headland shortly after the fire would be damning. But no one, man or woman, would choose to wear it on the cliff path. It was the quicker but the more difficult route and the habit would be a dangerously entangling garment. Certainly it would bear tell-tale traces of sandy earth or green stains from the seaweed-covered rocks on that difficult scramble to the beach. But perhaps that was what he was meant to believe. Had the habit, like Father Baddeley's letter, been planted for him to discover, so neatly, so precisely placed exactly where he might have expected to find it? Why abandon it at all? Thus rolled, it was hardly an impossible burden to manage on that slippery path to the shore.

The door of the tower was still ajar. Inside the smell of the fire still lingered but half pleasantly now in the first cool of the early evening, an evocative autumnal smell of burnt grass. The lower part of the rope banister had burnt away and hung from the iron rings in scorched and tattered fragments.

He switched on his torch and began systematically to search among the blackened threads of burnt straw. He found it within minutes, a battered, soot-covered and lidless tin which could once have held cocoa. He smelt it. It could have been his imagination that a trace of paraffin still lingered.

He made his way up the stone steps carefully hugging the fire-blackened wall. He found nothing in the middle chamber and was glad to climb out of this dark, windowless and claustrophobic cell into the upper room. The contrast with the chamber below was immediate and striking. The little room was filled with light. It was only six feet wide and the domed and ribbed ceiling gave it a charming, feminine and slightly formal air. Four of the eight compass point windows were without their glass and the air streamed in, cool and scented with the sea. Because the room was so small the height of the tower was accentuated. Dalgliesh had the sensation of being suspended in a decorative pepper pot between sky and sea. The quiet was absolute, a positive peace. He could hear nothing but the ticking of his watch and the ceaseless anodyne surge of the sea. Why, he wondered, hadn't that self-tormented Victorian Wilfred Anstey signalled his distress from one of these windows? Perhaps, by the time his will to endure had been broken by the tortures of hunger and thirst, the old man had been too weak to mount the stairs. Certainly nothing of his final terror and despair had penetrated to this miniature light-filled eyrie. Looking out of the southern window Dalgliesh could see the crinkled sea layered in azure and purple with one red triangle of sail stationary on the horizon. The other windows gave a panoramic view of the whole sunlit headland; Toynton Grange and its clutter of cottages could be identified only by the chimney of the house itself since they lay in the valley. Dalgliesh noticed too that the square of mossy turf, where Holroyd's wheelchair had rested before that final convulsive heave towards destruction, and the narrow sunken lane were also invisible. Whatever had happened on that fateful afternoon, no one could have seen it from the black tower.

The room was simply furnished. There was a wooden table and a chair set against the seaward window, a small oak cupboard, a rush mat on the floor, a slatted old-fashioned easy chair with cushions set in the middle of the room, a wooden cross nailed to the wall. He saw that the door of the cupboard was ajar and the key in the lock. Inside he found a small and unedifying collection of paperback pornography. Even allowing for the natural tendency – to which Dalgliesh admitted himself not immune – to be disdainful of the sexual tastes of others, this was not the pornography that he would have chosen. It was a paltry and pathetic little library of flagellation, titillation and salacity, incapable, he thought, of stimulating any emotion beyond ennui and vague disgust. True it contained *Lady Chatterley's Lover* – a novel which Dalgliesh considered overrated as literature and not qualifying as pornography – but the rest was hardly respectable by any standard. Even after a gap of over twenty years, it was difficult to believe that the gentle, aesthetic and fastidious Father Baddeley had developed a taste for this pathetic trivia. And if he had, why leave the cupboard unlocked or the key where Wilfred could find it? The obvious conclusion was that the books were Anstey's and that he had only just had time to unlock the cupboard before he smelt the fire. In the subsequent panic he had forgotten to lock away the evidence of his secret indulgence. He would probably return in some haste and confusion as soon as he was fit enough and got the opportunity. And, if this were true, it proved one thing: Anstey could not have started the fire.

Leaving the cupboard door ajar precisely as he had found it, Dalgliesh then carefully searched the floor. The rough mat of what looked like plaited hemp was torn in places and overlaid with dust. From the drag on its surface and the lie of the torn and minute filaments of fibre he deduced that Anstey had moved the table from the eastern to the southern window. He found, too, what looked like traces of two different kinds of tobacco ash, but they were too small to be collected without his magnifying glass and tweezers. But, a little to the right of the eastern window and resting between the interstices of the mat, he found something which could be identified easily with the naked eye. It was a single used yellow match identical with those in the booklet by Father Baddeley's bed, and it had been peeled down in five separate pieces to its blackened head.

IV

The front door of Toynton Grange was, as usual, open. Dalgliesh walked swiftly and silently up the main staircase to Wilfred's room. As he approached he could hear talking, Dot Moxon's expostulatory and belligerent voice dominating the broken murmur of male voices. Dalgliesh went in without knocking. Three pairs of eyes regarded him with wariness and, he thought, with some resentment. Wilfred was still lying propped up in his bed. Dennis Lerner quickly turned away to look fixedly out of the window, but not before Dalgliesh had seen that his face was blotched as if he had been crying. Dot was sitting by the side of the bed, stolid and immovable as a mother watching a sick child. Dennis muttered, as if Dalgliesh had asked for an explanation:

'Wilfred has told me what happened. It's unbelievable.'

Wilfred spoke with a mulish obstinacy which only emphasized his satisfaction at not being believed.

'It happened, and it was an accident.'

Dennis was beginning 'How could . . .' when Dalgliesh interrupted by laying the rolled habit on the foot of the bed. He said:

'I found this among the boulders by the black tower. If you hand it over to the police it may tell them something.'

'I'm not going to the police and I forbid anyone here – anyone – to go on my behalf.'

Dalgliesh said calmly:

'Don't worry; I've no intention of wasting their time. Given your determination to keep them out of it, they'd probably suspect that you lit the fire yourself. Did you?'

Wilfred cut swiftly into Dennis's gasp of incredulity and Dot's outraged protest.

'No, Dot, it's perfectly reasonable that Adam Dalgliesh should think as he does. He has been professionally trained in suspicion and scepticism. As it happens, I didn't attempt to burn myself to death. One family suicide in the black tower is enough. But I think I know who did light the fire and I shall deal with that person in my own time and in my own way. In the meantime nothing is to be said to the family, nothing. Thank God I can be sure of one thing, none of them can have had a hand in this. Now that I'm assured of that I shall know what to do. And now if you would all be kind enough to leave. . .'

Dalgliesh didn't wait to see if the others proposed to obey. He contented himself with one final word from the door.

'If you're thinking of private vengeance, then forget it. If you can't, or daren't, act within the law, then don't act at all.'

Anstey smiled his sweet infuriating smile.

'Vengeance, Commander? Vengeance? That word has no place in our philosophy at Toynton Grange.'

Dalgliesh saw and heard no one as he passed again through the main hall. The house might have been an empty shell. After a second's thought he walked briskly over the headland to Charity Cottage. The headland was deserted except for a solitary figure making its way down the slope from the cliff; Julius carrying what looked like a bottle in either hand. He held them aloft in a half-pugilistic, half-celebratory gesture. Dalgliesh lifted his hand in a brief salute and, turning, made his way up the stone path to the Hewsons' cottage.

The door was open and at first he heard no sign of life. He knocked, and getting no reply, stepped inside. Charity Cottage, standing on its own, was larger than the other two and the stone sitting-room, bathed now in sunshine from its two windows, was agreeably proportioned. But it looked dirty and unkempt, reflecting in its untidiness Maggie's dissatisfied and restless nature. His first impression was that she had proclaimed her intention that their stay would be brief by not bothering to unpack. The few items of furniture looked as if they still stood where the whim of the removal men had first deposited them. A grubby sofa faced the large television screen which dominated the room. Eric's meagre medical library was stacked flat on the shelves of the bookcase, which held also a miscellany of crockery, ornaments, records and crushed shoes. A standard lamp of repellent design was without its shade. Two pictures were propped with their faces against the wall, their cords hanging knotted and broken. There was a square table set in the middle of the room bearing what looked like the remains of a late lunch; a torn packet of water biscuits spilling crumbs; a lump of cheese on a chipped plate; butter oozing from its greasy wrapping; a topless bottle of tomato ketchup with the sauce congealed round the lip. Two bloated flies buzzed their intricate convolutions above the debris.

From the kitchen came the rush of water and the roar of a gas boiler. Eric and Maggie were washing up. Suddenly the boiler was turned off and he heard Maggie's voice:

'You're so bloody weak! You let them all use you. If you are poking that supercilious bitch – and don't think I care a damn either way – it's only because you can't say no to her. You don't really want her any more than you want me.'

Eric's reply was a low mutter. There was a crash of crockery. Then Maggie's voice rose again:

'For Christ's sake, you can't hide away here for ever! That trip to St Saviour's, it wasn't as bad as you feared. No one said anything.'

This time Eric's reply was perfectly intelligible:

'They didn't need to. Anyway, who did we see? Just the consultant in physical medicine and that medical records officer. She knew all right and let me see it. That's how it'd be in general practice, if I ever got a job. They'd never let me forget it. The practice delinquent. Every female patient under sixteen tactfully diverted to one of the partners, just in case. At least Wilfred treats me like a human being. I can make a contribution. I can do my job.'

Maggie almost yelled at him: 'What kind of a job, for God's

sake?' And then both their voices were lost in the roar from the boiler and the rush of water. Then it stopped and Dalgliesh heard Maggie's voice again, high, emphatic.

'All right! All right! All right! I've said I won't tell, and I won't. But if you keep on nagging about it, I may change my mind.'

Eric's reply was lost but it sounded like a long expostulatory murmur. Then Maggie spoke again:

'Well, what if I did? He wasn't a fool, you know. He could tell that something was up. And where's the harm? He's dead, isn't he? Dead. Dead. Dead.'

Dalgliesh suddenly realized that he was standing stock still, straining his ears to hear as if this were an official case, his case, and every surreptitiously stolen word was a vital clue. Irritated, he almost shook himself into action. He had taken a few steps back to the doorway and had raised his fist to knock again and more loudly when Maggie, carrying a small tin tray, emerged from the kitchen with Eric at her back. She recovered quickly from her surprise and gave a shout of almost genuine laughter.

'Oh God, don't say Wilfred has called in the Yard itself to grill me. The poor little man has got himself into a tizzy. What are you going to do, darling, warn me that anything I say will be taken down and may be given in evidence?'

The door darkened and Julius came in. He must, thought Dalgliesh, have run down the headland to arrive so quickly. Why the hurry, he wondered. Breathing heavily, Julius swung two bottles of whisky on to the table.

'A peace offering.'

'So I should think!' Maggie had become flirtatious. Her eyes brightened under the heavy lids and she slewed them from Dalgliesh to Julius as if uncertain where to bestow her favours. She spoke to Dalgliesh:

'Julius has been accusing me of attempting to roast Wilfred alive in the black tower. I know: I realize that it isn't funny. But Julius is, when he's trying to be pompous. And honestly, it's a nonsense. If I wanted to get my own back on St Wilfred I could do it without pussyfooting about the black tower in drag, couldn't I, darling?'

She checked her laughter and her glance at Julius was at once minatory and conspiratorial. It provoked no response. Julius said quickly:

'I didn't accuse you. I simply inquired with the utmost tact where you'd been since one o'clock.'

'On the beach, darling. I do go there occasionally. I know I can't prove it, but neither can you prove that I wasn't there.'

'That's rather a coincidence isn't it, your happening to walk on the beach?'

'No more a coincidence than your happening to drive along the coast road.'

'And you didn't see anyone?'

'I told you, darling, not a soul. Was I expected to? And now, Adam, it's your turn. Are you going to charm the truth out of me in the best Metropolitan tradition?'

'Not I. This is Court's case. That's one of the first principles of detection, never interfere with another man's conduct of his case.'

Julius said:

'Besides, Maggie dear, the Commander isn't interested in our paltry concerns. Strange as it may seem, he just doesn't care. He can't even pretend an interest in whether Dennis hurled Victor over the cliff and I'm covering up for him. Humiliating, isn't it?'

Maggie's laugh was uneasy. She glanced at her husband like an inexperienced hostess who fears that the party is getting out of control.

'Don't be silly, Julius. We know that you aren't covering up. Why should you? What would there be in it for you?'

'How well you know me, Maggie! Nothing. But then, I might have done it out of sheer good nature.' He looked at Dalgliesh with a sly smile and added:

'I believe in being accommodating to my friends.'

Eric said suddenly and with surprising authority:

'What was it you wanted, Mr Dalgliesh?'

'Just information. When I arrived at the cottage I found a booklet of matches by Father Baddeley's bed advertising the Olde Tudor Barn near Wareham. I thought I might try it for dinner tonight. Did he go there often, do you know?'

Maggie laughed:

'God, no! Never I should think. It's hardly Michael's scene. I gave him the matches. He liked trifles like that. But the Barn's not bad. Bob Loder took me there for lunch on my birthday and they did us quite well.'

Julius said:

'I'll describe it. Ambience: a chain of coloured fairy lights strung round an otherwise genuine and agreeable seventeenth-century barn. First course: tinned tomato soup with a slice of tomato to add verisimilitude and colour contrast; frozen prawns in bottled sauce on a bed of limp lettuce; half a melon – ripe if you're lucky; or the chef's own home-made pâté fresh from the local supermarket. The rest of the menu you may imagine. It's usually a variety of steak served with frozen vegetables and what they describe as french fried. If you must drink, stick to the red. I don't know whether the owner makes it or merely sticks the labels on the bottles but at least it's wine of a kind. The white is cat's pee.'

Maggie laughed indulgently.

'Oh, don't be such a snob, darling, it's not as bad as that. Bob and I had quite a decent meal. And whoever bottled the wine, it had the right effect as far as I was concerned.'

Dalgliesh said:

'But it may have deteriorated. You know how it is. The chef leaves and a restaurant changes almost overnight.'

Julius laughed:

'That's the advantage of the Olde Barn menu. The chef can and does change fortnightly but the tinned soup is guaranteed to taste the same.'

Maggie said:

'It won't have changed since my birthday. That was only 11th September. I'm Virgo, darlings. Appropriate, isn't it?'

Julius said:

'There are one or two decent places within driving distance. I can let you have a few names.'

He did so and Dalgliesh dutifully noted them at the back of his diary. But as he walked back to Hope Cottage his mind had already registered more important information.

So Maggie was on lunching terms with Bob Loder; the obliging

Loder, equally ready to alter Father Baddeley's will – or to dissuade him from altering it? – and to help Millicent cheat her brother out of half his capital from the sale of Toynton Grange. But that little ploy had, of course, been Holroyd's idea. Had Holroyd and Loder cooked it up between them? Maggie had told them about her luncheon date with sly satisfaction. If her husband neglected her on her birthday she wasn't without consolation. But what of Loder? Was his interest no more than a readiness to avail himself of a complaisant and dissatisfied woman, or had he a more sinister motive for keeping in touch with what happened at Toynton Grange? And the shredded match? Dalgliesh hadn't yet compared it with the stubs in the booklet still by Father Baddeley's bed, but he had no doubt that one of the stubs would match. He couldn't question Maggie further without rousing suspicion, but he didn't need to. She couldn't have given the booklet of matches to Father Baddeley before the afternoon of 11th September, the day before Holroyd's death. And on the afternoon of the eleventh, Father Baddeley had visited his solicitor. He couldn't, then, have received the booklet of matches until that evening at the earliest. And that meant that he must have been in the black tower on either the following morning or afternoon. It would be useful, when opportunity offered, to have a word with Miss Willison and ask whether Father Baddeley had been at the Grange on the Wednesday morning. According to the entries in his diary it had certainly been his invariable routine to visit the Grange every morning. And that meant that he had almost certainly been in the black tower on the afternoon of the twelfth, and, possibly, sitting at the eastern window. Those drag marks on the fibre matting had looked very recent. But even from that window, he couldn't have seen Holroyd's chair go over the cliff; couldn't even have watched the distant figures of Lerner and Holroyd making their way along the sunken lane to that patch of green turf. And, even if he could, what would his evidence be worth, an old man sitting alone, reading and probably dozing in the afternoon sun? It was surely ludicrous to search here for a motive for murder. But suppose Father Baddeley had known beyond doubt that he had neither dozed nor read? Then it wasn't a question of what he had seen, but of what he had singularly failed to see.

SIX

A Bloodless Murder

I

The next afternoon, on the last day of her life, Grace Willison sat in the courtyard in the afternoon sun. Its rays were still warm on her face but now they touched her parched skin with a gentler valedictory warmth. From time to time a cloud moved across the face of the sun and she found herself shivering with the first intimation of winter. The air smelt keener, the afternoons were darkening fast. There wouldn't be many more days warm enough for her to sit outside. Even today she was the only patient in the courtyard and she was grateful for the warmth of the rug across her knees.

She found herself thinking about Commander Dalgliesh. She wished that he had come more often to Toynton Grange. He was still at Hope Cottage apparently. Yesterday he had helped Julius rescue Wilfred from the fire in the black tower. Wilfred had bravely made light of his ordeal as one would expect. It had only been a small fire caused entirely by his own carelessness; he had never been in real danger. But, all the same, she thought, it was fortunate that the Commander had been on hand to help.

Would he leave Toynton, she wondered, without coming to say goodbye to her? She hoped not. She had liked him so much in their brief time together. How pleasant it would be if he could be sitting here with her now, talking about Father Baddeley. No one at Toynton Grange now ever mentioned his name. But, of course, the Commander couldn't be expected to give up his time.

The thought was entirely without bitterness or resentment. There really wasn't anything to interest him at Toynton Grange. And it wasn't as if she could issue a personal invitation. She allowed herself for one minute to indulge in regret for the retirement which she had hoped for and planned. Her small pension from the Society, a little cottage, sun-filled and bright with chintz and geraniums; her dear mother's possessions, the ones she had sold before she came to Toynton – the rose-patterned tea service; the rosewood writing table; the series of water-colours of English cathedrals. How lovely to be able to invite anyone she liked to her own home to take tea with her. Not a communal institutional tea at a bleak refectory table, but proper afternoon tea. Her table; her tea service; her food; her guest.

She became aware of the weight of the book on her lap. It was a paperback edition of Trollope's *Last Chronicle of Barset.* It had lain there all the afternoon. Why, she wondered, was she so strangely reluctant to read it? And then she remembered. This had been the book she was re-reading on that dreadful afternoon when Victor's body had been brought home. She hadn't opened it since. But that was ridiculous. She must put the thought out of her mind. It was stupid, no, it was wrong, to spoil a book she so loved – its leisurely world of cathedral intrigue, its sanity, its delicate moral sensibility – by contaminating it with images of violence, hatred and blood.

She curved her deformed left hand around the book and parted the pages with her right. There was a bookmark between the last pages she had read, a single pink antirrhinum pressed between a sheet of tissue. And then she remembered it. It was a flower from the small posy Father Baddeley had brought her on the afternoon of Victor's death. Normally he never picked wild flowers except for her. They hadn't lasted long, less than a day. But this single flower she had pressed at once between the leaves of her book. She gazed at it, motionless.

A shadow fell across the page. A voice said:

'Anything wrong?'

She looked up and smiled.

'Nothing. It's just that I've remembered something. Isn't it extraordinary how the mind rejects anything which it associates with horror or great distress? Commander Dalgliesh asked me if I knew what Father Baddeley did on the few days before he went into hospital. And, of course, I do know. I know what he did on the Wednesday afternoon. I don't suppose it's the least important, but it would be nice to tell him. I know that everyone here is terribly busy but do you think that . . .?'

'Don't worry. I'll find time to drop in at Hope Cottage. It's time he showed his face here if he proposes to stay on much longer. And now, don't you think it would be wise for you to come in? It's getting chilly.'

Miss Willison smiled her thanks. She would have preferred to have stayed out a little longer. But she didn't like to insist. It was meant kindly. She closed her book again and her murderer grasped the chair with strong hands and wheeled her to her death.

II

Ursula Hollis always asked her nurses to leave her curtains undrawn and tonight in the faint haze of light from her luminous bedside clock, she could still just discern the oblong frame which separated darkness outside from the darkness within. It was nearly midnight. The night was starless and very still. She lay in blackness so thick that it was almost a weight on her chest, a dense curtain descending to stifle breath. Outside, the headland was asleep, except, she supposed, for the small animals of the night scurrying among the rigid grasses. Inside Toynton Grange she could still hear distant sounds; brisk footsteps passing down a passage; the quiet closing of a door; the squeak of unoiled wheels as someone moved a hoist or a wheelchair; the mouselike scrabbling sounds from next door as Grace Willison moved restlessly in her bed; a sudden blare of music, instantly muted, as someone opened and shut the sitting-room door. Her bedside clock snatched at the seconds and ticked them into oblivion. She lay rigid, the warm tears flowing in a constant stream over her face to seep, suddenly cold and sticky, into her pillow. Under the pillow was Steve's letter. From time to time she folded her right arm painfully across her chest and insinuated her fingers under the pillow to feel the envelope's knife-sharp edge.

Mogg had moved into the flat; they were living together. Steve had written the news almost casually as if it were merely a temporary and mutually convenient arrangement for sharing the rent and the chores. Mogg was doing the cooking; Mogg had redecorated the sitting-room and put up more shelves; Mogg had found him a clerical job with his publishers which might lead to a permanent and better post. Mogg's new book of poems was due out in the spring. There was only a perfunctory inquiry after Ursula's health. He hadn't ever made the usual vague and insincere promises to visit. He had written no word about her return home, the planned new flat, his negotiations with the local authority. There was no need. She never would return. They both knew it. Mogg knew it.

She hadn't received the letter until teatime. Albert Philby had been unaccountably late in fetching the post and it was after four o'clock before it was placed in her hand. She was grateful that she had been alone in the sitting-room, that Grace Willison hadn't yet come in from the courtyard to get ready for tea. There had been no one to watch her face as she read it, no one to make tactful inquiries, or, more tactfully, to refrain. And anger and shock had carried her through until now. She had held on to anger, feeding it with memory and imagination, willing herself to eat her usual two slices of bread, to drink her tea, to contribute her sentences of platitude and small talk to the party. Only now, when Grace Willison's heavy breathing had settled into a gentle snoring, when there was no longer a risk that Helen or Dot might pay a last visit, when Toynton Grange was finally wrapping itself in silence for the night, could she give way to desolation and loss and indulge in what she knew was self-pity. And the tears, when once they started, would not stop. The grief once indulged was unassuageable. She had no control over her crying. It no longer even distressed her; it had nothing to do with grief or longing. It was a physical manifestation, involuntary as a hiccup, but silent and almost consoling; an interminable stream.

She knew what she had to do. She listened through the rhythm of her tears. There was no sound from next door except Grace Willison's snoring, which was now regular. She put out her hand and switched on the light. The bulb had the lowest wattage which Wilfred could buy but the brightness was still blinding. She imagined it, a dazzling oblong of light shining out to signal her intention to all the world. She knew that there was no one to see it, but in imagination the headland was suddenly full of running feet and loud with calling voices. She had stopped crying now but her swollen eyes saw the room as if it were a half-developed photograph, an image of bleared and distorted shapes, shifting and dissolving and seen through a stinging curtain pierced with needles of light.

She waited. Nothing happened. There was still no sound from next door but Grace's harsh and regular breathing. The next step was easy; she had done it twice before. She dropped both her pillows on the floor and, manoeuvring her body to the edge of the bed, let herself drop gently on top of their soft cushion. Even with the pillows to break her weight it seemed that the room shook. Again she waited. But there were no quick footsteps hurrying down the passage. She raised herself upwards on the pillows against the bed and began propelling herself towards its foot. It was an easy matter to stretch out her hand and withdraw the cord from her dressing-gown. Then she began her painful progress towards the door.

Her legs were powerless; what strength she had was in her arms. Her dead feet lay white and flabby as fish on the cold floor, the toes splayed like obscene excrescences vainly scrabbling for a grip. The linoleum was unpolished but smooth and she slid along with surprising speed. She remembered with what joy she had discovered that she could do this; that, ridiculous and humiliating as the trick might be, she could actually move around her room without the use of her chair.

But now she was going farther afield. It was lucky that the modern insubstantial doors of the annexe rooms were opened by depressing a handle and not turning a knob. She made the dressing-gown cord into a loop and, at the second attempt, managed to throw it over the handle. She tugged and the door quietly opened. Discarding one of the pillows, she edged her way into the silent passage. Her heart was thudding with such power it must surely betray her. Again she slipped the cord over the handle and, manoeuvring herself a few feet down the passage, heard the door click shut.

One single light-bulb, heavily shaded, was always kept burning at the far end of the corridor and she could see without difficulty where the short staircase led to the upper floor. This was her objective. Reaching it proved astonishingly easy. The linoleum in the passage, although never polished, seemed smoother than that in her room; or perhaps she had gained the knack of progress. She slid forward with almost exhilarating ease.

But the staircase was more difficult. She was relying on pulling herself up by the banisters, step by step. But it was necessary to take the pillow with her. She would need it on the floor above. And the pillow seemed to have swollen into a gigantic, soft, white encumbrance. The stairs were narrow and it was difficult to prop it safely. Twice it tumbled down and she had to slide after it to retrieve it. But after four steps had been painfully negotiated she worked out the best method of progress. She tied one end of the dressing-gown cord around her waist and the other tightly round the middle of the pillow. She wished she had put on the dressing-gown. It would have hampered her progress, but she was already shivering.

And so, step by step, grasping and sweating despite the cold, she pulled herself up, grasping the banisters with both hands. The stairs creaked alarmingly. She expected any minute to hear the faint summons of a bedside bell and hear from the distance Dot or Helen's hurrying footsteps.

She had no idea how long it took to reach the top of the stairs. But at last she was sitting crouched and shivering on the final step, grasping the banisters with both hands so convulsively that the wood shook, and peering down at the hall below. It was then that the cloaked figure appeared. There were no warning footsteps, no cough, no sound of human breath. One second the passage was empty. In the next a brown cloaked figure – head bent, hood drawn well over the face – had moved silently and swiftly beneath her, and disappeared down the passage. She waited terrified, hardly daring to breathe, huddling herself as far as possible out of view. It would come back. She knew that it would come back. Like the dreadful figure of death which she had seen in old books, carved on monumental tombs, it would pause beneath her and throw back the concealing hood to reveal the grinning skull, the eyeless sockets, would poke at her through the banisters its fleshless fingers. Her heart, beating in icy terror against the rib cage, seemed to have grown too large for her body. Surely its frantic thudding must betray her! It seemed an eternity, but she realized that it could only have been less than a minute before the figure reappeared and passed, beneath her terrified eyes, silently and swiftly into the main house.

Ursula realized then that she wasn't going to kill herself. It had only been Dot, or Helen, or Wilfred. Who else could it have been? But the shock of that silent figure, passing like a shadow, had restored in her the will to live. If she had really wanted to die, what was she doing here crouched in cold discomfort at the top of the stairs? She had her dressing-gown cord. Even now she could tie it round her neck and let herself slip unresisting down the stairs. But she wouldn't. The very thought of that last fall, the strangling cord biting into her neck, made her moan in agonized protest. No, she had never meant to kill herself. No one, not even Steve, was worth an eternity of damnation. Steve might not believe in Hell, but what did Steve really know about anything that mattered? But she had to complete her journey now. She had to get hold of that bottle of aspirin which she knew must be somewhere in the clinical room. She wouldn't use it, but she would keep it always within reach. She would know that, if life became intolerable, the means to end it was at hand. And perhaps, if she just took a handful and left the bottle by the bed, they would realize at least that she was unhappy. That was all she intended; all she had ever intended. They would send for Steve. They would take some notice of her misery. Perhaps they might even force Steve to take her back to London. Having come so far at such cost, she had to get to the clinical room.

The door presented no problem. But when she had sidled through, she realized that this was the end. She couldn't switch on the light. The low bulb in the corridor gave a faint diffused glow but, even with the door of the clinical room ajar, it was inadequate to show her the position of the light. And if she were to succeed in switching it on with the dressing-gown cord, she had to know accurately at what spot to aim. She stretched out her hand and felt along the wall. Nothing. She held the cord in a loop and flung it softly and repeatedly where she thought the switch might be. But it fell away uselessly. She began to cry again, defeated, desperately cold, suddenly realizing that she had the whole painful journey to do again in reverse, and that dragging herself back into bed would be the most difficult and painful of all.

And then, suddenly, a hand stretched out of the darkness and the light was switched on. Ursula gave a little scream of fright. She looked up. Framed in the doorway, wearing a brown habit open down the front and with the hood flung back was Helen Rainer. The two women, petrified, stared at each other speechlessly. And Ursula saw that the eyes bent on hers were as full of terror as her own.

III

Grace Willison's body jerked into wakefulness and immediately began to tremble uncontrollably as if a strong hand were shaking her into full consciousness. She listened in the darkness, raising her head with difficulty from the pillow; but she could hear nothing. Whatever noise, real or imagined, had woken her was now stilled. She switched on her bedside lamp; nearly midnight. She reached for her book. It was a pity that the paperback Trollope was so heavy. It meant that it had to be propped up on the coverlet and since, once stretched into her conventional attitude for sleep she couldn't easily bend her knees, the effort of slightly raising her head and peering down at the small print was tiring both to her eyes and to the muscles of her neck. The discomfort sometimes made her wonder whether reading in bed was the pleasant indulgence she had always believed it to be since those childhood days, when her father's parsimony over the electricity bill and her mother's anxiety about eye strain and eight hours' good sleep each night had denied her a bedside lamp.

Her left leg was jerking uncontrollably and she watched, detached and interested, the erratic jump of the coverlet as if an animal were loose among the bed clothes. To wake suddenly like this once she had first fallen asleep was always a bad sign. She was in for a restless night. She dreaded sleeplessness and for a moment was tempted to pray that she might be spared it just for tonight. But she had finished her prayers and it seemed pointless to pray again for a mercy which experience had taught her she wasn't going to receive. Pleading to God for something which he had already made it perfectly plain he wasn't disposed to give you was to behave like a peevish, importunate child. She watched her limb's antics with interest, vaguely comforted by the sensation which was now almost self-induced of being detached from her unruly body.

She lay down her book and decided instead to think about the pilgrimage to Lourdes in fourteen days' time. She pictured the happy bustle of departure – she had a new coat saved for the occasion – the drive across France with the party gay as a picnic; the first glimpse of the mists swirling around the foothills of the Pyrenees; the snowcapped peaks; Lourdes itself with its concentrated business, its air of being always *en fête*. The Toynton Grange party, except for the two Roman Catholics, Ursula Hollis and Georgie Allan, were not part of an official English pilgrimage, did not take Mass, grouped themselves with becoming humility at the back of the crowd when the bishops in their crimson robes made their slow way round Rosary Square, the golden monstrance held high before them. But how inspiring, how colourful, how splendid it all was! The candles weaving their patterns of light, the colours, the singing, the sense of belonging again to the outside world but a world in which sickness was honoured, no longer regarded as an alienation, a deformity of the spirit as well as of the body. Only thirteen more days now. She wondered what her father, implacably Protestant, would have said about this keenly awaited pleasure. But she had consulted Father Baddeley about the propriety of going on pilgrimage and his advice had been very clear. 'My dear child, you enjoy the change and the journey, and why not? And surely no one could believe themselves harmed by a visit to Lourdes. By all means help Wilfred to celebrate his bargain with the Almighty.'

She thought about Father Baddeley. It was still difficult to accept that she wouldn't ever again be talking with him in the patients' courtyard or praying with him in the quiet room. Dead; an inert, neutral, unattractive word. Short, uncompromising, a lump of a word. The same word, come to think of it, for a plant, an animal or a man. That was an interesting thought. One would have expected a distinctive, more impressive or momentous word for the death of a man. But why? He was only part of the same creation, sharing its universal life, dependent on the same air. Dead. She had hoped to be able to feel that Father Baddeley was close to her; but it hadn't happened, it just wasn't true. They are all gone into the world of light. Well, gone away; not interested any more in the living.

She ought to put out her light; electricity was expensive; if she didn't intend to read it was her duty to lie in the darkness. Lighten our darkness; her mother had always liked that Collect; and by Thy great mercy defend us from all the perils and dangers of this night. Only there was no peril here, only sleeplessness and pain; the familiar pain to be tolerated, almost welcomed as an old acquaintance because she knew that she could cope with the worst it could do; and this new frightening pain which, sometime soon, she would have to worry someone about.

The curtain trembled in the breeze. She heard a sudden click, unnaturally loud, so that for a second her heart thudded. There was a rasp of metal on wood. Maggie hadn't checked the window fastening before bedding her down for the night. It was too late now. Her chair was at the side of the bed but she couldn't get into it without help. But all would be well unless it were a stormy night. And she was perfectly safe, no one would climb in. There was nothing at Toynton Grange to steal. And beyond that fluttering curtain of white, nothing; nothing but a black void, dark cliffs stretching to the unsleeping sea.

The curtain billowed, bursting into a white sail, a curve of light. She exclaimed at the beauty of it. Cool air streamed across her face. She turned her eyes to the door and smiled a welcome. She began to say:

'The window – would you be good enough . . .?'

But she didn't finish. There were three seconds only left to her of earthly time. She saw the cloaked figure, hood well down obscuring the face, moving swiftly towards her on silent feet like an apparition, familiar but horribly different, ministering hands that held death, blackness bearing down on her. Unresisting, since that was her nature and how could she resist, she did not die ungently, feeling at the last through the thin veil of plastic only the strong, warm, oddly comforting lineaments of a human hand. Then the hand reached out and delicately, without touching the wooden stand, switched off the bedside lamp. Two seconds later the light was switched on again, and, as if by afterthought, the cloaked figure stretched out a hand for the Trollope, gently rustled the pages, found the pressed flower between the fold of tissue, and crumpled them both with strong fingers. Then the hand reached out for the lamp again and the light went out for the last time.

IV

At last they were back in Ursula's room. Helen Rainer closed the door with quiet firmness and leaned back momentarily against it as if exhausted. Then she went quickly over to the window and swept the curtains across in two swift gestures. Her heavy breathing filled the little room. It had been a difficult journey. Helen had left her in the clinical room briefly while she positioned Ursula's wheelchair at the foot of the stairs. Once they reached it all would be well. Even if they were seen together on the ground-floor corridor it would be assumed that Ursula had rung her night bell and was being helped to the bathroom. The stairs were the problem and the descent, with Helen half-supporting, half-carrying her, had been exhausting and noisy, five long minutes of laboured breathing, creaking banisters, hissed instructions, of Ursula's half-stifled moans of pain. It seemed now like a miracle that no one had appeared in the hall. It would have been quicker and easier to have moved into the main part of the Grange and used the lift, but the clanging metal grille and the noisy engine would have woken half the house.

But at last they were safely back and Helen, white faced but calm, pulled herself together and moved away from the door and began with professional competence to put Ursula to bed. Neither spoke until the task was completed and Ursula lay in rigid half-fearful silence.

Helen bent her face close to Ursula's, unpleasantly close. In the glare of the bedside lamp she could see the features magnified, coarsened, pores like miniature craters, two unplucked hairs standing like bristles at the corner of her mouth. Her breath smelt slightly sour. Odd, thought Ursula, that she hadn't noticed it before. The green eyes seemed to grow and protrude as she hissed her instructions, her dreadful warning.

'When the next patient goes, he'll have to start admitting from the waiting list or give in. He can't run this place on less than six patients. I've taken a look at the books when he's left them about in the business room and I know. He'll either sell out completely or hand over to the Ridgewell Trust. If you want to get out of here there are better ways than killing yourself. Help me to ensure that he sells out, and get back to London.'

'But how?'

Ursula found herself whispering back like a conspirator.

'He'll hold what he calls a family council. He always does when there's something important affecting all the household to decide. We all give our views. Then we go away to meditate in silence for one hour. Then we all vote. Don't let anyone persuade you to vote for the Ridgewell Trust. That way you'll be trapped here for life. It's hard enough for local authorities to find a place for the young chronic sick. Once they know you're being looked after, they'll never transfer you.'

'But if the Grange does close down, will they really send me home?'

'They'll have to, back to London anyway. That's still your permanent address. You're the responsibility of your own local authority, not of Dorset. And once back, at least you'll see him. He could visit you, take you out, you could go home for weekend leaves. Besides, the disease isn't really advanced yet. I don't see why you shouldn't manage together in one of those flats for disabled couples. After all he is married to you. He's got responsibilities, duties.'

Ursula tried to explain:

'I don't mind about responsibilities and duties. I want him to love me.'

Helen had laughed, a coarse, uncomfortable sound.

'Love. Is that all? Isn't that what we all want? Well he can't stay in love with someone he never sees, can he? It doesn't work like that with men. You've got to get back to him.'

'And you won't tell?'

'Not if you promise.'

'To vote your way?'

'And to keep your mouth shut about trying to kill yourself, about everything that's happened here tonight. If anyone mentions hearing a noise in the night, you rang for me and I was taking you to the lavatory. If Wilfred discovers the truth he'll send you to a mental hospital. You wouldn't want that, would you?'

No, she wouldn't want that. Helen was right. She had to get home. How simple it all was. She felt suddenly filled with gratitude, and struggled to hold out her arms towards Helen. But Helen had moved away. Firm hands were tucking in the bed clothes, rocking the mattress. The sheets were drawn taut. She felt imprisoned, but secure, a baby swaddled for the night. Helen stretched out her hand to the light. In the darkness a white blur moved towards the door. Ursula heard the soft click of the latch.

Lying there alone exhausted but strangely comforted she remembered that she hadn't told Helen about the cloaked figure. But it could be of no importance. It was probably Helen herself answering Grace's bell. Was that what Helen had meant when she warned, say nothing about anything that happened here tonight? Surely not. But she would say nothing. How could she speak without betraying that she had been crouching there on the stairs. And everything was going to be all right. She could sleep now. How lucky that Helen had gone to the clinical room to get a couple of aspirin for a headache and had found her! The house was blessedly unnaturally quiet. There was something strange, something different, about the silence. And then, smiling into the darkness, she remembered. It was Grace. No sound, no rasp of snoring breath came through the thin partition to disturb her. Tonight even Grace Willison was sleeping in peace.

V

Usually Julius Court fell asleep within minutes of turning out his bedside light. But tonight he turned in restless wakefulness, mind and nerves fidgety, his legs as cold and heavy as if it were winter. He rubbed them together, considering whether to dig out his electric blanket. But the bother of re-making the bed discouraged him. Alcohol seemed a better and quicker remedy both for sleeplessness and the cold.

He walked over to the window and looked out over the headland. The waning moon was obscured by scudding clouds; the darkness inland pierced only by a single oblong of yellow light. But as he watched, blackness was drawn like a shutter over the far window. Instantaneously the oblong became a square; then that, too, was extinguished. Toynton Grange lay, a faintly discerned shape etched in the darkness on the silent headland. Curious, he looked at his watch. The time was eighteen minutes past midnight.

VI

Dalgliesh awoke at first light, to the cold, quiet morning, and dragging on his dressing-gown, went downstairs to make tea. He wondered if Millicent was still at the Grange. Her television had been silent all the previous evening and now, although she was neither an early nor a noisy riser, Hope Cottage was wrapped in the slightly clandestine and unmistakable calm of complete isolation. He lit the lamp in the sitting-room, carried his cup to the table, and spread out his map. Today he would explore the north-east of the county aiming to arrive at Sherborne for lunch. But first it would be courteous to call at Toynton Grange and inquire after Wilfred. He felt no real concern; it was difficult to think of yesterday's charade without irritation. But it might be worth making one more attempt to persuade Wilfred to call in the police, or at least to take the attack on himself more seriously. And it was time that he paid some rent for the use of Hope Cottage. Toynton Grange could hardly be so prosperous that a tactful contribution wouldn't be welcome. Neither chore need keep him at the Grange for longer than ten minutes.

There was a knock on the door and Julius came in. He was fully dressed and, even at this early hour, gave his usual impression of slightly elegant informality. He said, calmly, and as if the news were hardly worth the trouble of telling:

'I'm glad you're up. I'm on my way to Toynton Grange. Wilfred has just rung. Apparently Grace Willison has died in her sleep and Eric is in a tizzy about the death certificate. I don't know what Wilfred thinks I can do about it. Restoring Eric to the medical register seems to have restored him also to the customary arrogance of his profession. Grace Willison wasn't due, in his opinion, to die for at least another eighteen months, possibly two years. That being so he's at a loss to put a name to this insubordination. As usual, they're all extracting the maximum drama from the situation. I shouldn't miss it if I were you.'

Dalgliesh glanced towards the adjacent cottage without speaking. Julius said cheerfully:

'Oh, you needn't worry about disturbing Millicent; I'm afraid she's there already. Apparently her television broke down last night so she went up to Toynton Grange to see a late programme and decided, for some unaccountable reason, to stay the night. Probably saw an opportunity of saving her own bed linen and bath water.'

Dalgliesh said:

'You go on, I'll follow you later.'

He drank his tea without haste and spent three minutes shaving. He wondered why he had been so reluctant to accompany Julius, why, if he had to go to Toynton Grange, he preferred to walk there on his own. He wondered, too, why he felt so keen a regret. He had no wish to involve himself in the controversy at Toynton. He had no particular curiosity about Grace Willison's death. He was aware of feeling nothing except an inexplicable unease amounting almost to grief for a woman he had barely known and a vague distaste that the start of a beautiful day should have been spoilt by the intimations of decay. And there was something else; a sense of guilt. It seemed to him both unreasonable and unfair. By dying she seemed to have allied herself with Father Baddeley. There were two accusing ghosts, not one. This was to be a double failure. It was by an effort of will that he set out for Toynton Grange.

He could be in no doubt which room was Grace Willison's, he could hear the raised voices even as he entered the annexe. When he opened the door he saw that Wilfred, Eric, Millicent, Dot and Julius were grouped around the bed with the desultory, uneasy air of strangers meeting fortuitously at the scene of an accident with which they would much prefer not to become involved but which they hardly like to leave.

Dorothy Moxon stood at the end of the bed, her heavy hands, red as hams, clasped to the rail. She was wearing her matron's cap. The effect, so far from providing a touch of professional reassurance, was grotesque. The high frilled pie crust of muslin looked like a morbid and bizarre celebration of death. Millicent was still in her dressing-gown, an enveloping plaid in heavy wool frogged like a ceremonial uniform which must once have belonged to her husband. In contrast, her slippers were insubstantial fripperies in pink fur. Wilfred and Eric were wearing their brown habits. They glanced briefly at the door when he entered, then immediately turned their attention back to the bed. Julius was saying:

'There was a light in one of the annexe rooms shortly after midnight. Isn't that when you say she died, Eric?'

'It could have been about then. I'm only going by the cooling of the body and the beginning of rigor mortis. I'm not an expert in these things.'

'How odd! I thought that death was the one thing you were expert at.'

Wilfred said quietly:

'The light was from Ursula's room. She rang shortly after midnight to be taken to the lavatory. Helen looked after her, but she didn't go in to Grace. There was no need. She didn't ring. No one saw her after Dot put her to bed. She made no complaint then.'

Julius turned to Eric Hewson:

'You haven't any option, have you? If you can't say what she died of, you can't write a certificate. Anyway, I should play for safety if I were you. After all, you've only recently been permitted to sign a death certificate. Better not take any chances of getting it wrong.'

Eric Hewson said:

'You keep out of it, Julius, I don't need your advice. I don't know why Wilfred rang you.'

But he spoke without conviction, like an insecure and frightened child, his eyes flicking to the door as if hoping for the arrival of an ally. Julius was unabashed:

'It seems to me that you need any advice that's going. What's worrying you anyway? Do you suspect foul play? What a ridiculous phrase that is, come to think of it, so delightfully British, compounded of the public school ethos and the boxing ring.'

Eric exerted himself to make a show of authority.

'Don't be ridiculous! Obviously it's a natural death. The difficulty is that I'm puzzled why it should have happened now. I know D.S. patients can go off quickly like that, but in her case I didn't expect it. And Dot says that she seemed just as usual when she put her to bed at ten o'clock. I'm wondering whether there was some other organic disease present which I missed.'

Julius went on happily:

'The police do not suspect foul play. Well, you've got a representative of them here if you want professional advice. Ask the Commander if he suspects foul play.'

They turned and looked at Dalgliesh as if fully aware of his presence for the first time. The window latch was rattling with irritating insistence. He went across to the window and glanced out. The ground close to the stone wall had been dug for a width of about four feet as if someone had intended to plant a border. The sandy earth was smooth and undisturbed. But of course it was! If a secret visitor had wanted to get into Grace's room unseen, why climb in at the window when the door of Toynton Grange was never locked?

He fastened the catch and, moving back to the bed, looked down at the body. The dead face looked not exactly peaceful, but slightly disapproving, the mouth a little open, the front teeth, more rabbity than in life, pressing against the lower lip. The eyelids had contracted showing a glimpse of the irises of the eye so that she seemed to be peering at her own two hands disposed so neatly over the taut coverlet. The strong right hand, blotched with the brown stigmata of age, was curved over the withered left as if instinctively protecting it from his pitying gaze. She was shrouded for her last sleep in an old-fashioned white nightdress of creased cotton with a child's bow in narrow blue ribbon tied incongruously under her chin. The long sleeves were gathered into frilled wrists. There was a fine darn about two inches from her elbow. His eyes fixed obsessively on it. Who today, he wondered, would take such trouble? Certainly her diseased tormented hands couldn't have woven that intricate pattern of repair. Why should he find that darn more pathetic, more heart-shaking, than the concentrated calm of the dead face?

He was aware that the company had stopped arguing, that they were looking at him in a half-wary silence. He picked up the two books on Miss Willison's bedside table, her prayer book and a paperback copy of *The Last Chronicle of Barset*. There was a bookmark in the prayer book. She had, he saw, been reading the Collect and Gospel for the day. The place was marked by one of those sentimental cards favoured by the pious, a coloured picture of a haloed St Francis surrounded by birds and apparently preaching to a motley and incongruous congregation of animals remote from their habitat and drawn with finicky precision. He wondered, irrelevantly, why there was no bookmark in the Trollope. She was not a woman to turn down the pages, and surely of the two volumes this was the one in which she would more easily lose her place. The omission vaguely worried him.

'Is there a next of kin?' he asked, and Anstey answered:

'No. She told me that her parents were only children. They were both over forty when she was born and they died within months of each other about fifteen years ago. She had an older brother but he was killed in the war in North Africa. El Alamein, I believe.'

'What about her estate?'

'Oh, nothing, nothing at all. After her parents' death she worked for several years for The Open Door, the discharged prisoners' charity, and had a small disability pension from them, a pittance merely. That, of course, dies with her. Her fees here were paid by the local authority.'

Julius Court said with sudden interest:

'The Open Door. Did she know Philby before you took him on?'

Anstey looked as if he found this irrelevant question in poor taste.

'She may have done; she certainly never said so. It was Grace who suggested that The Open Door might find us a handyman, that this was a way in which Toynton Grange could help the work of the charity. We have been very glad of Albert Philby. He's one of the family. I haven't repented my decision to take him on.'

Millicent broke in:

'And you got him cheap, of course. Besides it was Philby or no one wasn't it? You didn't have much luck with the labour exchange when the applicants found that you were offering £5 a week and all found. I sometimes wonder why Philby stays.'

Discussion of this point was prevented by the entrance of Philby himself. He must have been told of Miss Willison's death for he showed no surprise to find her room full of people and gave no explanation of his presence. Instead he stationed himself beside the door like an embarrassing and unpredictable guard dog. The company behaved as if they had decided that it would be prudent not to notice him. Wilfred turned to Eric Hewson:

'Can't you reach a diagnosis, without a post-mortem? I hate the idea of her being cut up, the indignity, the impersonality. She was so sensitive about her body, so modest in a way we don't understand nowadays. An autopsy is the last thing she herself would have wanted.'

Julius said coarsely:

'Well, it's the last thing she's going to get, isn't it?'

Dot Moxon spoke for the first time. She swung round on him in sudden anger, her heavy face blotched, hands clenched.

'How dare you! What has it to do with you? You didn't care about her dead or alive, her or any of the patients. You only use this place for your own purpose.'

'Use?' The grey eyes flickered and then widened; Dalgliesh could almost see the irises growing. Julius stared at Dot with incredulous anger.

'Yes, use! Exploit, if you like. It gives you a kick, doesn't it, to come visiting Toynton Grange when London begins to bore you, patronizing Wilfred, pretending to advise him, handing out treats to the inmates like Father Christmas? It makes you feel good, reinforces your ego to contrast your health with their deformity. But you take damned good care not to put yourself out. The kindness doesn't really cost you anything. No one but Henry gets invited to your cottage. But then Henry was quite important in his time wasn't he? He and you have things to gossip about. You're the only one here with a view of the sea, but we don't find you inviting us to wheel the chairs on to your patio. No bloody fear! That's one thing you could have done for Grace, take her to your place occasionally, let her sit quietly and look at the sea. She wasn't stupid, you know. You might even have enjoyed her conversation. But that would have spoilt the appearance of your elegant patio wouldn't it, an ugly middle-aged woman in a wheelchair? And now she's dead you come here pretending to advise Eric. Well, for God's sake, cut it out!'

Julius laughed uneasily. He seemed to have himself in hand but his voice was high and brittle.

'I don't know what I've done to deserve that outburst. I didn't realize that by buying a cottage from Wilfred I'd made myself responsible for Grace Willison or for anyone else at Toynton Grange for that matter. I've no doubt it's a shock for you, Dot, losing another patient so soon after Victor, but why take it out on me? We all know that you're in love with Wilfred and I've no doubt that's pretty unrewarding for you, but it's hardly my fault. I may be a little ambivalent in my sexual tastes but I'm not competing for him, I assure you.'

Suddenly she blundered up to him and threw back her arm to slap his face in a gesture at once theatrical and absurd. But before she could strike, Julius had caught her wrist. Dalgliesh was surprised at the quickness and effectiveness of his reaction. The taut hand, white and trembling with effort, held hers high in a muscled vice so that they looked like two ill-matched contestants locked in a tableau of conflict. Suddenly he laughed and dropped her hand. He lowered his hand more slowly, his eyes still on her face, and began massaging and twisting his wrist. Then he laughed again, a dangerous sound, and said softly:

'Careful! Careful! I'm not a helpless geriatric patient, you know.'

She gave a gasp and, bursting into tears, blundered sobbing from the room, an ungainly and pathetic but not a ridiculous figure. Philby slipped out after her. His departure caused as little interest as his arrival. Wilfred said softly:

'You shouldn't have said that, Julius, any of it.'

'I know. It was unforgivable. I'm sorry. I'll tell Dot so when we are feeling calmer.'

The brevity, the absence of self-justification and the apparent sincerity of the apology silenced them. Dalgliesh said quietly:

'I imagine that Miss Willison would have found this quarrelling over her body a great deal more shocking than anything that could happen to her on the mortuary slab.'

His words recalled Wilfred to the matter in hand; he turned to Eric Hewson:

'But we didn't have all this trouble with Michael, you gave a certificate without difficulty then.'

Dalgliesh could detect the first trace of peevishness in his voice.

Eric explained:

'I knew why Michael had died, I had seen him only that morning. It was only a matter of time for Michael after the last heart attack. He was a dying man.'

'As we all are,' said Wilfred. 'As we all are.'

The pious platitudes seemed to irritate his sister. She spoke for the first time.

'Don't be ridiculous, Wilfred. I'm certainly not dying and you would be very disconcerted to be told that you were. And as for Grace, she always looked to me a great deal sicker than anyone here seemed to understand. Now perhaps you will realize that it isn't always the ones who make the most fuss who need the most attention.'

She turned to Dalgliesh:

'What exactly will happen if Eric doesn't give a certificate? Does it mean that we'll have the police here again?'

'A policeman will probably come, yes; just an ordinary policeman. He'll be the coroner's officer and he will take charge of the body.'

'And then?'

'The coroner will arrange for a post-mortem. According to the result he will either issue a certificate for the registrar or he'll conduct an inquest.'

Wilfred said:

'It's all so horrible, so unnecessary.'

'It's the law and Dr Hewson knows that it is the law.'

'But what do you mean, it's the law? Grace died of D.S., we all know that. What if there was some other disease present? Eric can't treat her or do anything to help her now. What law are you talking about?'

Dalgliesh patiently explained:

'The doctor who attends a dead person during his last illness is required to sign and deliver to the registrar a certificate in a prescribed form stating the cause of death to the best of his knowledge and belief. At the same time he is required to deliver to a qualified informant, and that could be the occupant of the house where the death occurred, a notice to the effect that he has signed such a certificate. There is no statutory duty on a doctor to report any death to the coroner, but it's usual to do so where there is any doubt. When the doctor reports a death to a coroner he's not relieved of his duty to issue a certificate of the cause of death but there is provision for him to state on the form that he has reported the death so that the registrar will know that he must defer registration until he hears from the coroner. Under Section 3 of the Coroners Act 1887 a coroner has a duty to make inquiries whenever he is informed that there is lying within his jurisdiction the body of a person who there is reason to believe may have died a violent or unnatural death or a sudden death, the cause of which is unknown, or who has died in prison or in any place or circumstances which under another Act require an inquest to be held. That, since you have inquired – and in somewhat tedious detail – is the law. Grace Willison has died suddenly and in Dr Hewson's opinion the cause is at present unknown. His best course is to report the death to the coroner. It will mean a post-mortem, but not necessarily an inquest.'

'But I hate the thought of her lying mangled on an autopsy slab.' Wilfred was beginning to sound like an obstinate child. Dalgliesh said coolly:

'Mangled isn't exactly the word. A post-mortem is an organized and perfectly tidy procedure. And now if you will excuse me I'll get back to my breakfast.'

Suddenly Wilfred made an almost physical effort to pull himself together. He straightened up, and crossed his hands into the wide sleeves of his habit and stood for a moment in silent meditation.

Eric Hewson looked at him, puzzled, then glanced from Dalgliesh to Julius as if seeking guidance. Then Wilfred spoke:

'Eric, you had better ring the coroner's office now. Normally Dot would lay out the body but that had better wait until we get instructions. After you have telephoned, please let everyone know that I want to talk to all the family immediately after breakfast. Helen and Dennis are with them at present. Millicent, perhaps you could find Dot and see that she is all right. And now I should like to speak to you Julius, and to Adam Dalgliesh.'

He stood for a moment, eyes closed, at the foot of Grace's bed. Dalgliesh wondered whether he were praying. Then he led the way out. As they followed, Julius whispered with hardly a movement of his lips:

'Unpleasantly reminiscent of those summonses to the headmaster's study. We should have fortified ourselves with breakfast.'

In the business room Wilfred wasted no time.

'Grace's death means that I have to make my decision sooner than I'd hoped. We can't carry on with only four patients. On the other hand, I can hardly start admitting from the waiting list if the Grange isn't going to continue. I shall hold a family council on the afternoon Grace is buried. I think it would be right to wait until then. If there are no complications, that should be in less than a week's time. I should like you both to take part and help us to our decision.'

Julius said quickly:

'That's impossible, Wilfred. I've absolutely no interest; interest, I mean, in the legal or insurance sense. It just isn't my business.'

'You live here. I've always thought of you as one of the family.'

'Sweet of you, and I'm honoured. But it isn't true. I'm not one of the family and I have absolutely no right to vote on a decision that can't really affect me one way or the other. If you decide to sell out, and I wouldn't blame you, I probably shall too. I don't fancy living on Toynton Head once it's a caravan site. But it won't matter to me. I'll get a good price from some bright young executive from the Midlands who won't give a damn about peace and quiet but who will build a natty cocktail bar in the sitting-room and run up a flagpole on the patio. I shall probably look for my next cottage in the Dordogne after careful inquiries about any bargains which the owner may have made with God or the devil. Sorry, but it's a definite no.'

'And you, Adam?'

'I've even less right to an opinion than Court. This place is home to the patients. Why on earth should their future be decided, at least in part, by the vote of a casual visitor?'

'Because I greatly trust your judgement.'

'There's no reason why you should. In this matter, better trust your accountant.'

Julius asked:

'Are you inviting Millicent to the family council?

'Of course. She may not have always given me the support I hoped for from her, but she is one of the family.'

'And Maggie Hewson?'

Wilfred said curtly:

'No.'

'She's not going to like that. And isn't it a little hurtful to Eric?'

Wilfred said magisterially:

'As you have just made it plain that you don't consider yourself in any way concerned, why not leave me to decide what's hurtful to Eric. And now, if you will both excuse me, I shall join the family for breakfast.'

VII

As they left Wilfred's room, Julius said roughly and as if on impulse:

'Come up to the cottage and have breakfast. Have a drink anyway. Or if it's too early for alcohol, have coffee. Anyway, please come. I've started the day in a mood of self-disgust and I'm bad company for myself.'

It was too close to an appeal to be easily disregarded. Dalgliesh said:

'If you can give me about five minutes. There's someone I want to see. I'll meet you in the hall.'

He remembered from his first conducted tour of the Grange which was Jennie Pegram's room. There might, he thought, be a better time for this encounter but he couldn't wait for it. He knocked and heard the note of surprise in her answering 'come in'. She was sitting in her wheelchair in front of her dressing-table, her yellow hair flowing over her shoulders. Taking the poison pen letter from his wallet he walked up behind her and laid it in front of her. In the mirror their eyes met.

'Did you type that?'

She let her glance travel over it without picking it up. Her eyes flickered; a red stain began to travel like a wave over her neck. He heard the hiss of in-drawn breath, but her voice was calm.

'Why should I?'

'I can suggest reasons. But did you?'

'Of course not! I've never seen it before.'

She glanced at it again dismissively, contemptuously.

'It's . . . it's stupid, childish.'

'Yes, a poor effort. Done in a hurry, I imagine. I thought you might take rather a poor view of it. Not quite as exciting or imaginative as the others.'

'What others?'

'Come now, let's start with the one to Grace Willison. That did you credit. An imaginative effort, cleverly composed to spoil her pleasure in the only real friend she had made here, and nasty enough to ensure that she would be ashamed to show it to anyone. Except, of course, to a policeman. Even Miss Willison didn't mind showing it to a policeman. Where obscenity is concerned, we enjoy an almost medical dispensation.'

'She wouldn't dare! And I don't know what you're talking about.'

'Wouldn't she? It's a pity you can't ask her. You know that she's dead?'

'That's nothing to do with me.'

'Luckily for you, I don't think it is. She wasn't the suicidal type. I wonder if you were as lucky – or unlucky – with your other victims, with Victor Holroyd for example.'

There was no mistaking her terror now. The thin hands were twisting the handle of her hairbrush in a desperate pantomime.

'That wasn't my fault! I never wrote to Victor! I never wrote to anyone.'

'You aren't as clever as you think you are. You forget about fingerprints. Perhaps you didn't realize that forensic laboratories can detect them on writing paper. And then there's the timing. All the letters have been received since you arrived at Toynton Grange. The first was received before Ursula Hollis was admitted and I think we can rule out Henry Carwardine. I know that they've stopped since Mr Holroyd's death. Was that because you realized just how far you'd gone? Or did you hope that Mr Holroyd would be held responsible? But the police will know that those letters weren't written by a man. And then there's the saliva test. All except fifteen per cent of the population excrete their blood group in their saliva. It's a pity you didn't know that before you licked the envelope flaps.'

'The envelopes . . . but they weren't . . .'

She gasped at Dalgliesh. Her eyes widened with terror. The flush receded leaving her very pale.

'No, there weren't any envelopes. The notes were folded and placed in the victim's library book. But no one knows that except the recipients and you.'

She said, not looking at him:

'What are you going to do?'

'I don't know yet.'

And he didn't know. He felt a mixture, strange to him, of embarrassment, anger and some shame. It had been so easy to trick her, so easy and so contemptible. He saw himself as clearly as if he were an onlooker, healthy and able, sitting magisterially in judgement on her weakness, delivering the customary admonition from the bench, deferring sentence. The picture was distasteful. She had caused Grace Willison pain. But at least she could claim some psychological excuse. How much of his own anger and disgust had its roots in guilt? What had he done to make Grace Willison's last days happier? Yet something would have to be done about her. She was unlikely at present to make more mischief at Toynton Grange, but what of the future? And Henry Carwardine presumably had a right to know. So, one could argue, had Wilfred and the Ridgewell Trustees if they took over. Some people, too, would argue that she needed help. They would produce the orthodox contemporary solution, referral to a psychiatrist. He just didn't know. It wasn't a remedy in which he had much confidence. It would gratify her vanity, perhaps, and minister to her urge for self-importance to be taken seriously. But if the victims had resolved to keep silent, if only to protect Wilfred from worry, what right had he to deride their motive or break their confidence? He had been used in his job to working to rules. Even when he had taken an unorthodox decision, which wasn't seldom, the moral issues – if one could use that word and he never had – had been clear and unambiguous. His illness must have sapped his will and judgement as well as his physical strength for his paltry problem to defeat him. Ought he to leave a sealed note for Anstey or his successor to open in case of further trouble? Really it was ridiculous to be driven to such a weak and histrionic expedient. For God's sake, why couldn't he make a straight decision? He wished that Father Baddeley were alive, knowing on whose frail shoulders he could safely have lain this particular burden.

He said:

'I shall leave it to you to tell the victims, all of them, that you were responsible and that it won't happen again. You had better see that it doesn't. I leave it to your ingenuity to think out an excuse. I know that you must miss all the fuss and attention you had at your last hospital. But why compensate by making other people unhappy?'

'They hate me.'

'Of course they don't. You hate yourself. Did you write these notes to anyone else except Miss Willison and Mr Carwardine?'

She looked up at him slyly from under her eyelids.

'No. Only those two.'

It was probably a lie, he thought wearily. Ursula Hollis had probably had a letter. Would it do more harm or less if he asked her?

He heard Jennie Pegram's voice, stronger now, more confident. She lifted her left hand and began stroking her hair, drawing the strands across her face. She said:

'No one here cares about me. They all despise me. They never wanted me to come here. I didn't want it either. You could help me but you don't really care. You don't even want to listen.'

'Get Dr Hewson to refer you to a psychiatrist and confide in him. He's paid to listen to neurotics talking about themselves. I'm not.'

He regretted the unkindness as soon as the door was closed. He knew what had prompted it; the sudden remembrance of Grace Willison's shrunken, ugly body in its cheap nightdress. It was well, he thought, in a mood of self-disgust, that he was giving up his job if pity and anger could so destroy his detachment. Or was it Toynton Grange? This place, he thought, is getting on my nerves.

As he walked quickly down the passage the door next to Grace Willison's room opened and he saw Ursula Hollis. She beckoned him in, swivelling her wheelchair to clear the doorway.

'They've told us to wait in our rooms. Grace is dead.'

'Yes, I know.'

'What is it? What happened?'

'No one really knows yet. Dr Hewson is arranging for a post-mortem.'

'She didn't kill herself – or anything.'

'I'm not sure. It looked as if she died quietly in her sleep.'

'You mean like Father Baddeley?'

'Yes, just like Father Baddeley.'

They paused, staring at each other. Dalgliesh asked:

'You didn't hear anything last night?'

'Oh, no! Nothing! I slept very well, that is, after Helen had been in to me.'

'Would you have heard if she called out or if anyone went in to her?'

'Oh yes, if I wasn't asleep. Sometimes she kept me awake with her snoring. But I didn't hear her call out, and she went to sleep before I did. My light was out before twelve-thirty and I thought then how quiet she was.'

He moved towards the door and then paused, feeling that she was reluctant to see him go. He asked:

'Is anything worrying you?'

'Oh, no! Nothing. It was just the uncertainty about Grace, not knowing, everyone being so mysterious. But if they're going to do a post-mortem . . . I mean the post-mortem will tell us how she died.'

'Yes,' he said without conviction, as if reassuring himself as well as her, 'the post-mortem will tell us.'

VIII

Julius was waiting alone in the front hall and they left the Grange together walking through the bright morning air, abstracted, a little apart, their eyes fixed on the path. Neither spoke. As if yoked by an invisible cord, they paced, carefully distanced, towards the sea. Dalgliesh was glad of his companion's silence. He was thinking about Grace Willison, trying to understand and analyse the root of his concern and unrest, emotions which seemed to him illogical to the point of perversity. There had been no visible marks on the body; no lividity; no petechiae on the face or forehead; no sign of disturbance in her room; nothing unusual except an unlatched window. She had lain there stiffening in the quietus of natural death. Why then this irrational suspicion? He was a professional policeman, not a clairvoyant. He worked by evidence not by intuition. How many post-mortems were carried out in a year? Over 170,000 wasn't it? 170,000 deaths which required at least some preliminary investigation. Most of them could provide an obvious motive, at least for one person. Only the pathetic derelicts of society had nothing to leave, however meagre, however uncoveted to sophisticated eyes. Every death benefited someone, enfranchised someone, lifted a burden from someone's shoulders, whether of responsibility, the pain of vicarious suffering or the tyranny of love. Every death was a suspicious death if one looked only at motive, just as every death, at the last, was a natural death. Old Dr Blessington, one of the first and greatest of the forensic pathologists, had taught him that. It had, he remembered, been Blessington's last post-mortem, the young Detective Constable Dalgliesh's first. The hands of both had been shaking, but for very different reasons, although the old man had been as steady as a surgeon once the first incision was made. The body of a forty-two-year-old, red-haired prostitute was on the slab. The post-mortem assistant had with two strokes of his gloved hand wiped from her face the blood, the dirt, the pancake of paint and matted powder, leaving it pale, vulnerable, anonymous. His strong living hand, not death, had erased from it all personality. Old Blessington had demonstrated the cunning of his craft:

'You see, lad, the first blow, warded off by her hand, slipped down the neck and throat towards the right shoulder. A lot of blood, a lot of mess, but no great harm done. With the second, directed upwards and across, he severed the trachea. She died of shock, blood loss and asphyxia, probably in that order from the look of the thymus. When we get them on the slab, lad, there's no such thing as unnatural death.'

Natural or unnatural, he was through with it now. It was irritating that with a will so strong, his mind apparently needed this constant reassurance, that it was so obstinately reluctant to leave the problems alone. What possible justification, anyway, had he for going to the local police with a complaint that death was becoming a little too common at Toynton? An old priest dying of heart disease, without enemies, without possessions, except a modest fortune unexceptionally willed for charitable purposes to the man who had befriended him, a notable philanthropist whose character and reputation were beyond reproach. And Victor Holroyd? What could the police do about that death other than what they had already most competently done. The facts had been investigated, the inquest jury had pronounced their finding. Holroyd had been buried, Father Baddeley cremated. All that remained was a coffin of broken bones and decaying flesh and a fistful of grey, gritty dust in Toynton churchyard; two more secrets added to the store of secrets buried in that consecrated earth. All of them were beyond human solving now.

And now this third death, the one for which everyone at Toynton Grange had probably been superstitiously waiting, in thrall to the theurgy that death comes in threes. They could all relax now. He could relax. The coroner would order a post-mortem, and Dalgliesh had little doubt of the result. If Michael and Grace Willison had both been murdered, their killer was too clever to leave signs. And why should he? With a frail, sick, disease-ridden woman, it would have been only too easy, as simple and quick as a firm hand placed over nose and mouth. And there would be nothing to justify his interference. He couldn't say: I, Adam Dalgliesh, have had one of my famous hunches – I disagree with the coroner, with the pathologist, with the local police, with all the facts. I demand in the light of this new death that Father Baddeley's incinerated bones be resurrected and forced to yield up their secret.

They had reached Toynton Cottage. Dalgliesh followed Julius round to the seaward porch which led directly from the stone patio into the sitting-room. Julius had left the door unlocked. He pushed it open and stood a little aside so that Dalgliesh could go in first. Then they both stood stock still, stricken into immobility. Someone had been there before them. The marble bust of the smiling child had been smashed to pieces.

Still without speaking they moved together warily over the carpet. The head, hacked into anonymity, lay among a holocaust of marble fragments. The dark grey carpet was bejewelled with gleaming grits of stone. Broad ribbons of light from the windows and open door lay across the room and, in their rays, the jabbed slivers twinkled like a myriad of infinitesimal stars. It looked as if the destruction had at first been systematic. Both ears had been cleanly severed, and lay together, obscene objects oozing invisible blood, while the bouquet of flowers, so delicately carved that the lilies of the valley had seemed to tremble with life, lay a little distance from the hand as if tossed lightly aside. A miniature dagger of marble had lodged upright in the sofa, a microcosm of violence.

The room was very still; its ordered comfort, the measured ticking of the carriage clock on the mantelshelf, the insistent thudding of the sea, all heightened the sense of outrage, the crudity of destruction and hate.

Julius dropped to his knees and picked up a shapeless lump which had once been the child's head. After a second he let it drop from his loosened grasp. It rolled clumsily, obliquely, across the floor and came to rest against the foot of the sofa. Still without speaking, he reached over and picked up the posy of flowers cradling it gently in his hands. Dalgliesh saw that his body was shaking; he was very pale and his forehead, bent over the carving, glistened with sweat..He looked like a man in shock.

Dalgliesh went over to the side table which held a decanter

and poured out a generous measure of whisky. Silently he handed the glass to Julius. The man's silence and the dreadful shaking worried him. Anything, he thought, violence, a storm of rage, a spate of obscenity, would be better than this unnatural silence. But when Julius did speak his voice was perfectly steady. He shook his head at the offered glass.

'No, thank you. I don't need a drink. I want to know what I'm feeling, know it here in my belly not just in my head. I don't want my anger dulled, and by God, I don't need it stimulated! Think of it, Dalgliesh. He died three hundred years ago, this gentle boy. The marble must have been carved very shortly afterwards. It was of absolutely no practical use to anyone for three hundred years except to give comfort and pleasure and remind us that we are dust. Three hundred years. Three hundred years of war, revolution, violence, greed. But it survived. It survived until this year of grace. Drink that whisky yourself, Dalgliesh. Raise the glass and toast the age of the despoiler. He didn't know that this was here, unless he peers and pries when I am away. Anything of mine would have served. He could have destroyed anything. But when he saw this, he couldn't resist it. Nothing else could have given him quite such an exaltation of destruction. This isn't just hatred of me you know. Whoever did it, hated this too. Because it gave pleasure, was made with an intention, not just a lump of clay thrown against a wall, paint stamped into a canvas, a piece of stone smoothed into innocuous curves. It had gravity and integrity. It grew out of privilege and tradition, and contributed to it. God, I should have known better than to bring it here among these barbarians!'

Dalgliesh knelt beside him. He picked up two portions of a smashed forearm and fitted them together like a puzzle. He said:

'We know probably to within a few minutes when it was done. We know that it needed strength and that he – or she – probably used a hammer. There ought to be marks on that. And he couldn't have walked here and back in the time. Either he escaped down your path here to the shore, or he came by van and then went on to collect the post. It shouldn't be difficult to find out who is responsible.'

'My God, Dalgliesh, you have a policeman's soul haven't you? Is that thought supposed to comfort me?'

'It would me; but then, as you say, it's probably a matter of soul.'

'I'm not calling in the police if that's what you're suggesting. I don't need the local fuzz to tell me who did this. I know, and so do you, don't you?'

'No. I could give you a short list of suspects in order of probability, but that's not the same thing.'

'Spare yourself the trouble. I know and I'll deal with him in my own way.'

'And give him the added satisfaction of seeing you brought up on a charge of assault or G.B.H. I suppose.'

'I wouldn't get much sympathy from you would I, or from the local bench? Vengeance is mine saith Her Majesty's Commission of the Peace. Naughty, destructive boy, under-privileged lad! Five pounds fine and put him on probation. Oh! don't worry! I shan't do anything rash. I'll take my time, but I'll deal with it. You can keep your local pals out of it. They weren't exactly a flaming success when they investigated Holroyd's death were they? They can keep their clumsy fingers out of my mess.'

Getting to his feet he added with sulky obstinacy, almost as an afterthought:

'Besides, I don't want any more fuss here at present, not just after Grace Willison's death. Wilfred's got enough on his plate. I'll clear this mess away and tell Henry that I have taken the marble back to London. No one else from the Grange comes here, thank God, so I shall be spared the usual insincere condolences.'

Dalgliesh said:

'I find it interesting, this concern for Wilfred's peace of mind.'

'I thought you might. In your book I am a selfish bastard. You've got an identikit to selfish bastards, and I don't precisely fit. Ergo, find a reason. There has to be a first cause.'

'There's always a cause.'

'Well, what is it? Am I somehow in Wilfred's pay? Am I fiddling the books? Has he some hold over me? Is there perhaps some truth in Moxon's suspicions? Or perhaps I'm Wilfred's illegitimate son.'

'Even a legitimate son might reasonably feel that it was worth causing Wilfred some distress to discover who did this. Aren't you being too scrupulous? Wilfred must know that someone at Toynton Grange, probably one of his disciples, nearly killed him, intentionally or otherwise. My guess is that he'd take the loss of your marble fairly philosophically.'

'He doesn't have to take it. He's not going to know. I can't explain to you what I don't understand myself. But I am committed to Wilfred. He is so vulnerable and pathetic. And it is all so hopeless! If you must know, he reminds me in some way of my parents. They had a small general store in Southsea. Then when I was about fourteen, a large chain store opened next door. That was the end of them. They tried everything; they wouldn't give in. Extended credit when they weren't getting their money anyway; special offers when their profit margins were practically nil; hours spent after closing time rearranging the window; balloons given free to the local kids. It didn't matter, you see. It was all utterly pointless and futile. They couldn't succeed. I thought I could have borne their failure. What I couldn't bear was their hope.'

Dalgliesh thought that, in part, he did see. He knew what Julius was saying. Here am I, young, rich, healthy. I know how to be happy, if only the world were really as I want it to be. If only other people wouldn't persist in being sick, deformed, in pain, helpless, defeated, deluded. Or if only I could be just that bit more selfish so that I didn't care. If only there weren't the black tower. He heard Julius speaking:

'Don't worry about me. Remember I am bereaved. Don't they say that the bereaved always have to work through their grief? The appropriate treatment is a detached sympathy and plenty of good plain nourishment. We'd better get some breakfast.'

Dalgliesh said quietly:

'If you're not going to ring the police, then we might as well clear up this mess.'

'I'll get a dustpan. I can't bear the noise of the vacuum cleaner.'

He disappeared into his immaculate, fashionable over-equipped kitchen, and came back with a dustpan and two brushes. In an odd companionship they knelt together to their task. But the brushes were too soft to dislodge the slivers of marble, and in the end they had to pick them up laboriously one by one.

IX

The forensic pathologist was a locum tenens senior registrar, and if he had expected this three-week stint of duty in the agreeable West Country to be less arduous than his London job, he was disappointed. When the telephone rang for the tenth time that morning he peeled off his gloves, tried not to think about the fifteen naked cadavers still waiting on their refrigerated shelves and lifted the receiver philosophically. The confident masculine voice, except for its pleasant country burr, could have been the voice of any Metropolitan police officer, and the words, too, he had heard before.

'That you, Doc? We've got a body in a field three miles north of Blandford which we don't like the look of. Could you come to the scene?'

The summons seldom differed. They always had a body they didn't like the look of, in a ditch, a field, a gutter, in the tangled steel of a smashed car. He took up his message pad and asked the usual questions, heard the expected replies. He said to the mortuary assistant:

'OK, Bert, you can sew her up now. She's no twelve-guinea special. Tell the Coroner's office that he can issue the disposal order. I'm off to a scene. Get the next two ready for me, will you?'

He glanced for the last time at the emaciated body on the table. There had been nothing difficult about Grace Miriam Willison, spinster, aged 57. No external signs of violence, no internal evidence to justify sending the viscera for analysis. He had muttered to his assistant with some bitterness that if the local GPs were going to look to an over-stretched forensic pathology service to settle their differential diagnoses the service might as well pack up. But her doctor's hunch had been right. There was something he'd missed, the advanced neoplasm in the upper stomach. And much good that knowledge now would do him or her. That, or the D.S. or the heart condition had killed her. He wasn't God and he'd taken his choice. Or maybe she'd just decided that she had had enough and turned her face to the wall. In her state it was the mystery of continuing life not the fact of death that needed explaining. He was beginning to think that most patients died when they decided that it was their time to die. But you couldn't put that on a certificate.

He scribbled a final note on Grace Willison's record, called out a final instruction to his assistant, then pushed his way through the swing doors towards another death, another body, towards, he thought, with something like relief, his proper job.

SEVEN

Mist on the Headland

I

The church of All Saints at Toynton was an uninteresting Victorian reconstruction of an earlier building, the churchyard a triangular patch of swathed grass between the west wall, the road and a row of rather dull cottages. Victor Holroyd's grave, pointed out by Julius, was an oblong mound crudely patched with squares of weedy turf. Beside it, a simple wooden cross marked the spot where Father Baddeley's ashes had been buried. Grace Willison was to lie next to him. Everyone at Toynton Grange was at the funeral except Helen Rainer, who had been left to nurse Georgie Allan, and Maggie Hewson, whose absence, unremarked, was apparently taken for granted. But Dalgliesh, when he arrived alone, had been surprised to see Julius's Mercedes parked opposite the lych-gate beside the Toynton Grange bus.

The churchyard was encumbered and the path between the headstones narrow and overgrown so that it took some time to manoeuvre the three wheelchairs round the open grave.

The local vicar was taking a belated holiday and his substitute, who apparently knew nothing of Toynton Grange, was obviously surprised to see four mourners garbed in brown monk's habits. He asked if they were Anglican Franciscans, an inquiry which provoked a fit of nervous giggling from Jennie Pegram. Anstey's answer, unheard by Dalgliesh, apparently failed to reassure and the priest, puzzled and disapproving, took the service with carefully controlled speed as if anxious to free the churchyard as soon as possible from the risk of contamination by the imposters. The little party sang, at Wilfred's suggestion, Grace's favourite hymn, 'Ye Holy Angels Bright'. It was, thought Dalgliesh, a hymn peculiarly unsuited for amateur unaccompanied singing and their uncertain and discordant voices rose reed thin in the crisp autumnal air.

There were no flowers. Their absence, the rich smell of newly turned earth, the mellow autumn sunlight, the ubiquitous scent of burning wood, even the sense of unseen but inquisitive eyes peering morbidly from behind the hedges, brought back with stabbing pain the memory of another funeral.

He had been a fourteen-year-old schoolboy, at home for his half-term. His parents were in Italy and Father Baddeley was in charge of the parish. A local farmer's son, a shy, gentle, over-conscientious eighteen-year-old, home for the weekend from his first term at university, had taken his father's gun and shot dead both parents, his fifteen-year-old sister and, finally, himself. They were a devoted family, he a loving son. For the young Dalgliesh, who was beginning to imagine himself in love with the girl, it had been a horror eclipsing all subsequent horrors. The tragedy, unexplained, appalling, had at first stunned the village. But grief had quickly given way to a wave of superstitious anger, terror and repulsion. It was unthinkable that the boy should be buried in consecrated ground and Father Baddeley's gentle but inexorable insistence that all the family should lie together in one grave had made him temporarily an outcast. The funeral, boycotted by the village, had been held on such a day as this. The family had no close relatives. Only Father Baddeley, the sexton and Adam Dalgliesh had been there. The fourteen-year-old boy, rigid with uncomprehending grief, had concentrated on the responses willing himself to divorce the unbearably poignant words from their sense, to see them merely as black unmeaning symbols on the prayer book page, and to speak them with firmness, even with nonchalance, across the open grave. Now, when this unknown priest raised his hand to speak the final blessing over Grace Willison's body Dalgliesh saw instead the frail upright figure of Father Baddeley, the wind ruffling his hair. As the first sods fell on the coffin and he turned away he felt like a traitor. The memory of one occasion on which Father Baddeley had not relied on him in vain only reinforced his present nagging sense of failure.

It was probably this which made him reply tartly to Wilfred when he walked up to him and said:

'We are going back for luncheon now. We shall start the family council at half past two and the second session at about four. Are you quite sure you won't help us?'

Dalgliesh opened the door of his car.

'Can you give me one reason why it would be right that I should?' Wilfred turned away; for once he looked almost disconcerted. Dalgliesh heard Julius's low laugh.

'Silly old dear! Does he really think that we don't know that he wouldn't be holding a family council if he weren't confident that the decision would go his way. What are your plans for the day?'

Dalgliesh said that they were still uncertain. In fact he had decided to exercise away his self-disgust by walking along the cliff path as far as Weymouth and back. But he wasn't anxious to invite Julius's company.

He stopped at a nearby pub for a luncheon of cheese and beer, drove quickly back to Hope Cottage, changed into slacks and windcheater and set off eastwards along the cliff path. It was very different from that first early morning walk the day after his arrival when all his newly awakened senses had been alive to sound and colour and smell. Now he strode strongly forward, deep in thought, eyes on the path, hardly aware even of the laboured, sibilant breath of the sea. He would soon have to make a decision about his job; but that could wait for another couple of weeks. There were more immediate if less onerous decisions. How much longer should he stay at Toynton? He had little excuse to linger. The books had been sorted, the boxes were almost ready for cording. And he was making no progress with the problem which had kept him in Hope Cottage. There was small hope now of solving the mystery of Father Baddeley's summons. It was as if, living in Father Baddeley's cottage, sleeping in his bed, Dalgliesh had absorbed something of his personality. He could almost believe that he smelt the presence of evil. It was an alien faculty which he half resented and almost wholly distrusted. And yet it was increasingly strong. He was sure now that Father Baddeley had been murdered. And yet, when as a policeman he looked hard at the evidence, the case dissolved like smoke in his hand.

Perhaps because he was deep in unproductive thought the mist took him by surprise. It rode in from the sea, a sudden physical invasion of white obliterating clamminess. At one moment he was striding in the mellow afternoon sunlight with the breeze prickling the hairs on his neck and arms. The next, sun, colour and smell were blotted out and he stood stock still pushing at the mist as if it were an alien force. It hung on his hair, caught at his throat and swirled in grotesque patterns over the headland. He watched it, a writhing transparent veil passing over and through the brambles and bracken, magnifying and altering form, obscuring the path. With the mist came a sudden silence. He was only aware that the headland had been alive with birds now that their cries were mute. The silence was uncanny. In contrast, the sound of the sea swelled and became all-pervasive, disorganized, menacing, seeming to advance on him from all sides. It was like a chained animal, now moaning in sullen captivity, now breaking free to hurl itself with roars of impotent rage against the high shingles.

He turned back towards Toynton, uncertain of how far he had walked. The return journey was going to be difficult. He had no sense of direction except for the thread of trodden earth under his feet. But he thought that the danger would be slight if he went slowly. The path was barely visible but for most of the route it was fringed with brambles, a welcome if prickly barrier when, momentarily disorientated, he lost his way. Once the mist lifted slightly and he strode forward more confidently. But it was a mistake. Only just in time he realized that he was teetering on the edge of a wide crevice splitting the path and that what he had thought was a rising bank of moving mist was foam dying on the cliff face fifty feet below.

The black tower reared out of the mist so suddenly that his first realization of its presence was to scrape his palms – instinctively flung forward – against its cold infrangible scales. Then, suddenly, the mist rose and thinned and he saw the top of the tower. The base was still shrouded in swirls of white clamminess but the octagonal cupola with its three visible slits seemed to float gently from behind the last sinuous threads of mist to hang motionless in space, dramatic, menacingly solid, and yet unsubstantial as a dream. It moved with the mist, a fugitive vision, now descending so low that he could almost believe it within his reach, now rising, numinous and unobtainable, high over the thudding sea.

It could surely have no contact with the cold stones on which his palms rested or the firm earth beneath his feet. To steady his balance he rested his head against the tower and felt reality hard and sharp against his forehead. Here at least was a landmark. From here he thought he could remember the main twists and turns of the path.

It was then that he heard it; the spine-chilling scrape, unmistakable, of bone ends clawing against the stone. It came from inside the tower. Reason asserted itself over superstition so quickly that his mind hardly had time to recognize its terror. Only the painful thudding of his heart against the rib cage, the sudden ice in the blood, told him that for one second he had crossed the border into the unknowable world. For one second, perhaps less, childish nightmares long suppressed rose to confront him. And then the terror passed. He listened more carefully, and then explored. The sound was quickly identified. To the seaward side of the tower and hidden in the corner between the porch and the round wall was a sturdy bramble. The wind had snapped one of the branches and two sharp unleashed ends were scraping against the stone. Through some trick of acoustics the sound, distorted, seemed to come from within the tower. From such coincidences, he thought, smiling grimly, were ghosts and legends born.

Less than twenty minutes later he stood above the valley and looked down on Toynton Grange. The mist was thinning now and he could just discern the Grange itself – a substantial, dark shadow marked by blurs of lights from the windows. His watch showed that it was eight minutes past three. So they would all be closeted now in solitary meditation waiting for the four o'clock summons to announce their final votes. He wondered how, in fact, they were passing their time. But the result was hardly in doubt. Like Julius he thought it unlikely that Wilfred would have called a council unless he were sure of getting his way. And that, presumably, would mean handing over to the Ridgewell Trust. Dalgliesh assessed how the votes might go. Wilfred would no doubt have received an undertaking that all jobs would be safe. Given that assurance Dot Moxon, Eric Hewson and Dennis Lerner would probably vote for the take-over. Poor Georgie Allan would have little choice. The views of the other patients were less certain but he had the feeling that Carwardine would be content enough to stay, particularly with the increased comfort and professional skill which the Trust would bring. Millicent, of course, would want to sell out and she would have had an ally in Maggie Hewson, if Maggie had been allowed to participate.

Looking down on the valley he saw the twin squares of light from the windows of Charity Cottage where, excluded, Maggie waited alone for the return of Eric. There was a stronger and brighter haze from the edge of the cliff. Julius, when at home, was extravagant with electricity.

The lights, although temporarily obscured as the mist shifted and re-formed, were a useful beacon. He found himself almost running down the slope of the headland. And then, curiously, the light in the Hewson cottage windows went off and on again three times, deliberate as a signal.

He had such a strong impression of an individual call for help that he had to remind himself of reality. She couldn't know that he, or anyone, was on the headland. It could only be by chance if the signal were seen by anyone at Toynton Grange, preoccupied as they were with meditation and decision. Besides, most of the patients' rooms were at the back of the house. It had probably been no more than a fortuitous flickering of the lights; she had been uncertain, perhaps, whether to watch television in the dark.

But the twin smudges of yellow light, now shining more strongly as the mist thinned, drew him towards the Hewson cottage. It was only about three hundred yards out of his way. She was there alone. He might as well look in, even at the risk of becoming involved in an alcoholic recital of grievances and resentment.

The front door was unlocked. When no voice responded to his knock he pushed it open and went in. The sitting-room, dirty, untidy, with its grubby air of temporary occupation, was empty. All three bars of the portable electric fire were glowing red and the room struck very warm. The television screen was a blank. The single unshaded light-bulb in the middle of the ceiling shone down garishly on the square table, the opened and almost empty bottle of whisky, the upturned glass, the sheet of writing paper with its scrawl of black Biro, at first relatively firm, then erratic as an insect trail across the white surface. The telephone had been moved from its usual place on the top of the bookcase and stood now, cord taut, on the table, the receiver hanging loosely over the edge.

He didn't wait to read the message. The door into the back hall was ajar and he pushed it open. He knew, with the sick and certain premonition of disaster, what he would find. The hall was very narrow and the door swung against her legs. The body twisted so that the flushed face slowly turned and looked down at him with what seemed a deprecating, half-melancholy, half-rueful surprise at finding herself at such a disadvantage. The light in the hall, from a single bulb, was garish, and she hung elongated like a bizarre and gaudily painted doll strung up for sale. The scarlet tight-fitting slacks, the white satin overblouse, the painted toe and finger nails and the matching gash of mouth looked horrible but unreal. One thrust of a knife and the sawdust would surely spill out from the stuffed veins to pyramid at his feet.

The climber's rope, a smooth twist of red and fawn, gay as a bell rope, was made to take the weight of a man. It hadn't failed Maggie. She had used it simply. The rope had been doubled and the two ends passed through the loop to form a noose, before being fastened, clumsily but effectively, to the top banister. The surplus yards lay tangled on the upper landing.

A high kitchen stool fitted with two steps had fallen on its side obstructing the hallway as if she had kicked it from under her. Dalgliesh placed it beneath the body and, resting her knees on its cushioned plastic, mounted the steps and slipped the noose over her head. The whole weight of her inert body sagged against him. He let it slip through his arms to the floor and half carried it into the sitting-room. Laying her on the mat in front of the fireplace he forced his mouth over hers and began artificial respiration.

Her mouth was fumed with whisky. He could taste her lipstick, a sickly ointment on his tongue. His shirt, wet with sweat, stuck to her blouse, gumming together his thudding chest and her soft, still warm but silent body. He pumped his breath into her, fighting an atavistic repugnance. It was too like raping the dead. He felt the absence of her heartbeat as keenly as an ache in his chest.

He was aware that the door had opened only by the sudden chill of flowing air. A pair of feet stood beside the body. He heard Julius's voice.

'Oh, my God! Is she dead? What happened?'

The note of terror surprised Dalgliesh. He glanced up for one second into Court's stricken face. It hung over him like a disembodied mask, the features bleached and distorted with fear. The man was fighting for control. His whole body was shaking. Dalgliesh, intent on the desperate rhythm of resuscitation, jerked out his commands in a series of harsh disjointed phrases.

'Get Hewson. Hurry.'

Julius's voice was a high, monotonous mutter.

'I can't! Don't ask me. I'm no good at that sort of thing. He doesn't even like me. We've never been close. You go. I'd rather stay here with her than face Eric.'

'Then ring him. Then the police. Wrap the receiver in your handkerchief. May be prints.'

'But they won't answer! They never do when they are meditating.'

'Then for God's sake fetch him!'

'But her face! It's covered with blood!'

'Lipstick. Smudged. Phone Hewson.'

Julius stood unmoving. Then he said:

'I'll try. They will have finished meditating by now. It's just four. They may answer.'

He turned to the telephone. From the corner of his eye Dalgliesh glimpsed the lifted receiver shaking in his hands, and the flash of white handkerchief which Julius had wrapped around the instrument as awkwardly as if trying to bandage a self-inflicted wound. After two long minutes the telephone was answered. He couldn't guess by whom. Nor did he afterwards remember what Julius had said.

'I've told them. They're coming.'

'Now the police.'

'What shall I tell them?'

'The facts. They'll know what to do.'

'But oughtn't we to wait? Suppose she comes round?'

Dalgliesh straightened himself up. He knew that for the last five minutes he had been working on a dead body. He said:

'I don't think she's going to come round.'

Immediately he bent again to his task, his mouth clamped over hers, feeling with his right palm for the first pulse of life in the silent heart. The pendant light-bulb swung gently in the movement of air from the open door so that a shadow moved like a drawn curtain over the dead face. He was aware of the contrast between the inert flesh, the cool unresponsive lips bruised by his own, and her look of flushed intentness, a woman preoccupied in the act of love. The crimson stigmata of the rope was like a double-corded bracelet clasping the heavy throat. Remnants of cold mist stole in the door to twine themselves round the dust-encrusted legs of table and chairs. The mist stung his nostrils like an anaesthetic; his mouth tasted sour with the whisky-tainted breath.

Suddenly there was a rush of feet; the room was full of people and voices. Eric Hewson was edging him aside to kneel beside his wife; behind him Helen Rainer flicked open a medical bag. She handed him a stethoscope. He tore open his wife's blouse. Delicately, unemotionally, she lifted Maggie's left breast so that he could listen to the heart. He pulled off the stethoscope and threw it aside holding out his hand. This time, still without speaking, she handed him a syringe.

'What are you going to do?' It was Julius Court's hysterical voice.

Hewson looked up at Dalgliesh. His face was deathly white. The irises of his eyes were huge. He said:

'It's only digitalis.'

His voice, very low, was a plea for reassurance, for hope. But it sounded, too, like a plea for permission, a small abdication of responsibility. Dalgliesh nodded. If the stuff were digitalis it might work. And surely the man wouldn't be fool enough to inject anything lethal? To stop him now might be to kill her. Would it have been better to carry on with the artificial respiration? Probably not; in any case that was a decision for a doctor. And a doctor was here. But in his heart Dalgliesh knew that the argument was academic. She was as beyond harm as she was beyond help.

Helen Rainer now had a torch in her hand and was shining it

on Maggie's breast. The pores of the skin between the pendulous breasts looked huge, miniature craters clogged with powder and sweat. Hewson's hand began to shake. Suddenly she said:

'Here, let me do it.'

He handed over the syringe. Dalgliesh heard Julius Court's incredulous 'Oh, no! No!' and then watched the needle go in as cleanly and surely as a *coup de grâce.*

The slim hands didn't tremble as she withdrew the syringe, held a pad of cotton wool over the puncture mark and, without speaking, handed the syringe to Dalgliesh.

Suddenly Julius Court stumbled out of the room. He came back almost immediately holding a glass. Before anyone could stop him he had grasped the whisky bottle by the top of its neck and had poured out the last half inch. Jerking one of the chairs out from the table he sat down and slumped forward, his arms half circling the bottle.

Wilfred said:

'But Julius ... nothing should be touched until the police arrive!'

Julius took out his handkerchief and wiped it over his face.

'I needed that. And what the hell! I haven't interfered with her prints. And she's had a rope round her neck, or haven't you noticed? What d'you think she died of – alcoholism?'

The rest of them stood in a tableau round the body. Hewson still knelt at his wife's side; Helen cradled her head. Wilfred and Dennis stood one on each side, the folds of their habits hanging motionless in the still air. They looked, thought Dalgliesh, like a motley collection of actors posing for a contemporary diptych, their eyes fixed with wary anticipation on the bright body of the martyred saint.

Five minutes later Hewson stood up. He said dully:

'No response. Move her to the sofa. We can't leave her there on the floor.'

Julius Court rose from his chair and he and Dalgliesh together lifted the sagging body and placed it on the sofa. It was too short, and the scarlet-tipped feet, looking at once grotesque and pathetically vulnerable, stuck out stiffly over the end. Dalgliesh heard the company sigh gently, as if they had satisfied some obscure need to make the body comfortable. Julius looked round, apparently at a loss, searching for something with which to cover the corpse. It was Dennis Lerner who, surprisingly, produced a large white handkerchief, shook it free of its folds and placed it with ritual precision over Maggie's face. They all looked at it intently as if watching for the linen to stir with the first tentative breath.

Wilfred said:

'I find it a strange tradition that we cover the faces of the dead. Is it because we feel that they are at a disadvantage, exposed defenceless to our critical gaze? Or is it because we fear them? I think the latter.'

Ignoring him, Eric Hewson turned to Dalgliesh.

'Where . . .?'

'Out there in the hall.'

Hewson went to the door and stood silently surveying the dangling rope, the bright chrome and yellow kitchen stool. He turned towards the circle of watchful, compassionate faces.

'How did she get the rope?'

'It may be mine.' Wilfred's voice sounded interested, confident. He turned to Dalgliesh.

'It's newer-looking than Julius's rope. I bought it shortly after the old one was found frayed. I kept it on a hook in the business room. You may have noticed it. It was certainly hanging there when we left for Grace's funeral this morning. You remember, Dot?'

Dorothy Moxon moved forward from her shadowed refuge against the far wall. She spoke for the first time. They looked round as if surprised to find her in the company. Her voice sounded unnatural, high, truculent, uncertain.

'Yes, I noticed. I mean, I'm sure I would have noticed if it hadn't been there. Yes, I remember. The rope was there.'

'And when you got back from the funeral?' asked Dalgliesh.

'I went alone into the business room to hang up my cloak. I don't think it was there then. I'm almost sure not.'

'Didn't that worry you?' asked Julius.

'No, why should it? I'm not sure that I consciously noticed that the rope was missing at the time. It's only now, looking back, that I am fairly confident that it wasn't there. Its absence wouldn't have particularly concerned me even had I registered it. I should have assumed that Albert had borrowed it for some purpose. He couldn't have done so, of course. He came with us to the funeral, and got into the bus before me.'

Lerner said suddenly:

'The police have been telephoned?'

'Of course,' said Julius, 'I rang them.'

'What were you doing here?' Dorothy Moxon's didactic question sounded like an accusation, but Julius who seemed to have taken control of himself, answered calmly enough:

'She switched the light off and on three times before she died. I happened to see it through the mist from my bathroom window. I didn't come at once. I didn't think it was important or that she was really in trouble. Then I felt uneasy and decided to walk over. Dalgliesh was already here.'

Dalgliesh said:

'I saw the signal from the headland. Like Julius, I didn't feel more than slightly uneasy, but it seemed right to look in.'

Lerner had moved over to the table. He said:

'She's left a note.'

Dalgliesh said sharply:

'Don't touch it!'

Lerner withdrew his hand as if it had been stung. They moved round the table. The note was written in black Biro on the top sheet of a quarto-size pad of white writing paper. They read silently:

> 'Dear Eric, I've told you often
> enough that I couldn't stick it out
> in this lousy hole any longer. You
> thought it was just talk. You've been
> so busy fussing over your precious
> patients I could die of boredom and you
> wouldn't notice. Sorry if I've mucked
> up your little plans. I don't kid
> myself you'll miss me. You can have her
> now and by God you're welcome to each
> other. We had some good times. Remember

them. Try to miss me. Better dead. Sorry
Wilfred. The black tower.'

The first eight lines were plainly and strongly written, the last five were an almost illegible scrawl.

'Her handwriting?' asked Anstey.

Eric Hewson replied in a voice so low that they could barely hear him.

'Oh, yes. Her handwriting.'

Julius turned to Eric and said with sudden energy:

'Look, it's perfectly plain how it happened. Maggie never intended to kill herself. She wouldn't. She's not the type. For God's sake why should she? She's young enough, healthy, if she didn't like it here she could walk out. She's an SRN. She's not unemployable. This was all meant to frighten you. She tried to telephone Toynton Grange and get you over here – just in time, of course. When no one replied, she signalled with the lights. But by that time she was too drunk to know exactly what she was doing and the whole thing became horribly real. Take that note, does it read like a suicide note?'

'It does to me,' said Anstey. 'And I suspect it will to the coroner.'

'Well, it doesn't to me. It could just as well be the note of a woman planning to go away.'

Helen Rainer said calmly:

'Only she wasn't. She wouldn't be leaving Toynton wearing just a shirt and slacks. And where is her case? No woman plans to leave home without taking her make-up and nightwear.'

There was a capacious black shoulder bag beside a leg of the table. Julius picked it up and began rummaging in it. He said:

'There's nothing here. No nightdress or toilet bag.'

He continued his inspection. Then he glanced suddenly from Eric to Dalgliesh. An extraordinary succession of emotions crossed his face: surprise, embarrassment, interest. He closed the bag and placed it on the table.

'Wilfred's right. Nothing should be touched until the police arrive.'

They stood in silence. Then Anstey said:

'The police will want to know where we all were this afternoon, no doubt. Even in an obvious case of suicide these questions have to be asked. She must have died when we were nearly at the end of our meditation hour. That means, of course, that none of us has an alibi. Given the circumstances it is perhaps fortunate that Maggie chose to leave a suicide note.'

Helen Rainer said calmly:

'Eric and I were together in my room for the whole of the hour.'

Wilfred stared at her, disconcerted. For the first time since he had entered the cottage he seemed at a loss. He said:

'But we were holding a family council! The rules are that we meditate in silence and alone.'

'We didn't meditate and we weren't precisely silent. But we were alone – alone together.' She stared past him, defiant, almost triumphant, into the eyes of Eric Hewson. He gazed at her appalled.

Dennis Lerner, as if to dissociate himself from controversy, had moved over to stand by Dot Moxon by the door. Now he said quietly:

'I think I can hear cars. It must be the police.'

The mist had muffled the sound of their approach. Even as Lerner spoke Dalgliesh heard the dual slam of car doors. Eric's first reaction was to kneel by the sofa, shielding Maggie's body from the door. Then he scrambled clumsily to his feet as if afraid to be discovered in a compromising position. Dot, without looking round, moved her solid body away from the door.

The little room was suddenly as overcrowded as a bus shelter on a wet night, smelling of mist and damp raincoats. But there was no confusion. The new arrivals moved solidly and calmly in, bringing with them their equipment, moving as purposefully as encumbered members of an orchestra taking their appointed places. The group from Toynton Grange fell back and regarded them warily. No one spoke. Then Inspector Daniel's slow voice broke the silence.

'Well, now, and who found the poor lady?'

'I did,' said Dalgliesh. 'Court arrived about twelve minutes later.'

'Then I'll just have Mr Dalgliesh, Mr Court and Dr Hewson. That'll do to start with.'

Wilfred said:

'I should prefer to stay, if you please.'

'Well, Sir, I daresay. Mr Anstey isn't it? But we can't always have what we'd prefer. Now if you'll all go back to the Grange, Detective Constable Burroughs will accompany you and anything that's on your minds you can say to him. I'll be with you later.'

Without a further word, Wilfred led the way.

Inspector Daniel looked at Dalgliesh:

'Well, Sir, seemingly for you there's no convalescence from death at Toynton Head.'

II

When he had handed over the syringe and given his account of the finding of the body Dalgliesh didn't wait to watch the investigation. He had no wish to give the impression that he was keeping a critical eye on Inspector Daniel's handling of the case; he disliked the role of spectator, and he felt uncomfortably that he was getting in their way. None of the men present were getting in each other's. They moved confidently in the cramped space, each a specialist, yet giving the impression of a team. The photographer manoeuvred his portable lights into the narrow hall; the plain-clothes fingerprint expert, his case open to display the neatly arranged tools of his craft, settled down at the table, brush poised, to begin his methodical dusting of the whisky bottle; the police surgeon knelt, absorbed and judicial, beside the body and plucked at Maggie's mottled skin as if hoping to stimulate it into life. Inspector Daniel leaned over him and they conferred together. They looked, thought Dalgliesh, like two poulterers expertly assessing the qualities of a dead chicken. He was interested that Daniel had brought the police surgeon and not a forensic pathologist. But why not? A Home Office pathologist, given the huge areas which most of them had to cover, could seldom arrive promptly on the scene. And the initial medical examination here presented no obvious problems. There was no sense in committing more resources than were needed for the job. He wondered whether Daniel would have come himself if it hadn't been for the presence at Toynton Grange of a Metropolitan Police Commander.

Dalgliesh formally asked Daniel's permission to return to Hope Cottage. Eric Hewson had already left. Daniel had asked him only a few necessary brief and gentle questions before suggesting that he should join the others at Toynton Grange. Dalgliesh sensed the relief at his departure. Even these imperturbable experts moved more freely released from the inhibiting restraints of public grief. Now the Inspector exerted himself to do more than nod a curt dismissal. He said:

'Thank you, Sir. I'll call in for a word with you before I leave if I may,' and bent again to his contemplation of the body.

Whatever Dalgliesh had expected to find at Toynton Head it wasn't this; the old familiar routine commemoration of unnatural death. For a moment he saw it with Julius Court's eyes, an esoteric necromantic rite, carried out by its drab practitioners in silence or between grunts and muttered words as brief as incantations, a secret ministration to the dead. Certainly Julius seemed engrossed by the procedure. He made no move to leave but stood to one side of the door and, without taking his fascinated eyes from Inspector Daniel, held it open for Dalgliesh. Daniel didn't suggest that he, too, might now leave but Dalgliesh thought it unlikely that this was because the Inspector had forgotten his presence.

It was nearly three hours later before Inspector Daniel's car drove up to Hope Cottage. The Inspector was alone; Sergeant Varney and the others, he explained, had already left. He came in bringing with him remnants of mist like ectoplasm and a rush of cold damp air. His hair was jewelled with moisture and his long ruddy face glowed as if he had come in from a walk in the sun. At Dalgliesh's invitation he took off his trench coat and settled himself in the wheel-backed chair in front of the wood fire. His black lively eyes roamed over the cottage, taking in the scruffed rug, the meagre grate, the shabbiness of the wallpaper. He said:

'So this is where the old gentleman lived.'

'And died. You'll take whisky? Or there's coffee if you prefer it.'

'Whisky, thank you, Mr Dalgliesh. Mr Anstey didn't exactly make him comfortable, did he? But I daresay all the money goes on the patients, and very rightly no doubt.'

Some went on Anstey himself, thought Dalgliesh, remembering the sybaritic cell which was Wilfred's bedroom. He said:

'It's better than it looks. My packing cases don't exactly add to the cosiness. But I doubt whether Father Baddeley noticed the shabbiness or if he did, that he cared.'

'Well, it's warm enough anyway. This sea mist seems to seep into your bones. It's clearer inland, though, once you get beyond Toynton village. That's why we made good time.'

He sipped his whisky gratefully. After a minute's silence he said:

'This business tonight, Mr Dalgliesh. It looks straightforward enough. Her prints and Court's on the whisky bottle, and hers and Hewson's on the telephone. There's no hope of getting any dabs from the electric light switch, of course, and those on the Biro don't amount to anything. We found a couple of samples of her handwriting. The document chappies at the lab can take a look at them but it's clear enough to me – and Dr Hewson incidentally – that she wrote that suicide note. It's a strong distinctive scrawl for a woman.'

'Except for the last three lines.'

'The reference to the black tower? She was pretty far gone when she added that. Incidentally, Mr Anstey takes it as an admission that it was she who started the fire which nearly killed him. And that wasn't the first attempt according to him. You've heard, no doubt, about the frayed climbing rope? He gave me a full account of the incident in the black tower including your finding the brown habit.'

'Did he? He was anxious enough at the time to keep it from the police. So now it's to be laid very neatly at Maggie Hewson's door.'

'It always surprises me – although it shouldn't by now – how violent death unlooses tongues. He says that she was the one he suspected from the start; that she made no secret of her hatred of Toynton Grange or her resentment of him in particular.'

Dalgliesh said:

'Nor did she. I would be surprised if a woman who expressed her feelings with such uninhibited relish should feel the need for any other release. The fire; the frayed climbing rope; they strike me as being either part of a deliberate stratagem or the manifestations of frustrated hatred. Maggie Hewson was nothing if not candid about her dislike of Anstey.'

'Mr Anstey sees the fire as part of a deliberate stratagem. According to him she was trying to frighten him into selling out. She was desperate to get her husband away from Toynton Grange.'

'Then she'd misjudged her man. My guess is that Anstey isn't selling out. By tomorrow he'll have made up his mind to pass Toynton Grange to the Ridgewell Trust.'

'He's making up his mind now, Mr Dalgliesh. Apparently Mrs Hewson's death interrupted their final decision. He was anxious for me to interview all the inmates as quickly as possible so that they could get down to it. Not that it took much time, to get the basic facts, anyway. No one was seen leaving Toynton Grange after the party arrived back after the funeral. Apart from Dr Hewson and Nurse Rainer, who admit to having spent the meditation hour together in her room, all the others claim that they were alone. The patients' quarters, as you no doubt know, are at the back. Anyone, anyone not disabled that is, could have left the house. But there's no evidence that anyone did.'

Dalgliesh said:

'And even if someone did, this mist would have been an effective shield. Anyone could have walked about the headland unseen. Were you convinced, by the way, that Maggie Hewson did start the fire?'

'I'm not investigating arson or attempted murder, Mr Dalgliesh. Mr Anstey told me what he did in confidence and said that he wanted the whole subject dropped. She could have done it, but there is no real evidence. He could have done it himself.'

'I doubt that. But I did wonder if Henry Carwardine might have had a hand in it. He couldn't have started the fire himself, of course, but he might have paid an accomplice. I don't think he likes Anstey. But that's hardly a motive. He doesn't have to stay at Toynton Grange. But he's highly intelligent and, I should have thought, fastidious. It's difficult to imagine him embroiling himself with such childish mischief.'

'Ah, but he isn't using his intelligence is he, Mr Dalgliesh?

That's his trouble. He gave up too easily and too early, that one. And who can know the truth about motive? Sometimes I think not even the villain himself. I daresay it isn't easy for a man like that, living in such a restricted community, dependent always on others, having always to be grateful to Mr Anstey. Well, no doubt he is grateful to Mr Anstey; they all are. But gratitude can be the very devil sometimes, particularly if you have to be grateful for services you'd rather be without.'

'You're probably right. I know little of Carwardine's feelings, or of anyone else's at Toynton Grange. I've taken very good care not to know. Did the proximity of violent death induce any of the others to reveal their little secrets?'

'Mrs Hollis had a contribution. I don't know what she thought it proved, or why she thought it worth telling for that matter. But she may have wanted her little moment of importance. That blonde patient was the same – Miss Pegram isn't it? Kept hinting that she knew Dr Hewson and Nurse Rainer were lovers. No real evidence, of course, just spite and self-importance. I may have my ideas about those two, but I'd want more evidence than I heard tonight before I started thinking about conspiracy to murder. Mrs Hollis's story wasn't even particularly relevant to Maggie Hewson's death. She said that the night Grace Willison died she glimpsed Mrs Hewson passing along the dormitory corridor wearing a brown habit and with the hood drawn over her face. Apparently Mrs Hollis is in the habit of slipping out of bed at night and propelling herself round the room on her pillow. She says that it's a form of exercise, that she's trying to be more mobile and independent. Anyway on the night in question, she managed to get her door ajar – no doubt with the idea of taking a skid down the passage – and saw this cloaked figure. She thought afterwards that it must have been Maggie Hewson. Anyone with proper business – any of the staff – would have worn the hood down.'

'If they were about their proper business. When exactly was this?'

'A little after midnight she says. She closed the door again and got back into bed with some difficulty. She heard and saw nothing more.'

Dalgliesh said consideringly:

'I'm surprised from the little I've seen of her that she could manage to get back to bed unaided. Getting out is one thing, pulling herself back would be a great deal more difficult. Hardly worth the exercise, I should have thought.'

There was a short silence. Then Inspector Daniel asked, his black eyes full on Dalgliesh's face:

'Why did Dr Hewson refer that death to the coroner, Sir? If he had doubts about his medical diagnosis, why not ask the hospital pathologist, or one of his local chums to open her up for him?'

'Because I forced his hand and gave him no choice. He couldn't refuse to refer it without looking suspicious. And I don't think he has any local chums. He's not on those terms with his medical colleagues. How did you hear about it?'

'From Hewson. After hearing the girl's story I had another word with him. But Miss Willison's death was apparently straightforward.'

'Oh, yes. Just like this suicide. Just like Father Baddeley's death. All apparently straightforward. She died of cancer of the stomach. But this business tonight. Did you find out anything about the rope?'

'I forgot to mention that, Mr Dalgliesh. It's the rope which has clinched it. Nurse Rainer saw Mrs Hewson taking it from the business room at about half past eleven this morning. Nurse Rainer had been left behind to look after that bed-bound patient – Georgie Allan isn't it? – but everyone else was at Miss Willison's funeral. She was writing up the patient's medical record and needed a fresh sheet. All the stationery is kept in a filing cabinet in the business room. It's expensive and Mr Anstey doesn't like to issue it wholesale. He's afraid that people will use it as scribbling pads. When she reached the hall Nurse Rainer saw Mrs Hewson slipping out of the business room with the rope over her arm.'

'What explanation did Maggie give?'

'According to Nurse Rainer all she said was: "Don't worry, I'm not going to fray it. Quite the reverse. You'll get it back practically as good as new, if not from me." '

Dalgliesh said:

'Helen Rainer wasn't in any particular hurry to provide that information when we first found the body. But, assuming she isn't lying, it certainly completes your case.'

'I don't think she is lying, Mr Dalgliesh. But I did look at the boy's medical record. Nurse Rainer began a fresh sheet this afternoon. And there seems little doubt that the rope was hanging in the business room when Mr Anstey and Sister Moxon left for the funeral. Who else could have taken it? They were all at the funeral except Nurse Rainer, that very sick boy and Mrs Hammitt.'

Dalgliesh said:

'I'd forgotten about Mrs Hammitt. I noticed that almost everyone from Toynton Grange was at the cemetery. It didn't occur to me that she wasn't.'

'She says she disapproves of funerals. People ought to be cremated in what she calls decent privacy. She says that she spent the morning cleaning her gas stove. For what it's worth, the stove has certainly been cleaned.'

'And this evening?'

'Meditating at Toynton Grange with the others. They were all supposed to be separate and alone. Mr Anstey placed the small interviewing room at her disposal. According to Mrs Hammitt, she never left it until her brother rang the bell to summon them together just before four o'clock. Mr Court telephoned shortly afterwards. Mrs Hewson died sometime during the meditation hour, no doubt about that. And the police surgeon reckons nearer four than three.'

Was Millicent strong enough, Dalgliesh wondered, to have strung up Maggie's heavy body? Probably, with the help of the kitchen stool. And the strangling itself would have been easy enough once Maggie was drunk. A silent movement behind her chair, the noose dropped by gloved hands over the drooping head, the sudden upward jerk as the rope bit into the flesh. Any one of them could have done it, could have crept out unnoticed into the concealing mist towards the smudge of light marking the Hewson cottage. Helen Rainer was the slightest; but Helen was a nurse, skilful in lifting heavy bodies. And Helen Rainer might not have been alone. He heard Daniel speaking:

'We'll get that stuff in the syringe analysed and we had better ask the lab to take a look at the whisky. But those two little jobs shouldn't hold up the inquest. Mr Anstey is anxious to get that over as soon as possible so that it doesn't interfere with the pilgrimage to Lourdes on the twenty-third. None of them seems worried about the funeral. That can wait until they get back. I don't see why they shouldn't get away, if the lab can do the analysis quickly. And we know that the whisky's all right; Court still seems healthy enough. I was wondering, Mr Dalgliesh, just why he took that swig. Incidentally, he'd given her the whisky; half a dozen bottles for her birthday on 11th September. A generous gentleman.'

Dalgliesh said:

'I thought he might have been feeding her whisky. But I don't think Court took that drink to save the forensic boys trouble. He needed it.'

Daniel gazed consideringly into his half-empty glass:

'Court's been pressing his theory that she never intended killing herself, that the whole set-up was play-acting, a desperate plea for attention. She might well have chosen that moment. They were all at the Grange making an important decision which affected her future, and yet she'd been excluded. He could be right; the jury may buy it. But it won't provide much consolation for the husband.'

Hewson, thought Dalgliesh, might be looking elsewhere for consolation. He said:

'It seems out of character. I can see her making some dramatic *démarche* if only to relieve the monotony. What I can't see is her wanting to stay on at Toynton as a failed suicide, attracting the slightly pitying contempt that people feel for someone who can't even succeed in killing herself. My problem is that I find a genuine suicide attempt even less in character.'

Daniel said:

'Maybe she didn't expect to have to stay at Toynton. Maybe that was the idea, to convince her husband that she'd kill herself unless he found another job. I can't see many men taking that risk. But she did kill herself, Mr Dalgliesh, whether she intended to or not. This case rests on two bits of evidence: Nurse Rainer's story about the rope, and the suicide note. If Rainer convinces the jury, and the document examiner confirms that Mrs Hewson wrote that note, then I'll be taking no bets on the verdict. In character or not, you can't get away from the evidence.'

But there was other evidence, thought Dalgliesh, less strong but not uninteresting. He said:

'She looked as if she were going somewhere, or perhaps expecting a visitor. She'd recently had a bath, her pores were clogged with powder. Her face was made up and she'd painted her nails. And she wasn't dressed for a solitary evening at home.'

'So her husband said. I thought myself that it looked as if she'd dolled herself up. That could support the theory of a faked suicide attempt. If you're planning to be the centre of attraction you may as well dress for the show. There's no evidence that she did have a visitor, although it's true enough that no one would have seen him in the mist. I doubt whether he could have found his way once he'd left the road. And if she was planning to leave Toynton, then someone would have had to fetch her. The Hewsons have no car, Mr Anstey doesn't allow private transport; there's no bus today; and we've checked the car hire firms.'

'You've wasted no time.'

'A matter of a few telephone calls, Mr Dalgliesh. I like to get these details out of the way while they're in my mind.'

'I can't see Maggie sitting quietly at home while the rest of them settled her future. She was friendly with a solicitor in Wareham, Robert Loder. I suppose he wasn't calling for her?'

Daniel shifted his heavy weight forward and threw another plank of driftwood on the fire. The fire was burning sluggishly as if the chimney were blocked with mist. He said:

'The local boyfriend. You aren't the only one to suggest that, Mr Dalgliesh. I thought it as well to ring the gentleman's home and have a word. Mr Loder's in Poole General Hospital having his piles operated on. He was admitted yesterday and they gave him a week's notice. A nasty painful complaint. Hardly a comfortable time, you might say, to plan to run away with another man's wife.'

Dalgliesh asked:

'What about the one person at Toynton who did have his own car? Court?'

'It was an idea I had put to him, Mr Dalgliesh. I got a definite reply if not a very gentleman-like one. What it amounted to was that he'd do a great deal for dear Maggie but that self-preservation was the first law of nature and it just happens that his tastes don't run in that direction. Not that he was against the idea that she planned to leave Toynton. As a matter of fact, he suggested it, although I don't know how he thought it tied up with his previous view that Mrs Hewson faked a suicide attempt. Both theories can't be true.'

Dalgliesh asked:

'What was it that he found in her bag, a contraceptive?'

'Ah, you noticed that, did you? Yes, her Dutch cap. She wasn't on the pill seemingly. Court tried to be tactful about it, but as I told him, you can't be tactful about violent death. That's the one social catastrophe that the etiquette books can't help with. It's the strongest indication that she might have been planning to leave, that and her passport. They were both in the bag. You could say she was equipped for any eventuality.'

Dalgliesh said:

'She was equipped with the two items which she couldn't replace by a brief visit to the nearest chemist. I suppose you could argue that it's reasonable to keep the passport in her handbag. But the other?'

'Who's to know how long it was there. And women do keep things in odd places. No point in getting fanciful. And there's no reason to suppose that the two of them were set for a flit, she and Hewson. If you ask me he's as tied to Anstey and the Grange as any of the patients, poor devil. You know his story, I suppose?'

'Not really. I told you. I've taken good care not to become involved.'

'I had a sergeant like him once. The women couldn't leave him alone. It's that vulnerable, lost small boy look they have, I suppose. Name of Purkiss. Poor devil. He couldn't cope with the women and he couldn't cope without them. It did for his career. He runs a garage now, somewhere near Market Harborough, they tell me. And it's worse for Hewson. He doesn't even like his job. Forced into it, I gather, by one of those strong-minded mothers, a widow, determined to make her ewe lamb into a doctor. Appropriate enough, I suppose. It's the modern equivalent of the priesthood isn't it? He told me that the training wasn't so bad. He's got a phenomenal memory and can learn almost any facts. It's the responsibility he can't take. Well, there's not much of that at Toynton Grange. The patients are incurable and there's not much that they or anyone else expect him to do about it. Mr Anstey wrote to him and took him on, I gather, after he'd had his name removed from the Register by the G.M.C. He'd been having an affair with a patient, a girl of sixteen. There was a suggestion that it had started a year or so earlier, but he was lucky. The girl stuck to her story. He couldn't write prescriptions for dangerous drugs at Toynton Grange or sign death certificates, of course. Not until they restored his name to the Register six months ago. But they couldn't take away his medical knowledge and I've no doubt that Mr Anstey found him useful.'

'And cheap.'

'Well, there's that, of course. And now he doesn't want to leave. I suppose he might have killed his wife to stop her nagging him to go, but personally I don't believe it and neither will a jury. He's the sort of man who gets a woman to do his dirty work.'

'Helen Rainer?'

'That'd be daft, wouldn't it, Mr Dalgliesh? And where's the evidence?'

Dalgliesh wondered briefly whether to tell Daniel about the conversation between Maggie and her husband which he had overheard after the fire. But he put the thought from him. Hewson would either deny it or be able to explain it. There were probably a dozen petty secrets in a place like Toynton Grange. Daniel would feel bound to question him, of course. But he would see it as an irritating duty forced on him by an over-suspicious and officious intruder from the Met. determined to twist plain facts into a tangle of complicated conjecture. And what possible difference could it make? Daniel was right. If Helen stuck to her story about seeing Maggie collect the rope; if the document examiner confirmed that Maggie had written the suicide note; then the case was closed. He knew now what the inquest verdict would be, just as he had known that the post-mortem on Grace Willison would reveal nothing suspicious. Once again he saw himself, as if in a nightmare, watching impotently as the bizarre charabanc of facts and conjecture hurtled on its predestined course. He couldn't stop it because he had forgotten how. His illness seemed to have sapped his intelligence as well as his will.

The spar of driftwood, charred now into a blackened spear, jewelled with sparks, slowly toppled and died. Dalgliesh was aware that the room was very cold and that he was hungry. Perhaps because of the occluding mist smudging the twilight hour between day and night, the evening seemed to have lasted for ever. He wondered whether he ought to offer Daniel a meal. Presumably the man could eat an omelette. But even the effort of cooking seemed beyond him.

Suddenly the problem solved itself. Daniel got slowly to his feet and reached for his coat. He said:

'Thank you for the whisky, Mr Dalgliesh. And now I'd best be on my way. I'll see you at the inquest, of course. It'll mean your staying on here. But we'll get on with the case as quickly as we can.'

They shook hands. Dalgliesh almost winced at the grip. At the doorway Daniel paused, tugging on his coat.

'I saw Dr Hewson alone in that small interviewing room which they tell me Father Baddeley used to use. And if you ask me, he'd have been better off with a priest. No difficulty in getting him to talk. Trouble was to stop him. And then he began crying and it all came out. How could he go on living without her? He'd never stopped loving her, longing for her. Funny, the more they're feeling, the less sincere they sound. But you'll have noticed that, of course. And then he looked up at me, his face blubbered with tears and said:

' "She didn't lie for me because she cared. It was only a game to her. She never pretended to love me. It was just that she thought the G.M.C. committee were a set of pompous old bores who despised her and she wasn't going to give them the satisfaction of seeing me go to prison. And so she lied."

'Do you know, Mr Dalgliesh, it was only then that I realized that he wasn't speaking about his wife. He wasn't even thinking of her. Or of Nurse Rainer for that matter. Poor devil! Ah, well, it's an odd job we have, you and I.'

He shook hands again as if he had already forgotten that last crushing grip, and with a final keen-eyed survey of the sitting-room as if to reassure himself that everything was still in place, slipped out into the mist.

III

In the business room Dot Moxon stood with Anstey at the window and looked out of the curtain of misty darkness. She said bitterly:

'The Trust won't want either of us, you realize that? They may name the home after you, but they won't let you stay on as Warden, and they'll get rid of me.'

He laid his hand on her shoulder. She wondered how she could ever have longed for that touch or been comforted by it. He said with the controlled patience of a parent comforting a wilfully obtuse child:

'They've given me an undertaking. No one's job will be lost. And everyone will get a rise. From now on you'll all be paid National Health Service rates. And they have a contributory pension scheme, that's a big advantage. I've never been able to provide that.'

'And what about Albert Philby? You're not telling me that they've promised to keep Albert on, an established, respectable national charity like the Ridgewell Trust.'

'Philby does present a problem. But he'll be dealt with sympathetically.'

'Dealt with sympathetically! We all know what that means. That's what they said to me in my last job, before they forced me out! And this is his home! He trusts us. We've taught him to trust us! And we have a responsibility for him.'

'Not any longer, Dot.'

'So we betray Albert and exchange what you've tried to build up here for Health Service rates of pay and a pension scheme! And my position? Oh, they won't sack me, I know that. But it won't be the same. They'll make Helen matron. She knows that too. Why else did she vote for the take-over?'

He said quietly:

'Because she knew that Maggie was dead.'

Dot laughed bitterly: 'It's worked out very nicely for her hasn't it? For both of them.'

He said: 'Dot dear, you and I have to accept that we cannot always choose the way in which we are called to serve.'

She wondered how she had never noticed it before, that irritating note of unctuous reproof in his voice. She turned abruptly away. The hand, thus rejected, slipped heavily from her shoulders. She remembered suddenly what he reminded her of: the sugar Father Christmas on her first Christmas tree, so desirable, so passionately desired. And you bit into nothingness; a trace of sweetness on the tongue and then an empty cavity grained with white sand.

IV

Ursula Hollis and Jennie Pegram sat together in Jennie's room, the two wheelchairs side by side in front of the dressing table. Ursula was leaning across and brushing Jennie's hair. She wasn't sure how she came to be here, so oddly employed. Jennie had never asked her before. But tonight, waiting for Helen to put them to bed, Helen, who had never before been so late, it was comforting not to be alone with her thoughts, comforting even to watch the corn-gold hair rise with each brush stroke, to fall slowly, a delicate shining mist, over the hunched shoulders. The two women found themselves whispering, cosily, like conspiring schoolgirls. Ursula said:

'What do you think will happen now?'

'To Toynton Grange? The Trust will take over and Wilfred will go, I expect. I don't mind. At least there'll be more patients. It's boring here now with so few of us. And Wilfred told me that they plan to build a sun-lounge out on the cliff. I'll like that. And we're bound to get more treats, trips and so on. We haven't had many recently. As a matter of fact, I was thinking of leaving. They keep writing from my old hospital wanting me back.'

Ursula knew that they hadn't written. But it didn't matter. She contributed her own morsel of fantasy.

'So was I. Steve is keen for me to move nearer London so that he can visit. Just until he's found us a more suitable flat of course.'

'Well, the Ridgewell Trust have a home in London haven't they? You could be transferred there.'

How strange that Helen hadn't told her that! Ursula whispered:

'It's odd that Helen voted for the take-over. I thought she wanted Wilfred to sell out.'

'Probably she did until she knew that Maggie was dead. Now that she's got rid of Maggie, I suppose she feels she may as well stay on. I mean the field's clear now, isn't it?

Got rid of Maggie. But surely no one had got rid of Maggie but Maggie herself? And Helen couldn't have known that Maggie was going to die. Only six days ago she had been urging Ursula to vote for the sell-out. She couldn't have known then. Even at the preliminary family council, before they all parted for their meditation hour, she made it plain where her interests lay. And then during that meditation hour, she had changed her mind. No, Helen couldn't have known that Maggie was going to die. Ursula found the thought comforting. Everything was going to be all right. She had told Inspector Daniel about the hooded figure she had seen on the night of Grace's death, not the whole truth, of course, but enough to lift a weight of nagging and irrational worry from her mind. He hadn't thought it important. She had sensed that from the way he had listened, his few brief questions. And he was right, of course. It wasn't important. She wondered now how she could ever have lain awake fretted by inexplicable anxieties, haunted by images of evil and death, cloaked and hooded, stalking the silent corridors. And it must have been Maggie. With the news of Maggie's death she had suddenly become sure of it. It was difficult to know why, except that the figure had looked at once theatrical and surreptitious, so much a stranger, wearing the monk's robe with none of the slovenly familiarity of the Toynton Grange staff. But she had told the Inspector about it. There was no need to worry any more. Everything was going to be all right. Toynton Grange wouldn't close down after all. But it didn't matter. She would get a transfer to the London home, perhaps on exchange. Someone there was sure to want to come to the seaside. She heard Jennie's high childish voice.

'I'll let you into a secret about Maggie if you swear not to tell. Swear.'

'I swear.'

'She wrote poison pen letters. She sent one to me.'

Ursula's heart seemed to lurch. She said quickly:

'How do you know?'

'Because mine was typed on Grace Willison's typewriter and I actually saw Maggie typing it the evening before. The office door was ajar. She didn't know that I was watching.'

'What did she say?'

'It was all about a man who is in love with me. One of the television producers actually. He wanted to divorce his wife and take me away with him. It made a great deal of fuss and jealousy at the hospital at the time. That's partly why I had to leave. As a matter of fact I could still go to him if I chose.'

'But how did Maggie know?'

'She was a nurse, wasn't she? I think she knew one of the staff nurses at my old hospital. Maggie was clever at finding out things. I think she knew something about Victor Holroyd, too, but she didn't say what. I'm glad that she's dead. And if you had one of the letters, then you won't have any more now. Maggie's dead and the letters will stop. Brush a little harder and to the right, Ursula. That's lovely, lovely. We ought to be friends, you and me. When the new patients start arriving we must stick together. That's if I decide to stay, of course.'

Brush poised in mid-air, Ursula saw in the mirror the reflection of Jennie's sly, self-satisfied smile.

V

Shortly after ten o'clock, his supper eaten, Dalgliesh walked out into the night. The mist had lifted as mysteriously as it had appeared and the cool air, smelling of rain-washed grass, moved gently against his hot face. Standing in the absolute silence he could just hear the sibilant whisper of the sea.

A torch light, erratic as a will-o'-the-wisp, was weaving towards him from the direction of the Grange. Out of the darkness a bulky shadow emerged and took form. Millicent Hammitt had returned home. At the door of Faith Cottage she paused and called out to him.

'Goodnight, Commander. Your friends have left, then?'

Her voice was high, almost belligerent.

'The inspector has gone, yes.'

'You may have noticed that I didn't join the rush to participate in Maggie's ill-considered charade. I have no taste for these excitements. Eric has decided to sleep tonight at Toynton Grange. Much the best thing for him, no doubt. But, as I understand that the police have taken away the body, he needn't pretend to over-sensitivity. Incidentally, we've voted for the Ridgewell Trust take-over. What with one thing and another, quite an eventful evening.'

She turned to open the door. Then paused and called out again. 'They tell me that her nails were painted red.'

'Yes, Mrs Hammitt.'

'Her toe nails, too.'

He didn't reply. She said with sudden anger:

'Extraordinary woman!'

He heard the door close. A second later her light shone through the curtains. He went inside. Almost too weary to climb the stairs to bed, he stretched himself in Father Baddeley's chair staring into the dead fire. As he watched, the white ash shifted gently, a blackened spar of driftwood glowed momentarily into life, and he heard for the first time that night the familiar and comforting moan of the wind in the chimney. And then there followed another familiar sound. Faintly through the wall came a merry syncopated jingle. Millicent Hammitt had turned on the television.

EIGHT

The Black Tower

I

Next day Dalgliesh walked up to the Grange to explain to Wilfred that he must now stay on at Hope Cottage until after the inquest, and to pay his token rent. He found Wilfred alone in the business room. Surprisingly, there was no sign of Dot Moxon. Wilfred was studying a map of France spread out on the desk. A bundle of passports in a rubber band weighed down one corner. He seemed hardly to hear what his guest said. He replied, 'The inquest. Yes, of course,' as if it were a forgotten luncheon engagement, then bent again over the map. He made no mention of Maggie's death and Dalgliesh's formal condolences were coldly received as if they were in poor taste. It was as if by divesting himself of Toynton Grange, he had detached himself from further responsibility, even from concern. Now nothing remained but his twin obsessions, his miracle and the pilgrimage to Lourdes.

Inspector Daniel and the forensic laboratory worked quickly. The inquest was held exactly one week after Maggie's death, a week in which the inhabitants of Toynton Grange seemed as resolutely determined to keep out of Dalgliesh's way as he was to avoid them. No one, not even Julius, showed any inclination to chat over Maggie's death. It was as if they saw him now merely as a police officer, an unwelcome intruder of uncertain allegiance, a potential spy. He drove away from Toynton Head early every morning and returned late each night to darkness and silence. Neither the police activities nor the life at Toynton Grange touched him. He continued his daily, compulsive exploration of Dorset like a prisoner on licence and looked forward to the inquest as the final day of release.

It came at last. None of the patients from Toynton Grange attended except Henry Carwardine, surprisingly since he was not required to give evidence. As the company stood in whispering reverential groups outside the courthouse in the usual disorganized hiatus which follows attendance at the more sombre public rituals, he wheeled his chair with vigorous thrusts of the arms to where Dalgliesh stood. He looked and sounded euphoric.

'I realize that these ceremonial tidyings-up of legal loose ends aren't exactly a novelty to you as they are to me. But this one wasn't without interest, I thought. Less fascinating technically and forensically than Holroyd's, but with more human interest.'

'You sound like a connoisseur of inquests.'

'If we go on like this at Toynton Grange I soon shall be. Helen Rainer was the star turn today, I thought. That extraordinary suit and hat in which she chose to appear were, I take it, the dress uniform of a state registered nurse. A very wise choice. Hair up; the merest trace of make-up; a general air of dedicated professionalism. "Mrs Hewson may have believed that there was a relationship between me and her husband. She had too much free time to brood. Naturally Dr Hewson and I have to work closely together. I have a high opinion of his kindness and competence but there has never been anything improper between us. Dr Hewson was devoted to his wife." Nothing improper! I never believed that people actually used that expression.'

Dalgliesh said:

'At inquests they do. Did the jury believe her, do you suppose?'

'Oh, I think so, don't you? Difficult to imagine our lady with the lamp garbed as she was this afternoon in grey samite – gaberdine anyway – mystic, wonderful, romping between the sheets. She was wise, I think, to admit that she and Hewson had spent the meditation hour together in her room. But that, as she explained, was because both had already come to their decision and couldn't afford to waste sixty minutes mulling it over when they had so much to discuss professionally together.'

'They had to choose between their alibi, for what it was worth, and the risk to reputation. On the whole they chose wisely.'

Henry swung round his wheelchair with aggressive exuberance.

'It rather foxed the honest jurymen of Dorset, though. You could see the way their minds were working. If they aren't lovers why were they closeted together? But if they were together, then

Hewson couldn't have killed his wife. But unless they were lovers he wouldn't have had a motive for murdering his wife. But if he had such a motive, why admit that they were together? Obviously to give him an alibi. But he wouldn't need an alibi if he hadn't the usual motive. And if he had such a motive, then he and the girl would have been together. Very puzzling.'

Mildly amused, Dalgliesh asked:

'What did you think about Hewson's performance?'

'He did well too. Not quite the professional competence and detachment of yourself, my dear Commander, but quiet, sincere, some natural grief bravely under control. Sensible of him to admit that Maggie desperately wanted him to leave Toynton Grange but that he felt an obligation to Wilfred, "who took me on when I wasn't finding it easy to get a job". No mention, of course, of being struck off the Medical Register and no one tactless enough to bring it up.'

Dalgliesh said:

'And no one tactless enough to suggest that he and Helen may have been lying about their relationship.'

'What else do you expect? What people know and what they can legally prove – or care to state in a court of law – are two very different things. Besides, we must at all costs protect dear Wilfred from the contamination of truth. No, I thought it went very well. Suicide while the balance of mind, etc., etc. Poor Maggie! Stigmatized as a selfish, pleasure-seeking slut addicted to the bottle, out of sympathy with her husband's dedication to his noble profession and not even competent to make a comfortable home for him. Court's suggestion that it might have been an accidental death, play-acting which got out of hand, received no credence from the jury, did it? They took the view that a woman who drank the best part of a bottle of whisky, borrowed a rope and wrote a farewell letter was carrying play-acting a little far and did Maggie the compliment of believing that she intended what she did. I thought that the forensic scientist was extraordinarily definite in his opinion, given the basically subjective nature of document examination. There seems no doubt that Maggie did write the suicide note.'

'The first four lines of it, which were all he felt competent to pronounce on. What did you think of the verdict?'

'Oh, I agree with Julius. She was planning to be cut down just in time amidst general hullabaloo. But with the best part of a bottle of whisky inside her she wasn't even competent to stage-manage her own resurrection. Incidentally, Julius gave me a graphic description of the drama in Charity Cottage, including Helen's impressive debut in the role of Lady Macbeth;

> "Give me the syringe. The sleeping and the dead,
> Are but as pictures; 'tis the eye of childhood
> That fears a painted devil." '

There was no expression on Dalgliesh's face or in his voice. He said:

'How entertaining for you both. It's a pity Court wasn't as detached at the time. He might have made himself useful instead of behaving like a hysterical queer.'

Henry smiled, gratified to have provoked the response he wanted. He said:

'So you don't like him? Neither, I suspect, did your friend in holy orders.'

Dalgliesh spoke on impulse:

'I know that this is nothing to do with me, but isn't it time that you got away from Toynton Grange?'

'Got away? To where do you suggest?'

'There must be other places.'

'The world is full of places. But what do you suppose I could do, or be, or hope for in any of them? As a matter of fact, I did once plan to leave. It was a particularly foolish dream. No, I shall stay on at the Grange. The Ridgewell Trust have the professionalism and experience which Anstey lacks. I could do worse. Besides, Wilfred himself is to stay; and I still have a debt to pay Wilfred. In the meantime, this formality over, we can all relax and set off tomorrow to Lourdes in peace. You ought to come with us, Dalgliesh. You've hung around here so long that I suspect you rather enjoy our company. Besides, I don't think your convalescence has really done you a great deal of good. Why not come to Lourdes and see what the odour of incense and a change of scene can do for you?'

The Toynton Grange bus, driven by Philby, had drawn level with them now and the back ramp was being lowered. Dalgliesh watched in silence as Eric and Helen detached themselves from Wilfred, laid their hands simultaneously on the handlebars and wheeled Henry briskly into the bus. The ramp was raised, Wilfred took his seat in the front beside Philby, and the Toynton Grange bus disappeared from view.

Colonel Ridgewell and the trustees arrived after lunch. Dalgliesh watched as the car drew up and the sombre-suited party disappeared into the house. Later they emerged and walked with Wilfred over the headland towards the sea. Dalgliesh was a little surprised to see that Eric and Helen were with them but not Dorothy Moxon. He could see the Colonel's grey hair lifting in the breeze as he paused to swing his walking stick in wide explanatory sweeps or stood suddenly still conferring with the little group who quickly closed round him. No doubt, thought Dalgliesh, they would want to inspect the cottages. Well, Hope Cottage was ready for them. The bookshelves were empty and dusted, the packing cases corded and labelled for the carrier, his suitcase packed except for the few things he needed on this his last night. But he had no wish to get involved in introductions or to stand making small talk.

When the party finally turned back and made their way towards Charity Cottage, he got into his car and drove off, with no clear direction in mind, no particular aim, no intention except to keep driving long into the night.

II

The next morning was airless and sultry, inducing headache, the sky a tent of stained calico ponderous with unspilt rain. The pilgrimage party was due to set out at nine o'clock and at half past eight Millicent Hammitt barged in, without a preliminary knock, to say goodbye. She was wearing a blue-grey tweed suit badly seated, with a short double-breasted jacket; a blouse in a harsher and discordant blue adorned with a garish brooch at the neck; brogues; and a grey felt hat pulled down to cover the ears. She dumped a bulging airline bag and her shoulder bag at her feet, drew on a pair of fawn cotton gloves and held out her hand. Dalgliesh put down his coffee cup. His right hand was grasped in a crushing grip.

'Goodbye then, Commander. Odd, but I've never really got used to using your Christian name. You'll be gone, I understand, by the time we return?'

'I plan to drive back to London later this morning.'

'I hope you've enjoyed your stay. At least it has been eventful. One suicide, one natural death and the end of Toynton Grange as an independent institution. You can't have been bored.'

'And one attempted murder.'

'Wilfred in the burning tower? It sounds like the title of an *avant-garde* play. I've always had my doubts about that particular excitement. If you ask me, Wilfred set it up himself to justify handing over his responsibilities. No doubt that explanation occurred to you.'

'Several explanations occurred to me but none of them made much sense.'

'Little at Toynton Grange ever does. Well, the old order changeth yielding place to new and God fulfils Himself in many ways. We must hope that He will.'

Dalgliesh asked if Millicent had any plans.

'I shall stay on in the cottage. Wilfred's agreement with the Trust stipulates that I may live there for life, and I assure you, I've every intention of dying at my own convenience. It won't be the same, of course, knowing that the place belongs to strangers.'

Dalgliesh asked:

'How does your brother feel about the hand-over?'

'Relieved. Well, it's what he schemed for isn't it? He doesn't know what he's let himself in for, of course. Incidentally, he hasn't given this cottage to the Trust. This will continue to belong to him and he plans to move in after the place has been converted into something more civilized and comfortable. He's also offered to help at Toynton Grange in any capacity in which the Trust feel he can be of use. If he imagines that they'll let him stay on as Warden he's in for a shock. They've got their own plans for the Grange and I doubt whether they include Wilfred, even if they have agreed to pander to his vanity by naming the home after him. I suppose Wilfred imagines that everyone will defer to him as their benefactor and the original owner. I can assure you they won't. Now that the deed of gift – or whatever it is – is signed and the Trust are the legal owners, Wilfred counts for as little as Philby, less probably. It's his own fault. He should have sold out completely.'

'Wouldn't that have broken faith?'

'Superstitious nonsense! If Wilfred wanted to dress up in monk's garb and behave like a medieval abbot he should have applied for entry to a monastery. An Anglican one would have been perfectly respectable. The twice-yearly pilgrimage will go on, of course. That's one of Wilfred's stipulations. It's a pity you aren't coming with us, Commander. We stay at an agreeable little pension, really quite cheap and the food is excellent; and Lourdes is a cheerful little place. Quite an atmosphere. I don't say I wouldn't have preferred Wilfred to have had his miracle in Cannes, but it might have been worse. He could have got cured at Blackpool.'

She paused at the door to turn and say:

'I expect the bus will stop here so that the others can take leave of you.' She made it sound as if they would be conferring a privilege. Dalgliesh said that he would walk up with her and say goodbye at Toynton Grange. He had discovered one of Henry Carwardine's books on Father Baddeley's shelf and wanted to return it. There was also his bed linen to take back and some left-over tins of food which Toynton Grange could probably use.

'I'll take the tins later. Just leave them here. And you can return the linen any time. The Grange is never locked. Philby will be back later anyway. He only drives us to the port and sees us on the boat and then comes back to caretake and feed Jeoffrey and, of course, the hens. They're rather missing Grace's help with the hens although no one thought that she did anything very useful when she was alive. And it's not only the hens. They can't lay their hands on her list of the Friends. Actually, Wilfred wanted Dennis to stay at home this time. He's got one of his migraines and looks like death. But no one can make Dennis miss a pilgrimage.'

Dalgliesh walked up to the Grange with her. The bus was

drawn up outside the front door and the patients were already loaded. The pathetically depleted party had a bizarre air of slightly spurious joviality. Dalgliesh's first impression from their varied garb was that they proposed to pursue quite different and unrelated activities. Henry Carwardine, in a belted tweed coat and deerstalker hat, looked like an Edwardian gentleman on his way to the grouse moors. Philby, incongruously formal in a dark suit with high collar and black tie, was an undertaker's man loading a hearse. Ursula Hollis had dressed like a Pakistani immigrant in full fig whose only concession to the English climate was an ill-cut jacket in mock fur. Jennie Pegram, wearing a long blue headscarf, had apparently made an attempt to impersonate Saint Bernadette. Helen Rainer, dressed as she had been at the inquest, was a prison matron in charge of a group of unpredictable delinquents. She had already taken her seat at the head of Georgie Allan's stretcher. The boy's eyes were feverishly bright and Dalgliesh could hear his high frenetic chatter. He was wearing a blue and white striped woollen scarf and clutching an immense teddy bear, its neck adorned with pale-blue ribbon and what, to Dalgliesh's astounded eyes, looked like a pilgrimage medal. The party could have been an oddly assorted party of team supporters on their way to a football match, but one, Dalgliesh thought, that hardly expected the home side to win.

Wilfred was gently fussing over the remainder of the luggage. He, Eric Hewson and Dennis Lerner were wearing their monk's habits. Dennis looked desperately ill, his face was taut with pain and his eyes half closed as if even the dull morning light were intolerable. Dalgliesh heard Eric whisper to him:

'For God's sake, Dennis, give up and stay at home! With two wheelchairs less we can perfectly well manage.'

Lerner's high voice held a tinge of hysteria.

'I'll be all right. You know it never lasts more than twenty-four hours. For God's sake leave me alone!'

At last the medical paraphernalia, decently shrouded, was loaded, the ramp was raised, the rear door finally slammed and they were off. Dalgliesh waved in response to the frantically signalling hands and watched as the brightly painted bus lurched slowly over the headland looking, as it receded, as vulnerable and insubstantial as a child's toy. He was surprised, and a little saddened, that he could feel such pity and regret for people with whom he had taken such care not to become involved. He remained watching until the bus bumped slowly up the slope of the valley and finally tipped over the headland out of sight.

Now the headland was deserted, Toynton Grange and its cottages stood unlit and unpeopled under the heavy sky. It had grown darker in the last half-hour. There would be a storm before midday. Already his head ached with the premonition of thunder. The headland lay in the sinister anticipatory calm of a chosen battlefield. He could just hear the thudding of the sea, less a noise than a vibration on the dense air like the sullen menace of distant guns.

Restless and perversely reluctant to leave now that he was at last free to go, he walked up to the gate to collect his paper and any letters. The bus had obviously stopped for the Toynton Grange post and there was nothing in the box but the day's copy of *The Times*, an official-looking buff envelope for Julius Court and a square white one addressed to Father Baddeley. Tucking the newspaper under his arm he split open the stout linen-backed envelope and began to walk back, reading on his way. The letter was written in a firm, strong masculine hand; the printed address was a Midlands deanery. The writer was sorry not to have replied earlier to Father Baddeley's letter but it had been posted on to him in Italy, where he had taken a locum post for the summer. At the end of the conventional inquiries, the methodical recording of family and diocesan concerns, the perfunctory and predictable comments on public affairs, came the answer to the mystery of Father Baddeley's summons:

'I went at once to visit your young friend, Peter Bonnington, but he had, of course, been dead for some months. I am so very sorry. In the circumstances there seemed little point in inquiring whether he had been happy at the new home or had really wanted to move from Dorset. I hope that his friend at Toynton Grange managed to visit before he died. On your other problem, I don't think I can offer much guidance. Our experience in the diocese where, as you know, we are particularly interested in young offenders, is that providing residential care for ex-prisoners whether in a home or in the kind of self-supporting hostel you envisage requires a great deal more capital than you have available. You could probably buy a small house even at today's prices, but at least two experienced staff would be needed initially and you would have to support the venture until it became established. But there are a number of existing hostels and organizations who would very much welcome your help. There certainly couldn't be a better use for your money, if you have decided, as you obviously have, that it ought not now to go to Toynton Grange. I think that you were wise to call in your policeman friend. I'm sure that he will be best able to advise you.'

Dalgliesh almost laughed aloud. Here was an ironical and fitting end to failure. So that was how it had begun! There had been nothing sinister behind Father Baddeley's letter, no suspected crime, no conspiracy, no hidden homicide. He had simply wanted, poor, innocent, unworldly old man, some professional advice on how to buy, equip, staff and endow a hostel for young ex-offenders for the sum of £19,000. Given the present state of the property market and the level of inflation, what he had needed was a financial genius. But he had written to a policeman, probably the only one he knew. He had written to an expert in violent death. And why not? To Father Baddeley all policemen were fundamentally alike, experienced in crime and familiar with criminals, dedicated to prevention as well as detection. And I, thought Dalgliesh bitterly, have done neither. Father Baddeley had wanted professional advice, not advice on how to deal with evil. There he had his own infallible guidelines; there he was at home. For some reason, almost certainly connected with the transfer of that young, unknown patient, Peter Bonnington, he had become disenchanted with Toynton Grange. He had wanted advice on how else to use his money. How typical of my arrogance, thought Dalgliesh, to suppose that he wanted me for anything more.

He stuffed the letter into his jacket pocket and strolled on, letting his eyes glance over the folded newspaper. An advertisement stood out as clearly as if it had been marked, familiar words leaping to the eye.

'Toynton Grange. All our friends will wish to know that from the day of our return from the October Pilgrimage we shall be part of the larger family of the Ridgewell Trust. Please continue to remember us in your prayers at this time of change. As our list of Friends has unfortunately been mislaid will all those who wish to keep in touch please write to me urgently.

Wilfred Anstey, Warden.'

Of course! The list of Toynton Grange Friends, unaccountably mislaid since Grace Willison's death, those sixty-eight names which Grace had known by heart. He stood stock still under the menacing sky and read the notice again. Excitement gripped him, as violently physical as a twist of the stomach, a surge of the blood. He knew with immediate, with heart-lifting certainty that here at last was the end of the tangled skein. Pull gently on this one fact and the thread would begin, miraculously, to run free.

If Grace Willison had been murdered, as he obstinately believed, post-mortem result notwithstanding, it had been because of something she knew. But it must have been vital information, knowledge which she alone possessed. One did not kill merely to silence intriguing but evidentially useless suspicions about where Father Baddeley had been on the afternoon of Holroyd's death. He had been in the black tower. Dalgliesh knew it and could prove it; Grace Willison might have known it too. But the shredded match and Grace's testimony taken together could prove nothing. With Father Baddeley dead, the worst anyone could do would be to point out that it was strange that the old priest hadn't mentioned seeing Julius Court walking over the headland. And Dalgliesh could imagine Julius's contemptuous, sardonic smile. A sick, tired old man, sitting with his book at the eastern window. Who could say now that he hadn't slept the hours away before making his way back to Toynton Grange across the headland while, on the beach unseen below, the rescue party toiled with their burden? With Baddeley dead, his testimony silenced, no police force in the world would re-open the case on that second-hand evidence. The worst harm Grace could have done to herself might have been to betray that Dalgliesh wasn't just convalescing at Toynton, that he too was suspicious. That betrayal might just have tipped the scales for her from life to death. Then she might have become too dangerous to let live. Not because she knew that Father Baddeley had been in the black tower on the afternoon of 12th September, but because she possessed more specific, more valuable information. There was only one distribution list of the Friends of Toynton Grange and she could type it by heart. Julius had been present when she made that claim. The list could be torn up, burnt, utterly destroyed. But there was only one way in which those sixty-eight names could be erased from one frail woman's consciousness.

Dalgliesh quickened his pace. He found himself almost running down the headland. His headache seemed surprisingly to have lifted despite the lowering sky, the dense, storm-laden air. Change the metaphor, still trite but well proved. In this job it wasn't the last piece of jigsaw, the easiest of all, that was important. No, it was the neglected, uninteresting small segment which, slotted into place, suddenly made sense of so many other discarded pieces. Delusive colours, amorphous and ambiguous shapes came together as now to reveal the first recognizable outline of the finished picture.

And now, that piece in place, it was time to move the others speculatively over the board. For the present, forget proof, forget autopsy reports and the formal legal certainty of inquest verdicts; forget pride, the fear of ridicule, the reluctance to become involved. Get back to the first principle applied by any divisional detective constable when he smelt villainy on his patch. *Cui bono?* Who was living above his means? Who was in possession of more money than could reasonably be explained? There were two such people at Toynton Grange, and they were linked by Holroyd's death. Julius Court and Dennis Lerner. Julius, who had said that his answer to the black tower was money and the solace it could buy: beauty, leisure, friends, travel. How could a legacy of £30,000, however cleverly invested, enable him to live as he lived now? Julius, who helped Wilfred with the accounts and knew better than anyone how precarious were the finances of Toynton

Grange. Julius, who never went to Lourdes because it wasn't his scene, but who took care to be at his cottage to give a welcome home party for the pilgrims. Julius, who had been so untypically helpful when the pilgrimage bus had an accident, driving immediately to the scene, taking charge, buying a new and specially adapted bus so that the pilgrimages could be independent. Julius, who had provided the evidence to clear Dennis Lerner from any suspicion of Holroyd's murder.

Dot had accused Julius of using Toynton Grange. Dalgliesh recalled the scene at Grace's death bed; Dot's outburst, the man's first incredulous look, the quick reactive spite. But what if he were using the place for a more specific purpose than to gratify the insidious pleasure of patronage and easy generosity. Using Toynton Grange. Using the pilgrimage. Scheming to preserve them both because both were essential to him.

And what of Dennis Lerner? Dennis, who stayed on at Toynton Grange being paid less than the normal wages and who could yet support his mother in an expensive nursing home. Dennis, who resolutely overcame his fear so that he could go climbing with Julius. What better opportunity to meet and talk in absolute privacy without exciting suspicion? And how convenient that Wilfred had been frightened by the frayed rope into giving up rock climbing. Dennis, who could never bear to miss a pilgrimage even when, as today, he could hardly stand with migraine. Dennis, who was in charge of distributing the handcream and bath powder, who did most of the packing himself.

And it explained Father Baddeley's death. Dalgliesh had never been able to believe that his friend had been killed to prevent him disclosing that he hadn't glimpsed Julius walking over the headland on the afternoon of Holroyd's death. In the absence of clear proof that the old man hadn't, even momentarily, slumbered at his window, an allegation that Julius had lied, based on that evidence, would have been embarrassing perhaps but hardly dangerous. But what if Holroyd's death had been part of a larger and more sinister conspiracy? Then it might well have seemed necessary to snuff out – and how simply! – an obstinate, intelligent and ever-present watcher who could have been silenced in no other way once he smelt out the presence of evil. Father Baddeley had been taken to hospital before he learnt of Holroyd's death. But when he did learn, the significance of what he had so singularly failed to see must have struck him. He would have taken some action. And he had taken action. He made a telephone call to London, to a number he had needed to look up. He had made an appointment with his murderer.

Dalgliesh walked quickly on, past Hope Cottage and, almost without conscious decision, to Toynton Grange. The heavy front door opened to his touch. He smelt again the slightly intimidating spicy smell, masking more sinister, less agreeable odours. It was so dark that he had at once to switch on the light. The hall blazed like an empty film set. The black and white chequered floor was dazzling to the eye, a gigantic chess board, waiting for the pieces to move into place.

He paced through the empty rooms switching on the lights as he went. Room after room burst into brilliance. He found himself touching tables and chairs as he passed as if the wood were a talisman, looking intently around with the wary eye of a traveller returning unwelcomed to a deserted home. And his mind continued to shuffle the pieces of jigsaw. The attack on Anstey, the final and most dangerous attempt in the black tower. Anstey himself assumed that it was a final attempt to frighten him into selling out. But suppose it had had another purpose, not to close Toynton Grange but to make its future secure? And there was no other way, given Anstey's dwindling resources, than to pass it over to an organization financially sound and already well established. And Anstey hadn't sold out. Satisfied by the last, the most dangerous attack on him, that it couldn't have been the work of a patient and that his dream was still intact, he had given his inheritance away. Toynton Grange would go on. The pilgrimages would continue. Was that what someone – someone who knew only too well how financially precarious the home was – had always schemed for and intended?

Holroyd's visit to London. It was obvious that he had learnt something on that visit, had somehow acquired knowledge which had sent him back to Toynton Grange restless and elated. Was it also knowledge which had made him too dangerous to live? Dalgliesh had assumed that he had been told something by his solicitor, something perhaps about his own financial concerns or those of the Anstey family. But the visit to the solicitor hadn't been the main purpose of the trip. Holroyd and the Hewsons had also been to St Saviour's Hospital, the hospital where Anstey had been treated. And there, in addition to seeing the consultant in physical medicine with Holroyd, they had visited the medical records department. Hadn't Maggie said when she and Dalgliesh first met: 'He never went back to St Saviour's Hospital so that they could record the miraculous cure on his medical record. It would have been rather a joke if he had'? Suppose Holroyd had gained some knowledge in London but gained it, not directly, but through a confidence from Maggie Hewson given, perhaps, during one of their lonely periods together on the cliff edge. He remembered Maggie Hewson's words:

'I've said I won't tell. But if you keep on nagging about it I may change my mind.' And then: 'What if I did? He wasn't a fool you know. He could tell that something was up. And he's dead, dead, dead!' Father Baddeley was dead. But so was Holroyd. And so was Maggie. Was there any reason why Maggie had to die, and at that particular time?

But this was to go too fast. It was still all conjecture, all speculation. True, it was the only theory which fitted all the facts. But that wasn't evidence. He had still no proof that any of the deaths at Toynton Head had been murder. One fact was certain. If Maggie had been killed, then somehow she had been persuaded unwittingly to connive in her own death.

He became aware of a faint bubbling sound and detected the pungent smell of grease and hot soap from the direction of the kitchen. The kitchen itself stank like a Victorian workhouse laundry. A pail of teacloths was simmering on the old-fashioned gas stove. In the bustle of departure Dot Moxon must have forgotten to turn off the gas. The grey linen was billowing above the dark evil-smelling scum, the gas plate was splattered with sponges of dried foam. He turned off the gas and the teacloths subsided into their murky bath. With the extinguishing plop of the flame the silence was suddenly intensified; it was as if he had turned off the last evidence of human life.

He moved on into the activity room. The work tops were

shrouded with dust sheets. He could see the outline of the row of polythene bottles and the tins of bath powder waiting to be sieved and packed. Henry Carwardine's bust of Anstey still stood on its wooden plinth. It had been covered by a white plastic bag tied at the throat with what looked like one of Carwardine's old ties. The effect was peculiarly sinister; the nebulous features under the transparent shroud, the empty eye sockets, the sharp nose pointing the thin plastic made it as potent an image as a severed head.

In the office at the end of the annexe Grace Willison's desk still stood squarely under the north window, the typewriter under its grey cover. He pulled open the desk drawers. They were as he expected, immaculately tidy and ordered, banks of writing paper with Toynton Grange heading; envelopes carefully graded by size; typewriter ribbons; pencils; erasers; carbon paper still in its box; the sheets of perforated sticky labels on which she had typed the names and addresses of the Friends. Only the bound list of names was missing, the list of sixty-eight addresses; one of them in Marseilles. And here typed in that book and imprinted on Miss Willison's mind had been the vital link in the chain of greed and death.

The heroin had travelled far before it was finally packed at the bottom of a tin of bath powder in Toynton Grange. Dalgliesh could picture each stage of that journey as clearly as if he had travelled it himself. The fields of opium poppies on the high Anatolian plateau, the bulging pods oozing their milky sap. The secret rendering down of the raw opium into base morphine even before it left the hills. The long journey by mule train, rail, road or air towards Marseilles, one of the main distribution ports of the world. The refinement into pure heroin in one of a dozen clandestine laboratories. And then, the arranged rendezvous among the crowds at Lourdes, perhaps at Mass, the package slipped quickly into the waiting hand. He remembered wheeling Henry Carwardine across the headland on his first evening at Toynton, the thick rubber handgrips twisting beneath his hand. How simple to wrench one off, to insert a small plastic bag into the hollow strut, its drawstring taped to the metal. The whole operation would take less than a minute. And there would be plenty of opportunity. Philby didn't go on the pilgrimages. It would be Dennis Lerner who would have charge of the wheelchairs. What safer way for a drug smuggler to pass through customs than as the member of a recognized and respected pilgrimage. And the subsequent arrangements had been equally foolproof. The suppliers would need to know in advance the date of each pilgrimage, just as the customers and distributors would need to be told when the next consignment would come in. How more easily than by means of an innocuous newsletter from a respectable charity, a newsletter despatched so conscientiously and so innocently each quarter by Grace Willison.

And Julius's testimony in a French court, the alibi for a murderer. Had that been, not a reluctant yielding to blackmail, not a payment for services rendered, but payment in advance for services to come? Or had Julius, as Bill Moriarty's informant suggested, given Michonnet his alibi with no other motive than a perverse pleasure in thwarting the French police, gratuitously obliging a powerful family and causing his superiors the maximum of embarrassment? Possibly. He might neither have expected nor wanted any other reward. But if one were offered? If it were tactfully made known to him that a certain commodity could be supplied in strictly limited quantities if he could find a way to smuggle it into England? Would he later have been able to resist the temptation of Toynton Grange and its six-monthly pilgrimage?

And it was so easy, so simple, so foolproof. And so incredibly profitable. What was illegal heroin fetching now? Something like £4,000 an ounce. Julius had no need to deal in bulk or complicate his distribution arrangements beyond the one or two trusted agents to make himself secure for life. Ten ounces brought in each time would buy all the leisure and beauty that any man could desire. And with the Ridgewell Trust take-over the future was secure. Dennis Lerner would keep his job. The pilgrimages would continue. There would be other homes open to his exploitation, other pilgrimages. And Lerner was completely in his power. Even if the newsletter was discontinued and the home no longer needed to pack and sell its handcream and powder, the heroin would still come in. The arrangements for notification and distribution were a minor matter of logistics compared with the fundamental problem of getting the drug safely, reliably and regularly through the port.

There was as yet no proof. But with luck, and if he were right, there would be in three days' time. He could telephone the local police now and safely leave it to them to contact the central drug control branch. Better still, he could telephone Inspector Daniel and arrange to call in to see him on his way back to London. Secrecy was essential. There must be no risk of suspicion. It would take only one telephone call to Lourdes to cancel this consignment and leave him again with nothing but a hotchpotch of half-formulated suspicions, coincidences, unsubstantiated allegations.

The nearest telephone, he remembered, was in the dining-room. It had an external line, and he saw that this had been switched through to the exchange But when he lifted the receiver, the line was dead. He felt the usual momentary irritation that an instrument, taken for granted, should be reduced to a ridiculous and useless lump of plastic and metal, and reflected that a house with a dead telephone seemed always so much more isolated than one with no telephone at all. It was interesting, perhaps even significant, that the line was silent. But it didn't matter. He would get on his way and hope to find Inspector Daniel at police headquarters. At this stage when his theory was still little more than conjecture he was reluctant to talk to anyone else. He replaced the receiver. A voice from the doorway said:

'Having difficulty, Commander?'

Julius Court must have stepped through the house as delicately as a cat. He stood now, one shoulder resting lightly against the door post, both hands deep in his jacket pockets. The assumption of ease was deceptive. His body, poised on the balls of his feet as if to spring, was rigid with tension. The face above the high rolled collar of his sweater was as skeletal and defined as a carving, the muscles taut under the flushed skin. His eyes unblinking, unnaturally bright, were fixed on Dalgliesh with the speculative intentness of a gambler watching the spinning balls.

Dalgliesh said calmly:

'It's out of order apparently. It doesn't matter. My housekeeper will expect me when she sees me.'

'Do you usually roam about other people's houses to make your private calls? The main telephone is in the business room. Didn't you know?'

'I doubt whether I should have been any luckier.'

They looked at each other, silent in the greater silence. Across the length of the room Dalgliesh could recognize and follow the process of his adversary's thought as plainly as if it were registering visibly on a graph, the black needle tracing the pattern of decision. There was no struggle. It was the simple weighing of probabilities.

When Julius at last drew his hand slowly out of his pocket it was almost with relief that Dalgliesh saw the muzzle of the Luger. The die was cast. Now there was no going back, no more pretence, no more uncertainty.

Julius said quietly:

'Don't move, I'm an excellent shot. Sit down at the table. Hands on the top. Now, tell me how you found me out. I'm assuming that you have found me out. If not, then I've miscalculated. You will die and I shall be put to a great deal of trouble and inconvenience and we'll both be aggrieved to know that it wasn't after all necessary.'

With his left hand Dalgliesh took Father Baddeley's letter from his jacket pocket and slid it across the table.

'This will interest you. It came this morning addressed to Father Baddeley.'

The grey eyes did not move from his.

'Sorry. I'm sure it's fascinating but I have my mind on other matters. You read it to me.'

'It explains why he wanted to see me. You needn't have worried to concoct the poison pen letter or destroy his diary. His problem had nothing to do with you. Why kill him anyway? He was in the tower when Holroyd died; he knew perfectly well that he hadn't slept, that you hadn't come over the headland. But was that knowledge dangerous enough to snuff him out?'

'It was, in Baddeley's hands. The old man had a deep-rooted instinct for what he would describe as evil. That meant he had a deep-rooted suspicion of me, particularly of what he saw as my influence over Dennis. We were playing out our private comedy on a level which I don't think the procedures of the Metropolitan Police would recognize. It could only have one end. He telephoned me at my London flat from the hospital three days before he was discharged and asked me to come to see him on 26th September after nine o'clock. I went prepared. I drove down from London and left the Mercedes in that hollow behind the stone wall off the coast road. I took one of the habits from the business room while they were all at dinner. Then I walked to Hope Cottage. If anyone had seen me, then I should have had to change my plan. But no one did. He was sitting alone by the dying fire waiting for me. I think he knew about two minutes after I entered that I would kill him. There wasn't even a flicker of surprise when I pressed the plastic against his face. Plastic, you note. It wouldn't leave any tell-tale threads in the nostrils or windpipe. Not that Hewson would have noticed, poor fool. Baddeley's diary was on the table and I took it away with me just in case he'd made any incriminating entries. Just as well. He had, I discovered, a tedious habit of recording precisely where he'd been and when. But I didn't break into the bureau. I didn't need to. You can put that little peccadillo down to Wilfred. He must have been frantic to get his eyes on the old man's will. Incidentally, I never found your postcard and I suspect Wilfred looked no further once he'd found the will. Probably the old man tore it up. He disliked keeping trifles. Afterwards I went back and slept in some discomfort in the car. Next morning I rejoined the London road and arrived here when all the excitement was over. I saw in the diary that he had invited an A.D. to stay and that the visitor was expected on the first of October. It struck me as a bit odd. The old man didn't have visitors. So I planted the poison pen letter the evening before, just in case Baddeley had confided that something was on his mind. I must say, it was a bit disconcerting to discover that the mysterious A.D. was you, my dear Commander. Had I known, I might have tried for a little more subtlety.'

'And the stole? He was wearing his stole.'

'I should have removed it, but one can't remember everything. You see, he didn't believe I was protecting Dennis to save Wilfred grief or out of kindness to Dennis. He knew me too well.

When he accused me of corrupting Dennis, of using Toynton for some purpose of my own, I said that I would tell him the truth, that I wanted to make my confession. He must have known in his heart that this was death, that I was only amusing myself. But he couldn't take the risk. If he refused to take me seriously, then all his life would have been a lie. He hesitated for just two seconds, then he put the stole round his neck.'

'Didn't he even give you the gratification of a flicker of fear?'

'Oh, no! Why should he? We were alike in one thing. Neither of us feared death. I don't know where Baddeley thought he was going as he just had time to make that last archaic sign of his allegiance, but wherever it was he apparently saw nothing to fear. Neither do I. I know just as certainly as he did what will follow my death. Annihilation. It would be unreasonable to fear that. I'm not so unreasonable. Once you have lost the fear of death – absolutely lost it – then all other fears are meaningless. Nothing can touch you. All that is necessary is to keep the means of death to hand. Then one is invulnerable. I apologize for the fact that, in my case, it has to be a gun. I do realize that at the moment I look melodramatic, ridiculous. But I can't fancy killing myself any other way. Drowning? That onrush of suffocating water? Drugs? Some interfering fool might drag me back. Besides, I do fear that shadow land between life and death. A knife? Messy and uncertain. There are three bullets here, Dalgliesh. One for you, and two, in case they should be needed, for me.'

'If you trade in death as you do, it's as well no doubt to come to terms with it.'

'Everyone who takes hard drugs wants to die. You know that as well as I do. There is no other way they can do it with so little inconvenience and so much profit to others, and with such pleasure to themselves, at least initially.'

'And Lerner? I suppose you paid his mother's nursing home fees. What are they, about £200 a month? You got him cheap. Even so, he must have known what he was bringing in.'

'Will be bringing in, three days from now. Will go on bringing in. I told him that it was cannabis, a perfectly harmless drug; one which an over-sensitive government have chosen to make illegal but which my London friends happen to fancy and are prepared to pay highly for. He chooses to believe me. He knows the truth, but he won't admit to himself that he knows. That's reasonable, sensible, a necessary self-deception. It's how we all manage to go on living. You must know that your job is a dirty job, crooks catching crooks, and that you waste your intelligence by doing it. But it wouldn't exactly add to your peace of mind to admit the fact. And if you ever chuck it, you won't give that as your reason. Are you going to chuck it, by the way? Somehow I've gained the impression that you might be.'

'That shows some discernment. I did have it in mind. But not now.'

The decision to go on, arrived at when and why Dalgliesh didn't know, seemed to him as irrational as the decision to give up. It wasn't a victory. A kind of defeat even. But there would be time enough, if he lived, to analyse the vicissitudes of that personal conflict. Like Father Baddeley, a man lived and died as he had to. He heard Julius's amused voice.

'A pity. But as this seems likely to be your last job, why not tell me how you found me out.'

'Is there time? I don't relish spending my last five minutes in a recital of professional incompetence. It won't give me any satisfaction and I don't see why I should gratify your curiosity.'

'No. But it's more in your interests than mine. Oughtn't you to be playing for time? Besides, if it's fascinating enough I might relax my guard, might give you a chance to pounce or fling a chair at me or whatever they train you to do in this kind of situation. Or somebody may come, or I may even change my mind.'

'Will you?'

'No.'

'Then gratify my curiosity. I can guess about Grace Willison. You killed her in the same way you killed Father Baddeley once you decided that I was getting dangerously suspicious, because she could type by heart the list of Friends, the list which included your distributors. But Maggie Hewson, why did she have to die?'

'Because of something she knew. Haven't you guessed that? I've over-estimated you. She knew that Wilfred's miracle was a delusion. I drove the Hewsons and Victor to London for his appointment at St Saviour's Hospital. Eric and Maggie went to the medical records department to have a look at Wilfred's folder. I suppose they wanted to gratify a natural professional curiosity while they were there. They discovered that he'd never had disseminated sclerosis, that his latest tests had shown that it was a wrong diagnosis. All he'd suffered from was hysterical paralysis. But I must be shocking you, my dear Commander. You're a pseudo-scientist, aren't you? It must be hard for you to accept that medical technology can err.'

'No. I believe in the possibility of a wrong diagnosis.'

'Wilfred, apparently, doesn't share your healthy scepticism. He never returned to the hospital for his next check-up, so no one bothered to write to him about their little mistake. Why should they? But it was knowledge that the two Hewsons couldn't keep to themselves. They told me, and subsequently Maggie must have told Holroyd. He probably guessed on the drive back to Toynton that something was up. I tried to bribe her with whisky to keep the knowledge to herself – she actually believed in my solicitude for dear Wilfred – and it worked until Wilfred excluded her from the decision on the future of the home. She was furious. She told me that she planned to burst into the last session at the end of the meditation and publicly proclaim the truth. I couldn't risk that. It was the one fact, the only fact, that could have made him sell out. It would have stopped the hand-over to the Ridgewell Trust. Toynton Grange and the pilgrimage had to go on.

'She wasn't really looking forward to the fracas that would follow breaking the news and it was easy enough to persuade her to leave the party at Toynton Grange to indulge their various reactions to her news and escape up to town with me immediately afterwards. I suggested that she should leave a deliberately ambiguous note, one which could be read as a threat of suicide. Then she could return to Toynton if and when she felt like it and see how Eric was reacting as a presumptive widower. It was the kind of histrionic gesture which appealed to dear Maggie. It got her out of an awkward situation here, provided the maximum of worry and inconvenience to Wilfred and Eric, and provided her with a free holiday in my London flat and the prospect of plenty of excitement if and when she chose to return. She even volunteered to fetch the rope herself. We sat there drinking together until she was too fuddled to suspect me but still sober enough to write the note. The last scrawled lines, the reference to the black tower, were, of course, added by me.'

'So that was why she was bathed and dressed.'

'Of course. Tarted up to make an effective entrance at Toynton Grange, and also, I flatter myself, to impress me. I was gratified that I ranked clean underclothes and painted toe nails. I don't know what precisely she thought I had in mind for us when we reached London. Dear Maggie was never quite in touch with reality. To pack her contraceptive was perhaps more optimistic than discreet. But she may have had her plans. The dear girl was certainly delirious at the thought of leaving Toynton. She died happy I assure you.'

'And, before leaving the cottage, you gave the signal with the light.'

'I had to have some excuse for turning up and finding the body. It seemed prudent to add verisimilitude. Someone might have looked out of a window and been able to confirm my story. I didn't bargain for it being you. Finding you here busily doing your boy scout turn gave me a bad moment. And you were remarkably obstinate about not leaving the body.'

It must have been almost as bad a moment, thought Dalgliesh, as finding Wilfred so nearly choked to death. There had been nothing faked about Julius's terror either then or after Maggie's death. He asked:

'And was Holroyd pushed over the cliff for the same reason, to stop him talking?'

Julius laughed:

'Now this will amuse you; a delicious irony. I didn't even know that Maggie had confided in Holroyd until I challenged her with it after his death. And Dennis Lerner never knew. Holroyd began taunting Dennis as he usually did. Dennis was more or less inured to it and merely moved with his book a little way apart. Then Holroyd began on a more sinister line of torment. He began shouting at Dennis. He wondered what Wilfred would say when he learned that his precious pilgrimages were a fraud, that

Toynton Grange itself was founded on a lie. He told Dennis to make the most of the next pilgrimage; it would certainly be the last. Dennis panicked; he thought that Holroyd had discovered about the drug smuggling. He didn't pause to ask himself how in the hell Holroyd could have found out. He told me afterwards that he couldn't even remember scrambling to his feet, releasing the brakes and hurling the chair forward. But he did, of course. There was no one else to do it. It couldn't have landed where it did if it hadn't gone over the cliff with considerable force. I was on the beach beneath them when Holroyd came over. One of the irritating things about that murder was that I've never received any sympathy for the traumatic experience of having Holroyd smashed to death only twenty yards from me. I hope you will give it to me now.'

Dalgliesh reflected that the murder must have been doubly convenient for Julius. It removed Holroyd and his dangerous knowledge; it put Dennis Lerner finally in his power. He said:

'And you disposed of the two side pieces of the wheelchair while Lerner was fetching help.'

'About fifty yards away, down a deep cleft between two rocks. It seemed, at the time, a sensible way of complicating the case. Without the brakes no one could be sure that it wasn't an accident. On reflection I should have left well alone and let it be assumed that Holroyd killed himself. Essentially he did. That's what I've persuaded Dennis.'

Dalgliesh asked:

'What are you going to do now?'

'Put a bullet in your head, conceal your body in your own car and get rid of both together. It's a trite method of murder I know, but I understand that it works.'

Dalgliesh laughed. He was surprised that the sound could be so spontaneous.

'You propose to drive about sixty miles, I take it, in an easily identifiable car with the murdered body of a Commander of the Metropolitan Police in the boot – his own boot incidentally. A number of men of my acquaintance in the maximum security wings of Parkhurst and Durham would admire your nerve even while not exactly relishing the prospect of welcoming you to their company. They're a quarrelsome, uncivilized bunch. I don't think you're going to have a lot in common.'

'I shall be at risk. But you'll be dead.'

'Of course. So in effect will you from the moment the bullet enters my body, unless you count a life sentence as living. Even if you try to fake fingerprints on the trigger, they'll know that I was murdered. I'm not the type to kill myself or to drive my car into remote woods and quarries to put a bullet in my brain. And the forensic evidence will give the lab a field day.'

'If they find your body. How long before they even begin looking? Three weeks?'

'They'll be looking hard. If you can think of a suitable spot to dump me and the car, so can they. Don't assume that the police can't read an ordnance survey. And how do you propose to get back here? By picking up a train at Bournemouth or Winchester? By hitch-hiking, hiring a bicycle, walking through the night? You can hardly travel on to London by train, and pretend that you joined the train at Wareham. It's a small station and you're known there. Going or returning, you'll be remembered.'

Julius said consideringly:

'You're right, of course. Then it means the cliffs. They must fish you out of the sea.'

'With a bullet in my head? Or are you expecting me to walk over the cliff edge to suit your convenience? You could try physical force, of course, but then you'll have to come dangerously close, close enough for a fight. We're fairly evenly matched. I take it you don't intend to be dragged over with me? Once they find my body and that bullet, then you're finished. The trail begins here remember. I was last seen alive when the Toynton Grange bus left, and there's no one here but we two.'

It was then that, simultaneously, they heard the distant slam of the front door. The sound, sharp as a gunshot, was followed by the thud of footsteps, heavy and firm, crossing the front hall.

III

Julius said quickly:

'Call out, and I kill you both. Stand to the left of the door.'

The footsteps were crossing the central hall now unnaturally loud in the eerie silence. Both men held their breath. Philby stood in the doorway.

He saw the gun immediately. His eyes widened and then blinked rapidly. He looked from one man to the other. When he spoke he sounded hoarse, apologetic. He spoke directly to Dalgliesh like a child explaining a misdemeanour:

'Wilfred sent me back early. Dot thought she'd left the gas on.'

His eyes turned again to Julius. This time the terror was unmistakable. He said 'Oh, no!' Almost instantaneously, Julius fired. The crack of the revolver, although expected, was still shattering, still unbelievable. Philby's body stiffened, rocked, then fell backward like an axed tree with a crash which shook the room. The bullet had gone in precisely between the eyes. Dalgliesh knew that this was where Julius had intended it to go; that he had used this necessary killing to demonstrate that he knew how to use his gun. This had been target practice. He said calmly, his gun now turned on Dalgliesh again:

'Go over to him.'

Dalgliesh bent by the dead man. The eyes still seemed to hold their last look of wild surprise. The wound was a neat grumous slit in the low heavy forehead, so unremarkable that it could have been used for a forensic ballistics demonstration of the effect of discharge at six feet. There were no powder marks, as yet little blood, only the soiling of the skin by the spin of the bullet. It was a precise, almost decorative stigma giving no clue to the destructive tumult within.

Julius said:

'That settles the score for my smashed marble. Is there an exit wound?'

Gently Dalgliesh turned the heavy head.

'No. You must have hit a bone.'

'That's what I intended. Two bullets left. But this is a bonus, Commander. You were wrong about my being the last person to see you alive. I shall drive away to establish my alibi and, in the eyes of the police, the last person to see you alive will have been Philby, a criminal with a propensity to violence. Two bodies in the sea with bullet wounds. A pistol, licensed, I may say, stolen from my bedside drawer. Let the police concoct a theory to explain that. It shouldn't be difficult. Is there any blood?'

'Not yet. There will be. But not much.'

'I'll remember that. It will be easy enough to wipe it from this linoleum. Get that plastic hood from Carwardine's bust of Wilfred and tie it over his head. Use his own tie. And hurry. I shall be just six paces behind you. And if I get impatient I might feel it worthwhile doing my own work.'

Hooded with white plastic, his wound a third eye, Philby was transformed into an inert guy, its bulging body grotesquely stuffed into a dapper undersized suit, its tie askew under the clownish features. Julius said:

'Now get one of the lighter wheelchairs.'

He motioned Dalgliesh once again towards the workroom and followed, always a careful six feet behind. Three folded chairs were standing against the wall. Dalgliesh prized one open and wheeled it in beside the body. There would be fingerprints to find here. But what did they prove? This might even be the chair in which he had wheeled Grace Willison.

'Now get him into it.'

As Dalgliesh hesitated he said, allowing his voice a trace of controlled impatience:

'I don't want to have to manage two bodies alone. But I can if I need to. There's a hoist in the bathroom. If you can't lift him unaided, then get it. But I thought they taught policemen useful little knacks like this.'

Dalgliesh managed without the hoist. But it wasn't easy. The wheel brakes slid on the linoleum and it took more than two minutes before the heavy, unresponsive body slumped back against the canvas. Dalgliesh had succeeded in gaining some time but at a cost; he had lost strength. He knew that he would stay alive just as long as his mind, with its store of dreadfully appropriate experience, and his physical strength could be used by Julius. It would be inconvenient for Julius to have to carry two bodies to the cliff edge, but it could be done. Toynton Grange had facilities for moving inert bodies. At present Dalgliesh was less of an encumbrance alive than dead, but the margin was dangerously narrow; there was no sense in reducing it further. The optimum moment for action would come, and it would come for both of them. Both of them were waiting for it, Dalgliesh to attack, Julius to shoot. Both knew the cost of a mistake in recognizing that moment. Two bullets left and he had to ensure that neither of them ended in his body. And as long as Julius kept his distance and held the gun he was inviolable. Somehow Dalgliesh had to draw him close enough for physical contact. Somehow he had to divert that concentration if only for a fraction of a second.

Julius said: 'And now we'll take a walk together to Toynton Cottage.'

He still kept his careful distance behind as Dalgliesh wheeled the chair with its grotesque burden down the ramp of the front door and across the headland. The sky was a grey suffocating blanket pressing down on them. The close air was harsh and metallic on the tongue and smelt as strong as rotting seaweed. In the half-light the pebbles on the path glittered like semi-precious stones. Half-way across the headland Dalgliesh heard a high querulous wail and, looking back, saw that Jeoffrey was following them, tail erect. The cat padded behind Julius for another fifty yards and then, as unpredictably as he had appeared, turned tail and made off for home. Julius, his unblinking eyes on Dalgliesh's back, seemed to notice neither his arrival nor his departure. They walked on in silence. Philby's head had fallen back, his neck collared by the canvas of the chair. His cyclops wound, gummed to the plastic, stared into Dalgliesh's face in what seemed mute reproach. The path was dry. Looking down Dalgliesh saw that the wheels made only an imperceptible thread on the patches of dry turf and the dusty, gritty path. And behind him he could hear Julius's shoes scuffing the marks into oblivion. There would be no useful evidence left here.

And now they stood on the stone patio. It seemed to shake under their feet with the thunder of the waves as if earth and sea anticipated the coming storm. But the tide was ebbing. No curtain of spray rose between them and the cliff edge. Dalgliesh knew that it was the moment of great danger. He made himself laugh aloud, and wondered whether the sound rang as false to Julius's ears as it did to his own.

'Why so amused?'

'It's easy to see that your killing is normally done at a distance, a commercial transaction merely. You propose to hurl us into the sea at your own back door, a broad enough hint for even the stupidest detective constable. And they won't be putting stupid officers on this crime. Your cleaning woman is expected this morning isn't she? And this is one part of the coast with a beach, even at high tide. I thought you wanted to delay discovery of the bodies.'

'She won't come out here. She never does.'

'How do you know what she does when you aren't here? She may shake the dusters over the cliff. It may even be her habit to paddle. But have it your own way. I'm merely pointing out that your only hope of success – and I don't rate it high – is to delay discovery of our bodies. No one will start looking for Philby until the pilgrimage returns in three days' time. If you get rid of my car it will be even longer before they start looking for me. That gives you the opportunity to dispose of this consignment of heroin before the hunt is up, assuming you still intend to let Lerner bring it in. But don't let me interfere.'

Julius's hand on the gun did not waver. As if considering a proposition for a picnic site, he said:

'You're right, of course. You ought to go into deep water and further along the coast. The best place is the black tower. The sea will be still washing the cliffs there. We've got to get him to the tower.'

'How? He must weigh over twelve stone. I can't push him unaided up the cliff edge. You'll hardly be much help if you walk behind with a gun in my back. And what about the wheel marks?'

'The rain will finish those. And we shan't go up the headland. We'll drive along the coast road and approach the tower over the cliff as we did when we rescued Anstey. Once the couple of you are in the boot of the car I'll watch for Mrs Reynolds through my glasses. She cycles in from Toynton village, and she's always exactly on time. We ought to plan to meet her just outside the boundary gate. I'll stop and let her know that I shan't be back for dinner. That pleasant minute of ordinary conversation should impress the coroner if they ever get your bodies to an inquest. And eventually, the tedious business over, I'll drive off to Dorchester for an early luncheon.'

'With the wheelchair and the plastic hood in the boot?'

'With the chair and the hood locked in the boot. I shall establish an alibi for the whole of today and return to Toynton Grange this evening. And I shan't forget to wash the plastic hood before replacing it, dust the chair to remove your prints and examine the floor for bloodstains. And, of course, retrieve the cartridge case. Were you hoping I would overlook that? Don't worry, Commander. I do realize that, by then, I'll be planning without your valuable assistance, but thanks to you, I shall have a day or two to work out the details. One of two sophistications attract me. I'm wondering if I could make use of the smashed marble. Couldn't that be worked in to provide the motive for Philby's murderous attack on you?'

'I should keep it simple.'

'Perhaps you're right. My first two murders were models of simplicity and none the worse for it. Now get him into the boot of the Mercedes. It's parked at the back. But first through into the scullery. You'll find two sheets in the washing machine. Take the one from the top. I don't want fibres and shoe dust in the car.'

'Won't Mrs Reynolds notice that one is missing?'

'She washes and irons tomorrow. A woman of strict routine. By this evening I shall have replaced it. Don't waste time.'

Julius's mind must be registering every second, thought Dalgliesh, yet his voice betrayed no anxiety. Not once did he glance at his watch, or even at the clock on the kitchen wall. He kept his eyes and the muzzle of the Luger on his victim. Somehow that concentration had to be broken. And the time was running out.

The Mercedes was parked outside the stone garage. Under Julius's direction Dalgliesh raised the unlocked lid of the boot and spread the creased sheet over the floor. It was an easy matter to tumble Philby's body from the wheelchair. Dalgliesh folded the chair and placed it on top of the body. Julius said:

'Now get in beside him.'

Could this be the best opportunity, the last opportunity even, to act; here outside Julius's own cottage with the murdered man in his car and the evidence plain? But plain to whom? Dalgliesh knew that if he sprang on Julius now he would gain nothing but a second's release from frustration and anger before the bullet hit him. Two bodies instead of one would be driven to the black tower and tumbled into deep water. In his mind's eye he could see Julius poised in solitary triumph on the edge of the cliff, the gun curving through the air like a falling bird to cleave the tumbling waves, beneath which two bodies were being torn and tugged by the ebbing tide. The plan would go ahead. A little more tedious, taking longer since there would be two bodies to wheel unaided across the headland. But who was there to prevent it? Certainly not Mrs Reynolds even now cycling along the road from Toynton village. And if she suspected, if she even mentioned casually when she dismounted to greet Julius on the road that she had heard what sounded like a shot? Then there were still two bullets left in the gun. And he was no longer sure that Julius was sane.

But there was at least something he could do at this moment, something he had planned to do. But it wasn't going to be easy. He had hoped that, for a couple of seconds at least, the raised lid of the boot would have partly screened him from Julius's view. But Julius was standing immediately behind the car; Dalgliesh was in full view. But there was one advantage. The grey eyes never flickered, dared not flicker from his face. If he were quick and cunning, if he were lucky, he might bring it off. He placed his hands as if casually on his hips. He could feel the slight weight of his thin leather wallet in his back trouser pocket lying curved against his buttock. Julius said with dangerous quietness:

'I said get in on top of him. I'm not risking driving with you any closer.'

Dalgliesh's right thumb and forefinger twisted at the pocket button. Thank God the button hole was reasonably loose. He said:

'Then you'd better drive fast unless you want to have a corpse dead of suffocation to explain.'

'A night or two in the sea and your lungs will be too water-logged for that kind of diagnosis.'

The button was undone now. He insinuated his right forefinger and thumb gently into the top pocket and grasped the wallet. Everything now depended on its sliding out easily, on his being able to drop it unseen behind the wheel of the car. He said:

'They won't, you know. The P.M. will show perfectly clearly that I was dead before I hit the water.'

'And so you will be, with a bullet in your head. Given that, I doubt whether they'll look for signs of suffocation. But thank you for the warning. I'll drive fast. Now get in.'

Dalgliesh shrugged his shoulders and bent with sudden energy to get into the boot as if momentarily relinquishing hope. He rested his left hand on the bumper. Here, at least, there would be a palm mark which would be difficult to explain. But then he remembered. He had rested his palm on the bumper when loading the shepherd's crook, the sacks and the besom into the boot. It was only a small discouragement but it depressed him. He let his right hand dangle and the leather slipped from his finger and thumb to fall under the right wheel. No dangerously quiet word of command followed. Julius neither spoke nor moved, and he was still alive. With luck he would stay alive now until they reached the black tower. He smiled at the irony that his heart should now rejoice at a gift which a short month ago he had so grudgingly welcomed.

The boot lid slammed down. He was cramped in total blackness, total silence. He felt a second of claustrophobic panic, the irresistible urge to stretch his curled body and batter his clenched hands against the metal. The car did not move. Julius would be free now to check his timing. Philby's body lay heavily against him. He could smell the dead man as if he still breathed, an amalgam of grease, mothballs and sweat, the air of the boot was hot with his presence. He felt a moment of guilt that Philby was dead; he alive. Could he have saved him by calling out a warning? It could only have resulted, he knew, in both their deaths. Philby would have come on; must have come on. And even if he had turned and run, Julius would have followed and disposed of him. But now the feel of the cold moist flesh pressing against him, the hairs on the limp wrist sharp as bristles, pricked him like a reproach. The car rocked gently and began to move.

He had no means of knowing if Julius had seen the wallet and removed it; he thought it unlikely. But would Mrs Reynolds find it? It was lying in her path. She would almost certainly dismount from her bicycle outside the garage. If she did find it, then he guessed she would have no rest until it was returned. He thought of his own Mrs Mack, a Metropolitan police constable's widow who cleaned and occasionally cooked for him; of her almost obsessive honesty, her meticulous concern for her employer's belongings, the perpetual explanatory notes about missing laundry, the increased cost of shopping, a mislaid cufflink. No, Mrs Reynolds wouldn't rest with the wallet in her possession. He had cashed a cheque on his last visit to Dorchester; the three ten pound notes, the bundle of credit cards, his police warrant, all would particularly worry her. She would probably waste some time going to Hope Cottage. Not finding him there, what then? His guess was that she would ring the local police, terrified that he might discover his loss before she had reported it. And the police? If he were lucky they would see the incongruity of a wallet dropped so conveniently in her path. Suspicious or not, they would be courteous enough to get in touch with him at once. They might find it worthwhile ringing Toynton Grange since the cottage was not on the telephone. They would discover that the telephone was inexplicably out of order. It was at least an even chance that they would think it worthwhile sending a patrol car, and if one were reasonably close it could come quickly. Logically, one action must follow another. And he had one piece of luck. Mrs Reynolds, he remembered, was the village constable's widow. At least she wouldn't be afraid of using the telephone, would know whom to ring. His life depended on her seeing the wallet. A few square inches of brown leather on the paved courtyard. And the light was darkening under the storm-laden sky.

Julius was driving very fast even over the bumpy ground of the headland. The car stopped. Now he would be opening the boundary gate. Another few seconds of driving and the car stopped again. Now he must have met Mrs Reynolds and was exchanging that half-minute of conversation. Now they were off again, this time with smooth road under their wheels.

There was something else he could do. He moved his hand under his cheek and bit into his left thumb. The blood tasted warm and sweet. He smeared it across the roof of the boot and, scuffing aside the sheet, pressed his thumb into the carpet. Group AB rhesus negative. It was a rare enough group. And with any luck Julius would miss these minute tell-tale smears. He hoped the police searcher would be more perspicacious.

He began to feel stifled, his head thudded. He told himself that there was plenty of air, that this pressure on his chest was no more than psychological trauma. And then the car rocked gently and he knew that Julius was driving off the road and into the hollow behind the stone wall which divided the headland from the road. It was a convenient stopping place. Even if another car passed, and this was unlikely, the Mercedes wouldn't be visible. They had arrived. The final part of the journey was about to begin.

There were only about one hundred and fifty yards of rock-strewn and lumpy turf to where the black tower stood squat and malignant under the menacing sky. Dalgliesh knew that Julius would prefer to make a single journey. He would want to get as quickly as possible out of all sight of the road. He would want the business over so that he could get on his way. More important, he needed to make no physical contact with either victim. Their clothes would yield nothing when their bloated bodies were finally fished from the sea; but Julius would know how difficult to eradicate, without tell-tale cleaning, would be the infinitesimally small traces of hair, fibre or blood on his own clothes. So far he was absolutely clean. It would be one of his strongest cards. Dalgliesh would be allowed to live at least until they reached the shelter of the tower. He felt confident enough of this to take his time in getting Philby's body strapped into the chair. Afterwards he leaned for a moment over the handlebars breathing heavily, simulating more exhaustion than he felt. Somehow, despite the hard pushing ahead, he must conserve his strength. Julius slammed down the boot lid and said:

'Get a move on. The storm is almost on us.'

But he didn't shift his fixed gaze to glance at the sky, nor had he need. They could almost smell the rain in the freshening breeze.

Although the wheels of the chair were well oiled the going was hard. Dalgliesh's hands slid on the rubber handgrips. Philby's body, strapped like a recalcitrant child, jerked and rolled as the wheels struck stones or clumps of grass. Dalgliesh felt the sweat rolling into his eyes. It gave him the opportunity he needed to get rid of his jacket. When it came to the last physical struggle the man least encumbered would have an advantage. He stopped pushing and stood gasping. The feet behind him stopped too.

It might happen now. There was nothing he could do if it did. He comforted himself with the thought that he would know nothing. One press of Julius's finger on the trigger and his busy fearful mind would be stilled. He remembered Julius's words. 'I know what will happen to me when I die; annihilation. It would be unreasonable to fear that.' If only it were that simple! But Julius did not press. The dangerously quiet voice behind him said:

'Well?'

'I'm hot. May I take off my jacket?'

'Why not? Drape it over Philby's knees. I'll chuck it in the sea after you. It would be torn off your body by the tide anyway.'

Dalgliesh slid his arms from his jacket and placed it folded over Philby's knees. Without looking round he said:

'You'd be unwise to shoot me in the back. Philby was killed instantly. It has to look as if he shot me first but only to wound, before I wrenched the gun from him and finished him off. No fight with only one gun could reasonably result in two instantaneous killings, and one in the small of the back.'

'I know. Unlike you, I may be inexperienced in the cruder manifestations of violence but I'm not a fool and I do understand about firearms. Get on.'

They moved forward, carefully distanced, Dalgliesh pushing his macabre passenger and hearing behind him the soft rustle of the following feet. He found himself thinking about Peter Bonnington. It was because an unknown boy, now dead, had been moved from Toynton Grange that he, Adam Dalgliesh, was now walking across Toynton Head with a gun at his back. Father Baddeley had believed that there was a great underlying pattern. Given that assurance, all human perplexities were no more than exercises in spiritual geometry. Suddenly Julius began speaking. Dalgliesh could almost imagine that he felt the need to entertain his victim on this last tedious walk, that he was making some attempt at justification.

'I can't be poor again. I need money as I need oxygen. Not just enough; more than enough. Much more. Poverty kills. I don't fear death but I fear that particular slow and corrosive process of dying. You didn't believe me, did you – that story about my parents?'

'Not altogether. Was I expected to?'

'Yet that at least was true. I could take you to pubs in Westminster – Christ, you probably know them – and bring you face to face with what I fear; the pathetic elderly queens managing on their pensions. Or not managing. And they, poor sods, haven't even been used to having money. I have. I'm not ashamed of my nature. But if I'm to live at all, I have to be rich. Did you really expect me to let one sick old fool and a dying woman stand in my way?'

Dalgliesh didn't reply. Instead he asked:

'I suppose you came this way when you set fire to the tower.'

'Of course. I did as we've done now, drove to the hollow and came on foot. I knew when Wilfred, a creature of habit, was likely to be in the tower and I watched him walk over the headland through my binoculars. If it wasn't that day, it would be another. There was no difficulty in helping myself to the key and a habit. I saw to that a day in advance. Anyone who knows Toynton Grange can move about it undetected. Even if I were seen, I don't have to explain my presence there. As Wilfred says, I'm one of the family. That's why killing Grace Willison was so easy. I was home and in bed soon after midnight and with no worse effects than cold legs and a little difficulty in getting to sleep. By the way, I ought to say, in case you harbour any doubts, that Wilfred knows nothing of the smuggling. If I were about to die and you to live instead of the other way round you could look forward to the pleasure of breaking the news. Both pieces of news. His miracle a delusion and his abode of love a staging post for death. I should give a great deal to see his face.'

They were within feet now of the black tower. Without overtly changing direction Dalgliesh steered the wheelchair as close as he dared to the porch. The wind was gently rising in short moaning crescendos. But then, there would always be a breeze on this wind-scoured promontory of grass and rock. Suddenly he stopped. He held the chair with his left hand and half turned towards Julius, carefully balancing his weight. It was now. It had to be now.

Julius said sharply:

'Well, what is it?'

Time stopped. A second was stilled into infinity. In that brief, timeless lacuna, Dalgliesh's mind was drained free of tension and fear. It was as if he were detached from the past and the future, aware simultaneously of himself, of his adversary, of the sound, scent and colour of sky, cliff and sea. The pent-up anger at Father Baddeley's death, the frustration and indecision of the last few weeks, the controlled suspense of the past hour: all were calmed in this moment before their final release. He spoke, his voice, high and cracked, simulating terror. But, even to his own ears, the terror sounded horribly real.

'The tower! There's someone inside!'

It came again as he prayed it would, the bone ends, piercing the torn flesh, scrabbling frantically against unyielding stone. He sensed rather than heard the sharp hiss of Julius's intake of breath. Then time moved on, and in that second, Dalgliesh sprang.

As they fell, Julius's body beneath him, Dalgliesh felt the hammer blow on his right shoulder, the sudden numbness, the sticky warmth, soothing as a balm, flowing into his shirt. The shot echoed back from the black tower, and the headland came alive. A cloud of gulls rose screaming from the rock face. Sky and cliff were a tumult of wildly beating wings. And then as if the laden clouds had waited for this signal, the sky was ripped open with the sound of tearing canvas, and the rain fell.

They fought like famished animals clawing at their prey, without skill, eyes stung and blinded by rain, locked in a rigor of hate.

Dalgliesh, even with the weight of Julius's body beneath him, felt his strength ebbing. It had to be now, now while he was on top. And he still had the use of his good left shoulder. He twisted Julius's wrist into the clammy earth and pressed with all his strength on the beat of the pulse. He could feel Julius's breath like a hot blast on his face. They lay cheek to cheek in a horrible parody of exhausted love. And still the gun did not drop from those rigid fingers. Slowly, in painful spasms, Julius bent his right arm towards Dalgliesh's head. And then the gun went off. Dalgliesh felt the bullet pass over his hair to spend itself harmlessly in the sheeting rain.

And now they were rolling towards the cliff edge. Dalgliesh, weakening, felt himself clutching Julius as if for support. The rain was a stinging lance on his eyeballs. His nose was pressed suffocatingly into the sodden earth. Humus. A comforting and familiar last smell. His fingers clawed impotently at the turf as he rolled. It came apart in moist clumps in his hands. And suddenly Julius was kneeling over him, hands at his throat, forcing his head back over the cliff edge. The sky, the sea and the sheeting rain were one turbulent whiteness, one immense roaring in his ears. Julius's streaming face was out of his reach, the rigid arms pressing down the cruel encircling hands. He had to bring that face closer. Deliberately he slackened his muscles and loosened his already weakening hold on Julius's shoulders. It worked. Julius relaxed his grasp and instinctively bent his head forward to look into Dalgliesh's face. Then he screamed as Dalgliesh's thumbs gouged into his eyes. Their bodies fell apart. And Dalgliesh was on his feet and scrambling up the headland to fling himself behind the wheelchair.

He crouched behind it, heaving against the sagging canvas for support, watching Julius advance, hair streaming, eyes wild, the strong arms stretched forward, eager for that final clutch. Behind him the tower streamed black blood. The rain slashed like hail against the boulders, sending up a fine mist to mingle with his hoarse breath. Its painful rhythm tore at his chest and filled his ears like the death throes of some great animal. Suddenly he released the brakes and with his last strength hurled the chair forward. He saw his murderer's astonished and desperate eyes. For one second he thought that Julius would fling himself against the chair. But at the last moment he leapt aside, and the chair and its dreadful burden sailed over the cliff.

'Explain that when they fish it out!' Dalgliesh never knew whether he spoke to himself or shouted the words aloud. And then Julius was on him.

This was the end. He wasn't fighting now, only letting himself be rolled downwards towards death. He could hope for nothing except to carry Julius over with him. Hoarse, discordant cries were hurting his ears. The crowd were shouting for Julius. All the world was shouting. The headland was full of voices, of shapes.

Suddenly the weight on his chest lifted. He was free. He heard Julius whisper 'Oh, no!' Dalgliesh heard the sad despairing protest as clearly as if the voice had been his own. It wasn't the last horrified cry of a desperate man. The words were quiet, rueful, almost amused. Then the air was darkened by a shape, black as a great bird, passing spread-eagled over his head in what seemed slow motion. Earth and sky turned slowly together. A solitary seagull screamed. The earth thudded. A white ring of amorphous blobs was bending over him. But the ground was soft, irresistibly soft. He let his consciousness bleed away into it.

IV

The surgical registrar came out of Dalgliesh's room to where a group of large men were obstructing the corridor. He said: 'He'll be OK for questioning in about half an hour or so. We've extracted the bullet. I've handed it over to your chap. We've put up a drip but don't let that worry you. He's lost a fair amount of blood but there's no real damage. There's no harm now in your going in.'

Daniel asked:

'Is he conscious?'

'Barely. Your chap in there says he's been quoting King Lear. Something about Cordelia anyway. And he's fretting because he hasn't said thank you for the flowers.'

Daniel said:

'He won't be needing flowers this time, thank God. He can thank Mrs Reynolds's sharp eyes and common sense for that. And the storm helped. But it was a close thing. Court would have carried him over the cliff if we hadn't come up on them before he noticed us. Well, we may as well go in if you think it's OK.'

A uniformed constable appeared, helmet under his arm.

'Well?'

'The Chief Constable's on his way, Sir. And they've pulled out Philby's body half-strapped to a wheelchair.'

'And Court's?'

'Not yet, Sir. They reckon he'll be washed in further down the coast.'

Dalgliesh opened his eyes. His bed was ringed with black and white figures advancing and receding in a ritual dance. Nurses' caps floating like disembodied wings above the smudged faces as if uncertain where to settle. Then the picture cleared and he saw the circle of half-familiar faces. Sister was here, of course. And the consultant had got back early from his wedding. He wasn't wearing his rose any more. The faces broke simultaneously into wary smiles. He made himself smile back. So it wasn't acute leukaemia; it wasn't any kind of leukaemia. He was going to get better. And once they'd removed this heavy contraption which for some reason they'd fixed to his right arm he could get out of here and back to his job. Wrong diagnosis or not, it was nice of them, he thought sleepily, looking up into the ring of smiling eyes, to look so pleased that he wasn't going to die after all.

DEATH OF AN EXPERT WITNESS

CONTENTS

AUTHOR'S NOTE

There is no official forensic science laboratory in East Anglia and, even if there were, it is in the highest degree improbable that it would have anything in common with Hoggatt's Laboratory, whose staff, like all other characters in this story – even the most unpleasant – are purely imaginary and bear no resemblance to any person living or dead.

BOOK ONE

A Call to Murder

I

The call had come at six-twelve precisely. It was second nature to him now to note the time by the illuminated dial of his electric bedside clock before he had switched on his lamp, a second after he had felt for and silenced the raucous insistence of the telephone. It seldom had to ring more than once, but every time he dreaded that the peal might have woken Nell. The caller was familiar, the summons expected. It was Detective Inspector Doyle. The voice, with its softly intimidating suggestion of Irish burr, came to him strong and confident, as if Doyle's great bulk loomed over the bed.

'Doc Kerrison?' The interrogation was surely unnecessary. Who else in this half-empty, echoing house would be answering at six-twelve in the morning? He made no reply and the voice went on.

'We've got a body. On the wasteland – a clunch field – a mile north-east of Muddington. A girl. Strangulation by the look of it. It's probably pretty straightforward but as it's close . . .'

'All right, I'll come.'

The voice expressed neither relief nor gratitude. Why should it? Didn't he always come when summoned? He was paid well enough for his availability, but that wasn't the only reason why he was so obsessively conscientious. Doyle, he suspected, would have respected him more if he had occasionally been less accommodating. He would have respected himself more.

'It's the first turn off the A142 after you leave Gibbet's Cross. I'll have a man posted.'

He replaced the receiver, swung his legs out of bed and, reaching for his pencil and pad, noted the details while they were still fresh in his mind. In a clunch field. That probably meant mud, particularly after yesterday's rain. The window was slightly open at the bottom. He pushed it open, wincing at the rasp of the wood, and put out his head. The rich loamy smell of the fen autumn night washed over his face; strong, yet fresh. The rain had stopped and the sky was a tumult of grey clouds through which the moon, now almost full, reeled like a pale demented ghost. His mind stretched out over the deserted fields and the desolate dykes to the wide moon-bleached sands of the Wash and the creeping fringes of the North Sea. He could fancy that he smelt its medicinal tang in the rain-washed air. Somewhere out there in the darkness, surrounded by the paraphernalia of violent death, was a body. His mind recalled the familiar ambience of his trade: men moving like black shadows behind the glare of the arc-lights, the police cars tidily parked; the flap of the screens, desultory voices conferring as they watched for the first lights of his approaching car. Already they would be consulting their watches, calculating how long it would be before he could make it.

Shutting the window with careful hands, he tugged trousers over his pyjamas and pulled a polo-necked sweater over his head. Then he picked up his torch, switched off the bedside light and made his way downstairs, treading warily and keeping close to the wall to avoid the creaking treads. But there was no sound from Eleanor's room. He let his mind wander down the twenty yards of landing and the three stairs to the back bedroom where his sixteen-year-old daughter lay. She was always a light sleeper, uncannily sensitive even in sleep to the ring of the telephone. But she couldn't possibly have heard. He had no need to worry about three-year-old William. Once asleep, he never woke before morning.

Actions as well as thought were patterned. His routine never varied. He went first to the small washroom near the back door where his wellington boots, the thick red socks protruding like a pair of amputated feet, stood ready at the door. Pushing up his sleeves over the elbow, he swilled cold water over his hands and arms, then bent down and sluiced the whole of his head. He performed this act of almost ceremonial cleansing before and after every case. He had long ago ceased to ask himself why. It had become as comforting and necessary as a religious ritual, the brief preliminary washing which was like a dedication, the final ablution which was both a necessary chore and an absolution, as if by wiping the smell of his job from his body he could cleanse it from his mind. The water splashed heavily against the glass, and rising to fumble for a towel, he saw his face distorted, the mouth hanging, the heavily lidded eyes half hidden by glistening weeds of black hair like the surfacing visage of a drowned man. The melancholy of the early hours took hold of him. He thought:

'I'm forty-five next week and what have I achieved? This house, two children, a failed marriage, and a job which I'm frightened of losing, because it's the only thing I've made a success of.' The Old Rectory, inherited from his father, was unmortgaged, unencumbered. This wasn't true, he thought, of anything else in his anxiety-ridden life. Love, the lack of it, the growing need, the sudden terrifying hope of it, was only a burden. Even his job, the territory where he moved with most assurance, was hedged with anxiety.

As he dried his hands carefully, finger by finger, the old familiar worry returned, heavy as a morbid growth. He hadn't yet been appointed as Home Office Pathologist in succession to old Dr Stoddard and he very much wanted to be. The official appointment wouldn't give him more money. The police already employed him on an item of service basis, and paid generously enough for each case. That and the fees for coroner's post-mortems provided an income which was one of the reasons why his professional colleagues in the pathology department of the district general hospital both envied and resented his unpredictable absences on police work, the long days in court, the inevitable publicity.

Yes, the appointment was important to him. If the Home Office looked elsewhere it would be difficult to justify to the Area Health Authority a continuing private arrangement with the local Force. He wasn't even sure that they would want him. He knew himself to be a good forensic pathologist, reliable, more than competent professionally, almost obsessively thorough and painstaking, a convincing and unflappable witness. The Force knew that their meticulously erected edifices of proof wouldn't fall to pieces under cross-examination when he was in the witness box, although he sometimes suspected that they found him too scrupulous for complete comfort. But he hadn't the easy masculine camaraderie, the blend of cynicism and *machismo* which had bound old Doc Stoddard so strongly to the Force. If they had to do without him he wouldn't be greatly missed, and he doubted whether they would put themselves out to keep him.

The garage light was blinding. The overhead door swung up easily to his touch and the light splayed out over the gravel of the drive and the unkempt verges of silvered grass. But at least the light wouldn't wake Nell. Her bedroom was at the back of the house. Before switching on the engine he studied his maps. Muddington. It was a town on the edge of his area, about seventeen miles to the north-west, less than half an hour's drive each way if he were lucky. If the laboratory scientists were there already – and Lorrimer, the Senior Biologist, never missed a homicide if he could help it – then there mightn't be much for him to do. Allow, say, an hour at the scene, and with luck he would be home again before Nell woke and she need never know that he had been away. He switched off the garage light. Carefully, as if the gentleness of his touch could somehow silence the engine, he turned on the ignition. The Rover moved slowly into the night.

II

Standing motionless behind the curtains on the front landing, her right hand cupped round the pale flicker of her night-light, Eleanor Kerrison watched the sudden red blaze of the Rover's rear lights as the car stopped at the gate before turning left and accelerating out of sight. She waited until the glare of the headlights had finally faded from view. Then she turned and made her way along the corridor to William's room. She knew that he wouldn't have woken. His sleep was a sensuous gluttony of oblivion. And while he slept she knew that he was safe, that she could be free of anxiety. To watch him then was such a mingled joy of yearning and pity that sometimes, frightened of her waking thoughts but more afraid of the nightmares of sleep, she would carry her night-light into his bedroom and crouch by the cot for an hour or more, her eyes fixed on his sleeping face, her restlessness soothed by his peace.

Although she knew that he wouldn't wake, she turned the handle of the door as carefully as if expecting it to explode. The night-light, burning steadily in its saucer, was unnecessary, its yellow gleam extinguished by the moonlight which streamed through the uncurtained windows. William, bagged in his grubby sleeping suit, lay as always on his back, both arms flung above his head. His head had flopped to one side and the thin neck, stretched so still that she could see the pulse beat, looked too fragile to bear the weight of his head. His lips were slightly parted, and she could neither see nor hear the thin whisper of breath. As she watched he suddenly opened sightless eyes, rolled them upwards, then closed them with a sigh and fell again into his little semblance of death.

She closed the door softly behind her and went back to her own room next door. Dragging the eiderdown from her bed, she wrapped it round her shoulders and shuffled her way down the landing to the top of the stairs. The heavily studded oak banister curved down into the darkness of the hall from which the tick of the grandfather clock sounded as unnaturally loud and ominous as a time bomb. The atmosphere of the house came up to her nostrils, sour as a stale vacuum flask, redolent with the sad effluent of stodgy clerical dinners. Placing the night-light against the wall she sat down on the top stair, humping the eiderdown high over her shoulders and gazing into the darkness. The stair-carpet was gritty to her bare soles. Miss Willard never vacuumed it, pleading that her heart couldn't stand the strain of lugging the cleaner from step to step, and her father never appeared to notice the drabness or dirtiness of his house. He was, after all, so seldom there. Sitting rigid in the darkness she thought of her father. Perhaps he was already at the scene of crime. It depended how far he had to drive. If it were on the very fringe of his area he might not be back until lunch-time.

But what she hoped was that he would return before breakfast so that he would find her here, crouched lonely and exhausted on the top stair, waiting for him, frightened because he had left her alone. He would put away the car quietly, leaving the garage open in case the thud of the door woke her, then sneak in like a thief at the back door. She would hear the swirl of water from the downstairs washroom, his footsteps on the tessellated floor of the hall. Then he would look up and see her. He would come running up the stairs, torn between anxiety for her and fear of disturbing Miss Willard, his face suddenly old with weariness and concern as he put his arms round her trembling shoulders.

'Nell, darling, how long have you been here? You shouldn't be out of bed. You'll get cold. Come on, old girl, there's nothing to be frightened of now. I'm back. Look, I'll take you back to bed again and you try to get some sleep. I'll see to the breakfast. Suppose I bring it up on a tray in about half an hour. How would you like that?'

And he would guide her back to her room, cajoling, murmuring reassurance, trying to pretend that he wasn't frightened, frightened that she would start to cry for her mother, that Miss Willard would appear, censorious and whining, complaining that she had to get her sleep, that the precarious little household would fall apart and he would be parted from William. It was William he loved, William he couldn't bear to lose. And he could only keep William and stop the court from giving Mummy custody if she were at home to help care for her brother.

She thought about the day ahead. It was Wednesday, a grey day. Not a black day when she wouldn't see her father at all, but not a yellow day like Sunday, when, unless on call, he might be there most of the time. In the morning, immediately after breakfast, he would be at the public mortuary doing the post-mortem. There would be other autopsies too, those who had died in hospital, the old, the suicides, the accident victims. But the body he was probably examining now would be first on the mortuary table. Murder has priority. Wasn't that what they always said at the Lab? She mused, but without real curiosity, on what he might be doing at this very moment to that unknown cadaver, young or old, male or female. Whatever he was doing, the body wouldn't feel it, wouldn't know about it. The dead had nothing to be frightened of any more, and there was nothing to fear from them. It was the living who held the power to hurt. And suddenly two shadows moved in the darkness of the hall, and she heard her mother's voice, pitched high, frighteningly unfamiliar, a strained, cracked, alien voice.

'Always your job! Your bloody job! And my God, no wonder you're good at it. You haven't the guts to be a real doctor. You made one wrong diagnosis early on and that was the end, wasn't it? You couldn't take responsibility for living bodies, blood that can flow, nerves that can actually feel. All you're fit for is messing about with the dead. It makes you feel good, doesn't it, the way they defer to you? The phone calls at all hours of the day and night, the police escort. Never mind that I'm buried alive here in this bloody fen with your children. You don't even see me any more. I'd be more interesting to you if I were dead and laid out on your slab. At least you'd be forced to take some notice of me.'

Then the low defensive mumble of her father's voice, dispirited, abject. She had listened in the darkness and wanted to call out to him:

'Don't answer her like that! Don't sound so defeated! Can't you understand that it only makes her despise you more?'

His words had come to her in snatches, barely audible.

'It's my job. It's what I do best. It's all that I can do.' And then, more clearly. 'It's what keeps us.'

'Not me. Not any longer.'

And then the slam of the door.

The memory was so vivid that for a second she thought she heard the echo of the slam. She stumbled to her feet, clutching the eiderdown around her, and opened her mouth to call to them. But then she saw that the hall was empty. There was nothing but the faint image of the stained glass in the front door where the moonlight streamed through, the ticking of the clock, the bundle of coats hanging from the hallstand. She sank back again on to the stair.

And then she remembered. There was something she had to do. Slipping her hand into her dressing-gown pocket she felt the cold slippery plasticine of her model of Dr Lorrimer. Carefully she drew it out through the folds of the eiderdown and held it close to the flame of the night-light. The model was a little misshapen, the face furred with fluff from her pocket, but it was still intact. She straightened the long limbs and pressed the strands of black cotton she had used for hair more firmly into the scalp. The white coat, cut from an old handkerchief, was particularly successful, she thought. It was a pity that she hadn't been able to use one of his handkerchiefs, a strand of his hair. The model represented more than Dr Lorrimer, who had been unkind to her and William, who had practically thrown them out of the Laboratory. It stood for the whole of Hoggatt's Lab.

And now to kill it. Gently she knocked the head against the baluster. But the plasticine merely flattened, the head lost its identity. She remodelled it with careful fingers, then held it close to the flame. But the smell was disagreeable and she was afraid that the white linen would burst into flame. She dug the nail of her little finger deeply in behind the left ear. The cut was clean and sharp, right through to the brain. That was better. She sighed, satisfied. Holding the dead creature in her right palm she squeezed the pink plasticine, the white coat, the cotton hair into one amorphous lump. Then, huddling deep into the eiderdown, she sat and waited for the dawn.

III

The car, a green Morris Minor, had been toppled over the edge of a shallow depression in the wasteland, and had lurched to rest on a grassy plateau about ten feet from the ridge like a clumsy animal going to earth. It must have been there for years, abandoned to the plunderers, an illicit plaything for the local children, a welcome shelter for the occasional vagrant like the seventy-year-old alcoholic who had stumbled on the body. The two front wheels had been removed, and the rusted back wheels with their rotting tyres were firmly embedded in the chalky earth, the paintwork was battered and scratched, the interior stripped of instruments and steering wheel. Two mounted arc-lights, one directed downwards from the top of the bank and the other precariously planted on the edge of the plateau, illuminated its stark decrepitude. Thus brightly lit it looked, thought Kerrison, like some grotesque and pretentious modern sculpture, symbolically poised on the brink of chaos. The back seat, its padding springing from the slashed plastic, had been ripped out and hurled to one side.

In the front seat rested the body of a girl. Her legs were

decorously planted together, the glazed eyes were slyly half open, the mouth, devoid of lipstick, was fixed in a drool elongated by two small trickles of blood. They gave a face which must have been pretty, or at least childishly vulnerable, the vacuous look of an adult clown. The thin coat, too thin surely for a night in early November, was pulled waist-high. She was wearing stockings; and the suspender clips bit into plump white thighs.

Drawing close to the body, under the watchful eyes of Lorrimer and Doyle, he thought, as he often did at such a scene, that it looked unreal, an anomaly, so singularly and ridiculously out of place that he had to stifle a nervous impulse to laugh. He didn't feel this so strongly when a corpse was far advanced in decay. It was then as if the rotting maggot-infested flesh, or the tags of matted clothing, had already become part of the earth which clung to and enclosed them, no more unnatural or frightening than a clump of compost or a drift of decaying leaves. But here, colours and outlines intensified in the glare, the body, still outwardly so human, looked an absurd burlesque, the skin of the pallid cheek as artificial as the stained plastic of the car against which it rested. It seemed ridiculous that she should be beyond help. As always he had to fight the impulse to fasten his mouth over hers and begin resuscitation, to plunge a needle into the still warm heart.

He had been surprised to find Maxim Howarth, newly appointed director of the Forensic Science Laboratory, at the scene, until he remembered that Howarth had said something about following through the next murder case. He supposed that he was expected to instruct. Withdrawing his head from the open door he said:

'It's almost certainly a case of manual throttling. The slight bleeding from the mouth is caused by the tongue being caught between the teeth. Manual strangulation is invariably homicidal. She couldn't have done this herself.'

Howarth's voice was carefully controlled.

'I should have expected more bruising of the neck.'

'That's usual, certainly. There's always some damage to the tissues, although the extent of the bruised area depends on the position of the assailant and victim, the way in which the neck is grasped as well as the degree of pressure. I'd expect to find deep-seated internal bruising, but it's possible to get this without many superficial signs. This happens when the murderer has maintained pressure until death; the vessels have been emptied of blood and the heart stops beating before the hands are removed. The cause of death is asphyxia, and one expects to find the usual signs of this. What is so interesting here is the cadaveric spasm. You'll see that she's clutching the bamboo handle of her bag. The muscles are absolutely rigid, proof that the grasp occurred at or about the moment of death. I've never before seen cadaveric spasm in a case of homicidal manual throttling, and it's interesting. She must have died extraordinarily quickly. But you'll get a clearer idea of what exactly happened when you watch the post-mortem.'

Of course, thought Howarth, the post-mortem. He wondered how early Kerrison would expect to get down to that job. He wasn't afraid that his nerve would fail him, only his stomach, but he wished he hadn't said he would be there. There was no privacy for the dead; the most one could hope for was a certain reverence. It now seemed to him monstrous that tomorrow he, a stranger, would be looking unrebuked at her nakedness. But for the present he had seen enough. He could step aside now without loss of face. Turning up the collar of his Burberry against the chill morning air, he climbed up the slope to the rim of the hollow and stood looking down at the car. This must be what shooting a film was like: the brightly lit scene, the ennui of waiting for the chief actors to appear, the brief moments of activity, the concentrated attention to detail. The body could easily be that of an actress simulating death. He half expected one of the police to dart forward and rearrange her hair.

The night was nearly over. Behind him the eastern sky was already brightening, and the wasteland, which had been a formless void of darkness above the lumpy earth, was assuming an identity and a shape. To the west he could see the outline of houses, probably a council estate, a trim row of identical roofs and square slabs of darkness broken by patterned squares of yellow as the early risers switched on their lights. The track along which his car had bumped, rock-strewn and silver, alien as a moonscape in the glare of the head-lights, took shape and direction, became ordinary. Nothing was left mysterious. The place was an arid scrubland between the two ends of the town, litter-strewn and edged with sparse trees above a ditch. He knew that the ditch would be dank with nettles and sour with rotting rubbish, the trees wounded by vandals, the trunks carved with initials, the low branches hanging torn from the boughs. Here was an urban no-man's-land, fit territory for murder.

It was a mistake to have come, of course; he should have realized that the role of voyeur was always ignoble. Few things were more demoralizing than to stand uselessly by while other men demonstrated their professional competence: Kerrison, that connoisseur of death, literally sniffing at the body; the photographers, taciturn, preoccupied with lighting and angles; Inspector Doyle, in charge of a murder case at last, impresario of death, tense with the suppressed excitement of a child at Christmas gloating over a new toy. Once, while waiting for Kerrison to arrive, Doyle had actually laughed, a hearty guffaw, filling the hollow. And Lorrimer? Before touching the body he had briefly crossed himself. It was so small and precise a gesture that Howarth could have missed it, except that nothing Lorrimer did escaped him. The others seemed unsurprised at the eccentricity. Perhaps they were used to it. Domenica hadn't told him that Lorrimer was religious. But then his sister hadn't told him anything about her lover. She hadn't even told him that the affair was over. But he had needed only to look at Lorrimer's face during the past month to know that. Lorrimer's face, Lorrimer's hands. Odd that he hadn't noticed how long the fingers were or with what apparent gentleness they had taped the plastic bags over the girl's hand to preserve, as he had tonelessly explained, conscientious in his role of instructor, any evidence under the fingernails. He had taken a sample of blood from the plump flaccid arm, feeling for the vein as carefully as if she could still flinch at the needle's prick.

Lorrimer's hands. Howarth thrust the tormenting, brutally explicit images out of his mind. He had never before resented one of Domenica's lovers. He hadn't even been jealous of her dead husband. It had seemed to him perfectly reasonable that she should eventually wish to marry, just as she might choose, in a fit of boredon or acquisitiveness, to buy herself a fur coat or a new item of jewellery. He had even quite liked Charles Schofield. Why was it then that, even from the first moment, the thought of Lorrimer in his sister's bed had been intolerable. Not that he could ever have been in her bed, at least not at Leamings. He wondered yet again where they had managed to meet, how Domenica had contrived to take a new lover without the whole Laboratory and the whole village knowing. How could they have met and where?

It had begun, of course, at that disastrous dinner party twelve months ago. At the time it had seemed both natural and civilized to celebrate the taking up of his directorship with a small private party at his house for the senior staff. They had, he remembered, eaten melon, followed by *boeuf stroganoff* and a salad. He and Domenica liked good food and, occasionally, she enjoyed cooking it. He had opened the 1961 claret for them because that was the wine he and Dom had chosen to drink and it hadn't occurred to him to offer his guests less. He and Dom had changed because that was their habit. It amused them to dine in some style, formally separating the working day from their evenings together. It hadn't been his fault that Bill Morgan, the vehicle examiner, had chosen to come in open-necked shirt and corduroys; neither he nor Dom had cared a damn what their guests chose to wear. If Bill Morgan felt awkward about these unimportant shibboleths of taste, he should learn either to change his clothes or to develop more social confidence in his sartorial eccentricities.

It had never occurred to Howarth that the six senior staff sitting awkwardly around his table in the candlelight, unmellowed even by the wine, would see the whole occasion as an elaborate gastronomic charade designed to demonstrate his social and intellectual superiority. At least Paul Middlemass, the Principal Scientific Officer Document Examiner, had appreciated the wine, drawing the bottle across the table towards him and refilling his glass, his lazy ironic eyes watching his host. And Lorrimer? Lorrimer had eaten practically nothing, had drunk less, pushing his glass almost petulantly aside and fixing his great smouldering eyes on Domenica as if he had never before seen a woman. And that, presumably, had been the beginning of it. How it had progressed, when and how they had continued to meet, how it had ended, Domenica hadn't confided.

The dinner party had been a private and public fiasco. But what, he wondered, had the senior staff expected? An evening of solid drinking in the private snug in the Moonraker? A free-for-all jollification in the village hall for the whole Laboratory including the cleaner, Mrs Bidwell, and old Scobie, the Laboratory attendant? 'Knees Up Mother Brown' in the public bar? Perhaps they had thought that the first move should have come from their side. But that was to admit that there were two sides. The conventional sophistry was that the Laboratory worked as a team harnessed by a common purpose, reins lightly but firmly in the director's hands. That had worked well enough at Bruche. But there he had directed a research laboratory with a common discipline. How could you direct a team when your staff practised half a dozen different scientific disciplines, used their own methods, were responsible for their own results, stood finally alone to justify and defend them in the only place where the quality of a forensic scientist's work could properly be judged, the witness-box of a court of law? It was one of the loneliest places on earth, and he had never stood there.

Old Dr Mac, his predecessor, had, he knew, taken the occasional case, to keep his hand in as he would say, trotting out to a scene of crime like an old bloodhound happily sniffing after half-forgotten scents, doing the analysis himself, and finally appearing, like a resurrected Old Testament prophet, in the witness-box, greeted by the judge with dry judicial compliments, and boisterously welcomed in the bar by counsel like a long-missed old reprobate drinking comrade happily restored to them. But that could never be his way. He had been appointed to manage the Laboratory and he would manage it in his own style. He wondered, morbidly introspective in the cold light of dawn, whether his decision to see the next murder case through from the call to the scene of crime to the trial had really arisen from a desire to learn or merely from a craven wish to impress or, worse, to propitiate his staff, to show them that he valued their skills, that he wanted to be one of the team. If so, it had been one more error of judgement to add to the bleak arithmetic of failure since he had taken up his new job.

It looked as if they had nearly finished. The girl's rigid fingers had been prised from her handbag and Doyle's hands, gloved, were spreading out its few contents on a plastic sheet laid on the bonnet of the car. Howarth could just make out the shape of what looked like a small purse, a lipstick, a folded sheet of paper. A love letter probably, poor little wretch. Had Lorrimer written letters to Domenica? he wondered. He was always first at the door when the post arrived, and usually brought his sister her letters. Perhaps Lorrimer had known that. But he must have written. There must have been assignations. Lorrimer would hardly have risked telephoning from the Laboratory or from home in the evenings when he, Howarth, might have taken the call.

They were moving the body now. The mortuary van had moved closer to the rim of the hollow and the stretcher was being manoeuvred into place. The police were dragging out the screens from their van, ready to enclose the scene of crime. Soon there would be the little clutch of spectators, the curious children shooed away by the adults, the Press photographers. He could see Lorrimer and Kerrison conferring together a little way apart, their backs turned, the two dark heads close together. Doyle was closing his notebook and supervising the removal of the body as if it were a precious exhibit which he was frightened someone would break. The light was strengthening.

He waited while Kerrison climbed up beside him and together they walked towards the parked cars. Howarth's foot struck a beer-can. It clattered across the path and bounced against what looked like the battered frame of an old pram, with a bang like a pistol shot. The noise startled him. He said pettishly:

'What a place to die! Where in God's name are we exactly? I just followed the police cars.'

'It's called the clunch field. That's the local name for the soft chalk they mined here from the Middle Ages onwards. There isn't any hard building stone hereabouts, so they used clunch for most domestic building and even for some church interiors. There's an example in the Lady Chapel at Ely. Most villages had their clunch pits. They're overgrown now. Some are quite pretty in the spring and summer, little oases of wild flowers.'

He gave the information almost tonelessly, like a dutiful guide repeating by rote the official spiel. Suddenly he swayed and reached for the support of his car door. Howarth wondered if he were ill or whether this was the extremity of tiredness. Then the pathologist straightened himself and said, with an attempt at briskness:

'I'll do the P.M. at nine o'clock tomorrow at St Luke's. The hall porter will direct you. I'll leave a message.'

He nodded a goodbye, forced a smile, then eased himself into his car and slammed the door. The Rover bumped slowly towards the road.

Howarth was aware that Doyle and Lorrimer were beside him. Doyle's excitement was almost palpable. He turned to look across the clunch field to the distant row of houses, their yellow-brick walls and mean square windows now plainly visible.

'He's over there somewhere. In bed probably. That is, if he doesn't live alone. It wouldn't do to be up and about too early, would it? No, he'll be lying there wondering how to act ordinary, waiting for the anonymous car, the ring at the door. If he's on his own, it'll be different, of course. He'll be creeping about in the half-dark wondering if he ought to burn his suit, scraping the mud off his shoes. Only he won't be able to get it all off. Not every trace. And he won't have a boiler big enough for the suit. And even if he had, what will he say when we ask for it? So maybe he'll be doing nothing. Just lying there and waiting. He won't be asleep. He didn't sleep last night. And he won't be sleeping again for quite a time.'

Howarth felt slightly sick. He had eaten a small and early dinner and knew himself to be hungry. The sensation of nausea on an empty stomach was peculiarly unpleasant. He controlled his voice, betraying nothing but a casual interest.

'You think it's relatively straightforward then?'

'Domestic murder usually is. And I reckon that this is a domestic murder. Married kid, torn stump of a ticket for the local Oddfellows' hop, letter in her bag threatening her if she doesn't leave another bloke alone. A stranger wouldn't have known about this place. And she wouldn't have come here with him even if he had. By the look of her, they were sitting there cosily together before he got his hands on her throat. It's just a question of whether the two of them set off home together or whether he left early and waited for her.'

'Do you know yet who she is?'

'Not yet. There's no diary in the bag. That kind don't keep diaries. But I shall know in about half an hour.'

He turned to Lorrimer.

'The exhibits should be at the Lab by nine or thereabouts. You'll give this priority?'

Lorrimer's voice was harsh.

'Murder gets priority. You know that.'

Doyle's exultant, self-satisfied bellow jangled Howarth's nerves.

'Thank God something does! You're taking your time over the Gutteridge case. I was in the Biology Department yesterday and Bradley said the report wasn't ready; he was working on a case for the defence. We all know the great fiction that the Lab is independent of the police and I'm happy to go along with it most of the time. But old Hoggatt founded the place as a police lab, and when the chips are down that's what it's all about. So do me a favour. Get moving with this one for me. I want to get chummy and get him quickly.'

He was rocking gently on his heels, his smiling face uplifted to the dawn like a happy dog sniffing at the air, euphoric with the exhilaration of the hunt. It was odd, thought Howarth, that he didn't recognize the cold menace in Lorrimer's voice.

'Hoggatt's does an occasional examination for the defence if they ask us and if the exhibit is packed and submitted in the approved way. That's departmental policy. We're not yet a police lab even if you do walk in and out of the place as if it's your own kitchen. And I decide priorities in my Laboratory. You'll get your report as soon as it's ready. In the meantime, if you want to ask questions, come to me, not to my junior staff. And, unless you're invited, keep out of my Laboratory.'

Without waiting for an answer, he walked over to his car. Doyle looked after him in a kind of angry bewilderment.

'Bloody hell! His Lab! What's wrong with him? Lately, he's

been as touchy as a bitch on heat. He'll find himself on a brain-shrinker's couch or in the bin if he doesn't get a hold of himself.'

Howarth said coldly:

'He's right, of course. Any inquiry about the work should be made to him, not to a member of his staff. And it's usual to ask permission before walking into a laboratory.'

The rebuke stung. Doyle frowned. His face hardened. Howarth had a disconcerting glimpse of the barely controlled aggression beneath the mask of casual good humour. Doyle said:

'Old Dr Mac used to welcome the police in his Lab. He had this odd idea, you see, that helping the police was what it was all about. But if we're not wanted, you'd better talk to the chief. No doubt he'll issue his instructions.'

He turned on his heel and made off towards his car without waiting for a reply. Howarth thought:

'Damn Lorrimer! Everything he touches goes wrong for me.' He felt a spasm of hatred so intense, so physical that it made him retch. If only Lorrimer's body was sprawled at the bottom of the clunch pit. If only it were Lorrimer's cadaver which would be cradled in porcelain on the post-mortem table next day, laid out for ritual evisceration. He knew what was wrong with him. The diagnosis was as simple as it was humiliating: that self-infecting fever of the blood which could lie deceptively dormant, then flare now into torment. Jealousy, he thought, was as physical as fear; the same dryness of the mouth, the thudding heart, the restlessness which destroyed appetite and peace. And he knew now that, this time, the sickness was incurable. It made no difference that the affair was over, that Lorrimer, too, was suffering. Reason couldn't cure it, nor, he suspected, could distance, nor time. It could be ended only by death; Lorrimer's or his own.

IV

At half past six, in the front bedroom of 2 Acacia Close, Chevisham, Susan Bradley, wife of the Higher Scientific Officer in the Biology Department of Hoggatt's Laboratory, was welcomed by the faint, plaintive wail of her two-month-old baby, hungry for her first feed of the day. Susan switched on the bedside lamp, a pink glow under its frilled shade, and reaching for her dressing-gown, shuffled sleepily to the bathroom next door, and then to the nursery. It was a small room at the back of the house, little more than a box, but when she pressed down the switch of the low-voltage nursery light she felt again a glow of maternal, proprietorial pride. Even in her sleepy morning daze the first sight of the nursery lifted her heart: the nursing chair with its back decorated with rabbits; the matching changing-table fitted with drawers for the baby's things; the wicker cot in its stand which she had lined with a pink, blue and white flowered cotton to match the curtains; the bright fringe of nursery-rhyme characters which Clifford had pasted round the wall.

With the sound of her footsteps the cries became stronger. She picked up the warm, milky-smelling cocoon and crooned reassurance. Immediately the cries ceased and Debbie's moist mouth, opening and shutting like a fish, sought her breast, the small wrinkled fists freed from the blanket, unfurled to clutch against her crumpled nightdress. The books said to change baby first, but she could never bear to make Debbie wait. And there was another reason. The walls of the modern house were thin, and she didn't want the sound of crying to wake Cliff.

But suddenly he was at the door, swaying slightly, his pyjama jacket gaping open. Her heart sank. She made her voice sound bright, matter-of-fact.

'I hoped she hadn't woken you, darling. But it's after half past six. She slept over seven hours. Getting better.'

'I was awake already.'

'Go back to bed, Cliff. You can get in another hour's sleep.'

'I can't sleep.'

He looked round the little nursery with a puzzled frown, as if disconcerted not to find a chair. Susan said:

'Bring in the stool from the bathroom. And put on your dressing-gown. You'll catch cold.'

He placed the stool against the wall and crouched there in sullen misery. Susan raised her cheek from resting against the soft furriness of the baby's head. The small, snub-nosed leech latched on to her breast, fingers splayed in an ecstasy of content. Susan told herself that she must keep calm, mustn't let nerves and muscles knot themselves into the familiar ache of worry. Everyone said that it was bad for the milk. She said quietly:

'What's wrong, darling?'

But she knew what was wrong. She knew what he would say. She felt a new and frightening sense of resentment that she couldn't even feed Debbie in peace. And she wished he would do up his pyjamas. Sitting like that, slumped and half-naked, he looked almost dissolute. She wondered what was happening to her. She had never felt like this about Cliff before Debbie was born.

'I can't go on. I can't go into the Lab today.'

'Are you ill?'

But she knew that he wasn't ill, at least not yet. But he would be ill if something wasn't done about Edwin Lorrimer. The old misery descended on her. People wrote in books about a black weight of worry, and they were right, that was just how it felt, a perpetual physical burden which dragged at the shoulders and the heart, denying joy, even destroying, she thought bitterly, their pleasure in Debbie. Perhaps in the end it would destroy even love. She didn't speak but settled her small, warm burden more comfortably against her arm.

'I've got to give up the job. It's no use, Sue. I can't go on. He's got me in such a state that I'm as useless as he says I am.'

'But Cliff, you know that isn't true. You're a good worker. There were never complaints about you at your last lab.'

'I wasn't an H.S.O. then. Lorrimer thinks I ought never to have been promoted. He's right.'

'He isn't right. Darling, you mustn't let him sap your confidence. That's fatal. You're a conscientious, reliable forensic biologist. You mustn't worry if you're not as quick as the others. That isn't important. Dr Mac always said it's accuracy that counts. What does it matter if you take your time? You get the answer right in the end.'

'Not any longer. I can't even do a simple peroxidase test now without fumbling. If he comes within two feet of me my hands start shaking. And he's begun checking all my results. I've just finished examining the stains on the mallet from the suspected Pascoe murder. But he'll work late tonight doing it again. And he'll make sure that the whole Biology Department knows why.'

Cliff couldn't, she knew, stand up to bullying or sarcasm. Perhaps it was because of his father. The old man was paralysed now after a stroke and she supposed that she ought to feel sorry for him lying there in his hospital bed, useless as a felled tree, mouth slavering, only the angry eyes moving in impotent fury from face to watching face. But from what Cliff had let slip he had been a poor father, an unpopular and unsuccessful schoolmaster yet with unreasonable ambitions for his only son. Cliff had been terrified of him. What Cliff needed was encouragement and affection. Who cared if he never rose any higher than H.S.O.? He was kind and loving. He looked after her and Debbie. He was her husband and she loved him. But he mustn't resign. What other job could he get? What else was he suited for? Unemployment was as bad in East Anglia as it was elsewhere. There was the mortgage to pay and the electricity bill for the central heating – they couldn't economize there because of Debbie needing warmth – and the hire-purchase on the bedroom suite to find. Even the nursery furniture wasn't paid for yet. She had wanted everything nice and new for Debbie, but it had taken all their remaining savings. She said:

'Couldn't you apply to Establishment Department for a transfer?'

The despair in his voice tore at her heart.

'No one will want me if Lorrimer says I'm no good. He's probably the best forensic biologist in the service. If he thinks I'm useless, then I'm useless.'

It was this, too, which she was beginning to find irritating, the obsequious respect of the victim for his oppressor. Sometimes, appalled by her disloyalty, she could begin to understand Dr Lorrimer's contempt. She said:

'Why not have a word with the director?'

'I might have done if Dr Mac was still there. But Howarth wouldn't care. He's new. He doesn't want any trouble with the senior staff, particularly now when we're getting ready to move into the new Lab.'

And then she thought of Mr Middlemass. He was the Principal Scientific Officer Document Examiner, and she had worked for him as a young S.O. before her marriage. It was at Hoggatt's

Laboratory that she had met Cliff. Perhaps he could do something, could speak to Howarth for them, could use his influence with Estabs. She wasn't sure how she expected him to help, but the need to confide in someone was overwhelming. They couldn't go on like this. Cliff would have a breakdown. And how would she manage with the baby and Cliff ill and the future uncertain? But surely Mr Middlemass could do something. She believed in him because she needed to believe. She looked across at Cliff.

'Don't worry, darling, it's going to be all right. We're going to think of something. You go in today and we'll talk about it in the evening.'

'How can we? Your mother's coming to supper.'

'After supper then. She'll be catching the quarter to eight bus. We'll talk then.'

'I can't go on like this, Sue.'

'You won't have to. I'll think of something. It's going to be all right. I promise you, darling. It's going to be all right.'

V

'Mum, did you know that every human being is unique?'

'Of course I did. It stands to reason, doesn't it? There's only one of every person. You're you. I'm me. Pass your Dad the marmalade and keep your sleeves out of that butter.'

Brenda Pridmore, recently appointed Clerical Officer/receptionist at Hoggatt's Laboratory, pushed the marmalade across the breakfast table and began methodically slicing thin strips from the white of her fried egg, postponing, as she had from early childhood, that cataclysmic moment when she would plunge the fork into the glistening yellow dome. But indulgence in this small personal ritual was almost automatic. Her mind was preoccupied with the excitements and discoveries of her wonderful first job.

'I mean biologically unique. Inspector Blakelock, he's the Assistant Police Liaison Officer, told me that every human being has a unique fingerprint and no two types of blood are exactly the same. If the scientists had enough systems they could distinguish them all, the blood types I mean. He thinks that day may come in time. The forensic serologist will be able to say with certainty where the blood came from, even with a dried stain. It's dried blood that's difficult. If that blood is fresh we can do far more with it.'

'Funny job you've got yourself.' Mrs Pridmore refilled the teapot from the kettle on the Aga hob and eased herself back into her chair. The farmhouse kitchen, its flowered cretonne curtains still undrawn, was warm and cosily domestic, smelling of toast, fried bacon and hot strong tea.

'I don't know that I like the idea of you checking in bits of body and bloodstained clothes. I hope you wash your hands properly before you come home.'

'Oh Mum, it's not like that! The exhibits all arrive in plastic bags with identifying tags. We have to be ever so particular that all of them are labelled and properly entered in the book. It's a question of continuity of evidence, what Inspector Blakelock calls the integrity of the sample. And we don't get bits of body.'

Remembering suddenly the sealed bottles of stomach contents, the carefully dissected pieces of liver and intestines, looking, when you came to think of it, no more frightening than exhibits in the science laboratory at school, she said quickly:

'Well, not in the way you mean. Dr Kerrison does all the cutting up. He's a forensic pathologist attached to the Laboratory. Of course, some of the organs come to us for analysis.'

Inspector Blakelock, she remembered, had told her that the Laboratory refrigerator had once held a whole head. But that wasn't the kind of thing to tell Mum. She rather wished that the Inspector hadn't told her. The refrigerator, squat and gleaming like a surgical sarcophagus, had held a sinister fascination for her ever since. But Mrs Pridmore had seized gratefully on a familiar name.

'I know who Dr Kerrison is, I should hope. Lives at the Old Rectory at Chevisham alongside the church, doesn't he? His wife ran off with one of the doctors at the hospital, left him and the two kids, that odd-looking daughter and the small boy, poor little fellow. You remember all the talk there was at the time, Arthur?'

Her husband didn't reply, nor did she expect him to. It was an understood convention that Arthur Pridmore left breakfast conversation to his women. Brenda went happily on:

'Forensic science isn't just helping the police to discover who's guilty. We help clear the innocent too. People sometimes forget that. We had a case last month – of course, I can't mention names – when a sixteen-year-old choir girl accused her vicar of rape. Well, he was innocent.'

'So I should hope! Rape indeed!'

'But it looked very black against him. Only he was lucky. He was a secreter.'

'A what, for goodness' sake?'

'He secreted his blood group in all his body fluids. Not everyone does. So the biologist was able to examine his saliva and compare his blood group with the stains on the victim's . . .'

'Not at breakfast, Brenda, if you don't mind.'

Brenda, her eyes suddenly alighting on a round milk stain on the table cloth, herself thought that breakfast wasn't perhaps the most suitable time for a display of her recently acquired information about the investigation of rape. She went on to a safer subject.

'Dr Lorrimer – he's the Principal Scientific Officer in charge of the Biology Department – says that I ought to work for an 'A' level subject and try for a job as an Assistant Scientific Officer. He thinks that I could do better than just a clerical job. And once I got my A.S.O. I'd be on a scientific grade and could work myself up. Some of the most famous forensic scientists have started that way, he said. He's offered to give me a reading list, and he says he doesn't see why I shouldn't use some of the Laboratory equipment for my practical work.'

'I didn't know that you worked in the Biology Department.'

'I don't. I'm mainly on Reception with Inspector Blakelock, and sometimes I help out in the general office. But we got talking when I had to spend an afternoon in his Laboratory checking reports for courts with his staff, and he was ever so nice. A lot of people don't like him. They say he's too strict; but I think he's just shy. He might have been Director if the Home Office hadn't passed him over and appointed Dr Howarth.'

'He seems to be taking quite an interest in you, this Mr Lorrimer.'

'Dr Lorrimer, Mum.'

'Dr Lorrimer, then. Though why he wants to call himself a doctor beats me. You don't have any patients at the Lab.'

'He's a Ph.D., Mum. Doctor of Philosophy.'

'Oh, is he? I thought he was supposed to be a scientist. Anyway, you'd better watch your step.'

'Oh, Mum, don't be daft. He's old. He must be forty or more. Mum, did you know that our Lab is the oldest forensic science lab in the country? There are regional labs covering the whole country but ours was the first. Colonel Hoggatt started it in Chevisham Manor when he was Chief Constable in 1860, then left the manor house to his force when he died. Forensic science was in its infancy then, Inspector Blakelock says, and Colonel Hoggatt was one of the first Chief Constables to see its possibilities. We've got his portrait in the hall. We're the only lab with its founder's name. That's why the Home Office has agreed that the new Laboratory will still be called Hoggatt's. Other police forces send their exhibits to their regional laboratory. North-East or the Metropolitan and so on. But in East Anglia they say "Better send it to Hoggatt's."'

'You'd better send yourself to Hoggatt's if you want to get there by eight-thirty. And I don't want you taking any short cuts through the new Lab. It isn't safe, only half-built, especially these dark mornings. Like as not you'd fall into the foundations or get a brick down on your head. They're not safe, building sites aren't. Look what happened to your Uncle Will.'

'All right, Mum. We're not supposed to go through the new Lab anyway. Besides, I'm going by bike. Are these my sandwiches or Dad's?'

'Yours, of course. You know your Dad's home to dinner on Wednesdays. Cheese and tomato this morning, and I've put you in a boiled egg.'

When Brenda had waved goodbye, Mrs Pridmore sat down for her second cup of tea and looked across at her husband.

'I suppose it's all right, this job she's found for herself.'

Arthur Pridmore, when he did condescend to talk at breakfast, talked with the magisterial authority of head of his family, Mr Bowlem's bailiff and people's warden at the village church. He laid down his fork.

'It's a good job, and she was lucky to get it. Plenty of girls from the grammar school after it, weren't they? An established civil servant, isn't she? And look what they're paying her. More than the pigman gets at the farm. Pensionable too. She's a sensible girl and she'll be all right. There aren't many opportunities left locally for girls with good 'O' levels. And you didn't want her to take a job in London.'

No indeed, Mrs Pridmore hadn't wanted Brenda to go to London, a prey to muggers, I.R.A. terrorists and what the Press mysteriously called 'the drug scene'. None of her infrequent, but uneventful and pleasant, visits to the capital on Women's Institute theatre excursions or rare shopping trips had failed to shake her conviction that Liverpool Street was the cavernous entry to an urban jungle, where predators armed with bombs and syringes lurked in every Underground station, and seducers laid their snares for innocent provincials in every office. Brenda, thought her mother, was a very pretty girl. Well, no point in denying it, she took after her mother's side of the family for looks even if she had her dad's brains, and Mrs Pridmore had no intention of exposing her to the temptations of London. Brenda was walking out with Gerald Bowlem, younger son of her father's boss, and if that came off there's no denying it would be a very satisfactory marriage. He wouldn't get the main farm, of course, but there was a very nice little property over at Wisbech which would come to him. Mrs Pridmore couldn't see the sense of more examinations and all this talking about a career. This job at the Lab would do Brenda very well until she married. But it was a pity that there was all this emphasis on blood.

As if reading her thoughts, her husband said:

'Of course it's exciting for her. It's all new. But I daresay it's no different from other jobs, pretty dull most of the time. I don't reckon anything really frightening will happen to our Brenda at Hoggatt's Lab.'

This conversation about their only child's first job was one they'd had before, a comforting reiteration of mutual reassurance. In imagination Mrs Pridmore followed her daughter as she pedalled vigorously on her way; bumping down the rough farm track between Mr Bowlem's flat fields to Tenpenny Road, past old Mrs

Button's cottage where, as a child, she had been given rice-cake and home-made lemonade, by Tenpenny Dyke where she still picked cowslips in summer, then a right turn into Chevisham Road and the straight two miles skirting Captain Massey's land and into Chevisham village. Every yard of it was familiar, reassuring, unmenacing. And even Hoggatt's Laboratory, blood or no blood, had been part of the village for over seventy years, while Chevisham Manor had stood for nearly three times as long. Arthur was right. Nothing frightening could happen to their Brenda at Hoggatt's. Mrs Pridmore, comforted, drew back the curtains and settled down to enjoy her third cup of tea.

VI

At ten minutes to nine the post van stopped outside Sprogg's Cottage on the outskirts of Chevisham to deliver a single letter. It was addressed to Miss Stella Mawson, Lavender Cottage, Chevisham, but the postman was a local man and the difference in name caused him no confusion. There had been Sproggs living in the cottage for four generations, and the small triangle of green in front of the gate had been Sprogg's Green for almost as long. The present owner, having improved the cottage by the addition of a small brick garage and a modern bathroom and kitchen, had decided to celebrate the metamorphosis by planting a lavender hedge and renaming the property. But the villagers regarded the new name as no more than a foreigner's eccentric fancy which they were under no obligation either to use or recognize. The lavender hedge, as if in sympathy with their views, failed to survive the first fen winter and Sprogg's Cottage remained Sprogg's.

Angela Foley, the twenty-seven-year-old personal secretary to the Director of Hoggatt's Laboratory, picked up the envelope and guessed at once by the quality of the paper, the expertly typed address and the London postmark what it must be. It was a letter they had been expecting. She took it through to the kitchen where she and her friend were breakfasting and handed it over without speaking, then watched Stella's face as she read. After a minute she asked:

'Well?'

'It's what we feared. He can't wait any longer. He wants a quick sale, and there's a friend of his who thinks he might like it for a weekend cottage. As sitting tenants we get first refusal, but he must know by next Monday whether we're interested.'

She tossed the letter across the table. Angela said bitterly:

'Interested! Of course we're interested! He knows we are. We told him weeks ago that we were writing round trying to get a mortgage.'

'That's just lawyer's jargon. What his solicitor is asking is whether we're able to go ahead. And the answer is that we can't.'

The arithmetic was plain. Neither of them needed to discuss it. The owner wanted sixteen thousand pounds. None of the mortgage societies they had approached would advance them more than ten. Together they had a little over two thousand saved. Four thousand short. And, with no time left, it might just as well be forty.

Angela said:

'I suppose he wouldn't take less?'

'No. We've tried that. And why should he? It's a fully converted, reed-thatched seventeenth-century cottage. And we've improved it. We've made the garden. He'd be a fool to let it go for under sixteen even to a sitting tenant.'

'But, Star, we are sitting tenants! He's got to get us out first.'

'That's the only reason why he's given us as long as he has. He knows we could make it difficult for him. But I'm not prepared to stay on here under sufferance, knowing that we'd have to go in the end. I couldn't write under those conditions.'

'But we can't find four thousand in a week! And, with things as they are, we couldn't hope for a bank loan even if . . .'

'Even if I had a book coming out this year, which I haven't. And what I make from writing barely pays my part of the housekeeping. It was tactful of you not to say so.'

She hadn't been going to say it. Stella wasn't a conveyor-belt writer. You couldn't expect her novels to make money. What was it that last reviewer had said? Fastidious observation wedded to elegantly sensitive and oblique prose. Not surprisingly, Angela could quote all the reviews even if she sometimes wondered what exactly they were trying to say. Wasn't it she who pasted them with meticulous care into the cuttings-book which Stella so affected to despise! She watched while her friend began what they both called her tiger prowl, that compulsive pacing up and down, head lowered, hands sunk in her dressing-gown pockets. Then Stella said:

'It's a pity that cousin of yours is so disagreeable. Otherwise one might not have minded asking him for a loan. He wouldn't miss it.'

'But I've already asked him. Not about the cottage, of course. But I've asked him to lend me some money.'

It was ridiculous that this should be so difficult to say. After all, Edwin was her cousin. She had a right to ask him. And it was her grandmother's money after all. There was really no reason why Star should be cross. There were times when she didn't mind Star's anger, times even when she deliberately provoked it, waiting with half-shameful excitement for the extraordinary outburst of bitterness and despair of which she herself was less a victim than a privileged spectator, relishing even more the inevitable remorse and self-incrimination, the sweetness of reconciliation. But now for the first time she recognized the chill of fear.

'When?'

There was nothing for it now but to go on.

'Last Tuesday evening. It was after you decided that we'd have to cancel our bookings for Venice next March because of the exchange rate. I wanted it to be a birthday present, Venice I mean.'

She had pictured the scene. Herself handing over the tickets and the hotel reservations tucked into one of those extra-large birthday cards. Star trying to hide her surprise and pleasure. Both of them poring over maps and guide books, planning the itinerary of every marvellous day. To see for the first time and together that incomparable view of San Marco from the western end of the Piazza. Star had read to her Ruskin's description. 'A multitude of pillars and white domes, clustered into a long low pyramid of coloured light.' To stand together on the Piazzetta in the early morning and look across the shimmering water to San Giorgio Maggiore. It was a dream, as insubstantial as the crumbling city. But the hope of it had been worth steeling herself to ask Edwin for that loan.

'And what did he say?'

There was no chance now of softening that brutal negative, of erasing the whole humiliating episode from her memory.

'He said no.'

'I suppose you told him why you wanted it. It didn't occur to you that we go away from here to be private, that our holidays are our own affair, that it might humiliate me to have Edwin Lorrimer know that I can't afford to take you to Venice, even on a ten-day package tour.'

'I didn't.' She cried out in vehement protest, horrified to hear the crack in her voice, and feel the first hot, gritty tears. It was odd, she thought, that it was she who could cry. Star was the emotional, the vehement one. And yet Star never cried.

'I didn't tell him anything, except that I needed the money.'

'How much?'

She hesitated, wondering whether to lie. But she never lied to Star.

'Five hundred pounds. I thought we might as well do it properly. I just told him that I badly needed five hundred pounds.'

'So, not surprisingly, faced with that irrefutable argument, he declined to hand out. What exactly did he say?'

'Only that grandmother had made her intentions perfectly plain in her will and that he had no intention of upsetting them. Then I said that most of the money would come to me after his death, anyway – I mean, that's what he told me when the will was read – and it would be too late then. I'd be an old lady. I might die first. It was now that was important. But I didn't tell him why I wanted it. I swear that.'

'Swear? Don't be dramatic. You're not in a court of law. And then what did he say?'

If only Star would stop that agitated pacing, would only turn and look at her instead of questioning her in that cold, inquisitorial voice. And the new bit was even harder to tell. She couldn't explain to herself why it should be, but it was something which she had tried to put out of her mind, for the present anyway. One day she would tell Star, the moment when it was right to tell. She had never imagined being forced into confidence with such brutal suddenness.

'He said that I shouldn't rely on getting anything in his will. He said that he might acquire new obligations. Obligations was the word he used. And if he did, the will would no longer stand.'

And now Star swung round and faced her.

'New obligations. Marriage! No, that's too ridiculous. Marriage, that desiccated, pedantic, self-satisfied prude. I doubt whether he ever deliberately touches a human body except his own. Solitary, masochistic, surreptitious vice, that's all he understands. No, not vice, the word's too strong. But marriage! Wouldn't you have thought . . .'

She broke off. Angela said:

'He didn't mention marriage.'

'Why should he? But what else would automatically set aside an existing will unless he made a new one? Marriage cancels a will. Didn't you know that?'

'You mean that as soon as he married I should be disinherited?'

'Yes.'

'But that isn't fair!'

'Since when has life been noted for its fairness? It wasn't fair that your grandmother left her fortune to him instead of sharing it with you just because he's a man and she had an old-fashioned prejudice that women shouldn't own money. It isn't fair that you're only a secretary at Hoggatt's because no one bothered to educate you for anything else. It isn't fair, come to that, that you should have to support me.'

'I don't support you. In every way except the unimportant one, you support me.'

'It's humiliating to be worth more dead than alive. If my heart gave out tonight, then you'd be all right. You could use the life assurance money to buy the place and stay on. The bank would advance the money once they knew you were my legatee.'

'Without you I shouldn't want to stay on.'

'Well, if you do have to leave here, at least it will give you an excuse to live on your own, if that's what you want.'

Angela cried out in vehement protest:

'I shall never live with anyone else but you. I don't want to live anywhere but here, in this cottage. You know that. It's our home.'

It was their home. It was the only real home she'd ever known. She didn't need to look around her to fix with startling clarity each familiar loved possession. She could lie in bed at night and in imagination move confidently around the cottage touching them in a happy exploration of shared memories and reassurance. The two Victorian lustre plant pots on their matching pedestals, found in The Lanes at Brighton one summer weekend. The eighteenth-century oil of Wicken Fen by an artist whose indecipherable signature, peered at through a microscope, had provided so many shared moments of happy conjecture. The French sword in its decorated scabbard, found in a country sale room and now hanging above their fireplace. It wasn't just that their possessions, wood and porcelain, paint and linen, symbolized their joint life. The cottage, their belongings, were their joint life, adorned and gave reality to it just as the bushes and flowers they had planted in the garden staked out their territory of trust.

She had a sudden and terrifying memory of a recurrent nightmare. They were standing facing each other in an empty attic room, bare walls squared with the pale imprints of discarded pictures, floorboards harsh to the feet, two naked strangers in a void, herself trying to reach out her hands to touch Stella's fingers, but unable to lift the heavy monstrous bolsters of flesh that had become her arms. She shivered and then was recalled to the reality of the cold autumn morning by the sound of her friend's voice.

'How much did your grandmother leave? You did tell me, but I've forgotten.'

'About thirty thousand, I think.'

'And he can't have spent any of it, living with his old father in that poky cottage. He hasn't even renovated the windmill. His salary alone must be more than enough for the two of them, apart from the old man's pension. Lorrimer's a senior scientist, isn't he? What does he get?'

'He's a Principal Scientific Officer. The scale goes up to eight thousand.'

'God! More in a year than I could earn from four novels. I

suppose if he jibbed at five hundred he'd hardly part with four thousand, not at a rate of interest we could afford. But it wouldn't hurt him. I've a good mind to ask him for it after all.'

Stella was only teasing, of course; but she recognized this too late to control the panic in her voice.

'No, please, Star! No, you mustn't!'

'You really hate him, don't you?'

'Not hate. Indifference. I just don't want to be under an obligation to him.'

'Nor, come to that, do I. And you shan't be.'

Angela went out to the hall and came back pulling on her coat. She said:

'I'll be late at the Lab if I don't hurry. The casserole is in the oven. Try to remember to switch on at half-past five. And don't touch the regulator. I'll turn down the heat when I get back.'

'I think I can just about manage that.'

'I'm taking sandwiches for lunch, so I shan't be back. There's the cold ham and salad in the fridge. Will that be enough, Star?'

'No doubt I'll survive.'

'Yesterday evening's typing is in the folder, but I haven't read it through.'

'How remiss of you.'

Stella followed her friend out to the hall. At the door she said:

'I expect they think at the Lab that I exploit you.'

'They know nothing about you at the Lab. And I don't care what they think.'

'Is that what Edwin Lorrimer thinks, too, that I exploit you? Or what does he think?'

'I don't want to talk about him.'

She folded her scarf over her blonde hair. In the antique mirror with its frame of carved shells she saw both their faces distorted by a defect in the glass; the brown and green of Stella's huge luminous eyes smeared like wet paint into the deep clefts between nostrils and mouth; her own wide brow bulging like that of a hydrocephalic child. She said:

'I wonder what I'd feel if Edwin died this week; a heart attack, a car accident, a brain haemorrhage.'

'Life isn't as convenient as that.'

'Death isn't. Star, shall you reply today to that solicitor?'

'He doesn't expect an answer until Monday. I can ring him at the London office on Monday morning. That's another five days. Anything can happen in five days.'

VII

'But they're just like mine! The panties I mean. I've got a pair like that! I bought them from Marks and Spencer's in Cambridge with my first salary cheque.'

It was ten thirty-five and Brenda Pridmore, at the reception desk at the rear of the main hall of Hoggatt's Laboratory, watched wide-eyed while Inspector Blakelock drew towards him the first labelled bag of exhibits from the clunch pit murder. She put out a finger and tentatively slid it over the thin plastic through which the knickers, crumpled and stained round the crotch, were clearly visible. The detective constable who had brought in the exhibits had said that the girl had been to a dance. Funny, thought Brenda, that she hadn't bothered to put on clean underclothes. Perhaps she wasn't fastidious. Or perhaps she had been in too much of a hurry to change. And now the intimate clothes which she had put on so unthinkingly on the day of her death would be smoothed out by strange hands, scrutinized under ultra-violet light, perhaps be handed up, neatly docketed, to the judge and jury in the Crown Court.

Brenda knew that she would never again be able to wear her own panties, their prettiness contaminated for ever by the memory of this dead unknown girl. Perhaps they had even bought them together in the same store, on the same day. She could recall the excitement of spending for the first time money she had actually earned. It had been a Saturday afternoon and there had been a crush round the lingerie counter, eager hands rummaging among the panties. She had liked the pair with the sprays of pink machine-embroidered flowers across the front. So, too, had this unknown girl. Perhaps their hands had touched. She cried:

'Inspector. Isn't death terrible?'

'Murder is. Death isn't; at least, no more than birth is. You couldn't have one without the other or there'd be no room for us all. I reckon I won't worry overmuch when my time comes.'

'But that policeman who brought in the exhibits said that she was only eighteen. That's my age.'

He was making out the folder for the new case, meticulously transferring details from the police form to the file. And his head, with the cropped dry hair which reminded her so of corn-stubble, was bent low over the page so that she could not see his face. Suddenly she remembered being told that he had lost an only daughter, killed by a hit-and-run driver, and she wished the words unsaid. Her face flared and she turned her eyes away. But when he replied his voice was perfectly steady.

'Aye, poor lass. Led him on, I daresay. They never learn. What's that you've got?'

'It's the bag of male clothes, suit, shoes and underwear. Do you think these belong to the chief suspect?'

'They'll be the husband's, likely as not.'

'But what can they prove? She was strangled, wasn't she?'

'No telling for certain until we get Dr Kerrison's report. But they usually examine the chief suspect's clothes. There might be a trace of blood, a grain of sand or earth, paint, minute fibres from the victim's clothes, a trace of her saliva even. Or she could have been raped. All that bundle will go into the Biology Search Room with the victim's clothes.'

'But the policeman didn't say anything about rape! I thought you said this bundle belongs to the husband.'

'You don't want to let it worry you. You have to learn to be like a doctor or a nurse, detached, isn't it?'

'Is that how forensic scientists feel?'

'Likely as not. It's their job. They don't think about victims or suspects. That's for the police. They're only concerned with scientific facts.'

He was right, thought Brenda. She remembered the time only three days previously when the Senior Scientific Officer of the instrument section had let her look into the giant scanning electron microscope and watch the image of a minute pill of putty burst instantaneously into an exotic incandescent flower. He had explained.

'It's a coccolith, magnified six thousand times.'

'A what?'

'The skeleton of a micro-organism which lived in the ancient seas from which the chalk in the putty was deposited. They're different, depending on where the chalk was quarried. That's how you can differentiate one sample of putty from another.'

She had exclaimed:

'But it's so lovely!'

He had taken her place at the eyepiece of the instrument.

'Yes, nice, isn't it?'

But she had known that, while she looked back in wonder across a million years, his mind was on the minute scrape of putty from the heel of the suspect's shoe, the trace which might prove a man was a rapist or a murderer. And yet, she had thought, he doesn't really mind. All he cares about is getting the answer right. It would have been no use asking him whether he thought there was a unifying purpose in life, whether it could really be chance that an animal so small that it couldn't be seen by the naked eye could die millions of years ago in the depths of the sea and be resurrected by science to prove a man innocent or guilty. It was odd, she thought, that scientists so often weren't religious when their work revealed a world so variously marvellous and yet so mysteriously unified and at one. Dr Lorrimer seemed to be the only member of Hoggatt's who was known to go regularly to church. She wondered if she dared ask him about the coccolith and God. He had been very kind this morning about the murder. He had arrived at the Laboratory over an hour late, at ten o'clock, looking terribly tired because he had been up that night at the scene of crime, and had come over to the reception desk to collect his personal post. He had said:

'You'll be getting exhibits from your first murder case this morning. Don't let them worry you, Brenda. There's only one death we need to be frightened of, and that's our own.'

It was a strange thing to have said, an odd way to reassure her. But he was right. She was suddenly glad that Inspector Blakelock had done the documentation on the clunch pit murder. Now, with care, the owner of those stained panties would remain, for her, unknown, anonymous, a number in the biology series on a manila folder. Inspector Blakelock's voice broke into her thoughts:

'Have you got those court reports we checked yesterday ready for the post?'

'Yes, they've been entered in the book. I meant to ask you. Why do all the court statements have "Criminal Justice Act 1967 sections 2 and 9" printed on them?'

'That's the statutory authority for written evidence to be tendered at committal proceedings and the Crown Court. You can look up the sections in the library. Before the 1967 Act the labs had a hard time of it, I can tell you, when all scientific evidence had to be given orally. Mind you, the court-going officers still have to spend a fair amount of time attending trials. The defence doesn't always accept the scientific findings. That's the difficult part of the job, not the analysis but standing alone in the witness box to defend it under cross-examination. If a man's no good in the box, then all the careful work he does here goes for nothing.'

Brenda suddenly remembered something else that Mrs Mallett had told her, that the motorist who had killed his daughter had been acquitted because the scientist had crumbled under the cross-examination; something to do with the analysis of chips of paint found on the road which matched the suspect's car. It must be terrible to lose an only child; to lose any child. Perhaps that was the worst thing that could happen to a human being. No wonder Inspector Blakelock was often so quiet; that when the police officers came in with their hearty banter he answered only with that slow, gentle smile.

She glanced across at the Laboratory clock. Ten forty-five. Any minute now the scene-of-crime course would be arriving for their lecture on the collection and preservation of scientific evidence, and this brief spell of quiet would be over. She wondered what Colonel Hoggatt would think if he could visit his Laboratory now. Her eyes were drawn, as they so often were, to his portrait hanging just outside the Director's office. Even from her place at the desk she could read the gold lettering on the frame.

Colonel William Makepeace Hoggatt V.C.
Chief Constable 1894–1912
Founder of Hoggatt's Forensic Science Laboratory.

He was standing in the room which was still used as a library, his ruddy face stern and bewhiskered under the sprouting plumes of his hat, his braided, bemedalled tunic fastened with a row of gilt buttons. One proprietorial hand was laid, light as a priestly blessing, on an old-fashioned microscope in gleaming brass. But the minatory eyes weren't fixed on this latest scientific wonder; they were fixed on Brenda. Under his accusing gaze, recalled to duty, she bent again to her work.

VIII

By twelve o'clock the meeting of senior scientists in the Director's office to discuss the furniture and equipment for the new Laboratory was over, and Howarth rang for his secretary to clear the conference table. He watched her as she emptied and polished the ashtray (he didn't smoke and the smell of ash offended him), collected together the copies of the Laboratory plans and gathered up the strewn discarded papers. Even from his desk, Howarth could see Middlemass's complex geometrical doodles, and the crumpled agenda, ringed with coffee stains, of the Senior Vehicle Examiner, Bill Morgan.

He watched the girl as she moved with quiet competence about the table wondering, as always, what, if anything, was going on behind that extraordinarily wide brow, those slanted enigmatic eyes. He missed his old personal assistant, Marjory Faraker, more than he had expected. It had, he thought ruefully, been good for his self-conceit to find that her devotion didn't, after all, extend to leaving London where, surprisingly, she had been discovered to have a life of her own, to join him in the fens. Like all good secretaries she had acquired, or at least known how to simulate, some of the idealized attributes of wife, mother, mistress, confidante, servant and friend without being, or indeed expecting to be, any of these. She had flattered his self-esteem, protected him from the minor irritations of life, preserved his privacy with maternal pugnacity, had ensured, with infinite tact, that he knew all he needed to know about what was going on in his Laboratory.

He couldn't complain about Angela Foley. She was a more than competent shorthand typist and an efficient secretary. Nothing was left undone. It was just that for her he felt that he hardly existed, that his authority, meekly deferred to, was nevertheless a charade. The fact that she was Lorrimer's cousin was irrelevant. He had never heard her mention his name. He wondered from time to time what sort of a life she led in that remote cottage with her writer friend, how far it had satisfied her. But she told him nothing, not even about the Laboratory. He knew that Hoggatt's had a heartbeat – all institutions did – but the pulse eluded him. He said:

'The Foreign and Commonwealth Office want us to take a Danish biologist for two or three days next month. He's visiting England to look at the service. Fit him in, will you, when I'm free to give him some time. You'd better consult Dr Lorrimer about his diary commitments. Then let the F.C.O. know what days we can offer.'

'Yes, Dr Howarth.'

At least the autopsy was over. It had been worse than he had expected, but he had seen it through and without disgrace. He hadn't expected that the colours of the human body would be so vivid, so exotically beautiful. Now he saw again Kerrison's gloved fingers, sleek as eels, busying themselves at the body's orifices. Explaining, demonstrating, discarding. Presumably he had become as immune to disgust as he obviously was to the sweet-sour smell of his mortuary. And to all the experts in violent death, faced daily with the final disintegration of the personality, pity would be as irrelevant as disgust.

Miss Foley was ready to go now and had come up to the desk to clear his out-tray. He said:

'Has Inspector Blakelock worked out last month's average turn-round figures yet?'

'Yes, sir. The average for all exhibits is down to twelve days, and the blood alcohol has fallen to 1.2 days. But the figure for crimes against the person is up again. I'm just typing the figures now.'

'Let me have them as soon as they're ready, please.'

There were memories which, he suspected, would be even more insistent than Kerrison marking out with his cartilage knife on the milk-white body the long line of the primary incision.

Doyle, that great black bull, grinning at him in the washroom afterwards as, side by side, they washed their hands. And why, he wondered, had he felt it necessary to wash. His hands hadn't been contaminated.

'The performance was well up to standard. Neat, quick and thorough, that's Doc Kerrison. Sorry we shan't be able to call for you when we're ready to make the arrest. Not allowed. You'll have to imagine that bit. But there'll be the trial to attend, with any luck.'

Angela Foley was standing in front of the desk, looking at him strangely, he thought.

'Yes?'

'Scobie has had to go home, Dr Howarth. He's not at all well. He thinks it may be this two-day 'flu that's going about. And he says that the incinerator has broken down.'

'Presumably he telephoned for the mechanic before he left.'

'Yes, sir. He says it was all right yesterday morning when Inspector Doyle came with the court orders authorizing the destruction of the cannabis exhibits. It was working then.'

Howarth was irritated. This was one of those minor administrative details which Miss Faraker would never have dreamed of troubling him with. Miss Foley was, he guessed, expecting him to say something sympathetic about Scobie, to inquire whether the old man had been fit to cycle home. Dr MacIntyre had, no doubt, bleated like an anxious sheep when any of the staff were ill. He bent his head over his papers.

But Miss Foley was at the door. It had to be now. He made himself say:

'Ask Dr Lorrimer to come down for a few minutes, will you please?'

He could, perfectly casually, have asked Lorrimer to stay on after the meeting; why hadn't he? Probably because there might have been an echo of the headmaster in so public a request. Perhaps because this was an interview he had been glad to postpone, even temporarily.

Lorrimer came in and stood in front of the desk. Howarth took out Bradley's personal file from his right-hand drawer and said:

'Sit down will you, please. This annual report on Bradley.

You've given him an adverse marking. Have you told him?'

Lorrimer remained standing. He said:

'I'm required by the reporting rules to tell him. I saw him in my office at ten-thirty, as soon as I got back from the P.M.'

'It seems a bit hard. According to his file, it's the first adverse report he's had. We took him on probation eighteen months ago. Why hasn't he made out?'

'I should have thought that was obvious from my detailed markings. He's been promoted above his capacity.'

'In other words, the Board made a mistake?'

'That's not so unusual. Boards occasionally do. And not only when it comes to promotions.'

The allusion was blatant, a deliberate provocation, yet Howarth decided to ignore it. With an effort he kept his voice level.

'I'm not prepared to countersign this report as it stands. It's too early to judge him fairly.'

'I made that excuse for him last year when he'd been with us six months. But if you disagree with my assessment you'll presumably say so. There's a space provided.'

'I intend to use it. And I suggest that you try the effect of giving the boy some support and encouragement. There are two reasons for an inadequate performance. Some people are capable of doing better and will if judiciously kicked into it. Others aren't. To kick them is not only pointless, it destroys what confidence they have. You run an efficient department. But it might be more efficient and happier if you learned how to understand people. Management is largely a matter of personal relationships.'

He made himself look up. Lorrimer said through lips so stiff that the words sounded cracked:

'I hadn't realized that your family were noted for success in their personal relationships.'

'The fact that you can't take criticism without becoming as personal and spiteful as a neurotic girl is an example of what I mean.'

He never knew what Lorrimer was about to reply. The door opened and his sister came in. She was dressed in slacks and a sheepskin jacket, her blonde hair bound with a scarf. She looked at them both without embarrassment and said easily:

'Sorry, I didn't realize you were engaged. I ought to have asked Inspector Blakelock to ring.'

Without a word, Lorrimer, deathly pale, turned on his heels, walked past her and was gone. Domenica looked after him, smiled and shrugged. She said:

'Sorry if I interrupted something. It's just to say that I'm going to Norwich for a couple of hours to buy some materials. Is there anything you want?'

'Nothing, thank you.'

'I'll be back before dinner, but I think I'll give the village concert a miss. Without Claire Easterbrook the Mozart will be pretty insupportable. Oh, and I'm thinking of going up to London for the best part of next week.'

Her brother didn't reply. She looked at him and said:

'What's wrong?'

'How did Lorrimer know about Gina?'

He didn't need to ask her if it was she who had told him. Whatever else she may have confided, it would not have been that. She went across, ostensibly to study the Stanley Spencer set in the overmantel of the fireplace, and asked lightly:

'Why? He didn't mention your divorce, did he?'

'Not directly, but the allusion was intended.'

She turned to face him.

'He probably took the trouble to find out as much as possible about you when he knew that you were a candidate for the job here. It isn't such a large service after all.'

'But I came from outside it.'

'Even so, there would be contacts, gossip. A failed marriage is one of those unconsidered trifles he might expect to sniff out. And what of it? After all, it's not unusual. I thought forensic scientists were particularly at risk. All those late hours at scenes of crime and the unpredictable court attendances. They ought to be used to marital break-ups.'

He said, knowing that he sounded as petulant as an obstinate child:

'I don't want him in my Lab.'

'Your Lab? It isn't quite as simple as that, is it? I don't think the Stanley Spencer is right over the fireplace. It looks incongruous. It's strange that Father bought it. Not at all his kind of picture I should have said. Did you put it here to shock?'

Miraculously, his anger and misery were assuaged. But then she had always been able to do that for him.

'Merely to disconcert and confuse. It's intended to suggest that I may be a more complex character than they assume.'

'Oh, but you are! I've never needed "Assumption at Cookham" to prove it. Why not the Greuze? It would look good with that carved overmantel.'

'Too pretty.'

She laughed, and was gone. He picked up Clifford Bradley's report and, in the space provided, wrote:

'Mr Bradley's performance has been disappointing, but not all the difficulties are of his making. He lacks confidence and would benefit from more active encouragement and support than he has received. I have corrected the final marking to what I consider a more just assessment and have spoken to the senior biologist about the personnel management in his department.'

If he did finally decide, after all, this wasn't the job for him, that snide comment should go some way to ensure that Lorrimer stood no chance of succeeding him as Director of Hoggatt's.

IX

At one forty-eight precisely Paul Middlemass, the Document Examiner, opened his file on the clunch pit murder. The Document Examination Room, which occupied the whole of the front of the building immediately under the roof, smelled like a stationer's shop, a pungent amalgam of paper and ink, sharpened by the tang of chemicals. Middlemass breathed it as his native air. He was a tall, rangy, large-featured man with a mobile, wide-mouthed face of agreeable ugliness and iron-grey hair which fell in heavy swathes over parchment-coloured skin. Easy-going and seemingly indolent, he was in fact a prodigious worker with an obsession for his job. Paper in all its manifestations was his passion. Few men, in or outside the forensic science service, knew so much about it. He handled it with joy and with a kind of reverence, gloated over it, knew its provenance almost by its smell. Identification of the sizing and loading of a specimen by spectrographic or X-ray crystallography merely confirmed what touch and sight had already pronounced. The satisfaction of watching the emergence of an obscure water-mark under soft X-rays never palled, and the final pattern was as fascinating to his unsurprised eyes as the expected potter's mark to a collector of porcelain.

His father, long dead, had been a dentist, and his son had taken for his own use the old man's inordinately large store of self-designed surgical overalls. They were old-fashioned in cut, waisted and full-skirted as the coat of a Regency buck, and with crested metal buttons fastening high to the side of the throat. Although they were too short in the arm so that his lean wrists protruded like those of an overgrown schoolboy, he wore them with a certain panache, as if this unorthodox working garb, so different from the regulation white coats of the rest of the Laboratory staff, symbolized that unique blend of scientific skill, experience and flair which distinguishes the good Document Examiner.

He had just finished telephoning his wife, having remembered rather belatedly that he was due to help out that evening with the village concert. He liked women, and before his marriage had enjoyed a succession of casual, satisfactory and uncommitted affairs. He had married late, a buxom research scientist from Cambridge twenty years his junior, and drove back to their modern flat on the outskirts of the city each night in his Jaguar – his chief extravagance – frequently late, but seldom too late to bear her off to their local pub. Secure in his job, with a growing international reputation, and uxoriously contented with his comely Sophie, he knew himself to be successful and suspected himself to be happy.

The Document Examination Laboratory with its cabinets and range of monorail cameras took up what some of his colleagues, notably Edwin Lorrimer, regarded as more than its share of room. But the Laboratory, lit by rows of fluorescent lights and with its low ceiling, was stuffy and ill-ventilated, and this afternoon the central heating, unreliable at the best of times, had concentrated all its efforts on the top of the building. Usually he was oblivious of his working conditions, but a sub-tropical temperature was difficult to ignore. He opened the door to the passage. Opposite and a little to the right were the male and female lavatories, and he could hear the occasional feet, light or heavy, hurried or dilatory, of passing members of staff, and hear the swing of the two doors. The sounds didn't worry him. He applied himself to his task.

But the specimen he was now poring over held little mystery. If the crime had been other than murder he would have left it to his Scientific Officer assistant, not yet returned from a belated lunch. But murder invariably meant a court appearance and cross-examination – the defence seldom let the scientific evidence go unchallenged in this, the gravest of charges – and a court appearance put document examination in general, and Hoggatt's Laboratory in particular, on public trial. He made it a matter of principle always to take the murder cases himself. They were seldom the most interesting. What he most enjoyed were the historical investigations, the satisfaction of demonstrating, as he had only last month, that a document dated 1872 was printed on paper containing chemical wood-pulp which was first used in 1874, a discovery which had initiated a fascinating unravelling of complicated documentary fraud. There was nothing complicated and little of interest about the present job. Yet, only a few years ago, a man's neck could have depended upon his opinion. He seldom thought of the half-dozen men who had been hanged during the twenty years of his forensic experience, primarily because of his evidence, and when he did, it was not the strained but oddly anonymous faces in the dock which he remembered, or their names, but paper and ink, the thickened downward stroke, the peculiar formation of a letter. Now he spread out on his table the note taken from the dead girl's handbag, placing on each side the two specimens of the husband's handwriting which the police had been able to obtain. One was a letter to the suspect's mother written on holiday at Southend – how, he wondered, had they managed to extract that from her? The other was a brief telephoned message about a football match. The note taken from the victim's purse was even briefer.

'You've got your own chap so lay off Barry Taylor or you'll be sorry. It would be a pity to spoil a nice face like yours. Acid isn't pretty. Watch it. A Wellwisher.'

The style, he decided, was derived from a recent television thriller, the writing was obviously disguised. It was possible that the police would be able to provide him with some more samples of the suspect's handwriting when they visited the lad's place of work, but he didn't really need them. The similarities between the threatening note and the samples were unmistakable. The writer had tried to alter the slant of his hand and had changed the shape of the small r. But the lifts of the pen came regularly at every fourth letter – Middlemass had never found a forger who remembered to vary the interval at which he lifted pen from paper – and the dot above the i, high and slightly to the left, and the over-emphatic apostrophe were almost a trade-mark. He would analyse the paper sample, photograph and enlarge each individual letter and then mount them on a comparison chart, and the jury would pass it solemnly from hand to hand and wonder why it needed a highly-paid expert to come and explain what anyone could see with his own eyes.

The telephone rang. Middlemass stretched out a long arm and held the instrument to his left ear. Susan Bradley's voice, at first apologetic then conspiratorial and finally close to tears, squeaked into his ear in a long monologue of complaint and desperation. He listened, made soft encouraging noises, held the receiver an inch or two from his ear, and meanwhile noted that the writer, poor bastard, hadn't even thought of altering the distinctive cross-bar of his small letter t. Not that it would have done any good. And he couldn't have known, poor devil, that his effort would feature as an exhibit in his trial for murder.

'All right,' he said. 'Don't worry. Leave it to me.'

'And you won't let him know that I phoned you?'

'Of course not, Susan. Relax. I'll settle it.'

The voice crackled on.

'Then tell him not to be a fool, for God's sake. Hasn't he noticed that we've got one and a half million unemployed?

Lorrimer can't sack him. Tell Clifford to hang on to his job and stop being a bloody fool. I'll deal with Lorrimer.'

He replaced the receiver. He had liked Susan Moffat who, for two years, had worked for him as his S.O. She had both more brains and more guts than her husband, and he had wondered, without greatly caring, why she had married Bradley. Pity probably, and an over-developed maternal instinct. There were some women who simply had to take the unfortunate literally to their breast. Or perhaps it was just lack of choice, the need for a home of her own and a child. Well, it was too late to try and stop the marriage now, and it certainly hadn't occurred to him to try at the time. And at least she had the home and the kid. She had brought the baby to the Lab to see him only a fortnight ago. The visit of the prune-faced yelling bundle had done nothing to change his own resolution not to produce a child, but certainly Susan herself had seemed happy enough. And she would probably be happy again if something could be done about Lorrimer.

He thought that the time had perhaps come to do something about Lorrimer. And he had, after all, his own private reason for taking on the job. It was a small personal obligation, and to date it hadn't particularly fretted what he supposed other people called conscience. But Susan Bradley's call had reminded him. He listened. The footsteps were familiar. Well, it was a coincidence, but better now than later. Moving to the door he called at the retreating back:

'Lorrimer. I want a word with you.'

Lorrimer came and stood inside the door, tall, unsmiling in his carefully buttoned white coat, and regarded Middlemass with his dark, wary eyes. Middlemass made himself look into them, and then turned his glance away. The irises had seemed to dilate into black pools of despair. It was not an emotion he felt competent to deal with, and he felt discomforted. What on earth was eating the poor devil? He said, carefully casual:

'Look, Lorrimer, lay off Bradley will you? I know he's not exactly God's gift to forensic science, but he's a conscientious plodder and you're not going to stimulate either his brain or his speed by bullying the poor little beast. So cut it out.'

'Are you telling me how to manage my staff?'

Lorrimer's voice was perfectly controlled, but the pulse at the side of his temple had begun to beat visibly. Middlemass found it difficult not to fix his eyes on it.

'That's right, mate. This member of your staff anyway. I know damn well what you're up to and I don't like it. So stow it.'

'Is this meant to be some kind of a threat?'

'More friendly warning, reasonably friendly anyway. I don't pretend to like you, and I wouldn't have served under you if the Home Office had been daft enough to appoint you Director of this Lab. But I admit that what you do in your own department isn't normally my business, only this happens to be an exception. I know what's going on, I don't like it, and I'm making it my business to see that it stops.'

'I didn't realize that you had this tender regard for Bradley. But of course, Susan Bradley must have phoned you. He wouldn't have the guts to speak for himself. Did she telephone you, Middlemass?'

Middlemass ignored the question. He said:

'I haven't any particular regard for Bradley. But I did have a certain regard for Peter Ennalls, if you can remember him.'

'Ennalls drowned himself because his fiancée threw him over and he'd had a mental breakdown. He left a note explaining his action and it was read out at the inquest. Both things happened months after he'd left the Southern Laboratory; neither had anything to do with me.'

'What happened while he was at the Lab had a hell of a lot to do with you. He was a pleasant, rather ordinary lad with two good 'A' levels and an unaccountable wish to become a forensic biologist when he had the bad luck to begin to work under you. As it happens, he was my wife's cousin. I was the one who recommended him to try for the job. So I have a certain interest, you could say a certain responsibility.'

Lorrimer said:

'He never said that he was related to your wife. But I can't see what difference it makes. He was totally unsuited for the job. A forensic biologist who can't work accurately under pressure is no use to me or the Service and he'd better get out. We've no room for passengers. That's what I propose to tell Bradley.'

'Then you'd better have second thoughts.'

'And how are you going to make me?'

It was extraordinary that lips so tight could produce any sound, that Lorrimer's voice, high and distorted, could have forced itself through the vocal cords without splitting them.

'I shall make it plain to Howarth that you and I can't serve in the same Lab. He won't exactly welcome that. Trouble between senior staff is the last complication he wants just now. So he'll suggest to Establishment Department that one of us gets a transfer before we have the added complication of moving into a new Lab. I'm banking on Howarth – and Estabs come to that – concluding that it's easier to find a forensic biologist than a Document Examiner.'

Middlemass surprised himself. None of this rigmarole had occurred to him before he spoke. Not that it was unreasonable. There wasn't another Document Examiner of his calibre in the Service and Howarth knew it. If he categorically refused to work in the same Laboratory as Lorrimer, one of them would have to go. The quarrel wouldn't do either of them any good with the Establishment Department, but he thought he knew which one it would harm most.

Lorrimer said:

'You helped stop me getting the directorship, now you want to drive me out of the Lab.'

'Personally I don't care a damn whether you're here or not. But just lay off bullying Bradley.'

'If I were prepared to take advice about the way I run my Department from anyone, it wouldn't be a third-rate paper fetishist with a second-rate degree, who doesn't know the difference between scientific proof and intuition.'

The taunt was too absurd to puncture Middlemass's secure self-esteem. But at least it warranted a retort. He found that he was getting angry. And suddenly he saw light. He said:

'Look, mate, if you can't make it in bed, if she isn't finding you quite up to the mark, don't take your frustration out on the rest of us. Remember Chesterfield's advice. The expense is exorbitant, the position ridiculous, and the pleasure transitory.'

The result astounded him. Lorrimer gave a strangled cry and

lunged out. Middlemass's reaction was both instinctive and deeply satisfying. He shot out his right arm and landed a punch on Lorrimer's nose. There was a second's astonished silence in which the two men regarded each other. Then the blood spurted and Lorrimer tottered and fell forward. Middlemass caught him by the shoulders and felt the weight of his head against his chest. He thought: 'My God, he's going to faint.' He was aware of a tangle of emotion, surprise at himself, boyish gratification, pity and an impulse to laugh. He said:

'Are you all right?'

Lorrimer tore himself from his grasp and stood upright. He fumbled for his handkerchief and held it to his nose. The red stain grew. Looking down, Middlemass saw Lorrimer's blood spreading on his white overall, decorative as a rose. He said:

'Since we're engaging in histrionics, I believe your response ought now to be "By God, you swine, you'll pay for this." '

He was astounded by the sudden blaze of hate in the black eyes. Lorrimer's voice came to him muffled by the handkerchief.

'You will pay for it.' And then he was gone.

Middlemass was suddenly aware of Mrs Bidwell, the Laboratory cleaner, standing by the door, eyes large and excited behind her ridiculous upswept diamanté spectacles.

'Nice goings on, I don't think. Senior staff fighting each other. You ought to be ashamed of yourselves.'

'Oh, we are, Mrs Bidwell. We are.' Slowly Middlemass eased his long arms from his overall. He handed it to her.

'Drop this in the soiled linen, will you.'

'Now you know very well, Mr Middlemass, that I don't go into the gents' cloakroom, not in working hours. You put it in the basket yourself. And if you want a clean one now, you know where to find it. I'm putting out no more clean linen until tomorrow. Fighting, indeed. I might have known that Dr Lorrimer would be mixed up in it. But he's not a gentleman you'd expect to find using his fists. Wouldn't have the guts, that would be my view. But he's been odd in his manner these last few days, no doubt about that. You heard about that spot of bother in the front hall yesterday, I suppose? He practically pushed those kids of Dr Kerrison's out of the door. All they were doing was waiting for their dad. No harm in that, I suppose. There's a very nasty atmosphere in this Lab recently, and if a certain gentleman doesn't take a hold of himself there'll be a mischief done, you mark my words.'

X

It was nearly five o'clock and dark before Detective Inspector Doyle got back to his home in the village four miles to the north of Cambridge. He had tried to telephone his wife once, but without success: the line was engaged. Another of her interminable, secretive and expensive telephone calls to one of her old nursing friends, he thought, and, duly satisfied, made no further attempt. The wrought-iron gate, as usual, was open and he parked in front of the house. It wasn't worth garaging the car for a couple of hours, which was all the time he could allow himself.

Scoope House hardly looked its best in the late afternoon of a dark November evening. No wonder that the agents hadn't recently sent anyone to view. It was a bad time of the year. The house was, he thought, a monument to miscalculation. He had bought it for less than seventeen thousand and had spent five thousand on it to date, expecting to sell it for at least forty. But that was before the recession had upset the calculations of more expert speculators than he. Now, with the property market sluggish, there was nothing to do but wait. He could afford to hang on to the house until the market quickened. He wasn't sure that he would be given a chance to hold on to his wife. He wasn't even sure that he wanted to. The marriage, too, had been a miscalculation, but given the circumstances of the time, an understandable one. He wasted no time on regrets.

The two tall oblongs of light from the first-floor drawing-room window should have been a welcoming promise of warmth and comfort. Instead they were vaguely menacing; Maureen was at home. But where else, she would have argued, was there for her to go in this dreary East Anglian village on a dull November evening?

She had finished tea, and the tray was still at her side. The milk bottle, with its crushed top pressed back, a single mug, sliced bread spilling out of its wrapper, a slab of butter on a greasy dish, a bought fruit cake in its unopened carton. He felt the customary surge of irritation, but said nothing. Once when he had remonstrated at her sluttishness she had shrugged:

'Who sees, who cares?'

He saw and he cared, but it had been many months since he had counted with her. He said:

'I'm taking a couple of hours' kip. Wake me at seven, will you?'

'You mean we aren't going to the Chevisham concert?'

'For God's sake, Maureen, you were yelling yesterday that you couldn't be bothered with it. Kids' stuff. Remember?'

'It's not exactly The Talk of the Town, but at least we were going out. Out! Out of this dump. Together for a change. It was something to dress up for. And you said we'd have dinner afterwards at the Chinese restaurant at Ely.'

'Sorry. I couldn't know I'd be on a murder case.'

'When will you be back? If there's any point in asking?'

'God knows. I'm picking up Sergeant Beale. There are still one or two people we've got to see who were at the Muddington dance, notably a lad called Barry Taylor who has some explaining to do. Depending on what we get out of him, I may want to drop in on the husband again.'

'That'll please you, won't it, keeping him in a muck sweat. Is that why you became a cop – because you like frightening people?'

'That's about as stupid as saying you became a nurse because you get a kick out of emptying bed-pans.'

He flung himself in a chair and closed his eyes, giving way to sleep. He saw again the boy's terrified face, smelt again the sweat of fear. But he'd stood up well to that first interview, hindered rather than helped by the presence of his solicitor, who had never seen his client before and had made it painfully apparent that he would prefer never to see him again. He had stuck to his story, that they'd quarrelled at the dance and he had left early. That she hadn't arrived home by one o'clock. That he'd gone out to look for her on the road and across the clunch pit field, returning alone half an hour later. That he'd seen no one and hadn't been anywhere near the clunch pit or the derelict car. It was a good story, simple, unelaborated, possibly even true except in that one essential. But, with luck, the Lab report on her blood and the stain on his jacket cuff, the minute traces of sandy soil and dust from the car on his shoes, would be ready by Friday. If Lorrimer worked late tonight – and he usually did – the blood analysis might even be available by tomorrow. And then would come the elaborations, the inconsistencies, and finally the truth. She said:

'Who else was at the scene?'

It was something, he thought, that she had bothered to ask. He said sleepily:

'Lorrimer, of course. He never misses a murder scene. Doesn't trust any of us to know our jobs, I suppose. We had the usual half-hour hanging about for Kerrison. That maddened Lorrimer, of course. He's done all the work at the scene – all anyone can do – and then he has to cool his heels with the rest of us, waiting for God's gift to forensic pathology to come screaming up with a police escort and break the news to us that what we all thought was a corpse is – surprise, surprise – indeed a corpse, and that we can safely move the body.'

'The forensic pathologist does more than that.'

'Of course he does. But not all that much more, not at the actual scene. His job comes later.'

He added:

'Sorry I couldn't ring. I did try but you were engaged.'

'I expect that was Daddy. His offer still stands, the job of Security Officer in the Organization. But he can't wait much longer. If you don't accept by the end of the month, then he'll advertise.'

Oh God, he thought, not that again.

'I wish your dear Daddy wouldn't talk about the Organization. It makes the family business sound like the Mafia. If it were, I might be tempted to join. What Daddy's got are three cheap, shabby shops selling cheap, shabby suits to cheap shabby fools who wouldn't recognize a decent cloth if it were shoved down their throats. I might've considered coming into the business if dear Daddy hadn't already got Big Brother as a co-director, ready to take over from him, and if he didn't make it so plain hat he only tolerates me because I'm your husband. But I'm amned if I'm going to fart around like a pansy floor-walker vatching that no poor sod nicks the Y-fronts, even if I am ignified with the name security officer. I'm staying here.'

'Where you've got such useful contacts.'

And what exactly, he wondered, did she mean by that? He'd een careful not to tell her anything, but she wasn't altogether a ool. She could have guessed. He said:

'Where I've got a job. You knew what you were taking on vhen you married me.'

But no one ever does know that, he thought. Not really.

'Don't expect me to be here when you get back.'

That was an old threat. He said easily:

'Suit yourself. But if you're thinking of driving, forget it. I'm aking the Cortina, the clutch is playing up on the Renault. So if ou're planning on running home to Mummy before tomorrow norning, you'll have to phone Daddy to call for you, or take a axi.'

She was speaking, but her voice, peevishly insistent, was coming rom far away, no longer coherent words but waves of sound eating against his brain. Two hours. Whether or not she othered to rouse him, he knew that he would wake almost to the ninute. He closed his eyes and slept.

BOOK TWO

Death in a White Coat

I

It was very peaceful in the front hall of Hoggatt's at eight-forty in the morning. Brenda often thought that this was the part of the working day she liked best, the hour before the staff arrived and the work of the Lab got really under way, when she and Inspector Blakelock worked together in the quiet emptiness of the hall, still and solemn as a church, making up a supply of manila folders ready to register the day's new cases, repacking exhibits for collection by the police, making a final check of the Laboratory reports to courts to ensure that the examination was complete, that no relevant detail had been omitted. Immediately on arrival she would put on her white coat, and at once she felt different, no longer young and uncertain, but a professional woman, almost like a scientist, a recognized member of the Lab staff. Then she would go into the kitchen at the back of the house and make tea. After the dignification of the white coat this domestic chore was something of a let-down, and she didn't really need a drink so soon after breakfast. But Inspector Blakelock, who motored from Ely every day, was always ready for his tea, and she didn't mind making it.

'That's the stuff to give the troops,' he would invariably say, curving back moist lips to the mug's brim and gulping the hot liquid down as if his throat were asbestos. 'You make a nice cup of tea, Brenda, I'll say that for you.' And she would reply:

'Mum says the secret is always to warm the pot and let the tea brew for just five minutes.'

This small ritual exchange, so invariable that she could silently mouth his words and had to resist an impulse to giggle, the familiar domestic aroma of the tea, the gradual warmth as she curved her hands around the thick mug, constituted a reassuring and comforting beginning to the working day.

She liked Inspector Blakelock. He spoke seldom, but he was never impatient with her, always kind, a companionable father figure. Even her mother, when she visited the Lab before Brenda took up her post, had been happy about her working alone with him. Brenda's cheeks still burned with shame when she remembered her mother's insistence that she should visit Hoggatt's to see where her daughter was going to work, although Chief Inspector Martin, the Senior Police Liaison Officer, had apparently thought it perfectly reasonable. He had explained to her mother how it was an innovation for Hoggatt's having a clerical officer on the desk instead of a junior police officer. If she made a success of the job it would mean a permanent saving in police manpower as well as a useful training for her. As Chief Inspector Martin had told her mother: 'The reception desk is the heart of the Laboratory.' At present he was with a party of police officers visiting the United States and Inspector Blakelock was totally in charge doing the two jobs, not only receiving the exhibits, making out the register of court attendances and preparing the statistics, but discussing the cases with the detective in charge, explaining what the Laboratory could hope to do, rejecting those cases where the scientists couldn't help, and checking that the final statements for the court were complete. Brenda guessed that it was a big responsibility for him and was determined not to let him down.

Already, when she had been making the tea, the first exhibit of the day had arrived, brought in no doubt by a detective constable working on the case. It was another plastic bag of clothes from the clunch pit murder. As Inspector Blakelock turned it over in his large hands, she glimpsed through the plastic a pair of dark blue trousers with a greasy waistband, a wide-lapelled striped jacket, and a pair of black shoes with pointed toes and ornate buckles. Inspector Blakelock was studying the police report. He said:

'These belong to the boyfriend she was messing about with at the dance. You'll need a new file for the report, but register it to Biology under the Muddington reference with a sub-group number. Then attach one of the red Immediate slips. Murder gets priority.'

'But we might have two or three murders at the same time. Who decides the priority then?'

'The head of the department concerned. It's his job to allocate the work to his staff. After murder and rape, it's usual to give priority to those cases where the accused hasn't been bailed.'

Brenda said:

'I hope you don't mind my asking so many questions. Only I do want to learn. Dr Lorrimer told me that I ought to find out all I can and not just look on this job as routine.'

'You ask away, lass, I don't mind. Only you don't want to listen too much to Dr Lorrimer. He isn't the director here, even if he thinks he is. When you've registered that clobber, the bundle goes on the Biology shelf.'

Brenda entered the exhibit number carefully in the day-book and moved the plastic-shrouded bundle to the shelf of exhibits waiting to go into the Biology Search Room. It was good to be up to date with the entering. She glanced up at the clock. It was nearly eight-fifty. Soon the day's post would be delivered and the desk would be heaped with padded envelopes containing yesterday's blood samples from the drink and driving cases. Then the police cars would start arriving. Uniformed or plain-clothes policemen would bring in large envelopes of documents for Mr Middlemass, the Document Examiner; specially prepared kits issued by the Laboratory for the collection of saliva, blood and semen stains; unwieldy bags of stained and dirty bed linen and blankets; the ubiquitous blunt instruments; blood-stained knives carefully taped into their boxes.

And at any moment now the first members of staff would be arriving. Mrs Bidwell, the cleaner, should have been with them twenty minutes ago. Perhaps she had caught Scobie's influenza. The first of the scientific staff to arrive would probably be Clifford Bradley, the Higher Scientific Officer in the Biology Department, scurrying through the hall as if he had no right to be there, with his anxious hunted eyes and that stupid, drooping moustache, so preoccupied that he hardly noticed their greeting. Then Miss Foley, the Director's secretary, calm and self-possessed, wearing always that secret smile. Miss Foley reminded Brenda of Mona Rigby at school, who was always chosen to play the Madonna in the Christmas nativity play. She had never liked

Mona Rigby – who wouldn't have been chosen twice for the coveted role if the staff had known as much about her as did Brenda – and she wasn't sure that she really liked Miss Foley. Then someone she did like, Mr Middlemass, the Document Examiner, with his jacket slung over his shoulders, leaping up the stairs three steps at a time and calling out a greeting to the desk. After that they would come in almost any order. The hall would become alive with people, rather like a railway terminus, and at the heart of the seeming chaos, controlling and directing, helping and explaining, were the staff of the reception desk.

As if to signal that the working day was about to begin, the telephone rang. Inspector Blakelock's hand enveloped the receiver. He listened in silence for what seemed a longer period than normal, then she heard him speak.

'I don't think he's here, Mr Lorrimer. You say he never came home last night?'

Another silence, Inspector Blakelock half turned away from her and bent his head conspiratorially over the mouthpiece as if listening to a confidence. Then he rested the receiver on the counter and turned to Brenda:

'It's Dr Lorrimer's old dad. He's worried. Apparently Dr Lorrimer didn't take him his early tea this morning and it looks as if he didn't come home last night. His bed hasn't been slept in.'

'Well, he can't be here. I mean, we found the front door locked when we arrived.'

There could be no doubt about that. As she had come round the corner of the house from putting her bicycle in the old stable block, Inspector Blakelock had been standing at the front door almost as if he were waiting for her. Then, when she had joined him, he had shone his torch on the locks and inserted the three keys, first the Yale, and then the Ingersoll, and lastly the security lock which disconnected the electronic warning system from Guy's Marsh police station. Then they had stepped together into the unlighted hall. She had gone to the cloakroom at the back of the building to put on her white coat and he had gone to the box in Chief Inspector Martin's office to switch off the system which protected the inner doors of the main Laboratory rooms.

She giggled and said:

'Mrs Bidwell hasn't turned up to start the cleaning and now Dr Lorrimer's missing. Perhaps they've run away together. The great Hoggatt scandal.'

It wasn't a very funny joke, and she wasn't surprised when Inspector Blakelock didn't laugh. He said:

'The locked door doesn't necessarily signify. Dr Lorrimer has his own keys. And if he did make his bed and then come in extra early this morning, like as not he'd have relocked the door and set the internal alarms.'

'But how would he have got into the Biology Lab, then?'

'He'd have had to have opened the door and then left it open when he reset the alarms. It doesn't seem likely. When he's here alone he usually relies on the Yale.'

He put the receiver again to his ear and said:

'Hold on a moment will you, Mr Lorrimer. I don't think he's here, but I'll just check.'

'I'll go,' said Brenda, anxious to demonstrate helpfulness. Without waiting to lift the flap she slipped under the counter. As she turned she saw him with startling clarity, brightly instantaneous as a camera flash. Inspector Blakelock, with his mouth half-open in remonstrance, his arm flung out towards her in a gesture, stiff and histrionic, of protection or restraint. But now, uncomprehending, she laughed and ran up the wide stairs. The Biology Laboratory was at the back of the first floor, running with its adjoining search room almost the whole length of the building. The door was shut. She turned the knob and pushed it open, feeling along the wall for the light switch. Her fingers found it and she pressed it down. The two long fluorescent tubes suspended from the ceiling blinked, then glimmered, then glowed into steady light.

She saw the body immediately. He was lying in the space between the two large central examination tables, face downwards, his left hand seeming to claw at the floor, his right arm hunched beneath him. His legs were straight. She gave a curious little sound between a cry and a moan and knelt beside him. The hair above his left ear was matted and spiked like her kitten's fur after he had washed, but she couldn't see the blood against the dark hair. But she knew that it was blood. Already it had blackened on the collar of his white coat and a small pool had separated and congealed on the Lab floor. Only his left eye was visible, fixed and dull and retracted, like the eye of a dead calf. Tentatively she felt his cheek. It was cold. But she had known as soon as she had seen the glazed eye that this was death.

She had no memory of closing the Lab door or coming down the stairs. Inspector Blakelock was still behind the counter, rigid as a statue, the telephone receiver in his hand. She wanted to laugh at the sight of his face, he looked so funny. She tried to speak to him, but the words wouldn't come. Her jaw jabbered uncontrollably and her teeth clattered together. She made some kind of gesture. He said something that she couldn't catch, dropped the receiver on the counter and raced upstairs.

She staggered to the heavy Victorian armchair against the wall outside Chief Inspector Martin's office, Colonel Hoggatt's chair. The portrait looked down at her. As she watched, the left eye seemed to grow larger, the lips twisted to a leer.

Her whole body was seized with a terrible cold. Her heart seemed to have grown immense, thudding against the rib-cage. She was breathing in great gulps, but still there wasn't enough air. Then she became aware of the crackling from the telephone. Rising slowly like an automaton, she made her way over to the counter and picked up the receiver. Mr Lorrimer's voice, frail and querulous, was bleating at the other end. She tried to say the accustomed words 'Hoggatt's Laboratory here. Reception speaking.' But the words wouldn't come. She replaced the receiver in its cradle and walked back to her chair.

She had no memory of hearing the long peal of the doorbell, of moving stiffly across the hall to answer it. Suddenly the door crashed open and the hall was full of people, loud with voices. The light seemed to have brightened, which was odd, and she saw them all like actors on a stage, brightly lit, faces made grotesque and heightened by make-up, every word clear and comprehensible as if she were in the front row of the stalls. Mrs Bidwell, the cleaner, in her mackintosh with the imitation-fur collar, her eyes bright with indignation, her voice pitched high.

'What the hell's going on here! Some bloody fool phoned my old man and told him that I needn't come in today, that Mrs Schofield wanted me. Who's playing silly buggers?'

Inspector Blakelock was coming down the stairs, slowly and deliberately, the protagonist making his entrance. They stood in a small circle and looked up at him. Dr Howarth, Clifford Bradley, Miss Foley, Mrs Bidwell. The Director stepped forward. He looked as if he were going to faint. He said:

'Well, Blakelock?'

'It's Dr Lorrimer, sir. He's dead. Murdered.'

Surely they couldn't all have repeated that word in unison, turning their faces towards each other, like a Greek chorus. But it seemed to echo in the quiet of the hall, becoming meaningless, a sonorous groan of a word. Murder. Murder. Murder.

She saw Dr Howarth run towards the stairs. Inspector Blakelock turned to accompany him, but the Director said:

'No, you stay here. See that no one gets any further than the hall. Phone the Chief Constable and Dr Kerrison. Then get me the Home Office.'

Suddenly they seemed to notice Brenda for the first time. Mrs Bidwell came towards her. She said:

'Did you find him then? You poor little bugger!'

And suddenly it wasn't a play any more. The lights went out. The faces became amorphous, ordinary. Brenda gave a little gasp. She felt Mrs Bidwell's arms go round her shoulders. The smell of the mackintosh was pressed into her face. The fur was as soft as her kitten's paw. And, blessedly, Brenda began to cry.

II

In a London teaching hospital close by the river, from which he could in his more masochistic moments glimpse the window of his own office, Dr Charles Freeborn, Controller of the Forensic Science Service, all six foot four of him, lay rigidly in his narrow bed, his nose peaked high above the methodical fold of the sheet, his white hair a haze against the whiter pillow. The bed was too short for him, an inconvenience to which he had accommodated himself by neatly sticking out his toes over the foot-board. His bedside locker held the conglomerate of offerings, necessities and minor diversions considered indispensable to a brief spell in hospital. They included a vase of official-looking roses, scentless but florid, through whose funereal and unnatural blooms Commander Adam Dalgliesh glimpsed a face so immobile, upturned eyes fixed on the ceiling, that he was momentarily startled by the illusion that he was visiting the dead. Recalling that Freeborn was recovering from nothing more serious than a successful operation for varicose veins, he approached the bed and said tentatively:

'Hello!'

Freeborn, galvanized from his torpor, sprang up like a jack-in-the-box, scattering from his bedside locker a packet of tissues, two copies of the *Journal of the Forensic Science Society* and an open box of chocolates. He shot out a lean speckled arm encircled by the hospital identity bracelet and crushed Dalgliesh's hand.

'Adam! Don't creep up on me like that, damn you! God, am I glad to see you! The only good news I've had this morning is that you'll be in charge. I thought that you might have already left. How long can you spare? How are you getting there?'

Dalgliesh answered the questions in order.

'Ten minutes. By chopper from the Battersea heliport. I'm on my way now. How are you, Charles? Am I being a nuisance?'

'I'm the nuisance. This couldn't have happened at a worse time. And the maddening part of it is that it's my own fault. The op could have waited. Only the pain was getting rather tedious and Meg insisted that I had it done now before I retired, on the theory I suppose, that better in the Government's time than my own.'

Recalling what he knew of the ardours and achievements of Freeborn's forty-odd years in the Forensic Science Service, the difficult war years, the delayed retirement, the last five years when he had exchanged his directorship for the frustrations of bureaucracy, Dalgliesh said:

'Sensible of her. And there's nothing you could have done at Chevisham.'

'I know. It's ridiculous, this feeling of responsibility because one isn't actually in post when disaster strikes. They rang from the duty office to break the news to me just after nine. Better that than learning it from my visitors or this evening's paper, I suppose they thought. Decent of them. The Chief Constable must have called in the Yard within a few minutes of getting the news. How much do you know?'

'About as much as you, I imagine. I've spoken to the C.C. and to Howarth. They've given me the main facts. The skull smashed, apparently by a heavy mallet which Lorrimer had been examining. The Lab found properly locked when the Assistant Police Liaison Officer and the young C.O. arrived at eight-thirty this morning. Lorrimer's keys in his pocket. He often worked late and most of the Lab staff knew that he proposed to do so last night. No sign of a break-in. Four sets of keys. Lorrimer had one set as the Senior P.S.O. and Deputy Security Officer. The Assistant Police Liaison Officer has the second. Lorrimer or one of the Police Liaison Officers were the only people authorized to lock and open up the building. The Director keeps the third set of keys in his security cupboard, and the fourth are in a safe at Guy's Marsh police station in case the alarm rings in the night.'

Freeborn said:

'So either Lorrimer let in his murderer or the murderer had a key.'

There were, thought Dalgliesh, other possibilities, but now was not the time to discuss them. He asked:

'Lorrimer would have let in anyone from the Lab, I suppose?'

'Why not? He'd probably have admitted any of the local police whom he personally knew, particularly if it were a detective concerned with a recent case. Otherwise, I'm not so sure. He may have admitted a friend or relative, although that's even more doubtful. He was a punctilious blighter and I can't see him using the Lab as a convenient place for a rendezvous. And, of course, he would have let in the forensic pathologist.'

'That's a local man, Henry Kerrison, they tell me. The C.C. said that they called him in to look at the body. Well, they could hardly do anything else. I didn't know you'd found a successor to Death-House Donald.'

'Nor have we. Kerrison is doing it on an item of service basis. He's well thought of and we'll probably appoint him if we can get the Area Health Authority to agree. There's the usual difficulty about his hospital responsibilities. I wish to hell we could get the forensic pathology service sorted out before I go. But that's one headache I'll have to leave to my successor.'

Dalgliesh thought without affection of Death-House Donald with his ghoulish schoolboy humour – 'Not that cake-knife, my dear lady. I used it this morning on one of Slash Harry's victims and the edge is rather blunted' – his mania for self-advertisement and his intolerable bucolic laugh, and was grateful that at least he wouldn't be interrogating that redoubtable old phoney. He said:

'Tell me about Lorrimer. What was he like?'

This was the question which lay at the heart of every murder investigation; and yet he knew its absurdity before he asked it. It was the strangest part of a detective's job, this building up of a relationship with the dead, seen only as a crumpled corpse at the scene of crime or naked on the mortuary table. The victim was central to the mystery of his own death. He died because of what he was. Before the case was finished Dalgliesh would have received a dozen pictures of Lorrimer's personality, transferred like prints from other men's minds. From these amorphous and uncertain images he would create his own imaginings, superimposed and dominant, but essentially just as incomplete, just as distorted – as were the others – by his own preconceptions, his own personality. But the question had to be asked. And at least he could rely on Freeborn to answer it without initiating a philosophical discussion about the basis of the self. But their minds must for a moment have flowed together, for Freeborn said:

'It's odd how you always have to ask that question, that you'll only see him through other men's eyes. Aged about forty. Looks like John the Baptist without his beard and is about as uncompromising. Single. Lives with an elderly father in a cottage just outside the village. He is – was – an extremely competent forensic biologist, but I doubt whether he would have gone any higher. Obsessional, edgy, uncomfortable to be with. He applied for the job at Hoggatt's, of course, and was runner-up to Howarth.'

'How did he and the Lab take the new appointment?'

'Lorrimer took it pretty hard, I believe. The Lab wouldn't have welcomed his appointment. He was pretty unpopular with most of the senior staff. But there are always one or two who would have preferred a colleague to a stranger even if they hated his guts. And the Union made the expected noises about not appointing a forensic scientist.'

'Why did you appoint Howarth? I take it you were on the Board.'

'Oh, yes. I accept a share of the responsibility. That's not to say that I think we made a mistake. Old Doc Mac was one of the really great forensic scientists – we started together – but there's no denying that he'd let the reins slip a bit in recent years. Howarth has already increased the work turnover by ten per cent. And then there's the commissioning of the new Lab. It was a calculated risk to take a man without forensic experience, but we were looking for a manager primarily. At least, most of the Board were and the rest of us were persuaded that it would be no bad thing, without, I confess, being precisely clear what we meant by that blessed word. Management. The new science. We all make obeisance to it. In the old days we got on with the job, jollied staff along if they needed it, kicked the sluggards in the backside, encouraged the unconfident and persuaded a reluctant and sceptical police force to use us. Oh, and sent in an occasional statistical return to the Home Office just to remind them that we were there. It seemed to work all right. The service didn't collapse. Have you ever considered what exactly is the difference between administration and management, Adam?'

'Keep it as a question to confound the candidate at your next Board. Howarth was at the Bruche Research Institute wasn't he? Why did he want to leave? He must have taken a cut in pay.'

'Not more than about six hundred a year, and that wouldn't worry him. His father was rich, and it all came to him and his half-sister.'

'But it's a bigger place surely? And he can't be getting the research at Hoggatt's.'

'He gets some, but essentially, of course, it's a service laboratory. That worried us a bit on the Board. But you can hardly set out to persuade your most promising applicant that he's downgrading himself. Scientifically and academically – he's a pure physicist – he was well ahead of the rest of the field. Actually we did press him a bit and he gave the usual reasons. He was getting stale, wanted a new sphere of activity, was anxious to get away from London. Gossip has it that his wife had recently left him and he wanted to make a clean break. That was probably the reason. Thank God he didn't use that blasted word "challenge". If I have to listen to one more candidate telling me he sees the job as a challenge I'll throw up over the boardroom table. Adam, I'm getting old.'

He nodded his head towards the window.

'They're in a bit of a twitch over there, I need hardly say.'

'I know. I've had an exceedingly brief but tactful interview. They're brilliant at implying more than they actually say. But obviously it's important to get it solved quickly. Apart from confidence in the service, you'll all want to get the Lab back to work.'

'What's happening now? To the staff, I mean.'

'The local C.I.D. have locked all the interior doors and they're keeping the staff in the library and the reception area until I arrive. They're occupying themselves writing out an account of their movements since Lorrimer was last seen alive and the local force are getting on with the preliminary checking of alibis. That should save some time. I'm taking one officer, John Massingham, with me. The Met Lab will take on any of the forensic work. They're sending a chap down from Public Relations Branch to handle the publicity, so I won't have that on my plate. It's obliging of that pop group to break up so spectacularly. That and the Government's troubles should keep us off the front page for a day or two.'

Freeborn was looking down at his big toes with mild distaste as if they were errant members whose deficiencies had only now become apparent to him. From time to time he wriggled them, whether in obedience to some medical instruction or for his own private satisfaction, it was impossible to say. After a moment he spoke.

'I started my career at Hoggatt's, you know. That was before the war. All any of us had then was wet chemistry, test tubes, beakers, solutions. And girls weren't employed because it wasn't decent for them to be concerned with sex cases. Hoggatt's was old-fashioned even for the 1930 service. Not scientifically, though. We had a spectrograph when it was still the new wonder toy. The fens threw up some odd crimes. Do you remember the Mulligan case, old man who chopped up his brother and tied the remains to the Leamings' sluice-gates? There was some nice forensic evidence there.'

'Some fifty bloodstains on the pig-sty wall, weren't there? And Mulligan swore it was sow's blood.'

Freeborn's voice grew reminiscent.

'I liked that old villain. And they still drag out those photographs I took of the splashes and use them to illustrate lectures on bloodstains. Odd, the attraction Hoggatt's had – still has for that matter. An unsuitable Palladian mansion in an unexciting East Anglian village on the edge of the black fens. Ten miles to Ely, and that's hardly a centre of riotous activity for the young. Winters to freeze your marrow and a spring wind – the fen blow they call it – which whips up the peat and chokes your lungs like smog. And yet the staff, if they didn't leave after the first month, stayed for ever. Did you know that Hoggatt's has got a small Wren chapel in the Lab grounds? Architecturally it's much superior to the house because old Hoggatt never messed it about. He was almost entirely without aesthetic taste, I believe. He used it as a chemical store once it had been deconsecrated or whatever it is they do to unused churches. Howarth has got a string quartet going at the Lab and they gave a concert there. Apparently he's a noted amateur violinist. At the moment he's probably wishing that he'd stuck to music. This isn't a propitious start for him, poor devil. And it was always such a happy Lab. I suppose it was the isolation that gave us such a feeling of camaraderie.'

Dalgliesh said grimly:

'I doubt whether that will survive an hour of my arrival.'

'No. You chaps usually bring as much trouble with you as you solve. You can't help it. Murder is like that, a contaminating crime. Oh, you'll solve it, I know. You always do. But I'm wondering at what cost.'

Dalgliesh did not answer. He was both too honest and too fond of Freeborn to make comforting and platitudinous promises. Of course, he would be tactful. That didn't need saying. But he would be at Hoggatt's to solve a murder, and all other considerations would go down before that overriding task. Murder was always solved at a cost, sometimes to himself, more often to others. And Freeborn was right. It was a crime which contaminated everyone whom it touched, innocent and guilty alike. He didn't grudge the ten minutes he had spent with Freeborn. The old man believed, with simple patriotism, that the Service to which he had given the whole of his working life was the best in the world. He had helped to shape it, and he was probably right. Dalgliesh had learned what he had come to learn. But as he shook hands and said goodbye he knew that he left no comfort behind him.

III

The library at Hoggatt's was at the rear of the ground floor. Its three tall windows gave a view of the stone terrace and the double flight of steps going down to what had once been a lawn and formal gardens, but which was now a half-acre of neglected grass, bounded to the west by the brick annexe of the Vehicle Examination Department, and to the east by the old stable block, now converted into garages. The room was one of the few in the house spared by its former owner's transforming zeal. The original bookcases of carved oak still lined the walls, although they now housed the Laboratory's not inconsiderable scientific library, while extra shelf-room for bound copies of national and international journals had been provided by two steel movable units which divided the room into three bays. Under each of the three windows was a working table with four chairs; one table was almost completely covered by a model of the new Laboratory.

It was in this somewhat inadequate space that the staff were congregated. A detective sergeant from the local C.I.D. sat impassively near the door, a reminder of why they were so inconveniently incarcerated. They were allowed out to the ground-floor cloakroom under tactful escort, and had been told they could telephone home from the library. But the rest of the Laboratory was at present out of bounds.

They had all, on arrival, been asked to write a brief account of where they had been, and with whom, the previous evening and night. Patiently, they waited their turn at one of the three tables. The statements had been collected by the sergeant and handed out to his colleague on the reception desk, presumably so that the preliminary checking could begin. Those of the junior staff who could provide a satisfactory alibi were allowed home as soon as it had been checked; one by one and with some reluctance at missing the excitements to come they went their way. The less fortunate, together with those who had arrived first at the Laboratory that morning and all the senior scientists, had been told they must await the arrival of the team from Scotland Yard. The Director had put in only one brief appearance in the library. Earlier he had gone with Angela Foley to break the news of Lorrimer's death to his father. Since his return he had stayed in his own office with Detective Superintendent Mercer of the local C.I.D. It was rumoured that Dr Kerrison was with them.

The minutes dragged while they listened for the first hum of the approaching helicopter. Inhibited by the presence of the police, by prudence, delicacy or embarrassment from talking about the subject foremost in their minds, they spoke to each other with the wary politeness of uncongenial strangers stranded in an airport lounge. The women were, on the whole, better equipped for the tedium of the wait. Mrs Mallett, the typist from the general office, had brought her knitting to work and, fortified by an unshakeable alibi – she had sat between the postmistress and Mr Mason from the general store at the village concert – and with something to occupy her hands, sat clicking away with understandable if irritating complacency until given the order of release. Mrs Bidwell, the Laboratory cleaner, had insisted on visiting her broom cupboard, under escort, and had provided herself with a feather duster and a couple of rags with which she made a vigorous onslaught on the bookshelves. She was unusually silent, but the group of scientists at the tables could hear her muttering to herself as she punished the books at the end of one of the bays.

Brenda Pridmore had been allowed to collect the exhibits-received book from the counter and, white-faced but outwardly composed, was checking the previous month's figures. The book took more than its share of the available table space; but at least she had a legitimate job. Claire Easterbrook, Senior Scientific Officer in the Biology Department and, with Lorrimer's death, the senior biologist, had taken from her briefcase a scientific paper she had prepared on recent advances in blood grouping and settled down to revise it with as little apparent concern as if murder at Hoggatt's were a routine inconvenience for which, prudently, she was always provided.

The rest of the staff passed the time each in his own way. Those who preferred the pretence of business immersed themselves in a book and, from time to time, made an ostentatious note. The two Vehicle Examiners, who were reputed to have no conversation except about cars, squatted side by side, their backs against the steel book-racks, and talked cars together with desperate eagerness. Middlemass had finished *The Times* crossword by quarter to ten and had made the rest of the paper last as long as possible. But now even the deaths column was exhausted. He folded the paper and tossed it across the table to eagerly awaiting hands.

It was a relief when Stephen Copley, the Senior Chemist, arrived just before ten, bustling in as usual, his rubicund face with its tonsure and fringe of black curly hair glistening as if he had come in from the sun. Nothing was known to disconcert him, certainly not the death of a man he had disliked. But he was secure in his alibi, having spent the whole of the previous day in the Crown Court and the evening and night with friends at Norwich, only getting back to Chevisham in time for a late start that morning. His colleagues, relieved to find something to talk about, began questioning him about the case. They spoke rather too loudly to be natural. The rest of the company listened with simulated interest as if the conversation were a dramatic dialogue provided for their entertainment.

'Who did they call for the defence?' asked Middlemass.

'Charlie Pollard. He hung his great belly over the box and explained confidentially to the jury that they needn't be frightened of the so-called scientific expert witnesses because none of us, including himself of course, really know what we're talking about. They were immensely reassured, I need hardly say.'

'Juries hate scientific evidence.'

'They think they won't be able to understand it so naturally they can't understand it. As soon as you step into the box you see a curtain of obstinate incomprehension clanging down over their minds. What they want is certainty. Did this paint particle come from this car body? Answer Yes or No. None of those nasty mathematical probabilities we're so fond of.'

'If they hate scientific evidence they certainly hate arithmetic more. Give them a scientific opinion which depends on the ability to divide a factor by two-thirds and what do you get from counsel? "I'm afraid you'll have to explain yourself more simply, Mr Middlemass. The jury and I haven't got a higher degree in mathematics, you know." Inference: you're an arrogant bastard and the jury would be well advised not to believe a word you say.'

It was the old argument. Brenda had heard it all before when she ate her lunch-time sandwiches in the room, half-way between a kitchen and a sitting-room, which was still called the junior Mess. But now it seemed terrible that they should be able to talk so naturally while Dr Lorrimer lay there dead upstairs. Suddenly she had a need to speak his name. She looked up and made herself say:

'Dr Lorrimer thought that the service would end up with about three immense laboratories doing the work for the whole country with exhibits coming in by air. He said that he thought all the scientific evidence ought to be agreed by both sides before the trial.'

Middlemass said easily:

'That's an old argument. The police want a local lab nice and handy, and who's to blame them? Besides, three-quarters of forensic scientific work doesn't require all this sophisticated instrumentation. There's more of a case for highly equipped regional laboratories with local out-stations. But who'd want to work in the small labs if the more exciting stuff went elsewhere?'

Miss Easterbrook had apparently finished her revision. She said:

'Lorrimer knew that this idea of the lab as a scientific arbiter wouldn't work, not with the British accusatorial system. Anyway, scientific evidence ought to be tested like any other evidence.'

'But how?' asked Middlemass. 'By an ordinary jury? Suppose you're an expert document examiner outside the service and they call you for the defence. You and I disagree. How can the jury judge between us? They'll probably choose to believe you because you're better-looking.'

'Or you, more likely, because you're a man.'

'Or one of them – the crucial one – will reject me because I remind him of Uncle Ben and all the family know that Ben was the world's champion liar.'

'All right. All right.' Copley spread plump hands in a benediction of appeasement. 'It's the same as democracy. A fallible system but the best we've got.'

Middlemass said:

'It's extraordinary, though, how well it works. You look at the jury, sitting there politely attentive, like children on their best behaviour because they're visitors in an alien country and don't want to make fools of themselves or offend the natives. Yet how often do they come up with a verdict that's manifestly perverse having regard to the evidence?'

Claire Easterbrook said drily:

'Whether it's manifestly perverse having regard to the truth is another matter.'

'A criminal trial isn't a tribunal for eliciting the truth. At least we deal in facts. What about the emotion? Did you love your husband, Mrs B.? How can the poor woman explain that, probably like the majority of wives, she loved him most of the time, when he didn't snore in her ear all night or shout at the kids or keep her short of Bingo money.'

Copley said:

'She can't. If she's got any sense and if her counsel has briefed her properly, she'll get out her hankerchief and sob, "Oh yes, sir. A better husband never lived, as God's my witness." It's a game, isn't it? You win if you play by the rules.'

Claire Easterbrook shrugged:

'If you know them. Too often it's a game where the rules are known only to one side. Natural enough when that's the side which makes them up.'

Copley and Middlemass laughed.

Clifford Bradley had half hidden himself from the rest of the company behind the table holding the model of the new Laboratory. He had taken a book from the shelves at random but, for the last ten minutes, hadn't even bothered to turn the page.

They were laughing! They were actually laughing! Getting up from the table he groped his way down the furthest bay and replaced his book in the rack, leaning his forehead against the cold steel. Unobtrusively Middlemass strolled up beside him and, back to the company, reached up to take a book from the shelf. He said:

'Are you all right?'

'I wish to God they'd come.'

'So do we all. But the chopper should be here any minute now.'

'How can they laugh like that? Don't they care?'

'Of course they care. Murder is beastly, embarrassing and inconvenient. But I doubt whether anyone is feeling a purely personal grief. And other people's tragedies, other people's danger, always provoke a certain euphoria as long as one is safe oneself.' He looked at Bradley and said softly:

'There's always manslaughter, you know. Or even justified homicide. Though, come to think of it, one could hardly plead that.'

'You think I killed him, don't you?'

'I don't think anything. Anyway, you've got an alibi. Wasn't your mother-in-law with you yesterday evening?'

'Not all the evening. She caught the seven forty-five bus.'

'Well, with luck, there'll be evidence that he was dead by then.' And why, thought Middlemass, should Bradley assume that he wasn't? Bradley's dark and anxious eyes narrowed with suspicion.

'How did you know that Sue's mother was with us last night?'

'Susan told me. Actually, she telephoned me at the Lab just before two. It was about Lorrimer.' He thought and then said easily, 'She was wondering whether there was a chance he might ask for a transfer now that Howarth has been in his post a year. She thought I might have heard something. When you get home, tell her that I don't propose to tell the police about the call unless she does first. Oh, and you'd better reassure her that I didn't bash in his head for him. I'd do a lot for Sue, but a man has to draw the line somewhere.'

Bradley said with a note of resentment:

'Why should you worry? There's nothing wrong with your alibi. Weren't you at the village concert?'

'Not all the evening. And there's a certain slight embarrassment about my alibi even when I was ostensibly there.'

Bradley turned to him and said with sudden vehemence:

'I didn't do it! Oh God, I can't stand this waiting!'

'You've got to stand it. Pull yourself together, Cliff! You won't help yourself or Susan by going to pieces. They're English policemen, remember. We're not expecting the K.G.B.'

It was then that they heard the long-awaited sound, a distant grinding hum like that of an angry wasp. The desultory voices at the tables fell silent, heads were raised and, together, the company moved towards the windows. Mrs Bidwell rushed for a place of vantage. The red and white helicopter rattled into sight over the top of the trees and hovered, a noisy gadfly, above the terraces. No one spoke. Then Middlemass said:

'The Yard's wonder boy, appropriately, descends from the clouds. Well, let's hope that he works quickly. I want to get into my lab. Someone should tell him that he's not the only one with a murder on his hands.'

IV

Detective Inspector the Honourable John Massingham disliked helicopters, which he regarded as noisy, cramped and frighteningly unsafe. Since his physical courage was beyond question either by himself or anyone else, he would normally have had no objection to saying so. But he knew his chief's dislike of unnecessary chat, and strapped as they were side by side in uncomfortably close proximity in the Enstrom F28, he decided that the Chevisham case would get off to the most propitious start by a policy of disciplined silence. He noted with interest that the cockpit instrument panel was remarkably similar to a car dashboard; even the airspeed was shown in miles per hour instead of knots. He was only sorry that there the resemblance ended. He adjusted his earphones more comfortably and settled down to soothe his nerves by a concentrated study of his maps.

The red-brown tentacles of London's suburbs had at last been shaken off, and the chequered autumn landscape, multi-textured as a cloth collage, unrolled before them in a changing pattern of brown, green and gold, leading them on to Cambridge. The fitful sunshine moved in broad swathes across the neat, segmented villages, the trim municipal parks and open fields. Miniature tin cars, beetle-bright in the sun, pursued each other busily along the roads.

Dalgliesh glanced at his companion, at the strong, pale face, the spatter of freckles over the craggy nose and wide forehead, and the thatch of red hair springing under the headphones, and thought how like the boy was to his father, that redoubtable, thrice-decorated peer, whose courage was equalled only by his obstinacy and *naïveté*. The marvel of the Massinghams was that a lineage going back five hundred years could have produced so many generations of amiable nonentities. He remembered when he had last seen Lord Dungannon. It had been a debate in the House of Lords on juvenile delinquency, a subject on which His Lordship considered himself an expert since he had, indubitably, once been a boy and had, briefly, helped organize a youth club on his grandfather's estate. His thoughts, when they finally came, had been uttered in all their simplistic banality, in no particular order of logic or relevance, and in a curiously gentle voice punctuated by long pauses in which he had gazed thoughtfully at the throne and appeared to commune happily with some inner presence. Meanwhile, like lemmings who have smelt the sea, the noble lords streamed out of their chamber in a body to appear, as if summoned by telepathy, when Dungannon's speech drew to its close. But if the family had contributed nothing to statesmanship and little to the arts, they had died with spectacular gallantry for orthodox causes in every generation.

And now Dungannon's heir had chosen this far from orthodox job. It would be interesting to see if, for the first time and in so unusual a field, the family achieved distinction. What had led Massingham to choose the police service instead of his family's usual career of the Army as an outlet for his natural combativeness and unfashionable patriotism Dalgliesh had not inquired, partly because he was a respecter of other men's privacy, and partly because he wasn't sure that he wanted to hear the answer. So far Massingham had done exceptionally well. The police were a tolerant body and took the view that a man couldn't help who his father was. They accepted that Massingham had gained his promotion on merit although they were not so naïve as to suppose that being the elder son of a peer did any man harm. They called Massingham the Honjohn behind his back and occasionally to his face, and bore no malice.

Although the family was now impoverished and the estate sold – Lord Dungannon was bringing up his considerable family in a modest villa in Bayswater – the boy had still gone to his father's school. No doubt, thought Dalgliesh, the old warrier was unaware that other schools existed; like every other class, the aristocracy, however poor, could always find the money for the things they really wanted. But he was an odd product of that establishment, having none of the slightly *dégagé* elegance and ironic detachment which characterized its alumni. Dalgliesh, if he hadn't known his history, would have guessed that Massingham was the product of a sound, upper-middle-class family – a doctor or a solicitor, perhaps – and of an old established grammar school. It was only the second time they had worked together. The first time, Dalgliesh had been impressed by Massingham's intelligence and enormous capacity for work, and by his admirable ability to keep his mouth shut and to sense when his chief wanted to be alone. He had also been struck by a streak of ruthlessness in the boy which, he thought, ought not to have surprised him since he knew that, as with all good detectives, it must be present.

And now the Enstrom was rattling above the towers and spires of Cambridge, and they could see the shining curve of the river, the bright autumnal avenues leading down through green lawns to miniature hump-backed bridges, King's College Chapel upturned and slowly rotating beside its great striped square of green. And, almost immediately, the city was behind them and they saw, like a crinkled ebony sea, the black earth of the fens. Below them were straight roads ridged above the fields, with villages strung along them as if clinging to the security of high ground; isolated farms with their roofs so low that they looked half submerged in the peat; an occasional church tower standing majestically apart from its village with the gravestones planted round it like crooked teeth. They must be getting close now; already Dalgliesh could see the soaring west tower and pinnacles of Ely Cathedral to the east.

Massingham looked up from his map-reading and peered down. His voice cracked through Dalgliesh's earphones:

'This is it, sir.'

Chevisham was spread beneath them. It lay on a narrow plateau above the fens, the houses strung along the northerly of two converging roads. The tower of the impressive cruciform church was immediately identifiable, as was Chevisham Manor and, behind it, sprawling over the scarred field and linking the two roads, the brick and concrete of the new Laboratory building. They rattled along the main street of what looked like a typical East Anglian village. Dalgliesh glimpsed the ornate red-brick front of the local chapel, one or two prosperous-looking houses with Dutch gables, a small close of recently built, semi-detached boxes with the developer's board still in place, and what looked like the village general store and post office. There were few people about, but the noise of the engines brought figures from shops and houses and pale faces, their eyes shielded, strained up at them.

And now they were turning towards Hoggatt's Laboratory, coming in low over what must be the Wren chapel. It stood about a quarter of a mile from the house in a triple circle of beech trees, an isolated building so small and perfect that it looked like an architect's model precisely set in a fabricated landscape, or an elegant ecclesiastical folly, justifying itself only by its classical purity, as distanced from religion as it was from life. It was odd that it lay so far from the house. Dalgliesh thought that it had probably been built later, perhaps because the original owner of the mansion had quarrelled with the local parson and, in defiance, had decided to make his own arrangements for spiritual ministrations. Certainly the house hardly looked large enough to support a private chapel. For a few seconds as they descended, he had an unimpeded view through a gap in the trees of the west front of the chapel. He saw a single high-arched window with two balancing niches, the four Corinthian pilasters separating the bays, the whole crowned with a large decorated pediment and topped with a hexagonal lantern. The helicopter seemed almost to be brushing the trees. The brittle autumn leaves, shaken by the rush of air, flurried down like a shower of charred paper over the roof and the bright green of the grass.

And then, sickeningly, the helicopter soared, the chapel lurched out of sight and they were poised, engines rattling, ready to land on the wide terrace behind the house. Over its roof he could see the forecourt patterned with parking lots, the police cars tidily aligned and what looked like a mortuary van. A broad drive, bordered with straggling bushes and a few trees, led down to what the map showed as Stoney Piggott's Road. There was no gate to the driveway. Beyond it he could see the bright flag of a bus stop and the bus shelter. Then the helicopter began to descend and only the rear of the house was in view. From a ground-floor window he could see the smudges of watching faces.

There was a reception committee of three, their figures oddly foreshortened, the necks straining upwards. The thrash of the rotor blades had tugged their hair into grotesque shapes, flurried the legs of their trousers and flattened their jackets against their chests. Now, with the stilling of the engines, the sudden silence was so absolute that he saw the three motionless figures as if they were a tableau of dummies in a silent world. He and Massingham unclasped their seat belts and clambered to earth. For about five seconds the two groups stood regarding each other. Then, with a single gesture, the three waiting figures smoothed back their hair and advanced warily to meet him. Simultaneously his ears unblocked and the world again became audible. He turned to thank and speak briefly to the pilot. Then he and Massingham walked forward.

Dalgliesh already knew Superintendent Mercer of the local C.I.D.; they had met at a number of police conferences. Even at sixty feet his ox-like shoulders, the round comedian's face with the wide upturned mouth, and the button-bright eyes, had been instantly recognizable. Dalgliesh felt his hand crushed, and then Mercer made the introductions. Dr Howarth; a tall fair man, almost as tall as Dalgliesh himself, with widely spaced eyes of a remarkably deep blue and the lashes so long that they might have looked effeminate on any face less arrogantly male. He could, Dalgliesh thought, have been judged an outstandingly handsome man were it not for a certain incongruity of feature, perhaps the contrast being the fineness of the skin stretched over the flat cheekbones and the strong jutting jaw and uncompromising mouth. Dalgliesh would have known that he was rich. The blue eyes regarded the world with the slightly cynical assurance of a man accustomed to getting what he wanted when he wanted it by the simplest of expedients, that of paying for it. Beside him, Dr Henry Kerrison, although as tall, looked diminished. His creased, anxious face was bleached with weariness and there was a look in the dark, heavily-lidded eyes which was uncomfortably close to defeat. He grasped Dalgliesh's hand with a firm grip, but didn't speak. Howarth said:

'There's no entrance now to the back of the house; we have to go round to the front. This is the easiest way.'

Carrying their scene-of-crime cases, Dalgliesh and Massingham followed him round the side of the house. The faces at the ground-floor window had disappeared and it was extraordinarily quiet. Trudging through the leaves which had drifted over the path, sniffing the keen autumnal air with its hint of smokiness, and feeling the sun on his face, Massingham felt a surge of animal well-being. It was good to be out of London. This promised to be the kind of job he most liked. The little group turned the corner of the house and Dalgliesh and Massingham had their first clear view of the façade of Hoggatt's Laboratory.

V

The house was an excellent example of late seventeenth-century domestic architecture, a three-storey brick mansion with a hipped roof and four dormer windows, the centre three-bay projection surmounted by a pediment with a richly carved cornice and medallions. A flight of four wide, curved stone steps led to the doorway, imposing on its pilasters but solidly, unostentatiously, right. Dalgliesh paused momentarily to study the façade. Howarth said:

'Agreeable, isn't it? But wait till you see what the old man did to some of the interior.'

The front door, with its elegant but restrained brass door handle and knocker, was fitted with two security locks, a Chubb and an Ingersoll, in addition to the Yale. At a superficial glance there was no sign of forcing. It was opened almost before Howarth had lifted his hand to ring. The man who stood aside, unsmiling, for them to enter, although not in uniform, was immediately recognizable to Dalgliesh as a police officer. Howarth introduced him briefly as Inspector Blakelock, Assistant Police Liaison Officer. He added:

'All three locks were in order when Blakelock arrived this morning. The Chubb connects the electronic warning system to Guy's Marsh police station. The internal protection system is controlled from a panel in the Police Liaison Officer's room.'

Dalgliesh turned to Blakelock.

'And that was in order?'

'Yes, sir.'

'There is no other exit?'

It was Howarth who answered.

'No. My predecessor had the back door and one side door permanently barred. It was too complicated coping with a system of security locks for three doors. Everyone comes in and goes out by the front.'

'Except possibly one person last night,' thought Dalgliesh.

They passed through the entrance hall, which ran almost the whole length of the house, their feet suddenly loud on the marble tessellated floor. Dalgliesh was used to receiving impressions at a glance. The party did not pause on their way to the stairs, but he had a clear impression of the room, the high moulded ceiling, the two elegant pedimented doors to right and left, an oil painting of the Laboratory founder on the right-hand wall, the gleaming wood of the reception counter at the rear. A police officer with a sheaf of papers before him was using the desk telephone, presumably still checking alibis. He went on with his conversation without glancing up.

The staircase was remarkable. The balustrades were carved oak panels decorated with scrolls of acanthus foliage, each newel surmounted by a heavy oak pineapple. There was no carpet and the unpolished wood was heavily scarred. Dr Kerrison and Superintendent Mercer mounted behind Dalgliesh in silence. Howarth, leading the way, seemed to feel the need to talk:

'The ground floor is occupied with Reception and the Exhibits Store, my office, my secretary's room, the general office and the Police Liaison Officer's room. That's all, apart from the domestic quarters at the rear. Chief Inspector Martin is the chief P.L.O. but he's in the U.S.A. at the moment and we only have Blakelock on duty. On this floor we have Biology at the back, Criminalistics at the front and the Instrument Section at the end of the corridor. But I've put a plan of the Lab in my office for you. I thought you might like to take that over if it's convenient. But I haven't moved any of my things until you've examined the room. This is the Biology Lab.'

He glanced at Superintendent Mercer, who took the key from his pocket and unlocked the door. It was a long room obviously converted from two smaller ones, possibly a sitting-room or small drawing-room. The ceiling carvings had been removed, perhaps because Colonel Hoggatt had thought them inappropriate to a working laboratory, but the scars of the desecration remained. The original windows had been replaced by two long windows occupying almost the whole of the end wall. There was a range of benches and sinks under the windows, and two islands of work benches in the middle of the room, one fitted with sinks, the other with a number of microscopes. To the left was a small glass-partitioned office, to the right a dark-room. Beside the door was an immense refrigerator.

But the most bizarre objects in the room were a pair of unclothed window-dressers' dummies, one male and one female, standing between the windows. They were unclothed and denuded of their wigs. The pose of the bald egg-shaped heads, the jointed arms stiffly flexed in a parody of benediction, the staring eyes and curved arrow-like lips gave them the hieratic look of a couple of painted deities. And at their feet, a white-clad sacrificial victim, was the body.

Howarth stared at the two dummies as if he had never seen them before. He seemed to think that they required explanation. For the first time he had lost some of his assurance. He said:

'That's Liz and Burton. The staff dress them in a suspect's clothes so that they can match up bloodstains or slashes.' He added: 'Do you want me here?'

'For the moment, yes,' answered Dalgliesh.

He knelt by the body. Kerrison moved to stand beside him. Howarth and Mercer stayed one each side of the door.

After two minutes Dalgliesh said:

'Cause of death obvious. It looks as if he was struck by a single blow and died where he fell. There's surprisingly little bleeding.'

Kerrison said:

'That's not unusual. As you know, you can get serious inter-cranial injury from a simple fracture, particularly if there's extra-dural or subdural haemorrhage or actual laceration of the brain substance. I agree that he was probably killed by a single blow and that wooden mallet on the table seems the likely weapon. But Blain-Thomson will be able to tell you more when he gets him on the table. He'll be doing the P.M. this afternoon.'

'Rigor is almost complete. What sort of estimate did you make of the time of death?'

'I saw him just before nine and I thought then that he'd been dead about twelve hours, perhaps a little longer. Say between eight and nine p.m. The window is closed and the temperature pretty steady at sixty-five Fahrenheit. I usually estimate a fall in body temperature in these circumstances of about one-and-a-half degrees Fahrenheit an hour. I took it when I examined the body and, taken with the rigor which was almost fully established then, I'd say it was unlikely that he was alive much after nine p.m. But you know how unreliable these estimates can be. Better say between eight-thirty and midnight.'

Howarth said from the door:

'His father says that Lorrimer rang him at a quarter to nine. I went to see the old man this morning with Angela Foley to break the news to him. She's my secretary. Lorrimer was her cousin. But you'll be seeing the old man, of course. He seemed pretty confident about the time.'

Dalgliesh said to Kerrison:

'It looks as if the blood flowed fairly steadily, but without any preliminary splashing. Would you expect the assailant to be bloodstained?'

'Not necessarily, particularly if I'm right about the mallet being the weapon. It was probably a single swinging blow delivered when Lorrimer had turned his back. The fact that the murderer struck above the left ear doesn't seem particularly significant. He could have been left-handed, but there's no reason to suppose he was.'

'And it wouldn't have required particular force. A child could probably have done it.'

Kerrison hesitated, disconcerted.

'Well, a woman, certainly.'

There was one question which Dalgliesh had formally to ask although, from the position of the body and the flow of the blood, the answer was in little doubt.

'Did he die almost immediately, or is there any possibility that he could have walked about for a time, even locked the door and set the alarms?'

'That's not altogether unknown, of course, but in this case I'd say it was highly unlikely, virtually impossible. I did have a man only a month ago with an axe injury, a seven-inch depressed fracture of the parietal bone and extensive extradural haemorrhage. He went off to a pub, spent half an hour with his mates, and then reported to the casualty department and was dead within a quarter of an hour. Head injuries can be unpredictable, but not this one, I think?'

Dalgliesh turned to Howarth.

'Who found him?'

'Our clerical officer, Brenda Pridmore. She starts work at eight-thirty with Blakelock. Old Mr Lorrimer phoned to say that his son hadn't slept in his bed, so she went up to see if Lorrimer were here. I arrived almost immediately with the cleaner, Mrs Bidwell. Some woman had telephoned her husband early this morning to ask her to come to my house to help my sister, instead of to the Lab. It was a false call. I thought that it was probably some stupid village prank, but that I'd better get in as soon as possible in case something odd was happening. So I put her bicycle in the boot of my car and got here just after nine. My secretary, Angela Foley, and Clifford Bradley, the Higher Scientific Officer in the Biology Department, arrived at about the same time.'

'Who at any time has been alone with the body?'

'Brenda Pridmore, of course, but very briefly, I imagine. Then Inspector Blakelock came up on his own. Then I was here alone for no more than a few seconds. Then I locked the Laboratory door, kept all the staff in the main hall, and waited there until Dr Kerrison arrived. He was here within five minutes and examined the body. I stood by the door. Superintendent Mercer arrived shortly afterwards and I handed over the key of the Biology Lab to him.'

Mercer said:

'Dr Kerrison suggested that I call in Dr Greene – he's the local police surgeon – to confirm his preliminary findings. Dr Greene wasn't alone with the body. After he'd made a quick and fairly superficial examination I locked the door. It wasn't opened again until the photographers and the fingerprint officers arrived. They've taken his dabs and examined the mallet, but we left it at that when we knew the Yard had been called in and you were on your way. The print boys are still here, in the Police Liaison Officer's room, but I let the photographers go.'

Putting on his search gloves, Dalgliesh ran his hands over the body. Under his white coat Lorrimer was wearing grey slacks and a tweed jacket. In the inside pocket was a thin leather wallet containing six pound notes, his driving licence, a book of stamps, and two credit cards. The right outer pocket held a pouch with his car keys and three others, two Yale and a smaller intricate key, probably to a desk-top drawer. There were a couple of ballpoint pens clipped to the top left-hand pocket of his white coat. In the bottom right-hand pocket was a handkerchief, his bunch of Laboratory keys and, not on the bunch, a single heavy key which looked fairly new. There was nothing else on the body.

He went over to study two exhibits lying on the central work bench, the mallet and a man's jacket. The mallet was an unusual weapon, obviously hand-made. The handle of crudely carved oak was about eighteen inches long and might, he thought, have once been part of a heavy walking stick. The head, which he judged to weigh just over two pounds, was blackened on one side with congealed blood from which one or two coarse grey hairs sprouted like whiskers. It was impossible to detect in the dried slough a darker hair which might have come from Lorrimer's head, or with the naked eye to distinguish his blood. That would be a job for the Metropolitan Police Laboratory when the mallet, carefully packed and with two identifying exhibit tags instead of one, reached the Biology Department later in the day.

He said to the Superintendent:

'No prints?'

'None, except for old Pascoe's. He's the owner of the mallet. They weren't wiped away, so it looks as if this chap wore gloves.'

That, thought Dalgliesh, would point to premeditation, or to the instinctive precaution of a knowledgeable expert. But if he came prepared to kill it was odd that he had relied on seizing the first convenient weapon; unless, of course, he knew that the mallet would be ready to hand.

He bent low to study the jacket. It was the top half of a cheap mass-produced suit in a harsh shade of blue with a paler pinstripe, and with wide lapels. The sleeve had been carefully spread out and the cuff bore a trace of what could have been blood. It was apparent that Lorrimer had already begun the analysis. On the bench was the electrophoresis apparatus plugged into its power pack and with two columns of six paired small circles punched in the sheet of agar gel. Beside it was a test-tube holder with a series of blood samples. To the right lay a couple of buff-coloured laboratory files with biology registrations and, beside them, flat open on the bench, a quarto-sized loose-leaf notebook with a ring binding. The left-hand page, dated the previous day, was closely covered in hieroglyphics and formulae in a thin, black, upright hand. Although most of the scientific jottings meant little to him, Dalgliesh could see that the time at which Lorrimer had started and finished each analysis had been carefully noted. The right-hand page was blank.

He said to Howarth:

'Who is the Senior Biologist now that Lorrimer's dead?'

'Claire Easterbrook. Miss Easterbrook, but it's advisable to call her Ms.'

'Is she here?'

'With the others in the library. I believe she has a firm alibi for the whole of yesterday evening, but as she's a senior scientist she was asked to stay. And, of course, she'll want to get back to work as soon as the staff are allowed into the Laboratory. There was a murder two nights ago in a clunch pit at Muddington – that jacket is an exhibit – and she'll want to get on with that as well as coping with the usual heavy load.'

'I'd like to see her first, please, and here. Then Mrs Bidwell. Is there a sheet we could use to cover him?'

Howarth said:

'I imagine there's a dust-sheet or something of the kind in the linen-cupboard. That's on the next floor.'

'I'd be grateful if you'd go with Inspector Massingham and show him. Then if you'd wait in the library or your own office I'll be down to have a word when I've finished here.'

For a second he thought that Howarth was about to demur. He frowned, and the handsome face clouded momentarily, petulant as a child's. But he left with Massingham without a word. Kerrison was still standing by the body, rigid as a guard of honour. He gave a little start as if recalling himself to reality and said:

'If you don't want me any longer I ought to be on my way to the hospital. You can contact me at St Luke's at Ely or here at the Old Rectory. I've given the sergeant an account of my movements last night. I was at home all the evening. At nine o'clock, by arrangement, I rang one of my colleagues at the hospital, Dr J. D. Underwood, about a matter which is coming up at the next medical committee. I think he's already confirmed that we did speak. He hadn't got the information I was waiting for but he rang me back at about a quarter to ten.'

There was as little reason to delay Kerrison as there was at present to suspect him. After he had left, Mercer said:

'I thought of leaving two sergeants. Reynolds and Underhill, and a couple of constables, Cox and Warren, if that will suit you. They're all sound, experienced officers. The Chief said to ask for anyone and anything you need. He's at a meeting in London this morning, but he'll be back tonight. I'll send up the chaps from the mortuary van if you're ready for them to take him away.'

'Yes, I've finished with him. I'll have a word with your men as soon as I've seen Miss Easterbrook. But ask one of the sergeants to come up in ten minutes to pack up the mallet for the Yard lab, will you? The chopper pilot will want to get back.'

They spoke a few more words about the liaison arrangements with the local force, then Mercer left to supervise the removal of the body. He would wait to introduce Dalgliesh to his seconded officers; after that, his responsibility would end. The case was in Dalgliesh's hands.

VI

Two minutes later Claire Easterbrook was shown into the laboratory. She entered with an assurance which a less experienced investigator than Dalgliesh might have mistaken for arrogance or insensitivity. She was a thin, long-waisted girl of about thirty, with a bony, intelligent face and a cap of dark curling hair which had been layered by an obviously expert, and no doubt expensive, hand to lie in swathes across the forehead and to curl into the nape of her high-arched neck. She was wearing a chestnut-brown sweater in fine wool belted into a black skirt which swung calf length above high-heeled boots. Her hands, with the nails cut very short, were ringless and her only ornament was a necklace of large wooden beads strung on a silver chain. Even without her white coat the impression she gave – and no doubt intended – was of a slightly intimidating professional competence. Before Dalgliesh had a chance to speak she said, with a trace of belligerence:

'I'm afraid you'll be wasting your time with me. My lover and I dined last night in Cambridge at the Master's Lodge of his college. I was with five other people from eight-thirty until nearly midnight. I've already given their names to the constable in the library.'

Dalgliesh said mildly:

'I'm sorry, Ms Easterbrook, that I had to ask you to come up before we were able to remove Dr Lorrimer's body. And as it seems impertinent to invite you to sit down in your own laboratory, I won't. But this isn't going to take long.'

She flushed, as if he had caught her out in a social solecism. Glancing with reluctant distaste at the shrouded, lumpen shape on the floor, at the stiff protruding ankles, she said:

'He'd be more dignified if you'd left him uncovered. Like this he could be a sack of rubbish. It's a curious superstition, the universal instinct to cover up the recently dead. After all, we're the ones at a disadvantage.'

Massingham said lightly:

'Not, surely, with the Master and his wife to vouch for your alibi?'

Their eyes met, his coolly amused, hers dark with dislike.

Dalgliesh said:

'Dr Howarth tells me you're the senior biologist now. Could you explain to me, please, what Dr Lorrimer was doing here last night? Don't touch anything.'

She went at once over to the table and regarded the two exhibits, the files and the scientific paraphernalia. She said:

'Would you open this file, please?'

Dalgliesh's gloved hands slipped between the covers and flipped it open.

'He re-checked Clifford Bradley's result on the Pascoe case. The mallet belongs to a sixty-four-year-old fen labourer called Pascoe whose wife has disappeared. His story is that she's walked out on him, but there are one or two suspicious circumstances. The police sent in the mallet to see if the stains on it are human blood. They aren't. Pascoe says that he used it to put an injured dog out of his misery. Bradley found that the blood reacted to anti-dog serum and Dr Lorrimer has duplicated his result. So the dog it was that died.'

Too mean to waste a bullet or send for a vet, thought Massingham savagely. It struck him as odd that the death of this unknown mongrel should, for a moment, anger him more than the killing of Lorrimer.

Miss Easterbrook moved over to the open notebook. The two men waited. Then she frowned and said, obviously puzzled:

'That's odd. Edwin always noted the time he began and finished an analysis and the procedure he adopted. He's initialled

Bradley's result on the Pascoe file, but there's nothing in the book. And it's obvious that he's made a start with the clunch pit murder; but that isn't noted either. The last reference is five forty-five and the final note is unfinished. Someone must have torn out the right-hand page.'

'Why do you suppose anyone should do that?'

She looked straight into Dalgliesh's eyes and said calmly:

'To destroy the evidence of what he'd been doing, or the result of his analysis, or the time he'd spent on it. The first and second would be rather pointless. It's obvious from the apparatus what he's been doing, and any competent biologist could duplicate the work. So it's probably the last.'

So the appearance of intelligence wasn't misleading. Dalgliesh asked:

'How long would he take checking the Pascoe result?'

'Not long. Actually, he'd started on that before six and I think he'd finished when I left at six-fifteen. I was the last to leave. The junior staff had gone. It isn't usual for them to work after six. I usually stay later, but I had to dress for the dinner party.'

'And the work he's done on the clunch pit case – how long would that have taken?'

'Difficult to say. I should have thought it would have kept him busy until nine or later. He was grouping a sample of the victim's blood and the blood from the dried stain by the ABO blood group system, and using electrophoresis to identify the haptoglobins and PGM, the enzyme phosphoglucomutase. Electrophoresis is a technique for identifying the protein and enzyme constituents of the blood by placing the samples in a gel of starch or agar and applying an electric current. As you can see, he'd actually started the run.'

Dalgliesh was aware of the scientific principle of electrophoresis, but didn't think it necessary to mention the fact. He opened the clunch pit file, and said:

'There's nothing on the file.'

'He would write up the result on the file later. But he wouldn't have started the analysis without noting the details in his book.'

There were two pedal-bins against the wall. Massingham opened them. One, plastic-lined, was obviously for laboratory waste and broken glass. The other was for waste paper. He stirred the contents: paper tissues, a few torn envelopes, a discarded newspaper. There was nothing which resembled the missing page.

Dalgliesh said:

'Tell me about Lorrimer.'

'What do you want to know?'

'Anything which could throw light on why someone disliked him enough to smash in his skull.'

'I can't help you there, I'm afraid. I've no idea.'

'You liked him?'

'Not particularly. It's not a question I've given much thought to. I got on all right with him. He was a perfectionist who didn't suffer fools gladly. But he was all right to work with if you knew your job. I do.'

'So he wouldn't need to check your work. What about those who don't know their jobs?'

'You'd better ask them, Commander.'

'Was he popular with his staff?'

'What has popularity to do with it? I don't suppose I'm popular, but I don't go in fear of my life.'

She was silent for a moment, then said in a more conciliatory tone:

'I probably sound obstructive. I don't mean to be. It's just that I can't help. I've no idea who could have killed him or why. I only know that I didn't.'

'Had you noticed any change in him recently?'

'Change? You mean, in his mood or behaviour? Not really. He gave the impression of a man under strain; but then, he was that kind of man, solitary, obsessional, overworked. One rather odd thing. He's been interesting himself in the new C.O., Brenda Pridmore. She's a pretty child, but hardly his intellectual level, I should have thought. I don't think there was anything serious, but it caused a certain amount of amusement in the Lab. I think he was probably trying to prove something to someone, or, perhaps, to himself.'

'You've heard about the telephone call to Mrs Bidwell, of course?'

'I imagine the whole Lab knows. It wasn't I who rang her, if that's what you're thinking. In any case, I should have known that it wouldn't work.'

'How do you mean, it wouldn't work?'

'It depended, surely, on old Lorrimer not being at home yesterday. After all, the caller couldn't rely on his not noticing that Edwin hadn't come home last night until he didn't get his early tea brought to him. As it happens, he went off to bed quite happily. But the hoaxer couldn't have known that. Normally, Edwin would have been missed much earlier.'

'Was there any reason to suppose that old Mr Lorrimer wouldn't be at the cottage yesterday?'

'He was supposed to be admitted to Addenbrooke's hospital in the afternoon for treatment of a skin complaint. I think the whole Biology Lab knew. He used to telephone often enough, fretting about the arrangements and whether Edwin would get time off to drive him there. Yesterday, just after ten, he rang to say that the bed wouldn't be available for him after all.'

'Who took the call?'

'I did. It rang in his private office and I took it there. Edwin hadn't returned from the clunch pit autopsy. I told him as soon as he arrived.'

'Who else did you tell?'

'When I came out of the office I think I said something casually about old Mr Lorrimer not having to go into hospital after all. I'm not sure of the actual words. I don't think anyone made a comment or took much apparent notice.'

Suddenly she lost her composure. She flushed and hesitated, as if realizing for the first time where all this was leading. The two men waited. Then, angry with herself, she burst out, clumsily defensive:

'I'm sorry, but I can't remember. You'll have to ask them. It didn't seem important at the time and I was busy. We were all busy. I think everyone was there, but I can't be certain.'

'Thank you,' said Dalgliesh coolly. 'You've been remarkably helpful.'

VII

Mrs Bidwell arrived at the door as the two attendants from the mortuary van were carrying out the body. She seemed to regret its disappearance and looked at the chalk outline marked by Massingham on the floor as if this were a poor substitute for the real thing. Gazing after the covered metal container, she said:

'Poor devil! I never thought to see him carried out of his lab feet first. He were never popular, you know. Still, I don't suppose that's worrying him where he is now. Is that one of my dust-sheets you've had over him?'

She peered suspiciously at the sheet, now folded neatly at the end of one of the benches.

'It came from the laboratory linen-cupboard, yes.'

'Well, as long as it's put back where you found it. Come to that, it had better go straight into the soiled linen. But I don't want any of your chaps taking it away. Laundry disappears fast enough as it is.'

'Why wasn't he popular, Mrs Bidwell?'

'Too particular by half. Mind you, you've got to be these days if you want to get any work done. But from what I hear he was too fussy for his own good. And he'd been getting worse, no doubt about that. And very odd he'd been lately, too. Nervy. You heard about the unpleasantness in the reception hall the day before yesterday, I suppose? Oh well, you will. Ask Inspector Blakelock. Just before lunch it was. Dr Lorrimer had a real old tussle with that barmy daughter of Dr Kerrison's. Nearly pushed her out of the door. Screeching like a banshee, she was. I came into the hall just in time to see it. Her dad isn't going to like that, I said to Inspector Blakelock. He's crazy about those kids. Mark my words, I said, if Dr Lorrimer doesn't take a hold of himself there'll be murder done in this Lab. I said the same to Mr Middlemass.'

'I want you to tell me about the telephone call this morning, Mrs Bidwell. What time was it?'

'It was near enough seven o'clock. We was eating breakfast and I just filled the teapot for second cups. Had the kettle in me hand when it rang.'

'And who answered it?'

'Bidwell. Phone's in the hall and he got up and went out to it. Cursin' he was 'cos he'd just settled down to his kipper. He hates cold kipper, does Bidwell. We always has kippers on Thursday on account of Marshall's fish van coming from Ely Wednesday afternoons.'

'Does your husband usually answer the phone?'

'He always answers the phone. And if he's not in I lets it ring. I can't abide the dratted things. Never could. Wouldn't have it in the house if our Shirley hadn't paid to get it put in. She's married now and lives Mildenhall way and she likes to think we can ring her if we want her. Fat lot of use that is. I can't never hear what anyone says. And the ring is enough to put the fear of God in a soul. Telegrams and phone rings. I hate 'em both.'

'Who at the Lab would know that your husband always answered the phone?'

'Best part of them, more than likely. They knows I won't touch the thing. There's no secret about that. We're all as the good Lord made us and some of us a sight worse. Nothing to be ashamed of.'

'Of course not. Your husband's at work now, I expect?'

'That's right. Yeoman's Farm. Captain Massey's place. Tractor work mostly. Been there twenty years, near enough.'

Dalgliesh nodded almost imperceptibly to Massingham and the Inspector slipped out to have a quiet word with Sergeant Underhill. It would be as well to check with Mr Bidwell while his memory of the call was fresh. Dalgliesh went on:

'What happened then?'

'Bidwell came back. Said that I wasn't to go to the Lab this morning because Mrs Schofield wanted me over at Leamings particular. I was to bike there and she'd run me and the bike home afterwards. Sticking out of the back of that red Jaguar she's got, I suppose. I thought it was a bit of a cheek seeing as I'm due here mornings but I've nothing against Mrs Schofield and if she wanted me I wasn't above obliging. The Lab would just have to wait, I said to Bidwell. I can't be in two places at once, I said. What don't get done today will get done tomorrow.'

'You work here every morning?'

'Except weekends. Gets here as near eight-thirty as makes no odds, and works till about ten. Then back at twelve in case any of the gentlemen wants their lunch cooking. The girls mostly manage for themselves. Afterwards I washes up for them. I reckons to get away by two-thirty most days. Mind you, it's light work. Scobie – he's the Lab attendant – and I sees to the working labs but all the heavy cleaning is supposed to be done by the contractors. They comes on Mondays and Fridays only, from seven until nine, a whole van full of them from Ely, and does the main hall, the stairs and all the heavy polishing. Inspector Blakelock gets here early those mornings to let them in and Scobie keeps an eye on them. Not that you'd know they'd been most days. No personal interest, you see. Not like the old days when me and two women from the village did the lot.'

'So what would you normally have done as soon as you arrived if this had been an ordinary Thursday? I want you to think carefully, Mrs Bidwell. This may be very important.'

'No need to think. I'd do the same as I does every day.'

'Which is?'

'Take off me hat and coat in the downstairs cloakroom. Put on me overalls. Get cleaning bucket and powder and disinfectant from the broom cupboard. Clean the toilets, male and female. Then check dirty laundry and get it bagged up. Put out clean white coats where wanted. Then dust and tidy Director's office and general office.'

'Right,' said Dalgliesh. 'Let's do the rounds then, shall we?'

Three minutes later a curious little procession made its way up the stairs. Mrs Bidwell, clad now in a navy-blue working overall and carrying a plastic bucket in one hand and a mop in the other, led the way. Dalgliesh and Massingham followed. The two lavatories were on the second floor at the rear opposite the Document Examination Laboratory. They had obviously been converted from what had once been an elegant bedroom. But now a narrow passage leading to the single barred window had been constructed down the middle of the room. A mean-looking door gave entry to the women's cloakroom on the left and, a few yards down, a similar door led to the men's washroom on the right. Mrs Bidwell led the way into the left-hand room. It was larger than Dalgliesh had expected, but poorly lit from a single round window with pivoting opaque glass set about four feet from the floor. The window was open. There were three lavatory cubicles. The outer room contained two wash-hand basins with a paper-towel dispenser and, to the left of the door, a long Formica-covered counter with a glass above it which apparently served as a dressing-table. To the right were a wall-mounted gas-fired incinerator, a row of clothes-hooks, a large wicker laundry-basket and two rather battered cane chairs.

Dalgliesh said to Mrs Bidwell:

'Is this how you would expect to find it?'

Mrs Bidwell's sharp little eyes peered round. The doors to the three lavatories were open and she gave them a quick inspection.

'No better nor no worse. They're pretty good about the toilets. I'll say that for them.'

'And that window is usually kept open?'

'Winter and summer, except it's bitter cold. That's the only ventilation you see.'

'The incinerator is off. Is that usual?'

'That's right. Last girl to leave turns it off at night, then I puts it on next morning.'

Dalgliesh looked inside. The incinerator was empty except for a trace of carbon ash. He went over to the window. Rain had obviously driven in some time during the night and the dried splashes were clearly visible on the tiled floor. But even the inside pane, where no rain could have splashed, was remarkably clean and there was no discernible dust around the sill. He said:

'Did you clean the window yesterday, Mrs Bidwell?'

'Of course I did. It's like I told you. I cleans the lavatories every morning. And when I cleans, I cleans. Shall I get on with it now?'

'I'm afraid there'll be no cleaning done today. We'll pretend you've finished in here. Now what happens? What about the laundry?'

The laundry-basket contained only one overall, marked with the initials C.M.E. Mrs Bidwell said:

'I wouldn't expect many dirty coats, not on a Thursday. They usually manages to make them last a week and drop them in here on Friday before they go home. Monday's the busy day for laundry and putting out the new coats. Looks as though Miss

Easterbrook spilt her tea yesterday. That's not like her. But she's particular is Miss Easterbrook. You wouldn't find her going round with a dirty coat, no matter what day of the week.'

So there was at least one member of the Biology Department, thought Dalgliesh, who knew that Mrs Bidwell would make an early visit to the Lab to put out a clean white coat. It would be interesting to learn who had been present when the fastidious Miss Easterbrook had had her accident with the tea.

The male washroom, apart from the urinal stalls, differed very little from the women's. There was the same round open window, the same absence of any marks on the panes or sill. Dalgliesh carried over one of the chairs and, carefully avoiding any contact with the window or the sill, looked out. There was a drop of about six feet to the top of the window beneath, and an equal drop to that on the first floor. Below them both a paved terrace ran right up to the wall. The absence of soft earth, the rain in the night and Mrs Bidwell's efficient cleaning meant that they would be lucky to find any evidence of a climb. But a reasonably slim and sure-footed man or woman with enough nerve and a head for heights could certainly have got out this way. But if the murderer were a member of the Lab staff, why should he risk his neck when he must have known that the keys were on Lorrimer? And if the murderer were an outsider, then how account for the locked front door, the intact alarm system, and the fact that Lorrimer must have let him in?

He turned his attention to the wash-basins. None was particularly dirty, but near the rim of the one nearest the door there was a smear of porridge-like mucus. He bent his head over the basin and sniffed. His sense of smell was extremely acute and, from the plug-hole, he detected the faint but unmistakably disagreeable smell of human vomit.

Mrs Bidwell, meanwhile, had thrown open the lid of the laundry-basket. She gave an exclamation.

'That's funny. It's empty.'

Dalgliesh and Massingham turned. Dalgliesh asked:

'What were you expecting to find, Mrs Bidwell?'

'Mr Middlemass's white coat, that's what.'

She darted out of the room. Dalgliesh and Massingham followed. She flung open the door of the Document Examination room and glanced inside. Then she closed the door again and stood with her back against it. She said:

'It's gone! It's not hanging on the peg. So where is it? Where's Mr Middlemass's white coat?'

Dalgliesh asked:

'Why did you expect to find it in the laundry-basket?'

Mrs Bidwell's black eyes grew immense. She slewed her eyes furtively from side to side and then said with awed relish:

'Because it had blood on it, that's why. Lorrimer's blood!'

VIII

Lastly they went down the main staircase to the Director's office. From the library there was a broken murmur of voices, subdued and spasmodic as a funeral gathering. A detective constable was standing at the front door with the detached watchfulness of a man paid to endure boredom but ready to leap into action should, unaccountably, the boredom end.

Howarth had left his office unlocked and the key in the door. Dalgliesh was interested that the Director had chosen to wait with the rest of the staff in the library, and wondered whether this was intended to demonstrate solidarity with his colleagues, or was a tactful admission that his office was one of the rooms which had been due to receive Mrs Bidwell's early morning attention, and must, therefore, be of special interest to Dalgliesh. But that reasoning was surely too subtle. It was difficult to believe that Howarth hadn't entered his room since the discovery of the body. If there were anything to remove, he best of all must have had the chance to do it.

Dalgliesh had expected the room to be impressive, but it still surprised him. The plasterwork of the coved ceiling was splendid, a joyous riot of wreaths, shells, ribbons, and trailing vines, ornate and yet disciplined. The fireplace was of white and mottled marble with a finely carved frieze of nymphs and piping shepherds and a classical overmantel with open pediment. He guessed that the agreeably proportioned salon, too small to be partitioned and not large enough for a working laboratory, had escaped the fate of so much of the house more for administrative and scientific convenience than from any sensitivity on Colonel Hoggatt's part to its innate perfection. It was newly furnished in a style guaranteed not to offend, a nice compromise of bureaucratic orthodoxy and modern functionalism. There was a large glass-fronted bookcase to the left of the fireplace, and a personal locker and a coat-stand to the right. A rectangular conference table and four chairs, of a type provided for senior public servants, stood between the tall windows. Next to it was a steel security cupboard fitted with a combination lock. Howarth's desk, a plain contraption in the same wood as the conference table, faced the door. Apart from an inkstained blotter and a pen-stand it held a small wooden bookshelf containing the *Shorter Oxford Dictionary*, a dictionary of quotations, *Roget's Thesaurus* and *Fowler's Modern English Usage*. The choice seemed curious for a scientist. There were three metal trays marked 'In', 'Pending' and 'Out'. The 'Out' tray held two manila files, the top labelled 'Chapel – Proposals for transfer to Department of the Environment', and the second, a large, old and unwieldy file which had been much mended, was marked 'New Laboratory – Commissioning'.

Dalgliesh was struck by the emptiness and impersonality of the whole room. It had obviously been recently decorated for Howarth's arrival, and the pale grey-green carpet, with its matching square under the desk, was as yet unmarked, the curtains hung in pristine folds of dark green. There was only one picture, positioned in the overmantel, but this was an original, an early Stanley Spencer showing the Virgin's Assumption. Plump, foreshortened, varicosed thighs in red bloomers floated upwards from a circle of clutching work-worn hands to a reception committee of gaping cherubim. It was, he thought, an eccentric choice for the room, discordant both in date and style. It was the only object, apart from the books, which reflected a personal taste; Dalgliesh hardly supposed that it had been provided by a Government agency. Otherwise the office had the underfurnished, expectant atmosphere of a room refurbished to receive an unknown occupant, and still awaiting the imprint of his taste and personality. It was hard to believe that Howarth had worked here for almost a year. Mrs Bidwell, her tight little mouth pursed and eyes narrowed, regarded it with obvious disapproval. Dalgliesh asked:

'Is this how you would have expected to find it?'

'That's right. Every bloody morning. Nothing for me to do here really is there? Mind you, I dusts and polishes around and runs the Hoover over the carpet. But he's neat and tidy, there's no denying it. Not like old Dr MacIntyre. Oh, he was a lovely man! But messy! You should have seen his desk of a morning. And smoke! You couldn't hardly see across the room sometimes. He had this lovely skull on his desk to keep his pipes in. They dug it up when they was making the trench for the pipes to the new vehicle examination extension. Been in the ground more than two hundred years, Dr Mac said, and he showed me the crack – just like a cracked cup – where his skull had been bashed in. That's one murder they never solved. I miss that skull. Real lovely that used to look. And he had all these pictures of himself and his friends at university with oars crossed above them, and a coloured one of the Highlands with hairy cattle paddling in a lake, and one of his father with his dogs, and such a lovely picture of his wife – dead she was, poor soul – and another big picture of Venice with gondolas and a lot of foreigners in fancy dress, and a cartoon of Dr Mac done by one of his friends, showing the friend lying dead, and Dr Mac in his deerstalker hat looking for clues with his magnifying glass. That was a real laugh that was. Oh, I loved Dr Mac's pictures!' She looked at the Spencer with a marked lack of enthusiasm.

'And there's nothing unusual about the room this morning?'

'I told you, same as usual. Well, look for yourself. Clean as a new pin. It looks different in the day, mind you, when he's working here. But he always leaves it as if he isn't expecting to come back in the morning.'

There was nothing else to be learned from Mrs Bidwell. Dalgliesh thanked her and told her that she could go home as soon as she had checked with Detective Sergeant Reynolds in the library that he had all the necessary information about where she had spent the previous evening. He explained this with his usual tact, but tact was wasted on Mrs Bidwell. She said cheerfully and without rancour:

'No use trying to pin this on me, or Bidwell come to that. We was together at the village concert. Sat five rows back between

Joe Machin – he's the sexton – and Willie Barnes – he's the rector's warden, and we stayed there until the end of the show. No sneaking out at half-time like some I could mention.'

'Who sneaked out, Mrs Bidwell?'

'Ask him yourself. Sat at the end of the row in front of us, a gentleman whose office we might or might not be standing in at this very moment. Do you want to talk to him? Shall I ask him to step in?' She spoke hopefully and looked towards the door like an eager gun dog, ears pricked for the command to retrieve.

'We'll see to that, thank you, Mrs Bidwell. And if we want to talk to you again we'll get in touch. You've been very helpful.'

'I thought I might make coffee for them all before I go. No harm in that, I suppose?'

There was no point in warning her not to talk to the Lab staff, or, come to that, the whole village. Dalgliesh had no doubt that his search of the cloakrooms and the missing bloodstained coat would soon be common knowledge. But no great harm would be done. The murderer must know that the police would be immediately alive to the possible significance of that false early morning call to Mrs Bidwell. He was dealing with intelligent men and women, experienced, even if vicariously, in criminal investigation, knowledgeable about police procedure, aware of the rules which governed his every move. He had no doubt that, mentally, most of the group now waiting in the library to be interviewed were following his actions almost to the minute.

And among them, or known to them, was a murderer.

IX

Superintendent Mercer had selected his two sergeants with an eye to contrast or, perhaps, with a view to satisfying any prejudices which Dalgliesh might harbour about the age and experience of his subordinates. Sergeant Reynolds was near the end of his service, a stolid, broad-shouldered, slow-speaking officer of the old school and a native of the fens. Sergeant Underhill, recently promoted, looked young enough to be his son. His boyish, open face with its look of disciplined idealism was vaguely familiar to Massingham, who suspected that he might have seen it in a police recruitment pamphlet, but decided in the interest of harmonious co-operation to give Underhill the benefit of the doubt.

The four police officers were sitting at the conference table in the Director's office. Dalgliesh was briefing his team before he started on the preliminary interviews. He was, as always, restlessly aware of time passing. It was already after eleven and he was anxious to finish at the Laboratory and see old Mr Lorrimer. The physical clues to his son's murder might lie in the Laboratory; the clue to the man himself lay elsewhere. But neither his words nor his tone betrayed impatience.

'We start by assuming that the telephone call to Mrs Bidwell and Lorrimer's death are connected. That means the call was made by the murderer or an accomplice. We'll keep an open mind about the caller's sex until we get confirmation from Bidwell, but it was probably a woman, probably also someone who knew that old Mr Lorrimer was expected to be in hospital yesterday, and who didn't know that the appointment had been cancelled. If the old man had been home, the ruse could hardly hope to succeed. As Miss Easterbrook has pointed out, no one could rely on his going early to bed last night and not realizing until after the Lab opened this morning that his son hadn't come home.'

Massingham said:

'The killer would have made it his business to get here early this morning, assuming that he didn't know that his plan had misfired. And assuming, of course, the call wasn't a double bluff. It would be a neat ploy, wasting our time, confusing the investigation and diverting suspicion from everyone except the early arrivals.'

'But for one of the suspects, it could have been an even neater ploy,' thought Dalgliesh. It had been Mrs Bidwell's arrival at Howarth's house in obedience to the call which had given the Director himself the excuse for arriving so early. He wondered what time Howarth usually put in an appearance. That would be one of the questions to be asked. He said:

'We'll start by assuming that it wasn't a bluff, that the murderer, or his accomplice, made the call to delay Mrs Bidwell's arrival and the discovery of the body. So what was he hoping to do? Plant evidence or destroy it? Tidy up something which he'd overlooked; wipe the mallet clean; clear up the evidence of whatever it was he was doing here last night; replace the keys on the body? But Blakelock had the best opportunity to do that, and he wouldn't need to have taken them in the first place. The call would have given someone the chance to replace the spare set in the security cupboard here. But that would be perfectly possible without delaying Mrs Bidwell's arrival. And, of course, it may have been done.'

Underhill said:

'But is it really likely, sir, that the call was intended to delay the finding of the body and give the killer time to replace the keys? Admittedly Mrs Bidwell could be expected to be first in the Biology Department this morning when she put out the clean coats. But the murderer couldn't rely on that. Inspector Blakelock or Brenda Pridmore could easily have had occasion to go there.'

Dalgliesh thought it a risk that the murderer might well have thought worth taking. In his experience the early-morning routine in an institution seldom varied. Unless Blakelock had the early-morning job of checking on Lab security – and this was yet another of the questions to be asked – he and Brenda Pridmore would probably have got on with their normal work at the reception desk. In the ordinary course of events Mrs Bidwell would have been the one to find the body. Any member of staff who went into the Biology Lab before her would have needed a good excuse to explain his presence there, unless, of course, he was a member of the Biology Department.

Massingham said:

'It's odd about the missing white coat, sir. It can hardly have been removed or destroyed to prevent us learning about the fight between Middlemass and Lorrimer. That unedifying but intriguing little episode must have been round the Lab within minutes of its happening. Mrs Bidwell would see to that.'

Both Dalgliesh and Massingham wondered how far Mrs Bidwell's description of the quarrel, given with the maximum dramatic effect, had been accurate. It was obvious that she had come into the laboratory after the blow had been struck, and had in fact seen very little. Dalgliesh had recognized, with foreboding, a familiar phenomenon: the desire of a witness, aware of the paucity of her evidence, to make the most of it lest the police be disappointed, while remaining as far as possible within the confines of truth. Stripped of Mrs Bidwell's embellishments, the core of hard fact had been disappointingly small.

'What they were quarrelling about I couldn't take it on myself to say, except that it was about a lady, and that Dr Lorrimer was upset because she'd telephoned Mr Middlemass. The door was open and I did hear that much when I passed to go in to the ladies' toilet. I daresay she rang him to arrange a date and Dr Lorrimer didn't like it. I never saw a man more white. Like death he looked, with a handkerchief held up against his face all bloodied, and his black eyes glaring over the top of it. And Mr Middlemass was turkey red. Embarrassed, I daresay. Well, it's not what we're used to at Hoggatt's, senior staff knocking each other about. When proper gentlemen start in with the fists there's usually a woman at the bottom of it. Same with this murder if you ask me.'

Dalgliesh said:

'We'll be getting Middlemass's version of the affair. I'd like now to have a word with all the Lab staff in the library and then Inspector Massingham and I will start the preliminary interviews: Howarth, the two women, Angela Foley and Brenda Pridmore, Blakelock, Middlemass and any of the others without a firm alibi. I'd like you, Sergeant, to get on with organizing the usual routine. I shall want one of the senior staff in each department while the search is going on. They're the only ones who can tell whether anything in their lab has changed since yesterday. You'll be looking – admittedly without much hope – for the missing page of Lorrimer's notebook, any evidence of what he was doing here last night apart from working on the clunch pit murder, any sign of what happened to the missing coat. I want a thorough search of the whole building, particularly possible means of access and exit. The rain last night is a nuisance. You'll probably find the walls washed clean, but there may be some evidence that he got out through one of the lavatory windows.

'You'll need a couple of men on the grounds. The earth is fairly soft after the rain and if the murderer came by car or otorcycle there could be tyre-marks. Any we find can be checked gainst the tyre index here; we needn't waste time going to the Met Lab for that. There's a bus-stop immediately opposite the aboratory entrance. Find out what time the buses pass. There's lways the possibility that one of the passengers or crew noticed omething. I'd like the Laboratory building checked first, and as uickly as possible so that the staff can get back to work. They've new murder on their hands and we can't keep the place closed onger than is absolutely necessary. I'd like to give them access by omorrow morning.

'Then there's the smear of what looks like vomit on the first asin in the men's washroom. The smell from the pipe is still airly distinct. I want a sample of that to go to the Met Lab rgently. You'll probably have to unscrew the joint to get at the asin of the U-bend. We shall need to find out who used the oom last yesterday evening and whether he noticed the smear on he basin. If no one admits to having been sick during the day, or an't produce a witness that he was, we shall want to know what hey all ate for the evening meal. It could be Lorrimer's vomit, so we'll need some information on his stomach contents. I'd also like sample of his blood and hair to be left here at the Lab. But Dr Blain-Thomson will be seeing to that.'

Reynolds said:

'We take it that the crucial time is from six-fifteen, when he was ast seen alive in his lab, until midnight?'

'For the present. When I've seen his father and confirmed that ie made that call at eight forty-five we may be able to narrow it lown. And we shall get a clearer idea of the time of death when Dr Blain-Thomson has done the P.M. But judging from the state of rigor, Dr Kerrison wasn't far out.'

But Kerrison didn't need to be far out, if he were the murderer. Rigor mortis was notoriously unreliable, and if he wanted an alibi for himself, Kerrison could shift the time of death by up to an hour without suspicion. If the timing were tight he might not need even an hour. It had been prudent of him to call in the police surgeon to confirm his estimate of the time of death. But how likely was Dr Greene, experienced as he might be in viewing bodies, to disagree with the opinion of a consultant forensic pathologist unless the latter's judgement was manifestly perver If Kerrison were guilty, he had run little risk by calling in Gree

Dalgliesh got to his feet.

'Right,' he said. 'Let's get on with it, shall we?'

X

Dalgliesh disliked having more than one other officer pres with him at his preliminary and informal interview, so Massi ham was taking the notes. They were hardly necessary; Dalglie he knew, had almost total recall. But he still found the pract useful. They were sitting together at the conference table in t Director's office, but Howarth, perhaps because he objected sitting in his own room other than at his desk, preferred to sta He was leaning casually against the fireplace. From time to ti Massingham lifted an unobtrusive eyebrow to glance at the cle cut, dominant profile outlined against the classical frieze. Th were three bunches of keys on the table: the bunch taken fr Lorrimer's body, that handed over by Inspector Blakelock, a the set which Dr Howarth, manipulating the security lock, h taken from its box in the cupboard. Each set of keys was identic one Yale key and two security keys to the front door, and o smaller key on a plain metal ring. None was named, presumal for security reasons. Dalgliesh said:

'And these are the only three sets in existence?'

'Except for the set at Guy's Marsh police station, yes. Natural I checked earlier this morning that the police still have their s The keys are kept in the safe under the control of the stati officer, and they haven't been touched. They need a set at t police station in case the alarm goes off. There was no alarm l night.'

Dalgliesh already knew from Mercer that the station keys h been checked. He said:

'And the smallest key?'

'That's the one to the Exhibits Store. The system is for incoming exhibits, after they've been registered, to be stor there until they're issued to the head of the appropriate depa ment. It's his responsibility to allocate them to a specific offic

In addition, we store the exhibits which have been examined and are awaiting collection by the police, and those which have been presented to the court during the case and are returned to us for destruction. Those are mainly drugs. They're destroyed here in the incinerator and the destruction witnessed by one of the Laboratory staff and the officer in charge of the case. The Exhibits Store is also protected by the electronic alarm system, but, obviously, we need a key for internal security when the system hasn't been set.'

'And all the Laboratory internal doors and your office were protected last night once the internal alarm system was set? That means that an intruder could only have got out undetected through the top-floor lavatory windows. All the others are either barred or fitted with the electronic alarm?'

'That's right. He could have got in that way too, of course, which was what concerned us most. But it wouldn't have been an easy climb, and the alarm would have gone off as soon as he tried to gain access to any of the main rooms in the Laboratory. We did consider extending the alarm system to the lavatory suite soon after I arrived, but it seemed unnecessary. We haven't had a break-in in the seventy-odd years of the Lab's existence.'

'What are the precise arrangements about locking the Laboratory?'

'Only the two Police Liaison Officers and Lorrimer as the Deputy Security Officer were authorized to lock up. He or the Police Liaison Officer on duty was responsible for ensuring that no staff were left on the premises and that all the internal doors were shut before the alarm was set, and the front door finally locked for the night. The alarm system to Guy's Marsh police station is set whether the door is locked on the inside or the out.'

'And these other keys found on the body, the three in this leather pouch and the single key. Do you recognize any of those?'

'Not the three in the pouch. One is obviously his car keys. But the single one looks very like the key to the Wren chapel. If it is, I didn't know that Lorrimer had it. Not that it's important. But as far as I know, there's only one key to the chapel in existence and that's hanging on the board in the Chief Liaison Officer's room. It isn't a security lock and we're not particularly worried about the chapel. There's nothing left there of real value. But occasionally architects and archaeological societies want to view it, so we let them borrow the key and they sign for it in a book in the office. We don't allow them through the Laboratory grounds to get at it. They have to use the back entrance in Guy's Marsh Road. The contract cleaners take it once every two months to clean and check the heating – we have to keep it reasonably warm in winter because the ceiling and carving are rather fine – and Miss Willard goes there from time to time, to do some dusting. When her father was rector of Chevisham, he used occasionally to hold services in the chapel, and I think she has a sentimental regard for the place.'

Massingham went out to Chief Inspector Martin's office and brought in the chapel key. The two matched. The small notebook which he had found hanging with the key showed that it had last been collected by Miss Willard on Monday, 25th October. Howarth said:

'We're thinking of transferring the chapel to the Department of the Environment once we occupy the new Laboratory. It's a constant irritation to the Treasury that our funds are used to heat and maintain it. I've set up a string quartet here, and we held a concert on August 26th in the chapel, but otherwise it's completely unused. I expect you will want to take a look at it, and it's worth seeing in its own right. It's a very fine specimen of late seventeenth-century church architecture, although, in fact, it isn't by Wren but by Alexander Fort, who was strongly influenced by him.'

Dalgliesh asked suddenly:

'How well did you get on with Lorrimer?'

Howarth replied calmly:

'Not particularly well. I respected him as a biologist, and I certainly had no complaints either about his work or about his co-operation with me as Director. He wasn't an easy man to know, and I didn't find him particularly sympathetic. But he was probably one of the most respected serologists in the service, and we shall miss him. If he had a fault, it was a reluctance to delegate. He had two scientific officer serologists in his department for the grouping of liquid blood and stains, saliva and semen samples, but he invariably took the murder cases himself. Apart from his casework and attendance at trials and at scenes of crime, he did a considerable amount of lecturing to detective training courses, and police familiarization courses.'

Lorrimer's rough notebook was on the desk. Dalgliesh pushed it towards Howarth and said:

'Have you seen this before?'

'His rough notebook? Yes, I think I've noticed it in his department, or when he was carrying it with him. He was obsessively tidy and had a dislike of odd scraps of paper. Anything of importance was noted in that book, and subsequently transferred to the files. Claire Easterbrook tells me that the last page is missing.'

'That's why we're particularly anxious to know what he was doing here last night, apart from working on the clunch pit murder. He could have got into any of the other laboratories, of course?'

'If he'd switched off the internal alarm, yes. I believe it was his usual practice, when he was last on the premises, to rely on the Yale lock and the bolt on the front door and only check the internal doors and set the security alarm before he finally left. Obviously it's important not to set off the alarm accidentally.'

'Would he have been competent to undertake an examination in another department?'

'It depends on what he was trying to do. Essentially, of course, he was concerned with the identification and grouping of biological material, blood, body stains and the examination of fibres and animal and plant tissues. But he was a competent general scientist and his interests were wide – his scientific interests. Forensic biologists, particularly in the smaller laboratories, which this has been up to now, become pretty versatile. But he wouldn't attempt to use the more sophisticated instruments in the Instrument Section, the mass spectrometer, for example.'

'And you personally have no idea what he could have been doing?'

'None. I do know that he came into this office. I had to look up the name of a consultant surgeon who was giving evidence for the defence in one of our old cases, and I had the medical directory on my desk when I left last night. This morning, it was back in its place in the library. Few things irritated Lorrimer more than people removing books from the library. But if he was in this office last night, I hardly imagine it was merely to check on my carelessness with the reference books.'

Lastly, Dalgliesh asked him about his movements the previous night.

'I played the fiddle at the village concert. The rector had five minutes or so to fill in and asked me if the string quartet would play something which he described as short and cheerful. The players were myself, a chemist, one of the scientific officers from the document examination department, and a typist from the general office. Miss Easterbrook should have been the first 'cello, but she had a dinner engagement which she regarded as important, and couldn't make it. We played the Mozart Divertimento in D major and came third on the programme.'

'And you stayed for the rest of the concert?'

'I intended to. Actually, the hall was incredibly stuffy and just before the interval at eight-thirty I slipped out. I stayed out.'

Dalgliesh asked what precisely he'd done.

'Nothing. I sat on one of those flat tombstones for about twenty minutes, then I left.'

'Did you see anyone, or did anyone see you?'

'I saw a hobby-horse – I know now that it must have been Middlemass deputizing for Chief Inspector Martin – come out of the male dressing-room. He pranced around rather happily, I thought, and snapped his jaws at an angel on one of the graves. Then he was joined by the troupe of morris-dancers coming through the graveyard from the Moonraker. It was an extraordinary sight. There was the racing moon and these extraordinary figures with their bells jingling and their hats decked with evergreens moving through the swirl of ground mist out of the darkness towards me. It was like an *outré* film or a ballet. All it needed was second-rate background music, preferably Stravinsky. I was sitting motionless on the gravestone, some distance away, and I don't think they saw me. I certainly didn't make myself known. The hobby-horse joined them, and they went into the hall. Then I heard the fiddle start up. I suppose I stayed sitting there for about another ten minutes, and then I left. I walked for the rest of the evening along Leamings Dyke and got home about ten o'clock. My half-sister Domenica will be able to confirm the time.'

They spent a little time discussing the administrative arrangements for the investigation. Dr Howarth said that he would move into Miss Foley's room and make his office available to the police. There would be no chance of the Lab opening for the rest of the day, but Dalgliesh said that he hoped it would be possible for work to start again the next morning. Before Howarth left, Dalgliesh said:

'Everyone I've spoken to respected Dr Lorrimer as a forensic biologist. But what was he like as a man? What, for example, did you know about him except that he was a forensic biologist?'

Dr Howarth said coldly:

'Nothing. I wasn't aware there was anything to know, except that he was a forensic biologist. And now, if you've no more immediate questions, I must telephone Establishment Department and make sure that, in the excitement of his somewhat spectacular exit, they're not forgetting to send me a replacement.'

XI

With the resilience of youth, Brenda Pridmore had recovered quickly from the shock of finding Lorrimer's body. She had resolutely refused to be taken home and by the time Dalgliesh was ready to see her she was perfectly calm and, indeed, anxious to tell her story. With her cloud of rich auburn hair and her freckled wind-tanned face she looked the picture of bucolic health. But the grey eyes were intelligent, the mouth sensitive and gentle. She gazed across the desk at Dalgliesh as intently as a docile child and totally without fear. He guessed that all her young life she had been used to receiving an avuncular kindness from men and never doubted that she would receive it, too, from these unknown officers of police. In response to Dalgliesh's questioning, she described exactly what had happened from the moment of her arrival at the Laboratory that morning to the discovery of the body. Dalgliesh asked:

'Did you touch him?'

'Oh no! I knelt down and I think I did put out my hand to feel his cheek. But that was all. I knew that he was dead, you see.'

'And then?'

'I don't remember. I know I rushed downstairs and Inspector Blakelock was standing at the bottom looking up at me. I couldn't speak, but I suppose he saw by my face that something was wrong. Then I remember sitting on the chair outside Chief Inspector Martin's office and looking at Colonel Hoggatt's portrait. Then I don't remember anything until Dr Howarth and Mrs Bidwell arrived.'

'Do you think anyone could have got out of the building past you while you were sitting there?'

'The murderer, you mean? I don't see how he could have. I know I wasn't very alert, but I hadn't fainted or anything silly like that. I'm sure I would have noticed if anyone had come across the hall. And even if he did manage to slip past me, he would have bumped into Dr Howarth, wouldn't he?'

Dalgliesh asked her about her job at Hoggatt's, how well she had known Dr Lorrimer. She prattled away with artless confidence about her life, her colleagues, her fascinating job, Inspector Blakelock who was so good to her and who had lost his own only daughter, telling with every sentence more than she knew. It wasn't that she was stupid, thought Massingham, only honest and ingenuous. For the first time they heard Lorrimer spoken of with affection.

'He was always terribly kind to me, although I didn't work in the Biology Department. Of course, he was a very serious man. He had so many responsibilities. The Biology Department is terribly overworked and he used to work late nearly every night, checking results, catching up with the backlog. I think he was disappointed at not being chosen to succeed Dr Mac. Not that he ever said so to me – well he wouldn't, would he? – I'm far too junior and he was far too loyal.'

Dalgliesh asked:

'Do you think anyone could have misunderstood his interest in you, might have been a little jealous?'

'Jealous of Dr Lorrimer because he stopped sometimes at the desk to talk to me about my work and was kind to me? But he was old! That's just silly!'

Suppressing a grin as he bent over his notebook and penned a few staccato outlines, Massingham thought that it probably was.

Dalgliesh asked:

'It seems there was some trouble the day before he died when Dr Kerrison's children called at the Laboratory. Were you in the hall then?'

'You mean when he pushed Miss Kerrison out of the front hall? Well, he didn't actually push her, but he did speak very sharply. She had come with her small brother and they wanted to wait for Dr Kerrison. Dr Lorrimer looked at them, well, really as if he hated them. It wasn't at all like him. I think he's been under some terrible strain. Perhaps he had a premonition of his death. Do you know what he said to me after the clunch pit exhibits came in? He said that the only death we had to fear is our own. Don't you think that was an extraordinary remark?'

'Very strange,' agreed Dalgliesh.

'And that reminds me of another thing. You did say that anything might be important. Well, there was a funny kind of letter arrived for Dr Lorrimer yesterday morning. That's why he stopped at the desk, so that I could hand over any personal post. There was just this thin brown envelope with the address printed, printed by hand in capital letters, I mean. And it was just his name, no qualifications after it. Odd, wasn't it?'

'Did he receive many private letters here?'

'Oh, no, none really. The Lab writing-paper says that all communications have to be addressed to the Director. We deal at the desk with the exhibits received, but all the correspondence goes to the general office for sorting. We only hand over the personal letters, but there aren't many of those.'

In the quick preliminary examination which he and Massingham had made of Lorrimer's meticulously tidy office, Dalgliesh had found no personal correspondence. He asked whether Miss Pridmore knew if Dr Lorrimer had gone home for lunch. She said that he had. So it was possible that he had taken the letter home. It could mean anything, or nothing. It was just one more small fact which would have to be investigated.

He thanked Brenda Pridmore, and reminded her again to come back to him if she remembered anything which could be of importance, however small. Brenda was not used to dissembling. It was obvious that something had occurred to her. She blushed and dropped her eyes. The metamorphosis from happy confidante to guilty schoolgirl was pathetically comic. Dalgliesh said gently:

'Yes?'

She didn't speak, but made herself meet his eyes and shook her head. He waited for a moment, then said:

'The investigation of murder is never agreeable. Like most unpleasant things in life, it sometimes seems easier not to get involved, to keep oneself uncontaminated. But that isn't possible. In a murder investigation, to suppress a truth is sometimes to tell a lie.'

'But suppose one passes on information. Something private, perhaps, which one hasn't any real right to know – and it throws suspicion on the wrong person?'

Dalgliesh said gently:

'You have to trust us. Will you try to do that?'

She nodded, and whispered 'Yes', but she said nothing further. He judged that this was not the time to press her. He let her go, and sent for Angela Foley.

XII

In contrast to Brenda Pridmore's artless confiding, Angela Foley presented a bland inscrutable gaze. She was an unusual-looking girl with a heart-shaped face and a wide, exceedingly high forehead from which hair, baby fine, the colour of ripe grain, was strained back and plaited into a tight coil on top of her head. Her eyes were small, slanted, and so deeply set that Dalgliesh found it hard to guess their colour. Her mouth was small, pursed and uncommunicative above the pointed chin. She wore a dress in fine fawn wool, topped with an elaborately patterned, short-sleeved tabard, and short laced boots, a sophisticated and exotic contrast to Brenda's orthodox prettiness and neat hand-knitted twinset.

If she was distressed by her cousin's violent death, she concealed it admirably. She said that she had worked as Director's secretary for five years, first with Dr MacIntyre and now with Dr Howarth. Before that, she had been a shorthand typist in the general office of the Laboratory, having joined Hoggatt's straight from school. She was twenty-seven. Until two years ago, she lived in a bed-sitting-room in Ely, but now shared Sprogg's Cottage with a woman friend. They had spent the whole of the previous evening in each other's company. Edwin Lorrimer and his father had been her only living relatives, but they had seen very little of each other. The family, she explained as if this were the most natural thing in the world, had never been close.

'So you know very little of his private affairs, his will, for example?'

'No, nothing. When my grandmother left him all her money, and we were at the solicitor's office, he said that he would make me his heir. But I think he just felt guilty at the time that I wasn't named in the will. I don't suppose it meant anything. And, of course, he may have changed his mind.'

'Do you remember how much your grandmother left?'

She paused for a moment. Almost, he thought, as if calculating whether ignorance would sound more suspicious than knowledge. Then she said:

'I think about thirty thousand. I don't know how much it is now.'

He took her briefly but carefully through the events of the early morning. She and her friend ran a Mini, but she usually cycled to work. She had done so that morning, arriving at the Laboratory at her usual time, just before nine o'clock, and had been surprised to see Dr Howarth with Mrs Bidwell driving in before her. Brenda Pridmore had opened the door. Inspector Blakelock was coming downstairs and he had broken the news of the murder. They had all stayed in the hall together while Dr Howarth went up to the Biology Lab. Inspector Blakelock had telephoned for the police and for Dr Kerrison. When Dr Howarth returned to the hall he had asked her to go with Inspector Blakelock and check on the keys. She and the Director were the only two members of staff who knew the combination of his security cupboard. He had stayed in the hall, she thought talking to Brenda Pridmore. The keys had been in their box in the cupboard, and she and Inspector Blakelock had left them there. She had reset the combination lock and returned to the hall. Dr

Howarth had gone into his office to talk to the Home Office, telling the rest of the staff to wait in the hall. Later, after the police and Dr Kerrison had arrived, Dr Howarth had driven her in his car to break the news to old Mr Lorrimer. Then he had left her with the old man to return to the Laboratory, and she had telephoned for her friend. She and Miss Mawson had been there together until Mrs Swaffield, the rector's wife, and a constable arrived, about an hour later.

'What did you do at Postmill Cottage?'

'I made tea and took it in to my uncle. Miss Mawson stayed in the kitchen most of the time doing the washing-up for him. The kitchen was in a bit of a mess, mostly dirty crockery from the previous day.'

'How did your uncle seem?'

'Worried, and rather cross about having been left alone. I don't think he quite realized Edwin was dead.'

There seemed little else to be learned from her. As far as she knew, her cousin had had no enemies. She had no idea who could have killed him. Her voice, high, rather monotonous, the voice of a small girl, suggested that it was not a matter of much concern to her. She expressed no regret, advanced no theories, answered all his questions composedly in her high, unemphatic voice. He might have been a casual and unimportant visitor, gratifying a curiosity about the routine of the working of the Laboratory. He felt an instinctive antipathy towards her. He had no difficulty in concealing it, but it interested him since it was a long time since a murder suspect had provoked in him so immediate and physical a reaction. But he wondered whether it was prejudice that glimpsed in those deep and secretive eyes a flash of disdain, of contempt even, and he would have given a great deal to know what was going on behind that high, rather bumpy forehead.

When she had left, Massingham said:

'It's odd that Dr Howarth sent her and Blakelock to check on the keys. He must have immediately realized their importance. Access to the Lab is fundamental to this case. So why didn't he check on them himself? He knew the combination.'

'Too proud to take a witness, and too intelligent to go without one. And he may have thought it more important to supervise things in the hall. But at least he was careful to protect Angela Foley. He didn't send her alone. Well, let's see what Blakelock has to say about it.'

XIII

Like Dr Howarth, Inspector Blakelock chose not to sit. He stood at attention, facing Dalgliesh across Howarth's desk like a man on a disciplinary charge. Dalgliesh knew better than to try to get him to relax. Blakelock had first learned the technique of replying to questions in his detective constable days in the witness box. He gave the information he was asked for, no more and no less, his eyes fixed on some spot a foot above Dalgliesh's right shoulder. When he gave his name in a firm expressionless voice, Dalgliesh half expected him to reach out his right hand for the Book and take the oath.

In reply to Dalgliesh's questioning he described his movements since leaving his house in Ely to come to the Laboratory. His account of the finding of the body tallied with that of Brenda Pridmore. As soon as he had seen her face as she came down the stairs he had realized that something was wrong and he dashed up to the Biology Lab without waiting for her to speak. The door had been open and the light on. He described the position of the body as precisely as if its rigid contours were imprinted on the mind's retina. He had known at once that Lorrimer was dead. He hadn't touched the body except, instinctively, to slip his hand into the pocket of the white coat and feel that the keys were there.

Dalgliesh asked:

'When you arrived at the Laboratory this morning you waited for Miss Pridmore to catch you up before coming in. Why was that?'

'I saw her coming round the side of the building after having put her bicycle away, and it seemed courteous to wait, sir. And it saved me having to re-open the door to her.'

'And you found the three locks and the internal security system in good order?'

'Yes, sir.'

'Do you make a routine check of the Laboratory as soon as you arrive?'

'No, sir. Of course if I found that any of the locks or the security panel had been tampered with I should check at once. But everything was in order.'

'You said earlier that the telephone call from Mr Lorrimer senior was a surprise to you. Didn't you notice Dr Lorrimer's car when you arrived this morning?'

'No, sir. The senior scientific staff use the end garage.'

'Why did you send Miss Pridmore to see if Dr Lorrimer was here?'

'I didn't, sir. She slipped under the counter before I could stop her.'

'So you sensed that something was wrong?'

'Not really, sir. I didn't expect her to find him. But I think it did briefly occur to me that he might have been taken ill.'

'What sort of a man was Dr Lorrimer, Inspector?'

'He was the senior biologist, sir.'

'I know. I'm asking you what he was like as a man and a colleague.'

'I didn't really know him well, sir. He wasn't one for lingering at the reception desk to chat. But I got on all right with him. He was a good forensic scientist.'

'I've been told that he took an interest in Brenda Pridmore. Didn't that mean that he occasionally lingered at the desk?'

'Nor for more than a few minutes, sir. He liked to have a word with the girl from time to time. Everyone does. It's nice to have a young thing about the Lab. She's pretty and hard-working and enthusiastic, and I think Dr Lorrimer wanted to encourage her.'

'No more than that, Inspector?'

Blakelock said solidly:

'No, sir.'

Dalgliesh then asked him about his movements on the previous evening. He said that he and his wife had bought tickets for the village concert, although his wife was reluctant to go because of a bad headache. She suffered from sinus headaches which were occasionally disabling. But they had attended for the first half of the programme and, because her headache was worse, had left at the interval. He had driven back to Ely, arriving home about a quarter to nine. He and his wife lived in a modern bungalow on the outskirts of the city with no near neighbours and he thought it unlikely that anyone would have noticed their return. Dalgliesh said:

'There seems to have been a general reluctance on the part of everyone to stay for the second part of the programme. Why did you bother to go when you knew your wife was unwell?'

'Dr MacIntyre – he's the former Director, sir – liked the Laboratory staff to take part in village activities, and Chief Inspector Martin feels the same. So I'd got the tickets and my wife thought we might as well use them. She hoped that the concert might help her to forget her headache. But the first half was rather rowdy and, in fact, it got worse.'

'Did you go home and fetch her, or did she meet you here?'

'She came out earlier in the afternoon by the bus, sir, and spent the afternoon with Mrs Dean, wife of the Minister at the Chapel. She's an old friend. I went round to collect my wife when I left work at six o'clock. We had a fish and chip supper there before the concert.'

'That's your normal time for leaving?'

'Yes, sir.'

'And who locks up the Laboratory if the scientists are working after your time for leaving?'

'I always check who's left, sir. If there are junior staff working then I have to stay until they're finished. But that isn't usual. Dr Howarth has a set of keys and would check the alarm system and lock up if he worked late.'

'Did Dr Lorrimer normally work after you had left?'

'About three or four evenings a week, sir. But I had no anxiety about Dr Lorrimer locking up. He was very conscientious.'

'Would he let anyone into the Laboratory if he were alone?'

'No, sir, not unless they were members of the staff, or of the police force, maybe. But it would have to be an officer he knew. He wouldn't let anyone in who hadn't got proper business here. Dr Lorrimer was very particular about unauthorized people coming into the Laboratory.'

'Was that why he tried forcibly to remove Miss Kerrison the day before yesterday?'

Inspector Blakelock did not lose his composure. He said:

'I wouldn't describe it as a forcible removal, sir. He didn't lay hands on the girl.'

'Would you describe to me exactly what did happen, Inspector?'

'Miss Kerrison and her small brother came to meet their father. Dr Kerrison was lecturing that morning to the Inspector's training course. I suggested to Miss Kerrison that she sit down on the chair and wait, but Dr Lorrimer came down the stairs at that moment to see if the mallet had arrived for examination. He saw the children and asked rather peremptorily what they were doing there. He said that a forensic science lab wasn't a place for children. Miss Kerrison said that she didn't intend to leave, so he walked towards her as if he intended to put her out. He looked very white, very strange, I thought. He didn't lay a hand on her but I think she was frightened that he was going to. I believe she's very highly strung, sir. She started screeching and screaming "I hate you. I hate you." Dr Lorrimer turned and went back up the stairs and Brenda tried to comfort the girl.'

'And Miss Kerrison and her small brother left without waiting for their father?'

'Yes, sir. Dr Kerrison came down about fifteen minutes later and I told him that the children had come for him but had left.'

'You said nothing about the incident?'

'No, sir.'

'Was this typical of Dr Lorrimer's behaviour?'

'No, sir. But he hadn't been looking well in recent weeks. I think he's been under some strain.'

'And you've no idea what kind of strain?'

'No, sir.'

'Had he enemies?'

'Not to my knowledge, sir.'

'So you've no idea who might have wanted him dead?'

'No, sir.'

'After the discovery of Dr Lorrimer's body, Dr Howarth sent you with Miss Foley to check that his bunch of keys were in the security cupboard. Will you describe exactly what you and she did?'

'Miss Foley opened the cupboard. She and the Director are the only two people who know the combination.'

'And you watched?'

'Yes, sir, but I can't remember the figures. I watched her twisting and setting the dial.'

'And then?'

'She took out the metal cash box and opened it. It wasn't locked. The keys were inside.'

'You were watching her closely all the time, Inspector? Are you absolutely sure that Miss Foley couldn't have replaced the keys in the box without your seeing?'

'No, sir. That would have been quite impossible.'

'One last thing, Inspector. When you went up to the body Miss Pridmore was here alone. She told me that she's virtually certain that no one could have slipped out of the Laboratory during that time. Have you considered that possibility?'

'That he might have been here all night, sir? Yes. But he wasn't hiding in the Chief Liaison Officer's room because I would have seen him when I went to turn off the internal alarm. That's the room closest to the front door. I suppose he could have been in the Director's Office, but I don't see how he could have crossed the hall and opened the door without Miss Pridmore noticing even if she were in a state of shock. It isn't as if the door were ajar. He'd have had to turn the Yale lock.'

'And you are absolutely certain that your own set of keys never left your possession last night?'

'I'm certain, sir.'

'Thank you, Inspector. That's all for the present. Would you please ask Mr Middlemass to come in?'

XIV

The Document Examiner strolled into the office with easy assurance, arranged his long body without invitation in Howarth's armchair, crossed his right ankle over his left knee and raised an interrogatory eyebrow at Dalgliesh like a visitor expecting nothing from his host but boredom, but politely determined not to show it. He was wearing dark-brown corduroy slacks, a fawn turtle-necked sweater in fine wool and bright purple socks with leather slip-on shoes. The effect was of a *dégagé* informality, but Dalgliesh noticed that the slacks were tailored, the sweater cashmere, and the shoes hand-made. He glanced down at Middlemass's statement of his movements since seven o'clock the previous evening. Unlike the efforts of his colleagues, it was written with a pen, not a Biro, in a fine, high, italic script, which succeeded in being both decorative and virtually illegible. It was not the kind of hand he had expected. He said:

'Before we get down to this, could you tell me about your quarrel with Lorrimer?'

'My version of it, you mean, as opposed to Mrs Bidwell's?'

'The truth, as opposed to speculation.'

'It wasn't a particular edifying episode, and I can't say I'm proud of it. But it wasn't important. I'd just started on the clunch pit murder case when I heard Lorrimer coming out of the washroom. I had a private matter I wanted a word about so I called him in. We talked, quarrelled, he struck out at me and I reacted with a punch to his nose. It bled spectacularly over my overall. I apologized. He left.'

'What was the quarrel about? A woman?'

'Well, hardly, Commander, not with Lorrimer. I think Lorrimer knew that there were two sexes but I doubt whether he approved of the arrangement. It was a small private matter, something which happened a couple of years ago. Nothing to do with this Lab.'

'So we have the picture of your settling down to work on an exhibit from a murder case, an important exhibit since you chose to examine it yourself. You are not, however, so absorbed in this task that you can't listen to footsteps passing the door and identify those of Lorrimer. It seems to you a convenient moment to call him in and discuss something which happened two years ago, something which you've apparently been content to forget in the interim, but which now so incenses you both that you end by trying to knock each other down.'

'Put like that, it sounds eccentric.'

'Put like that, it sounds absurd.'

'I suppose it was absurd in a way. It was about a cousin of my wife's, Peter Ennals. He left school with two 'A' levels in science and seemed keen on coming into the Service. He came to me for advice and I told him how to go about it. He ended up as an S.O. under Lorrimer in the Southern Lab. It wasn't a success. I don't suppose it was entirely Lorrimer's fault, but he hasn't got the gift of managing young staff. Ennals ended up with a failed career, a broken engagement and what is euphemistically described as a nervous breakdown. He drowned himself. We heard rumours about what had happened at the Southern. It's a small service and these things get around. I didn't really know the boy; my wife was fond of him.

'I'm not blaming Lorrimer for Peter's death. A suicide is always ultimately responsible for his own destruction. But my wife believes that Lorrimer could have done more to help him. I telephoned her after lunch yesterday to explain that I'd be late home and our conversation reminded me that I'd always meant to speak to Lorrimer about Peter. By coincidence I heard his footsteps. So I called him in with the result that Mrs Bidwell has no doubt graphically described. Mrs Bidwell, I don't doubt, detects a woman at the bottom of any male quarrel. And if she did talk about a woman or a telephone call, then the woman was my wife and the telephone call was the one I've told you about.'

It sounded plausible, thought Dalgliesh. It might even be the truth. The Peter Ennals story would have to be checked. It was just another chore when they were already hard-pressed and the truth of it was hardly in doubt. But Middlemass had spoken in the present tense: 'Lorrimer hasn't the gift of managing junior staff.' Were there, perhaps, junior staff closer to home who had suffered at his hands? But he decided to leave it for now. Paul Middlemass was an intelligent man. Before he made a more formal statement he would have time to ponder about the effect on his career of putting his signature to a lie. Dalgliesh said:

'According to this statement you were playing the part of a hobby-horse for the morris-dancers at yesterday evening's village concert. Despite this, you say you can't give the name of anyone who could vouch for you. Presumably both the dancers and the audience could see the hobby-horse galumphing around, but not you inside it. But wasn't anyone there when you arrived at the hall, or when you left?'

'No one who saw me to recognize me. It's a nuisance but it

can't be helped. It happened rather oddly. I'm not a morris-dancer. I don't normally go in for these rustic rites and village concerts aren't my idea of entertainment. It was the Senior Liaison Officer's show, Chief Inspector Martin, but he had the chance of this U.S.A. visit unexpectedly and asked me to deputize. We're about the same size and I suppose he thought that the outfit would fit me. He needed someone fairly broad in the shoulders and strong enough to take the weight of the head: I owed him a favour – he had a tactful word with one of his mates on highway patrol when I was caught speeding a month ago – so I couldn't very well not oblige.

'I went to a rehearsal last week and all it amounted to was, as you say, galumphing round the dancers after they'd done their stuff, snapping my jaws at the audience, frisking my tail and generally making a fool of myself. That hardly seemed to matter since no one could recognize me. I'd no intention of spending the whole evening at the concert, so I asked Bob Gotobed, he's the leader of the troupe, to give me a ring from the hall about fifteen minutes before we were due to go on. We were scheduled to appear after the interval and they reckoned that that would be about eight-thirty. The concert, as you've probably been told, started at seven-thirty.'

'And you stayed working in your Lab until the call came?'

'That's right. My S.O. went out and got me a couple of beef and chutney sandwiches and I ate them at my desk. Bob phoned at eight-fifteen to say that they were running a bit ahead of time and that I'd better come over. The lads were dressed and were proposing to have a beer in the Moonraker. The hall hasn't a licence, so all the audience get in the interval is coffee or tea served by the Mothers' Union. I left the Lab at, I suppose, about eight-twenty.'

'You say here that Lorrimer was alive then as far as you know?'

'We know that he was alive twenty-five minutes later, if his dad is right about the telephone call. But actually I think I saw him. I went out of the front door because that's the only exit but I had to go round the back to the garages to get my car. The light was on then in the Biology Department and I saw a figure in a white coat move briefly across the window. I can't swear that it was Lorrimer. I can only say that it never occurred to me at the time that it wasn't. And I knew, of course, that he must be in the building. He was responsible for locking up and he was excessively tedious about security. He wouldn't have left without checking on all the departments, including Document Examination.'

'How was the front door locked?'

'Only with the Yale and a single bolt. That's what I expected. I let myself out.'

'What happened when you got to the hall?'

'To explain that I'll have to describe the architectural oddities of the place. It was put up cheaply five years ago by the village builder and the committee thought they'd save money by not employing an architect. They merely told the chap that they wanted a rectangular hall with a stage and two dressing-rooms and lavatories at one end, and a reception hall, cloakroom and a room for refreshments at the other. It was built by Harry Gotobed and his sons. Harry is a pillar of the Chapel and a model of Nonconformist rectitude. He doesn't hold with the theatre, amateur or otherwise, and I think they had some difficulty in persuading him even to build a stage. But he certainly didn't intend to have any communicating door between the male and female dressing-rooms. As a result what we've got is a stage with two rooms behind, each with its separate lavatory. There's an exit at each side into the graveyard, and two doors on to the stage, but there's literally no common space behind the stage. As a result the men dress in the right-hand dressing-room and come on to the stage from the prompt side, and the women from the left. Anyone who wants to enter from the opposite side has to leave the dressing-room, scurry in their costume and probably in the rain through the graveyard and, if they don't trip over a gravestone, break their ankle, or fall into an open grave, finally make a triumphant, if damp, appearance on the proper side.'

Suddenly he threw back his head and gave a shout of laughter, then recovered himself and said:

'Sorry, poor taste. It's just that I was remembering last year's performance by the dramatic society. They'd chosen one of those dated domestic comedies where the characters spend most of their time in evening dress making snappy small talk. Young Bridie Corrigan from the general store played the maid. Scurrying through the churchyard she thought she saw old Maggie Gotobed's ghost. She made her entrance screaming, cap awry, but remembered her part sufficiently to gasp: "Holy Mother of God, dinner is served!" Whereat the cast trooped dutifully off stage, the men to one side and the women to the other. Our hall adds considerably to the interest of the performances I can tell you.'

'So you went to the right-hand dressing-room?'

'That's right. It was a complete shambles. The cast have to hang up their outdoor coats as well as keeping the costumes there. There's a row of coat-hooks and a bench down the middle of the room, one rather small mirror and space for two people only to make up simultaneously. The single hand-basin is in the lavatory. Well, no doubt you'll be looking at the place for yourself. Last night it was chaotic with outdoor coats, costumes, boxes and props piled on the bench and overflowing on to the floor. The hobby-horse costume was hanging on one of the pegs, so I put it on.'

'There was no one there when you arrived?'

'No one in the room, but I could hear someone in the lavatory. I knew that most of the troupe were over at the Moonraker. When I had got myself into the costume the lavatory door opened and Harry Sprogg, he's a member of the troupe, came out. He was wearing his costume.'

Massingham made a note of the name: Harry Sprogg. Dalgliesh asked:

'Did you speak?'

'I didn't. He said something about being glad I'd made it and that the chaps were over at the Moonraker. He said he was just going to dig them out. He's the only teetotaller of the party so I suppose that's why he didn't go over with them. He left and I followed him out into the cemetery.'

'Without having spoken to him?'

'I can't remember that I said anything. We were only together for about a couple of seconds. I followed him out because the dressing-room was stuffy – actually it stank – and the costume was extraordinarily heavy and hot. I thought I'd wait outside where I could join the boys when they came across from the pub. And that's what I did.'

'Did you see anyone else?'

'No, but that doesn't mean there was no one there. Vision's a bit restricted through the headpiece. If someone had been standing motionless in the graveyard I could easily have missed him. I wasn't expecting to see anyone.'

'How long were you there?'

'Less than five minutes. I galumphed around a bit and tried a few trial snaps of the jaw and whisks of the tail. It must have looked daft if anyone was watching. There's a particularly repulsive memorial there, a marble angel with an expression of nauseating piety and a hand pointed upwards. I pranced around that once or twice and snapped my jaws at its asinine face. God knows why! Perhaps it was the joint effect of moonlight and the place itself. Then I saw the chaps coming across the graveyard from the Moonraker and joined up with them.'

'Did you say anything then?'

'I may have said good evening or hello, but I don't think so. They wouldn't have recognized my voice through the headpiece anyway. I raised the front right-hand hoof and made a mock obeisance and then tagged on behind. We went into the dressing-room together. We could hear the audience settling into their seats, and then the stage manager put his head in and said "Right, boys." Then the six dancers went on, and I could hear the violin strike up, the stamping of feet and the jangling of bells. Then the music changed and that was the signal for me to join them and do my bit. Part of the act was to go down the steps from the stage and frolic among the audience. It seemed to go down well enough to judge by the girlish shrieks, but if you're thinking of asking whether anyone recognized me, I shouldn't bother. I don't see how they could have.'

'But after the performance?'

'No one saw me after the performance. We came tumbling down the steps from the stage into the dressing-room, but the applause went on. Then I realized with considerable horror that some fools in the audience were calling out "encore". The lads in green needed no second invitation and they were up the stairs again like a troop of parched navvies who'd just been told that the bar's open. I took the view that my agreement with Bill Martin covered one performance, not including an encore, and that I'd made enough of a fool of myself for one evening. So when the fiddle struck up and the stamping began I got out of the costume, hung it back on the nail, and made off. As far as I know no one saw me leave and there was no one in the car-park when I unlocked my car. I was at home before ten and my wife can vouch for that if you're interested. But I don't suppose you are.'

'It would be more helpful if you could find someone to vouch for you between eight forty-five and midnight.'

'I know. Maddening, isn't it? If I'd known someone was proposing to murder Lorrimer during the evening I'd have taken good care not to put the headpiece on until the second before we went on stage. It's a pity the beast's head is so large. It's supported, as you'll discover, from the wearer's shoulders and doesn't actually touch the head or face. If it did you might find a hair or some biological evidence that I'd actually worn the thing. And prints are no good. I handled it at the rehearsals and so did a dozen other people. The whole incident is an example to me of the folly of indulging in good nature. If I'd only told old Bill just what he could do with his blasted hobby-horse I should have been home, and, quite literally, dry before eight o'clock with a nice cosy alibi at the Panton Arms for the rest of the evening.'

Dalgliesh ended the interview by asking about the missing white coat.

'It's a fairly distinctive design. I've got half a dozen of them, all inherited from my father. The other five are in the linen-cupboard here, if you want to have a look at them. They're waisted, in very heavy white linen, buttoning high to the neck with crested Royal Army Dental Corps buttons. Oh, and they've got no pockets. The old man thought pockets were unhygienic.'

Massingham thought that a coat already stained with Lorrimer's blood might be seen by a murderer as a particularly useful protective garment. Echoing his thought, Middlemass said:

'If it is found again I don't think I could say with certainty exactly what bloodstains resulted from our punch-up. There was one patch about four inches by two on the right shoulder, but there may have been other splashes. But presumably the serologists would be able to give you some idea of the comparative age of the stains.'

If the coat were ever found, thought Dalgliesh. It wouldn't be an easy thing to destroy completely. But the murderer, if he had taken it, would have had all night to dispose of the evidence. He asked:

'And you dropped this particular coat in the soiled-linen-basket in the men's washroom immediately after the quarrel?'

'I meant to, but then I thought better of it. The stain wasn't large and the sleeves were perfectly clean. I put it on again and dropped it in the soiled-linen-basket when I washed before leaving the Lab.'

'Do you remember what wash-basin you used?'

'The first one, nearest the door.'

'Was the basin clean?'

If Middlemass were surprised by the question, he concealed it.

'As clean as it ever is after a day's use. I wash fairly vigorously so it was clean enough when I left. And so was I.'

The picture came into Massingham's mind with startling clarity; Middlemass in his blood-spattered coat bending low over the wash-basin, both taps running full on, the water swirling and gurgling down the waste-pipe, water stained pink with Lorrimer's blood. But what about the timing? If old Lorrimer really had spoken to his son at eight forty-five then Middlemass must be in the clear, at least for the first part of the evening. And then he pictured another scene: Lorrimer's sprawled body, the raucous ring of the telephone. Middlemass's gloved hand slowly lifting the receiver. But could old Lorrimer really mistake another voice for that of his son?

When the Document Examiner had left Massingham said:

'At least he has one person to corroborate his story. Dr Howarth saw the hobby-horse prancing round the angel memorial in the churchyard. They've hardly had opportunity this morning to concoct that story together. And I don't see how else Howarth could have known about it.'

Dalgliesh said:

'Unless they concocted the story in the graveyard last night. Or unless it was Howarth, not Middlemass who was inside that hobby-horse.'

XV

'I didn't like him, and I was frightened of him, but I didn't kill him. I know everyone will think that I did, but it's not true. I couldn't kill anyone or anything; not an animal, let alone a man.'

Clifford Bradley had stood up fairly well to the long wait for questioning. He wasn't incoherent. He had tried to behave with dignity. But he had brought into the room with him the sour contagion of fear, that most difficult of all emotions to hide. His whole body twitched with it; the restless hands clasping and unclasping in his lap, the shuddering mouth, the anxious blinking eyes. He was not an impressive figure, and fear had made him pitiable. He would make an ineffective murderer, thought Massingham. Watching him, he felt some of the instinctive shame of the healthy in the presence of the diseased. It was easy to imagine him retching over that wash-basin, vomiting up his guilt and terror. It was less easy to envisage him tearing out the page of the notebook, destroying the white coat, organizing that early morning telephone call to Mrs Bidwell. Dalgliesh said mildly:

'No one is accusing you. You're familiar enough with Judge's Rules to know that we wouldn't be talking like this if I were about to caution you. You say that you didn't kill him. Have you any idea who did?'

'No. Why should I have? I don't know anything about him. All I know is that I was at home with my wife last night. My mother-in-law came to supper and I saw her off on the seven forty-five bus to Ely. Then I went straight home, and I was home all the evening. My mother-in-law telephoned about nine o'clock to say that she'd reached home safely. She didn't speak to me because I was having a bath. My wife told her that. But Sue can confirm that, except for taking her mother to the bus, I was home all the evening.'

Bradley admitted that he hadn't known that old Mr Lorrimer's hospital admission had been postponed. He thought he had been in the washroom when the old man's call came through. But he knew nothing of the early telephone call to Mrs Bidwell, the missing page from Lorrimer's notebook, or Paul Middlemass's missing white coat. Asked about his supper on Wednesday night, he said that they had eaten curry made with tinned beef, together with rice and tinned peas. Afterwards there had been a trifle which, he explained defensively, had been made with stale cake and custard. Massingham suppressed a shudder as he made a careful note of these details. He was glad when Dalgliesh said that Bradley could go. There seemed nothing else of importance to be learned from him in his present state; nothing more to be learned, indeed, from anyone at the Laboratory. He was fretting to see Lorrimer's house, Lorrimer's next of kin.

But before they left, Sergeant Reynolds had something to report. He was finding it difficult to keep the excitement from his voice.

'We've found some tyre-marks, sir, about half-way up the drive among the bushes. They look pretty fresh to me. We've got them protected until the photographer arrives and then we'll get a plaster cast made. It's difficult to be sure until we compare them with a tyre index, but it looks to me as if the two back tyres were a Dunlop and a Semperit. That's a pretty odd combination. It should help us to get the car.'

It was a pity, thought Dalgliesh, that Superintendent Mercer had told the photographers they could go. But it wasn't surprising. Given the present pressure of work on the Force, it was difficult to justify keeping men hanging about indefinitely. And at least the fingerprint officers were still here. He said:

'Have you been able to get in touch with Mr Bidwell yet?'

'Captain Massey says he's up on the five-acre raising sugar beet. He'll tell him you want to see him when he comes in for his dockey.'

'His what?'

'His dockey, sir. That's the meal break which we have in these parts at about half past ten or eleven.'

'I'm relieved that Captain Massey has a proper sense of priority between agriculture and murder.'

'They're a good bit behind with the five-acre, sir, but Captain

Massey will see that he calls in at Guy's Marsh station as soon as they've finished work this afternoon.'

'If he doesn't, you'd better dig him out, even if you have to borrow Captain Massey's tractor to do it. That telephone call is important. I'll have a word with the senior scientists in the library now and explain to them that I want them present in the departments when you do the internal search. The rest of them can go home. I'll tell them that we hope to have finished searching by the end of the day. It should be possible for the Lab to open again tomorrow morning. Inspector Massingham and I will be seeing Dr Lorrimer's father at Postmill Cottage. If anything breaks, you can contact us there or through the car radio control from Guy's Marsh.'

Less than ten minutes later, with Massingham at the wheel of the police Rover, they were on their way.

BOOK THREE

An Experimental Man

I

Postmill Cottage lay two miles to the west of the village at the junction of Stoney Piggott's Road and Tenpenny Lane, where the road curved gently upwards, but so imperceptibly that it was difficult for Dalgliesh to believe that he was on slightly higher ground until the car was parked on the grass verge and, turning to close the door, he saw the village strung out along the road below him. Under the turbulent painter's sky, with its changing clusters of white, grey and purple cumulus clouds massing against the pale azure blue of the upper air, and the sunlight moving fitfully across the fields and glittering on roofs and windows, it looked like an isolated frontier outpost, but welcoming, prosperous and secure. Violent death might lurk eastwards in the dark fenlands, but surely not under these neat domestic roofs. Hoggatt's Laboratory was hidden by its belt of trees, but the new building was immediately identifiable, its concrete stumps, ditches and half-built walls looking like the orderly excavation of some long-buried city.

The cottage, a low building of brick with a white wood-cladded front and with the rounded top and sails of the windmill visible behind, was separated from the road by a wide ditch. A wooden plank bridge and white-painted gate led to the front path and the latched door. The first impression of melancholy neglect, induced perhaps by the cottage's isolation and the bareness of outer walls and windows, proved on second glance illusory. The front garden had the dishevelled, overgrown look of autumn, but the roses in the two circular beds, one each side of the path, had been properly tended. The gravel path was clear of weeds, the paintwork on door and windows was shining. Twenty feet farther on two wide and sturdy planks bridged the ditch and led to a flagstoned yard and a brick garage.

There was an old and grubby red Mini already parked next to

a police car. Dalgliesh deduced from the bundle of parish magazines, a smaller one of what looked like concert programmes and the bunch of shaggy chrysanthemums and autumn foliage on the back seat, that the rector, or more probably his wife, was already at the cottage, probably on her way to help with the church decorations, although Thursday was an unusual day, surely, for this ecclesiastical chore. He had scarcely turned from this scrutiny of the rectory car when the door of the cottage opened and a woman bustled down the path towards them. No one who had been born and bred in a rectory could be in any doubt that here was Mrs Swaffield. She looked indeed like a prototype of a country rector's wife, large-bosomed, cheerful and energetic, exuding the slightly intimidating assurance of a woman adept at recognizing authority and competence at a glance, and making immediate use of them. She was wearing a tweed skirt covered with a flowered cotton apron, a hand-knitted twinset, thick brogues and open-work woollen stockings. A felt hat, shaped like a pork pie, its crown stabbed with a steel hatpin, was jammed uncompromisingly over a broad forehead.

'Good morning. Good morning. You're Commander Dalgliesh and Inspector Massingham. Winifred Swaffield. Come in, won't you. The old gentleman is upstairs changing. He insisted on putting on his suit when he heard you were on the way, although I assured him that it wasn't necessary. He'll be down in a minute. In the front parlour would be best I think, don't you? This is Constable Davis, but of course you know all about him. He tells me that he's been sent here to see that no one goes in to Dr Lorrimer's room and to stop any visitors from bothering the old gentleman. Well, we haven't had any so far except one reporter and I soon got rid of him, so that's all right. But the constable has really been very helpful to me in the kitchen. I've just been getting some lunch for Mr Lorrimer. It'll only be soup and an omelette, I'm afraid, but there doesn't seem to be much in the larder except tins and he might be glad of those in the future. One doesn't like to come laden from the rectory like a Victorian do-gooder.

'Simon and I wanted him to come back to the rectory at once but he doesn't seem anxious to leave, and really one mustn't badger people, especially the old. And perhaps it's just as well.

Simon's down with this two-day 'flu – that's why he can't be here – and we don't want the old gentleman to catch it. But we can't let him stay here alone tonight. I thought that he might like to have his niece here, Angela Foley, but he says no. So I'm hoping that Millie Gotobed from the Moonraker will be able to sleep here tonight, and we'll have to think again tomorrow. But I mustn't take up your time with my worries.'

At the end of this speech, Dalgliesh and Massingham found themselves ushered into the front living-room. At the sound of their footsteps in the narrow hall Constable Davis had emerged from what was presumably the kitchen, had sprung to attention, saluted, blushed and given Dalgliesh a glance of mingled appeal and slight desperation before disappearing again. The smell of home-made soup had wafted appetizingly through the door.

The sitting-room, which was stuffy and smelt strongly of tobacco, was adequately furnished, yet gave an impression of cheerless discomfort, a cluttered repository of the mementoes of ageing and its sad solaces. The chimney breast had been boarded up and an old-fashioned gas fire hissed out an uncomfortably fierce heat over a sofa in cut moquette with two greasy circles marking where innumerable heads had once rested. There was a square oak table with bulbous carved legs and four matching chairs with vinyl seats, and a large dresser set against the wall opposite the window, hung with the cracked remnants of long-smashed teasets. On the dresser were two bottles of Guinness and an unwashed glass. To the right of the fire was a high winged armchair and beside it a wicker table with a ramshackle lamp, a tobacco pouch, an ashtray bearing a picture of Brighton pier, and an open draught-board with the pieces set out, crusted with dried food and accumulated grime. The alcove to the left of the fire was filled with a large television set. Above it were a couple of shelves holding a collection of popular novels in identical sizes and bindings, issued by a book club to which Mr Lorrimer had once apparently briefly belonged. They looked as if they had been gummed together unopened and unread.

Dalgliesh and Massingham sat on the sofa. Mrs Swaffield perched upright on the edge of the armchair and smiled across at them encouragingly, bringing into the room's cheerlessness a reassuring ambience of home-made jam, well-conducted Sunday schools and massed women's choirs singing Blake's 'Jerusalem'. Both men felt immediately at home with her. Both in their different lives had met her kind before. It was not, thought Dalgliesh, that she was unaware of the frayed and ragged edges of life. She would merely iron them out with a firm hand and neatly hem them down.

Dalgliesh asked:

'How is he, Mrs Swaffield?'

'Surprisingly well. He keeps talking about his son in the present tense, which is a little disconcerting, but I think he realizes all right that Edwin is dead. I don't mean to imply that the old gentleman is senile. Not in the least. But it's difficult to know what the very old are feeling sometimes. It must have been a terrible shock, naturally. Appalling, isn't it? I suppose a criminal from one of those London gangs broke in to get his hands on an exhibit. They're saying in the village that there were no signs of a break-in, but a really determined burglar can get in anywhere, I've always been told. I know Father Gregory has had terrible trouble with break-ins at St Mary's at Guy's Marsh. The poor-box has been rifled twice and two pews of kneelers stolen, the ones the Mothers' Union had specially embroidered to celebrate their fiftieth anniversary. Goodness knows why anyone should want to take those. Luckily we've had no trouble of that kind here. Simon would hate to have to lock the church. Chevisham has always been a most law-abiding village, which is why this murder is so shocking.'

Dalgliesh wasn't surprised that the village already knew that there had been no break-in at the Lab. Presumably one of the staff, on the excuse of needing to telephone home and say that he wouldn't be back for luncheon and avid to break the exciting news, had been less than discreet. But it would be pointless to try to trace the culprit. In his experience news percolated through a village community by a process of verbal osmosis, and it would be a bold man who tried to control or stem that mysterious diffusion. Mrs Swaffield, like any proper rector's wife, had undoubtedly been one of the first to know. Dalgliesh said:

'It's a pity that Miss Foley and her uncle don't seem to get on.

If he could go to stay temporarily with her that would at least solve your immediate problem. She and her friend were here when you arrived this morning, I take it?'

'Yes, both of them. Dr Howarth came himself with Angela to break the news, which I think was thoughtful of him, then left her here when he went back to the Lab. He wouldn't want to be away for more than a short time, naturally. I think Angela phoned her friend and she came at once. Then the constable arrived and I was here shortly afterwards. There was no point in Angela and Miss Mawson staying on once I'd come, and Dr Howarth was anxious for most of the staff to be actually in the Lab when you arrived.'

'And there are no other relatives and no close friends, as far as you know?'

'None, I think. They kept themselves very much to themselves. Old Mr Lorrimer doesn't come to church or take part in village affairs, so that Simon and I never really got to know him. I know that people expect the clergy to come round knocking at doors and rooting people out, but Simon doesn't really believe it does much good, and I must say I think he's right. Dr Lorrimer, of course, went to St Mary's at Guy's Marsh. Father Gregory might be able to tell you something about him although I don't think he took a very active part in church life. He used to pick up Miss Willard from the Old Rectory and drive her over. She might be worth having a word with, although it seems unlikely that they were close. I imagine that he drove her to church because Father Gregory suggested it rather than from inclination. She's an odd woman, not really suitable to look after children, I should have thought. But here comes the one you really want to talk to.'

Death, thought Dalgliesh, obliterates family resemblance as it does personality; there is no affinity between the living and the dead. The man who came into the room, shuffling a little but still upright, had once been as tall as his son; the sparse hair brushed back from a high forehead still showed streaks of the black it had once been; the watery eyes, sunken under the creased lids, were as dark. But there was no kinship with that rigid body on the laboratory floor. Death, in separating them for ever, had robbed them even of their likeness.

Mrs Swaffield made the introductions in a voice of determined encouragement as if they had all suddenly gone deaf. Then she melted tactfully away, murmuring something about soup in the kitchen. Massingham sprang to help the old man to a chair, but Mr Lorrimer, with a stiff chopping motion of the hand, gestured him aside. Eventually, after some hesitation, as if the sitting-room were unfamiliar to him, he lowered himself into what was obviously his usual place, the shabby, high-backed armchair to the right of the fire, from which he regarded Dalgliesh steadily.

Sitting there, bolt upright, in his old-fashioned and badly cut dark blue suit, which smelt strongly of mothballs and now hung loosely on his diminished bones, he looked pathetic, almost grotesque, but not without dignity. Dalgliesh wondered why he had troubled to change. Was it a gesture of respect for his son, the need to formalize grief, a restless urge to find something to do? Or was it some atavistic belief that authority was on its way and should be propitiated by an outward show of deference? Dalgliesh was reminded of the funeral of a young detective constable killed on duty. What he had found almost unbearably pathetic had not been the sonorous beauty of the burial service, or even the young children walking hand in hand with careful solemnity behind their father's coffin. It had been the reception afterwards in the small police house, the carefully planned home-cooked food and the drink, ill-afforded, which the widow had prepared for the refreshment of her husband's colleagues and friends. Perhaps it had comforted her at the time, or solaced her in memory. Perhaps old Mr Lorrimer, too, felt happier because he had taken trouble.

Settling himself some distance from Dalgliesh on the extraordinarily lumpy sofa, Massingham opened his notebook. Thank God the old man was calm anyway. You could never tell how the relatives were going to take it. Dalgliesh, as he knew, had the reputation of being good with the bereaved. His condolences might be short, almost formal, but at least they sounded sincere. He took it for granted that the family would wish to co-operate with the police, but as a matter of justice, not of retribution. He didn't connive at the extraordinary psychological interdependence by which the detective and the bereaved were often supported, and which it was so fatally easy to exploit. He made no specious promises, never bullied the weak or indulged the sentimental. And yet they seem to like him, thought Massingham. God knows why. At times he's cold enough to be barely human.

He watched Dalgliesh stand up as old Mr Lorrimer came into the room; but he made no move to help the old man to his chair. Massingham had glanced briefly at his chief's face and seen the familiar look of speculative detached interest. What, if anything, he wondered, would move Dalgliesh to spontaneous pity? He remembered the other case they had worked on together a year previously, when he had been a detective sergeant; the death of a child. Dalgliesh had regarded the parents with just such a look of calm appraisal. But he had worked eighteen hours a day for a month until the case was solved. And his next book of poems had contained that extraordinary one about a murdered child which no one at the Yard, even those who professed to understand it, had had the temerity even to mention to its author. He said now:

'As Mrs Swaffield explained, my name is Dalgliesh and this is Inspector Massingham. I expect Dr Howarth told you that we would be coming. I'm very sorry about your son. Do you feel able to answer some questions?'

Mr Lorrimer nodded towards the kitchen.

'What's she doing in there?'

His voice was surprising; high timbred and with a trace of the querulousness of age, but extraordinarily strong for an old man.

'Mrs Swaffield? Making soup, I think.'

'I suppose she's used the onions and carrots we had in the vegetable rack. I thought I could smell carrots. Edwin knows I don't like carrots in soup.'

'Did he usually cook for you?'

'He does all the cooking if he isn't away at a scene of crime. I don't eat much dinner at midday, but he leaves me something to heat up, a stew from the night before or a bit of fish in sauce, maybe. He didn't leave anything this morning because he wasn't at home last night. I had to get my own breakfast. I fancied bacon, but I thought I'd better leave that in case he wants it for tonight. He usually cooks bacon and eggs if he's late home.'

Dalgliesh asked:

'Mr Lorrimer, have you any idea why anyone should want to murder your son? Had he any enemies?'

'Why should he have enemies? He didn't know anyone except at the Lab. Everyone had a great respect for him at the Lab. He told me so himself. Why would anyone want to harm him? Edwin lived for his work.'

He brought out the last sentence as if it were an original expression of which he was rather proud.

'You telephoned him last night at the Laboratory, didn't you? What time was that?'

'It was a quarter to nine. The telly went blank. It didn't blink and go zig-zag like it sometimes does. Edwin showed me how to adjust the knob at the back for that. It went blank with just one little circle of light and then that failed. I couldn't see the nine o'clock news, so I rang Edwin and asked him to send for the TV man. We rent the set, and they're supposed to come at any hour, but there's always some excuse. Last month when I telephoned they didn't come for two days.'

'Can you remember what your son said?'

'He said that it wasn't any use telephoning late at night. He'd do it first thing this morning before he went to work. But, of course, he hasn't. He didn't come home. It's still broken. I don't like to telephone myself. Edwin always sees to everything like that. Do you think Mrs Swaffield would ring?'

'I'm sure that she would. When you telephoned him did he say anything about expecting a visitor?'

'No. He seemed in a hurry, as if he didn't like it because I phoned. But he always said to ring the Lab up if I was in trouble.'

'And he said nothing else at all except that he'd ring the TV mechanic this morning?'

'What else would he say? He wasn't one for chatting over the telephone.'

'Did you ring him at the Laboratory yesterday about your hospital appointment?'

'That's right. I was supposed to go in to Addenbrooke's yesterday afternoon. Edwin was going to drive me in. It's my leg, you see. It's psoriasis. They're going to try a new treatment.'

He made as if to roll up his trouser leg. Dalgliesh said quickly:

'That's all right, Mr Lorrimer. When did you know the bed wasn't available after all?'

'About nine o'clock they rang. He'd only just left home. So I phoned the Lab. I know the number of the Biology Department, of course. That's where he works – the Biology Department. Miss Easterbrook answered the phone and said that Edwin was at the hospital attending a post-mortem but she would give him the message when he got in. Addenbrooke's said they'd probably send for me next Tuesday. Who's going to take me now?'

'I expect Mrs Swaffield will arrange something, or perhaps your niece could help. Wouldn't you like her to be here with you?'

'No. What can she do? She was here this morning with that friend of hers, the writing woman. Edwin doesn't like either of them. The friend – Miss Mawson, isn't it? – was rummaging around upstairs. I've got very good ears. I could hear her all right. I went out of the door and there she was coming down. She said she'd been to the bathroom. Why was she wearing washing-up gloves if she was going to the bathroom?'

Why indeed? thought Dalgliesh. He felt a spasm of irritation that Constable Davis hadn't arrived sooner. It was perfectly natural that Howarth should come with Angela Foley to break the news and should leave her with her uncle. Someone had to stay with him, and who more suitable than his only remaining relative? It was probably natural, too, that Angela Foley should send for the support of her friend. Probably both of them were interested in Lorrimer's will. Well, that too was natural enough. Massingham shifted on the sofa. Dalgliesh could sense his anxiety to get upstairs into Lorrimer's room. He shared it. But books and papers, the sad detritus of a dead life, could wait. The living witness might not again be so communicative. He asked:

'What did your son do with himself, Mr Lorrimer?'

'After work, do you mean? He stays in his room mostly. Reading, I suppose. He's got quite a library of books up there. He's a scholar, is Edwin. He doesn't care much about the television, so I sit down here. Sometimes I can hear the record-player. Then there's the garden most weekends, cleaning the car, cooking and shopping. He has quite a full life. And he doesn't get much time. He's at the Lab until seven o'clock most nights, sometimes later.'

'And friends?'

'No. He doesn't go in for friends. We keep ourselves to ourselves.'

'No weekends away?'

'Where would he want to go? And what would happen to me? Besides, there's the shopping. If he isn't on call for a scene-of-crime visit he drives me into Ely Saturday morning, and we go to the supermarket. Then we have lunch in the city. I enjoy that.'

'What telephone calls did he have?'

'From the Lab? Only when the Police Liaison Officer rings up to say that he's wanted at a murder scene. Sometimes that's in the middle of the night. But he never wakes me. There's a telephone extension in his room. He just leaves me a note and he's usually back in time to bring me a cup of tea at seven o'clock. He didn't do that this morning of course. That's why I rang the Lab. I rang his number first but there wasn't any reply so then I rang the reception desk. He gave me both numbers in case I couldn't get through to him in an emergency.'

'And no one else has telephoned him recently, no one has come to see him?'

'Who would want to come and see him? And no one has telephoned except that woman.'

Dalgliesh said, very quietly:

'What woman, Mr Lorrimer?'

'I don't know what woman. I only know she rang. Monday of last week it was. Edwin was having a bath and the phone kept on ringing so I thought I'd better answer it.'

'Can you remember exactly what happened and what was said, Mr Lorrimer, from the time you lifted the receiver? Take your time, there's no hurry. This may be very important.'

'There wasn't much to remember. I was going to say our number and ask her to hang on, but she didn't give me any time. She started speaking as soon as I lifted the receiver. She said: "We're right, there is something going on." Then she said something about the can being burned and that she'd got the numbers.'

'That the can had been burned and she'd got the numbers?'

'That's right. It doesn't sound sense now, but it was something like that. Then she gave me the numbers.'

'Can you remember them, Mr Lorrimer?'

'Only the last one, which was 1840. Or it may have been two numbers, 18 and 40. I remembered those because the first house we had after I was married was number 18 and the second was 40. It was quite a coincidence, really. Anyway, those numbers stuck in my mind. But I can't remember the others.'

'How many numbers altogether?'

'Three or four altogether, I think. There were two, and then the 18 and 40.'

'What did the numbers sound like, Mr Lorrimer? Did you think she was giving you a telephone number or a car registration, for example? Can you remember what impression they made on you at the time?'

'No impression. Why should they? More like a telephone number, I suppose. I don't think it was a car registration. There weren't any letters you see. It sounded like a date; eighteen forty.'

'Have you any idea who was telephoning?'

'No. I don't think it was anyone at the Lab. It didn't sound like one of the Lab staff.'

'How do you mean, Mr Lorrimer? How did the voice seem?'

The old man sat there, staring straight ahead. His hands, with the long fingers like those of his son, but with their skin dry and stained as withered leaves, hung heavily between his knees, grotesquely large for the brittle wrists. After a moment he spoke. He said:

'Excited.' There was another silence. Both detectives looked at him. Massingham thought that here again was an example of his chief's skill. He would have gone charging upstairs in search of the will and papers. But this evidence, so carefully elicited, was vital. After about a moment the old man spoke again. The word, when it came, was surprising. He said:

'Conspiratorial. That's what she sounded. Conspiratorial.'

They sat, still patiently waiting, but he said nothing else. Then they saw that he was crying. His face didn't change, but a single tear, bright as a pearl, dropped on to the parched hands. He looked at it as if wondering what it could be. Then he said:

'He was a good son to me. Time was, when he first went to

College up in London, that we lost touch. He wrote to his mother and me, but he didn't come home. But these last years, since I've been alone, he's taken care of me. I'm not complaining. I daresay he's left me a bit of money, and I've got my pension. But it's hard when the young go first. And who will look after me now?'

Dalgliesh said quietly:

'We need to look at his room, examine his papers. Is the room locked?'

'Locked? Why should it be locked? No one went into it but Edwin.'

Dalgliesh nodded to Massingham, who went out to call Mrs Swaffield. Then they made their way upstairs.

II

It was a long, low-ceilinged room with white walls and a casement window which gave a view of a rectangle of unmown grass, a couple of gnarled apple trees heavy with fruit burnished green and gold in the autumn sun, a straggling hedge beaded with berries and beyond it the windmill. Even in the genial light of afternoon the mill looked a melancholy wreck of its former puissance. The paint was peeling from the walls and the great sails, from which the slats had fallen like rotten teeth, hung heavy with inertia in the restless air. Behind the windmill, the acres of black fenland, newly sliced by the autumn ploughing, stretched in glistening clumps between the dykes.

Dalgliesh turned away from this picture of melancholy peace to examine the room. Massingham was already busy at the desk. Finding the lid unlocked, he rolled it back for a few inches, then let it drop again. Then he tried the drawers. Only the top left-hand one was locked. If he were impatient for Dalgliesh to take Lorrimer's keys from his pocket and open it, he concealed his eagerness. It was known that the older man, who could work faster than any of his colleagues, still liked occasionally to take his time. He was taking it now, regarding the room with his dark sombre eyes, standing very still as if he were picking up invisible waves.

The place held a curious peace. The proportions were right

and the furniture fitted where it had been placed. A man might have space to think in this uncluttered sanctum. A single bed, neatly covered with a red and brown blanket, stood against the opposite wall. A long wall shelf above the bed held an adjustable reading lamp, a radio, a record-player, a clock, a carafe of water and the Book of Common Prayer. In front of the window stood an oak working-table with a wheel-back chair. On the table was a blotter and a brown and blue pottery mug stacked with pencils and Biro pens. The only other items of furniture were a shabby, winged armchair with a low table beside it, a double wardrobe in oak to the left of the door, and to the right an old-fashioned desk with a roll-top. The telephone was fitted to the wall. There were no pictures and no mirror, no masculine impedimenta, no trivia on desk-top or table-ledge. Everything was functional, well used, unadorned. It was a room a man could be at home in.

Dalgliesh walked over to look at the books. He estimated that there must be about four hundred of them, completely covering the wall. There was little fiction, although the nineteenth-century English and Russian novelists were represented. Most of the books were histories or biographies, but there was a shelf of philosophy: Teilhard de Chardin's *Science and Christ*, Jean-Paul Sartre's *Being and Nothingness: A Humanist Outlook*, Simone Weil's *First and Last*, Plato's *Republic*, the *Cambridge History of Late Greek and Early Medieval Philosophy*. It looked as if Lorrimer had at one time been trying to teach himself Greek. The shelf held a Greek primer and a dictionary.

Massingham had taken down a book on comparative religion. He said:

'It looks as if he was one of those men who torment themselves trying to discover the meaning of existence.'

Dalgliesh replaced the Sartre he had been studying.

'You find that reprehensible?'

'I find it futile. Metaphysical speculation is about as pointless as a discussion on the meaning of one's lungs. They're for breathing.'

'And life is for living. You find that an adequate personal credo?'

'To maximize one's pleasures and minimize one's pain, yes, sir, I do. And I suppose, to bear with stoicism those miseries I can't avoid. To be human is to ensure enough of those without inventing them. Anyway, I don't believe you can hope to understand what you can't see or touch or measure.'

'A logical positivist. You're in respectable company. But he spent his life examining what he could see or touch or measure. It doesn't seem to have satisfied him. Well, let's see what his personal papers have to tell.'

He turned his attention to the desk, leaving the locked drawer to the last. He rolled back the top to reveal two small drawers and a number of pigeon-holes. And here, neatly docketed and compartmentalized, were the minutiae of Lorrimer's solitary life. A drawer with three bills waiting to be paid, and one for receipts. A labelled envelope containing his parents' marriage lines, his own birth and baptismal certificates. His passport, an anonymous face but with the eyes staring as if hypnotized, the neck muscles taut. The lens of the camera might have been the barrel of a gun. A life assurance certificate. Receipted bills for fuel, electricity and gas. The maintenance agreement for the central heating. The hire-purchase agreement for the television. A wallet with his bank statement. His portfolio of investments, sound, unexciting, orthodox.

There was nothing about his work. Obviously he kept his life as carefully compartmentalized as his filing system. Everything to do with his profession, the journals, the drafts of his scientific papers, were kept in his office at the Lab. They were probably written there. That might account for some of the late hours. It would certainly have been impossible to guess from the contents of his desk what his job had been.

His will was in a separate labelled envelope together with a brief letter from a firm of Ely solicitors, Messrs Pargeter, Coleby and Hunt. The will was very short and had been made five years earlier. Lorrimer had left Postmill Cottage and £10,000 to his father, and the rest of his estate absolutely to his cousin, Angela Maud Foley. To judge from the portfolio of investments, Miss Foley would inherit a useful capital sum.

Lastly, Dalgliesh took Lorrimer's bunch of keys from his pocket and unlocked the top left-hand drawer. The lock worked very easily. The drawer was crammed with papers covered with Lorimer's handwriting. Dalgliesh took them over to the table in front of the window and motioned Massingham to draw up the armchair. They sat there together. There were twenty-eight letters in all and they read them through without speaking. Massingham was aware of Dalgliesh's long fingers picking up each sheet, dropping it from his hand then shifting it across the desk towards him, then picking up the next. The clock seemed to him to be ticking unnaturally loudly and his own breathing to have become embarrassingly obtrusive. The letters were a liturgy of the bitter exfoliation of love. It was all here: the inability to accept that desire was no longer returned, the demand for explanations which, if attempted, could only increase the hurt, the excoriating self-pity, the spasms of irrational renewed hope, the petulant outbursts at the obtuseness of the lover unable to see where her happiness lay, the humiliating self-abasement.

'I realize that you won't want to live in the fens. But that needn't be a difficulty, darling. I could get a transfer to the Metropolitan Lab if you prefer London. Or we could find a house in Cambridge or Norwich, a choice of two civilized cities. You once said that you liked to live among the spires. Or if you wished, I could stay on here and we could have a flat in London for you, and I'd join you whenever I could. I ought to be able to make it most Sundays. The week without you would be an eternity, but anything would be bearable if I knew that you belonged to me. You do belong to me. All the books, all the seeking and the reading, what does it come to in the end? Until you taught me that the answer was so simple.'

Some of the letters were highly erotic. They were probably the most difficult of all love letters to write successfully, thought Massingham. Didn't the poor devil know that, once desire was dead, they could only disgust? Perhaps those lovers who used a private nursery talk for their most secret acts were the wisest. At least the eroticism was personal. Here the sexual descriptions were either embarrassingly Lawrentian in their intensity, or coldly clinical. He recognized with surprise an emotion that could only be shame. It wasn't just that some of the outpourings were brutally explicit. He was accustomed to perusing the privat pornography of murdered lives; but these letters, with thei mixture of crude desire and elevated sentiment, were outside hi experience. The naked suffering they expressed seemed to hin neurotic, irrational. Sex no longer had any power to shock him love, he decided, obviously could.

He was struck by the contrast between the tranquillity of th man's room and the turbulence of his mind. He thought: at leas this job teaches one not to hoard personal debris. Police work wa as effective as religion in teaching a man to live each day as if i were his last. And it wasn't only murder that violated privacy Any sudden death could do as much. If the helicopter hac crashed on landing, what sort of a picture would his leaving present to the world? A conformist, right-wing philistine, ob sessed with his physical fitness? *Homme moyen sensuel*, and *moyen* everything else for that matter? He thought of Emma, witl whom he slept whenever they got the opportunity, and who, h supposed, would eventually become Lady Dungannon unless, a seemed increasingly likely, she found an elder son with bette prospects and more time to devote to her. He wondered wha Emma, cheerful hedonist with her frank enjoyment of bed, woul have made of these self-indulgent, masturbatory fantasies, thi humiliating chronicle of the miseries of defeated love.

One half-sheet was covered with a single name. Domenica Domenica, Domenica. And then Domenica Lorrimer, a clumsy uneuphonic linking. Perhaps its infelicity had struck him, for h had written it only once. The letters looked laboured, tentative like those of a young girl practising in secret the hoped-fo married name. All the letters were undated, all without superscrip- tion and signature. A number were obviously first drafts, a painful seeking after the elusive world, the holograph scored witl deletions.

But now Dalgliesh was pushing towards him the final letter Here there were no alterations, no uncertainties, and if there hac been a previous draft, Lorrimer had destroyed it. This was as clea as an affirmation. The words, strongly written in Lorrimer's black upright script, were set out in even lines, neatly as an exercise in calligraphy. Perhaps this was one he had intended to post after all

'I have been seeking for the words to explain what has happened to me, what you have made happen. You know how difficult this is for me. There have been so many years of writing official reports, the same phrases, the same bleak conclusions. My mind was a computer programmed to death. I was like a man born in darkness, living in a deep cave, crouching for comfort by my small inadequate fire, watching the shadows flickering over the cave drawings and trying to find in their crude outlines some significance, a meaning to existence to help me endure the dark. And then you came and took me by the hand and led me out into the sunlight. And there was the real world, dazzling my eyes with its colour and its beauty And it needed only your hand and the courage to take a few small steps out of the shadows and imaginings into the light. *Ex umbris et imaginibus in veritatem.*'

Dalgliesh laid the letter down. He said:

'"Lord, let me know mine end, and the number of my days: that I may be certified how long I have to live." Given the choice, Lorrimer would probably have preferred his murder to go unavenged than for any eyes but his to have seen these letters. What do you think of them?'

Massingham was uncertain whether he was expected to comment on their subject matter or their style. He said cautiously:

'The passage about the cave is effective. It looks as if he worked over that one.'

'But not entirely original. An echo of Plato's *Republic*. And like Plato's caveman, the brightness dazzled and the light hurt his eyes. George Orwell wrote somewhere that murder, the unique crime, should result only from strong emotions. Well, here is the strong emotion. But we seem to have the wrong body.'

'Do you think Dr Howarth knew, sir?'

'Almost certainly. The wonder is that no one at the Lab apparently did. It's not the kind of information that Mrs Bidwell, for one, would keep to herself. First, I think, we check with the solicitors that this will still stands, and then we see the lady.'

But this programme was to be changed. The wall telephone rang, shattering the peace of the room. Massingham answered. It was Sergeant Underhill trying, but with small success, to keep the excitement out of his voice.

'There's a Major Hunt of Messrs Pargeter, Coleby and Hunt of Ely wants to see Mr Dalgliesh. He'd prefer not to talk over the telephone. He says could you ring and say when it would be convenient for Mr Dalgliesh to call. And sir, we've got a witness. He's over at Guy's Marsh police station now. The name's Alfred Goddard. He was a passenger last night passing the Lab in the nine-ten bus.'

III

'Running down drive he were like the devil out of hell.'

'Can you describe him, Mr Goddard?'

'Naw. He weren't old.'

'How young?'

'I never said 'e were young. I never seed 'im near enough to tell. But he didn't run like an old 'un.'

'Running for the bus, perhaps.'

'If 'e were 'e never catched it.'

'He wasn't waving?'

' 'Course he weren't. Driver couldn't see 'im. No point in waving at back of bloody bus.'

Guy's Marsh police station was a red-brick Victorian building with a white wooden pediment, which looked so like an early railway station that Dalgliesh suspected that the nineteenth-century police authority had economized by making use of the same architect and the same set of plans.

Mr Alfred Goddard, waiting comfortably in the interview room with a huge mug of steaming tea before him, looked perfectly at home, neither gratified nor impressed to find himself a key witness in a murder investigation. He was a nut-brown wrinkled, undersized countryman who smelt of strong tobacco alcohol and cow-dung. Dalgliesh recalled that the early fen settlers had been called 'yellow-bellies' by their highland neighbours because they crawled frog-like over their marshy fields or 'slodgers', splashing web-footed through the mud. Either would have suited Mr Goddard. Dalgliesh noticed with interest that he was wearing what looked like a leather thong bound round his left wrist, and guessed that this was dried eel-skin, the ancient harm to ward off rheumatism. The misshapen fingers stiffly radling the mug of tea suggested that the talisman had been less han efficacious.

Dalgliesh doubted whether he would have troubled to come orward if Bill Carney, the conductor of the bus, hadn't known im as a regular on the Wednesday evening service travelling rom Ely to Stoney Piggott via Chevisham, and had directed the nquiring police to his remote cottage. Having been summarily lug out of his lair, however, he displayed no particular resentment gainst Bill Carney or the police, and announced that he was repared to answer questions if, as he explained, they were put to im 'civil-like'. His main grievance in life was the Stoney Piggott bus: its lateness, infrequency, rising fares and, in particuar, the stupidity of the recent experiment of using doubleleckers on the Stoney Piggott route and his own subsequent anishment each Wednesday to the upper deck because of his pipe.

'But how fortunate for us that you were there,' Massingham ad pointed out. Mr Goddard had merely snorted into his tea.

Dalgliesh continued with the questioning:

'Is there anything at all you can remember about him, Mr Goddard? His height, his hair, how he was dressed?'

'Naw. Middling tall and wearing a shortish coat, or mac naybe. Flapping open, maybe.'

'Can you remember the colour?'

'Darkish, maybe. I never seed 'im for more'n a second, see. Then trees got in the way. Bus were moving off when I first set eyes on him.'

Massingham interposed:

'The driver didn't see him, nor did the conductor.'

'More than likely. They was on lower deck. Isn't likely they'd notice. And driver were driving bloody bus.'

Dalgliesh said:

'Mr Goddard, this is very important. Can you remember whether there were any lights on in the Lab?'

'What do you mean, Lab?'

'The house the figure was running from.'

'Lights in the house? If you mean house why not say house?'

Mr Goddard pantomimed the ardours of intensive thought,

pursing his lips into a grimace and half closing his eyes. They waited. After a nicely judged interval he announced:

'Faint lights, maybe. Not blazing out, mind you. I reckon I seed some lights from bottom windows.'

Massingham asked:

'You're quite sure it was a man?'

Mr Goddard bestowed on him the glance of mingled reproof and chagrin of a viva-voce candidate faced with what he obviously regards as an unfair question.

'Wearing trousers, wasn't he? If he weren't a man then he ought to have been.'

'But you can't be absolutely sure?'

'Can't be sure of nothing these days. Time was when folk dressed in a decent, God-fearing manner. Man or woman, it were human and it were running. That's all I seed.'

'So it could have been a woman in slacks?'

'Never run like a woman. Daft runners women be, keeping their knees tight together and kicking out ankles like bloody ducks. Pity they don't keep their knees together when they ain't running, I say.'

The deduction was fair enough, thought Dalgliesh. No woman ran precisely like a man. Goddard's first impression had been that of a youngish man running, and that was probably exactly what he had seen. Too much questioning now might only confuse him.

The driver and conductor, summoned from the bus depot and still in uniform, were unable to confirm Goddard's story, but what they were able to add was useful. It is not surprising that neither of them had seen the runner, since the six-foot wall and its overhanging trees cut off a view of the Laboratory from the bottom deck and they could only have glimpsed the house when the bus was passing the open drive and slowing down at the stop. But if Mr Goddard were right and the figure had only appeared when the bus was moving off, they still wouldn't have seen him.

It was helpful that they were both able to confirm that the bus, on that Wednesday evening at least, was running on time. Bill Carney had actually looked at his watch as they moved away. It had shown nine-twelve. The bus had halted at the stop for a ouple of seconds. None of the three passengers had made any reliminary moves to get off, but both the driver and the conduc-or had noticed a woman waiting in the shadows of the bus helter and had assumed that she would board. However, she adn't done so, but had turned away and moved back farther nto the shadow of the shelter as the bus drew up. The conductor ad thought it strange that she was waiting there, since there vasn't another bus that night. But it had been raining slightly nd he had assumed, without thinking about it very deeply, that he had been sheltering. It wasn't his job, as he reasonably ointed out, to drag passengers on the bus if they didn't want a ide.

Dalgliesh questioned them both closely about the woman, but here was little firm information they could give. Both agreed hat she had been wearing a headscarf and that the collar of her oat had been turned up at her ears. The driver thought that she ad been wearing slacks and a belted mackintosh. Bill Carney greed about the slacks but thought that she had been wearing a uffle-coat. Their only reason for assuming that the figure was a voman was the headscarf. Neither of them could describe it. They thought it unlikely that any of the three passengers on the ower deck would be able to help. Two of them were elderly egulars, both apparently asleep. The third was unknown to hem.

Dalgliesh knew that all three would have to be traced. This vas one of those time-consuming jobs which were necessary but vhich seldom produced any worthwhile information. But it was stonishing how much the most unlikely people did notice. The leepers might have been jogged awake by the slowing down of he bus and have had a clearer look at the woman than either the onductor or driver. Mr Goddard, not surprisingly, hadn't no-iced her. He inquired caustically how a chap was expected to ee through the roof of a bloody bus shelter and, in any case, he'd een looking the other way hadn't he, and a good job for them hat he had. Dalgliesh hastened to propitiate him and, when his tatement was at last completed to the old man's satisfaction, vatched him driven back to his cottage, sitting in some style, like a tiny upright manikin, in the back of the police car.

But it was another ten minutes before Dalgliesh and Massingham could set out for Ely. Albert Bidwell had presented himself conveniently if belatedly at the police station, bringing with him a hefty sample of the mud from the five-acre field and an air of sullen grievance. Massingham wondered how he and his wife had originally met and what had brought together two such dissimilar personalities. She, he felt sure, was born a cockney; he a fenman. He was taciturn where she was avid for gossip and excitement.

He admitted to taking the telephone call. It was a woman and the message was that Mrs Bidwell was to go to Leamings to give Mrs Schofield a hand instead of to the Lab. He couldn't remember if the caller had given her name but didn't think so. He had taken calls from Mrs Schofield once or twice before when she had rung to ask his wife to help with dinner parties or suchlike. Women's business. He couldn't say whether the voice sounded the same. Asked whether he had assumed that the caller was Mrs Schofield, he said that he hadn't assumed anything.

Dalgliesh asked:

'Can you remember whether the caller said that your wife was to come to Leamings or go to Leamings?'

The significance of this question obviously escaped him but he received it with surly suspicion and, after a long pause, said he didn't know. When Massingham asked whether it was possible that the caller hadn't been a woman but a man disguising his voice, he gave him a look of concentrated disgust as if deploring a mind that could imagine such sophisticated villainy. But the answer provoked his longest response. He said, in a tone of finality, that he didn't know whether it was a woman, or a man pretending to be a woman, or, maybe, a lass. All he knew was that he'd been asked to give his wife a message, and he'd given it to her. And if he'd known it would cause all this botheration he wouldn't have answered the phone.

And with that they had to be content.

IV

In Dalgliesh's experience, solicitors who practised in cathedral cities were invariably agreeably housed, and the office of Messrs

Pargeter, Coleby and Hunt was no exception. It was a well-preserved and maintained Regency house with a view of the Cathedral Green, an imposing front door whose ebony-black paint gleamed as if it were still wet, and whose brass knocker in the shape of a lion's head had been polished almost to whiteness. The door was opened by an elderly and very thin clerk, Dickensian in his old-fashioned black suit and stiff collar, whose appearance of lugubrious resignation brightened somewhat at seeing them, as if cheered by the prospect of trouble. He bowed slightly when Dalgliesh introduced himself and said:

'Major Hunt is, of course, expecting you, sir. He is just concluding his interview with a client. If you will step this way he won't keep you waiting more than a couple of minutes.'

The waiting-room into which they were shown resembled the sitting-room of a man's club in its comfort and air of controlled disorder. The chairs were leather and so wide and deep that it was difficult to imagine anyone over sixty rising from them without difficulty. Despite the heat from two old-fashioned radiators there was a coke fire burning in the grate. The large, circular mahogany table was spread with magazines devoted to the interests of the landed gentry, most of which looked very old. There was a glass-fronted bookcase packed with bound histories of the county and illustrated volumes on architecture and painting. The oil over the mantelpiece of a phaeton with horses and attendant grooms looked very like a Stubbs, and, thought Dalgliesh, probably was.

He only had time briefly to inspect the room, and had walked over to the window to look out towards the Lady Chapel of the cathedral when the door opened and the clerk reappeared to usher them into Major Hunt's office. The man who rose from behind his desk to receive them was in appearance the opposite of his clerk. He was a stocky, upright man in late middle age, dressed in a shabby but well-tailored tweed suit, ruddy-faced and balding, his eyes keen under the spiky, restless eyebrows. He gave Dalgliesh a frankly appraising glance as he shook hands, as if deciding where exactly to place him in some private scheme of things, then nodded as if satisfied. He still looked more like a soldier than a solicitor, and Dalgliesh guessed that the voice with which he greeted them had acquired its loud authoritative bar across the parade-grounds and in the messes of the Secon World War.

'Good morning, good morning. Please sit down, Commande You come on tragic business. I don't think we have ever lost on of our clients by murder before.'

The clerk coughed. It was just such a cough as Dalgliesh woul have expected, inoffensive but discreetly minatory and not to b ignored.

'There was Sir James Cummins, sir, in 1923. He was shot by hi neighbour, Captain Cartwright, because of the seduction of Mr Cartwright by Sir James, a grievance aggravated by some un pleasantness over fishing rights.'

'Quite right, Mitching. But that was in my father's time. The hanged poor Cartwright. A pity, my father always thought. H had a good war record – survived the Somme and Arras an ended on the scaffold. Battle-scarred, poor devil. The jur would probably have made a recommendation to mercy if h hadn't cut up the body. He did cut up the body, didn't he, Mitching?'

'Quite right, sir. They found the head buried in the orchard.'

'That's what did for Cartwright. English juries won't stand fo cutting up the body. Crippen would be alive today if he'd burie Belle Elmore in one piece.'

'Hardly, sir. Crippen was born in 1860.'

'Well he wouldn't have been long dead. It wouldn't surpris me if he'd reached his century. Only three years older than you father, Mitching, and much the same build, small, pop-eye and wiry. They live for ever, that type. Ah well, to our muttons You'll both take coffee, I hope. I can promise you it will b drinkable. Mitching has installed one of those glass retort affair and we grind our own fresh beans. Coffee then, please, Mitching.'

'Miss Makepeace is preparing it now, sir.'

Major Hunt exuded postprandial well-being, and Massinghan guessed, with some envy, that his business with his last client ha been chiefly done over a good lunch. He and Dalgliesh ha snatched a hurried sandwich and beer at a pub between Chevisham and Guy's Marsh. Dalgliesh, known to enjoy food an

ine, had an inconvenient habit of ignoring meal-times when in
ıe middle of a case. Massingham wasn't fussy about the quality;
was the quantity he deplored. But, at least, they were to get
offee.

Mitching had stationed himself near the door and showed no
ıclination to leave. This was apparently perfectly acceptable.
Dalgliesh thought that they were like a couple of comedians in
ıe process of perfecting their antiphonal patter, and reluctant to
ose any opportunity of practising it. Major Hunt said:

'You want to know about Lorrimer's will, of course.'

'And anything else you can tell us about him.'

'That won't be much, I'm afraid. I've only seen him twice
nce I dealt with his grandmother's estate. But of course I'll do
hat I can. When murder comes in at the window privacy goes
ut of the door. That's so, isn't it, Mitching?'

'There are no secrets, sir, in the fierce light that beats upon the
caffold.'

'I'm not sure that you've got that one right, Mitching. And we
on't have scaffolds now. Are you an abolitionist, Commander?'

Dalgliesh said:

'I'm bound to be until the day comes when we can be abso-
ıtely sure that we could never under any circumstances make a
ıistake.'

'That's the orthodox answer, but it begs quite a lot of questions,
oesn't it? Still you're not here to discuss capital punishment.
Mustn't waste time. Now the will. Where did I put Mr Lorrimer's
ox, Mitching?'

'It's here, sir.'

'Then bring it over, man. Bring it over.'

The clerk carried the black tin box from a side table and
laced it in front of Major Hunt. The Major opened it with some
eremony and took out the will.

Dalgliesh said:

'We've found one will in his desk. It's dated 3rd May 1971. It
ooks like the original.'

'So he didn't destroy it? That's interesting. It suggests that he
ıadn't finally made up his mind.'

'So there's a later will?'

'Oh, indeed there is, Commander. Indeed there is. That's wha I wanted to talk to you about. Signed by him only last Frida and both the original and the only copy left here with me. I hav them here. Perhaps you'd like to read it yourself.'

He handed over the will. It was very short. Lorrimer, in th accepted form, revoked all previous wills, proclaimed himself t be of sound mind and disposed of all his property in less than dozen lines. Postmill Cottage was left to his father together with sum of ten thousand pounds. One thousand pounds was left t Brenda Pridmore 'to enable her to buy any books required t further her scientific education'. All the rest of his estate was le to the Academy of Forensic Science to provide an annual cas prize of such amount as the Academy should see fit for a original essay on any aspect of the scientific investigation c crime, the essay to be judged by three judges selected by th Academy. There was no mention of Angela Foley.

Dalgliesh said:

'Did he give you any explanation why he left his cousir Angela Foley, out of the will?'

'As a matter of fact he did. I thought it right to point out tha in the event of his death his cousin, as his only surviving relativ apart from his father, might wish to contest the will. If she did, legal battle would cost money and might seriously deplete th estate. I didn't feel any obligation to press him to alter hi decision. I merely thought it right to point out the possibl consequences. You heard what he replied, didn't you, Mitching?'

'Yes, indeed, sir. The late Mr Lorrimer expressed his disappro bation of the way in which his cousin chose to live, in particula he deplored the relationship which, he alleged, subsisted betwee his cousin and the lady with whom I understand she makes he home, and said that he did not wish the said companion t benefit from his estate. If his cousin chose to contest the will, h was prepared to leave the matter to the courts. It would n longer be of any concern to himself. He would have made hi wishes clear. He also pointed out, if I remember rightly, sir, tha the will was intended to be transitional in its nature. He had it i mind to marry and if he did so the will would, of course, becom void. In the meantime he wished to guard against what he saw a he remote contingency of his cousin inheriting absolutely should e die unexpectedly before his personal affairs became clearer.'

'That's right, Mitching, that in effect is what he said. I must ay that it reconciled me somewhat to the new will. If he were roposing to get married obviously it would no longer stand and e could think again. Not that I thought it necessarily an unjust r unfair will. A man has the right to dispose of his property as he ees fit, if the state leaves him anything to dispose of. It struck me s a bit odd that, if he were engaged to be married, he didn't nention the lady in the interim will. But I suppose the principle's ound enough. If he'd left her a paltry sum she'd hardly have hanked him, and if he'd left her the lot, she'd probably promptly ave married another chap and it would all pass to him.'

Dalgliesh asked:

'He didn't tell you anything about the proposed marriage?'

'Not even the lady's name. And naturally I didn't ask. I'm not ven sure that he had anyone particular in mind. It could have een only a general intention or, perhaps, an excuse for altering he will. I merely congratulated him and pointed out that the ew will would be void as soon as the marriage took place. He aid that he understood that and would be coming to make a ew will in due course. In the meantime this was what he wanted nd this was what I drew up. Mitching signed it, with my ecretary as a second witness. Ah, here she is with the coffee. You emember signing Mr Lorrimer's will, eh?'

The thin, nervous-looking girl who had brought in the coffee ave a terrified nod in response to the Major's bark and hastened ut of the room. Major Hunt said with satisfaction:

'She remembers. She was so terrified that she could hardly ign. But she did sign. It's all there. All correct and in order. I ope we can draw up a valid will, eh, Mitching? But it will be nteresting to see if the little woman makes a fight for it.'

Dalgliesh asked how much Angela Foley would be making a ight for.

'The best part of £50,000, I daresay. Not a fortune these days ut useful, useful. The original capital was left to him absolutely y old Annie Lorrimer, his paternal grandmother. An extra-rdinary old woman. Born and bred in the fens. Kept a village store with her husband over at Low Willow. Tom Lorrimer drank himself into a comparatively early grave – couldn't stand the fen winters – and she carried on alone. Not all the money came from the shop, of course, although she sold out at a good time. No, she had a nose for the horses. Extraordinary thing. God knows where she got it from. Never mounted a horse in her life to my knowledge. Shut up the shop and went to Newmarket three times a year. Never lost a penny, so I've heard, and saved every pound she won.'

'What family had she? Was Lorrimer's father her only son?'

'That's right. She had one son and one daughter, Angela Foley's mother. Couldn't bear the sight of either of them, as far as I can see. The daughter got herself in the family way by the village sexton and the old woman cast her off in approved Victorian style. The marriage turned out badly and I don't think Maud Foley saw her mother again. She died of cancer about five years after the girl was born. The old woman wouldn't have her granddaughter back, so she ended up in local authority care. Most of her life's been spent in foster homes, I believe.'

'And the son?'

'Oh, he married the local schoolmistress, and that turned out reasonably well as far as I know. But the family were never close. The old lady wouldn't leave her money to her son because, she said, it would mean two lots of death duties. She was well over forty when he was born. But I think the real reason was simply that she didn't much like him. I don't think she saw much of the grandson, Edwin, either, but she had to leave the money somewhere and hers was a generation which believes that blood is thicker than charitable soup and male blood thicker than female. Apart from the fact she'd cast off her daughter and never taken any interest in her granddaughter, her generation didn't believe in leaving money outright to women. It only encourages seducers and fortune-hunters. So she left it absolutely to her grandson, Edwin Lorrimer. At the time of her death I think he had qualms of conscience about his cousin. As you know, the first will made her his legatee.'

Dalgliesh said:

'Do you know if Lorrimer told her that he intended to change his will?'

The solicitor looked at him sharply.

'He didn't say. In the circumstances it would be convenient for her if she could prove that he did.'

So convenient, thought Dalgliesh, that she would certainly have mentioned the fact when first interviewed. But even if she had believed herself to be her cousin's heir, that didn't necessarily make her a murderess. If she wanted a share of her grandmother's money, why wait until now to kill for it?'

The telephone rang. Major Hunt muttered an apology and reached for the receiver. Holding his palm over the mouthpiece, he said to Dalgliesh:

'It's Miss Foley, ringing from Postmill Cottage. Old Mr Lorrimer wants to have a word with me about the will. She says he's anxious to know whether the cottage now belongs to him. Do you want me to tell him?'

'That is for you. But he's the next of kin; he may as well know the terms of the will now as later. And so may she.'

Major Hunt hesitated. Then he spoke into the receiver.

'All right, Betty. Put Miss Foley on the line.'

He looked up again at Dalgliesh.

'This piece of news is going to put the cat among the pigeons in Chevisham.'

Dalgliesh had a sudden picture of Brenda Pridmore's eager young face shining across Howarth's desk at him.

'Yes.' he said grimly. 'Yes, I'm afraid it is.'

V

Howarth's house, Leamings, was three miles outside Chevisham village on the Cambridge road, a modern building of concrete, wood and glass cantilevered above the flat fenlands, with two white wings like folded sails. Even in the fading light it was impressive. The house stood in uncompromising and splendid isolation, depending for its effect on nothing but perfection of line and artful simplicity. No other building was in sight except a solitary black wooden cottage on stilts, desolate as an execution shed, and, dramatically, an intricate mirage hung above the eastern skyline, the marvellous single tower and octagon of Ely Cathedral.

From the rooms at the back one would see an immensity of sky and look out over vast unhedged fields dissected by Leamings' dykes changing with the seasons from black scarred earth, through the spring sowing to the harvest; would hear nothing but the wind and, in summer, the ceaseless susurration of the grain.

The site had been small and the architect had needed ingenuity. There was no garden, nothing but a short drive leading to a paved courtyard and the double garage. Outside the garage, a red Jaguar XJS stood beside Howarth's Triumph. Massingham cast envious eyes on the Jaguar and wondered how Mrs Schofield had managed to get such quick delivery. They drove in and parked beside it. Even before Dalgliesh had switched off the engine, Howarth had strolled out and was quietly waiting for them. He was wearing a butcher's long blue and white striped overall in which he seemed perfectly at ease, evidently seeing no need either to explain or remove it. As they made their way up the open-tread, carved wooden stairs Dalgliesh complimented him on the house. Howarth said:

'It was designed by a Swedish architect who did some of the modern additions at Cambridge. Actually it belongs to a university friend. He and his wife are spending a couple of years' sabbatical at Harvard. If they decide to stay on in the States they may sell. Anyway, we're settled for the next eighteen months and can then look around if we have to.'

They were mounting a wide circular wooden staircase rising from the well of the house. Upstairs someone was playing, very loudly, a record of the finale of the third Brandenburg Concerto. The glorious contrapuntal sound beat against the walls and surged through the house; Massingham could almost imagine it taking off on its white wings and rollicking joyously over the fens. Dalgliesh said, above the music:

'Mrs Schofield likes it here?'

Howarth's voice, carefully casual, came down to them. 'Oh she may have moved on by then. Domenica likes variety. My half-sister suffers from Baudelaire's *horreur de domicile* – she usually prefers to be elsewhere. Her natural habitat is London, but she's with me now because she's illustrating a new limited edition of Crabbe for the Paradine Press.'

The record came to an end. Howarth paused and said with a kind of roughness, as if regretting an impulse to confide:

'I think I ought to tell you that my sister was widowed just over eighteen months ago. Her husband was killed in a car crash. She was driving at the time but she was lucky. At least, I suppose she was lucky. She was scarcely scratched. Charles Schofield died three days later.'

'I'm sorry,' said Dalgliesh. The cynic in him wondered why he had been told. Howarth had struck him as essentially a private man, one not lightly to confide a personal or family tragedy. Was it an appeal to chivalry, a covert plea for him to treat her with special consideration? Or was Howarth warning him that she was still distraught with grief, unpredictable, unbalanced even? He could hardly be implying that, since the tragedy, she had indulged an irresistible impulse to kill her lovers.

They had reached the top of the stairs and were standing on a wide wooden balcony seemingly hung in space. Howarth pushed open a door and said:

'I'll leave you to it. I'm making an early start on cooking dinner tonight. She's in here.' He called:

'This is Commander Dalgliesh and Detective Inspector Massingham of the Met. The men about the murder. My sister, Domenica Schofield.'

The room was immense, with a triangular window from roof to floor jutting out over the fields like a ship's prow, and a high curved ceiling of pale pine. The furniture was scant and very modern. The room looked, in fact, more like a musician's studio than a sitting-room. Against the wall was a jangle of music stands and violin cases and, mounted above them, a bank of modern and obviously expensive stereo equipment. There was only one picture, a Sidney Nolan oil of Ned Kelly. The faceless metallic mask, with the two anonymous eyes gleaming through the slit, was appropriate to the austerity of the room, the stark blackness of the darkening fens. It was easy to imagine him, a grim latter-day Hereward, striding over the clogging acres.

Domenica Schofield was standing at a drawing desk placed in the middle of the room. She turned, unsmilingly, to look at them with her brother's eyes, and Dalgliesh encountered again those disconcerting pools of blue under the thick, curved brows. As always, in those increasingly rare moments when, unexpectedly, he came face to face with a beautiful woman, his heart jerked. It was a pleasure more sensual than sexual and he was glad that he could still feel it, even in the middle of a murder investigation.

But he wondered how studied was that smooth deliberate turn, that first gaze, remote yet speculative, from the remarkable eyes. In this light, the irises, like those of her brother, were almost purple, the whites stained with a paler blue. She had a pale, honey-coloured skin, with flaxen hair drawn back from the forehead and tied in a clump at the base of her neck. Her blue jeans were pulled tightly over the strong thighs and were topped with an open-necked shirt of checkered blue and green. Dalgliesh judged her to be about ten years younger than her half-brother. When she spoke, her voice was curiously low for a woman, with a hint of gruffness.

'Sit down.' She waved her right hand vaguely towards one of the chrome and leather chairs. 'You don't mind if I go on working?'

'Not if you don't mind being talked to while you do, and if you don't object to my sitting while you stand.'

He swung the chair closer to her easel, from where he could see both her face and her work, and settled himself. The chair was remarkably comfortable. He sensed that already she was regretting her lack of civility. In any confrontation the one standing has a psychological advantage, but not if the adversary is sitting very obviously at ease in a spot he has himself selected. Massingham, with an almost ostentatious quietness, had lifted a second chair for himself and placed it against the wall to the left of the door. She must have been aware of his presence at her back, but she gave no sign. She could hardly object to a situation she had herself contrived, but, as if sensing that the interview had started unpropitiously, she said:

'I'm sorry to seem so obsessively busy, but I have a deadline to meet. My brother's probably told you that I'm illustrating a new edition of Crabbe's poems for the Paradine Press. This drawing is for "Procrastination" – Dinah among her curious trifles.'

Dalgliesh had known that she must be a competent professional artist to have gained the commission, but he was impressed by the sensitivity and assurance of the line-drawing before him. It was remarkably detailed but unfinicky, a highly decorative and beautifully composed balance of the girl's slender figure and Crabbe's carefully enumerated objects of desire. They were all there, meticulously drawn: the figured wallpapers, the rose carpet, the mounted stag's head and the jewelled, enamelled clock. It was, he thought, a very English illustration of the most English of poets. She was taking trouble with the period details. On the right-hand wall was mounted a cork board on which was pinned what were obviously preliminary sketches: a tree, half-finished interiors, articles of furniture, small impressions of landscape. She said:

'It's as well one doesn't have to like a poet's work to illustrate him competently. Who was it called Crabbe "Pope in worsted stockings"? After twenty lines my brain begins to thud in rhymed couplets. But perhaps you're an Augustan. You write verse, don't you?'

She made it sound as if he collected cigarette cards for a hobby.

Dalgliesh said:

'I've respected Crabbe ever since I read as a boy that Jane Austen said she could have fancied being Mrs Crabbe. When he went to London for the first time he was so poor that he had to pawn all his clothes, and then he spent the money on an edition of Dryden's poems.'

'And you approve of that?'

'I find it appealing.' He quoted:

'"Miseries there were, and woes the world around,
But these had not her pleasant dwelling found;
She knew that mothers grieved and widows wept
And she was sorry, said her prayers and slept:
For she indulged, nor was her heart so small
That one strong passion should engross it all."'

She gave him a swift elliptical glance.

'In this case there is happily no mother to grieve nor widow to weep. And I gave up saying my prayers when I was nine. Or were you only proving that you could quote Crabbe?'

'That, of course,' replied Dalgliesh. 'Actually I came to talk to you about these.'

He took a bundle of the letters out of his coat pocket, opened one of the pages and held it out towards her. He asked:

'This is Lorrimer's handwriting?'

She glanced dismissively at the page.

'Of course. It's a pity he didn't send them. I should have liked to have read them, but not now perhaps.'

'I don't suppose they're so very different from the ones he did post.'

For a moment he thought that she was about to deny receiving any. He thought: 'She's remembered that we can easily check with the postman.' He watched the blue eyes grow wary. She said:

'That's how love ends, not with a bang, but a whimper.'

'Less a whimper than a cry of pain.'

She wasn't working, but stood still, scrutinizing the drawing. She said:

'It's extraordinary how unattractive misery is. He'd have done better to have tried honesty. "It means a lot to me, it doesn't mean very much to you. So why not be generous? It won't cost you anything except an occasional half-hour of your time." I'd have respected him more.'

'But he wasn't asking for a commercial arrangement,' said Dalgliesh. 'He was asking for love.'

'That's something I didn't have to give, and he had no right to expect.'

None of us, thought Dalgliesh, has a right to expect it. But we do. Irrelevantly a phrase of Plutarch fell into his mind. 'Boys throw stones at frogs in sport. But the frogs do not die in sport, they die in earnest.'

'When did you break it off?' he asked.

She looked surprised for a moment.

'I was going to ask you how you knew that I'd done the breaking. But, of course, you've got the letters. I suppose he was whining. I told him that I didn't want to see him again about two months ago. I haven't spoken to him since.'

'Did you give him a reason?'

'No. I'm not sure that there was a reason. Does there have to be? There wasn't another man if that's what you have in mind. What a beautifully simple view you must have of life. I suppose the police work produces a card-index mentality. Victim – Edwin Lorrimer. Crime – Murder. Accused – Domenica Schofield. Motive – Sex. Verdict – Guilty. What a pity that you can't any longer finish it off neatly with Sentence – Death. Let's say I was tired of him.'

'When you'd exhausted his possibilities, sexual and emotional?'

'Say intellectual, rather, if you'll forgive the arrogance. I find that one exhausts the physical possibilities fairly soon, don't you? But if a man has wit, intelligence, and his own peculiar enthusiasms, then there's some kind of purpose in the relationship. I knew a man once who was an authority on seventeenth-century church architecture. We used to drive for miles looking at churches. It was fascinating while it lasted, and I now know quite a lot about the late seventeenth century. That's something on the credit side.'

'Whereas Lorrimer's only intellectual enthusiasms were popular philosophy and forensic science.'

'Forensic biology. He was curiously inhibited about discussing it. The Official Secrets Act was probably engraved on what he would have described as his soul. Besides, he could be boring even about his job. Scientists invariably are, I've discovered. My brother is the only scientist I've ever met who doesn't bore me after the first ten minutes of his company.'

'Where did you make love?'

'That's impertinent. And is it relevant?'

'It could be – to the number of people who knew that you were lovers.'

'No one knew. I don't relish my private affairs being giggled over in the women's loo at Hoggatt's.'

'So no one knew except your brother and yourself?'

They must have decided in advance that it would be stupid and dangerous to deny that Howarth had known. She said:

'I hope you're not going to ask whether he approved.'

'No. I took it for granted that he disapproved.'

'Why the hell should you?' The tone was intended to be light, almost bantering, but Dalgliesh could detect the sharp edge of defensive anger. He said mildly:

'I am merely putting myself in his place. If I had just started a new job, and one of some difficulty, my half-sister's affair with a member of my own staff, and one who probably thought he'd been supplanted, would be a complication I'd prefer to do without.'

'Perhaps you lack my brother's confidence. He didn't need Edwin Lorrimer's support to run his Lab effectively.'

'You brought him here?'

'Seducing one of my brother's staff here in his own house? Had I disliked my brother, it might have given the affair extra piquancy. Towards the end I admit it could have done with it. But as I don't, it would merely have been in poor taste. We both have cars, and his is particularly roomy.'

'I thought that was the expedient of randy adolescents. It must have been uncomfortable and cold.'

'Very cold. Which was another reason for deciding to stop it.' She turned to him with sudden vehemence.

'Look, I'm not trying to shock you. I'm trying to be truthful. I hate death and waste and violence. Who doesn't? But I'm not grieving, in case you thought of offering condolences. There's only one man whose death has grieved me, and it isn't Edwin Lorrimer. And I don't feel responsible. Why should I? I'm not responsible. Even if he killed himself I shouldn't feel that it was my fault. As it is, I don't believe his death had anything to do with me. He might, I suppose, have felt like murdering me. I never had the slightest motive for murdering him.'

'Have you any idea who did?'

'A stranger, I imagine. Someone who broke into the Lab either to plant or to destroy some forensic evidence. Perhaps a drunken driver hoping to get his hands on his blood sample. Edwin surprised him and the intruder killed him.'

'The blood alcohol analysis isn't done in the Biology Department.'

'Then it could have been an enemy, someone with a grudge. Someone he'd given evidence against in the past. After all, he's probably well known in the witness box. Death of an expert witness.'

Dalgliesh said:

'There's the difficulty of how his killer got in and out of the Lab.'

'He probably gained entrance during the day and hid after the place was locked up for the night. I leave it to you to discover how he got away. Perhaps he slipped out after the Lab had been opened for the morning during the kerfuffle after that girl – Pridmore, isn't it? – discovered the body. I don't suppose that anyone was keeping an eye on the front door.'

'And the false telephone call to Mrs Bidwell?'

'Probably no connection, I'd say. Just someone trying to be funny. She's probably too scared to admit what happened. I should question the junior female staff of the Lab if I were you. It's the kind of joke a rather unintelligent adolescent might find amusing.'

Dalgliesh went on to ask her about her movements on the previous evening. She said that she hadn't accompanied her brother to the concert, having a dislike of rustic junketing, no wish to hear the Mozart indifferently played, and a couple of drawings to complete. They'd had an early supper at about six forty-five, and Howarth had left home at seven-twenty. She had continued working uninterrupted either by a telephone call or a visitor until her brother returned shortly after ten, when he had told her about his evening over a shared nightcap of hot whisky. Both of them had then gone early to bed.

She volunteered without being asked that her brother had seemed perfectly normal on his return, although both of them had been tired. He had attended a murder scene the night before and had lost some hours' sleep. She did occasionally make use of Mrs Bidwell, for example before and after a dinner party she and Howarth had given soon after their arrival, but certainly wouldn't call on her on a day when she was due at the Lab.

Dalgliesh asked:

'Did your brother tell you that he left the concert for a time after the interval?'

'He told me that he sat on a tombstone for about half an hour contemplating mortality. I imagine that, at that stage of the proceedings, he found the dead more entertaining than the living.'

Dalgliesh looked up at the immense curved wooden ceiling. He said:

'This place must be expensive to keep warm in winter. How is it heated?'

Again there was that swift elliptical flash of blue.

'By gas central heating. There isn't an open fire. That's one of the things we miss. So we couldn't have burnt Paul Middlemass's white coat. Actually, we'd have been fools to try. The most sensible plan would be to weigh it down with stones in the pockets and sling it into Leamings' sluice. You'd probably dredge it up in the end, but I don't see how that would help you to discover who put it there. That's what I would have done.'

'No, you wouldn't,' said Dalgliesh mildly. 'There weren't any pockets.'

She didn't offer to see them out, but Howarth was waiting for them at the foot of the stairs. Dalgliesh said:

'You didn't tell me that your sister was Lorrimer's mistress. Did you really convince yourself that it wasn't relevant?'

'To his death? Why should it be? It may have been relevant to his life. I very much doubt whether it was to hers. And I'm not my sister's keeper. She's capable of speaking for herself, as you've probably discovered.'

He walked with them out to the car, punctilious as a host speeding a couple of unwelcome guests. Dalgliesh said, his hand on the car door:

'Does the number 1840 mean anything to you?'

'In what context?'

'Any you choose.'

Howarth said calmly:

'Whewell published *Philosophy of the Inductive Sciences*; Tchaikovsky was born; Berlioz composed the *Symphonie Funèbre et Triomphale.* I think that's the limit of my knowledge of an unremarkable year. Or if you want a different context, the ratio of the mass of the proton to the mass of the electron.'

Massingham called from the other side of the Rover:

'I thought that was 1836, unless you're not fussy about rounding up. Good-night, sir.'

As they turned out of the drive, Dalgliesh asked:

'How do you come to remember that remarkably irrelevant piece of information?'

'From school. We may have been disadvantaged when it came to social mix, but the teaching wasn't bad. It's a figure which sticks in the mind.'

'Not in mine. What did you think of Mrs Schofield?'

'I didn't expect her to be like that.'

'As attractive, as talented, or as arrogant?'

'All three. Her face reminds me of someone, an actress. French I think.'

'Simone Signoret when she was young. I'm surprised that you're old enough to remember.'

'I saw a revival last year of *Casque d'Or*.'

Dalgliesh said: 'She told us at least one small lie.'

Apart, thought Massingham, from the one major lie which she may or may not have told. He was experienced enough to know that it was the central lie, the affirmation of innocence, which was the most difficult to detect, and the small, ingenious fabrications, so often unnecessary, which in the end confused and betrayed.

'Sir?'

'About where she and Lorrimer made love, in the back of his car. I don't believe that. Do you?'

It was rare for Dalgliesh to question a subordinate so directly. Massingham disconcertingly felt himself under test. He gave careful thought before replying.

'Psychologically it could be wrong. She's a fastidious, comfort-loving woman with a high opinion of her own dignity. And she must have watched the body of her husband being pulled from the wreckage of their car after that accident when she'd been driving. Somehow I don't think she'd fancy sex in the back of anyone's car. Unless, of course, she's trying to exorcize the memory. It could be that.'

Dalgliesh smiled. 'Actually I was thinking on less esoteric lines. A scarlet Jaguar, and the latest model, is hardly the most inconspicuous vehicle for driving round the country with a lover. And old Mr Lorrimer said that his son hardly left home in the evenings or at night, unless to a murder scene. These are unpredictable. On the other hand he was frequently late at the Lab. Not all the lateness could have been work. I think that he and Mrs Schofield had a rendezvous somewhere fairly close.'

'You think it important, sir?'

'Important enough to cause her to lie. Why should she care if we know where they chose to disport themselves? I could understand it if she told us to mind our own business. But why bother to lie? There was another moment, too, when very briefly she lost composure. It was when she talked about seventeenth-century church architecture. I got the impression that there was a small, almost undetectable moment of confusion when she realized that she'd stumbled into saying something indiscreet, or at least something she wished unsaid. When the interviews are out of the way tomorrow, I think we'll take a look at the chapel at Hoggatt's.'

'But Sergeant Reynolds had a look at it this morning, sir, after he'd searched the grounds. It's just a locked, empty chapel. He found nothing.'

'Probably because there's nothing to find. It's just a hunch. Now we'd better get back to Guy's Marsh for that Press conference and then I must have a word with the Chief Constable if he's back. After that I'd like to see Brenda Pridmore again; and I want to call later at the Old Rectory for a word with Dr Kerrison. But that can wait until we've seen what Mrs Gotobed at the Moonraker can do about dinner.'

VI

Twenty minutes later, in the kitchen at Leamings, an incongruous compromise between a laboratory and rustic domesticity, Howarth was mixing *sauce vinaigrette*. The sickly, pungent smell of the olive oil, curving in a thin golden stream from the bottle, brought back, as always, memories of Italy and of his father, that dilettante collector of trivia, who had spent most of each year in Tuscany or Venice, and whose self-indulgent, hypochondriacal, solitary life had ended, appropriately enough since he affected to dread old age, on his fiftieth birthday. He had been less a stranger to his two motherless children than an enigma, seldom with them in person, always present mysteriously to their minds.

Maxim recalled a memory of his dressing-gowned figure, patterned in mauve and gold, standing at the foot of his bed on that extraordinary night of muted voices, sudden running footsteps, inexplicable silences in which his stepmother had died. He had been home from prep-school for the holidays, eight years old. Ignored in the crisis of the illness, frightened and alone. He remembered clearly his father's thin, rather weary voice, already assuming the languors of grief.

'Your stepmother died ten minutes ago, Maxim. Evidently fate does not intend me to be a husband. I shall not again risk such grief. You, my boy, must look after your stepsister. I rely on you.' And then a cold hand casually laid on his shoulder as if conferring a burden. He had accepted it, literally, at eight years old, and had never laid it down. At first the immensity of the trust had appalled him. He remembered how he had lain there, terrified, staring into the darkness. Look after your sister. Domenica was three months old. How could he look after her? What ought he to feed her on? How dress her? What about his prep-school? They wouldn't let him stay at home to look after his sister. He smiled wryly, remembering his relief at discovering next morning that her nurse was, after all, to remain. He recalled his first efforts to assume responsibility, resolutely seizing the pram handles and straining to push it up the Broad Walk, struggling to lift Domenica into her high chair.

'Give over, Master Maxim, do. You're more of a hindrance than a help.'

But afterwards the nurse had begun to realize that he was becoming more of a help than a nuisance, that the child could safely be left with him while she and the only other servant pursued their own unsupervised devices. Most of his school holidays had been spent helping to look after Domenica. From Rome, Verona, Florence and Venice his father, through his solicitor, sent instructions about allowances and schools. It was he who helped buy the clothes, took her to school, comforted and advised. He had attempted to support her through the agonies and uncertainties of adolescence, even before he had outgrown his own. He had been her champion against the world. He smiled, remembering the telephone call to Cambridge from her boarding school, asking him to fetch her that very night 'outside the hockey pavilion – gruesome torture house – at midnight. I'll climb down the fire escape. Promise.' And then their private code of defiance and allegiance: *'Contra mundum.'*

'Contra mundum.'

His father's arrival from Italy, so little perturbed by the Reverend Mother's insistent summons that it was obvious that he had, in any case, been planning to return.

'Your sister's departure was unnecessarily eccentric, surely. Midnight assignation. Dramatic car drive across half England. Mother Superior seemed particularly pained that she had left her trunk behind, although I can appreciate that it would have been an encumbrance on the fire escape. And you must have been out of college all night. Your tutor can't have liked that.'

'I'm post-graduate now, Father. I took my degree eighteen months ago.'

'Indeed. Time passes so quickly at my age. Physics, wasn't it? A curious choice. Couldn't you have called for her after school in the orthodox way?'

'We wanted to get as far away from the place as possible before they noticed she'd gone and started looking.'

'A reasonable strategy, so far as it goes.'

'Dom hates school, Father. She's utterly miserable there.'

'So was I at school, but it never occurred to me to expect otherwise. Reverend Mother seems a charming woman. A tendency to halitosis when under stress, but I shouldn't have thought that would have troubled your sister. They can hardly have come into intimate contact. She isn't prepared to have Domenica back, by the way.'

'Need Dom go anywhere, Father? She's nearly fifteen. She doesn't have to go to school. And she wants to be a painter.'

'I suppose she could stay at home until she's old enough for art college, if that's what you advise. But it's hardly worth opening the London house just for one. I shall return to Venice next week. I'm only here to consult Dr Mavers-Brown.'

'Perhaps she could go back to Italy with you for a month or so. She'd love to see the Accademia. And she ought to see Florence.'

'Oh, I don't think that would do, my boy. Quite out of the question. She had much better take a room at Cambridge and you can keep an eye on her. They have some quite agreeable pictures in the Fitzwilliam Museum. Oh dear, what a responsibility children are! It's quite wrong that I should be troubled like this in my state of health. Mavers-Brown was insistent that I avoid anxiety.'

And now he lay coffined in his final self-sufficiency, in that most beautiful of burial grounds, the British Cemetery in Rome. He would have liked that, thought Maxim, if he could have borne the thought of his death at all, as much as he would have resented the over-aggressive Italian drivers whose ill-judged acceleration at the junction of the Via Vittoria and the Corso had placed him there.

He heard his sister's steps on the stairs.

'So they've gone.'

'Twenty minutes ago. We had a brief valedictory skirmish. Was Dalgliesh offensive?

'No more offensive than I to him. Honours even, I should have said. I don't think he liked me.'

'I don't think he likes anyone much. But he's considered highly intelligent. Did you find him attractive?'

She answered the unspoken question.

'It would be like making love to a public hangman.'

She dipped her finger in the vinaigrette dressing.

'Too much vinegar. What have you been doing?'

'Apart from cooking? Thinking about father. Do you know, Dom, when I was eleven I became absolutely convinced that he'd murdered our mothers.'

'Both of them? I mean yours and mine? What an odd idea. How could he have? Yours died of cancer and mine of pneumonia. He couldn't have fixed that.'

'I know. It's just that he seemed such a natural widower. I thought at the time that he'd done it to stop them having any more babies.'

'Well it would do that all right. Were you wondering whether a tendency to murder is inherited?'

'Not really. But so much is. Father's total inability to make relationships, for example. That incredible self-absorption. Do you know, he'd actually put me down for Stonyhurst before he remembered that it was your mother, not mine, who'd been RC.'

'A pity he did find out. I should like to have seen what the Jesuits made of you. The trouble with a religious education, if you're a pagan like me, is that you're left all your life feeling that you've lost something, not that it isn't there.'

She walked over to the table and stirred a bowl of mushrooms with her finger.

'I can make relationships. The trouble is that I get bored and they don't last. And I only seem to know one way to be kind. It's as well that we last, isn't it? You'll last for me until the day I die. Shall I change now or do you want me to see to the wine?'

'You'll last for me until the day I die.' *Contra mundum*. It was too late now to sever that cord even if he wanted to. He remembered Charles Schofield's gauze-cocooned head, the dying eyes still malicious behind two slits in the bandages, the swollen lips painfully moving.

'Congratulations, Giovanni. Remember me in your garden in Parma.'

What had been so astounding was not the lie itself, or that Schofield had believed it, or pretended to believe it, but that he had hated his brother-in-law enough to die with that taunt on his lips. Or had he taken it for granted that a physicist, poor philistine, wouldn't know his Jacobean dramatists? Even his wife, that indefatigable sexual sophisticate, had known better.

'I suppose you'd sleep together if Domenica happened to want it. A spot of incest wouldn't worry her. But you don't need to, do you? You don't need anything as normal as sex to be more to each other than you are. Neither of you wants anyone else. That's why I'm leaving. I'm getting out now while there's still something left of me to get out.'

'Max, what is it?'

Domenica's voice, sharpened with anxiety, recalled him to the present. His mind spun back through a kaleidoscope of spinning years, through superimposed swirling images of childhood and youth, to that last unforgettable image, still, perfectly in focus, patterned for ever in his memory, Lorrimer's dead fingers clawing at the floor of his laboratory, Lorrimer's dull, half-open eye, Lorrimer's blood. He said:

'You get changed. I'll see to the wine.'

VII

'What will people say?'

'That's all you ever think of, Mum, what will people say. What does it matter what they say? I haven't done anything to be ashamed of.'

'Of course not. If anyone says different your dad'll soon put them right. But you know what tongues they have in this village. A thousand pounds. I couldn't hardly believe it when that solicitor rang. It's a tidy sum. And by the time Lillie Pearce has passed the news around in the Stars and Plough it'll be ten thousand, more than likely.'

'Who cares about Lillie Pearce, silly old cow.'

'Brenda! I won't have that language. And we have to live in this village.'

'You may have to. I don't. And if that's the kind of minds they've got the sooner I move away the better. Oh, Mum, don't look like that! He only wanted to help me, he wanted to be kind. And he probably did it on impulse.'

'Not very considerate of him, though, was it? He might have talked it over with your dad or me.'

'But he didn't know that he was going to die.'

Brenda and her mother were alone in the farmhouse, Arthur Pridmore having left after supper for the monthly meeting of the Parochial Church Council. The washing-up was finished and the long evening stretched before them. Too restless to settle to the television and too preoccupied with the extraordinary events of the day to take up a book, they sat in the firelight, edgy, half excited and half afraid, missing Arthur Pridmore's reassuring bulk in his high-backed chair. Then Mrs Pridmore shook herself into normality and reached for her sewing basket.

'Well, at least it will help towards a nice wedding. If you have to take it, better put it in the Post Office. Then it'll add interest and be there when you want it.'

'I want it now. For books and a microscope like Dr Lorrimer intended. That's why he left it to me and that's what I'm going to do with it. Besides, if people leave money for a special purpose you can't use it for something else. And I don't want to. I'm going to ask Dad to put up a shelf and a work-bench in my bedroom and I'll start working for my science 'A' levels straight away.'

'He ought not to have thought of you. What about Angela Foley? She's had a terrible life, that girl. She never got a penny from her grandmother's will, and now this.'

'That's not our concern, Mum. It was up to him. Maybe he might have left it to her if they hadn't rowed.'

'How do you mean, rowed? When?'

'Last week sometime. Tuesday it was, I think. It was just before I came home and most of the staff had left. Inspector Blakelock sent me up to Biology with a query on one of the court reports. They were together in Dr Lorrimer's room and I heard them quarrelling. She was asking him for money and he said he wouldn't give her any and then he said something about changing his will.'

'You mean you stood there listening?'

'Well I couldn't help it, could I? They were talking quite loudly. He was saying terrible things about Stella Mawson, you know, that writer Angela Foley lives with. I wasn't eavesdropping on purpose. I didn't want to hear.'

'You could have gone away.'

'And come up again all the way from the front hall? Anyway, I had to ask him about the report for the Munnings case. I couldn't go back and tell Inspector Blakelock that I hadn't got the answer because Dr Lorrimer was having a row with his cousin. Besides, we always listened to secrets at school.'

'You're not at school now. Really, Brenda, you worry me sometimes. One moment you behave like a sensible adult, and the next anyone would think you were back in the fourth form. You're eighteen now, an adult. What has school to do with it?'

'I don't know why you're getting so het-up. I didn't tell anyone.'

'Well, you'll have to tell that detective from Scotland Yard.'

'Mum! I can't! It hasn't got anything to do with the murder.'

'Who's to say? You're supposed to tell the police anything that's important. Didn't he tell you that?'

He told her exactly that. Brenda remembered his look, her own guilty blush. He had known that she was keeping something back. She said, with stubborn defiance:

'Well, I can't accuse Angela Foley of murder, or as good as accuse her anyway. Besides,' she proclaimed triumphantly, remembering something Inspector Blakelock had told her, 'it would be hearsay, not proper evidence. He couldn't take any notice of it. And, Mum, there's another thing. Suppose she didn't really expect him to alter the will so soon? That solicitor told you that Dr Lorrimer made the new will last Friday, didn't he? Well that was probably because he had to go to a scene of crime in Ely on Friday morning. The police call only came through at ten o'clock. He must have gone into his solicitors then.'

'What do you mean?'

'Nothing. Only if people think that I had a motive, then so did she.'

'Of course you didn't have a motive! That's ridiculous. It's wicked! Oh, Brenda, if only you'd come to the concert with Dad and me.'

'No thank you. Miss Spencer singing "Pale Hands I Loved", and the Sunday School kids doing their boring old Maypole dance, and the W.I. with their hand-bells, and old Mr Matthews bashing away with the acoustic spoons. I've seen it all before.'

'But you'd have had an alibi.'

'So I would if you and Dad had stayed here at home with me.'

'It wouldn't have mattered where you'd been if it weren't for that thousand pounds. Well, let's hope Gerald Bowlem understands.'

'If he doesn't, he knows what he can do! I don't see what it's got to do with Gerald. I'm not married to him, nor engaged for that matter. He'd better not interfere.'

She looked across at her mother and was suddenly appalled. She had only seen her look like this once before, the night when she had had her second miscarriage and had been told by old Dr

Greene that there could never now be another baby. Brenda had only been twelve at the time. But her mother's face, suddenly remembered, had looked exactly as it did now, as if an obliterating hand had passed over it, wiping off brightness, blunting the contours of cheek and brow, dulling the eyes, leaving an amorphous mask of desolation.

She remembered and understood what before she had only felt, the anger and resentment that her mother, indestructible and comforting as a great rock in a weary land, should herself be vulnerable to pain. She was there to soothe Brenda's miseries, not to suffer herself, to comfort, not to seek comfort. But now Brenda was older and she was able to understand. She saw her mother clearly, like a stranger newly met. The cheap Crimplene dress, spotlessly clean as always, with the brooch Brenda had given her for her last birthday pinned to the lapel. The ankles thickening above the sensible low-heel shoes, the pudgy hands speckled with the brown stains of age, the wedding ring of dull gold biting into the flesh, the curly hair that had once been red-gold like her own, still brushed plainly to one side and held in a tortoiseshell slide, the fresh, almost unlined skin. She put her arms round her mother's shoulders.

'Oh, Mum, don't worry. It'll be all right. Commander Dalgliesh will find out who did it and then everything will be back to normal. Look, I'll make you some cocoa. Don't let's wait till Dad's back from the P.C.C. We'll have it now. Mum, it's all right. Really it is. It's all right.'

Simultaneously their ears caught the hum of the approaching car. They gazed at each other, speechless, guilty as conspirators. This wasn't their ancient Morris. And how could it be? The Parochial Church Council never finished their business before half past eight.

Brenda went to the window and peered out. The car stopped. She turned to her mother, white-faced.

'It's the police! It's Commander Dalgliesh!'

Without a word, Mrs Pridmore got resolutely to her feet. She placed a hand briefly on her daughter's shoulder, then went out into the passage and opened the door before Massingham had lifted his hand to knock. She said through stiff lips:

'Come in please. I'm glad that you're here. Brenda has something to tell you, something that I think you ought to know.'

VIII

The day was nearly over. Sitting in his dressing-gown at the small table in front of the window in his bedroom at the Moonraker, Dalgliesh heard the church clock strike half past eleven. He liked his room. It was the larger of the two which Mrs Gotobed had been able to offer. The single window looked out over the churchyard towards the village hall and beyond it the clerestory and square flint tower of St Nicholas's Church. There were only three rooms for guests at the inn. The smallest and noisiest, since it was over the public bar, had fallen to Massingham. The main guest-room had already been taken by an American couple touring East Anglia, perhaps in search of family records. They had sat at their table in the dining-parlour, happily occupied with maps and guidebooks, and if they had been told that their newly arrived fellow guests were police officers investigating a murder, they were too well bred to betray interest. After a brief smile and a good-evening in their soft transatlantic voices they had turned their attention again to Mrs Gotobed's excellent casserole of hare in cider.

It was very quiet. The muted voices from the bar had long since been silent. It was over an hour since he had heard the last shouted goodbyes. Massingham, he knew, had spent the evening in the public bar hoping, presumably, to pick up scraps of useful information. Dalgliesh hoped that the beer had been good. He had been born close enough to the fens to know that, otherwise, Massingham would have found it a frustrating evening.

He got up to stretch his legs and shoulders, looking around with approval at the room. The floorboards were of ancient oak, black and stout as ship's timbers. A fire of wood and turf burned in the iron Victorian grate, the pungent smoke curtseying under a decorated hood of wheat-ears and flower-posies tied with ribbons. The large double bed was of brass, high and ornate with four great knobs, large as polished cannon-balls, at the corners. Mrs Gotobed had earlier folded back the crocheted cover to reveal a feather mattress shaken to an inviting plumpness. In any four-star hotel he might have enjoyed greater luxury, but hardly such comfort.

He returned to his work. It had been a crowded day of interrogation and renewed interrogation, telephone calls to London, a hurriedly arranged and unsatisfactory Press conference, two consultations with the Chief Constable, the gathering of those odd-shaped pieces of information and conjecture which, in the end, would click together to form the completed picture. It might be a trite analogy, this comparison of detection with fitting together a jigsaw. But it was remarkably apt, not least because it was so often that tantalizing elusive piece with the vital segment of a human face that made the picture complete.

He turned the page to the last interview of the day, with Henry Kerrison at the Old Rectory. The smell of the house was still in his nostrils, an evocative smell of stale cooking and furniture polish, reminding him of childhood visits with his parents to over-large, ill-heated country vicarages. Kerrison's housekeeper and children had long been in bed and the house had held a melancholy, brooding silence as if all the tragedies and disappointments of its numerous incumbents still hung in the air.

Kerrison had answered the door himself and had shown him and Massingham into his study where he was occupied in sorting coloured slides of post-mortem injuries to illustrate a lecture he was to give the following week to the detection training school. On the desk was a framed photograph of himself as a boy with an older man, obviously his father. They were standing on a crag, climbing-ropes slung round their shoulders. What interested Dalgliesh as much as the photograph itself was the fact that Kerrison hadn't bothered to remove it.

He hadn't appeared to resent his visitors' late arrival. It was possible to believe that he welcomed their company. He had worked on in the light of his desk-lamp, fitting each slide into his view, then sorting it into the appropriate heap, intent as a schoolboy with a hobby. He had answered their questions quietly and precisely, but as if his mind were elsewhere. Dalgliesh asked him whether his daughter had talked to him about the incident with Lorrimer.

'Yes, she did tell me. When I got home for lunch from my lecture I found her crying in her room. It seems that Lorrimer was unnecessarily harsh. But Nell is a sensitive child and it's not always possible to know the precise truth of the matter.'

'You didn't talk to him about it?'

'I didn't talk to anyone. I did wonder whether I ought to, but it would have meant questioning Inspector Blakelock and Miss Pridmore, and I didn't wish to involve them. They had to work with Lorrimer. So, for that matter, did I. The effectiveness of an isolated institution like Hoggatt's largely depends on good relationships between the staff. I thought it was best not to take the matter further. That may have been prudence, or it may have been cowardice. I don't know.'

He had smiled sadly, and added:

'I only know that it wasn't a motive for murder.'

A motive for murder. Dalgliesh had discovered enough motive in this crowded but not very satisfactory day. But motive was the least important factor in a murder investigation. He would gladly have exchanged the psychological subtleties of motive for a single, solid, incontrovertible piece of physical evidence linking a suspect with the crime. And, so far, there was none. He still awaited the report from the Metropolitan Laboratory on the mallet and the vomit. The mysterious figure seen by old Goddard fleeing from Hoggatt's remained mysterious; no other person had yet been traced or had come forward to suggest that he wasn't a figment of the old man's imagination. The tyre-marks near the gate, now definitely identified from the tyre index at the laboratory, still hadn't been linked to a car. Not surprisingly, no trace had been found of Middlemass's white coat and no indication whether or how it had been disposed of. An examination of the village hall and the hobby-horse costumes had produced nothing to disprove Middlemass's account of his evening and it was apparent that the horse, a heavy all-enveloping contraption of canvas and serge, ensured that its wearer would be unidentifiable even, in Middlemass's case, to his elegant hand-made shoes.

The central mysteries of the case remained. Who was it who had telephoned the message to Lorrimer about the can being burned and the number 1840? Was it the same woman who had rung Mrs Bidwell? What had been written on the missing sheet from Lorrimer's rough notebook? What had prompted Lorrimer to make that extraordinary will?

Lifting his head from the files, he listened. There was a noise, faintly discernible, like the creeping of a myriad insects. He remembered it from his childhood nights, lying awake in the nursery of his father's Norfolk vicarage, a sound he had never heard in the noise of cities, the first gentle sibilant whisper of the night rain. Soon it was followed by a spatter of drops against the window and the rising moan of the wind in the chimney. The fire spluttered and then flared into sudden brightness. There was a violent flurry of rain against the pane and then, as quickly as it had begun, the brief storm was over. He opened the window to savour the smell of the damp night air, and gazed out into a blanket of darkness, black fen earth merging with the paler sky.

As his eyes became accustomed to the night, he could discern the low rectangle of the village hall and, beyond it, the great medieval tower of the church. Then the moon sailed out from behind the clouds and the churchyard became visible, the obelisks and gravestones gleaming pale as if they exuded their own mysterious light. Below him, faintly luminous, lay the gravel path along which, the previous night, the morris-dancers, bells jangling, had made their way through the rising mist. Staring out over the churchyard he pictured the hobby-horse pawing the ground to meet them, rearing its grotesque head among the gravestones and snapping the air with its great jaws. And he wondered again who had been inside its skin.

The door beneath his window opened and Mrs Gotobed appeared and crooned into the darkness, enticing in her cat: 'Snowball! Snowball! Good boy now.' There was a flash of white, and the door was closed. Dalgliesh latched his window and decided that he, too, would call it a day.

BOOK FOUR

Hanged by the Neck

I

Sprogg's Cottage, low-built and top-heavy under its low, occluding roof of thatch, wire-netted, strong against the fen winter gales, was almost invisible from the road. It lay about three-quarters of a mile north-east from the village and was fronted by Sprogg's Green, a wide triangular grass verge planted with willows. Pushing open the white wicker gate on which someone had optimistically but fruitlessly substituted the word 'Lavender' for Sprogg's, Dalgliesh and Massingham stepped into a front garden as brightly ordered and conventional as that of a suburban villa. An acacia tree in the middle of the lawn flaunted its autumn glory of red and gold, the yellow climbing roses trained over the door still gleamed with a faint illusion of summer and a massed bed of geraniums, fuchsia and dahlias, supported by stakes and carefully tended, flared in discordant glory against the bronze of the beech hedge. There was a hanging basket of pink geraniums beside the door, now past their best, but still bright with a few tattered blooms. The knocker was a highly polished brass fish, every scale gleaming.

The door was opened by a slight, almost fragile woman, bare-footed and wearing a cotton overblouse, patterned in greens and brown, above her corduroy slacks. She had coarse dark hair strongly streaked with grey and worn in a short bob, with a heavy fringe which curved low to meet her eyebrows. Her eyes were her most remarkable feature, immense, the irises brown speckled with green, translucently clear under the strongly curved brows. Her face was pale and taut, deeply etched with lines across the forehead and running from the widely springing nostrils to the corners of the mouth. It was the face, thought Dalgliesh, of a tortured masochist in a medieval triptych, the muscles bulging and knotted as if they had been racked. But no one coming under the gaze of those remarkable eyes could call it plain or ordinary. Dalgliesh said:

'Miss Mawson? I'm Adam Dalgliesh. This is Inspector Massingham.'

She gave him a direct, impersonal gaze and said without smiling:

'Come through into the study, will you? We don't light the sitting-room fire until the evening. If you want to speak to Angela, I'm afraid she's not here at present. She's over at Postmill Cottage with Mrs Swaffield meeting the Social Security people. They're trying to persuade old Lorrimer to go into an old people's home. Apparently he's being obstinately resistant to the blandishments of bureaucracy. Good luck to him.'

The front door opened directly into a sitting-room with a low, oak-beamed ceiling. The room surprised him. To enter it was like walking into an antique shop, but one where the proprietor had arranged his oddly assorted wares with an eye to the general effect. The mantelshelf and every ledge bore an ornament, three hanging cupboards held a variety of mugs, teapots, painted jugs and Staffordshire figures, and the walls were almost covered with prints, framed old maps, small oil-paintings and Victorian silhouettes in oval frames. Above the fireplace was the most spectacular object, a curved sword with a finely wrought scabbard. He wondered whether the room reflected merely an indiscriminate acquisitiveness, or whether these carefully disposed objects served as comforting talismans against the alien, undomesticated spirits of the encroaching fens. A wood fire was laid but not lit in the open hearth. Under the window a polished gate-legged table was already laid for two.

Miss Mawson led the way through to her study. It was a smaller, less cluttered room at the back with a latticed window giving a view of a stone terrace, a lawn with a sundial in the middle, and a wide field of sugar beet, still unharvested. He saw with interest that she wrote by hand. There was a typewriter, but it stood on a table by itself. The working-desk under the window held only a pad of unlined paper, covered with a black upright holograph in an elegant italic. The lines were carefully patterned on the paper, and even the marginal alterations were aligned.

Dalgliesh said:

'I'm sorry if we're interrupting your work.'

'You aren't. Sit down, won't you both. It isn't going well this morning. If it were I should have hung a "don't disturb" notice on the knocker and you wouldn't have got in. Still, it's nearly finished; only one chapter to do now. I suppose you want me to give Angela an alibi. Helping the police, isn't it called? What were we doing on Wednesday night; and when, and why, and where, and with whom?'

'We would like to ask you some questions, certainly.'

'But that one first, presumably. There's no difficulty. We spent the evening and night together from six-fifteen, which was the time she arrived home.'

'Doing what, Miss Mawson?'

'What we normally do. We separated the day from the evening, me with whisky, Angela with sherry. I asked about her day and she inquired about mine. Then she lit the fire and cooked the meal. We had avocado pear with *sauce vinaigrette*, chicken casserole and cheese and biscuits. We washed up together and then Angela typed my manuscript for me until nine. At nine we turned on the television and watched the news, followed by the play. That brought us to ten forty-five, cocoa for Angela, whisky for me, and bed.'

'Neither of you left the cottage?'

'No.'

Dalgliesh asked how long she had lived in the village.

'Me? Eight years. I was born in the fens – at Soham actually – and spent most of my childhood here. But I went up to London University when I was eighteen, took a second-class degree, and then worked, not particularly successfully, at various jobs in journalism and publishing. I came here eight years ago when I heard that the cottage was to let. That's when I first decided to give up my job and become a full-time writer.'

'And Miss Foley?'

'She came to live here two years ago. I advertised locally for a part-time typist and she replied. She was living in lodgings at Ely then and wasn't particularly happy there, so I suggested that she moved in. She had to depend on the bus to get to work. Living here is obviously much more convenient for the Lab.'

'So you've lived long enough in the village to get to know people?'

'As much as one ever does in the fens. But not well enough to point the finger at a murderer for you.'

'How well did you know Dr Lorrimer?'

'By sight. I wasn't told that Angela was his cousin until she came to live with me. They're not close and he never came here. I've met most of the Lab staff, of course. Dr Howarth started a string quartet soon after he arrived, and last August they gave a concert in the Wren chapel. Afterwards there was wine and cheese in the vestry. I met a number of the staff then. Actually, I already knew them by sight and name, as one does in a village. We use the same post office and the same pub. But if you're hoping for village and Lab gossip, it's no use coming to me.'

Dalgliesh said:

'Was the concert in the chapel successful?'

'Not particularly. Howarth is a very fine amateur violinist and Claire Easterbrook is a competent cellist, but the other two weren't up to much. He hasn't repeated the experiment. I gather that there was a certain amount of unkind comment about a new arrival who saw it as his duty to civilize the underprivileged natives, and it may have got to his ears. He does rather give the impression that he sees himself as bridging single-handed the culture-gap between the scientist and the artist. Or perhaps he wasn't satisfied with the acoustics. My own view is that the other three didn't want to go on playing with him. As a leader of a quartet he probably behaved with much the same arrogance as he does as Director. The Lab is certainly more efficient; the work output is up twenty per cent. Whether the staff are happy is another matter.'

So she wasn't altogether immune to Lab and village gossip, thought Dalgliesh. He wondered why she was being so frank. Equally frank, he asked bluntly:

'When you were at Postmill Cottage yesterday, did you go upstairs?'

'Fancy the old man telling you that! What did he think I was after, I wonder? I went up to the bathroom to see if there was a tin of scouring powder there to clean the sink. There wasn't.'

'You know about Dr Lorrimer's will, of course?'

'I imagine the whole village does. Actually I was probably the first to know. The old man was getting agitated to know whether there was any money coming, so Angela rang the solicitor. She'd met him at the time her grandmother's will was read. He told her that the cottage was to go to the old man with £10,000, so she was able to put his mind at rest.'

'And Miss Foley herself got nothing?'

'That's right. And that a new clerical officer at the Lab, whom Edwin had apparently taken a fancy to, gets a thousand pounds.'

'A not particularly just will.'

'Have you ever known beneficiaries who thought a will was just? His grandmother's will was worse. Angela lost the money then, when it could have made a difference to her life. Now she doesn't need it. We manage perfectly well here.'

'Presumably it wasn't a shock to her. Didn't he tell her of his intentions?'

'If that's meant to be a tactful way of finding out whether she had a motive for murder, you can ask her yourself. Here she is.'

Angela Foley came through the sitting-room, tugging off her head-scarf. Her face darkened at the sight of the visitors and she said with quick defensive annoyance:

'Miss Mawson likes to work in the mornings. You didn't say that you were coming.'

Her friend laughed.

'They haven't worried me. I've been getting a useful insight into police methods. They're effective without being crude. You're back early.'

'The social work department rang to say that they can't get over until after lunch. Uncle doesn't want to see them, but he wants to see me even less. He's having lunch with the Swaffields at the rectory, so I thought I might as well come home.'

Stella Mawson lit a cigarette.

'You've arrived at an opportune time. Mr Dalgliesh was inquiring tactfully whether you had a motive for murdering your cousin: in other words, did Edwin tell you that he was about to alter his will?'

Angela Foley looked at Dalgliesh and said calmly:

'No. He never discussed his affairs with me and I didn't discuss mine with him. I don't think I've spoken to him during the last two years except about Lab business.'

Dalgliesh said:

'It's surprising, surely, that he should want to change a long-standing will without talking to you about it?'

She shrugged, and then explained:

'It was nothing to do with me. He was only my cousin, not my brother. He transferred to Hoggatt's from the Southern Laboratory five years ago to live with his father, not because I was here. He didn't really know me. If he had, I doubt whether he would have liked me. He owed me nothing, not even justice.'

'Did you like him?'

She paused and thought, as if the question was one to which she herself wanted an answer. Stella Mawson, eyes narrowed, regarded her through the cigarette smoke. Then Miss Foley spoke:

'No, I didn't like him. I think I was even a little afraid of him. He was like a man psychologically burdened, unsure of his place in life. Lately the tension and unhappiness were almost palpable. I found it embarrassing and, well, somehow menacing. People who were really secure in their own personalities didn't seem to notice or be bothered by it. But the less secure felt threatened. I think that's why Clifford Bradley was so afraid of him.'

Stella Mawson said:

'Bradley probably reminded Edwin of himself when he was young. He was painfully insecure, even in his job, when he first started. D'you remember how he used to practise his evidence on the night before he went into the box; writing down all the possible questions the opposing counsel might ask, making sure that he was word perfect with the answers, learning all the scientific formulae by heart to impress the jury? He made a mess of one of his first cases, and never forgave himself.'

There was a strange little silence. Angela Foley seemed about to speak, then changed her mind. Her enigmatic gaze was fixed on her friend. Stella Mawson's eyes shifted. She walked over to her desk and stubbed out her cigarette. She said:

'Your aunt told you. She used to have to read out the questions for him over and over again; an evening of tension and incomprehensible boredom. Don't you remember?'

'Yes,' said Angela in her high, dispassionate voice. 'Yes, I remember.' She turned to Dalgliesh.

'If there's nothing else you want to ask me, there are things I need to get on with. Dr Howarth isn't expecting me at the Lab until this afternoon. And Stella will want to work.'

Both women showed them out, standing together in the doorway as if politely speeding departing guests. Dalgliesh almost expected them to wave goodbye. He hadn't questioned Miss Foley about the quarrel with her cousin. The time might come for that, but it wasn't yet. It had interested, but not surprised him that she had lied. But what had interested him more was Stella Mawson's story of Lorrimer rehearsing his evidence on the night before a trial. Whoever had told her this, he was fairly certain that it hadn't been Angela Foley.

As they drove away, Massingham said:

'Fifty thousand pounds could change her whole life, give her some independence, get her away from here. What sort of life is it for a young woman, just the two of them, stuck here in this isolated swamp? And she seems little more than a drudge.'

Dalgliesh, unusually, was driving. Massingham glanced at the sombre eyes in the mirror, the long hands laid lightly on the wheel. Dalgliesh said:

'I'm remembering what old George Greenall, the first detective sergeant I worked under, told me. He'd had twenty-five years in the C.I.D. Nothing about people surprised him, nothing shocked him. He said:

'"They'll tell you that the most destructive force in the world is hate. Don't you believe it, lad. It's love. And if you want to make a detective you'd better learn to recognize it when you meet it."'

II

Brenda was over an hour late at the Laboratory on Thursday morning. After the excitement of the previous day she had overslept and her mother had deliberately not called her. She had wanted to go without her breakfast, but Mrs Pridmore had placed the usual plate of bacon and egg before her, and had sai firmly that Brenda wouldn't leave the house until it was eaten Brenda, only too aware that both her parents would be happier i she never set foot in Hoggatt's again, knew better than to argue.

She arrived, breathless and apologetic, to find Inspector Blakelock trying to cope with a two days' intake of exhibits, a stead stream of arrivals and a constantly ringing telephone. She wondered how he would greet her, whether he had learned about th thousand pounds and, if so, whether it would make any difference But he seemed his usual stolid self. He said:

'As soon as you've taken off your things, you're to go to th Director. He's in Miss Foley's office. The police are using his Don't bother about making tea. Miss Foley will be out until afte lunch. She has to see someone from the local authority socia services about her uncle.'

Brenda was glad that she wouldn't have to face Angela Fole yet. Last night's admission to Commander Dalgliesh was too lik betrayal to be comfortable. She said:

'Everyone else is in, then?'

'Clifford Bradley hasn't made it. His wife telephoned to sa that he's not well. The police have been here since half pas eight. They've been checking all the exhibits, especially th drugs, and they've made another search of the whole Lab Apparently they've got the idea that there's something odd goin on.'

It was unusual for Inspector Blakelock to be so communicative Brenda asked:

'What do you mean, something odd?'

'They didn't say. But now they want to see every file in th Lab with a number 18 or 40 or 1840 in the registration.'

Brenda's eyes widened.

'Do you mean for this year only, or do we have to go back t those on microfilm?'

'I've got out this year's and last year's to begin with, an Sergeant Underhill and the constable are working on them now I don't know what they hope to find, and by the look of them neither do they. Better look nippy. Dr Howarth said that yo were to go into him as soon as you arrive.'

'But I can't do shorthand and typing! What do you think he wants me for?'

'He didn't say. Mostly getting out files, I imagine. And I daresay there'll be a bit of telephoning and fetching and carrying.'

'Where's Commander Dalgliesh? Isn't he here?'

'He and Inspector Massingham left about ten minutes ago. Off to interview someone, I daresay. Never mind about them. Our job's here, helping to keep this Lab working smoothly.'

It was as close as Inspector Blakelock ever got to a rebuke. Brenda hurried to Miss Foley's office. It was known that the Director didn't like people to knock on his door, so Brenda entered with what confidence she could muster. She thought, 'I can only do my best. If that's not good enough, he'll have to lump it.' He was sitting at the desk apparently studying a file. He looked up without smiling in response to her good-morning, and said:

'Inspector Blakelock has explained to you that I want some help this morning while Miss Foley's away? You can work with Mrs Mallett in the general office.'

'Yes, sir.'

'The police will be needing some more files. They're interested in particular numbers only. But I expect Inspector Blakelock has explained that.'

'Yes, sir.'

'They're working on the 1976 and '75 registrations now, so you'd better start getting out the 1974 series and any earlier years they want.'

He took his eyes from the files and looked directly at her for the first time.

'Dr Lorrimer left you some money, didn't he?'

'Yes, sir. One thousand pounds for books and apparatus.'

'You don't need to call me sir, Dr Howarth will do. You liked him?'

'Yes. Yes, I did.'

Dr Howarth had lowered his eyes again and was turning over the pages of the file.

'Odd, I shouldn't have thought that he would have appealed to women, or women to him.'

Brenda said resolutely:

'It wasn't like that.'

'What wasn't it like? Do you mean he didn't think of you as a woman?'

'I don't know. I mean, I didn't think that he was trying to . . .'

Her voice broke off. Dr Howarth turned a page. He said:

'To seduce you?'

Brenda took courage, helped by a spurt of anger. She said:

'Well, he couldn't, could he? Not here in the Lab. And I never saw him anywhere else. And if you'd known anything about him at all, you wouldn't talk like that.'

She was appalled at her own temerity. But the Director only said, rather sadly she thought:

'I expect you're right. I never knew him at all.'

She struggled to explain.

'He explained to me what science is about.'

'And what is science about?'

'He explained that scientists formulate theories about how the physical world works, and then test them out by experiments. As long as the experiments succeed, then the theories hold. If they fail, the scientists have to find another theory to explain the facts. He says that, with science, there's this exciting paradox, that disillusionment needn't be defeat. It's a step forward.'

'Didn't you do science at school? I thought you'd taken physics and chemistry at 'O' level.'

'No one ever explained it like that before.'

'No. I suppose they bored you with experiments about magnetism and the properties of carbon dioxide. By the way, Miss Foley has typed a paper on the ratio of staffing to workloads. I want the figures checked – Mrs Mallett will do it with you – and the paper circulated to all Directors before next week's meeting. She'll give you the list of addresses.'

'Yes, sir. Yes, Dr Howarth.'

'And I'd like you to take this file to Miss Easterbrook in the Biology Lab.'

He looked up at her, and she thought for the first time that he looked kind. He said, very gently:

'I know how you feel. I felt the same. But there's only a white outline on the floor, just a smudge of chalk. That's all.'

He handed her the file. It was a dismissal. At the door Brenda paused. The Director said:

'Well?'

'I was just thinking that detection must be like science. The detective formulates a theory, then tests it. If the facts he discovers fit, then the theory holds. If they don't, then he has to find another theory, another suspect.'

Dr Howarth said drily:

'It's a reasonable analogy. But the temptation to select the right facts is probably greater. And the detective is experimenting with human beings. Their properties are complex and not susceptible to accurate analysis.'

An hour later Brenda took her third set of files into Sergeant Underhill in the director's office. The pleasant-looking detective constable leaped forward to relieve her of her burden. The telephone rang on Dr Howarth's desk, and Sergeant Underhill went over to answer it. He replaced the receiver and looked across at his companion.

'That's the Met Lab. They've given me the result of the blood analysis. The mallet was the weapon all right. There's Lorrimer's blood on it. And they've analysed the vomit.'

He looked up, suddenly remembering that Brenda was still in the room, and waited until she had left and the door was closed. The detective constable said:

'Well?'

'It's what we thought. Think it out for yourself. A forensic scientist would know that the Lab can't determine a blood group from vomit. The stomach acids destroy the antibodies. What they can hope to say is what was in the food. So all you need to do, if it's your vomit and you're a suspect, is to lie about what you ate for supper. Who could disprove it?'

His companion said:

'Unless . . .'

Sergeant Underhill reached again for the phone.

'Exactly. As I said, think it out for yourself.'

III

After the last few days of intermittent rain and fitful autumn sunlight, the morning was cold but bright, the sun unexpectedly warm against their necks. But even in the mellow light, the Old Rectory, with its bricks the colour of raw liver under the encroaching ivy and its ponderous porch and carved overhanging eaves, was a depressing house. The open iron gate to the drive, half off its hinges, was embedded in a straggling hedge which bordered the garden. The gravel path needed weeding. The grass of the lawn was pulled and flattened where someone had made an inexpert attempt at mowing it, obviously with a blunt machine, and the two herbaceous borders were a tangle of overgrown chrysanthemums and stunted dahlias half choked with weeds. A child's wooden horse on wheels lay on its side at the edge of the lawn, but this was the only sign of human life.

As they approached the house, however, a girl and a small boy emerged from the porch and stood regarding them. They must, of course, be Kerrison's children, and as Dalgliesh and Massingham approached the likeness became apparent. The girl must, he supposed, be over school age, but she looked barely sixteen except for a certain adult wariness about the eyes. She had straight, dark hair drawn back from a high, spotty forehead into short dishevelled pigtails bound with elastic bands. She wore the ubiquitous faded blue jeans of her generation, topped with a fawn sweater, loose-fitting enough to be her father's. Round her neck Dalgliesh could glimpse what looked like a leather thong. Her grubby feet were bare and palely striped with the pattern of summer sandals.

The child, who moved closer to her at the sight of strangers, was about three or fours years old, a stocky, round-faced boy with a wide nose and a gentle, delicate mouth. His face was a softer miniature model of his father's, the brows straight and dark above the heavily lidded eyes. He was wearing a pair of tight blue shorts and an inexpertly knitted jumper against which he was clasping a large ball. His sturdy legs were planted in short red wellington boots. He tightened his hold on his ball and fixed on Dalgliesh an unblinking disconcertingly judgemental gaze.

Dalgliesh suddenly realized that he knew virtually nothing about children. Most of his friends were childless; those who were not had learned to invite him when their demanding, peace-disturbing, egotistical offspring were away at school. His only son had died, with his mother, just twenty-four hours after birth. Although he could now hardly recall his wife's face except in dreams, the picture of those waxen, doll-like features above the tiny swathed body, the gummed eyelids, the secret look of self-absorbed peace was so clear and immediate that he sometimes wondered whether the image was really that of his child, so briefly but intently regarded, or whether he had taken into himself a prototype of dead childhood. His son would now be older than this child, would be entering the traumatic years of adolescence. He had convinced himself long ago that he was glad to have been spared them.

But now it suddenly occurred to him that there was a whole territory of human experience on which, once repulsed, he had turned his back, and that this rejection somehow diminished him as a man. This transitory ache of loss surprised him by its intensity. He forced himself to consider a sensation so unfamiliar and unwelcome.

Suddenly the child smiled at him and held out the ball. The effect was as disconcertingly flattering as when a stray cat would stalk towards him, tail erect, and condescend to be stroked. They gazed at each other. Dalgliesh smiled back. Then Massingham sprang forward and whipped the ball from the chubby hands.

'Come on. Football!'

He began dribbling the blue and yellow ball across the lawn. Immediately the sturdy legs followed. The two of them disappeared round the side of the house and Dalgliesh could hear the boy's high, cracked laughter. The girl gazed after them, her face suddenly pinched with loving anxiety. She turned to Dalgliesh.

'I hope he knows not to kick it into the bonfire. It's almost out, but the embers are still very hot. I've been burning rubbish.'

'Don't worry. He's a careful chap. And he's got younger brothers.'

She regarded him carefully for the first time.

'You're Commander Dalgliesh, aren't you? We're Nell and William Kerrison. I'm afraid my father isn't here.'

'I know. We've come to see your housekeeper, Miss Willard, isn't it? Is she in?'

'I shouldn't take any notice of anything she says if I were you. She's a dreadful liar. And she steals Daddy's drink. Don't you want to question William and me?'

'A policewoman will be coming with us to talk to you both, sometime when your father's at home.'

'I won't see her. I don't mind talking to you, but I won't see a policewoman. I don't like social workers.'

'A policewoman isn't a social worker.'

'She's the same. She makes judgements on people, doesn't she? We had a social worker here after my mother left, before the custody case, and she looked at William and me as if we were a public nuisance which someone had left on her doorstep. She went round the house too, poking into things, pretending to admire, making out it was just a social visit.'

'Policewomen – and policemen – never pretend that they're just paying a social visit. No one would believe us, would they?'

They turned and walked together towards the house. The girl said:

'Are you going to discover who killed Dr Lorrimer?'

'I hope so. I expect so.'

'And then what will happen to him, the murderer, I mean?'

'He'll appear before the magistrates. Then, if they think tha the evidence is sufficient, they'll commit him to the Crown Cour for trial.'

'And then?'

'If he's found guilty of murder, the judge will pass the statutor penalty, imprisonment for life. That means that he'll be in priso for a long time, perhaps ten years or more.'

'But that's silly. That won't put things right. It won't bring D Lorrimer back.'

'It won't put anything right, but it isn't silly. Life is precious t nearly all of us. Even people who have little more than life sti want to live it to the last natural moment. No one has a right t take it away from them.'

'You talk as if life were like William's ball. If that's taken awa he knows what he's lost. Dr Lorrimer doesn't know that he's lost anything.'

'He's lost the years he might have had.'

'That's like taking away the ball that William might have had. It doesn't mean anything. It's just words. Suppose he was going to die next week anyway. Then he'd only have lost seven days. You don't put someone in prison for ten years to repay seven lost days. They might not even have been happy days.'

'Even if he were a very old man with one day left to him, the law says that he has a right to live it. Wilful killing would still be murder.'

The girl said thoughtfully:

'I suppose it was different when people believed in God. Then the murdered person might have died in mortal sin and gone to hell. The seven days could have made a difference then. He might have repented and had time for absolution.'

Dalgliesh said:

'All these problems are easier for people who believe in God. Those of us who don't or can't have to do the best we can. That's what the law is, the best we can do. Human justice is imperfect, but it's the only justice we have.'

'Are you sure you don't want to question me? I know that Daddy didn't kill him. He isn't a murderer. He was at home with William and me when Dr Lorrimer died. We put William to bed together at half past seven and then we stayed with him for twenty minutes and Daddy read Paddington Bear to him. Then I went to bed because I'd got a headache and wasn't feeling well, and Daddy brought me up a mug of cocoa which he'd made specially for me. He sat by me reading poetry from my school anthology until he thought I'd gone to sleep. But I hadn't really. I was just pretending. He crept away just before nine, but I was still awake then. Shall I tell you how I know?'

'If you want to.'

'Because I heard the church clock strike. Then Daddy left me and I lay there in the dark, just thinking. He came back to look in at me again about half an hour later, but I still pretended to be asleep. So that lets Daddy out, doesn't it?'

'We don't know exactly when Dr Lorrimer died but, yes, I think it probably does.'

'Unless I'm telling you a lie.'

'People very often do lie to the police. Are you?'

'No. But I expect I would if I thought it would save Daddy. I don't care about Dr Lorrimer, you see. I'm glad he's dead. He wasn't a nice man. The day before he died William and I went to the Lab to see Daddy. He was lecturing in the morning to the detective training course and we thought we'd call for him before lunch. Inspector Blakelock let us sit in the hall, and that girl who helps him at the desk, the pretty one, smiled at William and offered him an apple from her lunch box. And then Dr Lorrimer came down the stairs and saw us. I know it was he because the Inspector spoke to him by his name and he said: "What are those children doing in here? A lab isn't a place for children." I said: "I'm not a child. I'm Miss Eleanor Kerrison and this is my brother William, and we're waiting for our father." He stared at us as if he hated us, his face white and twitching. He said: "Well, you can't wait here." Then he spoke very unkindly to Inspector Blakelock. After Dr Lorrimer had gone, he said we'd better go but he told William not to mind and took a sweet out of his left ear. Did you know that the Inspector was a conjurer?'

'No. I didn't know that.'

'Would you like to see round the house before I take you to Miss Willard? Do you like seeing houses?'

'Very much, but I think perhaps not now.'

'See the drawing-room anyway. It's much the best room. There now, isn't it lovely?'

The drawing-room was in no sense lovely. It was a sombre, oak-panelled, over-furnished room which looked as if little had changed since the days when the bombazine-clad wife and daughters of the Victorian rector sat there piously occupied with their parish sewing. The mullioned windows, framed by dark-red, dirt-encrusted curtains, effectively excluded most of the daylight so that Dalgliesh stepped into a sombre chilliness which the sluggish fire did nothing to dispel. An immense mahogany table, bearing a jam-jar of chrysanthemums, stood against the far wall and the fireplace, an ornate edifice of marble, was almost hidden by two immense, sagging armchairs, and a dilapidated sofa. Eleanor said with unexpected formality, as if the room had recalled her to her duty as a hostess:

'I try to keep at least one room nice in case we have visitors. The flowers are pretty, aren't they? William arranged them. Please sit down. Can I get you some coffee?'

'That would be pleasant, but I don't think we ought to wait. We're really here to see Miss Willard.'

Massingham and William appeared in the doorway, flushed with their exercise, William with the ball tucked under his left arm. Eleanor led the way through a brass-studded, green-baize door and down a stone passage to the back of the house. William, deserting Massingham, trotted behind her, his plump hand clutching ineffectively at the skin-tight jeans. Pausing outside the door of unpolished oak, she said:

'She's in here. She doesn't like William and me to go in. Anyway, she smells, so we don't.'

And taking William by the hand, she left them.

Dalgliesh knocked. There was a rapid scrabbling noise inside the room, like an animal disturbed in its lair, and then the door was opened slightly and a dark and suspicious eye looked out at them through the narrow aperture. Dalgliesh said:

'Miss Willard? Commander Dalgliesh and Inspector Massingham from the Metropolitan Police. We're investigating Dr Lorimer's murder. May we come in?'

The eye softened. She gave a short, embarrassed gasp, rather like a snort, and opened the door wide.

'Of course. Of course. What must you think of me? I'm afraid I'm still in what my dear old nurse used to call my disability. But I wasn't expecting you, and I usually have a quiet moment to myself about this time of the morning.'

Eleanor was right, the room did smell. A smell, Massingham diagnosed after a curious sniff, composed of sweet sherry, unfresh body linen and cheap scent. It was very hot. A small blue flame licked the red-hot ovals of coal briquettes banked high in the Victorian grate. The window, which gave a view of the garage and the wilderness which was the back garden, was open for only an inch at the top despite the mildness of the day, and the air in the room pressed down on them, furred and heavy as a soiled blanket. The room itself had a dreadful and perverse femininity.

Everything looked moistly soft, the cretonne-covered seats of the two armchairs, the plump row of cushions along the back of a Victorian chaise-longue, the imitation fur rug before the fire. The mantelshelf was cluttered with photographs in silver frames, mostly of a cassocked clergyman and his wife, whom Dalgliesh took to be Miss Willard's parents, standing side by side but oddly dissociated outside a variety of rather dull churches. Pride of place was held by a studio photograph of Miss Willard herself, young, toothily coy, the thick hair in corrugated waves. On a wall shelf to the right of the door was a small woodcarving of an armless Madonna with the laughing Child perched on her shoulder. A night-light in a saucer was burning at her feet, casting a soft glow over the tender drooping head and the sightless eyes. Dalgliesh thought that it was probably a copy, and a good one, of a medieval museum piece. Its gentle beauty emphasized the tawdriness of the room, yet dignified it, seeming to say that there was more than one kind of human loneliness, human pain, and that the same mercy embraced them all.

Miss Willard waved them to the chaise-longue.

'My own little den,' she said gaily. 'I like to be private, you know. I explained to Dr Kerrison that I could only consider coming if I had my privacy. It's a rare and beautiful thing, don't you think? The human spirit wilts without it.'

Looking at her hands, Dalgliesh thought that she was probably in her middle forties, although her face looked older. The dark hair, dry and coarse and tightly curled, was at odds with her faded complexion. Two sausages of curls over the brow suggested that she had hurriedly snatched out the rollers when she heard their knock. But her face was already made up. There was a circle of rouge under each eye and the lipstick had seeped into the creases pursing her mouth. Her small, square, bony jaw was loose as a marionette's. She was not yet fully dressed and a padded dressing-gown of flowered nylon, stained with tea and what looked like egg, was corded over a nylon nightdress in bright blue with a grubby frill round the neck. Massingham was fascinated by a bulbous fold of limp cotton just above her shoes from which he found it difficult to avert his eyes, until he realized that she had put on her stockings back to front.

She said:

'You want to talk to me about Dr Kerrison's alibi, I expect. Of course, it's quite ridiculous that he should have to provide one, a man so gentle, totally incapable of violence. But I can help you, as it happens. He was certainly home until after nine, and I saw him again less than an hour later. But all this is just a waste of time. You bring a great reputation with you, Commander, but this is one crime which science can't solve. Not for nothing are they called the black fens. All through the centuries, evil has come out of this dank soil. We can fight evil, Commander, but not with your weapons.'

Massingham said:

'Well, suppose we begin by giving our weapons a chance.'

She looked at him and smiled pityingly.

'But all the doors were locked. All your clever scientific aids were intact. No one broke in, and no one could have got out. And yet he was struck down. That was no human hand, Inspector.'

Dalgliesh said:

'It was almost certainly a blunt weapon, Miss Willard, and I've no doubt there was a human hand at the end of it. It's our job to find out whose, and I hope that you may be able to help us. You housekeep for Dr Kerrison and his daughter, I believe?'

Miss Willard disposed on him a glance in which pity at such ignorance was mixed with gentle reproof.

'I'm not a housekeeper, Commander. Certainly not a housekeeper. Shall we say that I'm a working house-guest. Dr Kerrison needed someone to live in so that the children weren't left alone when he was called out to a murder scene. They're children of a broken marriage, I'm afraid. The old, sad story. You are not married, Commander?'

'No.'

'How wise.' She sighed, conveying in the sibilant release of breath infinite yearning, infinite regret. Dalgliesh persevered:

'So you live completely separately?'

'My own little quarters. This sitting-room and a bedroom next door. My own small kitchenette through this door here. I won't show it to you now because it's not quite as I should like it to be.'

'What precisely are the domestic arrangements, Miss Willard?'

'They get their own breakfast. The Doctor usually lunches at the hospital, of course; Nell and William have something on a tray when she bothers to prepare it, and I look after myself. Then I cook a little something in the evenings, quite simple, we're none of us large eaters. We eat very early because of William. It's more a high tea really. Nell and her father do all the cooking during the weekend. It really works out quite well.'

Quite well for you, thought Massingham. Certainly William had seemed sturdy and well nourished enough, but the girl looked as if she ought to be at school, not struggling, almost unaided, with this isolated and cheerless monstrosity of a house. He wondered how she got on with Miss Willard. As if reading his thoughts, Miss Willard said:

'William is a sweet little boy. Absolutely no trouble. I hardly see him really. But Nell is difficult, very difficult. Girls of her age usually are. She needs a mother's hand. You know, of course, that Mrs Kerrison walked out on her husband a year ago? She ran away with one of his colleagues at the hospital. It broke him up completely. Now she's trying to get the High Court to reverse the custody order and give her the children when the divorce is heard in a month's time, and I'm sure it'll be a good thing if they do. Children ought to be with their mother. Not that Nell's really a child any longer. It's the boy they're fighting over, not Nell. If you ask me, neither of them cares about her. She gives her father a terrible time of it. Nightmares, screaming attacks, asthma. He's going to London next Monday for a three-day conference on forensic pathology. I'm afraid she'll make him pay for that little jaunt when he gets back. Neurotic, you know. Punishing him for loving her brother more, although, of course, he can't see that.'

Dalgliesh wondered by what mental process she had arrived at that glib psychological assessment. Not, he thought, that it was necessarily wrong. He felt profoundly sorry for Kerrison.

Suddenly Massingham felt sick. The warmth and feculent smell of the room overpowered him. A blob of cold sweat dropped on his notebook. Muttering an apology, he strode over to the window and tugged at the frame. It resisted for a moment then slammed down. Great draughts of cool reviving air poured in

The frail light before the carved Madonna flickered and went out.

When he got back to his notebook, Dalgliesh was already asking about the previous evening. Miss Willard said that she had cooked a meal of minced beef, potatoes and frozen peas for supper, with a blancmange to follow. She had washed up alone and had then gone to say good-night to the family before returning to her sitting-room. They were then in the drawing-room, but Dr Kerrison and Nell were about to take William up to bed. She had seen and heard nothing else of the family until just after nine o'clock when she had gone to check that the front door was bolted. Dr Kerrison was sometimes careless about locking up and didn't always appreciate how nervous she felt, sleeping alone and on the ground floor. One read such terrible stories. She had passed the study door, which was ajar, and had heard Dr Kerrison speaking on the telephone. She had returned to her sitting-room and had switched on the television.

Dr Kerrison had looked in shortly before ten o'clock to talk to her about a small increase in her salary, but they had been interrupted by a telephone call. He had returned ten minutes or so later and they had been together for about half an hour. It had been pleasant to have the opportunity of a private chat without the children butting in. Then he had said good-night and left her. She had switched on the television again and had watched it until nearly midnight, when she had gone to bed. If Dr Kerrison had taken out the car, she felt fairly sure that she would have heard it since her sitting-room window looked out at the garage, which was built at the side of the house. Well, they could see that for themselves.

She had overslept the next morning and hadn't breakfasted until after nine. She had been woken by the telephone ringing, but it hadn't been until Dr Kerrison returned from the Laboratory that she knew about Dr Lorrimer's murder. Dr Kerrison had returned briefly to the house shortly after nine o'clock to tell her and Nell what had happened and to ring the hospital to say that any calls for him should be transferred to the reception desk at the Laboratory.

Dalgliesh said:

'I believe Dr Lorrimer used to drive you to the eleven o'clock service at St Mary's at Guy's Marsh. He seems to have been a solitary and not a very happy man. No one seems to have known him well. I was wondering whether he found in you the companionship and friendship he seems to have lacked in his working life.'

Massingham looked up, curious to see her response to this blatant invitation to self-revelation. She hooded her eyes like a bird, while a red blotch spread like a contagion over her throat. She said, with an attempt at archness:

'Now I'm afraid you're teasing me, Commander. It is Commander, isn't it? It seems so odd, just like a naval rank. My late brother-in-law was in the Navy, so I know a little of these matters. But you were talking of friendship. That implies confidence. I should like to have helped him, but he wasn't easy to know. And there was the age difference. I'm not so very much older, less than five years, I suppose. But it's a great deal to a comparatively young man. No, I'm afraid we were just two reprobate High Anglicans in this Evangelical swampland. We didn't even sit together in church. I've always sat in the third pew down from the pulpit and he liked to be right at the back.'

Dalgliesh persisted:

'But he must have enjoyed your company. He called for you every Sunday, didn't he?'

'Only because Father Gregory asked him. There is a bus to Guy's Marsh, but I have to wait half an hour and, as Dr Lorrimer drove past the Old Rectory, Father Gregory suggested that it would be a sensible arrangement if we travelled together. He never came in. I was always ready and waiting for him outside the drive. If his father were ill or he himself was out on a case, he'd telephone. Sometimes he wasn't able to let me know, which was inconvenient. But I knew that if he didn't drive up at twenty to eleven he wouldn't be coming, and then I'd set off for the bus. Usually, of course, he came, except during the first six months of this year when he gave up Mass. But he rang early in September to say that he would be stopping for me as he used to. Naturally I never questioned him about the break. One does go through these dark nights of the soul.'

So he had stopped going to Mass when the affair with Domenica Schofield began, and had resumed his churchgoing after the break. Dalgliesh asked:

'Did he take the Sacrament?'

She was unsurprised by the question.

'Not since he started coming to Mass again in mid-September. It worried me a little, I confess. I did wonder whether to suggest to him that if anything was troubling him he should have a talk with Father Gregory. But one is on very delicate ground. And it really wasn't any concern of mine.'

And she wouldn't want to offend him, thought Massingham. Those lifts in the car must have been very convenient. Dalgliesh asked:

'So he did very occasionally telephone you. Have you ever rung him?'

She turned away and fussed herself plumping up a cushion.

'Dear me, no! Why should I? I don't even know his number.'

Massingham said:

'It seems odd that he went to church at Guy's Marsh instead of in the village.'

Miss Willard looked at him severely.

'Not at all. Mr Swaffield is a very worthy man, but he's Low, very Low. The fens have always been strongly Evangelical. When my dear father was rector here, he had constant fights with the Parochial Church Council over Reservation. And then I think that Dr Lorrimer didn't want to get drawn into church and village activities. It's so difficult not to once you're known as a regular member of the congregation. Father Gregory didn't expect that; he realized that Dr Lorrimer had his own father to care for and a very demanding job. Incidentally, I was very distressed that the police didn't call for Father Gregory. Someone should have called a priest to the body.'

Dalgliesh said gently:

'He had been dead some hours when the body was discovered, Miss Willard.'

'Even so, he should have had a priest.'

She stood up as if signifying that the interview was at an end. Dalgliesh was glad enough to go. He said his formal thanks and asked Miss Willard to get in touch with him immediately if anything of interest occurred to her. He and Massingham were at the door when she suddenly called out imperiously:

'Young man!'

The two detectives turned to look at her. She spoke directly at Massingham, like an old-fashioned nurse admonishing a child:

'Would you please shut the window which you so inconsiderately opened, and relight the candle.'

Meekly, as if in obedience to long-forgotten nursery commands, Massingham did so. They were left to find their own way out of the house and saw no one. When they were in the car fastening their seat-belts, Massingham exploded:

'Good God, you'd think Kerrison could find someone more suitable than that old hag to care for his children. She's a slut, a dipsomaniac, and she's half-mad.'

'It's not so simple for Kerrison. A remote village, a large, cold house, and a daughter who can't be easy to cope with. Faced with the choice of that kind of job and the dole, most women today would probably opt for the dole. Did you take a look at the bonfire?'

'Nothing there. It looks as if they're periodically burning a lot of old furniture and garden rubbish which they've got stacked in one of the coach-houses. William said that Nell made a bonfire early this morning.'

'William can talk, then?' Dalgliesh asked.

'Oh William can talk. But I'm not sure that you'd be able to understand him, sir. Did you believe Miss Willard when she gave that alibi for Kerrison?'

'I'm as ready to believe her as I am Mrs Bradley or Mr Blakelock when they confirmed Bradley's and Blakelock's alibis. Who can tell? We know that Kerrison did ring Dr Underwood at nine and was here to receive his return call at about ten. If Miss Willard sticks to her story, he's in the clear for that hour, and I've a feeling that it's the crucial hour. But how did he know that? And if he did, why suppose that we should be able to pin down the time of death so precisely? Sitting with his daughter until nine and then calling on Miss Willard just before ten looks very like an attempt to establish that he was at home during the whole of that hour.'

Massingham said:

'He must have been, to take that ten o'clock call. And I don't see how he could have got to Hoggatt's, killed Lorrimer and returned home in less than sixty minutes, not if he went on foot. And Miss Willard seems confident that he didn't take the car. I suppose it would just be possible if he took a short cut through the new Laboratory, but it would be a close thing.'

Just then the car radio bleeped. Dalgliesh took the call. It was from the Guy's Marsh control tower to say that Sergeant Reynolds at the Lab wanted to contact them. The Met Lab report had been received.

IV

They opened the door together. Mrs Bradley held a sleeping child in her arms. Bradley said:

'Come in. It's about the vomit, isn't it? I've been expecting you.'

They moved into the sitting-room. He gestured Dalgliesh and Massingham to the two chairs and sat down on the sofa opposite them. His wife moved close to him, shifting the baby's weight against her shoulder. Dalgliesh asked:

'Do you want a solicitor?'

'No. Not yet, anyway. I'm ready to tell the whole truth and it can't hurt me. At least, I suppose it can lose me my job. But that's the worst it can do. And I think I'm almost beyond caring.'

Massingham opened his notebook. Dalgliesh said to Susan Bradley:

'Wouldn't you like to put the baby in her pram, Mrs Bradley?'

She gazed at Dalgliesh with blazing eyes, and shook her head vehemently, holding the child more tightly as if she expected them to tear her from her arms. Massingham was grateful that, at least, the child was asleep. But he wished that neither she nor her mother were there. He looked at the baby, bunched in her pink sleeping suit against her mother's shoulder, the fringe of longer hair above the tender hollowed neck, the round bare patch at the back of the head, the close shut eyes and ridiculous, snubbed nose. The frail mother with her milky bundle was more inhibiting than a whole firm of recalcitrant anti-police lawyers.

There was a lot to be said for bundling a suspect into the back of a police car and taking him off to the police station to make his statement in the functional anonymity of the interrogation room. Even the Bradleys' sitting-room provoked in him a mixture of irritation and pity. It still smelt new and unfinished. There was no fireplace, and the television held pride of place above the wall-mounted electric heater with, above it, a popular print of waves dashing against a rocky shore. The wall opposite had been papered to match the flowered curtains, but the other three were bare, the plaster already beginning to crack. There was a metal baby's high chair and, underneath it, a spread of plastic sheeting to protect the carpet. Everything looked new, as if they had brought to their marriage no accumulation of small personal impedimenta, had come spiritually naked into possession of this small, characterless room. Dalgliesh said:

'We'll take it that your previous account of your movements on Wednesday night wasn't true, or was incomplete. So what did happen?'

Massingham wondered for a moment why Dalgliesh wasn't cautioning Bradley; then he thought he knew. Bradley might have had the guts to kill if provoked beyond endurance, but he'd never have had the nerve to drop from that third-floor window. And if he didn't, how did he get out of the Laboratory? Lorrimer's killer had either used the keys or he had made that climb. All their investigations, all their careful and repeated examination of the building had confirmed that hypothesis. There was no other way.

Bradley looked at his wife. She gave him a brief, transforming smile and held out her free hand. He clasped it and they edged closer. He moistened his lips, and then began speaking as if the speech had been long rehearsed.

'On Tuesday Dr Lorrimer finished writing my annual confidential report. He told me he wanted to talk to me about it next day before he passed it to Dr Howarth, and he called me into his private room soon after he arrived in the Lab. He'd given me an adverse report and, according to the rules, he had to explain why. I wanted to defend myself, but I couldn't. And there wasn't any real privacy. I felt that the whole Laboratory knew what was happening and was listening and waiting. Besides, I was so frightened of him, I don't know why exactly. I can't explain it. He had such an effect on me that he'd only have to be working close to me in the Laboratory and I'd start shaking. When he was away at a scene of crime it was like heaven. I could work perfectly well then. The annual confidential report wasn't unjust. I knew that my work had deteriorated. But he was partly the reason why. He seemed to take my inadequacy as a personal denigration of himself. Poor work was intolerable to him. He was obsessed by mistakes. And because I was so terrified, I made them all the more.'

He paused for a moment. No one spoke. Then he went on:

'We weren't going to the village concert because we couldn't get a baby-sitter, and, anyway, Sue's mother was coming for supper. I got home just before six. After the meal – the curry and rice and peas – I saw her off on the seven forty-five bus. I came straight back here. But I kept thinking of the adverse report, what Dr Howarth would say, what I was going to do if he recommended a move, how we could possibly sell this house. We had to buy when prices were at their peak, and it's almost impossible to find buyers now, except at a loss. Besides, I didn't think another Lab would want me. After a time I thought I'd go back to the Laboratory and confront him. I think I had some idea that we might be able to communicate, that I could speak to him as another human being and make him understand how I felt. Anyway, I felt that I would go mad if I stayed indoors. I had to walk somewhere, and I walked towards Hoggatt's. I didn't tell Sue what I was going to do, and she tried to persuade me not to go out. But I went.'

He looked up at Dalgliesh and said:

'Can I have a drink of water?'

Without a word, Massingham got up and went to find the kitchen. He couldn't see the glasses, but there were two washed cups on the draining-board. He filled one with cold water and brought it back to Bradley. Bradley drained it. He drew his hand over his moist mouth and went on:

'I didn't see anyone on the way to the Laboratory. People

don't walk out in this village much after dark, and I suppose most of them were at the concert. There was a light on in the hall of the Laboratory. I rang the bell and Lorrimer came. He seemed surprised to see me but I said I wanted to speak to him. He looked at his watch and said he could only spare me five minutes. I followed him up to the Biology Lab.'

He looked across directly at Dalgliesh. He said:

'It was a strange sort of interview. I sensed that he was impatient and wanted to get rid of me, and part of the time I thought that he hardly listened to what I was saying, or even knew that I was there. I didn't make a good job of it. I tried to explain that I wasn't being careless on purpose, that I really liked the work and wanted to make a success of it and be a credit to the Department. I tried to explain the effect he had on me. I don't know whether he was listening. He stood there with his eyes fixed on the floor.

'And then he looked up and began speaking. He didn't really look at me, he was looking through me, almost as if I wasn't there. And he was saying things, terrible things, as if they were words in a play, nothing to do with me. I kept hearing the same words over and over again. Failure. Useless. Hopeless. Inadequate. He even said something about marriage, as if I were a sexual failure too. I think he was mad. I can't explain what it was like, all this hate pouring out, hate, and misery and despair. I stood there shaking with this stream of words pouring over me as if . . . as if it were filth. And then his eyes focused on me and I knew that he was seeing me, me, Clifford Bradley. His voice sounded quite different. He said:

'"You're a third-rate biologist and a fourth-rate forensic scientist. That's what you were when you came into this Department and you'll never change. I have two alternatives: to check every one of your results or to risk the Service and this Laboratory being discredited in the court. Neither is tolerable. So I suggest that you look for another job. And now I've things to do, so please leave."

'He turned his back on me and I went out. I knew that it was impossible. It would have been better not to have come. He'd never told me before exactly what he thought of me, not in those words, anyway. I felt sick and miserable, and I knew I was crying. That made me despise myself the more. I stumbled upstairs to the men's cloakroom and was just able to reach the first basin before I vomited. I don't remember how long I stood there, leaning over the basin, half crying and half vomiting. I suppose it could have been three or four minutes. After a time I put on the cold tap and swilled my face. Then I tried to pull myself together. But I was still shaking, and I still felt sick. I went and sat on one of the lavatory seats and sank my head in my hands.

'I don't know how long I was there. Ten minutes perhaps, but it could have been longer. I knew I could never change his opinion of me, never make him understand. He wasn't like a human being. I realized that he hated me. But now I began to hate him and in a different way. I'd have to leave; I knew he'd see to that. But at least I could tell him what I thought of him. I could behave like a man. So I went down the stairs and into the Biology Laboratory.'

Again he paused. The child stirred in her mother's arms and gave a little cry in her sleep. Susan Bradley began an automatic jogging and crooning, but kept her eyes on her husband. Then Bradley went on:

'He was lying between the two middle examination tables, face downwards. I didn't wait to see whether he was dead. I know that I ought to feel dreadful about that, about the fact that I left him without getting help. But I don't. I can't make myself feel sorry. But at the time I wasn't glad that he was dead. I wasn't aware of any feeling except terror. I hurled myself downstairs and out of the Laboratory as if his murderer were after me. The door was still on the Yale and I know that I must have drawn back the bottom bolt, but I can't remember. I raced down the drive. I think there was a bus passing, but it had started up before I reached the gate. When I got into the road it was disappearing. Then I saw a car approaching and, instinctively, I stood back into the shadows of the walls. The car slowed down and turned into the Laboratory drive. Then I made myself walk slowly and normally. And the next thing I remember was being home.'

Susan Bradley spoke for the first time:

'Clifford told me all about it. But, of course, he had to. He looked so terrible that I knew something awful must have happened. We decided together what we'd better do. We knew that he'd had nothing to do with what had happened to Dr Lorrimer. But who would believe Cliff? Everyone in the Department knew what Dr Lorrimer thought of him. He would be bound to be suspected anyway, and if you found out that he was there, in the Laboratory, and at the very moment it happened, then how could he hope to persuade you that he wasn't guilty? So we decided to say that we'd been together the whole evening. My mother did ring about nine o'clock to say that she'd got safely home, and I told her that Cliff was having a bath. She'd never really liked my marriage and I didn't want to admit to her that he was out. She'd only start criticizing him for leaving me and the baby. So we knew that she could confirm what I'd said, and that might be some help, even though she hadn't spoken to him. And then Cliff remembered about the vomit.'

Her husband went on, almost eagerly now, as if willing them to understand and believe:

'I knew I'd swilled cold water over my face, but I couldn't be certain that the bowl was clean. The more I thought about it, the more sure I was that it was stained with vomit. And I knew how much you could learn from that. I'm a secreter, but that didn't worry me. I knew that the stomach acids would destroy the antibodies and that the Lab wouldn't be able to determine my blood group. But there was the curry powder, the dye in the peas. They'd be able to say enough about that last meal to identify me. And I couldn't lie about what we'd had for supper because Sue's mother had been here sharing it with us.

'So we had this idea of trying to stop Mrs Bidwell going early to the Laboratory. I always get to work before nine, so I would be first on the scene quite naturally. If I went straight to the washroom as I normally would, and cleaned the bowl, then the only evidence that I was in the Lab the previous evening would be gone for ever. No one would ever know.'

Susan Bradley said:

'It was my idea to phone Mrs Bidwell, and I was the one who

spoke to her husband. We knew that she wouldn't answer the phone. She never did. But Cliff hadn't realized that old Mr Lorrimer wasn't entering hospital the previous day. He was out of the Department when old Mr Lorrimer rang. So the plan went all wrong. Mr Lorrimer telephoned Inspector Blakelock, and everyone arrived at the Lab almost as soon as Cliff. After that, there was nothing we could do but wait.'

Dalgliesh could imagine how terrible that time of waiting had been. No wonder that Bradley hadn't been able to face going in to the Lab. He asked:

'When you rang the bell at the Laboratory, how long was it before Dr Lorrimer answered?'

'Almost immediately. He couldn't have come down from the Biology Department. He must have been somewhere on the ground floor.'

'Did he say anything at all about expecting a visitor?'

The temptation was obvious. But Bradley said:

'No. He talked about having things to do, but I took it that he meant the analysis he was working on.'

'And when you found the body, you saw and heard nothing of the murderer?'

'No. I didn't wait to look, of course. But I'm sure he was there and very close. I don't know why.'

'Did you notice the position of the mallet, the fact that there was a page torn from Lorrimer's notebook?'

'No. Nothing. All I can remember is Lorrimer, the body and the thin stream of blood.'

'When you were in the washroom, did you hear the doorbell?'

'No, but I don't think I could have heard it, not above the first floor. And I'm sure I wouldn't have heard it while I was being sick.'

'When Dr Lorrimer opened the door to you, did anything strike you as unusual, apart from the fact that he had come so promptly?'

'Nothing, except that he was carrying his notebook.'

'Are you sure?'

'Yes, I'm sure. It was folded back.'

So Bradley's arrival had interrupted whatever it was that

Lorrimer had been doing. And he had been on the ground floor, the floor with the Director's office, the Records Department, the Exhibits Store.

Dalgliesh said:

'The car which turned into the drive as you left; what sort of car?'

'I didn't see. All I can remember are the headlights. We don't have a car and I'm not clever at recognizing the different models unless I get a clear look.'

'Can you remember how it was driven? Did the driver turn into the drive confidently as if he knew where he was going? Or did he hesitate as if he were looking for a convenient spot to stop and happened to see the open driveway?'

'He just slowed down a little and drove straight in. I think it was someone who knew the place. But I didn't wait to see if he drove up to the Lab. Next day, of course, I knew that it couldn't have been the police from Guy's Marsh or anyone with a key, or the body would have been discovered earlier.'

He looked at Dalgliesh with his anxious eyes.

'What will happen to me now? I can't face them at the Lab.'

'Inspector Massingham will drive you to Guy's Marsh police station so that you can make a formal statement and sign it. I'll explain to Dr Howarth what has happened. Whether you go back to the Lab and when must be for him and your Establishment Department to say. I imagine they may decide to give you special leave until this affair is settled.'

If it ever were settled. If Bradley were telling the truth, they now knew that Lorrimer had died between eight forty-five, when his father had telephoned him, and just before nine-eleven when the Guy's Marsh bus had moved away from the Chevisham stop. The clue of the vomit had fixed for them the time of death, had solved the mystery of the call to Mrs Bidwell. But it hadn't pointed them to a murderer. And if Bradley were innocent, what sort of life would he have, inside or outside the forensic science service, unless the case were solved? He watched Massingham and Bradley on their way, then set out to walk the half-mile back to Hoggatt's, not relishing the prospect of his interview with Howarth. Glancing back, he saw that Susan Bradley was still standing at the doorway looking after him, her baby in her arms.

V

Howarth said:

'I'm not going to trot out the usual platitude about blaming myself. I don't believe in that spurious acceptance of vicarious liability. All the same, I ought to have known that Bradley was near breaking point. I suspect that old Dr MacIntyre wouldn't have let this happen. And now I'd better telephone the Establishment Department. I expect they'll want him to stay at home for the present. It's particularly inconvenient from the point of view of the work. They need every pair of hands they can get in the Biology Department. Claire Easterbrook is taking on as much of Lorrimer's work as she can manage, but there's a limit to what she can do. At the moment she's busy with the clunch pit analysis. She's insisting on starting the electrophoresis again. I don't blame her; she's the one who'll have to give evidence. She can only speak for her own results.'

Dalgliesh asked what was likely to happen about Clifford Bradley.

'Oh, there'll be a regulation to cover the circumstances somewhere. There always is. He'll be dealt with by the usual compromise between expediency and humanity; unless, of course, you propose to arrest him for murder, in which case, administratively speaking, the problem will solve itself. By the way, the Public Relations Branch have rung. You probably haven't had time to see today's Press. Some of the papers are getting rather agitated about Lab security. "Are our blood samples safe?" And one of the Sundays has commissioned an article on science in the service of crime. They're sending someone to see me about three o'clock. Public Relations would like a word with you, incidentally. They're hoping to lay on another Press conference later this afternoon.'

When Howarth had left, Dalgliesh joined Sergeant Underhill and occupied himself with the four large bundles of files which Brenda Pridmore had provided. It was extraordinary how many of six thousand cases and nearly twenty-five thousand exhibits which the Laboratory dealt with each year had the numbers 18, 40 or 1840 in their registration. The cases came from all the departments: Biology, Toxicology, Criminalistics, Document Examination, Blood Alcohol Analysis, Vehicle Examination. Nearly every scientist in the Laboratory above the level of Higher Scientific Officer had been concerned in them. All of them seemed perfectly in order. He was still convinced that the mysterious telephone message to Lorrimer held the clue to the mystery of his death. But it seemed increasingly unlikely that the numbers, if old Mr Lorrimer had remembered them correctly, bore any reference to a file registration.

By three o'clock he had decided to put the task on one side and see if physical exercise would stimulate his brain. It was time, he thought, to walk through the grounds and take a look at the Wren chapel. He was reaching for his coat when the telephone rang. It was Massingham from Guy's Marsh station. The car which had parked in Hoggatt's drive on Wednesday night had at last been traced. It was a grey Cortina belonging to a Mrs Maureen Doyle. Mrs Doyle was at present staying with her parents in Ilford in Essex, but she had confirmed that the car was hers and that on the night of the murder it had been driven by her husband, Detective Inspector Doyle.

VI

The interview room at Guy's Marsh police station was small, stuffy and overcrowded. Superintendent Mercer, with his great bulk, was taking up more than his share of space and, it seemed to Massingham, breathing more than his share of the air. Of the five men present, including the shorthand writer, Doyle himself appeared both the most comfortable and the least concerned. Dalgliesh was questioning him. Mercer stood against the mullioned windows.

'You were at Hoggatt's last night. There are fresh tyre-marks in the earth under the trees to the right of the entrance, your tyre-marks. If you want to waste time for both of us, you can look at the casts.'

'I admit that they're my tyre-marks. I parked there, briefly, on Monday night.'

'Why?'

The question was so quiet, so reasonable, he might have had a genuine, human interest to know.

'I was with someone.' He paused and then added, 'Sir.'

'I hope, for your sake, that you were with someone last night. Even an embarrassing alibi is better than none. You quarrelled with Lorrimer. You're one of the few people he would have let into the Lab. And you parked your car under the trees. If you didn't murder him, why are you trying to persuade us that you did?'

'You don't really believe I killed him. Probably you already suspect or know who did. You can't frighten me, because I know you haven't any evidence. There isn't any to get. I was driving the Cortina because the clutch had gone on the Renault, not because I didn't want to be recognized. I was with Sergeant Beale until eight o'clock. We'd been to interview a man called Barry Taylor at Muddington, and then we went on to see one or two other people who'd been at the dance last Tuesday. From eight o'clock I was driving alone, and where I went was my own business.'

'Not when it's a case of murder. Isn't that what you tell your suspects when they come out with that good old bromide about the sanctity of their private lives? You can do better than that, Doyle.'

'I wasn't at the Lab on Wednesday night. Those tyre-marks were made when I parked there last Monday.'

'The Dunlop on the left-hand back wheel is new. It was fitted on Monday afternoon by Gorringe's garage, and your wife didn't collect the Cortina until ten o'clock on Wednesday morning. If you didn't drive to Hoggatt's to see Lorrimer, then what were you doing there? And if your business was legitimate, then why park just inside the entrance and under the trees?'

'If I'd been there to murder Lorrimer, I'd have parked in one of the garages at the back. That would have been safer than leaving the Cortina in the drive. And I didn't get to Hoggatt's until after nine. I knew that Lorrimer would be working late on the clunch pit case, but not that late. The Lab was in darkness. The truth, if you must know, is that I'd picked up a woman at the crossroads just outside Manea. I wasn't in any hurry to get home, and I wanted somewhere quiet and secluded to stop. The Lab seemed as good a place as any. We were there from about nine-fifteen until nine-fifty. No one left during that time.'

He had taken his time over what was presumably intended to be a quick one-night lay, thought Massingham. Dalgliesh asked:

'Did you trouble to find out who she was, exchange names?'

'I told her I was Ronny McDowell. It seemed as good a name as any. She said she was Dora Meakin. I don't suppose that more than one of us was lying.'

'And that's all, not where she lived or worked?'

'She said she worked at the sugar-beet factory and lived in a cottage near the ruined engine-house on Hunter's Fen. That's about three miles from Manea. She said she was a widow. Like a little gentleman, I dropped her at the bottom of the lane leading to Hunter's Fen. If she wasn't telling me a yarn, that should be enough to find her.'

Chief Superintendent Mercer said grimly:

'I hope for your sake that it is. You know what this means for you, of course?'

Doyle laughed. It was a surprisingly light-hearted sound.

'Oh I know, all right. But don't let that worry you. I'm handing in my resignation, and from now.'

Dalgliesh asked:

'Are you sure about the lights? The Lab was in darkness?'

'I shouldn't have stopped there if it hadn't been. There wasn't a light to be seen. And although I admit I was somewhat preoccupied for a minute or two, I could swear that no one came down that drive while we were there.'

'Or out of the front door?'

'That would be possible, I suppose. But the drive isn't more than forty yards long, I'd say. I think I'd have noticed, unless he slipped out very quickly. I doubt whether anyone would have risked it, not if he'd seen my headlights and knew that the car was there.'

Dalgliesh looked at Mercer. He said:

'We've got to get back to Chevisham. We'll take in Hunter's Fen on the way.'

VII

Leaning over the back of the Victorian chaise-longue, Angela Foley was massaging her friend's neck. The coarse hairs tickled the back of her hands as, firmly and gently, she kneaded the taut muscles, feeling for each separate vertebra under the hot, tense skin. Stella sat, head slumped forward in her hands. Neither spoke. Outside, a light scavenging wind was blowing fitfully over the fens, stirring the fallen leaves on the patio, and gusting the thin, white wood-smoke from the cottage chimney. But inside the sitting-room all was quiet, except for the crackling of the fire, the ticking of the grandfather clock, and the sound of their breathing. The cottage was full of the pungent, resinous aroma of burning apple wood, overlaid with the savoury smell from the kitchen of beef casserole reheated from yesterday's dinner.

After a few minutes Angela Foley said:

'Better? Would you like a cold compress on your forehead?'

'No, that's lovely. Almost gone in fact. Odd that I only get a headache on those days when the book has gone particularly well.'

'Another two minutes, then I'd better see about dinner.'

Angela flexed her fingers and bent again to her task. Stella's voice, muffled in her sweater, suddenly said:

'What was it like as a child, being in local authority care?'

'I'm not sure that I know. I mean, I wasn't in a Home or anything like that. They fostered me most of the time.'

'Well, what was that like? You've never really told me.'

'It was all right. No, that's not true. It was like living in a second-rate boarding house where they don't want you and you know that you won't be able to pay the bill. Until I met you and came here I felt like that all the time, not really at home in the world. I suppose my foster-parents were kind. They meant to be. But I wasn't pretty, and I wasn't grateful. It can't be much fun fostering other people's children, and I suppose one does rather look for gratitude. Looking back, I can see that I wasn't much joy for them, plain and surly. I once heard a neighbour say to my third foster-mother that I looked just like a foetus with my bulging forehead and tiny features. I resented the other children because they had mothers and I hadn't. I've never really outgrown that. It's despicable, but I even dislike Brenda Pridmore, the new girl on our reception desk, because she's so obviously a loved child, she's got a proper home.'

'So have you now. But I know what you mean. By the age of five you've either learned that the world is good, that everything and everyone in it stretches out towards you with love. Or you know that you're a reject. No one ever unlearns that first lesson.'

'I have, because of you. Star, don't you think we ought to start looking for another cottage, perhaps nearer Cambridge? There's bound to be a job there for a qualified secretary.'

'We're not going to need another cottage. I telephoned my publishers this afternoon, and I think it's going to be all right.'

'Hearne and Gollingwood? But how can it be all right? I thought you said . . .'

'It's going to be all right.'

Suddenly Stella shook herself free of the ministering hands and stood up. She went into the passage and came back, her duffle-coat over her shoulder, her boots in hand. She moved over to the fireside chair and began to pull them on. Angela Foley watched her without speaking. Then Stella took from her jacket pocket a brown opened envelope and tossed it across. It fell on the velvet of the chaise-longue.

'Oh, I meant to show you this.'

Puzzled, Angela took out the single folded sheet. She said:

'Where did you find this?'

'I took it from Edwin's desk when I was rummaging about for the will. I thought at the time that I might have a use for it. Now I've decided that I haven't.'

'But, Star, you should have left it for the police to find! It's a clue. They'll have to know. This was probably what Edwin was doing that night, checking up. It's important. We can't keep it to ourselves.'

'Then you'd better go back to Postmill Cottage and pretend to find it, otherwise it's going to be a bit embarrassing explaining how we came by it.'

'But the police aren't going to believe that; they wouldn't have missed it. I wonder when it arrived at the Lab. It's odd that he took it home with him and didn't even lock it up.'

'Why should he? There was only the one locked drawer in his desk. And I don't suppose anyone, even his father, ever went into that room.'

'But Star, this could explain why he was killed! This could be a motive for murder.'

'Oh, I don't think so. It's just a gratuitous bit of spite, anonymous, proving nothing. Edwin's death was both simpler, and more complicated, than that. Murder usually is. But the police might see it as a motive, and that would be convenient for us. I'm beginning to think I should have left it where it was.'

She had pulled on her boots and was ready to go. Angela Foley said:

'You know who killed him, don't you?'

'Does that shock you, that I haven't rushed to confide in that extraordinarily personable Commander?'

Angela whispered:

'What are you going to do?'

'Nothing. I've no proof. Let the police do the work they're paid for. I might have had more public spirit when we had the death penalty. I'm not afraid of the ghosts of hanged men. They can stand at the four corners of my bed and howl all night if it pleases them. But I couldn't go on living – I couldn't go on working, which amounts to the same thing for me – knowing that I'd put another human being in prison, and for life.'

'Not really for life. About ten years.'

'I couldn't stand it for ten days. I'm going out now. I shan't be long.'

'But, Star, it's nearly seven! We were going to eat.'

'The casserole won't spoil.'

Angela Foley watched silently as her friend went to the door. Then she said:

'Star, how did you know about Edwin practising his evidence the night before he had to go into the box?'

'If you didn't tell me, and you say that you didn't, then I must have invented it, I couldn't have learnt it from anyone else. You'd better put it down to creative imagination.'

Her hand was on the door. Angela cried out:

'Star, don't go out tonight. Stay with me. I'm afraid.'

'For yourself, or for me?'

'For both of us. Please don't go. Not tonight.'

Stella turned. She smiled and spread her hands in what could have been a gesture of resignation or a farewell. There was a howl of wind, a rush of cold air as the front door opened. Then the sound of its closing echoed through the cottage, and Stella was gone.

VIII

'My God, this is a dreary place!'

Massingham slammed the car door and gazed about in disbelief at the prospect before them. The lane, down which they had bumped in the fading light, had at last ended at a narrow iron bridge over a sluice, running grey and sluggish as oil, between high dykes. On the other bank was a derelict Victorian engine-house, the bricks tumbled in a disorderly heap beside the stagnant stream, the great wheel half visible through the ruined wall. Beside it were two cottages lying below water-level. Behind them the scarred and sullen acres of the hedgeless fields stretched to the red and purple of the evening sky. The carcass of a petrified tree, a bog-oak, struck by the plough and dredged from the depths of the peat, had been dumped beside the track to dry. It looked like some mutilated prehistoric creature raising its stumps to the uncomprehending sky. Although the last two days had been dry with some sun, the landscape looked saturated by the weeks of rain, the front gardens sour and waterlogged, the trunks of the few stunted trees sodden as pulp. It looked a country on which the sun could never shine. As their feet rang on the iron bridge a solitary duck rose with an agitated squawking, but otherwise the silence was absolute.

There was a light behind the drawn curtains of only one of the cottages, and they walked between wind-blown clumps of faded Michaelmas daisies to the front door. The paint was peeling, the iron knocker was so stiff that Dalgliesh raised it with difficulty. For a few minutes after the dull peremptory thud there was silence. Then the door was opened.

They saw a drab, shallow-faced woman, aged about forty, with pale anxious eyes and untidy straw-coloured hair strained back under two combs. She was wearing a brown checked Crimplene dress topped with a bulky cardigan in a harsh shade of blue. As soon as he saw her, Massingham instinctively drew back with an apology, but Dalgliesh said:

'Mrs Meakin? We're police officers. May we come in?'

She didn't trouble to look at his proffered identity card. She hardly seemed surprised even. Without speaking she pressed herself against the wall of the passage and they passed before her into the sitting-room. It was small and very plainly furnished, drearily tidy and uncluttered. The air smelt damp and chill. There was an electric reflector fire with one bar burning, and the single pendant bulb gave a harsh but inadequate light. A plain wooden table stood in the middle of the room, with four chairs. She was obviously about to start her supper. On a tray there was a plate of three fish fingers, a mound of mashed potato and peas. Beside it was an unopened carton containing an apple tart.

Dalgliesh said:

'I'm sorry that we're interrupting your meal. Would you like to take it into the kitchen to keep it warm?' She shook her head and motioned them to sit down. They settled themselves round the table like three card players, the tray of food between them. The peas were exuding a greenish liquid in which the fish fingers were slowly congealing. It was hard to believe that so small a meal could produce so strong a smell. After a few seconds, as if conscious of it, she pushed the tray to one side. Dalgliesh took out Doyle's photograph and passed it across to her. He said:

'I believe you spent some time yesterday evening with this man.'

'Mr McDowell. He's not in any trouble is he? You're not private detectives? He was kind, a real gentleman, I wouldn't like to get him into trouble.'

Her voice was low and rather toneless, Dalgliesh thought, a countrywoman's voice. He said:

'No, we're not private detectives. He is in some trouble, but not because of you. We're police officers. You can help him best by telling the truth. What we're really interested in is when you first met him and how long you were together.'

She looked across at him.

'You mean, a sort of alibi?'

'That's right. A sort of alibi.'

'He picked me up where I usually stand, at the crossroads, about half a mile from Manea. That must have been about seven. Then we drove to a pub. They nearly always start off by buying me a drink. That's the part I like, having someone to sit with in the pub, watching the people, hearing the voices and the noise. I usually have a sherry, or a port, maybe. If they ask me, I have a second. I never have got more than two drinks. Sometimes they're in a hurry to get away so I only get offered the one.'

Dalgliesh asked quietly:

'Where did he take you?'

'I don't know where it was, but it was about thirty minutes' drive. I could see him thinking where to go before he drove off. That's how I know he lives locally. They like to get clear of the district where they're known. I've noticed that, that and the quick look round they give before we go into the pub. The pub was called The Plough. I saw that from the illuminated sign outside. We were in the saloon bar, of course, quite nice really. They had a peat fire and there was a high shelf with a lot of different coloured plates round it and two vases of artificial roses behind the bar, and a black cat in front of the fire. The barman was called Joe. He was ginger-haired.'

'How long did you stay there?'

'Not long. I had two ports and he had two doubles of whisky. Then he said we ought to be going.'

'Where did he take you next, Mrs Meakin?'

'I think it was Chevisham. I glimpsed the signpost at the crossroads just before we got there. We turned into the drive of this big house and parked under the trees. I asked who lived there, and he said no one, it was just for Government offices. Then he put out the lights.'

Dalgliesh said gently:

'And you made love in the car. Did you get into the back seat, Mrs Meakin?'

She was neither surprised nor distressed at the question.

'No, we stayed in the front.'

'Mrs Meakin, this is very important. Can you remember how long you were there?'

'Oh yes, I could see the clock on the dashboard. It was nearly quarter past nine when we arrived and we stayed there until just before ten. I know because I was a bit worried wondering whether he'd drop me at the end of the lane. That's all I expected. I wouldn't have wanted him to come to the door. But it can be awkward if I'm just left, miles from home. Sometimes it isn't easy to get back.'

She spoke, thought Massingham, as if she were complaining about the local bus service. Dalgliesh said:

'Did anyone leave the house and come down the drive while you were in the car? Would you have noticed if they had?'

'Oh yes, I think so. I should have seen if they'd gone out through the space where the gate used to be. There's a street-light opposite and it shines on the drive.'

Massingham asked bluntly:

'But would you have noticed? Weren't you a bit occupied?'

Suddenly she laughed, a hoarse, discordant sound which startled them both.

'Do you think I was enjoying myself? Do you suppose I like it?' Then her voice again became toneless, almost subservient. She said obdurately:

'I should have noticed.'

Dalgliesh added:

'What did you talk about, Mrs Meakin?'

The question brightened her. She turned to Dalgliesh almost eagerly.

'Oh, he's got his troubles. Everyone has, haven't they? Sometimes it helps to talk to a stranger, someone you know you won't ever see again. They never do ask to see me again. He didn't. But he was kind, not in a rush to get away. Sometimes they almost push me out of the car. That isn't gentlemanly; it's hurtful. But he seemed glad to talk. It was about his wife really. Not wanting to live in the country. She's a London girl and keeps nagging him to get back there. She wants him to leave his job and go and work for her father. She's at home with her parents now and he doesn't know whether she'll come back.'

'He didn't tell you he was a police officer?'

'Oh no! He said he was a dealer in antiques. He seemed to know quite a lot about them. But I don't take much notice when they tell me about their jobs. Mostly they pretend.'

Dalgliesh said gently:

'Mrs Meakin, what you are doing is terribly risky. You know that, don't you? Some day a man will stop who wants more than an hour or so of your time, someone dangerous.'

'I know. Sometimes when the car slows down and I'm standing there waiting at the side of the road, wondering what he'll be like, I can hear my heart thudding. I know then that I'm afraid. But at least I'm feeling something. It's better to be afraid than alone.'

Massingham said:

'It's better to be alone than dead.'

She looked at him.

'You think so, sir? But then you don't know anything about it, do you?'

Five minutes later they left, having explained to Mrs Meakin that a police officer would call for her next day so that she could be taken to make a statement at Guy's Marsh station. She seemed perfectly happy about this, only asking whether anyone at the factory need know. Dalgliesh reassured her.

When they had crossed the bridge, Massingham turned to look back at the cottage. She was still standing at the door, a thin figure silhouetted against the light. He said angrily:

'God, it's all so hopeless. Why doesn't she get out of here, move to a town, Ely or Cambridge, see some life?'

'You sound like one of those professionals whose advice to the lonely is always the same: "Get out and meet people, join a club." Which, come to think of it, is precisely what she's doing.'

'It would help if she got away from this place, found herself a different job.'

'What job? She probably thinks that she's lucky to be employed. And this is at least a home. It takes youth, energy and money to change your whole life. She hasn't any of those. All she can do is to keep sane in the only way she knows.'

'But for what? To end up another corpse dumped in a clunch pit?'

'Perhaps. That's probably what she's subconsciously looking for. There's more than one way of courting death. She would argue that her way at least gives her the consolation of a warm, brightly lit bar and, always, the hope that, next time, it may be different. She isn't going to stop because a couple of intruding policemen tell her that it's dangerous. She knows about that. For God's sake let's get out of here.'

As they buckled their seat-belts, Massingham said:

'Who'd have thought that Doyle would have bothered with her. I can imagine him picking her up. As Lord Chesterfield said, all cats are grey in the dark. But to spend the best part of an hour telling her his troubles.'

'They each wanted something from the other. Let's hope they got it.'

'Doyle got something; an alibi. And we haven't done too badly out of their encounter. We know now who killed Lorrimer.'

Dalgliesh said:

'We think we know who and how. We may even think we know why. But we haven't a scintilla of proof and without evidence we can't move another step. At present, we haven't even enough facts to justify applying for a search warrant.'

'What now, sir?'

'Back to Guy's Marsh. When this Doyle affair is settled I want to hear Underhill's report and speak to the Chief Constable. Then back to Hoggatt's. We'll park where Doyle parked. I'd like to check whether it would be possible for someone to sneak down that drive without being seen.'

IX

By seven o'clock the work was at last up to date, the last court report had been checked, the last completed exhibit packed for the police to collect, the figures of cases and exhibits received had been calculated and checked. Brenda thought how tired Inspector Blakelock seemed. He had hardly spoken an unnecessary word during the last hour. She didn't feel that he was displeased with her, merely that he hardly knew she was there. She had talked little herself, and then in whispers, afraid to break the silence, eerie and almost palpable, of the empty hall. To her right the great staircase curved upwards into darkness. All day it had echoed to the feet of scientists, policemen, scene-of-crime officers arriving for their lecture. Now it had become as portentous and threatening as the staircase of a haunted house. She tried not to look at it, but it drew her eyes irresistibly. With every fleeting upward glance she half imagined that she could see Lorrimer's white face forming out of the amorphous shadows to hang imprinted on the still air, Lorrimer's black eyes gazing down at her in entreaty or despair.

At seven o'clock Inspector Blakelock said:

'Well, that's about all then. Your mum won't be best pleased that you've been kept late tonight.'

Brenda said with more confidence than she felt:

'Oh, Mum won't mind. She knew I was late starting. I rang her earlier and said not to expect me until half past.'

They went their separate ways to collect their coats. Then Brenda waited by the door until Inspector Blakelock had set and checked the internal alarm. All the doors of the separate laboratories had been closed and checked earlier in the evening. Lastly they went out by the front door and he turned the two final keys. Brenda's bicycle was kept in a shed by the side of the old stables, where the cars were garaged. Still together, they went round to the back. Inspector Blakelock waited to start his car until she had mounted, then followed her very slowly down the drive. At the gate he gave a valedictory hoot and turned to the left. Brenda waved and set off briskly, pedalling in the opposite direction. She thought she knew why the Inspector had waited so carefully until she was safely off the premises, and she felt grateful. Perhaps, she thought, I remind him of his dead daughter and that's why he's so kind to me.

And then, almost immediately, it happened. The sudden bump and the scrape of metal against tarmac were unmistakable. The bicycle lurched, almost throwing her into the ditch. Squeezing on both brakes she dismounted and examined the tyres by the light of the heavy torch which she always kept in her bicycle saddlebag. Both were flat. Her immediate reaction was one of intense irritation. This would happen on a late night! She swept the torchlight over the road behind her, trying to identify the source of the mishap. There must be glass or something sharp on the road somewhere. But she could see nothing, and realized that it wouldn't help if she did. There was no hope of repairing the punctures. The next bus home was the one due to pass the Laboratory just after nine o'clock, and there was no one left at the Lab to give her a lift. She spent very little time in thinking. The best plan was obviously to return the bicycle to its rack and then make her way home through the new Laboratory. It would cut off nearly a couple of miles and, if she walked fast, she could be home just after seven-thirty.

Anger, and ineffective railing against bad luck, is a powerful antidote to fear. So is hunger and the healthy tiredness that longs for its own fireside. Brenda had jerked the bicycle, now reduced to a ridiculously antiquated encumbrance, back into its stand and had walked briskly through the grounds of Hoggatt's and unbolted the wooden gate which led to the new site before she began to feel afraid. But now, alone in the darkness, the half-superstitious dread which it had seemed safe to stimulate in the Laboratory with Inspector Blakelock so reassuringly by her side, began to prick at her nerves. Before her the black bulk of the half-completed Laboratory loomed like some prehistoric monument, its great slabs bloodstained with ancient sacrifices, rearing upwards towards the implacable gods. The night was fitfully dark with a low ceiling of cloud obscuring the faint stars.

As she hesitated, the clouds parted like ponderous hands to unveil the full moon, frail and transparent as a Communion wafer. Gazing at it she could almost taste the remembered transitory dough, melting against the roof of her mouth. Then the clouds formed again and the darkness closed about her. And the wind was rising.

She held the torch more firmly. It was solidly reassuring and heavy in her hand. Resolutely she picked out her way between the tarpaulin-shrouded piles of bricks, the great girders laid in rows, the two neat huts on stilts which served as the contractor's office, towards the gap in the brickwork which marked the entrance to the main site. Then once again she hesitated. The gap seemed to narrow before her eyes, to become almost symbolically ominous and frightening, an entrance to darkness and the unknown. The fears of a childhood not so far distant reasserted themselves. She was tempted to turn back.

Then she admonished herself sternly not to be stupid. There was nothing strange or sinister about a half-completed building, an artefact of brick, concrete and steel, holding no memories of the past, concealing no secret miseries between ancient walls. Besides, she knew the site quite well. The Laboratory staff weren't supposed to take a short cut through the new buildings – Dr Howarth had pinned up a notice on the staff notice-board pointing out the dangers – but everyone knew that it was done. Before the building had been started there had been a footpath across Hoggatt's field. It was natural for people to behave as if it were still there. And she was tired and hungry. It was ridiculous to hesitate now.

Then she remembered her parents. No one at home could know about the punctures and her mother would soon begin worrying. She or her father would probably ring the Laboratory and, getting no reply, would know that everyone had left. They would imagine her dead or injured on the road, being lifted unconscious into an ambulance. Worse, they would see her lying crumpled on the floor of the Laboratory, a second victim. It had been difficult enough to persuade her parents to let her stay on in the job, and this final anxiety, growing with every minute she was overdue and culminating in the relief and reactive anger of her late appearance, might easily tip them into an unreasoned but obstinate insistence that she should leave. It really was the worst possible time to be late home. She shone her torch steadily on the entrance gap and moved resolutely into the darkness.

She tried to picture the model of the new Laboratory set up in the library. This large vestibule, still unroofed, must be the reception area from which the two main wings diverged. She must bear to the left through what would be the Biology Department for the quickest cut to the Guy's Marsh road. She swept the torch beam over the brick walls, then picked her way carefully across the uneven ground towards the left-hand aperture. The pool of light found another doorway, and then another. The darkness seemed to increase, heavy with the smell of brick dust and pressed earth. And now the pale haze of the night sky was extinguished and she was in the roofed area of the Laboratory. The silence was absolute.

She found herself creeping forward, breath held, eyes fixed in a stare on the small pool of light at her feet. And suddenly there was nothing, no sky above, no doorway, nothing but black blackness. She swept the torch over the walls. They were menacingly close. This room was surely far too small even for an office. She seemed to have stumbled into some kind of cupboard or storeroom. Somewhere, she knew, there must be a gap, the one by which she had entered. But disorientated in the claustrophobic darkness, she could no longer distinguish the ceiling from the walls. With every sweep of the torch the crude bricks seemed to be closing in on her, the ceiling to descend inexorably like the slowly closing lid of a tomb. Fighting for control, she inched gradually along one wall, telling herself that, soon, she must strike the open doorway.

Suddenly the torch jerked in her hand and the pool of light spilt over the floor. She stopped dead, appalled at her peril. In the middle of the room was a square well protected only by two planks thrown across it. One step in panic and she might have kicked them away, stumbled, and dropped into inky nothingness. In her imagination the well was fathomless, her body would never be found. She would lie there in the mud and darkness, too weak to make herself heard. And all she would hear would be the distant voices of the workmen as, brick on brick, they walled her up alive in her black tomb. And then another and more rational horror struck.

She thought about the punctured tyres. Could that really have been an accident? The tyres had been sound when she had parked the bicycle that morning. Perhaps it hadn't been glass on the road after all. Perhaps someone had done it purposely, someone who knew that she would be late leaving the Lab, that there would be no one left to give her a lift, that she would be bound to walk through the new building. She pictured him in the darkness of the early evening, slipping soundless into the bicycle shed, knife in hand, crouching down to the tyres, listening for the hiss of escaping air, calculating how big a rent would cause the tyres to collapse before she had cycled too far on her journey. And now he was waiting for her, knife in hand, somewhere in the darkness. He had smiled, fingering the blade, listening for her every step, watching for the light of her torch. He, too, would have a torch, of course. Soon it would blaze into her face, blinding her eyes, so that she couldn't see the cruel triumphant mouth, the flashing knife. Instinctively she switched off the light and listened, her heart pounding with such a thunder of blood that she felt that even the brick walls must shake.

And then she heard the noise, gentle as a single footfall, soft as the brush of a coat-sleeve against wood. He was coming. He was here. And now there was only panic. Sobbing, she threw herself from side to side against the walls, thudding her bruised palms against the gritty, unyielding brick. Suddenly there was a space. She fell through, tripped, and the torch spun out of her hands. Moaning she lay and waited for death. Then terror swooped with a wild screech of exultation and a thrashing of wings which lifted the hair from her scalp. She screamed, a thin wail of sound which was lost in the bird's cry as the owl found the paneless window and soared into the night.

She didn't know how long she lay there, her sore hands clutching the earth, her mouth choked with dust. But after a while she controlled her sobbing and lifted her head. She saw the window plainly, an immense square of luminous light, pricked with stars. And to the right of it gleamed the doorway. She scrambled to her feet. She didn't wait to search for the torch but made straight for that blessed aperture of light. Beyond it was another. And, suddenly, there were no more walls, only the spangled dome of the sky swinging above her.

Still sobbing, but now with relief, she ran unthinkingly in the moonlight, her hair streaming behind her, her feet hardly seeming to touch the earth. And now there was a belt of trees before her and, gleaming through the autumn branches, the Wren chapel, lit from within, beckoning and holy, shining like a picture on a Christmas card. She ran towards it, palms outstretched, as hundreds of her forebears in the dark fens must have rushed to their altars for sanctuary. The door was ajar and a shaft of light lay like an arrow on the path. She threw herself against the oak, and the great door swung inwards into a glory of light.

At first her mind, shocked into stupor, refused to recognize what her dazzled eyes so clearly saw. Uncomprehending, she put up a tentative hand and stroked the soft corduroy of the slacks, the limp moist hand. Slowly, as if by an act of will, her eyes travelled upwards and she both saw and understood. Stella Mawson's face, dreadful in death, drooped above her, the eyes half open, the palms disposed outward as if in a mute appeal for pity or for help. Circling her neck was a double cord of blue silk, its tasselled end tied to a hook on the wall. Beside it, wound on a second hook, was the single bell-rope. There was a low wooden chair upended close to the dangling feet. Brenda seized it. Moaning, she grasped at the rope and swung on it three times before it slipped from her loosening hands, and she fainted.

X

Less than a mile away across the field and the grounds of Hoggatt's, Massingham drove the Rover into the Laboratory drive and backed into the bushes. He switched off the car lights. The street-lamp opposite the entrance cast a soft glow over the path, and the door of the Laboratory was plainly visible in the moonlight. He said:

'I'd forgotten, sir, that tonight is the night of the full moon. He'd have had to wait until it moved behind a cloud. Even so, he could surely get out of the house and down the drive unseen if he chose a lucky moment. After all, Doyle had his mind – and not only his mind – on other things.'

'But the murderer wasn't to know that. If he saw the car arriving, I doubt whether he would have risked it. Well, we can at least find out if it's possible even without the co-operation of Mrs Meakin. This reminds me of a childhood game, Grandmother's Footsteps. Will you try first, or shall I?'

But the experiment was destined never to take place. It was at that moment that they heard, faint but unmistakable, three clear peals of the chapel bell.

XI

Massingham drove the car fast on to the grass verge and braked within inches of the hedge. Beyond them the road curved gently between a tattered fringe of windswept bushes, past what looked like a dilapidated barn of blackened wood and through the naked fens to Guy's Marsh. To the right was the black bulk of the new Laboratory. Massingham's torch picked out a stile, and, beyond it, a footpath leading across the field to a distant circle of trees, now no more than a dark smudge against the night sky. He said:

'Odd how remote from the house it is, and how secluded. You wouldn't know it was there. Anyone would think that the original family built it for some secret, necromantic rite.'

'More probably as a family mausoleum. They didn't plan for extinction.'

Neither of them spoke again. They had instinctively driven the mile and a half to the nearest access to the chapel from the Guy's Marsh road. Although less direct, this was quicker and easier than finding their way by foot through the Laboratory grounds and the new building. Their feet quickened and they found they were almost running, driven by some unacknowledged fear, towards the distant trees.

And now they were in the circle of loosely planted beeches, dipping their heads under the low branches, their feet scuffling noisily through the crackling drifts of fallen leaves, and could see at last the faintly gleaming windows of the chapel. At the half-open door Massingham instinctively turned as if to hurl his shoulder against it, then drew back with a grin.

'Sorry, I'm forgetting. No sense in precipitating myself in. It's probably only Miss Willard polishing the brass or the rector saying an obligatory prayer to keep the place sanctified.'

Gently, and with a slight flourish, he pushed open the door and stood aside; and Dalgliesh stepped before him into the lighted antechapel.

After that there was no speech, no conscious thought, only instinctive action. They moved as one. Massingham grasped and lifted the dangling legs and Dalgliesh, seizing the chair upturned by Brenda's slumping body, slipped the double loop of cord from

Stella Mawson's neck and lowered her to the floor. Massingham tore at the fastenings of her duffle jacket, forced back her head and, flinging himself beside her, closed his mouth over hers. The bundle huddled against the wall stirred and moaned, and Dalgliesh knelt beside her. At the touch of his arms on her shoulders she struggled madly for a moment, squealing like a kitten, then opened her eyes and recognized him. Her body relaxed against his. She said faintly:

'The murderer. In the new Lab. He was waiting for me. Has he gone?'

There was a panel of light switches to the left of the door. Dalgliesh clicked them on with a single gesture, and the inner chapel blazed into light. He stepped through the carved organ-screen into the chancel. It was empty. The door to the organ loft was ajar. He clattered up the narrow winding stairway into the gallery. It, too, was empty. Then he stood looking down at the quiet emptiness of the chancel, his eyes moving from the exquisite plaster ceiling, the chequered marble floor, the double row of elegantly carved stalls with their high-arched backs set against the north and south walls, the oak table, stripped of its altar-cloth, which stood before the reredos under the eastern window. All it now held were two silver candlesticks, the tall white candles burnt half down, the wicks blackened. And to the left of the altar, hanging incongruously, was a wooden hymnboard, showing four numbers:

29
10
18
40

He recalled old Mr Lorrimer's voice, 'She said something about the can being burned and that she'd got the numbers.' The last two numbers had been 18 and 40. And what had been burned was not a can, not cannabis, but two altar candles.

XII

Forty minutes later, Dalgliesh was alone in the chapel. Dr Greene had been sent for, had briefly pronounced Stella Mawson dead, and had departed. Massingham had left with him to take Brenda Pridmore home and to explain to her parents what had happened, to call at Sprogg's Cottage and to summon Dr Howarth. Dr Greene had given Brenda a sedative by injection, but had held out no hope that she would be fit to be questioned before morning. The forensic pathologist had been summoned and was on his way. The voices, the questions, the ringing footsteps, all for the moment were stilled.

Dalgliesh felt extraordinarily alone in the silence of the chapel, more alone because her body lay there, and he had the sense that someone – or something – had recently left, leaving bereft the unencumbered air. This isolation of the spirit was not new to him; he had felt it before in the company of the recently dead. Now he knelt and gazed intently at the dead woman. In life only her eyes had lent distinction to that haggard face. Now they were glazed and gummy as sticky sweetmeats forced under the half-opened lids. It was not a peaceful face. Her features, not yet settled in death, still bore the strain of life's inquietude. He had seen so many dead faces. He had become adept at reading the stigmata of violence. Sometimes they could tell him how, or where, or when. But essentially, as now, they told him nothing.

He lifted the end of the cord still looped loosely around her neck. It was made of woven silk in royal blue, long enough to drape a heavy curtain, and was finished with an ornate silver and blue tassel. There was a five-foot panelled chest against the wall and, putting on his gloves, he lifted the heavy lid. The smell of mothballs came up to him, pungent as an anaesthetic. Inside the chest was a folded pair of faded blue velvet curtains, a starched but crumpled surplice, the black and white of an M.A. hood, and, lying on top of this assorted bundle, a second tasselled cord. Whoever had put that cord round her neck – herself or another – had known in advance where it could be found.

He began to explore the chapel. He walked softly, yet his fee fell with portentous heaviness on the marbled floor. Slowly, h paced between the two rows of splendidly carved stalls toward the altar. In design and furnishing the building reminded him c his college chapel. Even the smell was the same, a scholasti smell, cold, austere, only faintly ecclesiastical. Now that the alta had been denuded of all its furnishing except the two candlesticks, the chapel looked purely secular, unconsecrated. Perhaps it always had. Its formal classicism rejected emotion. It enshrined man, not God; reason, not mystery. This was a place where certain reassuring rituals had been enacted, reaffirming its proprietor's view of the proper order of the universe and his own place in that order. He looked for some memento of that original owner and found it. To the right of the altar was the chapel's only memorial, a carved bust, half draped with a looped marble curtain, of a bewigged eighteenth-century gentleman, with the inscription:

Dieu aye merci de son ame.

This simple petition, unadorned, so out of period, was singularly inapposite to the formal confidence of the memorial, the proud tilt of the head, the self-satisfied smirk on the opulent marble lips. He had built his chapel and set it in a triple circle of trees, and death had not stayed its hand even long enough to give him time to make his carriage drive.

On either side of the organ-screen and facing the east window were two ornate stalls under carved canopies, each shielded from draughts by a blue velvet curtain similar to those in the chest. The seats were fitted with matching cushions; soft cushions with silver tassels at each corner lay on the book-rests. He climbed into the right-hand stall. On the cushion was a heavy black leather Book of Common Prayer which looked unused. The pages opened stiffly and the bold black and red lettering shone from the page.

> 'For I am a stranger with thee: and a sojourner, as all my fathers were. O spare me a little, that I may recover my strength: before I go hence, and be no more seen.'

He held the book by its spine and shook it. No paper fluttered from its rigid leaves. But where it had lain, four hairs, one fair and three dark, had adhered to the velvet pile. He took an envelope from his pocket and stuck them to the gummed flap. He knew how little the forensic scientists could hope to do with only four hairs, but it was possible that something could be learned.

The chapel, he thought, must have been ideal for them. Shielded by its trees, isolated, secure, warm even. The fen villages kept indoors once darkness fell and, even in the evening light, would have a half-superstitious dread of visiting this empty and alien shrine. Even without a key they need fear no casual intruder. She need only watch that she was unobserved when she drove the red Jaguar into Hoggatt's drive to park it out of sight in one of the garages in the stable block. And then what? Wait for the light in the Biology Department to go out at last, for the advancing gleam of light from Lorrimer's torch as he joined her for that walk through the Lab grounds and into the trees. He wondered whether she had dragged the velvet cushions to the sanctuary, whether it had added to the excitement to make love to Lorrimer in front of that denuded altar, the new passion triumphing over the old.

Massingham's flame of hair appeared in the doorway. He said:

'The girl's all right. Her mother got her straight to bed and she's asleep. I called next at Sprogg's Cottage. The door was open and the sitting-room light was on, but there's no one there. Howarth was at home when I rang, but not Mrs Schofield. He said he'd be along. Dr Kerrison is at the hospital at a medical committee meeting. His housekeeper said that he left just after seven. I didn't ring the hospital. If he is there, he'll be able to produce plenty of witnesses.'

'And Middlemass?'

'No answer. Out to dinner, or at the local perhaps. No answer either from the Blakelocks' number. Anything here, sir?'

'Nothing, except what we'd expect to find. You've got a man posted to direct Blain-Thomson when he arrives?'

'Yes, sir. And I think he's arriving now.'

XIII

Dr Reginald Blain-Thomson had a curious habit, before beginning his examination, of mincing round the body, eyes fixed on it with wary intensity as if half afraid that the corpse might spring into life and seize him by the throat. He minced now, immaculate in his grey pinstriped suit, the inevitable rose in i silver holder looking as fresh in his lapel as if it were a June blossom, newly plucked. He was a tall, lean-faced, aristocratic-looking bachelor with a skin as freshly pink and soft as that of a girl. He was never known to put on protective clothing before examining a body, and reminded Dalgliesh of one of those television cooks who prepare a four-course dinner in full evening dress for the pleasure of demonstrating the essential refinement of their craft. It was even rumoured, unjustly, that Blain-Thomson performed his autopsy in a lounge suit.

But, despite these personal idiosyncrasies, he was an excellent forensic pathologist. Juries loved him. When he stood in the box and recited, with slightly world-weary formality and in his actor's voice, the details of his formidable qualifications and experience, they gazed at him with the respectful admiration of men who know a distinguished consultant when they see one, and have no intention of being so disobliging as to disbelieve what he might choose to tell them.

Now he squatted by the body, listened, smelled and touched. Then he switched off his examination torch and got to his feet. He said:

'Yes, well. Obviously she's dead and it's very recent. Within the last two hours, if you press me. But you must have reached that conclusion yourselves or you wouldn't have cut her down. When did you say you found her? Three minutes after eight. Dead one and a half hours then, say. It's possible. You're going to ask me whether it's suicide or murder. All I can say at the moment is that there's only the double mark encircling the neck and the cord fits. But you can see that for yourselves. There's no sign of manual throttling, and it doesn't look as if the cord were superimposed on a finer ligature. She's a frail woman, little more than seven stone, I'd estimate, so it wouldn't need strength to overpower her. But there's no sign of a struggle and the nails look perfectly clean, so she probably didn't get the chance to scratch. If it is murder, he must have come up behind her very swiftly, dropped the looped cord over her head, and strung her up almost as soon as unconsciousness supervened. As for the cause of death – whether it's strangulation, broken neck or vagal inhibition – well, you'll have to wait until I get her on the table. I can take her away now if you're ready.'

'How soon can you do the P.M.?'

'Well, it had better be at once, hadn't it? You're keeping me busy, Commander. No questions about my report on Lorrimer, I suppose?'

Dalgliesh answered:

'None, thank you. I did try to get you on the phone.'

'I'm sorry I've been elusive. I've been incarcerated in committees practically all day. When's the Lorrimer inquest?'

'Tomorrow, at two o'clock.'

'I'll be there. They'll adjourn it, I suppose. And I'll give you a ring and a preliminary report as soon as I've got her sewn up.'

He drew on his gloves carefully, finger by finger, then left. They could hear him exchanging a few words with the constable who was waiting outside to light him across the field to his car. One of them laughed. Then the voices faded.

Massingham put his head outside the door. The two dark-uniformed attendants from the mortuary van, anonymous bureaucrats of death, manoeuvred their trolley through the door with nonchalant skill. Stella Mawson's body was lifted with impersonal gentleness. The men turned to trundle the trolley out through the door. But suddenly the way was blocked by two dark shadows, and Howarth and his sister stepped quietly and simultaneously into the light of the chapel. The figures with the trolley paused stock-still like ancient helots, unseeing, unhearing.

Massingham thought that their entrance seemed as dramatically contrived as that of a couple of film stars arriving at a première. They were dressed identically in slacks and fawn leather jackets, lined with shaggy fur, the collars upturned. And for the first time he was struck by their essential likeness. The impression of a film was reinforced. Gazing at the two pale, arrogant heads framed with fur, he thought that they looked like decadent twins, their fair, handsome profiles theatrically posed against the dark oak panelling. Again simultaneously, their eyes moved to the shrouded lump on the trolley, then fixed themselves on Dalgliesh. He said to Howarth:

'You took your time coming.'

'My sister was out driving and I waited for her to return. You said you wanted both of us. I wasn't given to understand that was of immediate urgency. What has happened? Inspector Massingham wasn't exactly forthcoming when he so peremptorily summoned us.'

'Stella Mawson is dead by hanging.'

He had no doubt that Howarth appreciated the significance of his careful use of words. Their eyes moved from the two hooks on the chapel wall, one with the bell-rope hitched over it, to the blue cord with its dangling tassel held lightly in Dalgliesh's hand. Howarth said:

'I wonder how she knew how to find the cord. And why choose here?'

'You recognize the cord?'

'Isn't it from the chest? There should be two identical cords. We had an idea of hanging the curtains at the entrance to the chancel when we held our concert on 26th August. As it happens, we decided against it. The evening was too hot to worry about draughts. There were two tasselled cords in the chest then.'

'Who could have seen them?'

'Almost anyone who was helping with the preparations: myself, my sister, Miss Foley, Martin, Blakelock. Middlemass gave a hand arranging the hired chairs, and so did a number of people from the Lab. Some of the women helped with the refreshments after the concert and they were fussing about here during the afternoon. The chest isn't locked. Anyone who felt curious could have looked inside. But I don't see how Miss Mawson could have known about the cord. She was at the concert, but she had no hand in the preparations.'

Dalgliesh nodded to the men with the trolley. They pushed it gently forward, and Howarth and Mrs Schofield stood aside to let it pass. Then Dalgliesh asked:

'How many keys are there to this place?'

'I told you yesterday. I know of only one. It's kept on a board in the Chief Liaison Officer's room.'

'And that's the one at present in the lock?' Howarth did not turn his head. He said:

'If it's got the Laboratory plastic tab – yes.'

'Do you know if it was handed out to anyone today?'

'No. That's hardly the sort of detail Blakelock would worry me with.'

Dalgliesh turned to Domenica Schofield:

'And that's the one, presumably, that you borrowed to get extra keys cut when you decided to use the chapel for your meetings with Lorrimer. How many keys?'

She said calmly:

'Two. One you found on his body. This is the second.'

She took it from her jacket pocket and held it out in the palm of her hand in a gesture of dismissive contempt. For a moment it appeared that she was about to tilt her palm and let it clatter on the floor.

'You don't deny that you came here?'

'Why should I? It's not illegal. We were both of age, in our right minds, and free. Not even adultery; merely fornication. You seem fascinated by my sex-life, Commander, even in the middle of your more normal preoccupations. Aren't you afraid it's becoming rather an obsession?'

Dalgliesh's voice didn't change. He went on:

'And you didn't ask for the key back when you broke with Lorrimer?'

'Again, why should I? I didn't need it. It wasn't an engagemen ring.'

Howarth hadn't looked at his half-sister during this exchange Suddenly he said harshly:

'Who found her?'

'Brenda Pridmore. She's been taken home. Dr Greene is wit her now.'

Domenica Schofield's voice was surprisingly gentle:

'Poor child. She seems to be making a habit of finding bodie doesn't she? Now that we've explained to you about the keys, there anything else you want us for tonight?'

'Only to ask you both where you've been since six o'clock.'

Howarth said:

'I left Hoggatt's at about a quarter to six and I've been home ever since. My sister's been out driving alone since seve o'clock. She likes to do that occasionally.'

Domenica Schofield said:

'I'm not sure if I can give you the precise route, but I did stop at an agreeable pub at Whittlesford for a drink and a meal shortly before eight o'clock. They'll probably remember me. I'm fairly well known there. Why? Are you telling us that this is murder?'

'It's an unexplained death.'

'And a suspicious one, presumably. But haven't you considered that she might have murdered Lorrimer and then taken her own life?'

'Can you give me one good reason why she should have?'

She laughed softly.

'Murdered Edwin? For the best and commonest of reasons, or so I've always read. Because she was once married to him. Hadn't you discovered that for yourself, Commander?'

'How did you know?'

'Because he told me. I'm probably the only person in the world he ever did tell. He said the marriage wasn't consummated and they got an annulment within two years. I suppose that's why he never brought his bride home. It's an embarrassing business, showing off one's new wife to one's parents and the village, particularly when she isn't a wife at all and one suspects that she never will be. I don't think his parents ever did know, so it's eally not so surprising if you didn't. But then, one expects you to erret out everything about people's private concerns.'

Before Dalgliesh could reply, their ears caught, simultaneously, he hurried footfall on the stone step, and Angela Foley stood nside the door. She was flushed with running. Looking wildly rom face to face, her body heaving, she gasped:

'Where is she? Where's Star?'

Dalgliesh moved forward, but she backed away as if terrified hat he might touch her. She said:

'Those men. Under the trees. Men with a torch. They're heeling something. What is it? What have you done with Star?'

Without looking at her half-brother, Domenica Schofield put ut her hand. His reached out to meet it. They didn't move oser together, but stood, distanced, rigidly linked by those clasped ands. Dalgliesh said:

'I'm sorry, Miss Foley. Your friend is dead.'

Four pairs of eyes watched as her own eyes turned, first to the blue loops of cord dangling from Dalgliesh's hand, then to the twin hooks, lastly to the wooden chair now tidily placed against the wall. She whispered:

'Oh no! Oh no!'

Massingham moved to take her arm, but she shook free. She threw back her head like a howling animal and wailed:

'Star! Star!' Before Massingham could restrain her she had run from the chapel and they could hear her wild, despairing cry borne back to them on the light wind.

Massingham ran after her. She was silent now, weaving through the trees, running fast. But he caught up with her easily before she reached the two distant figures with their dreadful burden. At first she fought madly; but suddenly, she collapsed in his arms and he was able to lift her and carry her to the car.

When he got back to the chapel, thirty minutes later, Dalgliesh was sitting quietly in one of the stalls, apparently engrossed with the Book of Common Prayer. He put it down and said:

'How is she?'

'Dr Greene's given her a sedative. He's arranged for the district nurse to stay the night. There's no one else he could think of. It looks as if neither she nor Brenda Pridmore will be fit to be questioned before morning.'

He looked at the small heap of numbered cards on the sea beside Dalgliesh. His chief said:

'I found them at the bottom of the chest. I suppose we can te these and those in the board for fingerprints. But we know wha we shall find.'

Massingham asked:

'Did you believe Mrs Schofield's story that Lorrimer and Stel Mawson were married?'

'Oh yes, I think so. Why lie when the facts can be so easi checked? And it explains so much: that extraordinary change will; even the outburst when he was talking to Bradley. The fir sexual failure must have gone deep. Even after all these years couldn't bear to think that she might benefit even indirectly from h will. Or was it the thought that unlike him, she had found happin – and found it with a woman – that he found so insupportable?'

Massingham said:

'So she and Angela Foley get nothing. But that's not a reason for killing herself. And why here, of all places?'

Dalgliesh got to his feet.

'I don't think she did kill herself. This was murder.'

BOOK FIVE

The Clunch Pit

I

They were at Bowlem's Farm before first light. Mrs Pridmore had begun her baking early. Already two large earthenware bowls covered with humped linen stood on the kitchen table, and the whole cottage was redolent with the warm, fecund smell of yeast. When Dalgliesh and Massingham arrived Dr Greene, a squat broad-shouldered man with the face of a benevolent toad, was folding his stethoscope into the depths of an old-fashioned Gladstone bag. It was less than twelve hours since Dalgliesh and he had last met, since, as police surgeon, he had been the first doctor to be called to Stella Mawson's body. He had examined i briefly and then pronounced:

'Is she dead? Answer: yes. Cause of death? Answer: hanging Time of death? About one hour ago. Now you'd better call in th expert and he'll explain to you why the first question is the onl one he's at present competent to answer.'

Now he wasted no time on civilities or questions but nodde briefly to the two detectives and continued talking to Mrs Prid more.

'The lass is fine. She's had a nasty shock but nothing that a goo night's sleep hasn't put right. She's young and healthy, and it' take more than a couple of corpses to turn her into a neurotic wrec if that's what you're frightened of. My family has been doctorin yours for three generations and there's none of you gone off yo heads yet.' He nodded to Dalgliesh. 'You can go up now.'

Arthur Pridmore was standing beside his wife, his hand gri ping her shoulder. No one had introduced him to Dalgliesh; n was there need. He said:

'She hasn't faced the worst yet, has she? This is the secon body. What do you think life in the village will be like for her these two deaths aren't solved?'

Dr Greene was impatient. He snapped shut his bag.

'Good grief, man, no one's going to suspect Brenda! She's lived here all her life. I brought her into the world.'

'That's no protection against slander, though, is it? I'm not saying they'll accuse her. But you know the fens. Folk here can be superstitious, unforgetting and unforgiving. There's such a thing as being tainted with bad luck.'

'Not for your pretty Brenda, there isn't. She'll be the local heroine, most likely. Shake off this morbid nonsense, Arthur. And come out to the car with me. I want a word about that business at the Parochial Church Council.' They went out together. Mrs Pridmore looked up at Dalgliesh. He thought that she had been crying. She said:

'And now you're going to question her, make her talk about it, raking it all up again.'

'Don't worry,' said Dalgliesh gently, 'talking about it will help.'

She made no move to accompany them upstairs, a tact for which Dalgliesh was grateful. He could hardly have objected, particularly as there hadn't been time to get a policewoman, but he had an idea that Brenda would be both more relaxed and more communicative in her mother's absence. She called out happily to his knock. The little bedroom with its low beams and its curtains drawn against the morning darkness was full of light and colour, and she was sitting up in bed fresh and bright-eyed, her aureole of hair tumbling around her shoulders. Dalgliesh wondered anew at the resilience of youth. Massingham, halted suddenly in the doorway, thought that she ought to be in the Uffizi, her feet floating above a meadow of spring flowers, the whole sunlit landscape of Italy stretching behind her into infinity.

It was still very much a schoolgirl's room. There were two shelves of schoolbooks, another with a collection of dolls in national costumes, and a cork board with cut-outs from the Sunday supplements and photographs of her friends. There was a wicker chair beside the bed holding a large teddy bear. Dalgliesh removed it and placed it on the bed beside her, then sat down. He said:

'How are you feeling? Better?'

She leaned impulsively towards him. The sleeve of her cream dressing-jacket fell over the freckled arm. She said:

'I'm so glad you've come. No one wants to talk about it. They can't realize that I've got to talk about it sometime and it's much better now while it's fresh in my mind. It was you who found me, wasn't it? I remember being picked up – rather like Marianne Dashwood in *Sense and Sensibility* – and the nice tweedy smell of your jacket. But I can't remember anything after that. I do remember ringing the bell, though.'

'That was clever of you. We were parked in Hoggatt's drive and heard it, otherwise it might have been hours before the body was found.'

'It wasn't clever really. It was just panic. I suppose you realize what happened? I got a puncture in my bike and decided to walk home through the new Lab. Then I got rather lost and panicked. I started thinking about Dr Lorrimer's murderer and imagining that he was lying in wait for me. I even imagined that he might have punctured the tyres on purpose. It seems silly now, but it didn't then.'

Dalgliesh said:

'We've examined the bicycle. There was a lorry-load of gri passing the Lab during the afternoon and some of the load wa shed. You had a sharp flint in each tyre. But it was a perfectl natural fear. Can you remember whether there really was some one in the building?'

'Not really. I didn't see anyone and I think I imagined most the sounds I heard. What really frightened me was an owl. The I got out of the building and rushed in a panic across a fiel straight towards the chapel.'

'Did you get the impression that anyone might be there ali in the chapel?'

'Well, there aren't any pillars to hide behind. It's a funn chapel, isn't it? Not really a holy place. Perhaps it hasn't bee prayed in enough. I've only been there once before when I Howarth and three of the staff from the Lab gave a concert, I know what it's like. Do you mean he could have be crouched down in one of the stalls watching me? It's a horrib idea.'

'It is rather. But now that you're safe, could you bear to think out it?'

'I can now you're here.' She paused. 'I don't think he was. I ln't see anyone, and I don't think I heard anyone. But I was so rified that I probably wouldn't have noticed. All I could see is this bundle of clothes strung up on the wall, and then the e drooping down at me.'

He didn't need to warn her of the importance of his next ques- n.

'Can you remember where you found the chair, its exact posi- n?'

'It was lying overturned just to the right of the body as if she d kicked it away. I think it had fallen backwards, but it might ve been on its side.'

'But you're quite sure that it had fallen?'

'Quite sure. I remember turning it upright so that I could ind on it to reach the bell-rope.' She looked at him, bright- ed.

'I shouldn't have done that, should I? Now you won't be able tell whether any marks or soil on the seat came from my shoes hers. Was that why Inspector Massingham took away my oes last night? Mummy told me.'

'Yes, that's why.'

The chair would be tested for prints, then sent for examination the Metropolitan Laboratory. But this murder, if it were urder, had been premeditated. Dalgliesh doubted whether, this ne, the killer would have made any mistakes.

Brenda said:

'One thing has struck me, though. It's odd, isn't it, that the ht was on?'

'That's another thing that I wanted to ask you. You're quite sure at the chapel was lit? You didn't switch on the light yourself?'

'I'm quite sure I didn't. I saw the lights gleaming through the ees. Rather like the City of God, you know. It would have been ore sensible to have run for the road once I'd got clear of the w building. But suddenly I saw the shape of the chapel and the ht shining faintly through the windows, and I ran towards it most by instinct.'

'I expect it was by instinct. Your ancestors did the same. O they would have run for sanctuary to St Nicholas's.'

'I've been thinking about the lights ever since I woke up. looks like suicide, doesn't it? I don't suppose people kill themsel in the dark. I know I wouldn't. I can't imagine killing myself all unless I was desperately ill and lonely and in terrible pain, someone was torturing me to make me give them vital inforn tion. But if I did, I wouldn't switch the lights off. I'd want to my last of the light before I went into the darkness, would you? But murderers always want to delay discovery of the bo don't they? So why didn't he turn off the light and lock door?'

She spoke with happy unconcern. The illness, the lonelin and the pain were as unreal and remote as was the tortu Dalgliesh said:

'Perhaps because he wanted it to look like suicide. Was t your first thought when you found the body, that she'd killed h self?'

'Not at the time. I was too frightened to think at all. But sir I've woken up and started considering it all – yes, I suppose I think it was suicide.'

'But you're not sure why you think that?'

'Perhaps because hanging is such a strange way of killi someone. But suicides often do hang themselves, don't they? Bowlem's previous pigman did – in the tithe-barn. And Annie Makepiece. I've noticed that, in the fens, people usua shoot themselves or hang themselves. You see, on a farm, ther always a gun or a rope.'

She spoke simply and without fear. She had lived on a farm her life. There was always birth and death, the birth and death animals and of humans too. And the long nights of the winters would bring their own miasma of madness or despair. B not to her. He said:

'You appal me. It sounds like a holocaust.'

'It doesn't happen often, but one remembers when it does. I j associate hanging with suicide. Do you think this time I'm wron

'I think you could be. But we shall find out. You've been ve helpful.'

He spent another five minutes talking to her, but there was ›thing that she could add. She hadn't gone with Inspector akelock to Chief Inspector Martin's office when he set the night arms, so couldn't say whether or not the key to the chapel was ll on its hook. She had only met Stella Mawson once before at e concert in the chapel, when she had sat in the same row as ngela Foley, Stella Mawson, Mrs Schofield and Dr Kerrison ıd his children.

As Dalgliesh and Massingham were leaving, she said:

'I don't think Mum and Dad will let me go back to the Lab ›w. In fact I'm sure they won't. They want me to marry Gerald ›wlem. I think I would like to marry Gerald, at least, I've never ought of marrying anyone else, but not just yet. It would be ce to be a scientist and have a proper career first. But Mum on't have an easy moment if I stay at the Lab. She loves me, ıd I'm all she's got. You can't hurt people when they love you.'

Dalgliesh recognized an appeal for help. He went back and sat gain in the chair. Massingham, pretending to look out of the indow, was intrigued. He wondered what they would think at e Yard if they could see the old man taking time from a murder vestigation to advise on the moral ambiguities of Women's Lib. ıt he rather wished that she had asked him. Since they had me into the room she had looked only at Dalgliesh. Now he ard him say:

'I suppose a scientific job isn't easy to combine with being a rmer's wife.'

'I don't think it would be fair to Gerald.'

'I used to think that we can have almost anything we want from e, that it's just a question of organization. But now I'm beginning think that we have to make a choice more often than we'd like. he important thing is to make sure that it's our choice, no one se's, and that we make it honestly. But one thing I'm sure of is that 's never a good thing to make a decision when you're not ›solutely well. Why not wait a little time, until we've solved Dr orrimer's murder anyway. Your mother may feel differently then.'

She said:

'I suppose this is what murder does, changes people's lives and ›oils them.'

'Changes, yes. But it needn't spoil. You're young and intellige and brave, so you won't let it spoil yours.'

Downstairs, in the farmhouse kitchen, Mrs Pridmore was san wiching fried rashers of bacon between generous slices of crus bread. She said gruffly:

'You both look as if you could do with some breakfast. Up night, I daresay. It won't hurt you to sit down and take a coup of minutes to eat these. And I've made fresh tea.'

Supper the previous night had been a couple of sandwich fetched by a constable from the Moonraker and eaten in t antechapel. Not until he smelt the bacon did Massingham reali how hungry he was. He bit gratefully into the warm bread to t oozing saltiness of home-cured bacon, and washed it down wi strong, hot tea. He felt cosseted by the warmth and friendliness the kitchen, this cosy womb-like shelter from the dark fens. Th the telephone rang. Mrs Pridmore went to answer it. She said:

'That was Dr Greene ringing from Sprogg's Cottage. He sa to tell you that Angela Foley is well enough to speak to you now

II

Angela Foley came slowly into the room. She was fully dressed a perfectly calm, but both men were shocked by the change in h She walked stiffly, and her face looked aged and bruised as if she h suffered all night a physical assault of grief. Her small eyes were pa and sunken behind the jutting bones, her cheeks were unhealthi mottled, the delicate mouth was swollen and there was a herp on the upper lip. Only her voice was unchanged; the childis unemphatic voice with which she had answered their first questio

The district nurse, who had spent the night at Sprogg's Cottag had lit the fire. Angela looked at the crackling wood and said:

'Stella never lit the fire until late in the afternoon. I used to l it in the morning before I went to the Lab, and she'd put match to it about half an hour before I was due home.'

Dalgliesh said:

'We found Miss Mawson's house-keys on her body. I'm afra we had to unlock her desk to examine her papers. You we asleep, so we weren't able to ask you.'

She said, dully:

'It wouldn't have made any difference, would it? You would have looked just the same. You had to.'

'Did you know that your friend once went through a form of marriage with Edwin Lorrimer? There wasn't a divorce; the marriage was annulled after two years because of non-consummation. Did she tell you?'

She turned to look at him, but it was impossible to gauge the expression in those small, pig-like eyes. If her voice held any emotion, it was closer to wry amusement than to surprise.

'Married? She and Edwin? So that's how she knew . . .' She broke off. 'No, she didn't tell me. When I came to live here it was a new beginning for both of us. I didn't want to talk about the past and I don't think she did either. She did sometimes tell me things, about her life at university, her job, odd people she knew. But that was one thing she didn't tell me.'

Dalgliesh asked gently:

'Do you feel able to tell me what happened last night?'

'She said that she was going for a walk. She often did, but usually after supper. That's when she thought about her books, worked out the plot and dialogue, striding along in the darkness on her own.'

'What time did she go?'

'Just before seven.'

'Did she have the key of the chapel with her?'

'She asked me for it yesterday, after lunch, just before I went back to the Lab. She said she wanted to describe a seventeenth-entury family chapel for the book, but I didn't know that she meant to visit it so soon. When she hadn't come home at half past ten, I got worried and went to look for her. I walked for early an hour before I thought of looking in the chapel.'

Then she spoke directly to Dalgliesh, patiently, as if explaining omething to an obtuse child:

'She did it for me. She killed herself so that I could have the money from her life assurance. She told me that I was her only gatee. You see, the owner wants to sell this cottage in a hurry; e needs the cash. We wanted to buy it, but we hadn't enough money for the deposit. Just before she went out, she asked me what it was like to be in local authority care, what it meant to have no real home. When Edwin was killed, we thought that there might be something for me in his will. But there wasn't. That's why she asked me for the key. It wasn't true that she needed to include a description of the chapel in her book, not this book anyway. It's set in London, and it's nearly finished. I know. I've been typing it. I thought at the time that it was odd that she wanted the key, but I learned never to ask Stella questions.

'But now I understand. She wanted to make life safe for me here, where we'd been happy, safe for ever. She knew what she was going to do. She knew she'd never come back. When I was massaging her neck to make her headache better, she knew that I should never touch her again.'

Dalgliesh asked:

'Would any writer, any writer who wasn't mentally ill, choose to kill herself just before a book was finished?'

She said dully:

'I don't now. I don't understand how a writer feels.'

Dalgliesh said:

'Well, I do. And she wouldn't.'

She didn't reply. He went on gently:

'Was she happy, living here with you?'

She looked up at him eagerly, and, for the first time, her voic became animated, as if she were willing him to understand.

'She said that she had never been as happy in all her life. Sh said that was what love is, knowing that you can make just on other person happy, and be made happy by them in return.'

'So why should she kill herself? Could she really have believe that you'd rather have her money than herself? Why should sh think that?'

'Stella always underrated herself. She may have thought tha I'd forget her in time, but the money and the security would g on for ever. She may even have thought that it was bad for me t be living with her – that the money would somehow set me fre She once said something very like that.'

Dalgliesh looked across at the slim, upright figure, sittin hands folded in her lap, opposite to him in the high winged chai He fixed his eyes on her face. Then he said quietly:

'But there isn't going to be any money. The life assurance policy had a suicide clause. If Miss Mawson did kill herself, then you get nothing.'

She hadn't known. He could be certain of that at least. The news surprised her, but it didn't shock. This was no murderess balked of her spoils.

She smiled and said gently:

'It doesn't matter.'

'It matters to this investigation. I've read one of your friend's novels. Miss Mawson was a highly intelligent writer, which means that she was an intelligent woman. Her heart wasn't strong and her life assurance premiums weren't cheap. It can't have been easy to meet them. Do you really think that she didn't know the terms of her policy?'

'What are you trying to tell me?'

'Miss Mawson knew, or thought she knew, who had killed Dr Lorrimer, didn't she?'

'Yes. She said so. But she didn't tell me who it was.'

'Not even whether it was a man or a woman?'

She thought.

'No, nothing. Only that she knew. I'm not sure that she said that, not in so many words. But when I asked her, she didn't deny it.'

She paused, and then went on with more animation:

'You're thinking that she went out to meet the murderer, aren't you? That she tried to blackmail him? But Stella wouldn't do that! Only a fool would run into that kind of danger, and she wasn't a fool. You said so yourself. She wouldn't voluntarily have gone alone to face a killer, not for any money. No sane woman would.'

'Even if the murderer were a woman?'

'Not alone and at night. Star was so small and fragile, and her heart wasn't strong. When I put my arms round her it was like holding a bird.' She looked into the fire and said, almost wonderingly:

'I shall never see her again. Never. She sat in this chair and pulled on her boots, just as she always did. I never offered to go with her in the evenings. I knew that she needed to be alone. It was all so ordinary, until she got to the door. And then I was frightened. I begged her not to go. And I shall never see her again. She won't ever speak again, not to me, not to anyone. She'll never write another word. I don't believe it yet. I know that it must be true or you wouldn't be here, but I still don't believe it. How shall I bear it when I do?'

Dalgliesh said:

'Miss Foley, we have to know if she went out on the night Dr Lorrimer was killed.'

She looked up at him.

'I know what you're trying to make me do. If I say that she did go out, then the case is finished for you, isn't it? It's all nicely tied up; means, motive, opportunity. He was her ex-husband and she hated him because of the will. She went to try to persuade him to help us with money. When he refused, she seized the first weapon to hand and struck him down.'

Dalgliesh said:

'He may have let her into the Laboratory, although it's unlikely. But how did she get out?'

'You'll say that I took the keys from Dr Howarth's security safe and lent them to her. Then I put them back next morning.'

'Did you?'

She shook her head.

'You could only have done that if you and Inspector Blakelock were in this together. And what reason has he for wishing Dr Lorrimer dead? When his only child was killed by a hit-and-run driver, the evidence of the forensic scientist helped secure an acquittal. But that was ten years ago, and the scientist wasn't Dr Lorrimer. When Miss Pridmore told me about the child we checked. That evidence was to do with paint particles, the job of a forensic chemist, not a biologist. Are you telling me that Inspector Blakelock lied when he said that the keys were in the security cupboard?'

'He didn't lie. The keys were there.'

'Then any case we might seek to build against Miss Mawson weakens, doesn't it? Could anyone really believe that she climbed out of a third-floor window? You must believe that we're here to find the truth, not to fabricate an easy solution.'

But she was right, thought Massingham. Once Angela Foley ad admitted that her friend had left Sprogg's Cottage that ight, it would be difficult to bring home the crime to anyone se. The solution she had propounded was neat enough and, hoever was brought to trial for Lorrimer's murder, the defence ould make the most of it. He watched his chief's face. Dalgliesh id:

'I agree that no sane woman would go out alone at night to eet a murderer. That's why I don't think she did. She thought e knew who had killed Edwin Lorrimer, and if she did have an ssignation last night, it wasn't with him. Miss Foley, please look t me. You must trust me. I don't know yet whether your friend illed herself or was killed. But if I'm to discover the truth, I'll ave to know whether she went out the night Dr Lorrimer died.'

She said dully:

'We were together all the evening. We told you.'

There was a silence. It seemed to Massingham to last for inutes. Then the wood fire flared and there was a crack like a istol shot. A log rolled out on the hearth. Dalgliesh knelt and ith the tongs eased it back into place. The silence went on. Then e said:

'Please tell me the truth first. Do you think Star was murered?'

'I can't be sure. I may never be able to prove it. But yes, I do.'

She said:

'Star did go out that night. She was out from half past eight ntil about half past nine. She didn't tell me where she'd been, nd she was perfectly ordinary, perfectly composed, when she got ome. She said nothing, but she did go out.'

he said at last:

'I'd like you to go now, please.'

'I think you should have someone with you.'

'I'm not a child. I don't want Mrs Swaffield or the district urse or any of the village do-gooders. And I don't need a olicewoman. I haven't committed a crime, so you've no right to rce yourselves on me. I've told you everything I know. You've cked her desk, so no one can get at Stella's things. I shan't do anything foolish – that's the expression people use when they' trying to ask tactfully if you're planning to kill yourself, isn't i Well, I'm not. I'm all right now. I just want to be left alone.'

Dalgliesh said:

'I'm afraid we shall need to force ourselves on you later again.

'Later is better than now.'

She wasn't trying to be offensive. It was a simple statement fact. She got up stiffly and walked towards the door, her he held rigidly high as if only the body's discipline could hold int the fragile integrity of the mind. Dalgliesh and Massingha exchanged glances. She was right. They couldn't force comfort company where neither was wanted. They had no legal authori either to stay or to compel her to leave. And there were things do.

She went over to the window and watched from behind t curtains as the car rounded Sprogg's Green and accelerat towards the village. Then she ran into the hall and dragged o the telephone directory from its shelf. It took only a few secon of feverishly leafing to find the number she wanted. She dialle waited and then spoke. Replacing the receiver she went back in the sitting-room. Slowly, with ceremony, she lifted the Fren sword from the wall and stood very still, holding out her arm the weapon resting across her palms. After a few seconds s curled her left hand round the scabbard, and with her rig slowly and deliberately withdrew the blade. Then she took h stand just inside the sitting-room door, naked sword in her han and measured the room with her eyes, regarding the dispositi of furniture and objects, intent as a stranger calculating h chances in some coming trial.

After a few minutes she moved into the study, and again sto silently surveying the room. There was a Victorian button-back chair beside the fireplace. She dragged it to the study door a hid the naked sword behind it, the tip resting against the floo then slid the scabbard under the chair. Satisfied that neith could be seen she returned to the sitting-room. She took her se beside the fire and sat motionless, waiting for the sound of t approaching car.

III

If Claire Easterbrook was surprised, on her arrival at the Laboratory just before nine o'clock, to be asked by Inspector Blakelock to see Commander Dalgliesh immediately, she concealed it. She changed first into her white coat, but otherwise did not delay in obeying the summons more than was strictly necessary to assert her independence. When she went into the Director's office, she saw the two detectives, the dark head and the red, quietly conferring together at the window almost, she thought, as if their business was ordinary, their presence unremarkable. There was an alien file on Dr Howarth's desk, and a plan of the Laboratory and an Ordnance Survey map of the village laid open on the conference table, but otherwise the room seemed unchanged. Dalgliesh moved to the desk and said:

'Good morning, Miss Easterbrook. You heard what happened last night?'

'No. Should I have? I was at the theatre after dinner, so people couldn't reach me, and I've spoken to no one but Inspector Blakelock. He hasn't told me anything.'

'Stella Mawson, Miss Foley's friend, was found hanged in the chapel.'

She frowned as if the news were personally offensive, and said with no more than polite interest:

'I see. I don't think I've met her. Oh yes, I remember. She was at the concert in the chapel. Grey-haired, with remarkable eyes. What happened? Did she kill herself?'

'That's one of two possibilities. It's unlikely to have been an accident.'

'Who found her?'

'Miss Pridmore.'

She said with surprising gentleness:

'Poor child.'

Dalgliesh opened the file, picked up two transparent exhibit envelopes, and said:

'I'd like you to have a look at these four hairs urgently for me. There's no time to get them to the Met Lab. I want to know, if possible, if the dark hairs came from the same head.'

'It's easier to say whether they don't. I can have a look under the microscope but I doubt whether I can help you. Hair identification is never easy, and I can't hope to do much with only three samples. Apart from microscopic examination, we'd normally use mass spectrometry to try to identify differences in the trace elements, but even that isn't possible with three hairs. If these were submitted to me, I'd have to say that I couldn't give an opinion.'

Dalgliesh said:

'I'd be grateful, all the same, if you'd take a look. It's just a hunch, and I want to know whether it's worth following up.'

Massingham said:

'I'd like to watch, if you don't mind.'

She gazed at him.

'Would it make any difference if I did?'

Then minutes later she lifted her head from the comparison microscope and said:

'If we're talking of hunches, mine, for what it's worth, is that they came from different heads. The cuticle, cortex and medulla are all significantly different. But I think they're both male. Look for yourself.'

Massingham bent his head to the eyepiece. He saw what looked like the sections of two logs, patterned and grained. And beside them were two other logs, their barks shredded. But he could see that they were different logs, and that they came from different trees. He said:

'Thank you. I'll let Mr Dalgliesh know.'

IV

There was nothing he could put between himself and that shining, razor-sharp blade. He thought wryly that a bullet would have been worse; but then he wondered. To use a gun at least required some skill, a preliminary aim. A bullet could go anywhere, and if her first shot was wide he could at least have ensured that she got no second chance. But she had three feet of cold steel in her hand and, in this confined space, she had only to lunge or slash and he would be cut to the bone. He knew now why she had shown him into the study. There was no room here to manoeuvre; no object within his range of sight which he could seize and hurl. And he knew that he mustn't look round, must keep his eyes firmly and without fear on her face. He tried to keep his voice calm, reasonable; one nervous smile, one hint of hostility or provocation and it might be too late to argue. He said:

'Look, don't you think we ought to talk about this? You've got the wrong man, believe me.'

She said:

'Read that note. The one on the desk behind you. Read it out loud.'

He didn't dare turn his head, but reached back and fumbled on the desk. His hand encountered a single sheet of paper. He read:

'You'd better check on the cannabis exhibits when Detective Inspector Doyle's around. How do you think he managed to afford his house?'

'Well?'

'Where did you get this?'

'From Edwin Lorrimer's desk. Stella found it and gave it to me. You killed her because she knew, because she tried to blackmail you. She arranged to meet you last night in the Wren chapel and you strangled her.'

He could have laughed at the irony of it, but he knew that laughter would be fatal. And at least they were talking. The longer she waited, the greater his chances.

'Are you saying that your friend thought that I killed Edwin Lorrimer?'

'She knew you didn't. She was out walking the night he died and I think she saw someone she recognized leaving the Laboratory. She knew that it wasn't you. She wouldn't have risked meeting you alone if she'd thought that you were the murderer. Mr Dalgliesh explained that to me. She went to the chapel thinking that she was safe, that she could come to some arrangement with you. But you killed her. That's why I'm going to kill you. Stella hated the thought of shutting people away in prison. I can't bear the thought of her murderer ever being free. Ten years in exchange for Stella's life. Why should you be alive when she's dead?'

He had no doubt that she meant what she said. He had dealt with people pushed over the brink of endurance into madness, had seen before that look of dedicated fanaticism. He stood very still, poised on the soles of his feet, waiting for the first instinctive tightening of the muscles before she struck. He tried to keep his voice low, calm, with no trace of facetiousness.

'That's a reasonable point of view. Don't think that I'm against it. I've never understood why people are squeamish about killing a convicted murderer instantaneously and resigned to killing him slowly over twenty years. But at least they have been convicted. There's the little matter of a trial. No execution without due process. And believe me, Miss Foley, you've got the wrong man. I didn't kill Lorrimer, and luckily for me I can prove it.'

'I don't care about Edwin Lorrimer. I only care about Stella. And you killed her.'

'I didn't even know that she was dead. But if she was killed yesterday any time between half past three and half past seven, then I'm in the clear. I've got the best possible alibi. I was at Guy's Marsh police station most of the time being interrogated by the Yard. And when Dalgliesh and Massingham left, I was there for another two hours. Ring them. Ask anyone. Look, you can lock me away in a cupboard – somewhere I can't escape – while you telephone Guy's Marsh. For God's sake, you don't want to make a mistake, do you? You know me. Do you want to kill me, messily, horribly, while the real murderer escapes? An unofficial execution is one thing; murder's another.'

He thought that the hand holding the sword lost some of its tension. But there was no change in the taut, white face. She said:

'And the note.'

'I know who sent the note – my wife. She wanted me to leave the Force, and she knew that there'd be nothing like a little official harassment to push me into resigning. I had a spot of trouble with the Force about two years ago. The disciplinary committee exonerated me, but I damn nearly resigned then. Can't you recognize feminine spite when you see it? That note proves nothing except that she wanted me disgraced and out of the Force.'

'But you have been stealing cannabis, substituting an inert substance?'

'Ah, that's a different question. But you're not killing me for that. You won't be able to prove it, you know. The last batch of cannabis exhibits I was concerned with had a destruction authorization from the court. I helped burn them myself. Just in time, luckily; the incinerator broke down immediately afterwards.'

'And the court exhibits you burned, were they cannabis?'

'Some of them were. But you'll never prove I made the substitution, even if you decide to make use of that note, not now. But what does it matter? I'm out of the Force. Look, you know that I've been working on the clunch pit murder. Do you really suppose that I'd have been sitting at home at this time of day, free to drive over here as soon as you rang me merely to satisfy my curiosity, if I were on a murder case, if I hadn't been suspended or resigned? I may not be a shining example of probity to the Force, but I'm not a murderer, and I can prove it. Ring Dalgliesh and ask him.'

There was no doubt about it now, her grip on the sword had relaxed. She stood there, very still, no longer looking at him, but with her gaze fixed out of the window. Her face didn't change, but he saw that she was crying. The tears were streaming out of the tight little eyes to roll unimpeded down her cheeks. He moved quietly forward and took the sword from her unresisting hand. He placed an arm on her shoulders. She didn't flinch. He said:

'Look, you've had a shock. You shouldn't have been left here on your own. Isn't it time we had a cup of tea? Show me where the kitchen is and I'll make it. Or better still, have you anything stronger?'

She said dully:

'There's whisky, but we keep that for Stella. I don't drink it.'

'Well, you're going to drink it now. It'll do you good. And, by God, I need it. And then you'd better sit down quietly and tell me all about it.'

She said:

'But if it wasn't you, who did kill Stella?'

'My guess is, the same person who killed Lorrimer. A couple of murderers loose in one small community is too much of a coincidence. But look, you've got to let the police know about that note. It can't hurt me, not now, and it might help them. If your friend found one incriminating piece of information in Lorrimer's desk, then she may have found another. She didn't use that note. She probably knew how little it was worth. But what about the information she did use?'

She said dully:

'You tell them, if you want to. It doesn't matter now.'

But he waited until he had made the tea. The tidiness and the good order of the kitchen pleased him, and he took trouble over the tray, setting it in front of her on a low table which he drew up before the fire. He replaced the sword above the fireplace, standing back to make sure that it hung correctly. Then he made up the fire. She had shaken her head when he had offered her the whisky, but he poured himself a generous measure and sat opposite to her on the other side of the fire. She didn't attract him. Even in their brief encounters at the Laboratory he had given her no more than a passing dismissive glance. It was unusual for him to put himself out for a woman from whom he wanted nothing, and the sensation of disinterested kindness was unfamiliar but agreeable. Sitting opposite to her in silence, the traumas of the day faded, and he felt a curious peace. They had some quite decent stuff in the cottage, he decided, looking around at the cosy, cluttered sitting-room. He wondered whether it was all coming to her.

It was ten minutes before he went out to telephone. When he returned the sight of his face roused her from her benumbed misery. She said:

'What is it? What did he say?'

He moved into the room, frowning. He said:

'He wasn't there. He and Massingham weren't at Guy's Marsh or at the Lab. They're at Muddington. They've gone to the clunch pit.'

V

They drove again over the route they had followed the previous night when they had heard the three clangs from the chapel bell, the mile and a half to the junction of Guy's Marsh road and then right through the main street of the village. Neither spoke. Massingham had taken one look at his chief's face and had decided that silence would be prudent. And it was certainly no time for self-congratulation. They still lacked proof, the one clinching fact that would break the case open. And Massingham wondered if they would ever get it. They were dealing with intelligent men and women who must know that they had only to keep their mouths shut and nothing could be proved.

In the village street, the first Saturday-morning shoppers were making their appearance. The gossiping groups of women turned their heads to glance briefly at the car as it passed. And now the houses were thinning and Hoggatt's field, with the new building, was on their right. Massingham had changed down to turn into the drive of the Old Rectory when it happened. The blue and yellow ball bounced out into the road in front of them, and after it, red wellingtons flashing, ran William. They were driving too slowly for danger, but Massingham cursed as he swerved and braked. And then came two seconds of horror.

Afterwards it seemed to Dalgliesh that time was suspended so that he saw in memory the whole accident like a film run slowly. The red Jaguar leaping and held suspended in the air; a blaze of blue from the terrified eyes; the mouth gaping in a soundless scream; the white knuckles wrenching at the wheel. Instinctively he cradled his head and braced himself for the impact. The Jaguar crashed the rear bumper of the Rover, ripping it away in a scream of torn metal. The car rocked wildly and spun round. There was a second of absolute silence. Then he and Massingham were out of their seat-belts and rushing across to the opposite verge to that small, motionless body. One boot lay in the road, and the ball trickled slowly towards the grass verge.

William had been tossed into a heap of hay left on the verge after the late summer scything. He lay spreadeagled, so relaxed in his perfect stillness that Massingham's first horrified thought was that his neck was broken. In the couple of seconds in which he was resisting the impulse to sweep the boy into his arms, and turning instead to telephone from the car for an ambulance, William recovered his wind and began struggling against the prickling dampness of the straw. Bereft both of dignity and his ball he began to cry. Domenica Schofield, hair streaming across her bleached face, stumbled up to them.

'Is he all right?'

Massingham ran his hands over William's body, then took the boy in his arms.

'I think so. He sounds all right.'

They had reached the drive of the Old Rectory when Eleanor Kerrison came running down the path towards them. She had obviously been washing her hair. It lay now in dank, dripping swathes across her shoulders. William, seeing her, redoubled his crying. As Massingham strode towards the house she ran clumsily beside him, clutching his arm. Drops of water sprayed from her hair to lie like pearls on William's face.

'Daddy's been called to a body. He said he'd take William and me to lunch at Cambridge when he got back. We were going to buy a grown-up bed for William. I was washing my hair specially. I left William with Miss Willard. He's all right, isn't he? Are you sure he's all right? Oughtn't we to take him to the hospital? What happened?'

'We didn't see. I think he was caught and tossed by the front bumper of the Jaguar. Luckily he landed on a heap of straw.'

'He could have been killed. I warned her about the road. He isn't supposed to play in the garden on his own. Are you sure we oughtn't to get Dr Greene?'

Massingham went straight through the house to the drawing-room and laid William on the sofa. He said:

'It might be as well, but I'm sure he's all right. Just listen to him.'

William, as if he understood, cut off his bawling instantaneously and struggled upright on the couch. He began hiccuping loudly but, apparently undistressed by the paroxysms which were jerking his body, he regarded the company with interest, then fixed his stare consideringly on his bootless left foot. Looking up at Dalgliesh he asked sternly:

'Where's William's ball?'

'At the edge of the road, presumably,' said Massingham. 'I'll fetch it. And you'll have to do something about fixing a gate for that drive.'

They heard footsteps in the hall, and Miss Willard stood, fluttering uneasily in the doorway. Eleanor had been sitting beside her brother on the sofa. Now she stood up and confronted the woman with a silent contempt so unmistakable that Miss Willard blushed. She glanced round the watching faces and said defensively:

'Quite a little party. I thought I heard voices.'

Then the girl spoke. The voice, thought Massingham, was as arrogant and cruel as that of a Victorian matron dismissing a kitchen maid. The confrontation would have been almost comic if it hadn't been at once pathetic and horrible.

'You can pack up your bags and get out. You're dismissed. I only asked you to watch William while I washed my hair. You couldn't even do that. He might have been killed. You're a useless, ugly, stupid old woman. You drink and you smell and we all hate you. We don't need you any more. So get out. Pack your beastly, horrible things and go. I can look after William and Daddy. He doesn't need anyone but me.'

The silly, ingratiating smile faded on Miss Willard's face. Two red weals appeared across her cheeks and forehead as if the words had been a physical whiplash. Then she was suddenly pale, her whole body shaking. She reached for the back of a chair for support and said, her voice high and distorted with pain:

'You! Do you think he needs you? I may be middle-aged and past my best but at least I'm not half-mad. And if I'm ugly, look at yourself! He only puts up with you because of William. You could leave tomorrow and he wouldn't care. He'd be glad. It's William he loves, not you. I've seen his face, I've heard him and I know. He's thinking of letting you go to your mother. You didn't know that, did you? And there's something else you don't know. What do you think your precious daddy gets up to when he's drugged you into sleep? He sneaks off to the Wren chapel and makes love to her.'

Eleanor turned and looked at Domenica Schofield. Then she spun round and spoke directly to Dalgliesh.

'She's lying! Tell me she's lying! It isn't true.'

There was a silence. It could only have lasted a couple of seconds while Dalgliesh's mind phrased the careful answer. Then, as if impatient to forestall him, not looking at his chief's face, Massingham said clearly:

'Yes, it's true.'

She looked from Dalgliesh to Domenica Schofield. Then she swayed as if she were about to faint. Dalgliesh went towards her, but she backed away. She said in a voice of dull calm:

'I thought he did it for me. I didn't drink the cocoa he made for me. I wasn't asleep when he came back. I went out and watched him in the garden, burning the white coat on the bonfire. I knew that there was blood on it. I thought he'd been to see Dr Lorrimer because he was unkind to William and me. I thought he did it for me, because he loves me.'

Suddenly she gave a high despairing wail like an animal in torment, and yet so human and so adult that Dalgliesh felt his blood run cold.

'Daddy! Daddy! Oh no!'

She put her hands to her throat and pulling the leather thong from beneath her sweater, struggled with it, twisting like a creature in a trap. And then the knot broke. Over the dark carpet they scattered and rolled, six newly polished brass buttons, bright as crested jewels.

Massingham stooped and carefully gathered them up into his handkerchief. Still no one spoke. William propelled himself off the sofa, trotted over to his sister and fastened his arms around her leg. His lip trembled. Domenica Schofield spoke directly to Dalgliesh.

'My God, yours is a filthy trade.'

Dalgliesh ignored her. He said to Massingham:

'Look after the children. I'll ring for a W.P.C. and we'd better get Mrs Swaffield. There's no one else I can think of. Don't leave her until they both arrive. I'll see to things here.'

Massingham turned to Domenica Schofield.

'Not a trade. Just a job. And are you saying that it's one you don't want done?'

He went up to the girl. She was trembling violently. Dalgliesh thought that she would cringe away from him. But she stood perfectly still. With three words he had destroyed her. But who else had she to turn to? Massingham took off his tweed coat and wrapped it round her. He said gently without touching her:

'Come with me. You show me where we can make some tea. And then you'll have a lie down and William and I will stay with you. I'll read to William.'

She went with him as meekly as a prisoner with a gaoler, without looking at him, the long coat trailing on the floor. Massingham took William's hand. The door closed after them. Dalgliesh wished never to see Massingham again. But he would see him again and, in time, without even caring or remembering. He never wanted to work with him again; but he knew that he would. He wasn't the man to destroy a subordinate's career simply because he had outraged susceptibilities to which he, Dalgliesh, had no right. What Massingham had done seemed to him now unforgivable. But life had taught him that the unforgivable was usually the most easily forgiven. It was possible to do police work honestly; there was, indeed, no other safe way to do it. But it wasn't possible to do it without giving pain.

Miss Willard had groped her way to the sofa. She muttered, as if trying to explain it to herself:

'I didn't mean it. She made me say it. I didn't mean it. I didn't want to hurt him.'

Domenica Schofield turned to go.

'No, one seldom does.' She said to Dalgliesh:

'If you want me, you know where I'll be.'

'We shall want a statement.'

'Of course. Don't you always? Longing and loneliness, terror and despair, all the human muddle, neatly documented, on one and a half sheets of official paper.'

'No, just the facts.'

He didn't ask her when it had begun. That wasn't really important; and he thought that he didn't need to ask. Brenda Pridmore had told him that she had sat in the same row as Mrs Schofield and Dr Kerrison and his children at the concert in the chapel. That had been held on Thursday, 26th August. And early in September, Domenica had broken with Edwin Lorrimer.

At the door she hesitated and turned. Dalgliesh asked:

'Did he telephone you the morning after the murder to let you know that he'd replaced the key on Lorrimer's body?'

'He never telephoned me. Neither of them did, ever. That was our arrangement. And I never rang him.' She paused and then said gruffly:

'I didn't know. I may have suspected, but I didn't know. We weren't – what's your expression? – in it together. I'm not responsible. It wasn't because of me.'

'No,' said Dalgliesh. 'I didn't suppose it was. A motive for murder is seldom so unimportant.'

She fixed on him her unforgettable eyes. She said:

'Why do you dislike me?'

The egotism which could ask such a question, and at such a time, astounded him. But it was his own self-knowledge which disgusted him more. He understood only too well what had driven those two men to creep guiltily like randy schoolboys to that rendezvous, to make themselves partners in her erotic, esoteric game. Given the opportunity, he would, he thought bitterly, have done the same.

She was gone. He went over to Miss Willard.

'Did you telephone Dr Lorrimer to tell him about the burnt candles, the numbers on the hymn-board?'

'I chatted to him when he drove me to Mass the Sunday before last. I had to talk about something on the journey; he never did. And I was worried about the altar candles. I first noticed that someone had lit them when I went to the chapel at the end of September. On my last visit they were burnt even lower. I thought that the chapel might be being used by devil-worshippers. I know it's been deconsecrated, but it's still a holy place. And it's so secluded. No one goes there. The fen people don't like to walk out after dark. I wondered if I ought to talk to the Rector or consult Father Gregory. Dr Lorrimer asked me to go to the chapel again next day and let him know the numbers on the hymn-board. I thought it was an odd thing to ask, but he seemed to think that it was important. I hadn't even noticed that they'd been altered. I could ask for the key, you see. He didn't like to.'

But he could have taken it without signing for it, thought Dalgliesh. So why hadn't he? Because of the risk that he might be seen? Because it was repugnant to his obsessional, conformist personality to break a Laboratory rule? Or, more likely, because he couldn't bear to enter the chapel again, to see with his own eyes the evidence of betrayal? She hadn't even bothered to change their meeting-place. She had still used the same ingenious code to fix the date of the next assignation. Even the key she had handed to Kerrison had been Lorrimer's key. And none better than he had known the significance of those four numbers. The twenty-ninth day of the tenth month at six-forty. He said:

'And you waited together last Friday in the shelter of the trees?'

'That was his idea. He needed a witness, you see. Oh, he was quite right to be worried. A woman like that, quite unsuitable to be a stepmother to William. One man after another, Dr Lorrimer said. That's why she had to leave London. She couldn't leave men alone. Any man would do. He knew about her, you see. He said the whole Lab knew. She'd even made advances to him once. Horrible. He was going to write to Mrs Kerrison and put a stop to it. I couldn't tell him the address. Dr Kerrison's so secretive about his letters and I'm not sure that even he knows exactly where his wife is. But we knew that she'd run away with a doctor, and we knew his name. It's quite a common name, but Dr Lorrimer said he could trace them from the Medical Directory.'

The Medical Directory. So that was why he had wanted to consult it, why he had opened the door so quickly when Bradley rang. He had only had to come from the Director's office on the ground floor. And he had been carrying his notebook. What was it that Howarth had said? He hated scraps of paper. He used the book to note down anything of importance. And this had been important. The names and addresses of Mrs Kerrison's possible lovers.

Miss Willard looked up at him. Dalgliesh saw that she was crying, the tears streaking her face and dropping unimpeded over the twisting hands. She said:

'What will happen to him? What will you do to him?'

The telephone rang. Dalgliesh strode across the hall and into the study and lifted the receiver. It was Clifford Bradley. His voice sounded as high and excited as a young girl's. He said:

'Commander Dalgliesh? They said at the police station you

might be there. I have to tell you at once. It's important. I've just remembered how I knew that the murderer was still in the Lab. I heard a sound as I got to the Lab door. I heard the same sound again two minutes ago coming downstairs from the bathroom. Sue had just finished telephoning her mother. What I heard was someone replacing the telephone receiver.'

It was no more than confirmation of what he had long ago suspected. He returned to the drawing-room and said to Miss Willard:

'Why did you tell us that you overheard Dr Kerrison making that nine o'clock telephone call from his study? Did he ask you to lie for him?'

The blotched face, the tear-stained eyes looked up at him.

'Oh, no, he'd never do that! All he asked was whether I'd happened to hear him. It was when he came back to the house after he'd been called to the body. I wanted to help him, to make him pleased with me. It was such a little, unimportant lie. And it wasn't really a lie. I thought that perhaps I did hear him. You might have suspected him, and I knew that he couldn't have done it. He's kind, and good and gentle. It seems such a venial sin to protect the innocent. That woman had got him into her clutches, but I knew he could never kill.'

He had probably always intended to telephone the hospital from the Laboratory if he wasn't back home in time. But, with Lorrimer lying dead, it must have taken nerve. He could hardly have put down the receiver before he heard the approaching footsteps. And what then? Into the darkroom to watch and wait? That must have been one of his worst moments, standing there rigidly in the darkness, breath held, his heart thudding, wondering who could be arriving at this late hour, how they could have got in. And it could have been Blakelock; Blakelock who would have rung at once for the police, who would have made an immediate search of the Lab.

But it had only been a terrified Bradley. There had been no telephone call, no summons for help, only the echo of panicking feet down the corridor. And now all he had to do was to follow, make his way quietly out of the Lab and home through the new Lab the way he had come. He had put out the light and reached the front door. And then he had seen the headlights of Doyle's car swinging into the drive and backing to park among the bushes. He no longer dared leave by that door. The way was barred. And he couldn't wait for them to drive off. There was Nell at home who might wake and ask for him. There was the return telephone call at ten o'clock. He had to get back.

But he had still kept his head. It had been a clever move to take Lorrimer's keys and lock the Laboratory. The police investigation would inevitably concentrate on the four sets of keys and the limited number of people who had access to them. And he knew the one way he could get out and had the skill and nerve to do it. He had put on Middlemass's jacket to protect his clothes; he knew how fatal a torn thread of cloth could be. But there had been no tear. And in the early hours of the morning a light rain had washed away any evidence on walls or windows which could have betrayed him.

He had reached home safely and made an excuse to call in on Miss Willard, establishing his alibi more firmly. No one had telephoned for him; no one had called. And he knew that, next day, he would be among the first to examine the body. Howarth had said that he had stood by the door while Kerrison made his examination. It must have been then that he had slipped the key into Lorrimer's pocket. But that had been one of his mistakes. Lorrimer carried his keys in a leather pouch, not loose in his pocket.

There was the crunch of tyres on the gravel of the drive. He looked out of the window and saw the police car with Detective Sergeant Reynolds and two women police constables in the back. The case had broken; except that it was never the case that broke, only the people. And now he and Massingham were free for the last interview, the most difficult of all.

At the edge of the clunch field a boy was flying a red kite. Tugged by the freshening wind it soared and dipped, weaving its convoluted tail against an azure sky as clear and bright as on a summer day. The clunch field was alive with voices and laughter. Even the discarded beer-cans glinted like bright toys and the waste paper bowled along merrily in the wind. The air was keen and smelt of the sea. It was possible to believe that the Saturday shoppers trailing with their children across the scrubland were carrying their picnics to the beach, that the clunch field led on to dunes and marram grass, to the child-loud fringes of the sea. Even the screen, which the police were fighting to erect against the wind, looked no more frightening than a Punch-and-Judy stand with a little group of curious people standing patiently at a distance, waiting for the show to begin.

It was Superintendent Mercer who came first up the slope of the clunch pit towards them. He said:

'It's a messy business; the husband of the girl who was found here on Wednesday. He's a butcher's assistant. Yesterday he took home one of the knives and came here last night to cut his throat. He left a note confessing to her murder, poor devil. It wouldn't have happened if we'd been able to arrest him yesterday. But Lorrimer's death and Doyle's suspension held us up. We only got the blood result late last night. Who is it you want to see?'

Mercer looked at Dalgliesh keenly, but he said only:

'Dr Kerrison.'

'He's finished here now. I'll let him know.'

Three minutes later Kerrison's figure appeared over the rim of the clunch pit and he walked towards them. He said:

'It was Nell, wasn't it?'

'Yes.'

He didn't ask how or when. He listened intently as Dalgliesh spoke the words of the caution, as if he hadn't heard them before and wanted to commit them to memory. Then he said, looking at Dalgliesh:

'I'd rather not go to Guy's Marsh police station, not yet. I want to tell you about it now, just you, no one else. There won't be any difficulty. I'll make a full confession. Whatever happens, I don't want Nell to have to give evidence. Can you promise me that?'

'You must know that I can't. But there's no reason why the Crown should call her if you intend to plead guilty.'

Dalgliesh opened the door of the car, but Kerrison shook his head. He said without a trace of self-pity:

'I'd rather stay outside. There'll be so many years of sitting when I shan't be able to walk under the sky. Perhaps for the rest of my life. If it were only Lorrimer's death, I might have hoped for a verdict of manslaughter. His killing wasn't premeditated. But the other was murder.'

Massingham stayed by the car while Dalgliesh and Kerrison walked together round the clunch pit. Kerrison said:

'It started here, at this very spot, only four days ago. It feels like an eternity. Another life, another time. We'd both been called to the clunch pit murder, and afterwards he drew me to one side and told me to meet him that evening at eight-thirty at the Laboratory. Not asked; told. And he told me, too, what he wanted to talk about. Domenica.'

Dalgliesh asked:

'Did you know that he was her lover before you?'

'Not until I met him that night. She had never talked about him to me, never once mentioned his name. But when he poured out his stream of hate and envy and jealousy, then, of course, I knew. I didn't ask him how he'd found out about me. I think he was mad. Perhaps we were both mad.'

'And he threatened to write to your wife and prevent your getting custody of the children unless you gave her up.'

'He was going to write anyway. He wanted her back, and I think, poor devil, that he actually believed that it might be possible. But he still wanted to punish me. I've only once before known such hate. He was standing there, white-faced, railing at me, taunting me, telling me that I'd lose the children, that I wasn't fit to be a father, that I'd never see them again. And suddenly it wasn't Lorrimer speaking. You see, I'd heard it all before from my wife. It was his voice, but her words. And I knew that I couldn't take any more. I'd been up for most of the night; I'd had a terrible scene with Nell when I got home; and I'd spent the day worrying what Lorrimer might have to tell me.

'It was then that the telephone rang. It was his father complaining about the television. He only spoke briefly, then he put down the receiver. But when he was speaking I saw the mallet. And I knew that I had gloves in my coat pocket. The call to his father seemed to have sobered him. He told me there was nothing else he wanted to say. It was when he turned his back on me dismissively that I seized the mallet and struck. He fell without a sound. I put the mallet back on the table, and it was then I saw the open notebook with the names and addresses of three doctors. One of them was my wife's lover. I tore out the page and crumpled it in my pocket. Then I went to the telephone and made my call. It was just nine o'clock. The rest, I think, you know.'

They had circled the clunch pit, pacing together, their eyes fixed on the bright grass. Now they turned and retraced their steps. Dalgliesh said:

'I think you'd better tell me.'

But there was nothing new to learn. It had happened just as Dalgliesh had reasoned. When Kerrison had finished describing the burning of the coat and the page from the notebook, Dalgliesh asked:

'And Stella Mawson?'

'She rang me at the hospital and asked me to meet her in the chapel at half past seven yesterday. She gave me an idea what it was about. She said that she had a draft letter which she wanted to discuss with me, one she'd found in a certain desk. I knew what it would say.'

She must have taken it with her to the chapel, thought Dalgliesh. It hadn't been found in her desk, neither the original nor the copy. It seemed to him extraordinary that she had actually risked letting Kerrison know that she had the letter on her. How could he be sure, when he killed her, that she hadn't left a copy? And how could she be sure that he wouldn't overpower her and take it?

Almost as if he knew what was going through Dalgliesh's mind, Kerrison said:

'It wasn't what you're thinking. She wasn't trying to sell me the letter. She wasn't selling anything. She told me that she'd taken it from Lorrimer's desk almost on impulse because she didn't want the police to find it. For some reason which she didn't explain, she hated Lorrimer, and she bore me no ill will. What she said was: "He caused enough misery in his life. Why should he cause misery after his death?" She said another extraordinary thing. "I was his victim once. I don't see why you should be his victim now." She saw herself as on my side, someone who'd done me a service. And now she was asking me for something in return, something quite simple and ordinary. Something she knew that I'd be able to afford.'

Dalgliesh said:

'The cash to buy Sprogg's Cottage, security for herself and Angela Foley.'

'Not even a gift, merely a loan. She wanted four thousand pounds over five years at a rate of interest she could afford. She needed the money desperately, and she had to find it quickly. She explained to me that there was no one else she could ask. She was perfectly ready to have a legal agreement drawn up. She was the gentlest, most reasonable of blackmailers.'

And she thought that she was dealing with the gentlest, most reasonable of men. She had been totally without fear, until that last hideous moment when he had drawn the cord from his coat pocket and she had realized that she was facing, not a fellow victim, but her murderer. Dalgliesh said:

'You must have had the cord ready. When did you decide she had to die?'

'Even that, like Lorrimer's death, was almost chance. She had got the key from Angela Foley and she arrived at the chapel first. She was sitting in the chancel, in one of the stalls. She had left the door open, and when I went into the antechapel I saw the chest. I knew the cord was inside it. I'd had plenty of time to explore the chapel when I'd been waiting for Domenica. So I took it out and put it in my pocket. Then I went through to her, and we talked. She had the letter with her, in her pocket. She took it out and showed it to me without the least fear. It wasn't the finished letter; just a draft that he'd been working on. He must have enjoyed writing it, must have taken a lot of trouble getting it right.

'She was an extraordinary woman. I said that I'd lend her the money, that I'd have a proper agreement drawn up by my solicitor. There was a Prayer Book in the chapel, and she made me put my hand on it and swear that I'd never tell anyone what had happened between us. I think she was terrified that Angela Foley would get to know. It was when I realized that she, and only she, held this dangerous knowledge, that I decided that she must die.'

He stopped walking. He turned to Dalgliesh and said:

'You see, I couldn't take a chance on her. I'm not trying to justify myself. I'm not even trying to make you understand. You aren't a father, so you never could understand. I couldn't risk giving my wife such a weapon against me when the custody case comes before the high court. They probably wouldn't worry overmuch that I had a mistress; that wouldn't make me unfit to care for my children. If it did, what chance would most parents have of getting custody? But a secret affair which I'd concealed from the police with a woman whose previous lover was murdered, a murder for which I had only a weak alibi and a strong motive. Wouldn't that tip the balance? My wife is attractive and plausible, outwardly perfectly sane. That's what makes it so impossible. Madness isn't so very difficult to diagnose, neurosis is less dramatic but just as lethal if you have to live with it. She tore us apart, Nell and me. I couldn't let her have William and Nell. When I stood in the chapel and faced Stella Mawson, I knew it was their lives against hers.

'And it was so easy. I slipped the double cord around her neck and pulled tight. She must have died at once. Then I carried her into the antechapel and strung her up on the hook. I remembered to scrape her boots on the chair seat and leave the chair overturned. I walked back across the field to where I'd left my car. I'd parked it where Domenica parks hers when we meet, in the shadow of an old barn on the edge of Guy's Marsh road. Even the timing was right for me. I was due at the hospital for a medical committee meeting, but I'd planned to go into my laboratory first and do some work. Even if someone at the hospital noted the time when I arrived, there was only about twenty minutes unaccounted for. And I could easily have spent an extra twenty minutes on the drive.'

They walked on in silence towards the car. Then Kerrison began speaking again:

'I still don't understand it. She's so beautiful. And it isn't only her beauty. She could have had any man she wanted. It was amazing that, for some extraordinary reason, she wanted me.

When we were together, lying by candlelight in all the quietness of the chapel after we'd made love, all the anxieties, all the tensions, all the responsibilities were forgotten. It was easy for us, because of the dark evenings. She could park her car by the barn in safety. No one walks on the Guy's Marsh road at night, and there are only a few cars. I knew it would be more difficult in the spring with the long evenings. But then, I didn't expect she would want me that long. It was a miracle that she wanted me at all. I never thought beyond the next meeting, the next date on the hymn-board. She wouldn't let me telephone her. I never saw or spoke to her except when we were alone in the chapel. I knew that she didn't love me, but that wasn't important. She gave what she could, and it was enough for me.'

They were back at the car now. Massingham was holding open the door. Kerrison turned to Dalgliesh and said:

'It wasn't love, but it was in its own way a kind of loving. And it was such peace. This is peace, too, knowing that there's nothing else I need do. There's an end of responsibility, an end of worry. A murderer sets himself aside from the whole of humanity for ever. It's a kind of death. I'm like a dying man now, the problems are still there, but I'm moving away from them into a new dimension. I forfeited so many things when I killed Stella Mawson, even the right to feel pain.'

He got into the back of the car without another word. Dalgliesh closed the door. Then his heart lurched. The blue and yellow ball came bounding across the clunch field towards him and after it, shouting with laughter, his mother calling after him, ran the child. For one dreadful second, Dalgliesh thought that it was William, William's dark fringe of hair, William's red wellingtons flashing in the sun.

READ MORE IN PENGUIN

ALSO BY P. D. JAMES IN PENGUIN

Her latest bestseller:

A Certain Justice

When Venetia Aldridge QC agrees to defend Garry Ashe, accused of the brutal murder of his aunt, it is one more opportunity to triumph in her career as a lawyer. But *Regina v. Ashe* initiates unpredictable events, and just four weeks later, Miss Aldridge is found dead . . .

'Fiendishly clever . . . an accomplished performance by a leader in her field' *Sunday Times*

'This is P. D. James at her highly impressive best' *Sunday Telegraph*

A Second Dalgliesh Trilogy

Contains *A Mind to Murder* • *A Taste for Death* • *Devices and Desires*

Trilogy of Death

Contains *An Unsuitable Job for a Woman* • *Innocent Blood* • *The Skull Beneath the Skin*

Also published:

Original Sin
Cover Her Face
Unnatural Causes
The Children of Men

and with T. A. Critchley:

The Maul and the Pear Tree

Cover Her Face *and* A Mind to Murder, *read by Roy Marsden,* Unnatural Causes, *read by Michael Jayston and* An Unsuitable Job for a Woman, *read by Tamara Ustinov, are available as Faber•Penguin Audiobooks*